Abel's Daughter
A Handful of Silver

Also by Meg Hutchinson

For the Sake of Her Child
No Place of Angels
A Promise Given
Bitter Seed
A Love Forbidden
Pit Bank Wench
Child of Sin
No Place for a Woman
The Judas Touch
Peppercorn Woman
Unholy Love
The Deverell Woman

Writing as Margaret Astbury
The Hitch-Hiker
The Seal

About the author

Meg Hutchinson left school at fifteen and didn't return to education until she was thirty-three, when she entered Teacher Training College and studied for her degree in the evenings. Ever since she was a child, she has loved telling stories and writing 'compositions'. She lived for sixty years in Wednesbury, where her parents and grandparents spent all their lives, but now has a quiet little cottage in Shropshire where she can indulge her passion for storytelling.

Meg Hutchinson

Abel's Daughter
A Handful of Silver

CORONET BOOKS
Hodder & Stoughton

First published as two separate volumes:
Abel's Daughter © 1996 Meg Hutchinson

First published in 1996 by Hodder & Stoughton
First published in paperback in 1996 by Hodder & Stoughton
A division of Hodder Headline
A Coronet paperback

A Handful of Silver © 1997 Meg Hutchinson
First published in 1997 by Hodder & Stoughton
First published in paperback in 1998 by Hodder & Stoughton
A division of Hodder Headline
A Coronet paperback
This paperback omnibus edition, 2003

1 3 5 7 9 10 8 6 4 2

A CIP catalogue record for this title is available from the British Library

ISBN 0 340 83086 7

Printed and bound in Great Britain by
Mackays of Chatham plc, Chatham, Kent

Hodder & Stoughton
A division of Hodder Headline
338 Euston Road
London NW1 3BH

ABEL'S DAUGHTER

For my husband, whose patient encouragement and faith in this work remained when my own had failed. Thank you, sweetheart.

Chapter One

'*Phoebe Pardoe, I find you guilty of wilful theft. I order you to be taken to a place of imprisonment where you will serve a term of fifteen years' hard labour.*'

Phoebe pushed the soiled rags into the hot tub, wincing as the soda bit into the raw flesh of her hands.

'. . . *you be taken to a place of detention . . .*'

She scrubbed the rags against the ribbed wooden board, the menstrual blood of her fellow inmates turning the water red.

'. . . *fifteen years' hard labour . . .*'

The words circled endlessly in her brain as they had for the past eight months.

'. . . *guilty of wilful theft . . .*'

'Put yer back into it, Pardoe!'

Phoebe gasped as the slim wooden cane sliced across her shoulders.

'. . . them bleedin' jam rags won't wash themselves – or p'raps you ain't used to washin'? Yeah, I forgot you once 'ad a laundry woman to do yer washin' for you. Well, you ain't got one now, you bloody thief, so get stuck in or you'll be sorry.'

Phoebe's teeth tightened on her lip; she knew better than to answer back to Sally Moreton, superintendent of the laundry. Built like a man, her mouth was twisted up at the side due to some childhood illness, and her insides were twisted to match. Beating other women seemed the only source of pleasure she had, the cane she carried cutting into their

1

flesh on the merest excuse, and often without any at all.

Squeezing the strips of cloth and dropping them into a cane basket, Phoebe pushed against her hair with a hand as bloody as the rags she had just scrubbed, then picking up the basket she carried it to one of the steaming boilers, dropping her load inside. Now she could take a recently removed batch to the yard and peg them on the lines stretched between the buildings. These were the only moments in her long days that she looked forward to. To see the sky, to feel the clean air on her face, to hear a bird sing . . .

'Leave them!' Sally Moreton's cane came down across Phoebe's raw hands, her cruel piggy eyes gleaming at the scream of pain it brought forth. 'Martha can peg them out. We don't want to risk yer delicate constitution by sending you out into the cold air, now do we?'

'But I always do the pegging out!' The thought of not going outside, even for the few minutes it took to peg the strips of torn sheeting to the lines, made Phoebe forget what so many blows of that cane had taught her. 'Martha does . . .'

The stinging cut of the cane across her mouth stilled the rest of the protest, sending Phoebe crashing backward against the cauldron of bubbling soapy water.

'Martha does what I tell 'er.' The cane rose again, swishing downward across Phoebe's legs, cutting through the worn grey calico. 'Same as all the rest of the thievin', murderin' scum in this place – same as you will, Miss High and Mighty Phoebe Pardoe! An' if you answer me back one more time you might find yerself missin' a tongue to answer back with. Now get that lot in.' Lashing out with her foot, she tipped over another basket of soiled cloths, stained crimson against the stone floor. 'An' get 'em clean. I don't want to see no mark on 'em when I come to inspect.'

'You better be ready to play tonight, you stuck up bitch!' Liza Spittle dropped a fresh basket of laundry at Phoebe's feet as the superintendent moved away. 'Or Steel Arsed

Sal might find a bundle of these pushed up a chimney somewhere.'

'She wouldn't . . .'

'Believe me,' Liza cut in, the beetroot birthmark staining the left side of her face seeming to swell suddenly as though about to burst, 'that wouldn't stop 'er usin' that cane if we was to give her a good excuse. Loves to use the cane does Steel Arse. It's 'er only pleasure. Does for 'er what no bloke would – not wi' a face like that.'

'You're disgusting!'

'Am I?' Liza's large hand grabbed the basket Phoebe had lifted and, bundling several stained cloths together, she shoved them beneath the hessian sack tied about her middle. 'So tonight will mek two of us, won't it?'

The rest of the long day stretched out between jibes and advice as to how to please Liza, but there was no sympathy, that was something these women had had removed from them as cleanly as amputation severed a limb. Please God, Phoebe prayed when at nine p.m. the one gaslamp was turned off, leaving the dormitory in darkness, please God don't let her come near me. But instinct told her that God was not listening.

'So, you've decided to be nice to Liza, 'ave you?'

Liza Spittle sat on the side of Phoebe's narrow mattress, her approach from the far end of the line of ten tight-spaced beds lost among the snuffles and coughs of the women who filled them.

The dim light from outside had faded almost to extinction by the time it touched the beds but Phoebe did not need light to tell her who sat beside her; the rancid stale fish smell that always accompanied Liza, despite the compulsory baths with carbolic soap, told her her prayers had gone unheeded.

'I thought as 'ow you'd see sense . . .'

Liza bent forward, one broad hand pulling away the rough woollen blanket, the miasmic stench of her closing Phoebe's throat.

'Leave me alone,' she choked, swallowing the smell of the other woman. 'Please, leave me alone.'

Liza snatched the blanket further down, revealing white calico a pale shadow in the darkness. 'Is that what you said to the bobbies when they come fer you, or did you let 'em do this?' One hand undid the row of flat calico-covered buttons while the other pressed heavily on Phoebe's shoulder, the snores and moans from the other beds indicating that none of the other women cared what was happening. 'In fer thievin', ain't you?' The nightgown opened to the waist, the older woman pulled it wide. 'A necklace so I 'ear, a very valible necklace . . . Look good over these pretty tits I've no doubt. Did the bobbies tell you you've got pretty tits? Did they feel 'em like Liza's doin'?' A scaly-skinned hand closed over Phoebe's breast.

'Stop . . . please!' Tears poured down Phoebe's cheeks, salting her lips. 'Please stop.'

Liza bent forward, the stale fish smell of her gagging the girl beneath her. 'You'll be a-sayin' please again soon enough but you won't be a-sayin' stop. You'll be begging Liza to go on . . .'

'Somebody'll be beggin' but it won't be 'er.'

The voice was a hiss in the darkness as Liza was jerked from the bed and flung face down on the floor.

'I told you to leave the kid be, keep yer filthy paws off 'er!'

One hand pressed to her mouth to stop the vomit spilling out, the other holding the edges of her nightgown together, Phoebe recognised the tones of Tilly Wood; serving a life sentence, the gaunt-featured woman was the only soul in the whole prison who had shown her the faintest semblance of kindness in all of the eight months she had spent in this hell hole.

'Seems as 'ow you don't understand plain English . . .'

Suddenly there were no snores, no groans. The silence from the other beds announced that each woman was awake and listening though none moved.

'. . . well, Liza Spittle, I can mek it plainer fer you . . .'

Lifting herself on one elbow, Phoebe peered through the gloom. Tilly Wood had one knee between Liza's shoulder blades with both hands cupped beneath the woman's chin, forcing her head back.

'Play yer dirty bloody games wi' any other of the pissants you fancies but this one you leaves be, an' if you doesn't then you's goin' to be found behind one o' them bilers wi' a jam rag stuck in yer gob!

'Y'see, Liza, I ain't got nuthin' to lose – I'm already behind these bars fer life an' there ain't nuthin' Steel Arse or the likes of 'er can do to me they ain't already done in ten years. That's a long time, Liza, but you put one more finger on that wench, just one finger, and *you'll* be 'ere for eternity.

'Oh, you knows I pushed my swine of a man down the stairs, they told you that did the wardresses, but what they didn't tell you was I broke 'is neck fust. It didn't tek much . . .'

Pressing her knee further into Liza's back, she pulled the chin upward, bringing a strangled cry from the woman on the floor. 'Just a quick jerk and the spine was broke at the base of the neck. You don't 'ave to be no big bloke to do that, Liza, you just need to spend yer life fightin' off ten brothers an' a bloke you wus never married to in fust place.' The cupped hands jerked again. 'It would be easy, Liza, an' pleasurable, an' you would never know when it was comin', so if you wants to live long enough to get out of 'ere, you'll think on what I says . . . leave this 'un be!'

Rising, Tilly waited while Liza picked herself up and slunk back to bed, hearing the disappointed grunts coming from the shadows; there were many in the room who would have welcomed the snapping of Liza Spittle's neck.

"Er won't mess wi' you any more,' Tilly said, covering Phoebe with the blanket, then louder, ''cos Tilly Wood don't tell the Good Lord 'isself more'n twice.'

I order you be taken to a place of imprisonment where you will serve a term of fifteen years.

Lying in the darkness, Phoebe knew her life would not stretch that far.

How had this happened to her? Phoebe closed her eyes, letting the darkness press against her lids, and in that darkness saw again the summer ball and herself in a pink rose-trimmed gown dancing with Montrose. Montrose Wheeler, son of Gaskell Wheeler, owner of the Monway Iron Foundry, had asked for her hand in marriage and her father had agreed. The ceremony had been planned to take place at Christmas, Montrose vowing he could hardly bear to wait until then. He was so handsome and tall, his sandy hair and light blue eyes so different from the coarse overfed features of his father or his thin, sharp-faced mother. Who would have dreamed that an evening so warm with music and moonlight, so soft with the promise of love, would be the last time she would see her fiancé, for in the space of weeks her own father lay dead and with his death all her own hopes were extinguished.

'It's bad news I'm afraid, my dear.' Alfred Dingley, her father's doctor and friend, had come to Brunswick House to tell her himself of the accident in which her father's chaise fell to the bottom of a vertical pit. Old mine workings, the coroner had said. Wednesbury was riddled with them and dangerous shafts regularly opened without warning.

The funeral had been a week later, a family affair with just her father's brother Samuel and sister Annie, no one being left of her dead mother's family.

Against the darkness of her lids, Phoebe saw again the finely drawn face of Uncle Samuel, a carbon copy of her own father, and the sad blue eyes that seemed to know more than they revealed. Phoebe realised it was the only time she had ever seen her uncle outside the house he shared with his sister, and even on her rare visits to them she was never left alone with him: 'Because of his stone deafness, dear,' was what she was always told when she had asked the reason he never went out, an answer that even as a child she'd found unconvincing. Her Aunt Annie in her customary black, shrouded in the perennial air of bitterness Phoebe had recognised from an early age, sat straight-backed in the carriage that followed the hearse, black-plumed horses walking slowly to St Bartholomew's Church and her father's final resting place.

His death had been a blow but there had been worse in store for her, much worse. The reading of Abel Pardoe's will took place in the drawing room of his home, Brunswick House, the following afternoon. James Siveter, her father's lawyer, in a long old-fashioned tail coat that gave him the appearance of a crow, rose from his seat at her father's heavy oak desk, ushering Phoebe to a chair beside her aunt. His impassive face as he resumed his seat betrayed nothing of what was to come.

"'I, Abel Pardoe, being of sound mind . . .'"

Siveter's expressionless voice droned on through the bequests to servants, only changing when he came to her father's provision for Phoebe herself.

"'Next I come to my beloved daughter, Phoebe Mary Pardoe. By the time of my death you will have been Mrs Montrose Wheeler for many years and as such mistress of your own home and in need of nothing. Therefore I leave you what you have always had and enjoyed: my love.

"'Lastly, to my brother Samuel, and my sister Annie who has imprisoned him for the last forty years – to you, Annie Maria Pardoe, I bequeath the sum of one thousand pounds annually and the house you live in for your lifetime. To my brother Samuel Isaac Pardoe I bequeath this house and all its contents together with Hobs Hill Coalmine, Dangerfield Lane, the Crown coalmine, Moxley, and all lands, property, goods and monies pertaining to me. May God give you the courage to use them to buy the freedom I never had the courage to give you.'"

The numbness she had felt since her father's death shielded Phoebe from the full impact of what the lawyer had said and she sat there while her aunt ushered him out. Mrs Banks, their cook-housekeeper, offered to help her upstairs.

Now, opening her eyes, Phoebe stared at the moon-filled squares of the windows, their regimented line like the yellow eyes of demons about to strike, while in the shadowed belly of the room figures from her nightmare continued to move.

'You understand, Phoebe, Uncle Samuel needs continual quiet. To have a young girl about the place, especially one with the comings and goings of a fiancé, would be much too upsetting for him,' her aunt had said not two weeks later. 'Therefore I am asking you to make other arrangements.'

'But Uncle Samuel is already in continual quietness, is he not, Aunt?' Phoebe remembered her own answer and the fulminating look that crossed the older woman's face as she added, 'Is he not chronically deaf?'

'And are you not chronically rude?' her aunt had retorted waspishly, then drawing black gloves over thin stick-like fingers, drove home her winning blow. 'I want you out of this house by one week from today, and be sure you take nothing that was paid for by your father.'

'But Father paid for everything,' Phoebe had protested. 'My clothes . . . everything.'

Her aunt moved to the door, waiting while the maid opened it. 'Then you will have less to carry. But your uncle would not want you to suffer any hardship. Therefore you may take two dresses and two changes of underwear, and to be certain you take no more, I will send my own housekeeper to pack them.'

'Surely I may take my jewellery?'

'All paid for by my brother, therefore part of his estate and now part of Samuel's.'

'Not all.' Phoebe followed the spare grey-haired woman, whom for all their family connection she hardly knew, out into the late-autumn sunshine. 'I have several pieces left me by my mother.'

8

Annie Pardoe did not hesitate in climbing into her pony trap. 'Paid for, no doubt, by my brother.' Picking up the reins, she clucked the horse forward. 'Unless you have a deed of gift you will be wise to leave any such pieces where they are.'

Phoebe concentrated hard on the tiny moon-filled spaces, willing the nightmare memories to go away, but on they went, passing before her eyes like some awful dance. She had been writing to Montrose when the Wheelers' carriage had arrived from Oakeswell Hall, and she had felt so relieved. Montrose had obviously been informed of what had happened and was arranging for her to be moved to his parents' home until after their marriage. Grabbing her bonnet and smiling at her maid, Lucy Baines, Phoebe rushed out of the house.

'Miss Pardoe . . .'

The formality of the greeting from Montrose's mother did not surprise Phoebe who had always found the woman cold if not positively unfriendly; neither did the absence of her husband who would be at his place of business at this hour of the day.

'Miss Pardoe,' Violet Wheeler sat stiff-backed facing Phoebe, 'have you written to my son informing him of your situation?'

'No.' Phoebe shook her head, wondering how such a sharp-featured, cold-natured woman could ever have been given the name of so lovely a flower.

'I thought perhaps you may not have, therefore I myself informed Montrose of your position. Under the circumstances I must inform you there can be no question of a marriage between you. As an officer in the Guards Montrose must be seen to make a good marriage – he cannot afford to tie himself to a wife unable to bring with her a good social standing.'

Phoebe remembered the physical sickness that had come over her at these words; how she had stuffed a gloved hand into her mouth.

'I know this must come as a disappointment to you,' Violet Wheeler went on with no more compassion than if she had been wishing her young visitor a pleasant walk about the gardens, 'but both Montrose's father and myself agree that it is for the best.'

Of course it was for the best – the best for Montrose.

'And your son, Mrs Wheeler,' Phoebe had managed, swallowing the sickness filling her throat, 'does he also think that breaking off our marriage is for the best?'

'Montrose will take the advice of his father,' Violet Wheeler's sharp features tightened, her nostrils flaring with controlled anger, 'whilst you would be wise to take mine and say no more than that you feel unable to go through with the marriage so soon after your father's death.'

Phoebe turned her head sideways, staring into the darkness of a room she shared with nine other women. In the space of three weeks she was orphaned, homeless and jilted. Violet Wheeler had said her son must have a wife who could bring with her a good social standing. What she really meant was Montrose must have a wife with a good financial standing.

Three days after Aunt Annie's visit her housekeeper Maudie Tranter arrived to supervise the packing of two dresses and two sets of underwear in a large carpet bag.

'Miss Annie says I am to see that all wardrobes and cupboards are locked in my presence and that I am to take the keys back with me.' The woman looked apologetically at Phoebe. 'She also said I was to take your jewellery box . . . I am sorry, Miss Pardoe, but that was what she said and I have to do it or lose my position.'

'Please don't worry, Mrs Tranter,' Phoebe had tried to reassure the woman, 'no one is blaming you, of course you must do as my aunt says.'

'I've made an inventory of everything in that box,' said Abel Pardoe's own housekeeper who had watched the packing. 'That sees us all safeguarded, Mrs Tranter. Your mistress can't go saying as how anything has gone astray. Tell her this sealing tape was set around the box in your presence and this here is the inventory I spoke of with a copy already sent to Lawyer Siveter's chambers in the High Street for her to check by.'

Fanny Banks's quick fingers passed brown sealing tape three times around the box before handing it to Annie's housekeeper. 'Now, as you've seen to all you came for, you best be off back to that crow you call your employer. As for me, I'll be leavin' when Miss Phoebe do.'

With Fanny Banks treading on her brown skirts, Maudie Tranter dropped Phoebe a quick bob and disappeared from the room, her footsteps almost at a run on the polished wood of the corridor and stairs.

Phoebe herself had left the next day, bidding goodbye to a tearful Mrs Banks who was joining her sister in Chester and a defiant Lucy who vowed to 'go into the workhouse rather than work for that sour-faced prune, Annie Pardoe'.

Try as she might Phoebe had never been able to remember more than walking down the long tree-lined drive away from the large house that had been her home since birth. She knew only that somehow or other she had walked the three miles across open grassland to Hobs Hill coalmine. There Joseph Leach had half carried her into the tiny brick building he called 'the office'. Injured in an explosion underground years before, her father had kept him on ostensibly as tally keeper, though the times her father had taken Phoebe with him on his regular visits to the pithead it seemed Joseph oversaw just about everything. Prising the carpet bag from her fingers, he sat her on the one chair, listening as tears and words poured from her.

'Joe . . . Joe . . .'

Even now, in the quiet of a prison cell punctured only by the breathing of its occupants, the shout seemed to throb against her ears.

'Joe . . . there's bin a cave in!'

'Christ Almighty!' Joseph Leach turned for the door as it burst open.

'Joe.' A figure black from head to foot with coal dust,

the white circles around his eyes the only patch of colour, announced, 'There's bin a fall – roof gone.'

'Where?' Joe asked tersely, all thoughts of Phoebe gone from his mind.

'North tunnel.'

'Bugger it!' he rasped. 'I knew that bastard would go, I said it would. Who's down there?'

'Manny Evans's gang.' The begrimed figure made no acknowledgement of Phoebe's presence.

'Eight men,' Joseph said instantly, with no reference to anything other than his own sharp brain. 'Right, you send young Billy for the doctor then meet me at the mouth.'

After that the girl was forgotten as Joseph organised the rescue.

Though no sound from the pit head told the women of the town what had occurred, the sight of the doctor's trap following the path across the heath told its own story and soon they stood just beyond the green-painted wooden gates with her father's name painted tall and white across them – Phoebe could see them clearly from the small office, women with chequered shawls about their heads, each face chalky with fear.

'How many, Joseph?' Alfred Dingley jumped from the trap, a black Gladstone bag in his hand.

'Eight, sir. Emanuel Evans, Evan Gittins, Charlie Norton and 'is lad Tommy, Sam Deeley, David Walker, Ben Corns and Meshac Speke.' Joseph reeled off the names as he swept papers and ledgers from the table that almost filled the office, clearing a space for the doctor to work on any injured men.

'Where?'

'North tunnel about thirty yards in. We can get to about ten yards of 'em at a guess. I've got a gang in now clearin' rest, but the shorin's be weak. We got to watch rest of roof don't come in atop of 'em.'

'You are sure there are no more than eight?'

Joseph had pointed to a line of nails hammered into the

brick wall of the office, each bearing a round metal plate the size of a penny. 'Tokens be all in an' Davy's be all gone for North tunnel an' there be nobody else in that part o' the mine. I'll 'ave the tokens checked again though, if you wants, for the other seams?'

'No need.' Alfred Dingley glanced at the wall where the Davy lamps were hung as each man checked in when coming from underground.

Phoebe ran out into the yard after the two men as a shout of 'They'm through' rang out, watching them make for the mouth of the mine. Her offer of help went unanswered.

Slowly, the iron cage was winched again and again to the surface, the cries of the women reaching across the yard as they recognised their men, but each in his turn waited for the raising of the cage until the last survivor, Charlie Norton, stepped out, his fifteen-year-old son carried in his arms.

In the darkness, Phoebe threw an arm across her face, desperate to obliterate the screams of the lad's mother. They had been lucky, Joseph had said later, but what use was that to Sally Norton?

'You did very well.' Dr Dingley had smiled at Phoebe as the last of the men's cuts were washed and bandaged. 'Now you'd better let me take you home, my girl.'

But Phoebe had refused, saying she preferred to walk, not wanting to admit the truth of having no home and Joseph said nothing of what she had told him.

'You'd better cum along o' me,' he said, watching the doctor drive horse and trap through the gates, 'my Sarah'll know what to do.'

And she had, leastways until Annie Pardoe landed on her doorstep.

It hadn't taken long. A fresh ripple of anger swept over Phoebe and she flung her arm from her face as if fending off an enemy. News had a way of travelling fast and it was news in the town that Sarah Leach had taken in Abel Pardoe's daughter. Days from the cave-in at Hobs Hill mine her aunt had driven down to the Leachs' cottage and marched in. The whole thing was over before it began: the house was part of Samuel's legacy, as were most others in this area, her aunt said, and either Phoebe went or they did – and with them Joseph's job at the mine.

'Yer father was good to me, I can't turn me back on 'is wench.'

Joseph's protest at her leaving echoed in Phoebe's mind. He and his family were reluctant to see her go but as Sarah admitted, jobs were hard come by, especially for 'a bloke wi' a bad leg'.

Phoebe stared upward. The light against the windows was changing as her life had changed, but where the sky was brightening her life grew ever darker. Turning on to her side she closed her eyes, squeezing the lids tight, fighting away a memory she could not escape . . . *fifteen years' hard labour.*

Chapter Two

Phoebe breathed deeply, savouring the warm July air, not wanting to return to the stifling steam-filled prison laundry. Last night had been only one more in a long line of sleepless nights but Liza Spittle's visit to her bed had left her terrified, too afraid to sleep even after Tilly Wood had half throttled the woman. Phoebe pegged the last cloth to the line, her hand shaking. Liza wasn't the sort to give in easily, sooner or later she would try again.

'Thinkin' of doin' a runner, Pardoe?'

Sally Moreton stood in the doorway of the laundry, the long cane swishing alongside her skirts.

Phoebe picked up the empty basket.

'Wait!'

The order cracked across the yard. Phoebe stood still, watching the other woman march the length of the washing line, her cane lifting each of the cloths in turn.

'Wot 'appened last night?'

'Last night?' Phoebe hedged, knowing Sally Moreton would already have been told everything.

'Don't play the innocent with me, you bloody thief! I want to 'ear wot 'appened.' The cane whistled past, close to Phoebe's ear.

'I didn't know anything had happened.' She waited for the blow she knew the lie would bring. 'We all sat as usual, mending linen after clearing the dining hall, then at eight-thirty we dispersed to the dormitories and prepared for bed. Then at nine the light was put out and everyone went to sleep – at least that is what happened in our dormitory.'

'"At least that is what happened in our dormitory,"' Sally

Moreton mimicked, bringing the cane down again. 'Listen to me, you little snot! If nothin' 'appened 'ow come Liza Spittle can 'ardly shift 'er 'ead on 'er neck this mornin'? An' 'ow come when 'er talks 'er sounds like a glede under a door? Got a touch of this new influenza as 'er or is it somethin' else grabbed 'er by the throat? Somethin' like another woman?'

The cane tapped warningly against the drab grey skirts of the laundry superintendent. Phoebe knew that it would take very little to bring it lashing across her face.

'Lost yer tongue, 'ave yer?' Sally Moreton grinned, showing large uneven teeth, bases blackening with decay. 'You nearly lost a lot more last night. 'Ad a visit from Liza so I 'ear. Enjoy it, did you?'

Phoebe gripped the empty basket, holding it close against her as Sally Moreton stepped nearer.

'Play wi' these, did 'er?' Sally's free hand closed over Phoebe's breast and squeezed. ''Er likes tits does Liza, especially young tits.' She smiled again, bringing her face close to Phoebe's. 'The sort that is still firm. But it ain't just tits satisfies Liza, 'er likes more, 'er likes a bit of what's down 'ere . . .' The hand holding the cane knocked the basket aside, allowing the other to press between Phoebe's legs. 'I know what Liza likes. We 'as the same tastes if you see what I mean!'

Dropping the basket, Phoebe pushed the woman, causing her to take several steps backward. 'You disgust me!' she spat.

'So I disgust you, do I?' Sally Moreton brought the cane to rest against the palm of her left hand, eyeing the girl whose mouth was still swollen from yesterday's blow. It was going to be more than her mouth would be swollen this time! 'Did Liza disgust you an' all . . . could it be we ain't good enough for Miss 'Igh and Mighty Pardoe? Or is it Tilly Wood 'as staked a claim?'

'Tilly Wood isn't like that!' Phoebe flared. 'She hasn't got your filthy ways . . .' She stopped as the cane found its mark, the force of it splitting her lower lip as it threw her backward.

'So Sally Moreton 'as filthy ways, 'as 'er?' The cane whistled through the air, slicing across Phoebe's shoulder. ''Er ain't to yer liking.' The cane struck again. ''Er disgusts you, do 'er?' The cane flashed downward, cutting across Phoebe's cheek, then lifted high into the air again.

'Stop that!' Agnes Marsh caught the superintendent's arm, halting the blows raining on to Phoebe. 'You bloody fool, Sally. Ain't you got more sense than to beat the kid senseless this time o' the day?'

'I don't let nobody mouth off at me!'

'Nor you should,' Agnes allowed, 'but daytime ain't the time to teach her a lesson, you should know that.'

'No, it ain't, Agnes.' Sally Moreton lowered the cane, her eyes on the girl still shielding her head with her arms. 'But it won't always be daytime, will it? Then this one will really find out what it means to mouth off at Sally Moreton.'

'That's it, Sally.' Agnes Marsh, deputy superintendent of the prison laundry, released the woman's arm. 'Do what you like in the dark – that way there's nobody can point the finger. As fer 'er,' she jerked her head towards Phoebe, 'Governess 'as sent fer 'er, wants 'er upstairs.'

'What for?' Sally looked quickly at the woman beside her.

'Didn't say, just sent Mary Pegleg to say as 'er wanted to see Prisoner Pardoe in 'er office, now.'

'You 'eard 'er.' Sally reached out with the cane, poking Phoebe in the ribs. 'Get yerself up there . . . an' mind, I'll 'ear of every word what's said so you better be careful what you tells our new lady Governess about yer little . . . accident.' She touched the cane to Phoebe's bleeding mouth then stood aside. 'Get yerself to the bathroom and wash afore you go upstairs.'

Her eyes clouded with pain Phoebe picked up the fallen basket, carrying it into the steam-filled laundry and depositing it beside her washtub. All eyes followed her as she walked from the laundry; all eyes registered the bloody mouth and weals like scarlet ribbons criss-crossing her cheek, among them the eyes of Tilly Wood.

'Wot did 'er say?'

The evening meal of bread and potatoes finished and the dining hall cleared, the women prisoners sat at the long wooden tables, each with a piece of mending.

'She said I wasn't to be assigned to the laundry from now on,' Phoebe answered in a whisper.

'A sined? Wot does that mean?'

'It means 'er don't 'ave to scrub no more bloody jam rags, that's what it means.' Mary Pegleg, her duties as general dogsbody for the prison Governess finished for the day, sat with the others, the wooden stump attached to her left knee thrust out beneath the table. Tilly Wood looked up from her place opposite Phoebe but said nothing.

''Ave you bin sprung, Pardoe?' a thin whippet-like woman asked.

'No,' Phoebe shook her head, 'I am not being released.'

''Er's goin' into the sewin' room.' Mary Pegleg supplied the information with an air of importance. 'I 'eard through the door. I 'as to sit outside Governess's room case I'm wanted, an' I 'eard 'er say as 'ow Pardoe was to work in the sewin' room from now on.'

'By all the Saints in Heaven, I wish it were me!'

'Governess ain't that daft,' the whippet-faced woman grinned. 'Tek you in there an' Christ knows 'ow many would get clobbered.'

'It's not bloody fair! A bloke lathers the 'ide off of a woman an' 'e gets away wi' it. A woman 'its a man an' 'er finishes up doin' twelve months in 'ell, washin' other folks' dirty linen.'

'That's true an' all, Bridie Trow,' came another whisper, 'but you hit the man with a wooden stool, nearly knocking his brains out!'

'Holy Mother o'God, an' that's a dirty lie.' Bridie looked up from the sheet she was mending. 'Oi could never 'ave knocked out the man's brain for 'e 'ad none in 'is 'ead to start with.'

'Hey up, Steel Arse is comin'.'

The sudden whisper stilled the women's giggles and all heads bent to the sewing.

''Alf-past eight . . . pack up.' The ever-present cane swished as the superintendent of the laundry surveyed two hundred silent women. 'Put the sewin' in its proper basket then prepare for bed. Each dormitory will be inspected before lights out at nine.' She stood watching the women file silently from the hall, her eyes following the thin figure of Phoebe Pardoe.

'So 'ow come the sewin' room . . . an' why you?'

Hands and face washed, a rough calico nightgown swamping her stringy body, Tilly Wood sat on the end of Phoebe's bed, the other occupants of the room covertly listening.

Phoebe glanced at her hands, encased in the white cotton gloves which Hannah Price, the prison Governess, had given her to protect them while they healed. 'It seems Mrs Price was invited to a friend's house at the weekend. While she was there they visited the Goose Fair at Wednesbury and Mrs Price purchased a petticoat from one of the stalls. She asked who had made it because she would like to buy more but was told that would not be possible for the girl who was responsible for the petticoat had been sent to prison in Birmingham. Being told the name "Phoebe Mary Pardoe", the governess guessed it might be me. When I told her my home was in Wednesbury she asked to see some of the sewing I had done here in Handsworth, then she said I was to be assigned to the sewing room but my duties would not begin until my hands were healed.'

'An' yer face?' Tilly asked, looking at the weals still red

against the swollen flesh. 'What 'ad the Governess to say about that?'

'She asked what had happened. I told her it was an accident, the drying racks had slipped and caught me on the face.'

'Best way,' Tilly nodded. 'This is a new government prison, it ain't like the old 'uns with everybody packed in a single stinkin' underground cell, an' Hannah Price is first woman to run a prison as I know of. It will be a 'ard job keepin' it if I know anythin' about men – one breath about 'er bein' unable to control we women an' 'er'll be out. Besides . . .' she threw a meaningful look at Liza Spittle '. . . we can sort out our own problems.'

'Find yer own bed, Tilly Wood.' Sally Moreton strode into the long room, her cane slapping the foot of each bed as she passed. Reaching Phoebe's, she paused. 'Seems you 'ave more than one visitin' yer bed at night, Pardoe.' She touched the cane to Phoebe's breast. 'Already gettin' more than tits to play with, are they? P'raps we better move you from more than the laundry.' She smiled, showing her blackened teeth. 'Mebbe that little room next to mine? Be nice an' private there you would, nobody to come pawin' you in the dark.'

In her bed, Tilly's strong fingers tightened on the rough blanket.

'Now the lot of you, listen!' The cane cracked against the iron frame of each bed like a series of pistol shots as Sally Moreton proceeded to the door. 'There'll be no lovers' meetin's tonight, no moonlight walks from bed to bed . . . you 'ear that, Liza Spittle? Each of you stays put where you am now. Ignore Sally's warnin' an' you'll wish yerselves dead!'

Turning off the one gaslamp, she left.

'Goodnight to you an all, Mrs Moreton,' Bridie Trow called softly after the departing wardress.

'An' arsehole to yer warnin',' another voice added, just loud enough to be heard.

'Ar, an' you can stick yer cane up that!' Mary Pegleg laughed in the darkness.

'Sure, Mary, an' that's not the place old Steel Arse will be pushin' 'er cane in 'er lonely room,' Bridie Trow said crudely. 'It's not that 'ole she'll be a pokin' stick into, may the Divil an' all 'is demons escort her into Hell!'

Tilly Wood pulled the blanket up to her chin, remembering the weals on Phoebe's face, the broken mouth swollen to four times its size. The Devil could have Sally Moreton but it would be Tilly Wood gave her to him.

Phoebe stared at the windows high above her bed. Why had her aunt turned her out of her own home? Why after that had she ordered Joseph Leach to turn her out of his? Why did her aunt hate her so much? Why had Montrose not come to see her or even sent a note? The questions kept sleep from her.

'. . . *I find you guilty of wilful theft* . . .'

The words seemed to echo through the quiet room.

'*I want you for my wife, Phoebe.*' The figure of Montrose Wheeler rose in her mind, so tall and handsome, so dashing and attentive. '*I want to take you to London . . . to Paris . . . I want to show you off to the world . . . I love you, Phoebe, and I want you to be my wife.*'

But he hadn't loved her enough to write, he hadn't wanted her badly enough to come for her when the home she thought hers forever had gone instead to her aunt and uncle.

And her aunt had made sure she went from it quickly, just as she had made sure she had also gone from Joseph's home.

But Joseph had not left her entirely without help. He had taken her to see Elias Webb, a stumpy irascible man who owned property on the edge of the town.

'I wants no truck wi' the Pardoes,' he had shouted, his face red and angry when Joseph told the reason for their visit. 'It was Abel Pardoe ruined my business when he sold Monway Field to an iron merchant – pulled my mill down, 'e did, a mill I'd ground flour in all me life, ar, an' me father afore that, an' then she . . . Annie Pardoe . . . I wasn't good enough fer 'er . . . wanted no mill owner fer a 'usband did that one . . . bloody stuck up bitch! No matter who got 'urt so long as it wasn't Annie Pardoe.'

'Then why let 'er 'urt another, Elias,' Joseph had asked, 'why when you can stop it?'

''Ow can my lettin' Abel Pardoe's wench 'ave my 'ouse 'urt that bitch of a sister of his'n?' Elias had demanded.

''Cos your 'ouses are about the only ones left in Wednesbury as don' belong to Pardoe or Foster or Platt, or else to folk who am beholden to 'em. Annie Pardoe not only turned 'er own brother's wench out of 'er father's 'ome, 'er turned 'er out o' mine. Said if 'er didn't go, I 'ad to – an' lose me job at the pit an' all. An' if Annie Pardoe 'as seen wench off two places, what meks you think 'er will let Abel's daughter rest in any if 'er can do anythin' about it?'

Elias had looked at her then, Phoebe remembered, his eyes bright and calculating in his red face.

'Why let the sins of the parents fall upon the children, Elias? Especially the sins of Annie Pardoe.' Joseph drove home the last nail.

'That 'un!' Elias had almost spat the words. 'Annie Pardoe is still the same heartless . . . done!' He struck the table palm down. 'You can 'ave the 'ouse but it will cost you two 'undred an' fifty guineas . . . tek it or tek yerself off.'

Joseph had tried to get Elias to lower his price but Phoebe had agreed. To own her own house, however small, a house her aunt could not turn her out of, would be worth two hundred and fifty of the three hundred guineas her maternal grandmother had left her.

Wiggins Mill stood some way out of the town, close to its own pool. Set in a hollow, it was sheltered from the winds blowing off the open heath, the Birmingham Navigation Canal at its rear. With a scullery, kitchen, large living room and smaller parlour, three fair-sized bedrooms, together with the usual outhouses and a stable, it had become hers the following day.

And a week later Annie Pardoe had arrived.

'And this is where you intend to live?' she had asked, looking down her nose at the furniture which the remainder of Phoebe's guineas had bought from John Kilvert's pawnbroker's shop in Union Street. 'And what do you intend to live on?'

Refusing the offer of tea, her aunt wiped a gloved finger across the chair Phoebe indicated then refused that too.

'. . . or is there someone prepared to keep you – for a price?'

Staring at the squares of moonlight high on the shadowed walls Phoebe felt again the heat that had risen to her face and the cold steady rise of anger in her stomach. She had despised Annie Pardoe then: before that moment she had held no real feelings for the woman who was her father's sister, but at that moment the seed of hate was sown.

'Aunt,' her voice had been steady though she was taut with fury, 'this house is my home and how I choose to make my living is my business and no one else's. My father's will did not name either you or Uncle Samuel my guardian, therefore you have no jurisdiction over me. That being so, you will not interfere in my affairs.'

Her aunt's face had twisted with what Phoebe had hoped was derision but knew to be hate.

'What do you expect people will say . . . a young woman living alone outside the town?'

'That I'm what you already think me,' Phoebe had answered, 'a whore.'

Sally Moreton strode through the prison laundry, thin cane swishing beside the skirts of her grey uniform, her hair scraped back to form a knot at her neck, adding to the severity of her features.

'Call them clean?' She stopped at a basket of cloths, their sides ragged where they had been torn into strips.

Martha Ames looked at the cloths she had scrubbed at for over an hour. 'They look clean to me, Mrs Moreton.'

'Well, they don't look clean to me. Look at 'em!' Sally Moreton's black-booted foot caught the wicker basket, tipping it over to one side. Poking the contents with the cane, she strewed them across the flagged floor. 'Look at this . . .' She ground a boot into a wet cloth. 'An' this . . .' Her boot came down on another, leaving a dirty mark on each. 'An' wot about these?' Hitching her skirts, she trampled the freshly scrubbed cloths, spreading a pool of water across the floor.

Martha Ames stared silently at the cloths that had had her knuckles bleeding. She knew better than to argue.

'They'm bloody filthy!' Sally Moreton shouted, her tall man-like frame towering over Martha. 'Filthy, like all o' you scum!' She glared at the other women, watching silently. Only Tilly Wood's eyes refused to fall before her glare. 'We'll 'ave 'em done again,' she shouted, kicking the cloths across the floor, 'we'll 'ave the 'ole bloody lot done again. You!' She pointed to Bridie Trow. 'Get them boilers emptied. An' you,' she bawled at the ferret-faced Nellie Bladen, 'get fresh water in them tubs. An' you lot . . .' she glared around the steam-filled laundry, '. . . you all do the same. You are going to start all over again.'

'But, Mrs Moreton . . .' The pale consumptive face of Nellie Bladen blanched further as the superintendent swung back to her. 'That'll tek the rest of the mornin'. It'll be afternoon afore we can start washin' agen.'

'Are you arguin' wi' me?' The cane lifted, coming down hard across Nellie's thin shoulders.

'Steel Arse ain't took kindly to Phoebe Pardoe bein' teken out of 'ere,' a voice whispered behind Tilly Wood, 'looks like we am all goin' to be made to pay.'

'When I tell you what to do, you do it . . .' The cane rose again, coming down across Nellie's bent back. 'You don't talk about it, you *do* it!'

Tilly's hand tightened about the thick wooden stick she used to lift clothes from the boiling water in the huge copper. 'You 'ear me, scum? You do it.'

Nellie was already on the floor when Sally Moreton fell across her, unconscious from the blow Tilly Wood struck to the back of her head.

'That bastard has dealt 'er last blow.' Tilly looked at the figure of the wardress almost covering the thin woman half-conscious beneath her. 'Quick, you lot, 'elp me get Nellie out from under this swine.'

Bridie Trow grabbed the shoulder of the woman who seconds before had seemed set to beat Nellie Bladen to death, and heaved her aside, rolling her on to her back.

'Christ Almighty!' Martha Ames breathed. 'What've you done, Tilly? We'll all be done for when Sally Moreton comes to.'

'Holy Mother an' all the Saints.' Bridie Trow crossed herself. 'We'll all be swingin' on the end of a rope, so we will, when 'er tells Justice about this.'

''Er won't be tellin' Magistrates nor nobody else,' Tilly said, grabbing a cloth from a basket standing ready to be taken to the washing lines in the yard. 'Steel Arse 'as caned the last woman 'er'll ever cane an' spoke the last words 'er'll ever say.'

The cloth stretched between her hands, Tilly sank to her knees at Sally Moreton's head. 'Sit on 'er,' she said, looking up at the women grouped around. 'Bridie, Martha, sit on 'er – an' one of you watch the door.'

Then as the two women sat on the unconscious wardress, Tilly placed the folded cloth over the woman's face and held it tightly until any sign of breathing had stopped.

'That's you got yer comeuppance,' Tilly breathed, getting to her feet.

'An' may the Divil 'ave the dealin' of it,' Bridie added, crossing herself again.

'We'll all be meetin' 'im when Governess sees that.' Martha

touched a foot to the dead woman. 'We'll all be as dead as this one.'

'No, we won't.' Tilly looked at the woman on the floor. 'Find Mary Pegleg an' tell 'er to report to the Governess there has been an accident in the laundry . . . an' tek your time.'

''Ow do we mek this look like an accident?' Martha asked. 'The woman's dead.'

'Sure an' 'as no one ever died of an accident before?' Bridie answered as the woman watching the door set off on her message. 'Try holdin' yer gob for a second, Martha Ames, an' listen to Tilly.'

'Leave 'er be.' Tilly held out a hand to the women who stepped forward, about to lift the whimpering Nellie. 'Let 'er lie. Now listen to me. Sally Moreton was tellin' Nellie to tek the cloths outside for peggin' out when 'er started to gasp. 'Er clutched 'er chest, staggerin' about knockin' that basket over, then 'er cried out, a funny stranglin' cry in 'er throat, an' then tumbled 'ead first over Nellie there, nearly knockin' 'er unconscious. You two,' she pointed to Bridie and Martha, 'an' meself rolled Sally over an' called out 'er name, but gettin' no answer thought we best send for the Governess.'

'What d'you reckon will 'appen then?'

Tilly looked at Liza Spittle who until that moment had remained a silent observer. 'Do you reckon as the Governess will believe you?'

'I do.' Tilly looked at the woman who revolted her. 'An' I reckon summat else, Liza, I reckon you'd better keep yer mouth shut, 'cos what Tilly Wood does once 'er can do again – only next time it will be *you* lyin' there.'

'Won't the Governess be after sendin' for the doctor though, Tilly?' Bridie's look was as anxious as her question.

'I'm bankin' on 'er doin' just that,' Tilly answered. 'That Poor Relief doctor as looks after this place is more interested in the bottle than in patients. 'E's drunk no matter when 'e's sent for, be it day or night. It's my guess 'e'll tek one look at Sally Moreton, listen to what we tells 'im 'appened, an' say 'er died of an 'eart attack.'

'Amen to that,' Martha murmured.

'Holy Mother o'God, smile on the man an' grant he be as drunk as a fiddler's bitch!' And Bridie Trow crossed herself again.

Chapter Three

'Are you all right?' Bridie Trow had watched Phoebe from the start of the evening meal. 'You've not touched your taties other than chase 'em round the plate like a bobby after a babby.'

'Yes . . . I'm all right.'

'Like my arse you're all right!' Martha Ames popped the last of her own potatoes into her mouth, speaking as she chewed. 'I seen you comin' from the sewin' room an' you was cryin'.'

'Cryin'!' Tilly Wood stopped eating. 'What about . . . 'as anybody 'ad a go at you?'

'No.' Phoebe didn't look up, unable to keep more tears from filling her eyes.

'Then what am you cryin' for, Phoebe?' Mary Pegleg eased her wooden leg to a more comfortable position under the long scrubbed table top.

''Er's cryin' for to go 'ome,' Liza Spittle laughed, the beetroot mark on her face seeming to darken. 'Well, you'll cry a long time, Pardoe – about fifteen year I'd say.'

'Shut yer gob, Liza Spittle!' Bridie's eyes flashed.

'"'As anybody said summat you didn't like, Phoebe? 'As anybody upset you, Phoebe?"' Liza Spittle minced, then laughed coarsely. 'You lot mek me sick the way you dance round 'er. 'Er ain't no different from the rest on we. 'Er was thievin' an' 'er was catched, now 'er's got to do time like we all 'ave so let 'er be . . . the more 'er cries the less 'er'll piddle.'

Tilly looked across the table, her thin face pinched with distaste. 'If you wants to chew yer next meal, Liza, then tek my advice and keep yer mouth closed.'

'Liza's right in a way, Tilly,' Mary Pegleg put in. 'Phoebe ain't no different. We all feel like 'avin' a cry at times, an' there be times when a good cry meks you feel better.'

'Give me half hour after lights out,' Liza smirked, 'then I'll mek 'er feel better. What Liza does is better for 'er than fartin' around wi' words. Ah bet you can remember 'ow it felt when that fiancy o' your'n touched you up, eh, Pardoe?'

Picking up her plate, Tilly tipped the remainder of her bread and potatoes on to Mary Pegleg's then swung the empty plate fast and hard, smashing it full into Liza Spittle's face.

'You was told to keep yer dirty mouth shut, Liza!' Tilly put the dented metal plate on the table as Sally Moreton's replacement began to move towards them. 'You should 'ave done just that, but then, they say there's no fool like an old fool.'

'What's going on here?'

Emily Pagett had been superintendent of the laundry for the month since Sally Moreton's death. She carried no cane but every prisoner in Handsworth gaol knew she was not to be played with.

'Phoebe . . . 'er's . . . 'er's a bit upset.' Nellie Bladen's consumptive face turned an even more sickly yellow.

'Why is that, Phoebe?'

Brushing at her cheeks with her fingers, Phoebe glanced up at the wardress. She had no occasion to see this woman other than at mealtimes, her place of labour being changed to the sewing room, but Tilly and the others had said she was not without sympathy.

'I . . . I was just remembering . . .'

''Er was saying that 'er father's bin dead twelve months today,' Tilly chipped in as Phoebe faltered. ''Er was very close to 'er father.'

'It happens to everybody, Pardoe.' Emily Pagett turned her

glance to Liza Spittle, trying to staunch the blood spurting crimson between her fingers. 'And what's happened to you, Spittle?'

'Sure an' 'tis the nose on 'er face, 'tis bleedin'.' Bridie Trow was angelic in her innocence. 'Sure an' it does that sometimes.'

'So her nose is bleeding. And what has happened to her tongue, why can't she use that? It's usually to be heard if she thinks none but inmates are around.'

'It'z juzt a doze bleed,' Liza snuffled through her fingers, 'it 'appenz zumtimes.'

'I see, just a nose bleed . . . not caused by anything specific like a snide remark or the promise of a midnight visit?' The wardress raised her voice so it carried over the clatter of forks. 'In the four weeks since my arrival in Handsworth I have come to know almost all of you women, and you have all come to know me and to know I will have no stepping out of line. Keep yourselves orderly, do your work well and there will be no trouble. That is *exactly* what I want and expect . . . no trouble.'

The clatter of forks resumed, no prisoner raising her head, each afraid that to catch the eye of the laundry superintendent might in some way constitute a challenge.

Her voice once more at a normal level Emily Pagett looked at Liza, blood smeared across her face, merging the beetroot mark into one red mask. 'Looks nasty, Spittle,' she said. 'Better get along to the washroom and get it cleaned up. You wouldn't want to get it knocked, now would you? That *would* be painful . . .' Then, her eyes still on the woman shuffling from the table, she added. 'And you, Tilly Wood, best try getting that plate back into shape. And next time, use your hand – there's less evidence that way.'

'How did you know?'

Phoebe slipped the rough calico nightgown over her head, fastening the flat cloth-covered buttons up to her throat.

31

'Took no guessin'.' Tilly fastened her hair in a plait, leaving it to lie across one shoulder. 'You've said one or two bits o' what 'appened afore you come 'ere, one o' em bein' as 'ow your father died sudden like.'

'God rest the puir man!' Bridie crossed herself.

'I never expected it.' Phoebe stared down at her hands, now lying in her lap. 'Father sometimes stayed away if his business took him to London or Southampton but he always told me first. I had no idea he had not come home that night until Mrs Banks announced his bed had not been slept in. Then when I heard about the accident . . .'

'Don't go over that.' Tilly fastened the buttons of her own nightgown. 'No use in rakin' spent coals.'

'Let 'er get it out if 'er wants to.' Martha Ames came to sit beside Phoebe on the low iron bed. 'Spit it out, wench, it'll feel better when you do.'

'It all happened so quickly,' Phoebe said quietly. 'Father dead, his will leaving me penniless, Montrose no longer wanting to marry me, and Aunt Annie turning me out of my own home . . .'

'By Patrick an' the Saints, ye puir girl! An' it's little wonder the Divil got his hooks into yous. So how did you manage, you never 'avin' to strike a blow yerself afore?' Bridie asked.

'I never would have managed without Joseph Leach and his family,' Phoebe answered. 'It was Joseph and his son Mathew who hired a horse and cart to transport the furniture from the shop to Wiggins Mill, and Sarah Leach and their daughter Miriam did most of the organising of the rooms. But it was providing food that gave me my worst moments. It was over an hour's walk from the house to the town and I would bring back only enough for one day. It was Sarah taught me to plan ahead, to buy in stones rather than in ounces, and it was she who got the carter to bring what I needed from the town and drop it at the crossroads on his way to and from Dudley. From the crossroads I had to carry it the half mile to the house. There were times I just wanted to give up . . .'

'I know that feelin'.' Nellie Bladen's sickly face looked death-like in the anaemic yellow light of the single gaslamp. 'But we keeps on goin' somehow.'

Phoebe smiled, recognising knowledge gained the hard way. 'Yes, Nellie, we keep going on. It didn't seem so bad once Miriam and Sarah finally taught me to cook . . . not so bad, that is, until I realised my very last pennies were gone.'

'Eeh, ma wench, 'ow did you manage?' Martha pressed a hand over Phoebe's, her eyes on the girl's face.

'I didn't know what to do,' Phoebe replied quietly, interrupted only by Liza Spittle's moans as the rough calico of her nightgown scraped her swollen nose. 'I only knew I wasn't going to take my trouble to Joseph and Sarah, they had done enough already and with my aunt only too ready to take their home . . . that was when Lucy Baines arrived. The carter had brought her to the crossroads then directed her to Wiggins Mill. I had not seen her since that last day at Brunswick House. She had found work at Sandwell Priory across the valley at West Bromwich. It was her first real day off, she said, and Sarah had told her how to find me.

'We talked a lot and laughed over some of the mistakes I had made while learning to fend for myself, then it came out about my last pennies being spent. She asked me about my jewellery, why didn't I sell it? I would get enough money to tide me over comfortably until I got work or was married.'

'But you said that fi-nancy o' your'n 'ad given you the push!' Mary Pegleg began, then stopped as Tilly's hand smacked against her backbone.

'Lucy seemed to think that was the least of my troubles.' Phoebe smiled again. 'I was better off without a "bloke with not enough oil in his lamp to light his way home", were her words, though what she meant exactly I don't know.'

'I do,' Tilly broke in for the first time since Phoebe had begun to speak. ''Er meant as 'ow your Montrose Wheeler 'adn't enough sense to hold on to a good thing when 'e'd got it, an' I fer one agrees wi' 'er. You be better off wi'out a bloke who only wants a woman for 'er money.'

'Tilly's right, Phoebe,' Mary Pegleg nodded. 'You be fortunate to 'ave found out what 'e was afore you married 'im. There be them among us as don't an' it's too late to do anythin' about it once you're wed. I know, that's 'ow I come to 'ave this.' She tapped her knuckles against the wooden stump below her left knee.

'So what did you do, Phoebe?' Martha asked, stealing Mary's moment of glory.

'I reminded Lucy of what my aunt had said. My mother's jewellery and mine must have been paid for by my father, and unless I had deeds of gift confirming they had been given to me, then they were part of the estate and as such belonged to Uncle Samuel.'

''Er sounds a proper old cow,' Nellie Bladen muttered. 'I wouldn't mind meetin' 'er one dark night. ''Er wouldn't bloody know 'er arse from 'er elbow when I'd finished wi' 'er.'

'An' the Lord give strength to ye,' Bridie Trow said fervently, 'an' the demons o' Hell be there to pick up the pieces.'

'And did you 'ave these deeds of gift?' It was Tilly who asked the question.

'No.' Phoebe shook her head. 'So when my aunt's house-keeper arrived to collect the keys to the house she was given both jewellery boxes, my mother's and my own.'

'So if your maid saw as 'ow the jewellery was took by your aunt's 'ousekeeper, 'ow come 'er asks you why you don't sell it?'

'I asked the same question,' Phoebe answered, 'then Lucy asked something else I found puzzling. What had I done with the dresses I had taken with me? I said I had not worn them since coming to Wiggins Mill, I had used only the underwear, the dresses were in a box in my bedroom. At that Lucy grabbed my hand and dragged me after her up the stairs. In the bedroom she flung open the box and threw the dresses across the bed. "Your bloody dried up fart of an auntie took your mother's jewellery but the old bag didn't get your'n," she said.' Phoebe halted. Less than a year ago she had never heard such words; now she could speak them without so much as a blush.

'But that 'ousekeeper of Annie's, 'er took both boxes, least tha's what you said.' Mary Pegleg sounded confused.

'So she did, Mary,' Phoebe answered, 'and I said the same to Lucy who laughed. She agreed Mrs Tranter had been given two boxes each containing pieces of jewellery – none of which, she said, was that given to me by my maternal grandmother. *That* she had removed from my box, replacing it with some of my mother's. She said Aunt Annie didn't know what jewellery my mother and I had so she would never know what or if any were missing.'

'Sure an' if that girl's brain is not the gift of the little people oi'll be after askin' what is?' Bridie Trow grinned. 'So tell me, what had she done wi' the trinkets an' all?'

'Sewn them in the hem of my dresses.' Phoebe looked at the women grouped around her. 'Mrs Banks and Lucy had taken my grandmother's jewellery out of my room as soon as Aunt Annie had left Brunswick House and together they had sewn it into the hem of two dresses, the two Lucy packed into a bag while Mrs Tranter watched.'

'Oi said it was the gift of the little people the girl had.' Bridie grinned again. 'Sure none but they have the guile to think of doin' the loike, sewin' baubles into a frock. Jesus, but Paddy O'Flaherty 'imself couldn't come up wi' better, an' him the smartest man in all Oirland.'

'So why 'adn't you sold the jewellery?' Tilly watched Phoebe's face, waiting for an answer.

'Because neither of them had told me what they had done. They both thought if I knew I would insist the jewellery go to my aunt, then Mrs Banks left for Chester, and with the worry of getting a new post and then not being allowed time off up until she came to see me that day, Lucy could do nothing but hope I'd found them.'

Seated on her own bed, Liza Spittle touched a finger to her broken mouth. 'If you found you 'ad jewellery to sell,' she said, trying hard to speak without moving lips swollen beyond recognition, "ow come you was 'ad up fer thievin'? 'Ow come you am in 'ere doin' fifteen years?'

'You sew very nicely, Pardoe.' The prison Governess examined the stitches Phoebe had put into a church Psalter. 'Father Heywood will be pleased with these, I'm sure. Tell me . . . who taught you to sew like this?'

Hannah Price's office was at the front of the plain purpose-built prison and from where she was standing Phoebe could see out across the heath, out where people were living ordinary lives, where they could walk with soft meadow earth beneath their feet, where they could stand with the sun and wind on their faces, out where her own life had once been worth living.

'Mrs Banks, Ma'am.'

'Mrs Banks was your tutor?'

'No, Ma'am.' Reluctantly Phoebe turned from her view of the outside world. 'She was my father's housekeeper. I did have a tutor,' she explained, seeing the Governess's enquiring look. 'Mr Caleb Priest was my tutor until I reached the age of thirteen then my father thought my education needed a woman's hand. He engaged Miss Stephenson who did not think I would need the skill of needlework, but I enjoyed it. When she left I used to sit with Mrs Banks and Lucy. That was when I learned to sew.'

'I see.' Hannah Price returned the Psalter. 'Tell me, Pardoe, do you prefer to work out your sentence in the sewing room, or would you rather be in the laundry or the kitchens?'

Phoebe's hand tightened on the beautifully embroidered Psalter. To have to return to the laundry, even without the presence of Sally Moreton . . . a cold sickness rose in her stomach; fifteen years' hard labour, the Magistrate had said, and the woman watching her across the room had the power to return her to a labour that paralysed the soul.

'I . . . I prefer the sewing room, Ma'am.' Phoebe swallowed the sickness of despair. 'I . . . I hope my work is satisfactory?'

'It is.' Hannah Price nodded, the slant of sun through the window catching the chestnut brown hair she had coiled into a knot on the back of her head. 'And so is your behaviour. Your superintendent tells me you have given no trouble while you have been here and I have received no report of any disturbance in your dormitory.' Crossing to the table that served as a desk, she sat down, her hands clasped on its surface. 'In view of that, Pardoe, and of the excellence of your work, I am placing you in charge of the work of the prisoners in the sewing room. I hope you realise the trust I am placing in you?'

'I do, Ma'am.' It took Phoebe long seconds to find her voice, the sickness of fear subsiding into relief. 'And I will do my best to honour it.'

She had not been returned to the steamy hell hole of the prison laundry and to the hated task of washing menstrual cloths, a task Sally Moreton had taken particular joy in making totally hers. Phoebe looked at the Psalter she was embroidering. Fifteen years . . . how many Psalters would she sew in that time?

'Eeh, Joseph, I can't believe it!' Sarah Leach looked across at her husband. 'I can't believe Abel Pardoe 'as bin dead over a year.'

'You can believe it all right.' Joseph peeled off his moleskin trousers, dropping them beside shirt and waistcoat on the floor of the tiny scullery of the one up, one down that housed them, their twenty-year-old son and fifteen-year-old daughter. There was little enough room to move in the place but there would have been less had the rest of his seven children lived beyond babyhood.

'I 'elped to gerrim out an' our Mathew 'elped to carry 'im 'ome.' He slipped into the tin bath Sarah had prepared for him, the warm water easing his crippled left leg, that being the only thing that had prevented him helping to carry Abel Pardoe's body.

''Ow did it 'appen?'

Reaching for the Sunlight soap Sarah kept on a cracked saucer, Joseph lathered his face, blowing like a seal breaking the surface. 'Crownin' in,' he spluttered, 'along of Bilston Road, I told you.'

'I know you did, but I still can't believe it.'

Picking up her husband's clothes, she carried them into the small yard they shared with five other families and threw them across the rope Joseph had fastened for her between two slim tree trunks he had trimmed and hammered into the earth. Proceeding to beat them with a cane carpet beater, she coughed, catching some of the billowing coal dust in her throat. There were those in Wednesbury did this once a week, same as their men took a weekly bath, but in her house it was a nightly affair. Sarah gave the finishing whacks then gathered the clothes, carrying them back to the scullery. Wealthy they were not, but clean they would be.

'Did anybody see it 'appen?' She took up the conversation from where she had left it.

'Don't think so, not many comings and goings up that end during the week.' Joseph scooped handfuls of water, throwing it over his hair, revealing brown beneath the black. 'Folks is all at work 'ceptin' fer Sunday, an' most o' that is spent in Chapel.'

'What did Miss Phoebe 'ave to say?' Sarah had heard it all before but felt the need to go over it again.

'Not a lot, too shocked I reckon, though 'er did say as 'ow 'er father didn't go 'ome at all that night.'

'Oh!' Sarah placed trousers, jacket and waistcoat across a wooden stool. Then, 'Joseph . . . do you reckon 'e wuz theer all night . . . in that 'ole?'

'I doubt it, Joby Hackwood would 'ave found 'im. Them dogs o' his'n could find anythin' – sharp as a razor be them dogs an' Joby 'isself not far off. No, if Abel Pardoe 'ad met wi' that 'ole that night, Joby would 'ave found 'im.' His bath finished Joseph dressed. ''Sides, 'e were facing wrong way.'

Carrying the tin bath out the back, Sarah emptied it into the communal drain that ran through the street of miners' houses then brought it back into the scullery against the arrival of her son.

'What do you mean, 'e were facin' the wrong way?' In the tiny living room she passed Joseph his clay pipe from the mantle then the precious tin with the last few strands of shag tobacco.

Joseph packed the tiny white bowl of the home-made pipe, pressing the tobacco firmly down with his thumb, testing the draw of it with loud sucking breaths before holding a taper to the fire. 'It were soft Johnnie as found 'em . . .'

'Wot! Minnie Pritchard's lad? I thought 'er kept 'im close, not let 'im roam about?'

'Lad 'as fits, Sarah,' Joseph held the lighted taper to the bowl, answering through short puffs, 'that . . . that don' . . . that don' mean as 'e's daft. Lad 'as a brain . . . it's folk around 'im as is daft . . . too daft to let lad be.' Knocking the taper against the bars of the grate blackleaded to a shine like silver, he extinguished the flame, dropping the taper back into a clay pot in the hearth. 'If that mother o' his'n let lad out to work . . .'

''Ow can 'er?' Sarah was quick to defend the woman. 'Lad 'as fits . . . 'e ain't responsible. 'E can't be trusted to act proper.'

'It's folk who believe that am the daft 'uns, Sarah.' Joseph leaned back into the chair set close to the fire, pulling heavily on the small pipe. 'Lad were responsible enough to come straight to pit an' tell me what 'e'd found. If that ain't actin' proper then I don' know wot is. Seems right responsible way of carryin' on to me, an' don' 'e always put isself down somewhere when 'e feels a turn comin' on?'

'I feel sorry for 'em both,' Sarah added coals to the fire, 'the lad an' 'is mother. What the good Lord was thinkin' on the day 'e was got . . .'

'Nobody knows the ways o' the Lord, Sarah, an' it's a wise 'ead that don' puzzle over 'em.'

'That be true enough.' Picking up her mending, Sarah carried it to the hard-backed settle beneath the small window. 'Any road up, it were lad found 'im, you say?'

Joseph tapped the white bowl against the palm of his hand, loosening the tobacco. 'Ar, leastways nobody else 'ad, not to my knowledge anyway.' He replaced the slender stem in his mouth, holding it between his teeth. 'Along about three o'clock he come runnin' into yard like a bat out of 'ell, babbling on about Bilston Road cavin' in and oss an' cart at bottom of 'ole.'

Sarah waited while Joseph tapped his pipe.

'I could see lad was upset,' a wisp of grey smoke curled from Joseph's lips, 'so I left office to Manny Whitehouse an' went wi' 'im.'

'What if gaffer 'ad come an' you not at the pit? You could 'ave lost yer job.'

'No fear o' that 'appening seein' it was 'im at bottom of that 'ole!'

You didn't know that at the time, tekin' off after soft Johnnie, Sarah thought, though was wise enough not to say it.

'Any road,' Joseph puffed, 'soon as I seen trap I knowed who it was 'ad gone in. I sent Johnnie 'ome an' went back to pit for men to raise Abel.'

'So, what about 'is facin' wrong way?' Sarah asked again as Joseph settled into silence.

'Well,' he removed the pipe from his mouth, his gaze on the glowing coals, 'if gaffer 'ad bin on his way from pit to the 'ouse, as Miss Phoebe thought, then oss would 'ave bin facin' t'other way, but it were facin' *toward* Bilston with its back end toward Brummagem.'

Sarah held the needle in mid-air, a puzzled frown drawing her brows together. 'What's wrong wi' that?'

'Think on it,' he answered. 'Abel Pardoe left 'ome that mornin' fer pit only 'e didn't come to pit that day. Miss Phoebe said 'e 'adn't come 'ome from pit in the afternoon nor 'ad 'e bin 'ome all night. Joby Hackwood is certain sure there was no 'ole in Bilston Road that night nor up to eleven o'clock next mornin' when he says 'e was runnin' 'is dogs along the edge o' cornfield . . .'

'Seein' 'ow many rabbits was runnin' likely,' Sarah said drily.

'Whatever 'e was doin', there was no 'ole in Bilston Road at that time or 'e would 'ave seen it, so Abel must 'ave run into it between eleven an' two. It would tek the hour between then an' three for young Johnnie Pritchard to sort out what to do then get isself over to the pit to get me.'

'I still don't see what you reckon is wrong?' Sarah stabbed the needle into her mending.

Joseph blew another stream of blue-grey smoke, the smell of shag tobacco mingling with the smell of coal. 'What's wrong is this. Oss 'ad its back end toward Brummagem,' he said, using the local term for Birmingham, 'that means Abel Pardoe was on 'is way back from there.'

'But 'ow can you be sure?' Sarah asked.

'I'm sure enough,' Joseph replied, his glance still deep in the heart of the fire. 'I 'appens to know Abel spent a deal of time there.'

'Doin' what . . . business?'

'Of a sort.' Joseph sucked on his pipe.

'What sort?' Sarah removed the thread from the needle, using the eye end to unpick an untidy stitch.

'Use yer 'ead, woman.' Joseph bit on the stem of the clay pipe. 'What sort of business does a man do at night? Not the sort 'e does in any office! It's my belief Abel Pardoe 'ad a kept woman – either that or he med regular visits to some knockin' shop.'

41

Sarah almost dropped the needle. 'Eeeh, Joseph! You mean Abel Pardoe . . .'

'That's just what I mean,' Joseph continued where Sarah's shocked voice left off. 'I mean Abel Pardoe had spent that night in Brummagem with a prostitute.'

'Thank the good Lord that never came out.' Sarah held the needle poised in mid-air. 'Phoebe Pardoe went through enough with that aunt of hers wi'out 'earin' such things about 'er father.'

'Seems nobody else figured it,' Joseph sucked once more on the slim white stem of his clay pipe, 'or, if they did then they'm keepin' quiet about it same as we 'ave.'

'That poor girl in prison these twelve months,' Sarah sighed, resuming her mending. 'I can't believe that neither, 'er would never steal anythin'.'

'Magistrate said 'er did.'

'Magistrate don't know everythin',' Sarah snapped, a catch in her voice. ''E don't know what a nice carin' wench young Phoebe was.'

'Magistrate don't need to know.' Joseph stared into the glowing heart of the grate. ''E knowed only what somebody wanted 'im to know an' in my opinion that somebody be Annie Pardoe. My guess is it be 'er as supplied that evidence, if what was said in that court could be called evidence, an' that were just enough to put Abel's daughter down the line for fifteen years.'

Chapter Four

"Er's sewin' what!' Martha Ames's face creased with a mixture of amusement and disbelief. 'Hey, Phoebe, you 'ear that? Mary Pegleg reckons you be sewin' salt cellars.'

'Psalters.' Phoebe joined the laughter of the women. Apart from a half-hour break for the midday meal she didn't see them until evening. 'I'm sewing Psalters . . .'

'That another of 'er new ideas?' Liza interrupted scathingly. 'Gets a good many of them does new Governess.'

'An' all of 'em to the good so far.' Martha looked at her fellow prisoner, the beetroot stain livid on her cheek. 'Though I reckon I could suggest one we'd all find to our liking.'

'Oh, ar, an' what's that, Martha Smart Arse?'

'That 'er 'as you put down.'

'What them Psalterers for then, Phoebe?' Nellie Bladen asked as the second flush of laughter died away.

'Jesus, Joseph and Mary!' Bridie exclaimed, making the regular sign on her chest. 'Sure an oi can't be after believin' what my own ears be tellin' me, Nellie Bladen.'

'So what am they tellin' you?' Nellie's ferret features tightened. 'One thing they ain't tellin' you for all the sign o' the cross you keep mekin' . . . they ain't tellin' you Bridie Trow is an angel nor ever likely to be!'

'That's where you be wrong altogether, so you be.' Bridie's native brogue thickened. 'If oi'm not after bein' an angel when oi'm dead it would be meanin' oi was to spend the rest of me after loif with the loikes of you – an' the good Lord will never be permittin' the loike of that.'

'And what is it the good Lord will not permit?'

The women's smiles faded as Agnes Marsh halted her patrol at their end of the long table.

Bridie, eyes still malignant, half turned on the bench seat. 'Nellie Bladen was after sayin' that oi'll be livin' wi' the loike of herself after oi be dead.'

'Well, you both have one consolation.' The wardress smiled spitefully. 'After you've finished in Handsworth you'll be used to each other . . . and to the place you'll both finish up in when you're dead. Now get this lot cleared and get ready for lights out or you might be wishing yourselves there now.'

'Sour-faced cow!' Nellie muttered, watching the wardress move down the room toward its one door. 'I know what 'er could do with.'

'An' p'raps you would like to tell 'er,' Liza Spittle dropped the apron she had been mending into the large basket set beside the table, 'to 'er face.'

'Why don't you when you am doin' it wi' 'er in the store room, you dirty bugger. Don't think we don't know what goes on in there.'

'It don't bother me what you think, none of you, I'll do what it teks to get by in this place.'

'An' that means mauling the tits off any woman who'll let you an' a few that's bin too frightened to refuse.' Martha Ames dropped her own mending into the basket then turned a disdainful glance on Liza. 'Yer nothing but a filthy swine, Liza Spittle, no wonder the Devil marked you one of his'n.'

'You still didn't tell me what a Psalterer was?' Nellie Bladen whispered to Phoebe as they left the dining hall.

'It is a book of Psalms.'

'A book! But you can't sew a book, Phoebe.'

'No, of course I can't.' She smiled, following Nellie out of the dining hall. 'What Mary should have said was that I am embroidering covers for Psalters.'

'Trust Mary Pegleg to get it wrong.' Nellie turned toward

the washroom. 'That woman couldn't get anythin' right, not if 'Ell fetched 'er.'

Soaping her hands and face with carbolic, Phoebe thought of the events of the morning. Hannah Price had sent for her, asking that she make two Psalter covers. She wanted them as a gift for the Vicar of St James's church in Wednesbury. Now Phoebe felt the same tug at her stomach she had felt when the Governess told her of her visit to a friend she had in the town. How long before *she* could visit friends? Phoebe buried her face in the rough cotton that served the prisoners as towels. She knew how long . . . fifteen years.

Phoebe stared at the familiar rectangles of moonlight, her brain refusing her the sanctuary of sleep. She had thought her troubles were ending when Lucy gave her the jewellery. If only she had known . . . her troubles were just beginning.

She had pawned a ruby ring first, choosing to take it to John Kilvert, the pawnbroker who had sold her the furniture, hoping to redeem it in a few weeks.

What a hope! Phoebe turned her face to the wall, finding no solace in the well of shadows.

The ring had been followed by a marcasite brooch and that by a cornelian bracelet. One by one the pieces had gone, John Kilvert giving her a fraction of their worth and that fraction swallowed by the purchase of food and the small amount of cotton she bought to make garments to sell, garments that brought her even less than her jewellery. Finally it was her grandmother's sapphire necklace. John Kilvert's eyes had glowed when she unwrapped it from her handkerchief and laid it on his counter. He had scrutinised it carefully then said, 'Two pounds ten, tek it or leave it.'

She had had to take it as the pawnbroker well knew. Two pounds ten shillings . . . careful as she had desperately tried to be, it had lasted less than six weeks.

Too proud to tell Sarah and Joseph of her circumstances, she had agreed to go with them to the Advent Fayre one

Saturday evening. 'The gentry will be there,' Sarah had said, 'mebbe they might buy some of your petticoats. Heaven knows they'm pretty enough.'

Only she had no material to sew petticoats and no money to buy more. But she would be expected to take something that could be sold to benefit the church. She hadn't thought about her two dresses until she went to bed. The next morning she had chosen the white one sprigged with tiny red flowers and carefully taken it to pieces, using the cloth to make two dresses for a child, trimming one with red ribbons and the other with pink.

Standing behind the stall allotted to her and Sarah Leach, Phoebe had seen Montrose's mother sweep into the market place and saw the doffed caps and bobbed curtsies of the townsfolk as the woman and her companions halted a few moments at each stall. Maybe they would pass her and Sarah by, maybe Violet Wheeler would not recognise her in the flickering light of candles set in jars, but even as she pressed into the shadows Phoebe knew it would not happen.

'Mama, look, how delightful.'

The two women and a girl Phoebe guessed to be around her own age paused at her stall, the cold November breeze fluttering the feathers of their bonnets.

'Look, Mama.' The girl touched a gloved hand to the dresses Phoebe had made. 'Don't you think they are pretty?'

'I do, my dear.' Lady Dartmouth smiled at her daughter then asked, 'Who made these?'

'I did, Your Ladyship,' Phoebe answered, aware of the warning in Violet Wheeler's eyes.

'They are very pretty and well stitched.' Lady Dartmouth held one of the dresses closer to the lighted candles. 'Don't you agree, Mrs Wheeler?'

Montrose's mother made a pretence of examining the stitches. 'Yes,' she answered, already turning in the direction of the next stall, 'quite.'

'Mama,' the girl picked up the second dress, 'do you not think these would make the most admirable Christmas gifts for the children of the servants? You know how much you enjoy the giving of something useful.'

'They would indeed be admirable, my dear, always provided the children are not boys, eh, Mrs Wheeler?'

Forced to turn back Violet Wheeler managed an acid smile. 'As you say, Your Ladyship, useful only if they are not boys.'

'Tell me,' Lady Dartmouth returned her hand to the warmth of her fur muff, 'have you more of these?'

Phoebe shook her head. 'No, Your Ladyship.'

'Pity.' Lady Dartmouth made to move on but her daughter stayed.

'But you could make more.' The girl's cheeks glowed red in the cold of the November night. 'How many could you make before Christmas?'

'Two would be all I had cloth for.' Phoebe avoided the glare of Violet Wheeler. 'You see, Your Ladyship, I made those from a gown of my own and I have only one more.'

'You mean you made something as pretty as this out of an old gown?'

Not so old, Phoebe thought, that particular dress had been a gift from her father on her last birthday.

'Then there is no problem.' The girl turned to her mother. 'I have lots of dresses I do not wear any more. I may give them to be used may I not, Mama?'

'Of course, Sophie,' Lady Dartmouth nodded, 'that is a very good suggestion.' Then turning her glance on Phoebe added, 'My daughter and I will be returning to the Manor on Thursday of this week. You may call whenever my daughter wishes.'

'Oh, come the next afternoon.' The girl turned to Montrose's mother. 'I'm sure you too will find a few dresses for such a worthy cause, Mrs Wheeler. After all, the proceeds will go to the church, so when may she call upon you?'

Even in the darkness of the November evening Phoebe saw the colour drain from the woman's face. 'I . . . she . . . she may call Thursday afternoon of this week at three o'clock.'

'So,' Lady Dartmouth was clearly to be delayed no longer, 'bring the dresses to the Manor one day before Christmas Eve. I will send a list of how many and what sizes to the Vicar.' She turned to her daughter. 'And now, Sophie, I insist on returning to Oakeswell Hall, this night air is much too cold for either of us.'

'Looks like Violet Wheeler 'as designs, invitin' 'er Ladyship to Oakeswell.' Sarah Leach watched the departing trio.

'Designs,' Phoebe breathed, relieved when the carriage drove away, 'how do you mean?'

'Mean!' Sarah handed over a pot of her preserve, taking a threepenny piece and handing back a penny and a halfpenny to a woman with five children hanging on her skirts. 'A man wi' half an eye can see what I mean. Violet Wheeler 'as set 'er sights on that young un for 'er lad.'

'You can't mean . . .'

'I can an' I do,' Sarah said. 'That woman intends for 'er son to wed Lady Sophie, daughter of Sir William and Lady Amelia Dartmouth of Sandwell Priory.'

Phoebe remembered the feeling that coursed through her then; it wasn't pain, no, she couldn't call it pain, it was more like pity . . . pity for a young girl being prepared like a lamb for the slaughter.

She had gone to Oakeswell Hall at the appointed time to find a servant waiting for her at the gate, the dresses, two of them, draped across her arms. Phoebe Pardoe was not to be admitted even to the grounds of her former fiancé's home.

The visit to Sandwell Priory had been so different. Phoebe turned her eyes back to the greyish-yellow rectangles high up on the wall. She had looked down from the ridge of high ground on to the house nestling in the valley, its tall windows reflecting the pale watery November sunlight, windows that seemed to go on and on along the expanse of the huge building. Brunswick House was by no means small but it would fit a hundred times over into that house. She had stared until a flurry of snow blew across her face then set off down the path to the valley. A mile or so further on she had stepped aside, hearing the rumble of an approaching carriage.

'It is you, isn't it?' Lady Sophie leaned from the window, calling for the carriage to stop. 'You are the girl I spoke to at the Fayre, are you not? The girl who is to call today?'

'I am, Your Ladyship.' Phoebe bobbed a curtsy.

'Edward,' she went on to someone in the carriage, 'this is the girl I told you about, the one who makes such delightfully pretty dresses.'

The carriage door had opened then and a tall blond man of about twenty or so had jumped out.

'Forgive my sister,' he said, 'it is a failing of hers to keep people standing in the cold.' He smiled, a smile that lit deep blue eyes. 'Allow me to assist you into the carriage?'

'No.' Phoebe took a step backward. 'No, thank you, I . . . I'll walk.'

'Nonsense.' The man smiled again. 'I will not hear of such a thing, the day is far too cold. And besides,' he held out a hand, 'it is coming on to snow.'

'Of course you must ride with us.' Lady Sophie added her smile and voice to her brother's. 'There is plenty of room.'

Phoebe had made no more demur, accepting the man's hand as she climbed into the carriage.

'My sister told me of meeting you but she failed to tell me your name?'

Across the carriage the blue eyes had smiled deep into hers.

'My name is Phoebe . . . Phoebe Pardoe.'

'How do you do, Phoebe?' He said her name slowly as if wanting to hold it in his mouth, to keep it inside of him, a part of himself.

'My sister you have met already, allow me to present myself – Edward Dartmouth.'

He had introduced himself simply. Phoebe knew he was Edward Albert Richard Dartmouth whose family had owned the Priory for nearly five hundred years, but he had given himself no airs and graces.

At the Priory Sophie had heaped dresses into her arms, their colours mixing like some exotic rainbow, then laughed as Phoebe gradually disappeared beneath them.

She had not seen Lady Dartmouth, Sophie apologising for her absence, explaining that her mother's evening visit to the market had given her a chill. 'Poor Mama,' Sophie had laughed. 'She says the things she does for the church should guarantee her a healthy eternity, though she does wish it would do the same for her earthly existence.'

Four maids had eventually carried the dresses down the great staircase. Phoebe watched for a glimpse of Lucy as they passed but she was not among the servants who crossed the vast marble hall and down a wide fan of steps to the carriage Sophie insisted Phoebe should travel home in. Edward stood beside it.

'I could not forgive myself should I let you go home alone.' He had helped her into the carriage then, his eyes never leaving her face. Phoebe had not wanted him to accompany her, ashamed for him to see her dilapidated home and the tumbling outhouses, but once there he had kept her hand in his while the coachman carried the dresses indoors. 'You must allow me to call you Phoebe,' he had said softly. 'Please tell me I may?'

Phoebe closed her eyes but the face of Edward Dartmouth was printed on the lids. A handsome face, a face with more than admiration revealed in those deep blue eyes.

Lucy had been at Wiggins Mill one day when Edward paid a visit, one of many since Phoebe's going to Sandwell Priory.

'You wants to be careful, Miss.' Phoebe remembered Lucy's warning. 'Could be 'e's here after more than you should give 'im.'

'He's a friend, Lucy.'

'There's friends and friends.' Lucy's reply had been tempered with the same warning. 'The sons of gentry is no friend to the likes of us, Miss. Not unless they want a special sort of friendship. You take a tip from me an' tell 'im not to call 'ere no more.'

But Edward had not tried to take advantage of her. He had been so courteous and yet so full of life, insisting on her going out for walks along the canal bank, teaching her to skim stones across the water, piling logs on to the fire then sitting at her feet as she sewed. She had known he loved her, known even before he told her. In the darkness of the quiet dormitory, Phoebe remembered.

Samuel Pardoe put down his brush, turning from his latest landscape painting. 'It has been a year now since Abel died.' He spelled out the words on his fingers as he had been taught in childhood. 'It seems so very long, Annie.'

Annie Pardoe watched the brother she had lived with all of his fifty-two years. He had always been slight of build even as a child but of late had become markedly more frail, seeming to dwindle into himself, fading a little more each day.

'Twelve months is a long time,' she signed in return, 'but there it is. Abel is gone and we must learn to live with the fact.'

'But Phoebe is not gone,' Samuel's fingers moved quickly, 'yet we have not seen her since her father died. Why is that, Annie? Why does Phoebe not come to see us?'

'I told you, Samuel . . .' Annie walked to the window of the room that had been turned into a studio for her brother, avoiding the need to look into the face that was so like that of Abel, then after a moment turned to sign: 'Phoebe said she never wanted to see either of us again.'

'But I think perhaps if we went to see her . . .'

'No, Samuel!' Annie Pardoe signed rapidly then dropped one hand to her side as if the movement gave her pain. 'We will not go to see her. She made the decision to leave this house, hers was the choice and we must abide by it. If it be that she changes her mind then she will be welcome to return. Until that time we will have to wait and pray.'

Samuel applied another touch of paint to the canvas, his thin hand almost transparent, then signed again. 'I wonder why Abel left everything to us? It seems so very strange.'

'I see nothing strange in a man entrusting his business and property to someone old enough and wise enough to look after it.' Annie breathed deeply, holding her hand tight against the spot beneath her rib cage, then released it to sign, 'Phoebe was very young. Abel thought we would be the better guardian of what was his until she married.'

'The better guardian of what was his . . .' Samuel left off painting. 'Phoebe was his but he did not name either of us her guardian, did he, Annie?' His eyes reflected a sadness he could not voice.

'Our brother did not appoint anyone as guardian to his daughter,' Annie crossed to the door, 'simply because he thought to see her married long before he died. I have called to see our niece several times, Samuel, hoping to persuade her to come and live with us, but each time I have been met with hostility. It hurts us both to know that she has cut herself off from her family, those who have loved her from her birth, but we cannot force her to come home, my dear.'

'Annie,' Samuel signed as she opened the door, 'what happened to the idea of her marrying Gaskell Wheeler's son?'

She hesitated, the hand on her ribs pressing a little harder, then, 'I'm afraid she took the same headstrong, foolish action she took toward us,' she answered. 'She said she had been pressured into accepting Montrose Wheeler against her will, and now her father was no longer here to enforce the marriage, she would not do so. The Wheelers were understandably upset but agreed to say that following the unforeseen death of her father, Phoebe felt she could not marry so soon, therefore a postponement had taken place.'

'Is she alone?' Samuel's fingers fluttered like wounded butterflies.

Annie looked into the thin face and sad grey eyes of her brother and the pain beneath her hand worsened. It had not been his fault, he was not to blame for what fate had ordained for him or the life Abel Pardoe had ordained for her – he was not to blame yet she could not forgive him.

'No, she is not alone.' Her answer was sharpened by the pain. 'Abel's housekeeper went with her and so did her maid. They are all well cared for, I instructed Lawyer Siveter to pay an annual allowance. Phoebe might have turned her back on us, Samuel, but we will never turn ours upon her.'

Leaving the room before he could ask any more questions, Annie paused outside the door, her eyes closed, her hand pressed to the pain that refused to be ignored. Samuel had asked the same questions before and she had told the same lies.

Opening her eyes she walked to her bedroom, taking a small cardboard box from a drawer in the table that stood beside the heavy fourposter bed. Abel had slept in that bed, Abel and his pretty wife; so many nights, so much happiness. Taking the lid from the box, she put two of the white tablets it held into her mouth, swallowing them with water from the carafe on the table. Yes, Abel had shared this bed, this room with a wife while she . . . what had she had . . . what love had Annie Pardoe known, whose bed had she shared?

Putting the lid back on the box, she replaced it in the drawer, covering it with a layer of lace-edged handkerchiefs.

She had shared neither love nor bed with any man thanks to her brother. Abel could never be made to pay while he was living and death had carried him beyond her reach. No, Abel would not pay for a life he'd snatched away, a life he had destroyed so he could live his own. But Abel's daughter would . . .

Is she alone?

Samuel's question echoed in her mind, and in her mind she answered but this time with all the truth of vengeance. No, Phoebe was not alone. Some two hundred women shared her home, a home she would inhabit for the next fifteen years.

'Well, if it ain't the Governess's little pet.'

Liza Spittle's narrow eyes watched Phoebe coming along the corridor that led to the kitchens, a tray balanced in her hands. 'Ain't you goin' to stop an' 'ave a chat wi' Liza?'

'Move out the way, Liza,' Phoebe said as the other woman moved her large frame, blocking the narrow passage. 'You know prisoners must not hang around the corridors.'

'There's a lot of things not allowed in this bloody place,' Liza grinned, showing discoloured teeth, 'but the bastards 'ave to catch you at it first.'

'I have no wish to be caught,' Phoebe edged to one side in an attempt to pass, 'especially talking to you.'

'We don't 'ave to talk.' Liza stepped closer, the beetroot mark pulsing like some living thing on her cheek. 'You don't need to talk for what I want.'

'Liza, please move.' Phoebe was becoming alarmed. Why wasn't Liza in the laundry?

'Lucky me, bein' given the job of clearin' dinner plates,' she grinned as if answering Phoebe's unspoken question, 'otherwise we wouldn't 'ave this chance.'

'Chance?' Phoebe tried to control her trembling. She knew Liza Spittle had not given up in her twisted desire and for that reason took care never to be in her company without Bridie or Tilly.

Liza stepped forward again, wedging Phoebe against the wall. 'The chance for me to show you what you missed 'cos of that interferin' bitch Tilly Wood.' She leaned forward, pressing the tray into Phoebe's middle, her hand lifting the skirts of Phoebe's prison uniform, sliding high up over her thigh.

'Leave me alone!' Phoebe tried to use the tray in an effort to push the woman away from her, turning her face from the sour fumes of her breath. 'Please, for God's sake, don't!'

Liza laughed, a husky sound deep in her throat. 'They all says that first time.' Her voice was deep as a man's, her mouth touching the side of Phoebe's neck. 'But then it changes – it changes to, for God's sake, please do.'

'Stop!' Phoebe's cry cracked on a sob. 'Please, I . . . I'm not like that . . .'

'You will be.' Liza's tongue licked upward against Phoebe's ear, her hand moving toward the vee between her legs. 'You will be when Liza gets through.'

'No, please.' Phoebe's control had gone, the tears spilling down her cheeks. 'Please leave me alone. Please, for God's sake!'

'If you won't do it for God, then do it for me!'

Tilly Wood's voice rang out behind Liza as she was swung away, one arm twisted high up her back.

'I warned you,' Tilly snarled, her gaunt face twisted with contempt. 'I warned you afore, Tilly Wood tells not even the Lord 'imself twice . . .'

Grabbing the collar of Liza's grey calico frock, she spun her backward against the opposite wall.

'. . . but you don't tek a tellin', do you, Liza Spittle?'

Tilly struck out, the back of her hand slamming hard across Liza's face.

'. . . so yer goin' to 'ave to be shown that 'ands off means what it says.'

Across the narrow corridor Liza's small eyes glittered with a feral light as they flicked from Tilly to Phoebe then back to Tilly. 'I'm goin' to do fer you, Tilly Wood,' she breathed, wiping the blood from her mouth with the back of a hand. 'This time I'm goin' to kill you.'

She lunged forward, her large masculine frame threatening to obliterate Tilly who turned aside, thrusting a foot in her way. Liza stumbled but the force of her attack carried her forward, the sickening crunch of bone against brick covering Phoebe's sobs as she hit the wall beside her. Then Liza was falling, slipping sideways as she went down, her cracked skull sliding slowly over Phoebe's shoulder and breast, down along her skirt, trailing a long slow smear of red across grey.

'What did the Governess 'ave to say about it?' Martha Ames asked as the women prepared for the nine o'clock light out.

'I couldn't 'ear all that well,' Mary Pegleg answered. 'But 'er sent me to get Agnes Marsh an' that one looked none too 'appy when 'er went into the Governess's office, an' 'er looked a damn' sight less when 'er come out again.'

'But sure an' you must have heard somethin'?' Bridie said, slipping her nightgown over her head then folding the drab grey prison dress before placing it regulation fashion across the foot of her low iron bed.

Mary Pegleg unfastened the straps that held the wooden stump below her left knee, balancing it against the wall beside her bed. 'Well, I 'eard 'er tell Agnes as 'ow this was the first prison to 'ave a woman in charge an' that it would only tek summat like a brawl between the inmates to convince the Board that a woman wasn't fit for the job an' that 'er would be replaced wi' a man.'

'Sure an' that would be a black day for all,' Bridie said, buttoning her nightgown. 'Hannah Price has been fair in her dealin's with us women an' all. Could be we might have had a Governess the loike of Steel Arsed Sally Moreton, God rest her puir soul.'

'Did 'er say anythin' about Tilly?' Nellie Bladen looked across to Phoebe, sitting silent on her bed, her face pale and empty, then whispered, 'Is 'er still locked away on 'er own?'

Mary Pegleg rubbed a hand over the rounded nub of bone where her leg had been amputated. 'I 'eard summat about police, but I don't know if Governess said 'er was sendin' fer 'em or keepin' thing quiet from 'em.'

'Get the bobbies in 'ere an' it'll be more than Hannah Price will be teken out.' Martha Ames looked from one to the other of the women, their faces mirroring the tension that had held them all afternoon and evening. 'We'll all go, an' there's some of us in 'ere knows where to. 'Ell itself would be a better place.'

'Do you think Liza will die?' Nellie's normally yellow skin took on a deathly gleam under the sullen glow of the one gaslamp.

''Er looked near enough to it when we carried 'er to the infirmary,' Martha answered. 'Reckon 'er'll be lucky to last the night.'

'Holy Mother of God!' Bridie's hand lifted, making the sign of the cross several times in rapid succession.

'Did Agnes Marsh send fer the doctor, does anybody know?'

''Er couldn't.' Mary Pegleg eased her thin body into her bed, covering it with the one rough blanket before answering the question. ''Er 'ad to wait till Hannah Price got back from meeting with the Board an' that wasn't till after seven o'clock gone. 'Er said it was too late to get the doctor out then, that it would 'ave to wait till mornin'.'

'Too late my arse!' Martha spat. 'What 'er meant was the bloody doctor was too blind drunk by that time of the night even to stand up, let alone treat anybody.'

'Well, whatever 'er meant, 'er didn't send fer 'im,' Mary Pegleg stated flatly.

'Oi wonder what he will be makin' of it when he does come?' Bridie said.

'I don't know,' Martha shook her head, 'but this much I can say – drunk or sober there be no way 'e can call this a 'eart attack.'

'What will 'e call it . . . will it be murder?'

'Liza Spittle ain't dead,' Martha shot a glance at Phoebe but Nellie's words seemed to have passed over her head, 'so 'ow can 'e call what 'appened murder?'

Crossing to Phoebe's bed she pressed her back on the pillow, pulling the coarse blanket up to her chin before going back to her own place.

'But what if Liza do die?' Nellie persisted.

'If 'er does then any tears I shed won't be for 'er,' Martha said acridly. ''Er was nothin' but a filthy bitch sniffin' round women, 'er 'ad it comin' to 'er an' I fer one ain't sorry as 'er's copped it. The one I'm sorry fer is Tilly Wood.'

'What's goin' to 'appen to Tilly would you say, Martha?'

'Lord knows!' She looked at the other woman, death marked plain across her thin consumptive features. 'Depends on what the doctor and the Governess 'as ter say ter the Prison Board.'

Bridie crossed herself fervently. 'Then may the sweet Mother o'Jesus be puttin' the words into their mouths.'

Chapter Five

Phoebe lay awake in the hard narrow bed. She had not spoken since the affair in the corridor, she had not joined the discussions of the women, her mind empty, somehow detached, hearing nothing yet registering everything.

Tilly had offered no resistance when Agnes Marsh ordered two wardresses to take her away, only the eyes that had long forgotten laughter staying on Phoebe's face as they took her. What would they do to Tilly? She was already serving a life sentence for manslaughter . . . if Liza Spittle died Tilly would be accused of murder and it was certain she would hang. But she was no murderer; she had told Sally Moreton a lie about snapping her husband's neck to frighten her, it was the push down the stairs had broken it. No, Tilly Wood was not quite guilty of murder . . . yet.

Oh Lord! In the darkness, listening to the breathing of the sleeping women and the consumptive coughing of Nellie Biaden, Phoebe prayed, 'Oh Lord, don't let Liza die.'

High on the wall the windows showed a paler shade of darkness. Why was I sent to return that tray to the kitchen? Why was Liza Spittle clearing the dinner plates? Why was she in the corridor at that precise moment? Why was there no one else clearing the dining hall?

Questions vied for prominence in her brain. Lord, if only her father had not met with that terrible accident, if only her Aunt Annie had not acted as she had, if only she had never made those children's dresses, Lord if only . . . but how often had the Lord heard those words?

Above her the small rectangular windows lightened with infinite slowness, like lids lifting to reveal strange hypnotic eyes, and she turned her head away. But out of the shadows Lucy danced towards her, Lucy with eyes glowing and lips smiling.

'I'm getting wed.'

Phoebe heard the laughing happy voice rise from the depths of buried thoughts. 'Mathew an' me, we are goin' to be wed.'

Phoebe had joined in the girl's delight, returning the hug Lucy enfolded her in. They had talked a long time in the kitchen of the mill house, Lucy baking scones and mixing an amount of bread dough Phoebe thought must last a year at least, then she had asked about a wedding dress.

'I hadn't thought about it,' Lucy answered, setting the cloth-covered dough to rise besides the hearth. 'Well, not really thought about it, though I would like somethin' nice, somethin' new, I suppose, if the truth be told. But that's out of the question on what I get paid at the Priory.'

'And Mathew?' Phoebe had asked.

'Can't really ask him to sport me a dress from the money he makes, Miss Phoebe.' Lucy collected wooden mixing spoons, dropping them into the large brown earthenware bowl. 'Mathew had his wages docked same as the rest of 'em at the pit.'

'Docked?' Phoebe remembered the surprise she felt, but had it been surprise or disgust? 'Do you mean my aunt has reduced the wages of the men working at the mine?'

'Yes, Miss Phoebe, I do,' Lucy answered. 'Both of 'em, the Hobs Hill pit and the Crown mine at Moxley, and the folks who depend on it am feelin' the pinch real bad.'

'But why?' Phoebe asked. 'For what reason?'

'Annie Pardoe said as how price of coal had fallen an' men could take lower wages or take their hook.'

'She said that!'

'Well, not in them exact words.' Lucy carried the utensils

she had used in her baking to the long shallow sink in the scullery, returning for the kettle singing softly over the fire. 'But that was what 'er meant: the men could either accept a lower wage for a day's work or they could leave the pit altogether. And as you know, Miss Phoebe, that would leave them without a home as well as a job 'cos most houses in Wednesbury belong to Annie Pardoe, least at that end of the town they do.'

Phoebe might have asked what part her uncle had played in all of this but deep down she knew Samuel would know nothing of it.

'Mind you,' Lucy carried the kettle into the scullery, pouring hot water over a bowl and spoons then putting the kettle aside to be filled later at the pump in the yard, 'some of 'em couldn't be much worse off if they did leave. They 'ave little enough in their tins to feed a family *and* pay rent, and Annie Pardoe ain't one to let rent man call twice and get nothin', so some of the women an' kids am goin' more than hungry.'

'What of Joseph and Sarah?' Phoebe reached for a cloth to dry the dishes but it hung forgotten in her hands.

Lucy placed the freshly washed baking bowl on the wooden board Mathew had made to stand beside the sink. 'They are fairin' up to now though Joseph had his wage docked same as others, but they only manage 'cos Sarah can do most things herself.'

Sarah was a marvel, Phoebe thought, cook, housekeeper and gardener rolled into one, growing vegetables Joseph could no longer tend after the accident that had left him lame. But how long could she manage now money was short?

'So how will you and Mathew be fixed with him not earning as much?'

'It's going to be harder.' Lucy took the cloth from Phoebe and set about drying the bowls and spoons. 'There be no use in my denyin' that, but I'll have my position at the Priory and Mathew will 'ave his job at Hobs Hill. We can afford to rent a little house . . . just.'

'But you said yourself the wage at the pits had been reduced and what if you start a family? They won't keep you on at the Priory if you have children to care for. And if the situation at the pit gets any worse . . .'

'We've thought of that, Miss Phoebe, and we both know that if we wait for things to be perfect we will never be wed so we decided to go ahead. There will be hard times and worry for us whether we wed or not so we have little to lose except each other.'

Why had her aunt reduced the wages of the miners? Had the market price for coal really dropped or was there some other reason for her action? Phoebe picked up the bowls and spoons, carrying them back into the kitchen, replacing them on the rough wooden dresser set along one wall. Could it in some way have anything to do with her aunt's obvious dislike of Phoebe herself?

'So when will you and Mathew be married?' she asked as Lucy bustled into the kitchen, setting the freshly filled kettle over the glowing coals.

'Next month, the fifteenth,' Lucy's face radiated her joy, 'that's my birthday. Mathew said to have the wedding on that day then we would have two things to be happy for. Ooh, I am looking forward to it.'

Just as I was looking forward to my own wedding, Phoebe thought, watching the happiness light the other girl's eyes, only mine never took place.

'We want the ceremony to be at St Bart's.' Lucy lifted the bread dough on to the table, scoring it with a knife before placing it in the oven to bake. 'Just family and a few friends. We both hoped you would come, Miss? It won't be grand or anything.'

'I'm hardly grand myself, Lucy,' Phoebe smiled at the half apology, 'and I would like to come very much.'

'Would you?' Lucy placed the cooled scones on to a prettily flowered plate, embarrassment touching her cheeks with pink. 'I mean, could . . . ?'

'Would I . . . could I what?' Phoebe laughed.

'Well, Miss, me and Mathew thought . . . we hoped you might be my attendant.'

'Bridesmaid!' Phoebe grabbed the young girl, hugging her. 'Lucy, I would be absolutely delighted, and I think I have something upstairs you might be delighted with too.'

Holding on to Lucy's hand, Phoebe raced through the sitting room and up the stairs to a bedroom draped with the dresses Sophie had given her and which as yet she had not taken to pieces to make up into garments for children.

'What about one of these for a wedding dress?' she asked.

Lucy stood quite still, her eyes wide. 'You mean . . . you mean I could have one of these . . . to keep?'

'Of course to keep,' Phoebe laughed. 'Try them, I'm sure they will fit. You and Sophie are much the same size, and if need be we can soon make a few adjustments.'

'Which one?' Lucy stepped forward, touching first one and then another of the dresses. 'Which one can I try?'

'Try them all.' Phoebe snatched up a blue muslin gown trimmed with silk forget-me-nots, pressing it into Lucy's hands. 'And take whichever you wish.'

'Ooh, Miss Phoebe,' Lucy held the gown almost reverently, her eyes playing over the others, 'do you think I should?'

'No, I do not think you should!' Phoebe answered emphatically. 'I *know* you should. Now get out of that skirt and blouse and try every one of those dresses.'

Trying the blue gown, Lucy preened before a long cheval mirror that had come from Kilvert's pawn shop, then discarded it for one of pale creamy yellow, the skirt caught around the hem in half hoops of yellow tea roses.

'That looks lovely, Lucy,' Phoebe said, scooping up the girl's dark hair into a yellow silk ribbon, 'and we could make some silk rose-buds to dress your hair. The whole effect would be marvellous.'

'Oh, I do like it, Miss Phoebe,' Lucy breathed, touching a hand to the high waist, 'it's so pretty.'

'Then it's yours,' Phoebe smiled.

'But what if Miss Sophie should see me?' Lucy turned, her eyes filled with concern. 'Wouldn't 'er get mad seein' as how 'er give you these to make kids' frocks?'

Phoebe knelt, smoothing the creamy folds about Lucy's feet. 'I really don't expect the Dartmouths to turn up at Wednesbury Parish Church to witness the marriage of Mr Mathew Leach to Miss Lucy Baines, even though she'll be the prettiest bride in the country. And even if they should, I'm sure Miss Sophie would be delighted you chose to wear her gift on the most special day of your life.'

'Then if you be sure, Miss, I think I would like it to be this one. Only . . .'

'Only what?' Phoebe stood up.

'Only it do seem a shame not to try them others on, I'll not be gettin' another chance to wear such frocks!' Lucy grinned.

'And I will not be getting another chance to rescue the bread from burning.' Phoebe sniffed then dashed out of the bedroom. 'You carry on,' she called, hurrying downstairs to the kitchen, 'I'll be back in a minute.'

'Am the loaves all right, Miss?' Lucy asked when Phoebe returned a few minutes later.

'They look delicious. You are so good at cooking, Lucy.'

'Like you with sewing, Miss.' Lucy paraded a pale green sprigged dress. 'Those little frocks you've made for the kids look real pretty, I reckon Lady Dartmouth will be right pleased wi' them.'

'I hope I can get them all done in time for Christmas.' Phoebe helped to extricate Lucy from the swathes of pale green. 'There are more than I had expected.'

'Then you mustn't use your time making rose-buds or nothin' for my wedding frock,' Lucy mumbled from beneath layers of muslin.

'I shall make just as many rose-buds as it takes, Lucy Baines.' Phoebe took the dress, draping it across a chair.

'And anything else we think is necessary to make your day perfect.'

'P'raps I can 'elp, on my day off? I ain't much wi' a needle but I'm willing to try.'

'You already help enough, Lucy, I don't know how I would manage without your coming here. Sarah and Miriam tried hard to teach me to cook but I am still not very good, I'm afraid, so your help in that department is invaluable.'

'Mathew says my scones are as good as his mother's.' Lucy beamed.

'And Mathew is right.' Phoebe draped the green dress higher on the chair, leaving its folds free of the floor. 'Their only drawback being you want to go on eating them and that is not so good for a girl's shape.'

'Eeh, Miss, you need 'ave no worries in that direction.' Standing in white frilled bloomers and chemise, Lucy looked at her former employer. 'It might not be my place to say it but I reckon as you could be doin' wi' a bit more meat on your bones. You be gettin' to look right scrawny, beggin' your pardon.'

'Well, all that delicious bread of yours will soon remedy that.' Phoebe picked up the last of the dresses Sophie had given her and one which Lucy had so far refrained from touching. 'Now, Miss Lucy, I think you should try this on.'

Lucy looked at the gown, its folds streaming to the floor like a jade waterfall. 'Ooh, no, I couldn't, not that one . . . it's much too grand.'

'Nonsense.' Phoebe held it out. 'I agree it might not be as suitable to your colouring as the yellow but try it anyway. You will never know unless you try.'

'I . . . I don't think I should . . .' Lucy hesitated, a longing to feel the rich taffeta against her skin pulling her one way; a reluctance to dare try anything so grand and costly pulling her in the opposite direction.

'Oh, come on, Lucy.' Phoebe held out the dress, its fabric gleaming in the wintry sunlight, entering the tiny window sheltered by the eaves. 'Where is your sense of adventure?'

'Well, if you say so.' Lucy held up her arms for Phoebe to slip the gown over her head. 'Though I don't think it's goin' to suit me.'

'We will see.' Phoebe pulled the heavy fabric down over Lucy's shoulders then stopped as the girl cried out.

'It's somethin' in the frock,' she said, pushing the gown right down to the floor and stepping out of it. 'Somethin' cold and . . . and . . .'

'And what?' Phoebe put an arm around the frightened girl, leading her away from the dress folded in upon itself like a green island on the bare wooden floor.

'I don't know,' Lucy answered shakily, 'it . . . it felt cold and . . . and hard . . . across my chest.'

Phoebe stared at the mound of taffeta. She couldn't just leave it, she had to find out what it was lying coiled inside that dress.

'Stay here.' She pushed Lucy into the open doorway of the bedroom then, her own heart thumping, walked back to where the gown lay heaped.

'Eeh, don't touch it, Miss,' Lucy said, fear making her voice sound hollow, 'don't touch it!'

'Don't be silly, Lucy, it's probably nothing more than a dressmaker's pin that has been overlooked.' Sounding far more confident than she felt, Phoebe reached for the gown. Teeth gripped together she shook the material, then as nothing happened, lifted the dress, holding it at arm's length.

'Eeh, I could 'ave sworn there was somethin' in that frock,' Lucy said, courage returning sufficiently for her to step back inside the bedroom. 'I could swear I felt somethin'.'

'Well, let us look.' Phoebe laid the taffeta gown atop the pale green muslin draped over the room's one chair.

'I'll look.' Lucy came to stand beside her. 'I know whereabouts it was.'

Opening the bodice wide, she examined the inside of it. 'Oh my Good God!' she exclaimed, drawing back as though from the hand of death. 'Oh my Good God, will you look at that!'

'I want you to tell me exactly what happened.' The Governess of Handsworth Prison for Women looked at the thin figure of the girl standing in front of her desk. 'You were in the corridor at the time Liza Spittle was injured, were you not?'

'Yes, Ma'am,' Phoebe answered, her voice little more than a whisper.

'What were you doing there?'

Phoebe looked across the desk at the woman she knew held Tilly's life in her hands. 'I was returning a lunch tray to the kitchen, Liza blocked my way, she would not move when I asked her to let me pass . . . then . . . then she tried to force herself upon me.'

'She tried to do what?' The Governess's face blanched, her mouth pinched with disgust. 'Are you telling me Liza Spittle tried to behave like . . . like a man?'

'Yes, Ma'am,' Phoebe whispered, looking down at her feet. 'It happened once before and Tilly Wood helped me then.'

'As she did yesterday?' The Governess spoke as though she held a bad taste in her mouth. 'Tell me, Pardoe, where were the wardresses whilst all of this was going on?'

'Mrs Marsh accompanied me almost to the kitchens,' Phoebe lied, aware of Agnes Marsh standing just behind her, aware also that the woman had been asleep in her room instead of being on duty and knowing that to say so would bring vengeance not only upon herself but also on Tilly and the others. 'Then we heard the noise of a bucket being dropped on the stairs and she went to see what had happened.'

The Governess raised an enquiring glance to the wardress.

'It was one of the new intake, Ma'am,' Agnes Marsh took up the lie. 'She was scrubbing the top landing and knocked over the bucket, sending it down the stairs. I stayed to see to her mopping up before anybody could slip on the wet stairs, then I saw to her getting fresh water and soda to start again, and when I got to go to the kitchen Liza Spittle was lying unconscious in the corridor.'

'I see.' The Governess returned to Phoebe. 'You say Tilly Wood helped you? How come she was in that part of the building and not in the laundry?'

'I checked on that, Ma'am,' Agnes Marsh put in swiftly. 'She'd been sent to fetch the cooking cloths and towels from the kitchens ready for the afternoon wash.'

'Allow Pardoe to answer my next question,' Hannah Price answered coldly. 'Tell me, what assistance did Wood give?'

Phoebe swallowed hard, her eyes still on her shoes. Please God, help me to answer without making things worse for Tilly, she thought. Don't let me put her in greater danger than she is in now.

'She pulled Liza away, then when Liza tried to attack her, stepped aside. Liza crashed her head into the wall. It all happened so quickly, Ma'am, then Mrs Marsh came and had Liza taken to the infirmary and Tilly was locked away. That is all I know.'

Hannah Price glanced at the blank sheet of paper lying on her desk. Was that all the girl knew, or was it all she was prepared to say she knew?

'Have you seen Spittle this morning, Mrs Marsh?' she asked without looking up.

'Yes, Ma'am,' Agnes answered. 'There is no change from last night. She is still unconscious.'

'In that case there is no sense in sending for the doctor.' The Governess picked up a pen, dipping the nib into a glass ink-well and beginning to write on the paper before her. 'I will send an interim report informing the Prison Board that one of the inmates is unwell, and this evening I will ask the doctor to call. Spittle should have recovered sufficiently well by that time to relate to him what occurred.'

Spittle should have recovered by that time, Agnes Marsh thought, beginning to usher Phoebe from the Governess's office, or was Hannah Price giving the doctor time to drink away his senses? Either way it suited them both. The last thing the Governess or Agnes Marsh wanted was a murder inside the prison, and if Liza didn't make it then that would be another bonus.

'Excuse me, Ma'am.' Phoebe ignored Agnes Marsh pushing her towards the door. 'May I please ask a question?'

Hannah Price paused in the writing of her report and looked up at the young girl whose eyes no longer studied her own shoes but were on her, steady and unblinking. Was she truly a thief? Had she really robbed the home of Sir William Dartmouth? In all honesty Hannah could not bring herself to believe so; this girl was very different from all the other prisoners in Handsworth, so well mannered and polite, so obviously well bred it would be hard for anyone to believe her a criminal, but the law had pronounced her such and the law must always be upheld.

'Yes, Pardoe, what is it?' She signed to the wardress to wait.

'It is Tilly Wood, Ma'am,' Phoebe said, showing no trace of her true feelings. 'What is to happen to her?'

The Governess balanced the pen back and forth between thumb and forefinger as though testing its weight, her lips pursed tightly together. Phoebe waited, each tick of the tiny carriage clock sounding like the boom of a cannon in the still room.

'Ah, yes, Wood.' The balancing of the pen stopped as if some decision had finally been reached. 'I do not think it necessary to mention the involvement of any other prisoner at this stage, so for the time being Prisoner Wood will return to the laundry.'

'Thank you, Ma'am.'

Hannah Price looked up at the quiet answer and knew it was more than a simple thank you. Much, much more.

Chapter Six

Phoebe pushed the needle tiredly into the cloth, her eyes aching from a sleepless night, a night that had followed the pattern of so many since her confinement to Handsworth Prison, for though her body rested her brain refused to sleep. But last night it had not been for herself she had worried but for Tilly: locked up in solitary isolation, a place Phoebe herself had only heard of, a place the mention of which reduced the rest of the women to hushed tones.

But Tilly was free of that for the moment at least. Phoebe pulled the gold wire thread through the cloth, seating it with the tip of a finger. And what of Liza . . . would the Governess send for the doctor this evening, and if so . . . ?

'May I see?'

Phoebe looked up as a voice broke into her thoughts. She placed her needlework in the prison Governess's outstretched hand.

'This is very fine.' Hannah Price examined the Psalter cover. 'You sew very well, and such an elegant choice of colour, I know Phi— Father Heywood will be pleased when he receives them. You should be able to place yourself in some dressmaking or millinery establishment upon your release.'

Phoebe took the piece back as the Governess moved on along the line of sewing women. She should be able to secure a position. It was so easily said but who would employ a convicted thief?

'I find you guilty of wilful theft . . . you will serve a term of fifteen years . . .'

She pushed the needle through the cloth. Fifteen years for a crime of which she was innocent.

'Oh my Good God, will you look at that!' Lucy's shocked words rose to the surface of her mind and Phoebe saw again the bodice of the jade taffeta gown spread wide, revealing the necklace caught up inside it.

''Ow do you reckon that got there?'

Lucy's words replaced the quiet hum of the sewing women's conversations.

'I don't know,' Phoebe had replied, 'but we must return it to the Priory.'

'How come it hasn't been missed?' Lucy looked up from the floor of the bedroom. 'And it can't 'ave been or I would 'ave heard about it. Word gets round fast in that house.'

'It must have become caught when Sophie removed the dress,' Phoebe said, seeing how the mounting had become hooked into the dress lining. 'She probably wouldn't feel it through her petticoats, but surely when her maid came to put the gown away she would inspect it first for any mark or stain?'

'Not that one, Miss.' Lucy watched her free the necklace. 'I know 'er and lazy isn't the word I'd be using to describe 'er. She would 'ave had 'er marching orders long since but Miss Sophie is too soft. Everybody downstairs says they don't know how 'er gets away with half of the things she gets up to, but get away with it she does.'

'Maybe, Lucy, but to overlook something as valuable as this must be more than careless.'

Lucy looked at the necklace, emeralds dripping like huge green tears through Phoebe's fingers.

'Aye, Miss,' she said thoughtfully. 'Like you says, more than careless.'

They had taken the necklace to the kitchen where they both sat looking at it spread on the table, its stones gleaming in the pale sunlight, the gold of its setting turned red by the glow of the fire.

'Eeh, it's so beautiful,' Lucy sighed. 'A girl would feel like a queen with that round 'er neck.'

Phoebe glanced up, her mouth curved in a smile. 'Much as I want you to look and feel like a queen on your wedding day, Lucy, I couldn't offer to let you wear this.'

'Would make no difference if you could,' Lucy drew back as if the necklace were a living thing, 'I wouldn't dare to. Why, I'd be scared to death!'

'And rob Mathew of his pretty bride? Then it is as well this does not belong to me.'

'What *will* you do with it, Miss Phoebe?'

'Return it to Sophie as I said.'

'I 'ave to return to the Priory, do you want me to take it for you?'

'No, Lucy,' Phoebe answered as the girl reached for the cloak she had hung on a nail set into the kitchen door, 'I would not want to put such a responsibility upon you. The dresses were given to me and I must be the one to return the necklace. Not to do so personally would be most impolite.'

'If you say so, Miss Phoebe.' Lucy tied the ribbon of her bonnet beneath her chin. 'But you be careful you say nothin' to anybody as to why you be visiting the Priory. There's folk about these parts as can't be trusted.'

Lucy had left Wiggins Mill then, and for the first time since making it her home Phoebe had felt truly afraid of being alone. The next day she had wrapped the necklace in a piece of white linen, pushing it deep into the pocket of her skirt, then wrapping her cloak tight about her had set off across the heath toward the Sandwell Valley.

She had reached the rise above the Lyng Fields, so called for their covering of tiny purple wild flowers, when Edward had caught up with her.

'Couldn't you have sent someone with word?' he said, dismounting from the huge bay horse and listening to her reason for visiting the Priory. 'I would have sent the carriage for you.'

'I have no one to send.' For some reason Phoebe did not mention Lucy and her connection with his home. 'Besides I have no wish to impose, your family has already been very kind to me.'

'Yes, but out here all alone,' Edward took her hand, concern loud in his voice, 'there's nothing out here for miles around . . . anything might happen.'

'And nothing.' Phoebe smiled. 'Really, I am quite safe.'

'I suppose I know that,' he touched her hand to his lips, 'but I would prefer you didn't walk the heath alone, Phoebe. I only wish I could accompany you but I have an appointment with my father at two and it is almost that now.'

'I would not want to be the reason for your being late for Sir William.' Phoebe withdrew her hand. 'Please go, I will be all right.'

'Well, at least let me take the blamed trinket for you. It's near enough an hour's walk from here to the Priory and I can send a carriage to take you home.'

'No, Edward,' Phoebe returned firmly. 'No carriage. I want to walk back to Wiggins Mill. The fresh air will do me good.'

'If it doesn't kill you from cold first, and it will be dark before you get there.' He glanced at the grey snow clouds gathering over the valley.

'Then hadn't you better take this so I can be on my way home?' Phoebe drew the linen bundle from her pocket, unwrapping the necklace and handing it to Edward. 'Please would you give my apology to your sister and explain I did not know this was caught inside one of the gowns she gave me until yesterday evening?'

'My sister would lose her head were someone not there to fasten it to her neck.'

Edward tossed the necklace up into the air and Phoebe watched the tiny flashes of green flame dance circles in the light as it descended into his palm.

'I still wish you would let me send a carriage out to you.'

He dropped the necklace into his pocket before swinging easily into the saddle.

'I shall be perfectly safe, Edward.' Phoebe stepped back from the horse, a sudden breeze catching the animal's nostrils and causing it to prance restlessly.

Edward reined the bay, speaking softly and touching the animal's neck. 'Sophie will certainly wish to thank you herself.' He looked down at Phoebe, the breeze fanning her sherry-gold hair about her cheeks. 'May I bring her to Wiggins Mill tomorrow?'

The horse neighed loudly, its hooves stamping restlessly at being held in check, and Phoebe raised a hand to wave, relieved at not having to answer.

One week later she had been arrested.

'Governess wants to see Phoebe.'

Mary Pegleg limped into the sewing room, delivering her message to Agnes Marsh.

'What for?' The wardress's voice was sharper than usual and as she looked at Phoebe her eyes held a touch of concern and a heavier touch of warning. Whatever the Governess wanted, Agnes Marsh had better come out of it white as snow if she were to keep the promotion of Superintendent to the sewing room and not be sent back to that hell hole of a laundry.

''Er didn't say.' Mary Pegleg leaned against the door jamb easing her weight from the wooden stump attached to her left knee. ''Er just said to tell you 'er wanted to see Phoebe right away.'

'You better get yerself to the office then, Pardoe.' Phoebe put her sewing on the end of the long trestle table, feeling the eyes of the other prisoners on her as she went towards the door.

'Pardoe!' Agnes Marsh came close, her mouth merely a slit as she breathed, 'Mind what you tell 'er. Things could be made pretty bad for you . . . there are worse places inside this prison than the laundry.'

Mary Pegleg limping alongside her and Agnes Marsh marching behind, Phoebe walked along the gloomy corridors that led to the Governess's office. How many more years would she spend locked away? Her fingers curled tightly as the memory of flashes of green fire darted across her brain. She had not stolen Sophie's necklace, they had found it caught up inside a dress, she and Lucy, but neither she nor the maid had been believed.

Edward and his sister had not called the next day or any day. She had seen no one until the day the constable arrived. She had to go with him to the Magistrates' Court, he said, and no, he could not tell her why, the Magistrate would tell her that.

They had walked the several miles to Wednesbury where she had been taken to the Green Dragon Inn at the entrance to the Shambles. It was in an upstairs room there that the Magistrate had heard evidence against her.

It was alleged that she had visited Sandwell Priory and taken away several dresses, the gift of Miss Sophie Dartmouth; in the process she had stolen an emerald necklace, the property of the said Miss Sophie.

That had been the point at which John Kilvert had been asked if she was the woman who had pawned several pieces of jewellery at his shop.

'She is, Your Honour.' The pawnbroker's shifty eyes had fastened on her and his high-pitched reedy voice carried around the room. 'Some very valible jewellery, and where could the likes of 'er get such from lessen 'er stole it?'

'We will decide that, Kilvert.'

But the Magistrate's voice had held no rebuke and the pawnbroker had smirked at Phoebe as she stood up from her seat.

'Are you now prepared to tell us what you have done with the necklace?'

She had not been asked if she had taken Sophie's necklace, she had been told she had, told she had stolen from a girl who had helped her.

'The necklace you speak of,' Phoebe tried to stay calm, to keep the mounting fear out of her voice, 'I . . . we found it hooked inside a gown given to me by Miss Sophie.'

'We?' The Magistrate had looked at her over heavy spectacles. 'Do I take it someone else was with you?'

'Yes,' Phoebe answered, the trembling in her stomach increasing as she realised Lucy was not present and neither was Edward. Did he know she was being accused of stealing the necklace she had given to him? Of course he must know, the complaint must have come from the Priory, so where was he? Why wasn't he here to tell them it was a mistake . . . to tell them she had been returning Sophie's property when he had overtaken her, that he himself took the necklace from her?

'Well, was someone else involved in this theft?' The Magistrate leaned across the table that served as a desk.

'There was no theft.' Phoebe stared at the other three people in the room: the constable sent to bring her here, John Kilvert her accuser, and a woman dressed in black, her face hidden behind a heavy veil. 'Please, you must believe me, I am telling the truth. We found the necklace caught up in the bodice of the gown and . . .'

'*We* found?' The Magistrate leaned back in his high wing chair. 'You had better say who it is besides yourself makes up this we.'

'It was Lucy, my mai— my friend. She was visiting me and we decided to try on the dresses before taking them apart. We found the necklace inside a green gown. We guessed it belonged to Miss Sophie, seeing she had given me the gowns, and Lucy asked if she could return it that day when she went back to the Priory.'

'And did she?'

'No, Sir.' Phoebe swallowed hard, seeing the look of satisfaction cross the hard features of the man facing her. 'I thought that as the gowns had been given to me, mine was the responsibility of returning the necklace.'

'Which you obviously did not or we would not be here today.'

'I did not return it to the Priory.' Phoebe felt a cold desperation take hold of her: they did not want to believe her, this man had already decided she was guilty. 'The . . . the day after finding the necklace, I went to return it. I had crossed the Lyng Fields and was about to go on when Edward Dartmouth overtook me. I told him the reason for my journey and he offered to take the necklace for me as the weather was worsening and it would take me several hours to get home.'

For several minutes the room remained silent except for the anxious fidgeting of the pawnbroker. Across the table the Magistrate fingered long white whiskers then, leaning forward, he glared at Phoebe.

'You are saying that you returned a valuable emerald necklace to Edward Dartmouth, that he did not return it to his sister, and that therefore he is in fact the thief?'

'No! No, I . . . I'm not . . . Edward wouldn't . . .'

'No more.' The Magistrate's palm came down hard on the table. 'I have heard enough. You stole a necklace and now try to place the blame upon the son of a respected family, a family who have held their seat in West Bromwich for hundreds of years. You accuse a man who is not present to answer for himself against your lies. Well, I will answer for him. Edward Dartmouth would never commit such treachery against his own. You are a liar and a thief, and it is only out of regard for the young man's father, Sir William Dartmouth, that I will exercise leniency and not inform him of what you have said here, for to do so would result in your incurring a far heavier penalty than the one I am about to pass.'

He then reached out a hand to the wooden gavel lying in front of him.

'Phoebe Pardoe, I find you guilty of wilful theft. I order you be taken to a place of imprisonment . . .'

A rustle of black skirts told of the woman's leaving the

room as the gavel struck hard against the table. Behind her black veil Annie Pardoe almost smiled. Her meeting with Sophie Dartmouth's personal maid had paid off. That girl's attempt to extract money in return for her silence regarding a missing emerald necklace had failed, but the charge of theft Annie had forced her to lay against Phoebe had not. The Magistrate's final words followed her through the door. '. . . you will serve a term of fifteen years' hard labour.'

'Wait there, Pardoe.'

Agnes Marsh held out a hand as they reached the Governess's office. Mary Pegleg limped to the stool set against one wall where she was allowed to sit between running messages.

'Why has she asked to see me, Mary, do you know?'

'No idea.' Mary Pegleg answered the question in a whisper. 'I ain't bin 'ere the whole time though I knows there be someone in there with 'er 'cos I 'eard 'em talkin' when I come up from the kitchen. Sounded deep, the other voice, like a man's.'

'Is it the doctor?' Phoebe asked worriedly. 'Has the Governess sent for the doctor, is Liza worse?'

'I don't know,' Mary hissed. 'Was some shemozzle goin' on downstairs, summat about a visitor, but I didn't 'ave chance to find out who it was. Though like I said, it sounded like a man an' 'er in there seemed in a right tizzy, 'er voice all excited, what I could hear.'

'Maybe it is Father Heywood.' Phoebe's reply was almost a prayer. 'Perhaps he has called regarding the covers for the Psalters.'

'Let's 'ope it is.' Mary Pegleg shifted position on the stool, one hand rubbing her amputated leg where it sat in the cup of the wooden stump. 'At least let's pray to God it ain't the doctor. We don't want to see 'im 'ere while 'is brains is still in 'is skull.'

The door to the Governess's room opened and Agnes Marsh stepped out, her mouth tight with resentment.

'You're wanted inside, Pardoe,' she said, barely allowing her lips to free the words. 'And you, Pegleg, get your arse off that stool and get down to the kitchen. Tell them Her Highness is wanting a tray of tea sent up to her office – *now*.'

Waiting for an answer to her tap on the Governess's door, Phoebe remembered the Magistrate's words: 'Out of regard for the young man's father I will exercise leniency and not inform him of what you have said here, for to do so would result in your incurring a far heavier penalty.'

Chapter Seven

Inside the Governess's office, its desk lit by a larger window than elsewhere in the prison and set about with comfortable leather high wing armchairs, Phoebe bobbed a curtsy to the woman standing behind the desk.

'Pardoe, this is Sir William Dartmouth.'

'*A far heavier penalty*'. The words screamed in Phoebe's brain, the room whirling around her in a mad dance of chairs, desk and people. '*A far heavier penalty* . . .'

'Are you all right, Miss Pardoe?'

Phoebe felt hands to either side of her as her legs began to crumple.

'Sit here,' the distant voice commanded. Then, 'Have you sal volatile, Mrs Price?'

'Smelling salts, Sir William.' Somewhere above the void that threatened to swallow her, Phoebe heard the Governess answer, 'I have smelling salts,' then coughed as a small bottle was held beneath her nostrils.

'No, do not get up!' Sir William Dartmouth touched a hand to her shoulder then walked to the fireplace that held a fire both winter and summer. 'I have something I wish to say to you.'

He hesitated, waiting for Hannah Price to acknowledge the tap on the door. A woman in the drab grey dress that marked her as an inmate entered carrying a tray, depositing it on a small oval table set against one of the wing back chairs. She glanced at Phoebe before leaving.

He had been told. Phoebe's fingers curled, pressing her

nails hard into her palms. He had been told she had accused Edward of not returning the necklace to his sister. But she had made no such accusation. Why hadn't Edward told them he had the necklace, and why after so many months had his father decided to seek his own revenge?

'You will take some tea, Miss Pardoe?' he said as Hannah Price poured the steaming liquid into a china cup. 'My presence here has seemingly upset you.'

A china cup! She had not drunk from a china cup in over twelve months. Phoebe made no move to accept the tea the Governess held out to her. A tin mug was all she had to drink from now and would be all she would have for fifteen years – and how many more? How many more years had this man demanded be added to her sentence?

'You were accused of stealing a necklace from my daughter . . .'

Phoebe raised her gaze, her soul in her eyes. 'I did not steal it,' she said softly, 'I was returning it to the Priory.'

'So I understand.'

Hannah Price returned the cup to the tray, leaving her own untouched as she studied the girl who had already served a year in Handsworth gaol.

'I gave it to Ed— to your son. He said he would give it to Miss Sophie together with my apology. They were both to call at Wiggins Mill the next day, but they never came.'

'Miss Pardoe . . .' Sir William hesitated, looking into the fire for several moments then faced her again, squaring his shoulders as if preparing for an unpleasant task he would have preferred to leave to someone else.

Frightened of what she knew was about to come Phoebe stared at Edward's father, standing tall against the fireplace, tan knee-length coat accentuating his powerful physique, hair that had once been black crested with a dusting of grey above the temples, and eyes that in the dim light of the room might have been grey or even black.

'Miss Pardoe,' he said again, as if searching for words, 'I

was told of what passed between yourself and the Magistrate the day after you were sentenced, but yesterday I was told more . . .'

Phoebe's throat closed and her head began to pound. Yesterday he had been told more and today he would have retribution.

'Yesterday,' he went on, 'I spoke to Lucy Baines, or I should say I spoke to Mrs Mathew Leach. She told me you would not allow her to return my daughter's necklace but said that you yourself would do so.' Breaking off, he turned towards the Governess. 'We will not go on with this any longer. Mrs Price, you have the Magistrate's signed document?'

'Yes, Sir William.' She touched the folded sheet of white paper lying on her desk as he moved to take up his hat and gloves lying on a small table just inside the door of the room.

'Then I will say good day.' He inclined his head the merest fraction as Hannah Price dropped a curtsy. 'Miss Pardoe.' The same slight movement of the head and he was gone.

He had spoken to Lucy. The pounding of her head mounting to a sickening crescendo, Phoebe gripped the arms of the chair. Why had he not mentioned Edward? Why had he not spoken to his son?

'Sir William took the trouble to bring this himself.' Hannah Price picked up the sheet of paper, holding it unopened in her hand.

Phoebe stared at it, the world slowly dropping away from her. He had taken the trouble to bring it himself, to see the girl who had attempted to accuse his son of theft, attempted to blacken the character of his family, to see the girl whose life he was taking away. How many more years were written on that paper? How many more years to serve in hell?

'It seems a mistake has been made . . .'

Hannah Price's face swam before Phoebe's eyes.

'. . . the necklace you were accused of stealing has been

found. This,' she tapped the paper against her fingers, 'is an authorisation from the Magistrate. You are free to go.'

'Sir William Dartmouth himself?' Sarah Leach looked in disbelief at her son and his wife seated in her tiny living room. 'Billy-me-Lord in your 'ouse? Eeh, it's not to be believed.'

'What did 'e say?' Joseph tapped his pipe against the bars of the fire.

''E said as how his family had returned from Europe the day before and 'e had asked his son if he knew anything of Sophie's missing emerald necklace,' Lucy answered. 'It seemed at first as though he knew nothing of it then he remembered taking it from Phoebe and dropping it in the pocket of his riding habit.'

'So?' Sarah urged as her daughter-in-law paused for breath.

'So 'e says 'e sent a footman or some such to search the coat an' 'e comes back wi' the necklace in 'is hands,' Mathew took up the story.

'Oh, thank God . . . thank God!' Sarah wiped her eyes on her apron. 'Now she'll be free – Abel's daughter will be free to come 'ome.'

'Oh, aye, I reckon as Phoebe will be free to come 'ome,' Mathew went on, 'but what sort of freedom will it be? Nobody will want to know a gaolbird, innocent or not. I reckon as Phoebe Pardoe ain't gonna be a whole lot better off outside o' that prison than she were inside of it, 'specially if that aunt of 'ers can do anythin' about it.'

'What does that mean?' Joseph scraped the bowl of his clay pipe with a slender bladed knife then blew down the stem.

Mathew looked over to where his father sat beside the shiny blackleaded grate. 'I mean that in my opinion Annie Pardoe is somewheres to be found in this business. She 'olds something against Phoebe, the facts tell that themselves – turnin' her out of her father's house, tekin everythin' that was hers 'cept what Lucy saved for her – an' it's my guess it was her in that Magistrates' Court in the Green Dragon.'

"Ow can you tell that?'

'I can't really, Mother.' Mathew turned his glance to Sarah, scalding tea in a large brown earthenware teapot. 'But I got talkin' to the bobby as fetched Phoebe to the Magistrate . . . 'e gets into the Gladstone most evenings when 'e ain't on duty . . . an' 'e said the woman come in a carriage – a carriage wi' A.P. on the door.'

'A.P.' Sarah held up the teapot, the first cup half filled. 'Abel Pardoe.'

'Yes, Abel Pardoe,' Mathew said. 'The carriage was Abel Pardoe's an' the woman as rode in it were Annie Pardoe. An' 'er went to the Green Dragon to hear 'er own niece sentenced to fifteen years an' never lifted a finger to stop it!'

'God 'elp us,' Sarah murmured.

'Ar, an' 'e will 'ave to an' all if anybody 'ears you goin' on like that.' Joseph glared at his son. 'Keep yer opinions to yerself, my lad. Annie Pardoe 'as done thee badly as it is but 'er's capable of doin' a damn' sight more so be ruled by one older and wiser an' keep yer tongue between yer teeth.'

'Did 'Is Lordship say what was to be done about Phoebe?' Sarah resumed filling the cups, handing a larger mug to Joseph.

'He said he would see to everything himself,' Lucy accepted the cup from her, 'but he didn't say what it would be.'

'Billy-me-Lord be a fair man,' Joseph said, using the name by which the locals addressed Sir William. 'If 'e 'as said 'e will see to things then see to 'em 'e will. Reckon we will just 'ave to bide our time til' Abel's daughter be 'ome.'

'There's no telling when that will be,' Lucy said, swallowing her tea, 'but when she does come I want to have a fire going and something hot ready for the table. So drink up your tea, Mathew Leach, it's a long walk to Wiggins Mill.'

'Aye, the wench will be wantin' a bit o' comfort,' Joseph nodded as Lucy dropped a kiss on his head. 'If you can let we know when 'er is back, Mother an' me will walk over to the mill.'

'I'll do that, Father.' Mathew grabbed his cap from one of the several nails hammered into the door that opened on to the street, respectfully holding it until he was out of the house. 'Bye, Mother.' He folded Sarah in his arms, feeling the thinness that had come in the last few months, and in his soul cursed Annie Pardoe afresh. Her money grubbing was robbing his mother of her life as surely as Phoebe had been robbed of hers. 'We will be back to see you on Sunday.'

Reaching the corner where the road curved away out of sight of the house, he turned to wave to his mother and in his heart he made a wish: May Annie Pardoe not live to see Sunday!

The heavy door banged behind Phoebe. She was free! There would be no more days locked inside Handsworth Prison for Women, no more backbreaking hours in that laundry or sewing until she could barely see the needle, no more wardresses barking orders at her. Closing her eyes she breathed deeply, feeling the fresh air bite at her throat. She was free, free to go home, but Tilly Wood would never go home.

Phoebe had not been allowed to say goodbye to any of the women who had shared her existence for more than a year; even Mary Pegleg had not been sitting on her stool outside the Governess's office when she had come out. Given the clothes she had arrived at the prison in, she had changed, Agnes Marsh in attendance, then had been taken to the door of the prison, passing no other prisoner on the way.

'Excuse me, Miss . . .'

Phoebe opened her eyes to see the man who had come to stand at her side, wearing a high black hat and knee-length boots teamed with deep blue coat.

'Sir William asks if you would be good enough to ride home in the carriage?'

'*Sir William took the trouble to bring this himself.*' The

words echoed in her mind. But he had not come to lengthen her eternity, he had come to bring her freedom.

'Miss!'

'What . . . what did you say?'

The coachman looked at the girl in the shabby brown dress and cloak, her bonnet tied over lifeless hair snatched back from a drawn pallid face. This was not the usual kind to ride in the Dartmouth coach, but then again it was certain sure she wouldn't get far on foot. 'Sir William, Miss,' he said again, 'asks if you would kindly take the carriage home?'

Phoebe glanced about her, seeing for the first time the outside of the high prison building. She had not seen where they had brought her in that black-painted cart with its iron-grilled window, nor even known apart from hearing 'the women's gaol in Birmingham'. Now she saw a bare stretch of heath broken only by a group of scraggy trees some distance to the left and a path leading to the right, and realised she had no idea in which direction home lay.

'Yes . . . yes, thank you.'

Holding both hands to her skirt, feeling every sharp stone through the worn soles of her boots, she half stumbled to where the carriage stood waiting. Then the door closed and she was on her way home. Home! Leaning her head against the cushioned upholstery, she allowed the pent up tears of months to flood her cheeks.

'Allow me!'

Phoebe felt the soft cloth pressed into her ungloved hands and opened her eyes to see Sir William Dartmouth.

Across the narrow space that separated them he saw the sudden fear return to her eyes and felt disgusted at a system that treated a young girl in such a way as almost to destroy her; but it was a system he himself had long upheld.

'Forgive me for not giving you an explanation,' he said quietly, 'but I felt the sooner you were out of that place, the better.' He glanced at her hands, nervously twisting the white lawn handkerchief, then went on, 'I was informed of the outcome of your appearance before Gideon Speke, and of the term of imprisonment to which he had sentenced you, and I felt no regret. My family's friendship seemed to have been abused and my daughter's property stolen. But yesterday I found that nothing had been stolen and that I had been wrong. Because of my action you have been made to suffer great hardship. I can only offer my most sincere apology. I will, of course, make reparation in any way you wish.'

Reparation! Phoebe stared out of the window but the passing streets and imposing buildings of Birmingham went unseen. How could any reparation make up for what she had been through . . . for what she knew was yet to come?

'Your home is at Wednesbury, I believe,' he resumed, covering her silence. 'If you will tell me where I will have Aston take us there.'

'Brunswick House,' she answered, only half registering what he had said.

'Brunswick House!' He leaned forward slightly, a small frown creasing his brow. 'You live at Brunswick House?'

'No . . . I . . . I'm sorry.' Phoebe forced her mind to attend her words. 'I do not live at Brunswick House. My home is Wiggins Mill on the outskirts of the town.'

'Then why say Brunswick House?'

For a moment Phoebe thought she heard the note of accusation so many voices had held over the past months and her head rose defensively. 'Possibly, Sir William,' she said clearly, 'because I once did live there.'

'Brunswick House?' The frown deepened, his eyes narrowing in concentration. 'That was Abel Pardoe's house . . . his sister got it if I remember rightly. And you . . . your name is Pardoe . . .'

'Yes, Sir William.' Phoebe looked straight into his dark eyes. 'Phoebe Pardoe. I am Abel's daughter.'

'So she is to be set free?' Annie Pardoe looked at the man

seated in her drawing room, one hand tugging nervously at long white side whiskers.

'There was nothing I could do,' he answered. 'Sir William Dartmouth himself came to withdraw the charge, said the necklace had been found and demanded the girl be set free at once.'

'And you signed the document of release?'

'I had to, Annie.' Gideon Speke had been unnerved at Sir William's appearance in his office; he was a powerful man and not only in West Bromwich, there was no telling what he would do if he found out.

'Yes, I suppose you did.' Annie stood up, black skirts rustling. 'But hear me, Gideon Speke. You took my hundred pounds to put her away and if anything comes of her being found innocent 'tis you will bear the brunt. I will swear before God I paid you one hundred pounds to try buying her freedom, and that you pocketed that money while hearing no evidence in her defence. One word, Gideon . . . just one word and you will never sit on the Magistrates' bench again!'

So Abel's girl was free! Annie Pardoe closed the door on the departing Magistrate. She had been denied little more than one year of her life while she, Annie, had had no life at all. Slowly she walked through the house and out into the garden. She would not let it rest here. She had taken her niece's home and all she possessed save the paltry sum her maternal grandmother had left her, but all that would not pay for what her own brother had taken from her. Revenge tasted sweet and Annie craved its sweetness. There was more yet to be had and she would drink it to the very last drop.

Turning, she walked back into the house and up the stairs to her room. Putting on her cloak and settling a black bonnet on her head, she went to the room Samuel used as a studio.

'I have to go out for a while,' she signed on her fingers. 'I do not expect to be very long. Is there anything I can get for you while I am in the town?'

Samuel shook his head, his mouth unsmiling as he regarded his sister. Annie had always worn a look of bitterness but of late that look had changed; to what he could not rightly say but it was a look he liked even less.

'Has Tranter brought your hot drink?'

Samuel rested his brush on the palette. 'No,' he signed back, his fingers moving rapidly, 'I told her not to.'

Annie did not question his answer, knowing that in the years Maudie Tranter had spent with them she too had learned the sign language that enabled Samuel to speak.

'Then we will have one together when I return.' Annie Pardoe looked at the brother she had cared for for so many years. His features were thinned and gaunt compared to a year ago but they were still a carbon copy of the man who had been a brother to them both, still with the same keen eyes, 'Take care not to get cold, dear.' Her gloved fingers fluttered like the black wings of a crow. 'You know how unwell you have been of late.'

Samuel picked up his brush, watching his sister leave the room. The house always felt easier when she was not in it.

Annie drove the small trap, guiding the mare along the Holyhead Road that linked Wednesbury to its neighbouring towns. Passing the Monway Steel Mill of which Samuel, thanks to their brother, was part-owner, she turned off across the heath towards Hobs Hill mine, stopping at the huddle of small houses some half-mile away.

'I will say what I came to say.' She had marched straight into Joseph Leach's cottage, ownership relieving her of the necessity of waiting to be asked. 'My niece has besmirched her father's name, she has been imprisoned for theft, therefore she will be unwelcome in any house of standing.'

'But my Mathew's wife says Miss Phoebe is to be set free.' Sarah Leach stared at the woman who seemed to fill her small room with darkness. ''Er says as 'ow they 'ave found out Miss Phoebe never done it, 'er never stole no necklace.'

'Nevertheless,' Annie drew in a long breath, the effort flaring her nostrils, 'the slur remains, my brother's good name has been stained, and I will not have it perpetuated by accepting the girl's presence in any property I and my brother Samuel own. And this house forms part of that property. I tell you, Sarah Leach, you have Phoebe inside this house for one minute and you are out, bag and baggage. What's more, I will see to it that the cripple you call a husband will get no job in Wednesbury.'

'There be only one thief in Abel's family,' Sarah muttered, watching the trap pull away, 'an' that be you, Annie Pardoe. You 'ave teken everythin' that should 'ave bin his daughter's an' may the Good Lord pay you for it!'

Chapter Eight

Sir William Dartmouth watched the face of the girl he had
just seen released from prison. Its pallor and thinness did not
completely hide its fine-boned quality, or the unhappiness
shading her green eyes detract from their lovely almond
shape. He had known Abel Pardoe for many years, they
had done business together on a regular basis, he buying
much of the coal Abel's mines produced together with steel
from his Monway works, but they had not mixed socially.
Now he was looking at the daughter he had not realised the
other man had, a daughter whom he guessed bore a quiet
beauty beneath the mark of Handsworth Prison.

She had not spoken since telling him she had once lived
at Brunswick House and though she had stared out of the
window for the rest of their journey he guessed it was not
the passing scenery that held her attention.

'Is this Wiggins Mill?' he asked as the carriage rumbled
over a stony path worn by the carter's wagon. 'Miss Pardoe?'
He leaned across, touching a hand to hers, still twisting the
handkerchief, then withdrew as Phoebe jerked backward,
the shadow in her eyes deepening. 'I asked, is this your
home?'

'Yes.' Phoebe looked across to where the old house began
to rise out of the hollow that sheltered it, the stilled windmill
standing sentinel on the adjoining high ground. 'Yes, this is
Wiggins Mill.'

The coach drew to a halt and almost immediately the
coachman was opening the door.

'Miss Pardoe,' Sir William waited until she stepped down, 'you are no doubt in need of rest but perhaps you will do me the courtesy of calling at the Priory as soon as you feel able? There is a lot I still have not said and we must discuss how you may be compensated.'

Phoebe looked at her home. She was free, she did not have to bite back her words any longer and never again would man or woman order her life.

'Sir William,' she turned back to him, a cool gleam of assurance clearing the shadows from her eyes, 'I will call at the Priory but only to return your handkerchief. As for compensation, there is no need of any. A mistake has been made and a mistake has been rectified, we need say no more on the subject. Will the day after tomorrow be convenient for me to return your handkerchief?'

'I will send the carriage for you at eleven.' Then, as Phoebe made to reject the offer, he smiled. 'And *you* need say no more on *that* subject.'

'Miss Phoebe . . . oh, Miss Phoebe, you're home!' Lucy raced around the corner of the house as the carriage drove away. 'Oh, it's so good to see you.'

'And you, Lucy,' she breathed as her friend's hug threatened to stifle her.

'Welcome home, Miss Phoebe.' Mathew Leach smiled at the two women, laughing and crying at the same time.

'Mathew!' Phoebe broke free to hug the man she had known from childhood. 'But . . . but shouldn't you be at the pit?'

'Come in, Miss Phoebe.' Lucy's voice lost some of its joy. 'There's a fire in the grate an' tea on the hob an' I'm dyin' to butter you one of my scones.

'You see, Miss Phoebe,' she said when at last Phoebe stopped wandering through the rooms of her home and settled in the warm kitchen, 'when I was sacked from the Priory and Mathew was given the sack from the pit we had nowhere to go like an' . . . well, I thought the mill could do wi' being kept an eye on an' you wouldn't mind us being in one of the outhouses. We never used the 'ouse, Miss, honest we didn't. I just come in every day to dust and keep the rooms aired.'

'You mean, you were both removed from your employment?' Phoebe left the scone untouched. 'But why? For what reason?'

'Mathew was sacked for questioning the reason for your aunt reducing the wages at the pit an' meself? Well miss, Sophie's maid said I must 'ave put the necklace in one of the dresses sent to Wiggins Mill, that I knowed you as a friend and would be able to retrieve it when I visited you and then sell it. So the housekeeper up and sacks me. Matters of the servants is left to 'er when 'er Ladyship is away, Sir William is never bothered with little things like sacking a maid.'

'They don't 'ave to give a reason,' Mathew said sourly. 'Pit owner or gentry, meks no difference – when either of 'em wants you out it's a case of pick up yer tin and go.'

'But how have you managed with no wage between you?'

'Well, like I said, Miss,' Lucy took up the thread, 'we had nowhere to go. We thought yer aunt might turn nasty if we lived with Mathew's parents an' we couldn't live here without being wed so we just got Father Heywood to say the words over us then we come here. Oh, Miss, I hopes you don't mind?'

'Of course I don't mind, but Lucy . . . your lovely wedding? Didn't you get it after all?'

'No, Miss.' Lucy smiled at her husband. 'But I got the man and that's all that matters.'

'We'll be gone in the mornin', Miss.' Mathew turned towards the door. 'I'll go see to our bits an' pieces an' when Lucy is finished over 'ere 'er'll pack the beddin'.'

'She will do no such thing!' Phoebe answered vehemently. 'And neither will you. You will stay here and glad I'll be of your company. I . . . I wouldn't want to stay here alone . . .'

'We understand, Miss, and we thank you,' Lucy cut in, seeing the shadow return to Phoebe's eyes. 'Mathew and me we'll mek it up to you, really we will.'

'There is nothing to make up.' Phoebe smiled. 'We are friends, and wage or no wage will survive somehow. In fact, you two seem to have found a way already, judging by the food on this table.'

'That's Mathew, Miss,' Lucy beamed. 'You remember he was quite handy with hammer and saw? Well, he gets a few odd jobs from folk in the town, mending a chair or mekin' a stool, little things like but they buy flour and vegetables. And I do a bit of sewing like you used to only I don't get no dresses from the nobs.'

'Neither will I again, Lucy.' Phoebe sipped the hot tea she had poured. 'Those doors are closed forever, I'm afraid.'

'But you didn't never tek anything!' Lucy's glance was bright with anger. 'Them at the Priory knows you never and so does Magistrate.'

'I don't think that will make any difference.' Phoebe shook her head as the other girl offered more tea. 'The very fact that I have been in prison will be sufficient for the nobs, as you called them, to reject my company.'

'Then bloody nobs ain't worth associatin' wi'.'

'Mathew!' Lucy glared at her husband. 'Language.'

'Beg your pardon, Miss Phoebe,' Mathew pulled open the door that led on to the yard, 'but that's the way I feel,' he said, going outside.

'Please don't tek no notice of Mathew.' Lucy gathered the used cups on to a wooden tray. 'But the losin' of his job 'as made 'im bitter. I keep tellin' 'im it's no use his feelin' that way but I might as well bang my 'ead against a brick wall for all the good it does. ''E just won't take a tellin', says all moneyed folk am the same: all out for themselves an' sod the likes of folk who grind for 'em. There be times I think he'll never be the same as he was.'

Never be the same. The thought lingered as Phoebe followed the other girl into the scullery. She understood Mathew's feelings. Things might never be the same for any of them. She was free, but what freedom would Wednesbury allow a girl who had been in prison?

Phoebe came up the rise from Lyng Fields, feeling the softness of the earth beneath her feet, and stood on the crest of the high ground cradling Sandwell Valley, looking down on the ancient Priory. Cool air fanned her brow and she lifted her face to it, revelling in its touch. She had deliberately not waited for the carriage as Sir William had told her to, ignoring his instruction. Never again, she told herself, closing her eyes to the delicious taste of freedom, never again would any man or woman order her life.

A breeze lifting out of the valley caught her skirts, lifting them like unseen fingers, and she pressed a hand to them, delighting in the touch of the brown bombazine after so many months of wearing drab grey calico. But the women who had been her companions of those months were still wearing grey uniforms. Her mind flashed to Tilly. She would be dressed in grey calico the rest of her life. If only they had given her time to say goodbye to the woman who had befriended her . . . but she had been rushed from Handsworth Prison as though she carried the plague and now she would never be able to tell Tilly how glad she was to have known her and to have been her friend.

Opening her eyes, she looked down at the house nestling on the floor of the valley, its mullioned windows seeming to stare back at her. Sir William Dartmouth had waited outside that prison, waited until she emerged through its heavy door; he had brought her home in his carriage, but for what reason? Reparation for what his son had caused to happen to her? Maybe, but any such feeling would be momentary, passed and forgotten in a week. As Mathew had said yesterday, all moneyed folk were out for themselves, they and they alone were all that mattered to them, and the more money they had the less those without it counted for. Well, she had none but she would count for something. Lifting her skirt, she set off down into the valley. Somehow, some way, Phoebe Pardoe would count for something.

At the foot of the high ground the valley widened into a flat swathe, the grass-covered earth rolling away to green eternity. It had been green around Brunswick House, Phoebe remembered, the lawns edged with beds bright with flowers, a shaded arbour leading to her favourite rose garden, but there had been nothing like these vast acres spreading endlessly, the ancient house at their heart.

Passing at last beneath a great stone arch, she began to walk along the sweeping approach, itself lined with magnificent beeches, their arched branches almost meeting overhead as if in imitation of the stone.

'Hey!'

The shout coming from the hushed silence of the morning took her unawares and she stopped, both hands clutched to her brown cloak.

'Where do you think you be goin'?'

A man in late middle age, his shoulders hunched, stepped from behind a tree.

'Don't you know this 'ere be private property?'

He stepped towards her and Phoebe saw his earth-stained hands move toward the heavy buckle belt fastened about his breeches.

'Of course I know.' Phoebe lifted her chin, putting every ounce of her failing confidence into her voice. There was no one around; in fact there might only be herself and this man in the world, so empty was the spread of ground. 'This is Sandwell Priory and I am here by appointment.'

'Appointment, eh!'

The man's hands still hovered about the fastener of his belt and Phoebe felt her heart jerk. What did he intend to do? Whatever it was there was no one to see.

'Yes, by appointment.' Phoebe stood her ground as he came closer. 'I am here to see Sir William . . .'

'*You*, 'ere to see Billy-me-Lord?' The man sniffed derisively, eyeing her plain brown dress. 'You'll be tellin' me 'as 'ow you be a personal friend of 'is next.'

'Hardly.' Phoebe stared into the man's eyes, pale rheumy eyes that seemed to swim in a mist of water. 'Though I do wish to return this.'

Thrusting a hand into the pocket of her cloak, she pulled out the freshly laundered handkerchief, its crested initial worked in pale blue, and held it towards him.

'Oh!' He stared at the handkerchief, his manner changing as if the owner himself had suddenly appeared. 'It's . . . it's just that 'er Ladyship don't like town folk using the main drive, an' with you not bein' in a carriage like I thought as you . . .'

'That I was one of the town folk?' Phoebe returned the handkerchief to her pocket. 'You thought correctly, I am.'

'In that case . . .' the hands stopped hovering, dropping instead to the man's sides '. . . you should 'ave come by the back way, up against Ice Pool. That way there would be less chance of them up at the 'ouse seein' you. You best go back. There be a path around to the left of the arch will lead you to the stables. You can get to the servants' quarters that way.'

'Thank you.' Phoebe's mouth did not relax.

'I ain't seen you afore,' the man went on as she turned away. 'You be the new maid?'

'No.' Phoebe halted then swung around to face the lovely stone mansion. 'I am not the new maid and neither do I enter a house via the servants' quarters.'

Feeling those watery eyes on her back she marched up the arrow-straight drive, her mouth set in a straight line. Her home might be a hovel in comparison to that of Sir William Dartmouth but she was mistress of it and servant to no man, and that was the way her life would remain.

She had almost reached the steps that led from left and right, forming an arc up to the main entrance of the Priory, when a footman in dark blue livery appeared as if from nowhere.

'You shouldn't have come this way.'

His voice was hushed, almost reverential; no servant in her father's house had been expected to speak this way.

'So I have been told,' Phoebe answered loudly.

Closing the space between them, the man glanced at the house before grabbing her elbow. 'Then why did yer? You must 'ave been told 'er Ladyship don't like servants usin' the main drive. C'mon, out of it, there'll be trouble if 'er sees you 'ere.'

The hand on her elbow tightened and for a fleeting second Phoebe was back inside that corridor with Liza Spittle's hand pushing her back against the wall, the old sickness rising in her throat.

'What is going on here?'

The words were not loud but they acted upon the footman like a starting pistol. His hand fell away from Phoebe's elbow and he stepped back as Sir William Dartmouth rounded the corner of the house.

'I asked what is going on here?'

The sickness that memory had provoked faded as he approached. Glancing at the footman, Phoebe saw the pale line of anxiety now lining that man's lips. So it was the same here in West Bromwich as it was in Wednesbury! Positions once lost would be hard to replace, especially if a man were to be dismissed with no references.

'I have a stone in my shoe,' Phoebe lied, 'your footman was about to assist me.'

'I see.'

I know you do, thought Phoebe, catching the look of gratitude in the servant's eye as he was dismissed. First you think me a thief, now you see me as a liar.

'I will send for one of the maids.'

'Please don't bother.' Phoebe bent, and removing a shoe, shook it, displacing the imaginary stone. Then she slipped her foot back into it. 'A woman learns to do these things for herself in Handsworth Gaol.'

'Take him back to the stable.' Sir William turned to the groom who had followed him from the back of the house. The man began to lead away the magnificent black horse and its master turned back to Phoebe.

'That will keep them in conversation for a few days.' He smiled.

Phoebe glanced at the departing groom, remembering how the slightest deviation from the usual could set the women's prison humming for days. The slightest deviation! What Tilly had done to Liza Spittle was no slight deviation . . . what would happen now to Tilly . . . what would the Prison Board do to her?

'Shall we go inside?'

The question cut across those thoughts spinning in Phoebe's mind, bringing her attention back to the man half smiling at her.

'There is no need.' She fished in her pocket then held out the folded square of white lawn. 'I can return this to you here. It is all I came for.'

'But that is not the only reason I wished you to come.' He regarded her from deep grey eyes. 'You have not yet been given a full explanation of the facts of what happened on that day, nor have you received my family's apology.'

'I have received my freedom,' Phoebe answered, her own gaze clear and steady, 'that is enough. Nothing more is necessary or wanted, therefore I wish you good day, Sir William.'

'Maybe it is enough for you,' his voice was suddenly hard, cutting through the quietness covering the beautiful valley, 'but what of my son? All he can do is apologise, Miss Pardoe. Would you deprive him of what little solace that can give him?'

Edward! How many times had he filled her thoughts during those long nights, how many times had she seen in her mind that handsome face, those vividly blue eyes? Yet strangely she had not once thought of him since meeting his father.

'Will you not at least let the boy speak for himself?'

Only a brief nod indicating her agreement, Phoebe followed him into the Priory. Dismissing all offers of attention, Sir William led her through the spacious rooms, each exquisite in its furnishings, until he came to a door concealed in an alcove in a corridor lined with portraits.

'My wife will be in here,' he said, pushing open the door and waiting until Phoebe passed inside.

Much smaller than the rooms through which she had already walked, this held a more intimate feel, the home of laughing children and shared secrets. Phoebe glanced quickly at the photographs in silver frames dotted on tables, the deep chairs carelessly scattered with bright cushions, the spectacles beside the newspapers that marked this a family room.

'Amelia, my dear, Miss Pardoe is here.'

Lady Amelia Dartmouth laid aside the book she had been reading. 'Miss Pardoe, do forgive my not welcoming you but I was not informed . . . William, why did no one tell me of Miss Pardoe's arrival?'

'Never mind that for now,' he replied as his wife drew Phoebe to a chair, 'ring for Edward and Sophie.'

'You will take tea, my dear?'

Phoebe looked at the elegant woman, remembering her from the evening market, only then her bonnet had hidden the traces of gold that still shone among the carefully dressed fading hair and her cloak had covered the stately, tightly corseted figure.

'Thank you,' she murmured as Amelia Dartmouth issued softly spoken orders to the man who responded almost immediately to the pull of a bell cord.

'Phoebe!' Edward was first into the room, rushing to where she sat in a deep brocade chair. 'Oh, Phoebe, I'm so sorry.'

'Edward!' his father cautioned as a maid entered with a silver tray. 'We will wait for your sister.'

He had grown. Phoebe glanced over to where Edward stood beside his father. He was taller than she remembered but still lacked three or four inches beside the older man. He had the same blue eyes and golden hair of his mother but the stance of his father, the assurance that a life of wealth and position bestows.

'Phoebe . . . Phoebe, I'm so happy to see you!' Sophie burst into the room like a boisterous puppy, grabbing both of Phoebe's hands and pulling her out of the chair. 'Was it positively awful in that prison?'

'Sophie!' Lady Amelia's voice was sharp.

'Sorry, Mama,' she said, giving Phoebe's hands a squeeze before releasing them.

'Miss Pardoe,' Sir William said as Phoebe accepted the delicate porcelain cup Sophie handed her, 'my son has something to say to you.'

'Yes, Phoebe.' Edward's blue eyes clouded. 'That day I met you coming here to return a necklace you told me you had found caught up inside a dress that Sophie had given you, I said I would return it in your stead.' He looked at his mother and Phoebe thought that despite his height he seemed just like a little boy, seeking encouragement in making a confession.

'Go on, Edward.' His mother smiled, a world of understanding in her eyes.

'Well, after I left you, The Prince caught his foot in a root or something and came down heavily.'

'The Prince?' Phoebe questioned.

'The bay I was riding,' Edward replied, 'he was a son of Satan, my father's black, and sometimes he showed it. He did that day anyway . . .'

'He was restless, I remember.' Phoebe put the delicate cup and saucer aside, her tea untouched.

'He always reacted to a sudden breeze that way.' Edward glanced at his father, still standing before the Adam fireplace. 'As if he wanted to race the wind. Anyway he got the bit between his teeth and set off like a bat out of hell. We were half across the valley when he came down, and when I couldn't get him to his feet I went for help. By the time it was all sorted out I had completely forgotten about the necklace in my pocket.'

'The Prince was a particular favourite of Edward's.' Amelia Dartmouth stretched a hand toward the tall young man who was her son. 'His father gave him the foal when it was born, you could say they grew up together were it not to sound so sentimental.'

'Edward was devastated when they had to shoot The Prince,' Sophie put in. 'It was days before he could bring himself to speak to anyone.'

'By that time,' Lady Dartmouth took up the explanation, 'the chill I had caught that evening at the street market had worsened, and it was decided we should leave for Europe earlier than originally intended. So you see, Miss Pardoe, both Sophie and Edward were out of the country when you . . .' The explanation trailed off, his mother holding on to Edward's hand.

'What my wife was about to say was that she and our son and daughter were abroad when you were arrested and imprisoned, and I did not acquaint them with that information in my letters to them. Therefore the fault is mine . . .'

'William,' Amelia Dartmouth's brow creased in a small frown as she turned to her husband, 'my dear, you were not to know the necklace would be found.'

'As you say, Amelia,' he nodded, 'but that does not excuse my behaviour. When James Siveter informed me that a young woman had been found guilty of stealing the necklace, I did nothing to ascertain the truth of what had happened.'

'But what could you have done?' his wife asked. 'You must accept the law.'

'As we all must,' his already dark eyes seemed to darken further, 'but we need not accept that the law has been presented with the true facts. I should have set in motion my own investigation.' He turned to Phoebe. 'As it was I did not, and therein lies my guilt. I was too ready to believe the friendship of my family had been abused and for that I offer my profound apology, Miss Pardoe, and ask in what manner I may make reparation?'

Phoebe rose, her plain brown garments a stark contrast to the elegant testimony to wealth that lay all about her.

'Sir William,' she said quietly, 'I told you yesterday that a mistake had been made. It was a mistake for which I attribute no blame and require no reparation. I know that as soon as you were told the truth you lost no time in securing my release. I know also that neither your son nor daughter would have wished for such a thing as my imprisonment, but now the truth is out and the necklace retrieved there is no need for the subject to be raised again.'

She turned to the woman who still clutched her son's hand, as if thinking he might be marched away to some prison. 'Thank you for receiving me, Lady Dartmouth. Now I must return home.'

'May I come to see you tomorrow, Phoebe?' Sophie was on her feet. 'I do so enjoy talking to you.'

'Sophie,' Lady Dartmouth smiled for the first time, 'Miss Pardoe may wish to rest for a few days before being concerned with callers.'

'I should be happy for Sophie to call at Wiggins Mill whenever you feel she may, Lady Dartmouth.' Phoebe dropped a polite curtsy.

'Does that invitation hold for me too?' Edward released his hand from that of his mother.

'Again, only when your mother permits it.'

'Don't bother ringing for Compson.' Sir William stepped forward as his wife made to pull the bell that would ring for a servant. 'If Miss Pardoe will allow, I will see her out myself.

'I really cannot permit you to refuse to take some form of compensation for what we have done to you.'

They had passed once again through rooms Phoebe would have loved to linger in and stood now at the foot of the curving stone steps that fronted the great house.

'You can't force me to accept either.'

'As it seems I could not force you into waiting for my carriage to collect you this morning.' William Dartmouth looked down into a face too pale and too thin but one that nevertheless whispered of beauty and character, and he smiled. 'Perhaps you will permit it to take you home?'

'Thank you, Sir William, but I prefer to walk.'

'What!' He laughed then, low in his throat. 'And get another stone in your shoe?'

'I may even take them off and walk barefoot.' Suddenly Phoebe too was smiling. 'That would give your servants even more cause for conversation. Good day, Sir William.'

Sir William Dartmouth watched the slight brown-clad figure walk away and found himself admiring the courage and honesty of the girl, the resilience that had brought her through months of imprisonment yet blaming no one at the end of it. He remembered the astuteness and honesty of the man he had known in the world of business.

'Yes, Miss Phoebe Pardoe,' he murmured, watching her disappear along the drive, 'you are truly Abel's daughter.'

Chapter Nine

Phoebe put the last of the breakfast dishes back on the kitchen dresser then settled the kettle over the coals. She would make a broth later against Lucy and Mathew's return from town. They were both trying so hard to make a living, Mathew trudging the streets in search of odd jobs and Lucy baking every night then selling scones and pies in the market place by day, while she . . . Phoebe looked around the small kitchen, its red flagstones boasting a pegged rug against the door, dresser arrayed with an assortment of plates and cups, the table whose twice-daily scrub had the wood almost white . . . apart from keeping the house clean, what was she doing?

She turned back to the fire, staring into its red heart. She couldn't go on like this, she couldn't continue to live off Lucy and her husband. In prison she had dreamed of being home, of earning her own living, of being beholden to none save herself yet . . . 'Why?' she whispered to the flames. 'Why can't I do it, why can't I at least try?'

The coals settled, sending a small glowing ember sliding between the bars of the grate. Phoebe watched the trail of sparks it made as it fell against the fender, sparks that glittered and then faded into nothing, as her life had once glittered only to fade.

If only her father's death had not come so soon, if she had been married to Montrose, her life would have been so different. Different! Reaching the tongs from the companion set that stood beside the range, she picked up the fallen ember, replacing it on the fire. Yes, her life would have been different but her world would still be empty for how long would happiness have lasted once she'd found out that Montrose's real reason for marrying her was her father's money? And now it seemed Sophie had been earmarked to become Mrs Montrose Wheeler.

Replacing the tongs, she walked restlessly into the small living room with its meagre pawnshop furnishings. Mrs Montrose Wheeler! Phoebe touched a finger to the blue glass top of the oil lamp sitting in the centre of the round chenille-covered table and knew which she would rather have.

The skirts of her brown dress swishing, she ran up the stairs and into the bedroom she had once used as a workroom, the lethargy that had lain over her since leaving prison falling away like a discarded shawl. She knew how she could make a living. Opening a chest that stood against the window wall she took out the small dresses she had made for Lady Dartmouth, dresses that had never been given as the presents they were intended for. They were pretty. She lifted them one at a time, holding them against the light from the window. There were women in Wednesbury who either hadn't the skill to make their children's clothes or else were too busy working to keep them to have the time to try. Lucy said there were customers for her baking, maybe some of those customers would buy clothing. Draping the dresses across a table she used for cutting out her patterns, she counted them. There were eight ready for sale now and she still had some of the dresses Sophie had given her.

Turning to a larger chest standing on the opposite wall she raised the domed lid and stood stock still. The pale green gown stared up at her.

'. . . *I find you guilty of wilful theft* . . .' Phoebe's hand tightened on the mahogany lid as the room swam away from her.

'. . . *I sentence you to be taken to a place of imprisonment and there you will serve a term of fifteen years' hard labour . . .'*

Hard labour . . . imprisonment . . . fifteen years . . . wilful theft . . . I sentence . . . fifteen years. . . . The words twisted and turned in her mind, louder and louder until they screamed in her head; life draining out of her, Phoebe's fingers loosed the heavy lid and it fell with a bang, the noise of it chasing away the ghosts of the past. She stood for several seconds, her breathing rapid and short. She was free of the walls but not yet free of the prison. But she would be free, determinedly she lifted the lid of the chest and took out the green gown, totally free.

Laying the gown across the one chair the room still held she hesitated at a sound from downstairs. Sophie? Edward? It couldn't be Lucy or Mathew, they would not return before evening. She crossed to the window and looked out to where the Dartmouth carriage would be standing . . . only there was no carriage.

It could have driven up unheard but it could not have left the same way. Maybe she had imagined the sound? She stood listening until the crash of breaking china told her she had not imagined it.

Maybe it was Lucy, maybe she was unwell. 'Lucy!' she called, running from the room and downstairs to the kitchen. 'Lucy, are you all right?'

'It ain't Lucy . . .' a voice behind her halted her progress toward the scullery '. . . it's me!'

Phoebe turned toward the voice. A man stood inside the kitchen, blocking the doorway to the living room. He was about five feet ten and aged around thirty, and eyed her brazenly.

'Who are you? What do you want?' Phoebe asked, suddenly knowing a new fear as his eyes wandered over her.

'Who I be don't matter.' He spoke through lips that seemed too thick for his narrow face. 'What I want, though, that be a different matter.'

'I have no work to give you.'

He smiled, spreading the thick lips, showing teeth that were strong but in need of a rub with baking soda. 'It ain't work I'm after.'

'I . . . I don't live alone here.'

'Oh, I know you don't.' His eyes glittered, he knew her fear and was feeding on it. 'I know about Lucy and 'er 'usband, same as I know about you and your visit to Sandwell Priory last week. 'Ow much did 'e give you?'

'I don't understand.' Phoebe tried to move into the scullery but the man was at her side before she had taken two steps.

'Don't play me for a fool, Miss Bloody Fancy Pardoe,' he grated. 'You understands all right an' comin' on all innocent won't pull the wool. My eyes am wide open. I knows the Dartmouths won't be lettin' things go wi'out payin' you somethin' . . . now wheer is it?'

'I did go to the Priory last week.' The fear in her was stronger now and she knew he sensed it as an animal senses fear. What would he do when he found nothing here of value? 'But I went there only to return a handkerchief Sir William had lent to me, nothing more. I . . . I took nothing from them.'

'So Phoebe Pardoe got nothing?' He moved closer. 'Look, I warned you, don't play clever wi' me. I know you done twelve months an' more on account of Mr Bloody 'igh falutin' Edward Dartmouth an' that last week you went to the Priory to collect. You talked to the 'ole bloody lot of 'em . . . compensation is what you talked and compensation is money. You got money an' it's that money I've come for . . . now wheer is it?'

One hand flashed upward, grabbing her hair, snatching her head backward. 'You might as well tell me,' he brought his face close, the thick lips only inches away, "cos I'll find out one way or another and one of them ways you're gonna find very painful.'

'I . . . told . . . you,' Phoebe fought to speak against the constriction of her neck being pulled backward, 'I was given nothing . . . the Dartmouth family . . . they gave me . . . no . . . no money.'

'Lyin' bitch!' He released her hair, the same hand smacking viciously across her face, knocking her against the dresser, sending plates hurtling to the floor. Grabbing a poker, he thrust it deep into the glowing fire. 'If you ain't told me wheer you 'ave the money 'id by the time that's 'ot, you'll 'ave a face nobody will bear the lookin' at.'

He wouldn't believe her, he was convinced she had been given money by the Dartmouths and nothing she said would alter that. Phoebe swallowed hard, her thoughts unnaturally clear. If she could get out of the house she might be able to make a run for it.

'All right,' she said, wiping a hand across her smarting eyes, 'Sir William did give me money but it's not here . . .'

'Then wheer is it?'

He grabbed at her again, cinching her arm, pulling her forward. There was no smell of coal dust, Phoebe thought, and no tiny burn holes in his trousers so he was not a miner nor did he work in an iron foundry. That meant he wasn't local for there was little for men to do otherwise around Wednesbury. So how did he know about her being in prison or about her visit to the Priory?

'I said, wheer is it?' He reached his free hand to the poker, its steel tip indistinguishable from the crimson coals. 'But you can take yer time, it's gonna be a pleasure gettin' you to say.'

'It's outside.' Phoebe prayed her words would convince him. 'I thought it better not to bring it into the house. No one would expect so much money to be left out there.'

'Wheer outside?' He drew the poker out of the fire.

'In the old mill.'

'That's better.'

He dropped the poker, letting it rattle down the bars of the grate on to the stone hearth, dragging Phoebe with him out of the house and across the yard to where the windmill stood on a little rise.

'Wheer abouts did you put it?'

Phoebe winced as he jerked her arm. 'Up in the corn loft. There's a pile of empty sacks against the wall, I hid the money under them.'

'Yer best be tellin' the truth,' he threatened, almost frog marching her towards the door of the disused mill, 'yer'll regret it if you ain't.'

If only he would release her arm! Phoebe tried to form a plan: she could run back into the house and bolt the doors. But he did not release her. Kicking open the wooden door, he pushed her before him into the mill.

'The corn loft, you said?' He glanced upward then down to where a rickety ladder lay half buried in the dust of the floor. Holding her with one hand, he struggled to raise the ladder then rest it against the floor of the loft.

'You first.' He leered, his almost canine teeth taking on a yellower hue in the light streaming from the doorway.

Phoebe struggled up the ladder, her feet catching in her skirts, threatening to throw her off the narrow uneven struts.

'Stop there an' don't go movin' . . . if you know what's best for you.'

Pushing her as he followed from the topmost rung of the ladder, he kicked it aside, laughing as he made for the heap of sacks lying in a corner.

This would be her only chance. There would be no more tricking him when he found there was no money under those sacks. Moving slowly, holding her skirts so they wouldn't rustle, she got to her feet, inching towards the edge of the corn loft floor. He had kicked away the ladder but that wouldn't stop her.

'Go on . . . jump! Makes no odds.'

Despite her caution he had heard and was watching her, on his knees among the empty corn sacks.

'You'll break one leg at least, mebbe both, but you won't need legs for what I'm gonna do to you . . . after I've got yer money, that is. Go on, jump . . . you won't crawl far.'

He began to laugh again, a laugh that had her spine crawling. 'What I'm gonna do to you . . .' She had heard those words before; the image of Liza Spittle's birthmarked face floated before her eyes and the sour smell of her filled Phoebe's nostrils. Closing her eyes, she jumped.

Annie Pardoe slipped the key into her black bag and left her bedroom, going to her brother's studio.

'I am going into the town,' she signed, the movement of her hands setting her bag swinging from her arm. 'Doctor Dingley has prescribed a medicine for your headaches and I do not trust Isaac Jackson to send it before teatime. That man is not nearly the chemist his father was.'

Samuel put his brush on a table beside a palette smeared with paints and looked at his sister. He could hardly remember seeing her dressed in any colour other than black, as though she were in constant mourning; neither could he remember seeing her smile, he could only recall the bitterness that had eaten away at her over the years, a bitterness of her own making. Yes, Annie *was* in perpetual mourning, grieving for a life she thought duty had required her to forgo and nurturing bitterness against the brother she blamed for taking it.

'There is no need for you to go,' he signed, his long fingers moving in rapid succession, 'my headache is quite gone.'

'Yes, it is now,' Annie's fingers relayed words of care she had never truly felt, 'but what of the night-time, dear? You know how sometimes you cannot sleep for the pain in your head. I think it better I fetch your medicine myself.'

'If that is what you wish.' Samuel's fingers seemed to flow into each other, one sign blending into another with the practice of years. 'I will take a turn in the garden until you return.'

Going into the adjoining room that was her brother's bedroom, Annie took a lightweight coat from the panelled wardrobe. Returning to the studio, she held it out to Samuel.

'You must take care,' she signed as he took the coat and slipped it on, 'you know how quickly you take the influenza.'

Yes, he knew. Samuel followed her out of the studio, making his separate way into the garden. He also knew how much he wished the influenza would take him.

Annie drove her small trap along Walsall Road turning off when she reached Oakeswell End, directing the horse toward the chemist's shop that topped Dudley Street. She would collect the medicine Alfred Dingley had prescribed and then she would complete what she had intended all along.

Ignoring the sidelong glances of the women and the looks of dislike from men she had laid off from the pits on one pretext or another, and whom the iron foundries would not take on, she trotted the horse a roundabout route, avoiding where possible the more heavily frequented roads until she came to Bescot Fields. This part of Wednesbury was still mostly pasture with only a few farms holding out against the industrialisation that had engulfed the town like the black plague; here she had lived so many years before coming to Brunswick House, here at the end of a beaten track hidden by high hedges was the house Abel had given to her and Samuel. It had not been sold or let to tenants and neither would it be until her use for it was gone. Samuel took no interest in the property or businesses left to him by Abel and none in this house: his painting was his only interest, which suited her. She turned the horse off the track, driving round to the back of the house where the trap would be screened. Yes, it suited her very well.

Leaving the horse to crop at the overgrown flower border she took the key from her bag, letting herself into the house. She would not open the shutters. The years had taught her the geography of this house and she moved easily through its shadowed dimness. In her old bedroom she drew a box from the back of a narrow shelf obscured by a marble-topped washstand set in front of it.

A finger of daylight poked between the heavy velvet curtains. Annie carried the box over to it. She removed the lid and breathed deeply, a feeling of satisfaction coursing through her. It was still there. From the depths of the box she withdrew a small finely wrought glass bottle. By the finger of daylight she read the label: 'D'Amour'. Elias Webb had thought her his the day he gave her the bottle of French perfume. But the perfume and its giver had long gone from her life.

Discarding the box, she thrust the bottle into her bag and left the house, locking it securely before climbing into the trap and leaving her former prison to its silence.

Phoebe struck the packed earth with a jarring thud and lay still. Above her, his narrow face pulled into a grin, the man watched, then satisfied she was either unconscious or worse, turned back to searching the heap of sacks.

Hearing his movements above her, Phoebe knew he had not followed. Carefully, a prayer in every move, she pushed herself to her knees, then to her feet. By what miracle she had not broken her legs she didn't know and didn't stop to reason, her one thought was to make it back to the house and bolt herself in. Gathering her skirts in both hands she tiptoed toward the open door and was almost through it when she heard him shout.

Running the last few yards, she hurled herself out of the door, slamming it behind her, eyes skimming it in search of a bolt or securing bar. But there was no way of locking it; there had been no need for locks at Wiggins Mill.

'Hey! Come here, you bloody bitch . . .'

The shout was followed by a grunt. He was down from the corn loft, had jumped as she had.

'Think you could fool me, did you? You'll 'ave nuthin' to think with when I catch you!'

Phoebe heard the scuffle as he got to his feet. She was already halfway across the open ground separating the mill from the house when she heard the door slam open against the wall.

'You won't bloody get away . . .'

The shout followed her as she ran.

'You've got that money somewheers an' I'm gettin' it!'

The last came out in a gasp as he threw himself at Phoebe's back, his hands fastening in her skirts and dragging her to the ground.

'Would 'ave gone a lot better wi' you if you had just told me wheer the money is 'cos now I'm gonna knock the truth outa you . . .'

'I told you the truth.' Phoebe tried to move but his weight sprawled half across her was too much. Her face pressed against the earth, she went on, 'I was given no money at the Priory.' It would not be enough. Her brain began to work calmly; she had to be more convincing, tell him something his thieving mind would accept. 'They . . . they offered me a hundred pounds . . .'

She stopped as he rolled off her then snatched her over on to her back, a hand about her throat. "Undred pounds!' His fingers tightened on her neck, lifting her head then banging it hard down on the ground. 'An' you told me you got nuthin', you bloody lyin' cow!'

'I . . . I didn't take it.' His fingers tightened about her throat and behind her eyes tiny fireworks began to explode. 'I . . . I told them . . . it . . . it wasn't enough.'

His fingers relaxed but stayed about her neck; above her his thick lips drew back. 'Not enough! You told 'im a 'undred pounds wasn't enough?'

'Y . . . Yes . . .' Phoebe coughed.

'You! You told the 'igh an' mighty Billy-me-Lord Dartmouth that a 'undred pounds wasn't enough?' He laughed. 'What a bloody cheek . . . I bet 'e 'ad near enough an' 'eart attack.'

'He . . . he wasn't pleased.'

'Pleased!' Her attacker laughed again, the sound rolling off the walls of the old windmill and away toward the canal. 'I bet 'e wasn't bloody pleased, 'is sort ain't used to bein' refused, not no way. So . . .' he stopped laughing '. . . if you didn't take 'is 'undred quid, what did you tek?'

Phoebe lifted her hands to the one still holding her by the neck and pushed. 'Nothing.'

The fingers tightened again, banging her head twice against the hard earth. 'You keep arsin' around wi' me an' you gets yer brains knocked out,' he hissed. 'I don't believe you didn't get summat, you was one of a sort once till that sister of yer father's took the lot from you . . . oh, I know all about that.' He grinned down at her, his yellow teeth parted. 'Same as I know you to be too smart to miss the chance of gettin' your 'ands on some of Billy's money, so don't tell me you got none.'

'I got a lot *more* than a hundred.'

The flicker of greed in his eyes told Phoebe this was what he wanted to hear, this would convince him, this he might just accept. Pushing against his wrist, she stared up at him.

Holding her stare for a full minute, he tried to gauge the truth of what she had just said then dropped his hand.

"Ow much more?'

'A lot.' She sat up, coughing as a stream of air gained free passage to her lungs. 'Only I don't get it until this afternoon.'

'Go on.' He watched her rub her throat, his eyes lowering to her breasts.

'They were all there, like you said,' Phoebe tried to ignore his look, 'Sir William and Lady Dartmouth and their son and daughter. They said they were sorry I had been inconvenienced . . .'

'Incon-bloody-venienced.' He laughed again, the noise of it rolling in waves from the mill to its outhouses before washing out over the low embankment that bordered the canal. 'That sounds just like 'im – somebody does twelve months in the shit an' 'e calls it a inconvenience!'

Taking her chance, Phoebe got to her feet, brushing spears of dried grass from her skirts. 'I told him much the same. I also told him that this particular inconvenience was going to cost him ten thousand pounds or I would go to the newspapers. I said I was sure they would relish reporting how so prominent a member of the gentry had allowed an innocent girl to take the blame for a crime his son had committed.'

'But the necklace was found!' His eyes glittered up at her.

'Was it?' Phoebe flicked a dried straw from her sleeve, trying to guess how long she could stall him. Maybe Sophie or Edward would call and maybe not, reason told her, they had called only two days before. 'Or was it a replica? After all, who would know? And who would really care? The public's interest would not be in the recovery of the necklace but in the suffering of a young girl, and that suffering would only increase in the telling.'

'An' 'e went for it?'

He stood up, his tongue skimming his thick lips, and Phoebe stepped backwards, making a breathing space between them.

'Not at first. He argued that I would never be believed, but I argued that the damage to his family's reputation would be already done and that he might never be quite believed again in anything he tried to do. I said the aristocracy is a cautious breed. It cares to take no chances with the unreliable in case its own unreliability is brought to light.'

'Clever.' He smiled his approval. 'I said you was one of 'is own sort, y'ave brains as well as looks.'

Deep inside Phoebe shuddered at the glance he played over her but forced herself to stay calm. 'Clever enough,' she said, avoiding his eyes, 'to turn a hundred pounds into ten thousand.'

'Christ Almighty,' he breathed, 'ten thousand quid . . . it's a bloody king's ransom!'

'But it's a king's ransom I earned,' Phoebe said, 'over twelve months in hell I earned that money, and I told them either they pay what I ask or I tell the whole story plus more . . . much more.'

'So 'e agreed?' His eyes slid again to her breasts. 'Billy-me-Lord is payin' you ten thousand quid.'

'This afternoon.' Phoebe turned towards the house. 'He had to go to the bank. He said that he never kept that much money in the house, so if you come back around four o'clock you can have half.'

'Why go?' He grabbed at her, pulling her hard against him. 'It will be more pleasurable to wait 'ere . . .'

He pressed his face to the side of her neck, pulling at her flesh with his thick lips, and this time Phoebe could not hold her shudder inside. Grasping his hands, she tried to force them away, a sob of terror escaping her as he turned her in his arms. 'I . . . I'll give it all to you if you go.'

'I intend 'avin' it all,' he grinned, thick lips shining wetly, 'an' the money besides.'

Hooking one foot behind her ankle he brought her down, her spine hitting the ground hard, driving the wind out of her.

Already unbuckling the belt holding up his trousers, he looked down at her. 'Relax,' he grinned again, 'you'll enjoy what I've got fer you.'

Their hold released, his trousers fell around his ankles, revealing the naked flesh beneath, then he was on top of her, one hand clawing at her breast while the other slid her skirts above her hips.

'You'll enjoy what Liza's got fer you.'

Once more Phoebe was against that prison wall, the stink of Liza Spittle in her nostrils, the vileness of her touch rising like gall in her throat.

'Stop!' She struggled to push him away, to rid herself of the threat of his body. 'Please stop!'

'It ain't stop you'll be sayin' in a minute,' he said thickly, his hands fumbling at her underwear, 'you'll be sayin' more . . . please, more.'

'No . . .' Phoebe screamed as his fingers touched against her bare skin. 'Liza, no . . . o . . . o!'

Chapter Ten

Maudie Tranter slipped out of the back entrance of Brunswick House, her cloak covering a wicker basket.

Annie Pardoe would be gone most of the afternoon and there was little likelihood of Samuel's needing anything, poor man. Maudie shook her head. He seemed to become more drawn into himself every day, eating hardly enough to keep a sparrow alive, and those headaches! She reached the lane that backed the house, turning left towards Hall End. Yes, Samuel Pardoe's headaches just seemed to get worse despite the medicines Alfred Dingley regularly prescribed.

'Come in, Maudie.' Sarah Leach left off scraping the potatoes she had freshly pulled from the vegetable patch, wiping her hands on a square of white huckaback. 'It's good to see you, the seein' ain't often enough.'

'An' likely to be less.' Maudie followed her through to the kitchen, letting the basket on to the table with a groan. 'It gets to be a longer walk out 'ere each time a body comes, or at least that's the way it feels.'

'Give us yer cloak.' Sarah took the heavy woollen cloak, her eye on the basket.

'Eeh, ma wench!' Maudie dropped heavily on to a hoop-backed chair, its cane seat welcoming to her thin frame. 'Why do you still go on livin' out 'ere? You would be better off nearer the town an' Joseph wouldn't 'ave near so far to trot to the pit.'

'Try tellin' 'im that.' Sarah smiled, lifting the kettle from its bracket above the fire and scalding the tea in her brown earthenware pot. "E says 'e is 'ere till they carries 'im up Church Hill an' settles 'im agen 'is mother and father.'

'P'raps 'e's got the right idea 'spite what I says.' Maudie watched the flow of dark brown liquid being poured into Sarah's china cups, kept for visitors. 'Wednesbury ain't the place it once was – all steel foundries wi' their smoke an' dirt messin' place up, an' now them newfangled toob works.'

'Toob works?' Sarah asked, adding milk to the tea before passing one of the cups to her visitor. 'What do toob works be?'

'They be factories as meks toobs – 'ollow stems of steel. All sizes they can mek – long an' fat, short an' thin, big or little.'

'What they be for then?' Sarah pointed to a small glass bowl filled with sugar. 'These toobs.'

'I'm buggered if I know!' Maudie spooned sugar into her tea. 'But I reckon 'er up at Brunswick 'Ouse does. Seems as 'er's dabblin' in a lot of things lately.'

'Is 'er buyin' these 'ere toobs then?' Sarah asked over her cup.

'Not buyin' 'em.' Maudie sipped her tea, savouring both it and the moment; she didn't see much of folk and when she did she enjoyed the glory of imparting news of the doings of Annie Pardoe. 'But I reckon 'er's puttin' money into the mekin' of 'em.'

'Well, 'er certainly ain't puttin' any into them pits o' their'n,' Sarah answered, placing home-cooked scones and a jar of her own damson jam on the table. 'Joseph says that Hobs Hill mine is near to cavin' in just about everywheer and that the Crown mine up at Moxley ain't much safer. What wi' all that an' their pay bein' docked, the men would pack in tomorrer if they could get set on anywheers else. Eeh, wench, what changes we've seen since Abel went!'

'There's been changes all right,' Maudie lifted a scone to the plate Sarah passed her, 'an' not all in them pits neither.' She sliced the scone, ladling it with thick dark jam. 'You knows 'ow long I've been wi' Annie Pardoe an' 'er brother, an' in all them years I ain't known 'er 'ave doin's wi' nobody other than tradesmen, but now . . . well, all I knows is summat is goin' on.'

"Ow do you mean?' Sarah helped herself to a scone.

'There's bin a caller to Brunswick 'Ouse several times over the last few weeks an' always when Samuel be sleepin' . . . 'e sleeps quite a bit, 'e does, these days.'

She paused but Sarah did not speak, not wanting to put her visitor off her stride. Maudie was easily diverted and any news of Annie Pardoe's doings was too good to miss.

Maudie drank the last of her tea and waited while the cup was refilled. Spooning sugar into it, she went on, 'It's always the same man: Clinton Harforth-Darby 'e says 'is name is, an' you should see Annie when 'e comes. All sweetness an' light 'er is, apologisin' for Samuel's absence sayin' as 'e regrets bein' unable to come down . . .' she stirred her tea vigorously as though the action would ease some of the contempt her words roused '. . . as if 'er would ever suffer the poor bugger to come downstairs. Keeps 'im up theer like a rooster in a pen, 'cept Samuel will never get to perform like no rooster.'

'Does 'e know what's going on?' Sarah chanced Maudie changing tack. 'I mean, the say-so in all business matters be wi' 'im surely? 'E must sign papers an' things, Annie can't do that.'

'That's what you think.' Maudie accepted a second scone. 'It's what a lot of folk think seein' as 'ow the lot was left to Samuel, but Maudie Tranter knows better . . .' Sinking her teeth into the light scone, her eyes fastened on Sarah's, relishing the interest she saw in them. 'I heard 'er tell this Harforth-Darby that 'er could sign in 'er brother's stead, that 'e 'ad given 'er power of a tur . . . I can't remember the exact word but it must be legal like 'cos Harforth-Darby passed her some papers an' I seen 'er sign meself.'

'You seen Annie Pardoe write 'er name on papers that man give 'er? Eeh, I wonder what they was for?'

Maudie touched a finger to each side of her lips checking for stray crumbs before sipping her tea. 'That I don't know,' she shook her head, 'but it was summat that set a smile on that man's face that stretched from ear to ear. An' there's another thing.' Maudie finished her tea, refusing a third cup with a shake of her head. 'Last time 'er went out, 'er bought a new frock . . .'

'Who, Annie Pardoe!' Sarah asked, disbelief plain in her voice.

Maudie nodded. 'Ar, an' not just a new frock but a new lavender-coloured frock.'

'God luv me, I don't believe it.' Sarah stared at the other woman. 'After all these years, Annie Pardoe in a frock that ain't black? I can't remember last time I seen 'er outa black.'

'Oh, 'er ain't wore it, it's hangin' in 'er wardrobe. 'Er don't know I've seen it – but then, there's one or two things as Annie Pardoe ain't knowin'.'

'P'raps they be goin' somewheer special?' Sarah swung the kettle on its bracket away from the fire as the hiss of steam became louder. ''Er an' Samuel, I mean.'

'Oh, ar,' Maudie smiled acidly, 'an' pigs might fly. That one never goes out nowheer, and garden is as far as 'e goes, an' I can't see as Annie 'as bought 'erself a new frock to saunter round the roses.'

'I never could understand that, Maudie,' Sarah said, sitting down again. 'From a babby 'e never went anywheer on 'is own, 'e was always wi' his mother, an' after 'er went 'e was only seen wi' Annie – an' that weren't often, poor sod. 'E was always kept close to their skirts an' yet from what I remembers of 'im 'e was a good-lookin' lad, same as Abel. Would 'ave been the mekin' of 'im to 'ave wed.'

'Ar, well,' Maudie sighed heavily, 'it be too late fer that now even if 'e 'ad the mind. That sister of his'n wouldn't 'arbour no other woman in the 'ouse an' I can't see Samuel goin' against 'er, not now.'

'Poor soul,' Sarah shook her head in unspoken sympathy,

'but whatever the reason 'e's been kept close all 'is life it couldn't a' been 'is brain or Abel would never 'ave left 'im everythin'.'

'It ain't 'is brain,' Maudie agreed, 'there be nuthin' wrong up top. 'E might not go out of that 'ouse but it ain't 'cos 'e's short of 'is marbles.' She tapped a finger to her forehead. "E's just got no interest in nuthin' 'cept for 'is paintin'.'

'Seems to me 'e ain't never been allowed no interests. Eeh, that family am goin' to 'ave a lot to answer for, an' not only on account of Samuel neither. There's young Phoebe an' what they've done to 'er.'

'That were all Annie's doin', an' all,' Maudie replied. 'I tell you, Sarah, Abel Pardoe would turn in 'is grave if 'e knowed what 'ad 'appened to that girl of 'is'n.'

'There was no call to go turnin' the wench out of 'er own 'ome,' Sarah said, 'that were nuthin' short of vicious. Surely Samuel 'ad summat to say about that?'

"E might 'ave done,' Maudie rose reaching her cloak from the nail in the door, 'supposin' 'e knowed the truth of it but I 'ave me doubts about that. More likely 'is sister 'as filled 'im up wi' all sorts of lies.' She fastened the cloak about her throat. 'But like I said, Annie Pardoe don't know all. Might be as one day 'er will 'ave one or two surprises comin'.'

"Ow do you mean, Maudie?' Sarah waited for Annie's housekeeper to finish fastening her cloak.

'I ain't sayin'.' Maudie dropped a hand to the wicker basket still on a corner of the table; she wasn't one to give all her news in one sitting. If it were worth the telling it were worth the holding, for a while longer anyway. 'But mark my words, Annie Pardoe be in for a shock.'

'No . . . Liza, don't . . . no . . . o . . . o!'

Phoebe's screams ricocheted off the walls of the mill and its outhouses as she struggled to push the man away.

'You won't be sayin' no fer long,' he grunted, snatching at her drawers, the cotton of them tearing in his hand. 'You won't be sayin' anythin', you'll just be moanin' wi' pleasure when you gets this up you . . .'

'Somebody is goin' to get summat up 'em but I don't think it's goin' to be no woman!'

'What the bloody 'ell . . . ?'

'Is this yer 'usband, Missis?'

Her movements jerky, like a badly controlled puppet, Phoebe sat up, pushing her skirts down over her legs, grasping the torn bodice of her dress and holding it across her breasts, fear still bubbling in her throat. The man who had attacked her was jerked to his feet by the scruff of his neck.

'Am you married to 'im?'

'No!' Phoebe looked up at the figure dangling like a rag doll in the grip of a tall, broad-shouldered man.

'So you ain't 'er 'usband!' The tall man shook her attacker effortlessly. 'Then how come you be sprawled across 'er wi' your bare arse to the sun?'

'Let go, you interferin' bastard . . .'

Phoebe made to get to her feet as her attacker struggled to free himself, wanting only to get inside the mill house and lock herself away, but fell back as her legs refused to hold her.

'Oh, I'll let you go.' Placing two fingers in his mouth, the tall man gave a series of sharp whistles. 'When I've done wi' you.'

'You'll be sorry, you bloody canal rat.' The man who had come to rob Phoebe tried to kick backward but the trousers draped around his ankles prevented him. 'I've got mates . . .'

'An' do they all go around doin' what you intended doin' 'ere?' The tall man twisted the other around. 'You call attackin' a woman fun, I suppose? Well, I call punchin' the daylights out of scum like you fun – an' I'm goin' to 'ave me some fun right now!' One hand holding Phoebe's attacker by the throat, the other smacked into his yellow teeth with the force of a sledge hammer.

Her face turned away, Phoebe heard the cries as fists found their mark again and again.

'Bert . . . Bert, no more . . . you'm like to 'ave killed 'im!'

'I could bloody kill 'im lief as look at 'im.' Anger darkening his face, the tall man answered a woman in black skirts, a white cotton poke bonnet fastened over her brown hair, as she ran up to him. 'Makin' too free wi' what God give 'im.'

'Well, 'e won't make too free wi' it no more for a while.' The woman looked at the semi-conscious figure lying on his back, legs sprawled apart. 'Mind, the Lord weren't too lavish in first place wi' what he give this one.'

''E can still do more than enough harm wi' it all the same.' He dropped a hand to the handle of a knife tucked in his wide leather belt. 'I've a mind to cut the bugger off. That way 'e won't force it up no other woman as don't want it.'

'No, Bert!' The woman put a restraining hand over the one fondling the knife. 'I reckon 'e'll 'ave learned 'is lesson by the time 'e gets round to usin' that again. Best you do what you always do when you've knocked a man senseless an' I'll see to the wench.'

Turning away as the tall man caught the other by the collar, dragging him away, trousers about his ankles, the bare flesh of his buttocks scraping the rough ground, she moved to where Phoebe still sat, arms huddled across her chest.

'It's all right, ma wench,' she said softly, going down beside Phoebe and drawing her into her arms. 'It's all right, it's all over now.'

'Tilly . . .' Phoebe sobbed against the woman's shoulder. 'Oh, Tilly.'

'That's it,' the woman murmured soothingly, 'cry it up, wench, cry it up. You'll be better for gettin' it out.'

'We best get 'er inside.'

The man called Bert returned and stood looking at the two women huddled together on the ground.

'You be right.' The woman got to her feet, gently urging Phoebe to follow suit. 'A cup of sweet tea is what 'er's wantin'.' Then, seeing Phoebe flinch as the man made to help her up,

'It's all right, me luv, my Bert won't 'arm you, you'll be safe wi' us.'

"Er don't look as though 'er can make it on 'er own.' Bert stood still a moment then, reaching out, swept Phoebe up in his arms.

'Not in there, Bert,' the woman cautioned as he turned toward the house, its rear door still wide, 'we don't know what that bloke might 'ave taken out of there an' we don't want stickin' wi' the blame. We'll take 'er wi' us till 'er feels better. Might be somebody will be lookin' for 'er by then.'

'Try to drink some of that, ma wench, it'll do you good. You be in my 'ome.' Phoebe felt the cup held against her mouth.

'Tilly,' she cried, turning her face away, 'Tilly . . . it was Liza, oh God, it was Liza!'

'I ain't Tilly.' The woman placed the cup on top of a low cupboard built against a wall. 'An' it weren't no Liza as was 'avin' a go at you, it was a man.'

'Tilly . . . ?' Phoebe opened her eyes, looking for the first time at the woman who had helped her.

'No, ma wench, like I told you, I ain't Tilly an' it was no Liza sprawled across you, it were a man.' The woman smiled, her face kind beneath its bonnet. 'But you be all right, 'e's gone, an' after what my Bert give 'im I don't think 'e'll be back – not unless 'e be glutton for punishment.' Taking the heavy cup from the cupboard top she held it out to Phoebe. 'Try drinkin' this. It's only tea, but then our means don't stretch to alcohol.'

'Thank you.' Phoebe took the thick cup, swallowing the hot sweet liquid.

'Theer you go, Mam.'

Phoebe looked up as a lad of around nine years old squeezed into the narrow room, placing a prettily painted tin jug on the cupboard top.

'The water you wanted.'

'Eh!' The woman glanced at Phoebe. 'I 'ope as you don't

mind but I sent the lad for water from your yard. That was what brought Bert to your place earlier. 'E was supposed to be comin' to ask if we could 'ave a jug of water, this in canal be none too clean for drinkin'.'

Phoebe handed the cup back, her tea finished. 'What happened?'

'Me dad kicked the shit outa some bloke as was attackin' you,' the boy answered, eyes gleaming.

'An' you will get it belted out of you when I tells 'im what you've just said!' The woman aimed a swift blow to the side of the lad's head. 'What've I told you about that sort of language? You might live on a barge but you ain't no canal rat an' I ain't 'avin' you talk like one.'

'Sorry, Mam, sorry Miss.' The lad smiled, his face proud beneath a shock of brown hair. 'But me dad still kicked the s . . . stuffin' outa that bloke. Says 'e won't be maulin' no women for many a day.'

'Out!' The woman aimed a hand at the boy who ducked expertly. 'Get out and help yer father. Eeh!' She turned to Phoebe, 'Kids today. Their mouth be grown up afore their backsides be free of the napkin.'

'Was it your husband who . . . who pulled him off me?'

'Ar.' The woman nodded. ''E could tell from your screamin' that what that one was about 'ad none of your consentin' so 'e dragged 'im off you and give 'im a punchin' 'e won't forget in a 'urry.'

'Where is he now?'

'Who? The one as 'ad you pinned beneath 'is tackle?' The woman made a noise of contempt in her throat. 'Bert will 'ave chucked 'im where it'll go rusty if 'e don't get 'isself out, an' sharpish. 'E'll be in the cut, an' if 'e drowns I 'ope there's none to mourn 'im.' She poured more tea from a tall pot, pink roses and green leaves bright against its black enamelled body. 'I thought we should bring you 'ere to the barge, I didn't want nobody thinkin' we was in any place we shouldn't be, 'sides . . .' she placed the heavy platter cup on the cupboard top near to Phoebe '. . . if anythin' be missin' from your place, could be folk might think we took it.'

'He . . . he didn't take anything.' Phoebe picked up the cup, glad of something to do with her hands. 'He came for money, had the idea I had some hidden at the mill, and it was his intention to rob me of it.'

'An' did 'e?'

'No.' Phoebe shook her head. 'I didn't have any money at all, much less the amount he expected me to have.'

'You don't 'ave to say any more if you don't feel you want to,' the woman sipped her own tea, 'though usually it feels better to get it out like.'

'I was upstairs.' Phoebe stared into the tea. 'I heard him downstairs and thought it was Edward or Sophie. When I went to see he grabbed me and threatened to burn my face with a poker if I didn't give him the money.'

'But you 'adn't got any?'

'No.' Phoebe went on staring into her cup as if the events of the past few hours were being played out in its depths. 'But he wouldn't believe me. I thought if I could get him across to the mill I might be able to run away while he was searching it so I told him I had hidden the money in the old corn loft, but he forced me up there with him.'

'But you was outside when Bert come across you.'

'He kicked the ladder away,' Phoebe ignored the interruption, 'so I jumped. He didn't come straight down. I slipped out and made a run for the house.'

'An' that's when 'e catched you?'

'Yes.' It was little more than a whisper. 'I told him then that the money he thought I already had was to be brought to the mill that afternoon. I said if he would leave right away I would hand it all over to him when he returned.'

'An' 'e said 'e would 'ave the money an' a bit more besides,' the woman finished for her. 'The dirty swine! 'E deserves all my Bert give 'im an' more. The rope is too good for the likes of that one, but it ain't always the ones that am guilty as pays the price.'

'*I find you guilty of wilful theft . . . you will serve a term of fifteen years . . .*'

The Magistrate's words rang in Phoebe's ears. The woman was right: it was not always the guilty who paid the price.

Maudie Tranter let herself in at the rear entrance of Brunswick House and stood for a while in the kitchen, her ear registering the silence. The mistress wasn't back yet. Removing her cloak, she hung it in a cupboard in the scullery, sitting her bonnet on a shelf above.

She had timed her visit well as always, arriving back before Annie returned. Running her hands over her tight-drawn hair, she returned to the kitchen, a bitter smile touching the corners of her mouth as she replaced the wicker basket in its place beside the large pine dresser. Annie Pardoe had cut the wages of the miners to the bone; it was only fitting that some of the contents of her larder had gone to one of them.

Going out of the kitchen she crossed the hall, the slow tick of a longcase clock measuring her steps as she climbed the stairs. Halting outside Samuel's bedroom she listened for movement but, hearing nothing, moved along the corridor to the room used as a studio. Tapping the door out of respect for the man whose ears had been sealed in the womb, she went in. Samuel was not there. Maudie breathed more easily. He was still sleeping, so neither of them would know she had been out of the house.

She was halfway down the staircase when Annie let herself in at the front door. 'Mister Samuel must still be sleeping. I have just been to see if he wanted anything but he is not in his studio.'

'Has he woken at all while I have been out?'

'No, Ma'am,' Maudie answered. 'There 'asn't been a sound out of 'im the whole afternoon.'

'Bring his tray in about five minutes,' Annie turned towards the staircase, 'we will be in the sitting room.'

In her room she removed her cloak and bonnet, hanging them in a large wardrobe, letting her fingers caress the lavender silk of the gown the cloak would conceal. Soon she would wear no more black, soon she would wear the colours her lost youth had never known, soon now . . . very soon she would share a bed as Abel had shared his. Her body would know the touches his had known. Soon now . . . soon.

Opening her bag she took out the pretty glass bottle, holding it to where the light from the window caught the faintly golden contents, then crossing to a chest of drawers she placed the bottle in the bottom one, covering it with a layer of silk petticoats carefully wrapped in blue tissue paper.

Pushing to her feet, she gasped, clutching at a point below her left breast as a pain ripped through her. Her breathing rapid, she stumbled to the bed and sat for several minutes before taking the bottle of tablets from the drawer of the side table. Pouring a little water from the carafe that always stood beside her bed, she swallowed a couple of small white tablets. Two minutes later she made her way to her brother's bedroom, the medicine she had collected from the chemist in her hand.

In the kitchen Maudie laid a tray with tea and thinly cut sandwiches of salmon and cucumber. Samuel had taken salmon and cucumber for tea almost daily for the fifteen years she had served as housekeeper; in fact, everything remained the same in Annie Pardoe's household – or at least it had until Harforth-Darby had arrived on the scene. She scalded the tea, setting the white china pot on the tray. She didn't trust Harforth-Darby with his smarmy ways, he was buttering Annie Pardoe up sure as shooting, and just as sure she was in for a disappointment. Maudie set milk and sugar on the tray. If Annie thought she was going to get that one to the altar then she was shouting into an empty gulley, lavender frock or no lavender frock!

Carrying the tray to the sitting room, she set it beside Annie, her eyes taking in the tired sunken features and thin frame of the man who sat opposite.

'You be on your last legs, Samuel Pardoe,' she murmured, closing the door on brother and sister, 'an' it's my idea there be them as is ready to kick 'em out from under you.'

Waiting until the door closed, Annie poured tea, handing one of the cups to Samuel.

'It is just as well I went to collect your medicine,' she signed. 'I swear that Isaac Jackson took near enough an hour to prepare it. Seems tradesmen don't care how long they keep you waiting these days. I tell you, dear, things are no longer the same.'

Samuel smiled wearily. 'Things have not been the same since Abel died.'

Annie watched the rapid flickering of his fingers. 'What do you mean, not been the same?' Her own fingers formed the question.

'Let us not try to delude each other. You have always seen to my welfare, Annie, and I thank you for that though it has not been in the best of ways. It was our parents' thinking that turned my home into a prison. You have merely carried on where they left off. Oh, I know I could physically have forced my way out of this or our former home but what good would that have done? So in that way things have not changed.

'No, Annie, things changed when we heard Abel's will, when we came to Brunswick House. Feelings between you and me have never been what our brother thought them to be. You have always been bitter, blamed Abel for putting you in the position of nursemaid to me, blamed him for your never having married and saw his leaving me his fortune as a means of repayment for what he did. I can't blame you for those feelings, Annie, but since Abel died the bitterness in you has grown. I can never give you back the years you have spent with me but there are some things I can do . . .'

Annie sat stock still, her eyes on Samuel's dancing fingers, a feeling of alarm, fear almost, beginning to rise in her throat.

'. . . you see, I too feel that Abel acted wrongly, that your life was yours to do with as you wished and not as his money dictated. I know I should have told you this twenty years ago but I never found the way. That was my mistake and I'm sorry for it. I also think it was wrong of him to leave everything to us, literally denying his own daughter what was rightfully hers. That was Abel's mistake but it is one I can do something about . . .'

Samuel saw the apprehension on his sister's face deepen into something more at his mention of Abel's daughter and he felt a sudden deep pity. Annie had fed on her bitterness for years. What would she do when she heard all he had to say?

'It is my intention to return Brunswick House to Phoebe,' the movement of his fingers continued, 'together with the mines and partnerships in the Monway steel works and everything else her father willed to me, except a sum of money large enough to keep you comfortably for your lifetime and maybe recompense you somewhat for the years you have spent with me. You do, of course, have the house at Bescot. Whether or not you choose to live in it will be your decision.'

Annie stared at her brother, her brain numbed by what he had told her.

'As for myself,' he went on, 'I don't think Abel or Phoebe would object to my buying a small house somewhere. And not to worry,' the same weary smile touched his lips but the old sadness remained in his eyes, 'you and my parents can rest easily – I am not about to break my bonds. The shame I brought to the family will die a secret.'

The sharp sting of pain below her breast broke the numbness encircling her and Annie stood up, her glance sweeping the now empty room. Samuel was going to give everything back to their niece. She pressed a hand to the pain, will-power forcing the nausea out of her throat. But it was not only Samuel's to give, it was *hers*; she had spent half a lifetime earning that money, earning the power it brought, and Samuel would not take it from her.

"Ave you finished with the tray, Ma'am?' Maudie entered the room, one look at her employer telling her that the suspicion she had held for some time had proved correct, Annie Pardoe had been given a nasty shock. She smiled over the tray as Annie swept out.

'Ar, you've 'ad a shock, Annie Pardoe,' she whispered, carrying the tray to the kitchen, 'a big 'un. But there be more to come yet . . . much more.'

'Excuse me, Sir, but might you be Lucy's 'usband?'

'Who are you?' Edward Dartmouth looked at the tall well-built man coming toward him across the mill yard.

'My name is Bertram . . . Bertram Ingles.'

The reply was polite but there was none of the deference men usually adopted when addressing Edward.

'Might I ask what you are doing here?'

Edward looked at the man standing inches above himself, shirt sleeves rolled halfway between wrist and elbow, trousers held up by a broad leather belt blackened with wear, brass-studded clogs on his feet.

'I've come for water.' He lifted the black enamelled bucket painted around with a band of brightly coloured flowers. 'An' I asks you agen, Sir, be you Lucy's 'usband?'

'I am not Lucy's husband.' Edward's gaze circled the outbuildings. 'How do you know of her?' The gaze came back to the man now almost barring his way. 'And where is Miss Pardoe?'

'If Miss Pardoe be the young woman as lives 'ere then 'er is on my barge.'

'Your barge?' Edward said sharply. 'And how does she come to be there?'

'You've no need to come out fightin'.' Bert saw the flame kindle in the younger man's eyes. ''Er be wi' my Lizzie. I come for to ask permission to draw drinkin' water from the pump there earlier on today an' I found a young woman wi' a bloke sprawled across 'er, 'is trousers round 'is ankles . . .'

'Phoebe!' Edward interrupted. 'Did he . . . ?'

'Rape 'er?' Bert shook his head. 'Though it weren't for the want of tryin', an' 'e would 'ave an' all 'ad I not come across 'im when I did.'

'This man,' Edward brought his riding crop across the palm of his left hand, anger drawing his mouth in to a tight line, 'where is he now?'

'Coolin' what's left of 'is ardour in the cut,' Bert said, a nod of his head indicating the canal, 'though I doubt there was much of that left after I'd finished lettin' daylight into 'is guts.'

'You didn't give him enough!' Edward's eyes glistened with rage. 'You should have killed the swine, and even *that* would have been too good for him.'

'I think I near enough did do for 'im.' Bert smiled grimly. 'Leastways 'e won't be botherin' no woman for a long time yet.'

'More likely never again if I can find him, and I will!' Edward slapped his palm with the crop. 'I'll find the man and finish what you started . . . in the meantime, take this for your trouble.'

Bert Ingles looked at the sovereigns Edward drew from his waistcoat pocket and his face hardened.

'Any trouble I took on young wench's behalf was a trouble I would tek for any woman,' he said angrily, 'an' if it were a trouble then it be one I don't need payment for. You put your money back in your pocket, lad, an' put this bit of advice wi' it: next time you offer payment to a barge man for preventin' a wench bein' raped, mek sure you steps away pretty sharpish or you be likely to find yourself in the cut wi' the light shinin' on *your* innards.'

Edward stared. What was it with these people? First Phoebe and now this man. Both had refused money though it was obvious neither had any: both had almost nothing to support them but both burned with the same fierce pride.

'My apologies, Mr Ingles.' He slipped the coins back into his pocket. 'I had no wish to offend.'

'None teken, lad.' Bert smiled. 'Now if you'll wait till this bucket be filled, I'll tek you to . . . what did you say wench was called?'

'Miss Pardoe,' Edward answered, a liking for the tall rough-mannered man already formed. 'Miss Phoebe Pardoe.'

Edward followed, stepping gingerly from the narrow towpath on to the moored barge, picking his way through an assortment of buckets and ropes clustered into the small space between the prow and the cabin, almost three-quarters of the barge housing a cargo of coal on top of which sat a young boy and an even younger girl, both watching his progress through solemn eyes.

'You pair stop on top,' Bert said to them as he led the way down four steep steps that gave on to the family's living quarters.

'Phoebe,' said Edward blinking against the gloom, 'are you all right?'

''Er's all right.' Lizzie glanced at her husband standing on the steps, the confined space not enough to hold them all. 'Though 'er's 'ad a bad fright.'

Head and shoulders stooped against the low roof, Edward squeezed down the cabin that seemed barely a yard wide. 'Let me take you home, Phoebe.'

'I don't think much of you doin' that,' Lizzie said firmly. 'That wench 'as 'ad a shakin' up an' the last thing 'er needs is to be left on 'er own, so lessen there be somebody wi' 'er in that place of 'er'n then I says 'er's best left 'ere.'

'I think perhaps that would be best.' Edward looked at the bargee's wife, a white poke bonnet still covering her head even though she was in what was her sitting room. 'It would not be proper if I stay alone with her and neither can she be left on her own whilst I fetch Lucy from the town.' He touched a hand to Phoebe's, resting in her lap.

'Don't fetch Lucy, Edward.' She looked up at him. 'I have

suffered no harm and don't want her worried. If it is all right with Mr and Mrs Ingles I would prefer to stay with them until Lucy and Mathew return. They are always home about seven.'

'That ain't no bother to me nor Bert.' Lizzie caught the nod from her husband.

'Thank you.' Edward squeezed Phoebe's fingers gently before turning towards the hatchway. 'You may have refused my money, Mr Ingles,' he said when they both stood once more on the towpath, 'but surely you will not refuse my thanks for your solicitousness.'

'I won't refuse.' Bert took the hand the younger man extended, shaking it warmly. 'An' though it don't be necessary, it be appreciated.'

'Surprised me, that 'as,' he said, half to himself, watching Edward stride away towards the mill, its redundant windmill standing sentinel on the low rise that hid the house from the canalside.

'What 'as, Dad?'

'That one,' Bert answered his son, eyes following the figure moving rapidly away. ''E don't come from no miner nor no foundryman neither, that one 'as a different breedin', yet I thought all moneyed folk was above thankin' the likes of we. But 'e ain't.'

'Dad,' the boy asked as his father stepped aboard the barge, 'what's titty us ness?'

'Eh?' Bert glanced sharply across the expanse of coal.

'Titty us ness,' the boy's eyes gleamed roguishly, 'that's what that bloke thanked you for ain't it?'

'They ears been flappin' agen?' Bert picked up a nut of coal, 'they need a set o' doors fastened to 'em.' He threw the coal laughing as his son rolled clear, 'Cheeky young bugger,' he muttered fondly.

Chapter Eleven

Phoebe looked up from the small dress she was sewing, waves of fear flooding through her at the sound from outside the house. Putting her work aside she tiptoed to the window that looked out towards the track leading to the town, breathing her relief when she saw the trap she knew to be Sophie's.

Running swiftly downstairs she opened the door, her smile of welcome fading when she saw her caller.

'Good afternoon, Miss Pardoe.' Sir William Dartmouth inclined his head with a slight, barely perceptible movement. 'I hope I am not inconveniencing you by calling?'

'No . . . not at all.' Phoebe could not entirely hide her surprise.

'Edward told me of the unfortunate incident that took place yesterday,' he said when she did not ask him into the house. 'I trust you were not injured . . . in any way?'

'No.' The tiny pause so significant in its meaning was not lost on Phoebe; he had been told not only of the assault upon herself but also the nature of that assault. 'I was not injured . . . in any way.'

'I am relieved to hear it,' he said, watching the colour rise to her cheeks. 'My wife and I were concerned to hear of what happened to you, as was Sophie. Both of them were anxious to call upon you but my wife is ill with influenza and Sophie is not happy to leave her mother at the moment. But given your permission they will call once Amelia is well again.'

'I shall be happy to see them.' Phoebe stepped aside,

clearing the doorway. 'Forgive me, Sir William, won't you come in?'

Stepping inside, he allowed her to take his gloves, and when she set them on a small mahogany stand, followed her to the tiny parlour.

'Will you take some tea?' Phoebe asked when he was seated. 'I am afraid I have nothing in the way of wine.'

Tea. William Dartmouth smiled inwardly. It was every Englishwoman's placebo. 'No, thank you,' he said. 'I will not detain you. I came only to assure myself and my womenfolk that you had taken no harm.'

'None, I assure you.'

'That is as well, for the fellow who attacked you will pay hard enough when he is caught, and he will be, you have my word on that.'

'I think he has probably paid enough already,' Phoebe said, 'judging by what I hear Bert Ingles did to him.'

'Ah, yes, Edward told me of him. A bit of a rough diamond if I'm not mistaken.'

'You're not!' Phoebe's eyes flashed green fire. 'But then, diamonds are valuable rough or cut, are they not? And the Ingleses will always be highly valued friends to me.'

He glanced around the small room with its tired, well-worn furniture. This child of Abel Pardoe's might have little in the way of worldly goods but courage and integrity she had in plenty.

'You are not here alone, Miss Pardoe?'

'Of course I am, this is my home, where else would I be?'

'But I understood a woman and her husband were here with you.'

'Lucy and Mathew,' Phoebe nodded, 'but they go into Wednesbury every day.'

'Leaving you in this place by yourself?'

'Sir William, I am not a child.'

'That much is obvious,' he replied tersely, 'and therefore

the greater the danger. This Lucy . . . she must stay home, you must not be alone here again.'

'Sir William,' Phoebe said coolly, 'Lucy is the mainstay of this house at the moment. Her earnings provide most of their living and all of mine. Mathew works hard but odd jobs pay little in Wednesbury, so you see it is impossible for Lucy to stay here all day. My explanation is more for Lucy's sake than for yours. I would not have you think she left me on my own from choice.

'There is one more thing I have to say and it is this: do not ever use the word "must" to me. I have earned the right to be my own mistress and no man or woman will ever dictate to me again.'

William Dartmouth glanced at the down-at-heel furniture. 'Accept the money I still offer and neither of you would need to work again.'

'Don't seek to still your conscience with money.' Anger made Phoebe's voice sharp. 'I asked for none and I shall take none.'

'That is your prerogative.' He smiled. 'As will be your answer to my next question, always supposing you choose to give one for of course I should not dream of saying you must.'

'You can ask.' Phoebe caught the hint of amusement behind his grey eyes and her own mouth relaxed into a smile.

'This Ingles fellow – he told Edward that when he came upon that man attacking you, you were screaming about someone called Liza, and a little later you thought you were talking to a Tilly. Neither is a suitable name for a man. Tell me, was anyone else involved? Did the one who assaulted you have an accomplice?'

Phoebe's smile faded. 'No,' she said, looking to her lap where her fingers had automatically twined together at the memory of Handsworth Women's Prison. 'At least, there was no one with him when he . . . when he came here.'

'So who are the women whose names you called?'

She didn't have to tell him, Phoebe thought, he had no claim upon her, no right to ask questions. She could tell him that and then ask him to leave.

'Liza Spittle was a prisoner in Handsworth,' she said, surprised by the decision she could not recall making. 'She . . . she had certain tendencies . . . she . . . she tried . . .'

'You mean, she tried to force herself on you much the same as a man?'

'Yes,' Phoebe said, not knowing why she wanted him to know what Liza had done and grateful when he spared her the strain of the telling. 'And Tilly helped me . . . twice. She warned Liza not to touch me in . . . in that way again, and when she did try a second time Tilly tripped her up and Liza hit her head against the wall. I think she was hurt quite badly . . . she . . . she may even have died, and if so the Governors might say it was murder and Tilly would hang. But it wasn't! Tilly couldn't . . .'

'Is Tilly an inmate of the prison also?'

Phoebe nodded. 'She always will be. She is serving a lifetime sentence for manslaughter. They . . . they said she killed her husband but . . .' She looked up, her eyes defiant behind their cloud of unhappiness. 'I don't think she did. Tilly is no murderess no matter what any judge may have said.'

He rose, collecting his gloves from the small stand where Phoebe had placed them and opening the door himself.

'You are a very stubborn young woman,' he said, smiling. 'You refuse my offer of compensation, then you tell me never to use the word "must" to you again, and now you say you do not believe the verdict of a court.'

'It would not be the first time a court had been wrong, would it, Sir William?'

Pulling on his gloves, William Dartmouth looked at the girl whom he knew would openly defy him on any matter she felt to be right. 'Yes,' he inclined his head in a gesture of farewell, 'a very stubborn young woman, but one I admire. Good afternoon, Miss Phoebe Pardoe.'

• • •

'Me mam says to ask can I fill this from your pump?'

Phoebe smiled at the lad, his grin cheeky, his toffeedrop eyes bright beneath tumbling brown hair.

'Of course,' she answered. 'And when you're done come into the kitchen. I've got a big fat scone that is just asking to be eaten.'

''As it got sultanas in it?'

'Yes, big ones . . . this size.' She made a circle with thumb and forefinger.

'Oooh, bostin'.' His eyes gleamed with anticipation. 'I like sultanas. Our Ruth don't, 'er picks 'em out when we 'ave cake. Me mam says 'er shouldn't, it's bad manners to pick, but I don't mind 'cos our Ruth, 'er gives 'em to me.'

'I might be able to find one without sultanas for Ruth.' Phoebe recognised the barge man's word for something good or pleasant.

'Eh, don't do that, Miss!' He grinned, putting down the large flower-painted jug then wiping his palms against the sides of his trousers. ''Er enjoys picking 'em out as much as 'er does the eatin' of the rest.'

'In that case, we will find her one with extra sultanas.'

'We am leavin' tomorrer,' he said, perched on a stool in the kitchen, pulling sultanas from a scone and squashing them between his teeth, savouring each one before swallowing it. 'We as to tek them coals to London.'

'London?' Phoebe watched him work his way around the edge of the scone, the plate she had offered it on forgotten on the table. 'That's a good way off.'

'Ar, it is,' he nodded, recovering a crumb from his knee and stuffing it in his mouth beside a sultana. 'You ever been there, Miss?'

'No, I haven't.'

'I don't know as you'd like it.' He surveyed her over the scone. 'It's quite a big place, an' dirty the parts I've seen of it, an' folks pushin' an' shovin' as if they don't 'ave a minute to live.'

'It can't be much dirtier than Wednesbury.'

'It is, Miss, you can tek it from me. Wednesbury is a picture compared to London. Oh, the buildin's 'ere am black wi' smoke an' soot but the streets, well, they ain't filled wi' everybody's rubbish like, am they? I mean, they don't drop their paper on the roads or throw the peelin's out the windows here, do they?'

'They don't do that in London, do they?'

One foot tapping a half-laced boot against the leg of the stool, he considered a partly concealed sultana. 'I don't know about the places the nobs live in,' he twisted the scone, considering the sultana from all angles, 'but the ones we dock in, the basins like, well, you finds all sorts o' stuff throwed down there. Me mam, 'er don't like London an' I don't think you would either.'

'In that case I shan't go.' Phoebe placed several scones in a dark blue paper bag that had once held sugar. 'But I do quite fancy the seaside.'

'Me an' all.' He gave way to temptation, pulling the sultana free. 'An' our Ruth. Me dad says we might pick up a load that 'as to go to a port one day . . . a port is like the seaside, ain't it, Miss?'

'Mmmm.' Phoebe twisted the top of the bag to make a fastening. 'I imagine so. A port has ships and ships sail on the sea, so a port must be the seaside.'

''Ave you been to the seaside?'

Settling the bag of scones on the table, Phoebe went into the scullery, fetching a jug of milk from a bowl half filled with water to keep it cool.

'Not since I was a very small girl.' She filled a glass with the frothy white milk, setting the linen cover back over the jug before returning it to the scullery.

'Didn't your parents 'ave the money to tek you more than once?'

'It wasn't the money,' Phoebe placed the glass of milk before him, 'my mother died while I was still quite young and my father was too busy with his business to take me to the seaside.'

'Never mind, Miss.' He looked across at her, his eyes round and brown as a well-used penny, a seriousness in them that outstripped his years. 'Like me mam says, we all 'ave our cross to bear, but when we get that load for a port you can come with we. Mam an' Dad won't mind.'

'Speaking of your mother, Mark Ingles, she is not going to be at all pleased if you keep her waiting much longer for that jug of water.'

'Bugger me! I'd forgot all about the water.' He jumped from the stool, shoving the desecrated scone into his mouth.

Phoebe followed him into the yard, handing him the bag of scones as he finished filling the jug.

'An' you'll forget me language, won't you, Miss?' He grinned up at her, crumbs edging his lips. 'Go on, Miss, be a pal, say you ain't 'eard me say what I said?'

'All right,' Phoebe laughed, 'I didn't hear you say what you said.'

'Ta, Miss.' He sauntered off across the yard, raising the bag of scones above his head. 'Tara for now.'

'Miss Phoebe,' Lucy said thoughtfully, 'whoever it was come 'ere to rob you, 'e knowed about you bein' up at the Priory, 'e even knowed as you seen all of the family together, so it seems to me 'e is either a footman or else somebody who works in the 'ouse told 'im about you bein' there.'

'I . . . I hadn't thought about it.' It was true she had not thought of how the man had known of her visit, or of the fact she had been in prison, but she had lived through the nightmare of his attack again and again through the long night, jangles of fear setting her nerves dancing at every sound, only the knowledge that Lucy and Mathew were staying in the house preventing her from screaming.

'Well, I 'ave.' Lucy went on talking as she tipped flour into a bowl. 'An' if I 'ave then Sir William is sure to 'ave an' all. 'E ain't no fool that one, 'e can put two an' two together an' come up with 'alf a dozen.'

'Do you think that was the real reason for his coming here today?'

'Don't know.' Lucy spooned a small amount of salt into the flour. ''E didn't ask any questions about 'ow anybody might know, did 'e? But that don't mean anythin'. 'E might not 'ave said as much but you can take it from me 'e 'ad thought of it.'

He might have thought about it but Phoebe wanted only to put the whole episode behind her. She wouldn't forget, she would never forget, but right now she wanted only to leave it, to talk of anything except that.

Phoebe reached for the tongs settling fresh coals on the fire, then rinsed her hands and set about greasing pie tins with a dab of lard on a scrap of cloth.

'He asked whether I had suffered any harm from being attacked.'

'What the 'ell did 'e think? It certainly ain't done you no good. Bloody soft question to ask!' Lucy exploded.

'He said Sophie and Lady Amelia were concerned and that they would call later.'

'Huh!' Reaching a small shallow basin from the dresser, Lucy pressed it into the pastry, making a series of circles. 'Why didn't they come with him?'

'Lady Amelia has the influenza.'

Taking the circles she had cut from the pastry, Lucy pressed them into the tins. 'It was their son's fault you was gaoled but even so their sort don't usually call on the likes o' we.'

'The likes of us are as good as any Dartmouths, Lucy,' Phoebe answered, pounding a pot of boiled potatoes with a wooden spoon. 'The only difference is they have money and we do not.'

'*You* could have.' Lucy scooped the remnants of the circles together, rolling them with quick deft movements, making a further mat of soft pastry. 'You was offered it an' I think you should take it. It's nothin' you don't deserve.'

Phoebe lifted the large pot of mutton from the fireplace where it had stewed gently from early morning. Draining the stock into a bowl, she added the meat to the mashed potato. 'Accepting money will not alter what happened. I prefer to earn my living.'

'Well, I think you'm daft.' Tasting the mixture of meat and potato, Lucy nodded and Phoebe began filling the pastry-lined tins.

Finishing the filling of a dozen pie tins, she draped a cloth over the unused mixture, setting the pan in the hearth. 'Lucy,' she asked, passing a smaller basin the other girl had pointed to, 'do you think my dresses would sell in the town?'

Lucy pressed the basin into the pastry, cutting out smaller circles. 'The bits an' pieces I've managed to make 'ave gone well enough an' they ain't near so good as your'n. Mind, I couldn't make much, what wi' the baking.'

Phoebe watched smaller circles of pastry being placed over each pie tin, Lucy fluting the edges between finger and thumb. 'But what you did make sold each time?'

'Ar.' Lucy nodded. 'Could 'ave sold more but like I says, it's 'avin' the time to sew.'

Dipping two fingers into an egg she had beaten, Phoebe traced the lid of each pie. 'What about your pies and my dresses?'

'What you mean, Miss?' Lucy was already busy with the next batch of pastry.

'Put them together.'

'Eh?' Lucy paused.

'Well, not together as such.' Phoebe began to load the oven with pies. 'What I meant was, if you bake and I sew we could pool the money we make.'

'No, Miss Phoebe,' Lucy began, cutting out larger circles, 'your little frocks is worth much more than mutton pies.'

Closing the oven, Phoebe straightened. 'Your mutton pies have fed me since I came home, Lucy.'

'Oh, ar!' Looking up she ran her eyes over the girl she had once worked for. 'Well, they ain't made you much fatter. Anyway you give Mathew an' me a place to stay . . . well, you did in a manner o' speakin' 'cept you wasn't 'ere to speak to, an' then when you come out you didn't make we go. Way I sees things, a mutton pie an' the odd scone don't count for much against that.'

'It counts for a great deal with me,' Phoebe said, oiling more pie tins with a knob of lard, 'so we are equal, neither of us owes the other anything.' Lifting the pan from the hearth, she spooned the remainder of the filling into the pastry-lined tins then carried the empty pot into the scullery to be washed later.

'Do you really think my clothes would sell?' She asked again, uncertainty edging her question. 'Money is not all that plentiful in Wednesbury, is it?'

'Not in all quarters it ain't.' Lucy finished fluting the edge of the last pie. 'But then everybody don't work for Annie Pardoe. Some o' the men 'er finished at the pits as got taken on at Hampstead mine. Seem to be doin' all right an' all judgin' by the number of pies them women o' their'n buy.'

'But everyone has to have food,' Phoebe said, moistening pastry lids with beaten egg.

'Ar, an' they 'ave to wear clothes an' all or they gets a slow walk to Wednesbury police station wi' a bobby on each arm.' Lucy stretched her aching back. 'Tell you what . . . why don't I take them little frocks you made for Lady Dartmouth an' see if they sell?'

'I had thought of trying, I was getting them out of the trunk when . . .' Despite the heat of the kitchen Phoebe's face paled. The fear of what had happened was still vivid. It haunted her nights and filled her days but she knew if she admitted as much her friend would stay home and that would mean very little money coming in, and Mathew and Lucy had things hard enough. Going to the oven, she took out the cooked pies, hoping the action would cover her hesitation, masking what she could not say.

Lucy rattled the cooking utensils, gathering them for washing. If that bastard hasn't drowned in the cut then I hope he's dropped down a mine shaft! she thought. Either way may he rot in hell for attacking a woman. 'I will just get this lot shifted an' we'll 'ave us a cup of tea,' she said, rubbing her hands in the bowl of warm water on the hob. 'Put the kettle back over the fire, Miss.'

Phoebe swung the iron bracket, bringing the kettle to rest over the hot coals, then picking up the basin of water, followed to where Lucy had carried bowls and dishes to the scullery.

'I'll empty this in the yard,' she said, going to the scullery door. 'Will I give Mathew a shout?'

'If you will, Miss.' Lucy set the dishes against the large brownstone sink. ''E'll be just about gaspin' for a cup of tea.'

'Lucy . . .' The three of them were sitting in the kitchen of the mill house, cosy with the glow of the fire and the smell of fresh-baked pies and scones. 'What did you mean when you said not everyone in Wednesbury works for Annie Pardoe?'

'What do you mean, what do I mean?' Lucy asked in the tongue-twisting Black Country style.

'It seemed strange your using my aunt's name. She can't have anything to do with the business, that is solely Uncle Samuel's responsibility.'

'P'raps yer father thought it would be,' Mathew looked up from the fire, 'but Annie soon put the mockers on that. It's 'er as 'as all the say in what is or what isn't to be done, an' who is to be finished an' who ain't.'

'Aunt Annie might say things,' Phoebe nursed her cup between her hands, 'but she can't do more than that, she cannot sign her name to anything. Only Uncle Samuel can do that.'

'Seems like 'er can,' Mathew replied. 'I called in me mam's afore I come 'ome an' 'er said Maudie Tranter 'ad visited earlier. Maudie told 'er that Annie be gettin' a gentleman visitor . . . quite reglar it seems . . . an' Maudie 'eard 'er tellin' 'im Samuel 'ad given 'er some sort of power . . . power of a turn summat or other, me mam couldn't rightly say, but whatever it be it means Annie Pardoe can sign any business paper in place o' her brother.'

'Power of Attorney,' Phoebe said, suddenly understanding the sacking of men and the reduction in wages. 'My aunt has Uncle Samuel's Power of Attorney.'

'What does that mean, Miss?' Lucy asked.

Phoebe let her head sink tiredly against the back of her chair. 'It means my aunt has control of everything my father left to Samuel.'

'An' that means 'alf of Wednesbury,' Mathew said. ''E might just as well 'ave left it to the Devil.'

A loud knock on the scullery door jangled Phoebe's frayed nerves and the jerk of her hands set the tea dancing madly in her cup.

'You be all right, Miss,' Mathew said calmly. 'Just stop you theer, I'll see who that be.'

'I would like a word wi' Miss Pardoe, would you ask 'er if 'er will see me?'

Phoebe breathed out long and slow, feeling the tension loosen from her stomach as she recognised the voice of Bert Ingles.

'Come in, Mr Ingles,' she said, going to the scullery. 'I hope you don't mind the kitchen? It's a bit cramped but it's warmer than the sitting room.'

'I'm used wi' being cramped, there's not much living space on a barge.' Bert Ingles nodded to Lucy and Mathew as Phoebe introduced them.

'What can I do for you?' Phoebe smiled.

'I come to bring you these.' He fished in the pocket of a jacket that should have had a decent burial long ago, pulling out two brass locks. 'Me an' Lizzie got to talkin' after we brought you back 'ere yesterday evenin' . . . well, like we said, you can bolt these doors from the inside but we couldn't see 'ow you would fasten 'em on the outside, not so as nobody could get in like, an' Lizzie said there was bound to come times when you 'ad to leave the place, so we thought if you put these on the doors you would at least be certain nobody had got in while you was away. You would 'ave no more nasty surprises waitin' for you, if you follow what I mean.'

'That is very kind of you, Mr Ingles, I am most grateful to you and to your wife. It will be a great relief to me knowing the doors of the house are securely fastened.'

'They will be with these.' He looked proudly at the locks he held, one in each hand. 'Nobody will get them open wi'out the keys. These am no ordinary locks, I made these meself.'

'You made 'em?' Mathew took one of the locks, turning it over in his hands. ''Ow could you do that on a barge?'

'I didn't make them on the barge.'

'Oh,' Mathew looked up, 'then where?'

Shaking his head at Phoebe's offer of a chair, Bert Ingles went on, a strong hint of pride lacing his explanation: 'Them locks be my own design. You can't buy them in no ironmonger's. I made them just before me father died. You see, Miss. . .' he looked at Phoebe '. . . me father was a lockmaker out at Willenhall, an' 'e taught me the locksmithing.'

'But the barge,' Phoebe said, 'I thought you worked the barge?'

'So I do, Miss,' he answered, 'but I ain't always done that. I worked wi' me father up to three years ago. It wasn't until 'e died though that I found 'e had run at such a loss I couldn't pay the brass founders an' everybody else that claimed 'e owed them wi'out selling up.' He shrugged. 'So that is what I did. There were nothing for it after that but to get a job, any job that would feed the wife and kids. That's how I come to be working the canal.'

'What be so different about this?' Mathew turned the lock he was holding, sending darts of gold flickering from the polished brass.

'I'll show you.' Fishing a key from his jacket, Bert took the lock, inserted the key in it. 'See?' He turned the key, the action shooting out a metal bar.

'Ar, it's locked,' Mathew said, a quizzical frown pulling his brows together. 'I don't see nothin' different in that.'

'But it's not locked, not altogether.' Bert Ingles smiled. 'You see, this is a doubler.'

'A whater?' Lucy asked.

'A doubler, Missis.' Bert passed her the lock. 'Least that's what I call it. You see, it's a double barrel lock.' He took the lock back, turning the key a second time, and another bar shot out. 'Now,' he handed the lock to Mathew, 'try openin' it.'

Mathew tried turning the key but it wouldn't budge. He tried again then looked at the man watching him. 'It's stuck,' he said. 'The key must be jammed or summat.'

'It's not the key nor the lock that be jammed.' Bert retrieved the lock. 'That's what you are meant to think. You see, anybody not knowing how it works would think the same, and thinking they had got the key stuck would leave off trying to get in.'

'Well, if a burglar couldn't get in, all supposin' 'e managed to get 'old of the key, 'ow do you expect we to do it?'

'Like this.' Bert laid the lock on the table so they could each follow what he did. 'You turned the key anti-clockwise to operate the bolt,' he said, glancing at Mathew, 'that would be the normal way to operate a lock, but I reversed the mechanism. On this the key has to be turned clockwise to lock it.'

'Clever.' Mathew pursed his lips admiringly. 'But what about the doubler bit?'

'This is where the key does get stuck,' Bert answered, 'least you would think it had 'cos you won't pull it out at this stage. You 'ave to turn the key once more, that releases a second bolt an' also the key; it's a double safeguard. Even if a burglar cottoned on to the fact the key had to be turned back way round from usual, its getting stuck would cause him a bit of a headache.'

'An' pickin' the lock an' then findin' it still didn't open, 'e would likely pack in tryin' altogether?' Mathew grinned. 'That's what I calls useful.'

'It is a very good way of locking doors,' Phoebe said. 'They will save me a deal of concern whenever I have to go anywhere. How much do I owe you, Mr Ingles?'

'You don't owe me anything.' He laid three more keys beside the locks on the table. 'Me and Lizzie be just glad we could be of help.'

'But I couldn't . . .'

'Ar you could,' Bert Ingles looked suddenly embarrassed, 'just show me where you keep your screwdrivers and such and I'll have them locks on the doors in no time.'

'I'll give you a hand.' Mathew picked up the locks. 'Tools am in the barn.'

'Eh! What do you reckon to that?' Lucy asked as the two men left the kitchen.

'I reckon you are going to have to pay for those locks, Mrs Leach.'

'Me!' Lucy gasped. 'I ain't got but ninepence in me purse.'

'Bert Ingles won't take money,' Phoebe handed her a clean cloth from the airer strung across the fireplace, 'but I don't think he would refuse four of your mutton pies.'

Chapter Twelve

'I said to sell them . . . both of them.'

Annie Pardoe sat in James Siveter's office in his chambers in Lower High Street, her voluminous black skirts entirely hiding the small chair beneath her.

'You will have no trouble, I have been asked to sell them on several occasions.'

'Miss Pardoe,' the solicitor cleared his throat, 'does your brother know of this intended sale?'

Annie's eyes narrowed and her mouth tightened. 'If you want to continue to be our solicitor, James Siveter, I advise you to do as I instruct. My brother gave me his full Power of Attorney and that means I can act as I see fit, and I see fit to sell the Hobs Hill coal mine and the Crown. It also means I can replace you in your capacity as Samuel's solicitor. Your sort are two a penny.'

James Siveter rolled his long-handled pen between his fingers, experiencing a strong desire to tell the woman sitting opposite his heavy desk to take her business with her to the nearest canal and jump in with it! But it was a desire he curbed; she was right when she said she could replace him, and while not exactly two a penny solicitors were not hard to come by. He could not afford to lose business, however wrong he felt it to be.

'I will bring the necessary papers to Brunswick House first thing tomorrow.'

'No!' Annie's tight mouth showed no sign of slackening. 'You will not come to Brunswick House. I will sign an agreement of sale while I am here. You can get the purchaser's signature today – we have already agreed the price. I shall call here again tomorrow at three and I expect the business to be concluded.'

Why the rush? James Siveter thought, filling out the necessary documents. And why was Annie Pardoe here instead of sending for him to come to Brunswick House as he had always done? Power of Attorney or not, she obviously didn't intend Samuel knowing of today's doings.

'I will get this to the purchaser as soon as . . .'

'You will take it to him now!' Annie snapped. 'I want this finished and done. Three o'clock tomorrow.'

Holding the door for her to pass, the solicitor watched as she swept into the street. So she was selling both coal mines, and quickly . . . too quickly even for Annie Pardoe. Yes, it was a safe bet Samuel knew nothing of it, just as he likely knew nothing of what she had sold already: the shares in the Monway steel foundry, the Moxley iron works, together with a string of smaller businesses and houses. And what was she doing with the money she'd had for them? He had drawn up no new contracts. Whatever she had done, he, James Siveter, had not been consulted. Closing the door, he returned to his desk. 'I wonder?' he mused, taking up the papers Annie had signed and putting them into a small valise. 'I wonder, Samuel, do you have any idea just how close you are to having nothing?'

Leaving the solicitor's office Annie had turned her trap left along the bottom end of Lower High Street, guiding the horse left again into Finchpath Lane. This way she could avoid the wheels of the trap becoming caught in the tramlines. There was also less likelihood of her being seen by going back to the house via the heath. She flicked the reins, urging the horse into a trot. What the folk of Wednesbury didn't see they couldn't talk about, and she wanted no talk of what she had been about today.

Samuel had spoken of reverting his legacy to Phoebe, of

giving back what his sister's sacrifices had earned. How easily, she thought bitterly, how *easily* her brothers disposed of her life, ordering hers to the comfort of their own. Abel had enjoyed that comfort, enjoyed the pleasures of his pretty wife, and now Samuel wanted the comfort of a conscience cleared of taking Phoebe's inheritance and his sister was to have no part in that decision. But she would not let it happen again; she had been given a second chance at living, a chance to have all Abel had had in every sense of the word, and this time she would not let it go. Tomorrow she would have the money from the sale of the mines and the next day she would give it to Clinton.

She clicked her tongue, encouraging the horse, seeing the figure of Clinton Harforth-Darby in her mind. In his mid-forties, he was a handsome man, tall, always well dressed, his dark hair just hinting at grey, with clear intense eyes and a manner only real breeding bestowed. Calling to see Violet Wheeler at Oakeswell Hall she had first been introduced to Gaskell's cousin, and the next afternoon he had come to Brunswick House.

The reins forgotten in her hands, she let her mind play over the events of the past weeks, events that had led her to the threshold of a new life. With the death of his wife a year ago Clinton had sold his sugar plantation in the West Indies to return to England. Interested in the manufacture of the new metal tubes, he had come to Wednesbury to discuss with Gaskell the possibility of starting up a business. That was when he and Annie had met. From that moment she had, for the first time in twenty years, been treated like a woman and not a servile catspaw. Clinton was not like her father had been, nor Abel, treating women as though they didn't have the capacity to understand anything beyond the kitchen. He had talked to her about going into the manufacture of tubes, how he saw the business expanding over the years; he had told her how Gaskell had wanted to be a partner in the venture but Clinton had refused him. He had more than enough money to finance any business, he said. He did not want a partner, what he wanted was *her*.

Annie's heart gave the same crazy bounce it had when Clinton had said those words two weeks ago. He wanted to marry her, to make her his wife. She, Annie Pardoe, would become Mrs Clinton Harforth-Darby, *she* would marry into the Wheeler family not Phoebe, and she would take the Pardoe money with her. Clinton had brushed it aside when she had told him that Samuel owned everything. It was of no consequence, he had said, he wanted her for his wife not the paltry amount her brother might have bequeathed. However, if it interested her, she could go on being the legal representative for Samuel. It was then he had given her the ring, placing it on the third finger of her left hand, a square-cut amethyst the size of her thumbnail.

It was kept in a drawer in her bedroom. Annie thought now of the lovely ring hidden beneath layers of petticoats, the same petticoats that covered the perfume bottle that had been Elias Webb's gift to her. Clinton would announce their engagement at the Wheelers' house during the party they were giving before their son's regiment left for India. Until then she would not wear it, and by then everything that had once been Abel's would be hers.

They had often talked of the new premises he would build for the making of metal tubes during Clinton's visits, her interest seeming to fire his own as she suggested sites in or near the town, pointing out their nearness to the canal that would be needed to transport the tubes. That was when Clinton had said she would have made an ideal partner for his business except she was to be his wife, refusing to entertain the idea she could be both; it had taken her some time to get him to agree, Clinton eventually suggesting she become a steel tube manufacturer in her own right; the premises, the machinery, the raw steel, everything in her name. Only that way would he be happy.

And now the coal mines, the mainstay of all that had

once constituted Abel's wealth and then Samuel's were gone. Tomorrow she would have the money that would start her in her own business and the beginning of a new life.

'I was pleased to hear Sophie's news.' Phoebe glanced at Edward walking beside her. 'She was so excited when she called on Thursday.'

'Her coming engagement to Montrose Wheeler, you mean?' He stopped, picking up a stone and skimming it into the canal. 'I wish I could feel as happy for her.'

'But you don't?' Phoebe knew she was stating the obvious.

'No.' He sent a second stone winging after the first. 'The Wheelers are simply intent on making a good match, just as they were with . . .' He stopped awkwardly. 'I . . . I beg your pardon, Phoebe.'

'Just as they were with Abel Pardoe's daughter?' She smiled. 'You don't need to apologise for telling the truth, Edward.'

'You knew!' He turned to her, surprise lifting his fair eyebrows. 'You knew they wanted you for your father's money rather than for . . . for . . .'

'For myself?' She gazed at the circles spreading on the surface where the stones had struck the water. 'No, not at the time. I only realised that when his mother told me she had written to tell him of my Uncle Samuel's inheriting everything that was my father's, and he did nothing . . . he never even wrote to me to tell me he no longer wished to marry me.'

'He left that to his mother also?'

She nodded. 'It was a shock then but at least I have been saved from a marriage that could have brought me no real love, and I am grateful for that.'

'But what will save Sophie?' He kicked a boot savagely into the spongy earth. 'Her dowry will not be signed away to an uncle, she will be handed over like so much coal or wheat, she and all she has will become the property of Montrose Wheeler – and it will be God help her after that.'

'Does your mother know how you feel about Sophie's marrying Montrose?'

'My mother thinks that it is a good match. I truly believe she is of the opinion that love grows only after marriage.'

'And Sophie . . .' Phoebe watched the circles spread into nothing. 'Have you said anything of your feelings to her?'

'No, how could I when she is so happy? I can't tell her, Phoebe, I can't be the one to hurt her.'

Far better the bubble be burst now, Phoebe thought, than let it carry her to the moon only to break there.

'What of your father?' she asked. 'Have you confided in him?'

Edward plucked a blade of grass, twisting it between his fingers. 'I have said nothing to him but I think he knows I feel such a marriage would be wrong, and that like myself he would rather Sophie widened her social circle, met other young men before making her choice. But like myself Father could never bring himself to hurt her.'

'So Sophie will marry regardless of how you and Sir William feel?'

'Maybe not.' He rolled the blade of grass between his fingers then flicked it out over the water. 'My father has no wish to see Sophie hurt and that is why he has set the date for her betrothal to Wheeler to take place when we return from Europe, which puts it several months into next year. At least that way he is giving her a little time to find out if her emotion is love or not. And who knows? She may meet someone she would rather marry than Gaskell Wheeler's son . . . anyway that is what I hope, and I think it is my father's hope too.'

And mine, thought Phoebe, no trace of jealousy colouring it. No girl should marry a man only to discover his passion was for her money. She had been saved from that. Pray God Sophie would be too.

Returning the wave of a small girl on a passing barge, Phoebe turned from the peaceful lure of the water. Sophie's visits once a fortnight were not so disruptive to her work but Edward had begun to call at Wiggins Mill weekly and sometimes more than that. She had to find a way of telling him she could not spend a couple of afternoons a week out walking with him. 'I really must return, Edward,' she began. 'I ought not to be here, it's not fair on Lucy and Mathew.'

'How do you mean, not fair?'

'Surely you must see it is not right for me to be out walking when both of them are at work? I should be working too. I have a living to make as they do.'

'There's no need for any of this,' he waved a hand in the direction of the mill, 'you should not have to work for your living.'

'Then how would I manage?' Phoebe's laugh held more irony than humour. 'People need money to live, Edward, and it does not grow on trees.'

'You would not need money,' he caught her hand, his blue eyes intense, 'not if you became my wife. I love you, Phoebe. I have since that moment I helped you into the carriage the day you came to the Priory to collect those dresses. Marry me . . . say you will be my wife?'

What would that hold for both of them? Phoebe looked into his face, so like his mother's, and knew the answer. Sir William Dartmouth's son and heir married to a woman who had been in prison . . . what gossip that would provide! What houses would receive them merely to see his gaolbird wife, only to ignore them politely from then on. She knew Edward would argue his love was strong enough to withstand the attitudes of others, but would it be? Yes, he loved her now, she had seen it in his eyes each time they met, but was it real or just the misguided infatuation of a young man attempting to right a wrong he had caused, and would a year from now see him regretting such a marriage?

Gently she released her hands. She could not take that risk. She had too much respect for his parents, Edward carried too old a family line, too ancient a name, to have anything threaten it. And marriage to her, a woman accused and convicted of theft, however wrongly, would do him no good in the eyes of society.

'I won't marry you, Edward,' she said softly. 'I will not marry anyone yet.' She smiled up at him. 'Perhaps in a year or so, providing you feel as you do now, you will ask me again.' She turned away, the cloud of disappointment on his face hurting her too. Trying hard to sound matter-of-fact, hoping that way to lighten any embarrassment her refusal of his offer might have caused him, she went on, 'In the meantime, whether we like it or not, I have work to do.'

'Phoebe,' he said as she would have walked on, 'is there anyone else?'

'No, Edward,' she replied, the truth of it shining from her eyes, 'there is no one else.'

'Eeh, what a to do in the town today!' Lucy dropped into a chair as Phoebe dished up the evening meal she had prepared. 'You know Charles West, the jeweller in the High Street . . . well, 'e was robbed the night afore.'

'Robbed!' Phoebe stopped filling Mathew's bowl with the soup she had simmered all day. 'Who did it?'

'Nobody knows,' Mathew answered. 'It 'appened durin' the night by what I 'eard.'

'Heavens!' Phoebe finished filling his bowl then ladled soup into her own. 'Was anyone hurt?'

Mathew took a chunk of crusty bread, dipping it into his soup. 'No,' he said between bites, 'nobody 'eard anythin', not a sound. Charlie West never knowed it 'ad 'appened till he went for 'is cash this mornin'.'

'But the money from the shop,' Phoebe looked up from her meal, 'surely he doesn't leave the takings in the shop overnight?'

'No, 'e don't,' Mathew helped himself to more bread, 'an' 'e don't put it in no bank neither. Seems whoever broke into 'is 'ouse last night knowed that, 'cos money was all was took.'

'Were the police called?' Phoebe asked.

Lucy nodded but it was Mathew answered. 'Ar, they was called but them bobbies don't seem to know whether they be comin' or whether they've been. It seems Charlie West wasn't the only one to get 'is pocket lightened last night. Hollingsworth the pork butcher, 'e was 'ad, an' so was Samuel Platt the iron founder up on King's Hill.'

'All on the same night? No wonder the police were at their wit's end. I don't remember anything like this ever happening in Wednesbury before.'

'I don't either.' Lucy spooned her soup. 'Me mam says nothin' like it *as* ever 'appened, least not as long as 'er's been alive.'

'Which is from the time of Adam, ain't it?'

'Watch it, Mathew Leach!' Lucy waved her spoon at her husband. 'You ain't so big 'er can't tan your arse.'

'Now *that* we would have to watch.' Phoebe joined in their laughter.

'Do you think it could be somebody local? The burglar, I means,' Lucy said finishing her soup.

'Won't know that till 'e be found.' Mathew cut a wedge of cheese from the block Phoebe placed on the table. 'An' Lord only knows if that'll ever 'appen. 'E could be miles away by now.'

Her sweet tooth preferring a sultana scone instead of cheese, Lucy spread it with the dark red damson jam Mathew's mother had sent from last summer's bottling. ''E could be,' she agreed, sinking her teeth into the scone, 'or 'e be down a disused mine shaft like that murderer we 'ad some years back. You know, 'e killed that woman Mary . . . Mary summat or other.'

'Mary Carter?' Mathew placed his cheese between two slices of bread, pressing the whole together with the heel of his hand. 'Bad business was that by what I've 'eard me mam an' dad say.'

'Any murder is a bad business.' Lucy popped the last of her scone into her mouth.

'Ar, that's right an' it ain't wrong, but that particular murder ended more'n one life, so it seemed, an' there was folks in Wednesbury was party to it 'appenin'. Me dad reckons there was no nicer bloke you would wish to meet than Joseph Bradly.'

'My father never spoke of a murder taking place in Wednesbury,' Phoebe said. 'At least, I never heard him speak of one. What happened?'

'Sit you down, Miss.' Lucy bustled up from the table. 'I'll get the teapot.'

Taking his cue, Mathew stayed silent but as the tea was poured Phoebe asked again.

'You don't want to be 'earin' about no murder, Miss Phoebe.' Lucy set the teapot firmly on the table. 'Anyway it all 'appened long ago.'

'Then my knowing can't hurt anyone,' Phoebe replied gently, realising Lucy wanted to protect her from anything she might find painful. 'Really, Mathew, I would like to know. There seems to be such a lot to this town I never knew of before.'

'If yer sure . . .' Mathew glanced at Lucy who lifted her shoulders resignedly. 'Joseph Bradly lived up along Church Hill, right against the old church. 'Is wife 'ad died while their daughter Anna was no more'n a babby an' Mary Carter used to go up to the 'ouse every day to do for 'em like. Well, 'er went missin' an' when 'er was found drownded in Millfields Pool folk said as 'ow Jos Bradly was one who done it; seems they kept on sayin' it till the poor bugger 'ad more'n 'e could stand.'

'What did he do?'

Mathew looked across the table at Phoebe then away to his mug of tea, his tongue stilled by sudden embarrassment.

'What did Joseph Bradly do, Mathew?'

''E . . . 'e got pie-eyed,' Mathew stared resolutely into the mug, 'too drunk to know what the 'ell 'e was about, then 'e . . . 'e went 'ome an' raped 'is own daughter.' The last came out in a rush. If he didn't say it quickly, he wouldn't say it at all.

'What a dreadful thing to happen!' Phoebe breathed.

'Ar,' Mathew nodded, "er couldn't 'ave been more'n sixteen or seventeen accordin' to what was said. Left Wednesbury 'er did, left a babby . . . a lad, Aaron 'e was called . . . don't know what 'appened to 'er after that.'

'And her father, did he stay in Wednesbury?' Phoebe stirred milk into her own tea.

'Me mam said 'e couldn't do no other, not wi' a babby.'

"E could've put it into the workhouse,' Lucy joined the conversation.

'Me mam said that an' all.' Mathew leaned back, his meal finished. 'But me dad said 'e was too fine a bloke to leave a babby in the workhouse, no matter 'ow it was got.'

'Was anything ever proved?'

'Seems years after a bloke was brought up from a shaft 'e 'ad dropped into, and 'e said it was 'im killed Mary Carter.'

'So Joseph Bradly was cleared of suspicion of murder?'

'Cleared of suspicion by law but not by folk of Wednesbury,' Lucy said, collecting dishes into a pile. 'They 'ad got their claws into 'im an' wouldn't let go. Me mam said the same old tales kept flyin' around.'

'Did his daughter return?' Phoebe helped with clearing the table.

Lucy glanced at Mathew. 'Ar, 'er returned,' he said. 'At least Mam says 'er did, but only after 'er father 'ung 'isself.'

'Oh, how awful!' Phoebe looked from one to the other. 'What an awful thing to happen to a family.'

'Ar.' Mathew rose from the table, preparing to go to the workshop he had fashioned from one of the smaller outbuildings. 'First murder an' now these burglaries, there be some right crackpotical things goes on in Wednesbury.'

Burglaries! Phoebe helped carry the dishes to the scullery for washing. She had almost forgotten them. Thank God for the locks Bert Ingles had given her!

•　•　•

Samuel was sleeping. Annie had given him the draught Alfred Dingley had prescribed against wakeful nights, doubling the dose he had recommended. She wanted no interruptions. Everything had gone smoothly; her prices for both mines had been accepted, as she'd known they would be, and the cash for them paid without question. Siveter had wanted to ask questions, she knew, but had thought better of it; there wasn't much of Samuel's inheritance left for him to have the legal handling of, but words from her could still harm the lawyer's reputation and he would not risk that.

Reaching a box from beneath the fourposter bed Annie opened it, setting the contents in neat white piles on the counterpane. The last of everything of value apart from this house and the one at Bescot was gone, everything that had once been Abel's was sold and the money for it lay staring up at her. 'Everything!' Annie scooped the money together, the wads of notes thick in her hands. 'Everything you had, Abel.' She laughed low in her throat. 'Everything you ever owned is here in my hands, and tomorrow it will buy back my life.'

Leaving the money scattering the bed like a sudden snowstorm, she crossed the bedroom to the chest of drawers. Opening the bottom one, she took out the amethyst ring. Soon it would be on her finger for all to see, soon the whole town would know she was to be Clinton's wife. Carefully she replaced it, her fingers touching the perfume bottle, almost stroking it, before drawing one of the silk petticoats from its blue tissue paper.

Closing the drawer, she dropped the petticoat on the bed, watching several banknotes rise in the draught of air as it landed then settled back on the silk. That would be her life from now on, surrounded in money, covered in money . . . Abel's money.

Unbuttoning her black grosgrain town dress she stepped out of it. Throwing it across a chair, she slipped off her heavy cotton petticoat. She would not wear black for Clinton's coming . . . she would never wear black again.

Sliding the silk over her head, Annie let it down over her hips, her hands caressing the soft luxury of it. No, she wouldn't wear black again nor cotton either. Clinton would see her in nothing but silks and satins. Going to the wardrobe, she took out the lavender dress. She would wear it for his coming this afternoon.

The last of the tiny self-covered buttons fastened, she took a lavender fichu from her bag. She had bought it from Fosbrook's in Union Street before going to the solicitor's. Setting it on her head, she secured it with hairpins then stood looking at her reflection in the full-length cheval mirror. Stylish the dress might be but it did not give her back her youth, it could not remove the lines that bordered her mouth nor return the bloom to her skin.

Why was Clinton marrying her? She asked herself the question she knew others would ask. It wasn't for her looks. Annie touched a hand to her face. She had never been blessed with them; what there had been in the way of looks had been given to Abel and Samuel, not that they had done Samuel a lot of good. She turned away from the mirror. He had not fared much better with his life than she had with her own.

Annie gathered the banknotes, putting them neatly into the box and closing it. Looks and life, fate had denied her both, and Samuel had ideas of taking the latter away again, of returning everything to Phoebe. 'But you are too late,' she breathed, picking up the box. 'Just as it's too late for Abel's daughter.'

Chapter Thirteen

Phoebe put down her sewing, stretching her aching back, listening to the quietness of the old mill house. Handsworth Prison had been quiet, every voice hushed to whispers save those of the wardresses, but it had been a harsh jarring quiet that left the brain reeling from its unsung staccato melody. Here it was gentle, its touch lenient to the mind, settling courteously over mill and heath. Here the quiet soothed and healed.

It wanted over an hour before Mathew and Lucy returned from their day's work, the meal was simmering in the oven, she had time for a walk. Running downstairs, cheating herself of time to change her mind, she slipped out of the back door, securing the lock Bert had fitted before slipping the brass key into the pocket of her brown dress.

Refusing to let her eyes linger on the brooding pile of the corn barn she turned in the direction of the canal. It would be pleasant there with the barges passing on the way to the ports Mark Ingles dreamed of.

Coming up out of the hollow that sheltered the mill house she looked toward the ribbon of water. There was no passing barge, only a finger of smoke spiralling toward the sky, the air too lazy to spread it. Shading her eyes from the remains of the sun, she stared. It had been an extra warm day but by no means hot enough to set the heath ablaze, so how come the smoke?

''Ow do, Miss?' The shout accompanied by a wave brought a smile to Phoebe's face and she walked on to where the

Ingleses sat grouped about a small fire above the towpath.

'I didn't know you were back.'

'Got back yesterday.' Bert took the shawl his wife handed to him, spreading it on the grass and gesturing Phoebe to sit down. 'Fetched a load of timber up from London way an' dropped it off at Moxley, shoring for the coalmine there.'

'But the barge,' Phoebe glanced to the empty waterway then back to Bert, 'where is it? You don't usually leave it while it's being reloaded.'

'Ain't no barge, Miss,' Lizzie said, staring at the fire trying its best to boil the kettle of water balanced over it, 'an' there ain't no load – least not for we there ain't.'

'No barge? I don't understand . . . what has happened to it?'

'Nothing 'as 'appened to the barge,' Bert poked the fire with a stick, 'barge is loaded an' off.'

'Mr Ingles,' Phoebe looked from one to the other, 'Lizzie, will you tell me what has happened, if not to the barge then to you . . . why are the four of you sitting here?'

'We come up yesterday . . . early on . . . wi' a load of timber for Moxley like Bert said,' Lizzie answered. 'We was expectin' to load coals for London like we usually does only the gaffer at the mine, 'e said there was no load for we an' that we was to get our things off the barge right away. There was already another bargee wantin' to take 'er off up to London.'

'But I thought the barge was yours . . . your home?'

'Our 'ome, yes,' Bert turned away, his face to the canal, 'but not our property. Now the owner 'as done a deal wi' new mine gaffer to put only 'is men on the barges.'

'New?' Phoebe looked at the man, his back still toward her. 'Do you mean Moxley mine has a new manager?'

'Not only a new manager.' Bert kicked out, sending a shower of grit from the path, spraying into the water. 'A new owner, an' that new owner 'as no place for Bert Ingles.'

The mine was sold! Phoebe sat back on her heels. Uncle Samuel had sold Moxley mine, and what of Hobs Hill? Was that also sold, was Joseph Leach too out of a job and a home?

'We would 'ave been further along but totin' our stuff as well as Bert's tools 'as slowed we more than we thought,' Lizzie said. "Sides the walkin' is a bit tough on the little 'un. The lad 'e can manage it but the babby . . . 'er just ain't used to it.'

'Further on to where?' Phoebe asked, watching the boy go to stand beside his father. 'Where will you go? Where will you live?'

Lizzie glanced at her husband, his shoulders slumped forward. 'It ain't too bad, sleepin' out is quite pleasant, an' anyway Bert will find work soon.'

She smiled but behind the expression Phoebe read a different story. Sleeping out? They had slept out last night, and would again for how many nights? And what about food? No job meant no money and that in turn no food. She looked at the tiny girl huddled against her mother's skirts. How in God's name could people behave in such a way as to throw a man and his family out of their home? What sort of man was it who had bought her father's mine?

'Mr Ingles,' she got to her feet, 'why not stay here for a few days, give yourself a chance to try for work in Wednesbury? There must be something there.'

'An' if there ain't?'

'Then you have gained a few nights' rest and lost nothing.' She picked up the shawl, shaking it free of dried grass and handing it to Lizzie.

'I could go wi' you, Dad, mebbe we could both find work.'

Bert dropped a hand to his son's shoulder but remained gazing into the green depths of the canal.

'Best we stop alongside o' the cut, Miss,' he said. 'That way I can keep in touch, ask if barges 'ave 'eard of work to be 'ad in other parts. News travels fast along the cut.'

'A couple o' days wouldn't make no odds, Bert,' Lizzie

said gently. 'You need not traipse into the town, you could come down 'ere 'an wait o' the barges passin', but the little un . . . 'er could do wi' a few nights restin' in one place.'

'The barn is dry and there are plenty of corn sacks in the loft,' Phoebe said. 'It isn't much, I know, but you would be more comfortable than sleeping beside the canal.'

'Thank you, Miss.' Bert's gratitude was plain to see. 'We be grateful for your kindness. A few days an' then we'll be off . . . the Ingleses will be a nuisance to none.'

'I'm all for 'elpin' folk but four more mouths to feed . . . eeh, Miss Phoebe, 'ow we goin' to manage that?'

'It will be difficult, I know, but the clothes I have made sold well . . . I have the money from those.'

'True,' Lucy heaped flour into a bowl, 'but it won't last long spread over four of 'em.'

'I couldn't let them go any further, Lucy, that little girl of theirs looks far from well.'

'I noticed.' She rubbed fat into the flour. 'It can't be 'ealthy on them barges, all cooped up like rabbits in a hutch, an' the damp . . . it's a wonder they ain't all sprouted fins.'

'So can we manage?'

'Reckon so,' Lucy answered, 'but not for long.'

Phoebe began the ritual of greasing pie tins. 'We won't have to for long.'

Lucy looked up from rolling pastry. 'It won't be no easier, Miss Phoebe, watchin' 'em go, I mean, whether they be 'ere a short span or a longer.'

Phoebe took each circle of pastry as Lucy pressed it out, positioning it in its tin. 'Maybe they won't need to go.'

'Look,' Lucy stopped cutting circles, her eyes on Phoebe filling pastry cases with meat and potato, 'I wouldn't bank on Bert Ingles findin' work in Wednesbury. Joseph told Mathew that there might be quite a few men lookin' for jobs, wi' Moxley mine changin' 'ands.'

'Who has bought it?' Phoebe put the heavy pan of meat and potato in the hearth, covering it with a cloth.

Lucy reached for the smaller dish with which to cut pastry lids. 'Joseph couldn't say. Told Mathew nobody 'ad wind of the buyer, not yet. Let's just 'ope that whoever it is keeps 'em workin' . . . like Joseph says, there might be a few others lookin' for work in Wednesbury so don't go ratin' Bert Ingles's chances too 'igh.'

Waiting while Lucy placed the lids on the pies, Phoebe dipped her fingers in milk, spreading each with a thin film of moisture. 'Maybe he won't need to go to the town for work.'

Lucy refilled the bowl with flour, a fine white cloud mushrooming up to settle along her brows and lashes. 'What do you mean?' she asked. 'What you thinkin'?'

Phoebe turned from stocking the oven, her cheeks red from the fire. 'Locks,' she said simply, 'I'm thinking of locks.'

'I ain't with you, Miss.'

'I have been thinking a lot about those burglaries in the town.' Phoebe came to stand beside the table.

'Me an' all. They worry me they do. Who knows where 'e might strike next? Makes you scared to go to bed nights.'

'Well, if they worry us here . . .' Phoebe glanced around the kitchen with its worn chairs and mongrel assortment of second hand pots and dishes '. . . imagine how worried some folk in the town must be.'

Lucy began to make her second batch of pastry. 'Ar, there be plenty like we. An' if *they* be frightened, 'ow must all the nobs be feelin'?'

'Exactly! How must they be feeling . . . mine owners, iron and steel founders, brewers, grocers, tavern keepers? Think of it, Lucy, the list is endless and Wednesbury has plenty of them as well as plenty like us. All these people have something to lose, and all of them, rich or not so rich, would pay to make their home secure, don't you agree?'

"Course I do, but I still ain't wi' you.'

'People will pay for security.' Phoebe covered the batch of pies waiting their turn in the oven. 'We can give them that security.'

'We!' Lucy exclaimed. ''Ow?'

'Wait.' Phoebe wiped her hands on the white huckaback cloth kept 'specially for the baking then went out through the scullery, running across the yard to the barn where Mathew was helping the Ingleses settle in.

'Mr Ingles.'

Lizzie Ingles looked up from covering a heap of straw with her shawl, her face clouding with disappointment as she saw Phoebe standing in the doorway,cheeks red and arms crossed over her breasts.

'It's all right, Miss.' She picked up the shawl and began to fold it, the children watching from a corner. 'We understand, you can't let we stop 'ere after all. Just give we a minute to get we things an' we'll be gone.'

'I did not come to ask you to leave, Lizzie, I said you could stay here and you can. I . . . I only wish it were more like a home.'

'It could be.' Lizzie looked around the barn, at the rusting implements and unused flour sacks. 'If only . . .'

'If you ain't askin' we to go then what was you wantin' to ask, Miss?'

Phoebe smiled at the children, each sitting on a broken quern, then looked to where Bert stood watching her. 'Mr Ingles . . . Lizzie, would you come to the house, please? And you too, Mathew, I have something I wish to discuss with the three of you.'

'You two mind what you be about,' Lizzie pushed to her feet as she spoke to her children, 'no messin' wi' anything an' no larkin' around. You can finish makin' up this bed for the pair o' you.'

In the kitchen Lucy had finished her evening baking, the bowls and basins already stacked against the scullery sink and the brown earthenware teapot filled and waiting.

'What be all this about, Miss?' Bert asked as Phoebe reached cups from the dresser.

'It's about your locks, Mr Ingles.'

'Locks?'

'Locks, the ones you made for me.'

'They ain't broke, am they?'

'No, they are not broken,' Phoebe said, 'they work very well. I was wondering if you could make more?'

'I could,' he looked puzzled, 'but for what reason? Beggin' your pardon, you 'ave the doors to the 'ouse secured an' them barns don't 'old nought save a few old tools. An' if it's Mathew's place you was thinkin' of I already 'as a lock made for 'im, made it on me last trip to London. We intended leavin' it on your doorstep afore we moved on from the cut.'

'Thanks, Bert, that's good o' you,' Mathew said. 'I knows missis was worried about 'er bits an' pieces, we bein' out all day.'

'I wasn't wanting locks for myself . . . well, not for my own use.' Phoebe passed round the tea. 'The point is, do you think you could make . . . say a dozen . . . of the same sort as you fixed to my doors?'

'A dozen!' Bert set his mug on the table. 'That's a few locks, Miss.'

'Could you make them?' She asked, emphasising her words.

'Reckon I could,' he mused, 'I 'ave me patterns an' me files. I brought them wi' me.'

'What else would you need?' Phoebe caught the look of enquiry that flashed from Mathew to Lucy and the shrug of the shoulders she returned.

Bert pursed his lips. 'Brass or steel . . . place to work . . . a fire . . . an anvil . . . then you could manage.'

'How long would it take to make them?'

'Depends.' Bert thought for several moments. 'A week, p'raps, depends on 'ow much time you 'ave to give to the work.'

'If you had nothing else to do,' Phoebe asked, 'could you make a dozen locks in one week?'

'Ar,' he nodded, 'supposin' I 'ad a week.'

'Mathew,' Phoebe turned her attention to Lucy's husband, 'where could we get the metal Mr Ingles would need?'

'Bagnall's,' Mathew answered, his tone revealing the puzzlement this conversation was causing him. 'Bagnall's in Dudley Street will 'ave what 'e needs. I could tek 'im in wi' me an' Lucy tomorrow . . .'

'That be easy to say,' Bert interrupted, 'but money be needed to buy metals an' I've got precious little o' that.'

'Don't worry about money, Mr Ingles . . .'

'That's all right for you to say, Miss,' Lizzie put in, the same cloud of anxiety that Phoebe had seen in the barn settling over her eyes, 'but we 'ave the kids to feed an' no prospect of work to fetch more money in. I don't want to sound ungrateful, God forbid, but what bit o' money we got can't go bein' spent on makin' locks.'

'I think you have every prospect of work, Lizzie,' Phoebe smiled, 'or at least your husband has.'

Standing behind his wife's chair, Bert dropped a hand to her shoulder. 'What do you mean, Miss, I 'ave the prospect o' work?'

Phoebe looked at each of the people grouped in her small kitchen. 'I have a proposition to make, a proposition that will involve all of us. I will provide the necessary materials for the making of a dozen double barrel locks and a place for Mr Ingles to work. Food and keep for himself and his family will be his wage for the time it takes. For your part, Mathew, if you are willing, I would like you to show the lock to as many shopkeepers and tradesmen as you can. Given the recent robberies I don't think they will take much persuading to buy one, and the fitting of them could provide you with extra work.' She paused then. 'So both of you, what do you say, will you give it a try?'

'I'm game.' Mathew grinned.

'And what about you, Mr Ingles?' Phoebe smiled at the man who looked as though he had been kissed with a pole axe. 'Are you game?'

'A week off the road . . . food for the kids?' Bert grinned. 'Game? I'll say I'm bloody game . . . thanks, Miss, thanks for everythin'. I . . . I'll make you the best bloody locks ever to come out of Willenhall!'

Phoebe held out a hand. 'Then we are in business, Mr Ingles, and if things go as I hope, we will discuss a more usual wage for your labour.' She smiled at Lizzie. 'All, of course, provided your wife agrees to your settling here?'

'Oh, I agree, Miss.' Lizzie laid a hand over the one resting on her shoulder. 'An' my Bert will make you the best locks you ever seen.'

'You said your proposition included all o' we?' Lucy spoke for the first time since the Ingleses had entered the kitchen. 'So where be my part in all o' this?'

'You have the most important part.' Phoebe threw an arm around her one-time maid. 'Even the strongest of men can't work without food. We need your cooking to pay Mr Ingles's wages. What I have to ask you, Mrs Leach, is this . . . are you up to it?'

Picking up a pie warm from the oven, Lucy passed it to Bert. 'Here,' she laughed, 'you tell me, Bert . . . am I up to it?'

'Didn't you hear anything . . . anything at all?'

Maudie Tranter looked at the woman she had worked twelve years for, twelve years and not one good word in all of them. Annie Pardoe was a woman twisted with jealousy and spite, a woman who deserved all she got and more. And more she would get, Maudie could feel it in her bones.

'No, Miss Pardoe,' she said, her feelings well hidden. 'I slept all through the night, never 'eard nothing.'

Annie glanced around the dishevelled room, the mantelpiece relieved of its silver candlesticks and silver framed miniatures of her mother and father, and the desk littered with papers snatched from their drawers, strewn like white confetti over the carpet.

'You am a light sleeper, Miss, didn't you 'ear nothin' neither?'

Annie looked sharply at her thin angular housekeeper, standing with hands clasped together over a white apron that reached to the hem of her black skirts, unsure whether the woman's voice held a note of sarcasm.

'No, I did not!' she snapped. 'Mr Samuel has slept badly for several nights and I have stayed up with him. Last night I took a draught in order to get some sleep myself.'

''Course, Mr Samuel wouldn't 'ear anything, not the way 'e is.'

'Precisely.' Annie glanced once more at the room, just this one, the one with the desk and little else of interest or value apart from the few bits of silver. No other room had been disturbed, so what was the thief looking for? Whatever it was he'd expected to find it in the desk and had almost torn it apart in the search. 'Whoever it was must have come in through there.' She pointed to a door still open on to the garden. 'The Leathern Bottle gives right on to this property. He was probably drinking in there all night. I knew we should have had that dividing wall heightened.' She crossed the room, slamming the door shut. 'Go at once and bring the constables.'

Much good they'll do, Maudie thought, returning to the scullery and reaching her cloak from the cupboard. Whoever had been rummaging in that desk I doubt the bobbies will find him. That lot ain't sharp enough to catch a cold!

In the room Abel had used as a study Annie gathered up the strewn papers. Bills of sale for property that had once been Abel's but none that pointed to what had become of the proceeds of those sales. There had not been time yet for her to receive the title deeds for her tube works but, thank God, she had already given the money to Clinton.

'Sergeant down the station says as constables be out,'

Maudie said an hour later. She would have liked to take the time to call on Sarah but commonsense had warned against it. Annie Pardoe could time a walk to the police station and back almost to the minute; she would know for certain if there had been any gossiping on the way.

'Out!' Annie glared at the impudence of the man. 'What did he mean, the constables were out?'

''E meant they wasn't in,' Maudie enjoyed replying.

This time Annie was sure of the sarcasm. 'As you will be out of a position if you try your lip on me, Maudie Tranter,' she said, anger barely held in check. 'Now, if you don't want to go from this house a sight quicker than you came into it, you will tell me exactly what that fool at the station told you.'

I know what I'd like to tell you, you bad-tempered old cow, and one day, with God's help or the Devil's, I will! Maudie's thoughts gave her little consolation and she answered sullenly. ''E said as constables were out 'vestigatin' a break in up at Julia Hanson's place an' across at William Purchase, top end o' Chapel Street; said 'e would send 'em along 'ere when they reported back to the station, but 'e couldn't say 'ow long that was like to be.'

Julia Hanson and William Purchase, Annie mused as her housekeeper left the room, one a brewer, the other a grocer and general dealer, both likely to have money and like as not that money kept in the house. But what was the motive for breaking into Brunswick House? Unless . . . she touched a hand to the papers she had sorted ready to replace in relevant drawers of the desk. Unless someone knew of the cash she had got from James Siveter. She made her way to Samuel's room. And if they did, who but James Siveter could have told them?

'No, there has been no damage,' she signed in answer to her brother's question. 'Some papers scattered about the desk and the silver taken from the study. I have informed the constables. They will be here later.'

'Later?' Samuel's question flicked from his fingers.

'Two more houses were robbed last night,' Annie answered, 'Julia Hanson's and William Purchase's.'

'A brewer and a general dealer.' Samuel's fingers moved with the transient fluidity of a mayfly. 'Our burglar chooses his victims well, though why us?'

Annie shrugged. 'Who knows?' she replied her own fingers having none of the grace of movement her brother's held. 'Perhaps he thought to find money here. Thank heaven we keep little but petty cash, enough for small unforeseen events, no more.'

'This event was certainly unforeseen but nothing was taken that cannot be replaced – except, of course, for the miniatures of our parents and there is the possibility they will be returned.'

'We can always hope, but I do have my doubts.'

'No one was harmed, that is truly all that matters.'

All that mattered! Annie turned away, unable to disguise the contempt she knew must show in her face. How like Samuel to adopt that attitude . . . how typical of the weakness and ineffectuality he had shown all his life, the incapacity born of relying first upon their mother to attend to all then transferring that reliance to herself. And what of that reliance once she was married? And what of the condition that had kept Samuel confined to one house or the other for the greater part of his life? How would Clinton accept that? Would he accept it or would he . . . ?

'I must prepare for the constables' arrival,' she signed, quickly leaving the room before Samuel could answer. Clinton would not have to accept, Clinton would never know; no more would she be her brother's keeper.

Chapter Fourteen

'Ar, sold 'em both.' Sarah Leach looked at the young woman seated at her table. The years since her father's death had left their mark but it was the mark of confidence, of a sureness in herself; that prison had taught her a valuable lesson and not one any Magistrate would have expected: it had taught her that even in 1900 a woman had to fight and fight hard for any sort of life of her own. Many would have gone under given what this one had been dealt, but Abel Pardoe's daughter had learned how to fight.

'For what reason?' Phoebe's question caused the older woman to shake her head in a slow rhythm. 'Were the coal seams running out?'

'Joseph says they be gettin' thinner, but they 'ave a few years left in 'em yet.'

'Then why?'

'God knows, ma wench, an' 'e ain't tellin'.' Sarah stirred the tea she had poured. 'Who can tell what they at Brunswick 'Ouse might do next?'

'I can't understand Uncle Samuel's actions . . . to sell the coal mines!'

Sarah went on stirring, the spoon rattling against the cup. 'Who's to say it be yer uncle doin' the sellin'? Maudie Tranter said that aunt o' your'n 'ad the legal power to sign in 'er brother's stead, an' the Lord knows 'er would do it, tek 'er spite out on any 'er can. There's a few poor buggers lost their livin' 'cos of Annie Pardoe.'

Such as Bert Ingles, Phoebe thought, though he was one

of the lucky ones. The locks he made were selling as fast as he could produce them, there need be no more tramping the country in search of work for him and Lizzie had the comfort of a permanent place to make a home . . . but there were others not so fortunate.

'Sarah!' She pulled back from her thoughts, sudden agitation in her voice. 'Joseph . . . he hasn't . . .'

'Been given 'is tin?' Sarah intervened. 'No, ma wench, 'e still 'as 'is job at Hobs Hill. Seems to be just cut people as 'as been laid off . . . eh, what will them wimmin an' their babbies 'ave to live on? Meks my 'eart bleed to think on 'em.'

'Then you think my aunt is the one who has sold the mines?'

Twisting in her chair, Sarah swung the kettle from the fire, stilling its shrill hiss of steam. 'Think o' it,' she said, turning back to face Phoebe. 'Like you said you can't imagine yer uncle actin' in such a way as to put men an' their families on the streets, an' neither can I. It's true nobody 'as seen much o' him but 'e were a caring soul, never a bad word for nobody an' wouldn't 'arm a fly. But the other 'un, that Annie, 'er was a bad bugger from the start. No . . . if it was me 'ad to say who was the back of all this then it would be 'er as I'd name.'

Phoebe fingered her cup, looking at the tea she had not touched. 'Do you think Uncle Samuel knows what is happening?'

'If 'e don't then you ain't the one to tell 'im,' Sarah said sharply. 'That woman 'as 'armed you enough wi'out you givin' 'er the opportunity to do more. 'Er turned you out o' yer father's 'ouse, not carin' twopence where you went, an' naught but two frocks an' two pairs o' bloomers to go in.' She could have added that she had suspicions it was her aunt who had got her sent down for fifteen years, but bit this back. 'Mark my words an' keep well away from 'er, that woman is poison.'

What Sarah had said was true, her aunt had turned her out with virtually nothing, so perhaps it was true she was the one who'd sold off the mines. Phoebe stared at her tea, now cold in the cup. If only she could speak to Uncle Samuel, but she knew there was little chance of getting past his sister.

'So 'ow is it wi' you?' Sarah took the cup from Phoebe, going into the scullery and tipping the contents into the slop pail standing beneath the shallow ironstone sink.

'I am well, Sarah.' Phoebe watched a second cup of tea being poured.

'No after effects?'

Phoebe took the cup, adding sugar and milk. She knew what lay behind the question, knew it referred to the attack that had been made upon her, and knew also it was asked out of genuine feeling for her welfare and not morbid curiosity. 'No,' she answered, 'no after effects, though I am glad Mathew and Lucy are at Wiggins Mill with me.'

'And not only them, I 'ear.'

'You mean the Ingleses.' Phoebe sipped her tea, more from politeness than thirst. 'They were one of the families laid off. It seems the new owners had their own bargees. Mr Ingles and his wife and children were on the road when I came across them, I'm only thankful I could help them.'

'Turned out well for both of you so our Mathew tells me, but tek care, ma wench, don't get in so deep as you can't get out. 'Elpin' others is all well an' good so long as you don't get drownded in your own pity.'

'I'll try not to.' Phoebe smiled. 'And you and Joseph are always there to give me advice.'

'As long as you don't get too uppity to ask for it.'

'Joseph won't allow that.' Phoebe's smile widened. 'He never would allow Abel Pardoe's little girl to get above herself, and to him I am still a little girl.'

'Ar, Joseph always 'ad a soft spot for you.' Her tea finished, Sarah set her cup to one side. 'An' to 'im you always will be naught but a babby, but I knows an' you knows babbies 'ave a way o' growin', an' you be growin' to a beauty.'

'Has Joseph said yet who bought the mines?' Phoebe reached into the bag she had brought with her, her cheeks pink from the older woman's compliment.

'Nobody really knows, though Billy-me-Lord's agents 'ave been nosin' around for the last few days.'

'Sir William Dartmouth bought them!' Phoebe straightened up, her embarrassment forgotten.

'Like I says, nobody 'as spoke of 'im but I think as the facts says it theirselves. I reckon Billy-me-Lord be the new owner of the Crown and the Hobs Hill mines.'

Phoebe held the paper she had taken from her bag, her hand resting on the table, worry in her eyes as she looked at Sarah. 'I hope he doesn't make any more changes,' she said, 'people in the town need their jobs.'

'That be right an' don't be wrong,' Sarah agreed, taking two pots of damson jam from a cupboard. 'Pity that aunt o' your'n didn't 'ave the same feelin'.'

'What will happen . . . to men who might be finished, I mean?'

Sarah hesitated, a pot in each hand. 'Be my guess as young 'uns . . . they wi' no family to keep . . . will move on, the others'll like to stand the line.'

'Stand the line?'

'Ar,' Sarah nodded again, the movement slow and deliberate, 'men wantin' work gathers in the market place every mornin' an' stands in line 'opin' that any with work to be done will choose them. Some gets lucky and some goes wi'out . . .'

'The ones who are not chosen,' Phoebe's words dropped into the pause, 'what happens to them?'

Sarah sighed heavily. 'Work'ouse like as not, poor buggers.'

'Oh, no!' Phoebe's eyes widened. 'There must be something else.'

'Ain't nothin' else.' Sarah put the pots on the table. 'If you don't work you don't eat, not in this town. It's the work'ouse or starve, there be no such thing as charity in Wednesbury . . . things be too 'ard for them wi' next to nothin', an' them as 'ave plenty keep it to theirselves. That's the way of it, ma wench, an' you heed what I've told you an' don't go thinkin' you can tek on every man as gets 'is tin. That business o' your'n is doin' well enough but you ain't your father, you ain't Abel Pardoe.'

'No, I'm not Abel Pardoe,' Phoebe said quietly, 'but I am Abel's daughter.'

Phoebe walked toward Upper High Street, the pots of jam alongside the papers in her bag. She didn't get to visit Sarah as often as she would have liked and Joseph would be disappointed she had not waited to see him but as she had explained she was still not up to walking home alone, crossing the heath in darkness. This way she would finish her business and walk home with Mathew and Lucy.

She thought again of Sarah's pleased expression when she had shown her the poster now rolled up in her bag and told her how every shopkeeper she'd asked had agreed to display one in their premises. 'The Invincible', it proclaimed in two-inch type, 'Pardoe's Patent Locks'. They would be seen by all who used the shops, and for those who didn't she was on her way to the office of the *Express and Star*, an advertisement in the newspaper would reach every businessman in the town.

'Good day, Miss Pardoe.'

Phoebe turned at the sound of her name. She glanced first at the figure in tall hat and dark knee-length coat, then at the building he was vacating, and couldn't quite repress a shudder. The Magistrate had sentenced her to fifteen years from that building. 'Good afternoon, Sir William,' she returned.

'It was my intention to call upon you later in the day.' He replaced the hat held raised as he spoke.

'Perhaps I can save you the bother of the journey.' Phoebe wanted to move on, move away from that building and the memories it evoked.

'It is no bother, Miss Pardoe.' Grey eyes that could so easily be black regarded her evenly.

'Nevertheless it is some distance and an uncalled for journey if I can help you here.'

'I wished to tell you the man who attacked you has been gaoled. But we can't talk here . . .' He glanced at the women, their heads draped in shawls, who'd turned to look in their direction as Phoebe caught her breath sharply, a hand touching her throat. 'My carriage is to the rear.'

Gaol! Phoebe tried to breathe past the lump filling her throat. She would not wish a gaol sentence on any man, but for what he had tried to do to her . . .

'May I drive you home? I will give you the details on the way.'

'Home? No . . .' The spectres of that man's attack and of Handsworth Women's Prison fused together in her mind. 'I . . . I am not going home.'

'Then maybe we can talk inside.'

'No!' Phoebe's cry as he indicated the Green Dragon Hotel drew fresh inquisitive stares. 'I . . . I'm sorry, Sir William,' she said, 'I have no wish ever to enter that place again.'

He glanced first at the hotel and then at her, realisation dawning. The Magistrates' Court. Of course, she must have been sentenced from here. 'My apologies,' he said, 'I had not thought.'

'It is of no consequence.' Phoebe looked up, not all traces of fear gone from her face. 'If you have finished what you had to say . . .'

'I have not finished.' William Dartmouth interrupted what he knew to be a dismissal. 'If you will not allow us to speak somewhere else then it will be said here on the street. It seems one of my wife's maids overheard Sophie and her mother discussing our meeting that morning at the Priory. She presumed I had given you money and said as much to a man she was walking out with. He in turn thought to take it from you. That man is now in custody and will be spending a very substantial part of his life behind bars.'

'And the maid?' Phoebe asked. 'Is she to be dismissed her position as Lucy was?'

'Lucy?' He drew his brows together enquiringly.

'Mrs Leach, the girl you questioned at Wiggins Mill.'

'Why did she not come to me sooner with what she knew of what had happened to the necklace? Why say nothing until I questioned her?'

'Because she was warned not to.'

'Warned not to?' He frowned. 'Just what exactly does that mean?'

Phoebe looked straight at him. 'It means,' she said, her voice calm and clear, 'that Lucy was warned that to involve Ed— your son – in the affair would prove disastrous for her. She tried telling Lawyer Siveter what she knew but he said you would see to it she came to regret bringing the Dartmouth name under suspicion, then she was dismissed your wife's services.'

'She was in service at the Priory?' he asked, then before Phoebe answered, added, 'I was unaware of that, it had not occurred to me. Perhaps you will be good enough to tell Mrs Leach she will be reinstated immediately.'

No apology, Phoebe thought, no word of regret for what had happened to Lucy, just a calm proposal of her reinstatement.

'Does it not occur to you that she may have no wish to return to your employment?' she asked coldly.

Sir William Dartmouth looked at the young woman, her eyes cool and steady, and found the admiration he had first felt at their earlier meetings re-kindling in him. Not many men would speak to him as she did: his title and his money made no impression upon her and certainly did not intimidate her.

'That must be her prerogative – if you will forgive the use of the word "must".' The faintest hint of a smile appeared at the corners of his mouth. 'I wish you good day Miss Pardoe.'

'You said that?' Lucy asked later when Phoebe told her of her encounter. 'You said that to Billy-me-Lord?'

'I did,' Phoebe smiled broadly. 'Naughty of me, wasn't it?'

'Naughty or no, I bet it took the wind out o' 'is sails.'

'He did look somewhat surprised,' Phoebe said, still smiling.

'What did 'e 'ave to say to that?'

Waiting while Lucy served a customer to the last of her scones, giving her change from a sixpenny piece, Phoebe answered, 'He said that must be your prerogative.'

'My what?' Lucy shook her head as a woman, shawl drawn tight about her shoulders, enquired after a meat pie. 'What on earth does that mean?'

'It means that yours must be the choice. You can return to work at the Priory tomorrow if you wish, his wife will return you to the position you held there before.'

'Oh, ar.' Lucy sniffed scornfully. 'I'll be there bright an' early in me best cardi an' me boots blacked . . . like bloody 'ell I will! Go back to skivvyin' for the Dartmouths? I'd sooner go on the roads.'

'Were they unkind to you?' Phoebe watched the hurrying women pass from stall to stall, their purchases shoved into deep-bottomed baskets draped over one arm.

'The Dartmouths?' Lucy handed a broken scone she had placed to the side of her own stall to a small girl, her face pinched and thin, a ragged dress hanging from her bony shoulders, receiving a smile in payment. 'Not Miss Sophie or 'er mother, an' I never 'ardly seen Edward or the master. No, it was that lot below stairs. Talk about mean! They'd take the sugar out o' your tea an' then come back for the milk . . . no, I ain't goin' back there no more.'

''Ow much for this?'

A woman in skirts that had parted from their colour long ago and now hung like panels of rust from below her chequered shawl touched a finger to a child's white dress, its full skirts edged with a ribbon of cornflower blue, another of the same caught around the waist.

'Six an' eleven to you, luv.' Lucy smiled encouragingly. 'It's a lovely little frock an' all muslin.'

'It be pretty enough,' the woman ran a wistful eye over

the dress, 'an' my Ginny would look a picture in that come Sunday.' She looked at Lucy. ''Er's to be confirmed.'

Holding the dress closer to the woman, Lucy spread its skirts. 'Bein' confirmed, is 'er? Well, 'er couldn't 'ave a prettier frock for it than this.'

'That's right enough,' the woman fingered the dainty material, 'but 'er wouldn't get much wear out o' it after. It ain't the stuff to stand up to wear.'

'Muslin is stronger than it seems,' Lucy said, 'an' it's so easy to wash. You only needs to show this to the wash tub an' the dirt drops out o' it nor it needs no ironin' neither.'

'It *is* a special day.' The woman lingered. ''Er won't never get confirmed again, but near enough seven shillin' for a frock . . . that'd keep the kids for a week.'

'It might do,' Lucy withdrew the dress a fraction, 'but which would your little wench remember longest – a meal or the lovely frock 'er mother bought for 'er confirmation?'

'You'm right!' The woman drew a purse from the depths of her rusty skirts. 'I'll tek it, an' what me old man don't know 'e can't grieve over.'

Lucy wrapped the dress in a piece of brown paper, religiously saved from cloth Phoebe had bought from the draper and haberdasher in Upper High Street. ''Er'll do you proud in this,' she said, handing the woman a penny change.

'You know,' the woman wedged her package on top of those already in her basket, 'if I was the one made these frocks you wouldn't find me in Wednesbury for long.'

''Ow do you mean?' Lucy shot a sidelong glance at Phoebe.

'Well, they'm so pretty, ain't they? I tell you, if I 'ad the touch in me fingers to make such I would be in one o' they big fancy places like Brummagem or London. Folk there would pay twice as much for summat like this.' Returning the purse to her pocket, the woman turned away.

'You know, Miss Phoebe,' Lucy watched the customer, her old-fashioned black bonnet set on top of hair turned prematurely grey, disappear among the shoppers, 'I reckon there be some Wednesbury folk got more in their 'eads than coal dust.'

'But there is one at least with six shillings and elevenpence less in her purse,' Phoebe answered solemnly. 'Do you really think she should have spent so much on a dress? She said it would have kept the children for a week.'

'Don't you worry about that one,' Lucy said, after selling a woman a pink petticoat. 'If 'er couldn't 'ave afforded it 'er wouldn't 'ave bought it. 'Sides, 'er will sell it for four or five shillin' once 'er own kid be finished wi' it an' then when next one be too big for it, it will fetch a couple o' bob from somebody else, an' after they be done it'll still fetch a tanner or so from old Kilvert. There's always customers at the pawnshop either pledging bundles in or buying.'

'As I bought this.' Phoebe touched one hand to her jade green suit, the jacket trimmed with darker green frogging.

'You paid for it, didn't you?' Lucy said, a slightly indignant note in her voice. 'You didn't beg from nobody so you 'ave nothin' to feel 'shamed over. 'Sides it suits you, it really does. You look lovely, Miss.'

'Lovely enough to impress the printer?' Phoebe smiled.

'You'll knock 'is eyes out.' Lucy grinned. 'Just don't let 'im charge too much for that 'eaded notepaper an' order forms you be goin' to get 'im to print for you.'

'I won't.' Phoebe took the pots of jam from her bag. 'But could I leave these with you? I don't think Mr Simpson will be too impressed by my handing him two pots of damson jam with the designs for my bill headings.'

''E might take a bit off the price if you gives 'im a pot o' me mother-in-law's damson.' Lucy took the jam, setting it to the side of her stall. 'You never knows your luck.'

'I know I had better be off.' Phoebe closed her bag. 'I am putting off your customers.'

'Miss Phoebe,' Lucy said as she made to leave, 'mebbe you should wait for Mathew to come, let 'im go with you like? Might be best for a man to do the talkin'. After all, you ain't used to talkin' prices.'

'Then the sooner I get used to it, the better,' Phoebe said. 'I intend to be talking quite a lot of prices in the future and not all of them to a printer.'

Well, let's 'ope you stands up a bit stronger to that printer than you would to that woman just bought the frock, thought Lucy as Phoebe walked away. If I 'adn't been 'ere you would 'ave finished up givin' it to 'er. There's such a thing as bein' too soft . . .

'What did Simpson sting you for?' Mathew asked as the three of them walked home.

'A shilling a dozen.'

'A shilling a dozen!' Mathew was clearly disgusted. 'Why, that be pure bloody thievery. I'll go see 'im tomorrow an' tell 'im 'e can stick 'is bleedin' printin' wheer the monkey sticks its nuts. A shillin' a dozen! Who does 'e think 'e is coddin'?'

'He wasn't fooling me, Mathew.' Phoebe switched her bag from one arm to the other. Crammed now with butter and cheese, a pork hock wedged between the pots of jam, it weighed heavily.

'But a shillin' a dozen, Miss!' Lucy came in on Mathew's side. 'That does seem a bit steep.'

'I did not accept that price unconditionally.' Phoebe winced as her foot twisted against a stone. 'We came to an agreement.'

'An agreement?' Mathew sounded far from reassured. 'Like what?'

'Like fourpence a dozen when I order a gross or more.'

'Well, that's more like it.' Mathew hitched the hessian sack of potatoes higher on his shoulder. 'But will you ever be orderin' a gross?'

'I will be ordering many gross,' Phoebe answered, 'order forms, bill forms, receipts and notepaper, and the price will be the same for all of them.'

'Phew, steady on, Miss!' Mathew laughed. 'Lock business

191

be goin' well enough but I can't see it goin' on. After all, Wednesbury ain't all that big a town, it will only buy so many.'

'Mathew be right, Miss,' Lucy said. 'It don't pay to get carried away. Don't spend your money on fancy 'eaded paper you might never get to use.'

'Mathew *is* right,' Phoebe agreed, 'Wednesbury is not all that big a town. But then it is not the only town, and what we have sold in one town we can sell in another.'

'But 'ow?' Lucy made a detour, avoiding a puddle in the track. 'I mean, it takes folk to sell locks an' we . . . well, we all be busy doin' what we be doin'.'

'I have thought of that,' Phoebe said confidently. 'When the time comes I shall find somebody.'

'Always supposin' you find somebody to sell locks for you, Bert couldn't mek no more,' Mathew pressed home his point. ''E is workin' flat out now.'

'To say nothin' of 'avin' to buy in more metal,' Lucy supported her husband. 'An' that might be the 'orse you can't ride. Brass founders don't let stuff out on the strap, least not to likes of we they don't. You got to be big in business to get things first and pay later.'

What they were saying was perfectly reasonable. Phoebe trudged on in silence, but she had taken a gamble, made her play as her father would have said, and now she must follow it through.

Across the heath the windmill stood silent witness to one such as herself, Elias Webb, who had sold her Wiggins Mill, had made his play but for him the cards of fortune had not followed through. But hers would. Phoebe clenched her teeth, defying the laughter of the fates. One way or another she would win through, she had to if the Ingleses were not to be put back on the road.

''Ello, Miss, 'ello, Mrs Leach.' From the edge of the yard the Ingles children waved then raced to meet them, the boy leaving his sister in his wake.

'I will take that for you, Miss.' The boy took the bag from Phoebe, easing it on to his shoulder in imitation of Mathew before going to walk beside him, matching his step, in his own mind at least very much the man.

'I can carry summat as well as our Mark.' The girl looked up with serious eyes. 'I'm as strong as 'im.'

'No, you ain't.' Her brother sniffed scathingly. 'You be only a girl an' they ain't as strong as men, am they, Mr Leach?'

'They ain't that, lad.' Mathew grinned. 'But I reckon most of 'em be prettier an' our Ruthie be prettiest o' the lot.'

'But I am strong, me mother says my 'elp be in . . . in . . . invalible.'

'Well, I could certainly do wi' some 'elp,' Lucy said tactfully, 'this basket be fair breakin' my arm.' Lowering it to the ground, she took out a shank end of mutton wrapped in paper tied round with string, handing it to the child. 'If you could take that it would be a powerful 'elp.' She smiled at the small girl, the meat cradled like a doll in her arms. 'But you 'ave only to say if it gets to be too 'eavy. We 'ave two strong men 'ere can carry it.'

'I can carry it, Mrs Leach,' the child said proudly. 'I can do lots of things. I 'elped Mother make a 'ot pot today, peelin' 'tatoes an' carrots, an' 'er let me 'elp wi' jam roly poly.'

'That sounds like a real meal for a workin' man,' Mathew said. 'Jam roly poly, that's my favourite puddin', you'll 'ave to show Mrs Leach how it's done.'

'I will.' She looked up at Lucy, her little face wreathed in smiles. 'It's real easy.'

'I 'opes as you ain't fond o' too much jam in your roly poly,' the boy said, hitching the bag on his shoulder as Mathew hitched the potato sack.

'I like jam, the more the better,' Mathew answered.

'A pity that.'

'Why, don't you have any more jam?'

'Oh, ar, Miss,' the answer was jaunty, 'me mother 'as

another pot o' jam, but we don't get much on a roly poly. Least there won't be much on this'n.'

'Why not?' Phoebe asked as they crossed the yard to the house.

"Cos our Ruth keeps eatin' it!'

'So that's what meks 'er such a little sweet'eart.' Mathew lowered the sack of potatoes to the ground, sweeping the child into his arms and whirling round with her. 'Who wants jam when we 'ave our Ruthie?'

'It's time our Ruthie was in bed.' Lizzie Ingles came from the barn she had turned into a home, smiling at her daughter's delighted squeals. 'An' you too, my lad,' she said, looking at her son. 'I told the pair o' you more'n half an hour gone.' She turned to Phoebe. 'I never can get 'em to bed afore you all be back.'

'I wonder why?' Taking her bag from the boy, she drew out two fat round lollipops. 'It couldn't have something to do with these, could it?'

Shoving the joint of meat into Lucy's hands, the little girl jigged up and down, eyes shining at the promise of the sweet. 'I wants the red one.' She pulled at Phoebe's arm. 'It's my turn to 'ave the red one. Our Mark 'ad it last time.'

'Then if Mark had the red one last time it must be your turn to have it this time.' Phoebe handed her the sweet.

'I've got the red one!' The child jigged away, holding the lollipop in the air like some coveted trophy. 'I've got the red one!'

'You'll 'ave a red bottom, Ruth Ingles, if you don't say thank you,' Lizzie said sternly. 'You know better'n to take what somebody gives an' return no thanks. Whatever 'as 'appened to your manners, girl!'

The child stopped dancing. 'Beg pardon, Miss.' She came to Phoebe, her pretty mouth drooping. 'I'm mortal sorry.'

'That's all right, Ruth.' Phoebe caught the twitching of Lucy's mouth. 'I was always forgetting to say thank you when I was a little girl, and to tell you the truth I sometimes forget now.'

'Do you, Miss, do you honest?'

'Honest.' Licking a forefinger, Phoebe made the sign of the cross over her heart. 'Cross my heart and hope to die if what I have said is just a lie.'

'Ooh, you knows that an' all, you can't never say that if you 'ave told a lie.' The child's mouth lost its droop, turning upward in a smile. 'So you must be tellin' the truth, Miss, you do forget sometimes.'

We all do, Phoebe thought, bending to hug Lizzie's daughter, remembering playing the same scene so many times with her father. We all do.

'Now say goodnight.' Lizzie caught her daughter's hand as Phoebe released her.

'Goodnight.' The child lifted her face to each in turn, receiving a kiss on the cheek. 'Thank you, Mrs Leach, an' you, Mr Leach.'

'Why can't we make that Aunty Lucy and Uncle Mathew?' Lucy said, her face on a level with that of the child.

'I don't know if we could,' the answer came solemnly, 'it might not be 'lowed 'cos you ain't a real aunt, am you?'

'No,' Lucy said softly, 'but I love you as much as a real aunt, and Mr Leach loves you as much as a real uncle.'

'I'd like to,' the child said pensively, 'but I don't know if it's 'lowed.'

'Why don't we ask your mother?' Lucy looked up at the face of Lizzie Ingles.

'It's allowed.' The woman smiled, her eyes cloudy behind tears. 'It's allowed.'

Clasping her red lollipop in one hand, the other held by her mother, the girl walked away then stopped to look back at the three adults. 'I do love you all,' she said simply. 'I'm so glad we come to live 'ere.'

'I would like to call you Aunt and Uncle an' all if it's all right wi' you?'

Mathew looked at the face turned up towards his own, seeing the disappointments and knocks life had already dealt the young son of Bert Ingles, seeing apprehension of another. He held out his hand, shaking that of the boy offered to meet it. 'It's a sight more'n all right, Mark,' he answered huskily. 'That would mean more to me than a medal from the Queen.'

'*I'm so glad we come to live 'ere.*' The words echoed in her mind as later Phoebe prepared for bed. She was glad too. Having people about the place during the day gave her a feeling of security, and the knowledge they were close, combined with the locks on her doors, had given her confidence to sleep alone in the house, freeing Lucy and Mathew to go back to sleeping in their own home.

Yes, she was glad they had all come to live at Wiggins Mill. Picking up her nightgown from the bed, she held the soft cotton to her face, the memory of rough calico vivid in her mind. She was glad they were all here, Lucy and Mathew, the Ingleses with their children . . . if only she could have brought one more. If only she could have brought Tilly . . .

Chapter Fifteen

Annie Pardoe sat in the neat parlour of Brunswick House its graceful bay window overlooking well-kept lawns. She paid a man twice a week to see to the upkeep of the gardens and made sure he earned his money. Annie Pardoe paid no one to sit around. There had been little alteration since Abel's time though she had seen to it that no laburnum or yew grew there and had grubbed them out herself from the garden of the house at Bescot years before. She caught her breath, holding it till the twinge of pain below her left breast subsided. Yes, she had grubbed them out – but not until she had made good use of them.

'Papers, Miss.' Maudie Tranter entered the room, a newspaper neatly folded on a cloth-covered tray. Wait till you reads that, she thought as Annie took the newspaper, you'll have another shock. Making her way back to the kitchen Maudie thought of what she had seen in the *Express and Star* and how the woman in the parlour would react in the knowledge that her housekeeper always read the newspaper before taking it into her. Maudie enjoyed her thoughts.

In the parlour Annie spread the newspaper on the oval mahogany table, fixing on to her nose the reading glasses that hung on a silk string about her neck. She had made a lifetime's habit of taking the papers, reading thoroughly through them before allowing them to go to her brother.

'Hmmph!' she snorted, reading of certain elections to the town council. 'Not an ounce of brain between the lot of them.' Slowly she turned the pages, finding some reports of interest to her, others not, but reading them all until her eye caught the advertisement.

Annie's fingers dropped to the corner of the page she had been about to turn, her eyes devouring the large caption: 'The Invincible'. The heading topped a representation of a lock under the sub-heading 'Pardoe's Patent Locks'. She read the advert through once and then again. Phoebe! She pressed a hand to her side but it did not still the pain biting beneath her breast. It could only be Phoebe!

Her thoughts flew to the man who had promised to make her his wife. What if he saw the advertisement? The name was the same, Pardoe, how long would it take him to wonder if it carried with it any relationship to her? He was no fool, he would put two and two together sharp enough, then how long before he found Pardoe's Patent Locks was run by her niece?

The pain jabbed viciously, bringing her teeth together, nostrils flaring with the effort of controlling it as she read the advert through again. If he should find out . . . if he discovered her niece had not quit Brunswick House of her own choice but had been virtually thrown out . . . And what of Samuel? What would his reaction be to seeing that piece in the newspaper? He had already made clear his intention of returning everything to Abel's daughter, what would he do when he found there was almost nothing to return? But it didn't matter what Samuel thought. Annie's eyes stayed glued to the advertisement. She had taken care her brother would never carry out his threat. No, it did not matter what Samuel knew, but Clinton . . . Clinton must never know. She would kill this lock business stone dead before it got started.

Leaving the newspaper on the table she walked upstairs to her bedroom. Slipping a smart grey day coat over her matching dress, she pinned a feathered bonnet over her hair. Clutching her bag, she went downstairs without calling in on her brother.

'I am going out,' she said as Maudie appeared from the kitchen, 'I don't know what time I shall be back.'

Maudie watched her mistress wriggle her fingers into grey chamois gloves. I was right, she thought, closing the door after the departing Annie, you've had a shock right enough and it won't be the last. And you taking to dressing up in fine colours won't ward them off. There be others waiting on you, Annie Pardoe, ones you won't walk away from.

Annie walked briskly along Spring Head, following it into the market place cutting across toward Great Western Street. She had not taken the horse and trap, they would be too conspicuous left standing outside the Great Western Railway Station, for today she meant to take the train to Birmingham.

'You can sit in the ladies' waitin' room, Mum, it's the next door along the platform. There be a nice fire burnin' in there.'

The man in the tiny ticket office touched a finger to the peak of his dark green cap as he handed Annie a ticket.

Putting it carefully into her bag, she nodded. It might be best to sit in the room set aside for women, there would not be many of them using the train, not when the steam tram was a cheaper way to travel. But today the train suited Annie. The fewer folk to see where she headed, the better pleased she felt.

Choosing a seat that gave a clear view of the door and of any who might choose to enter, Annie sat in the empty room. It was a bind having to go to Birmingham but it was safest. She would not be known there and there would be few in Wednesbury who knew that town in any detail. The advertisement she had read only an hour before lodged in her mind, till she felt her mouth tightening like a trap. The hundred pounds she had paid the Magistrate had been a total waste of money. What had it bought . . . a fifteen-year sentence that had been set aside after little more than one! What had that fool been about? He should have made the sentence one that couldn't so easily be revoked. It was a pity they had ceased transportation, that way Phoebe would have been out of the country, but now her niece was free and broadcasting her presence by way of advertisements, one at least published in the *Express and Star* and God only knew how many in other publications and places. Annie pressed her hands together in her lap. If you want a thing doing right, do it yourself. This time she would do it herself, and this time it would be done right.

The conductor's call of 'Snow Hill' told of having reached Birmingham and Annie alighted. Who was stupid enough to give a name like Snow Hill to this place? she wondered, taking in the soot-grimed archways of the railway station. Black Hill would have been more appropriate. Leaving the station, she followed the line of shops beside it; tailor, draper, grocer, milliner, each jostled the other, elbowing for room in the narrow streets, but she passed them by without a second look at the overcrowded windows. Pie shop, beer hall. Annie walked on, her eye scanning signs painted over shop fronts proclaiming the name of the proprietor and the wares he sold until she read: James Greaves, Hardware and Ironmongery.

Annie caught the train back to Wednesbury, six pot menders and six mousetraps in her bag. The purchase of these would raise no eyebrows in Brunswick House: pot menders were often used in her kitchen to close small holes worn in iron pots and pans and mousetraps were always set in the cellar. Mousetrap! She gazed through the window at the dingy houses set regimentally close alongside the railway line. The trap she was setting would catch more than a mouse . . .

'Has Mr Samuel been downstairs?' she asked when she reached the house.

'No, Ma'am,' Maudie answered. ''E took 'is lunch in 'is room though 'e didn't touch it none, an' when I popped in the studio about three o'clock 'e was asleep in 'is chair. 'E seems to 'ave slept more than ever these past few days.'

'That will be his medicine.' Annie took the pot menders and mousetraps from her bag, handing them to her housekeeper.

'The doctor increased the strength a little . . . you have been careful only to give him the prescribed dose?'

'Two teaspoonfuls, measured 'em out meself, Ma'am, an' 'e swallowed 'em right off, then 'e sat in 'is chair an' 'as been there all day far as I know.'

'And he ate nothing?'

'Nothin' at all,' Maudie shook her head, 'not even a bite. I carried 'is tray down same as I carried it up . . . nothin' 'ad been touched at all.'

'Perhaps a cucumber sandwich will tempt him?' Annie turned to the stairs. 'I will go in to him when I have removed my coat. Prepare a tray now.'

'Perhaps a cucumber sandwich will tempt him,' Maudie mimicked under her breath as Annie went up the stairs. 'As if she cares whether he eats anything or not. It's all bloody top show wi' that one an' underneath it all 'er couldn't care twopence whether the poor bugger lives or dies!'

In the kitchen Maudie put the hardware on the dresser and stood looking at it. Pot menders and mousetraps, nothing unusual in that – 'cept Annie Pardoe never bought anything without it had been asked for a dozen times and she, Maudie, hadn't asked for either. And why walk into the town, why hadn't she taken the horse and trap as always? And why jaunt off down into Wednesbury to get them herself when she could have had them sent up with provisions? Taking out a tray she spread it with a freshly laundered cloth and set it with china. Annie Pardoe was up to summat as sure as God made little apples, Maudie told herself, and like as not Samuel wouldn't come out of it too well.

In her room Annie spread the newspaper she had brought up from the parlour. She had spent a couple of hours with her brother before leaving him for the night. She turned a page. He had not eaten a cucumber sandwich earlier and neither had he taken any dinner, but she had expected that. She turned a second page. She had told Maudie Tranter she would go herself tomorrow and ask the doctor to call. But that would do nothing for Samuel. Her eyes scanned the columns of print, coming to rest on the advertisement for Pardoe's Patent Locks. No, nothing would help Samuel.

Going to the marble-topped washstand she slid open the narrow drawer that ran almost the full width of it, taking a sheet of paper from beneath the pile of towels. Returning to the table, she placed it beside the newspaper then took from her bag the bottle of ink and the cheap pen she had bought before taking the train back to Wednesbury. Reading the advert through one last time, Annie dipped the pen into the ink and began to write.

Phoebe heard the crunch of carriage wheels along the track and put aside the dress she had almost finished making. Going to the window, she watched it drive to the front of the house, her feelings mixed. She liked Edward, liked him very much, and was happy for him to call . . . but if only he would call less often. She had tried to tell him of her need to work, to explain the strong necessity for it, but he only said to marry him and be done with tiresome necessities.

She watched him climb from the carriage, the light glinting on his fair hair. She knew he loved her and that he would do his best to make marriage to him happy . . . so why couldn't she say yes? Why wouldn't she marry Edward Dartmouth? Turning from the window, Phoebe left the room. She didn't know why.

'Phoebe, I am so glad you are home. I told Edward we ought to send a card before we visited.'

'Sophie, how nice.' Phoebe's smile was a mixture of pleasure and relief. She had turned from the window before seeing Sophie and now the pleasure of her visit brought the added relief of not having to walk with Edward.

'Don't bother with tea,' Sophie said when Phoebe offered refreshments, 'just sit down and listen. You are invited to a farewell ball.'

'A ball?' Phoebe was surprised. 'Where?'

'At the Priory.' Sophie's face glowed with delight. 'Where else did you think!'

'That's just it,' Phoebe said, 'you gave me no time to think.'

'What is there to think of?' Sophie rushed on. 'Father is giving a ball and you are invited. There is nothing to be thought about.'

Phoebe looked from Sophie to Edward. 'You said a farewell ball?'

'My mother is to leave for Europe sooner than had been intended.' He smiled, misreading the reason for the question in her eyes. 'The influenza she suffered recently has not cleared as we would have hoped and her physician has recommended a warmer climate.'

'I am sorry to hear your mother is not yet fully recovered,' Phoebe returned her gaze to Sophie, 'please give her my regards.'

'Oh, Mother is not too ill,' Sophie burst out with the thoughtless disloyalty of youth, 'she simply has an over-fondness for Italy, and of course we have to go too which means I will not see Montrose for several more months. The whole thing would be totally unbearable were it not for the shopping en route. You really can buy the most exquisite lace in Paris. I intend to buy my whole trousseau there. Montrose . . .'

'My mother and sister cannot travel alone,' Edward put in as his sister paused for breath, 'I am to travel with them to our villa in Tuscany then I shall return.'

'Will that not be doubling a journey?' Phoebe asked, knowing he had interrupted Sophie because he hated to think of her with Montrose Wheeler and wanting to spare him as much as possible. 'To have to return to Italy again to escort your mother home will be very tiring.'

He smiled, the thought of her concern for him deepening the vivid blue of his eyes. 'I will not be returning there a second time,' he explained. 'My father will be joining Sophie and Mother after Christmas. He will bring them home.'

'With us leaving in two weeks there will be no Advent Ball at the Priory this year,' Sophie burbled on, 'hence the idea of a farewell ball. Mother has sent invitations to absolutely everybody and here is yours.' She took a cream vellum envelope from her bag, handing it to Phoebe. 'It will be absolutely wonderful and I hope to persuade Father to let Montrose announce . . .'

'It is kind of your parents to invite me,' Phoebe cut in but this time it was not to spare Edward, 'though I cannot accept.' She could not attend a ball at the Priory, she hadn't a suitable gown for one thing, and to ask her to one which Montrose would be attending . . . hadn't anyone told Sophie the man she wanted to marry had already been engaged to the daughter of Abel Pardoe, and had broken that engagement when he found out she had no money?

'But why?' Sophie demanded. 'Is it because of Montrose? You have no cause for worry there, Phoebe. He told me what happened himself. Told me you asked to be freed from your engagement to him – that after the shock of your father's death you felt you could not marry for some time, and later you found you no longer loved him and begged him not to hold you to your promise so of course he did not. But now he loves me and we are to be married. And you,' she squeezed Phoebe's hand, 'are not to worry over my feelings. You are to accept Mother's invitation and that is that!'

So Montrose had told Sophie! Phoebe glanced at Edward, reading the distaste in his face. It was not her recollection of events she had just heard but what effect would it have on Sophie should she ever find out the true story? And what effect would it have should she discover Montrose was marrying her purely and simply for her money; that for him love played no part in marriage.

'I'm so excited,' Sophie trilled on, 'I am to have a new gown, pink, Montrose says I look ravishing in pink . . .'

I wore a pink gown on our last evening together. Phoebe's thoughts suppressed Sophie's voice, drowning it in waves of memory. Montrose said I too looked ravishing in the colour. He held me in his arms while he vowed his love for me, while he told me he could not wait for our marriage, while he told me the same lies.

'. . . he is to get leave from his regiment . . .'

Wrenching her thoughts back to the present, Phoebe glanced across to where Edward sat.

'Sophie dear,' he rose, 'we really must not take any more of Phoebe's time.'

The girl jumped to her feet, colour rising to her cheeks. 'I'm sorry, Phoebe, I do prattle on. Mother is always telling me about it.'

'And so am I,' Edward laughed, 'to say nothing of Father's efforts in that direction, all of which are wasted.

'You will come, Phoebe?' He hung back as Sophie reached the carriage.

'It's not possible, Edward.'

'Why not?' The intensity of his question was echoed in the pressure of the hands he placed on her arms. 'Is it because of my forgetting that damned necklace?'

Releasing herself from his grip, Phoebe glanced at his sister but her back was still turned to them.

'You know it isn't, Edward.'

He looked at her, frustration and the need to know lending his eyes a desperation she had not seen before. 'Then why, Phoebe?' he asked hoarsely. 'Why?'

'Edward,' she smiled patiently as though dealing with a demanding child, 'for a single girl to attend a ball she requires a female chaperone or a male escort. It might have escaped your notice that I have neither of these, on top of which I own no gown suitable for a ball.'

'The escort part might have eluded me,' Edward admitted, his eyes clearing, 'but it had not escaped my father. He has expressed the wish that you give your permission for me to be your escort for the evening, and I sincerely hope you will agree. As for a gown, I . . .'

'No.' Phoebe cut short the offer she knew would follow. She would take none of the Dartmouths' money, not even enough to buy a gown to attend their ball; she wanted no reparation and she certainly did not want their charity. 'Thank you, Edward, but I prefer to provide my own gown.'

'Then you will come!'

'I think you had better be going.' Phoebe avoided answering what was more statement than question. 'Your sister is waiting.'

'A ball, and with Edward Dartmouth your escort!' Lucy held the cream card with its gold edging as though it were a priceless object. 'Eeh, Miss Phoebe, how lovely. What will you wear?'

'Nothing.' Phoebe took the card, putting it behind a jug that held pride of place on the dresser.

'Well, that'll give the women the vapours and the men a rare treat, though I 'adn't thought it of you, to go 'ob nobbin' in naught but that you were born in, Miss Phoebe.' Mathew stood in the doorway of the scullery.

'Trust a man to be there with 'is ears flappin'.' Lucy turned a reproving look as her husband grinned. 'What you be in 'ere after anyway, Mathew Leach?'

Phoebe smiled, joining in with his infectious grin. 'Yes, what do you be in 'ere after?' she asked, using the same lazy dialect, 'listenin' to wenches gossipin'.'

'Well, you be wi' one can do that all right.'

'Don't push your luck, me lad.' Lucy stretched a hand ominously towards an iron pot set on the hob.

'All right, all right.' Mathew raised both hands in a gesture of surrender. 'Bert says to tell you, Miss, as brass for locks be runnin' pretty low.'

'He knows he can get more whenever he needs it.'

'Ar, 'e do know,' Mathew answered, 'but 'e still reckons to tell you beforehand like, says that's the way it should be.'

'Tell him to get what he thinks necessary,' Phoebe said.

'I will come see him myself as soon as I finish helping Lucy with tomorrow's baking.'

'What did you mean when you said you would wear nothing to the Priory ball?' Lucy whisked about the kitchen gathering utensils.

'What I said.' Phoebe lifted the pot from the hob, placing it on a cloth she had set on a corner of the well-scrubbed table, then set about pounding the boiled potatoes with a wooden spoon. 'I will be wearing nothing to the Dartmouths' ball for the simple reason that I will not be going.'

'Eeh, Miss Phoebe, whyever not?' Lucy was already wrist-deep in flour.

'I can't Lucy.' Phoebe attacked the potatoes with a new savagery. 'I . . . I wouldn't feel right. Everyone there will know what my aunt did.'

Lucy banged lard indignantly into the flour, sending it surging upward in a cloud. 'Ar, they will, an' they'll know what an old bitch 'er is an' all.'

Phoebe ladled cubes of mutton into the mashed potato, folding them in with the spoon. 'They will also know about the business of the necklace.'

'That an' all.' Lucy rolled the pastry. 'An' they'll see that the Dartmouths 'old nothin' against you . . . not that there be anythin' for 'em to 'old . . . but you see what I mean. Billy-me-Lord can't be apologisin' any more clear, an' that's what 'e be doin'. In front of the 'ole bloomin' county 'e's apologisin', an' your refusin' to go to that ball be like chuckin' 'is apology right back in 'is face. It do an' all, Miss Phoebe.'

She had not thought of it in those terms. Phoebe watched Lucy working dexterously at her pie-making. This could well be Sir William and Lady Dartmouth's way of proclaiming the fact she had been wrongly accused of stealing their daughter's necklace and that despite her lack of fortune she was accepted in their home. For her to refuse would be seen as churlish, and worse, in her own eyes, would rank as rudeness. But to attend . . .

'I realise how my refusal may be received, Lucy, but it can't be helped. I haven't a dress anywhere near grand enough for such an occasion.'

'Is that all? Lord, it would take a bloody sight more than that to keep me from goin' to a grand do like that. Surely you ain't gonna let a frock keep you from it?'

'Not a frock, more the lack of one.'

'That be nothin' as can't be remedied,' Lucy said, watching Phoebe carry pies to the oven and load them in. 'You can buy a frock easy as winkin'.'

'You can if you have money, which I have not . . . well, not to spend on ball gowns anyway. They cost a small fortune.'

'Spendin' some on yourself won't 'urt for once.'

'Spending that much would. I need that money to buy metal if we are to go on producing locks. I will not throw it away on a gown I will never wear again.'

'I seen a lovely bolt o' satin in Underwood's window,' Lucy sounded almost matter-of-fact, 'the loveliest shade of pale yellow you ever did see – just like butter cream. Make a bostin' frock it would.'

'Make!' Phoebe stopped filling pies to stare at Lucy. 'I couldn't make a ball gown.'

'O' course you could.' Lucy loaded her bowl with a fresh helping of flour, adding salt and lard. 'You already makes frocks, don't you?'

'Little ones, yes.'

Lucy looked up from rubbing fat into flour. 'Well, then! this will be the same 'cept bigger.'

Phoebe half smiled. Lucy made it all sound so easy, make herself a gown . . . as if nothing were simpler. Supposing she did manage to make a gown, that would only be a part of what she would need. There were other things.

'A dress is not the whole of it, Lucy,' she said. 'Given that I had one, I would also require gloves and shoes . . . a bag . . . a fan. And jewellery, what of jewellery? I have absolutely nothing in that line at all. The last of Grandmother's pieces went before . . . before . . .'

'Before you were sent to prison,' Lucy finished for her. 'Jewellery be a bit o' a sticky 'un. Wonder if Bert could make anything?'

Phoebe set the second batch of pies aside, spreading the white huckaback cloth over them until there was room in the oven. 'Mr Ingles is not a jeweller.'

'I know 'e ain't.' Lucy paused from mixing dough. 'But 'e makes things out o' brass, don't 'e?'

'Brass is not gold. If it were we would be quite wealthy for there is several pounds of it in the workshop.'

'Pity it isn't,' Lucy floured the wooden pin and board then scooped the dough from the bowl a few quick light movements rolling it into a creamy mat, 'I wouldn't mind bein' wealthy . . . not too much, mind you,' she grinned cheekily, 'just enough to make the 'ole of Wednesbury sit up and take notice.'

'Oh, I understand,' Phoebe laughed, 'nothing too blatant . . . just the odd million would do.'

'I just thought as seein' Bert was so 'andy with the brass like 'e might be able to make summat as would pass for jewellery,' Lucy said when they both stopped laughing.

'And how would I explain my neck turning a delicate shade of green halfway through the evening?'

'Oh, ar!' Lucy grimaced wryly but her eyes were laughing still. 'I 'adn't thought o' that. Mind, that would put you one up over the nobs . . . you'd 'ave summat they 'adn't got.'

'How very true. But I think I prefer to do without a green neck. It doesn't seem me somehow.'

'No! Well, p'raps you be right.' Taking the last remnants of dough Lucy shaped it into the figure of a man, giving it sultana eyes and four sultana buttons.

'Ruth doesn't like sultanas,' Phoebe said as Lucy blobbed jam where a nose would be.

'I know, but Mark does!' Lucy sprinkled the figure with

a coating of sugar before placing it in the tin alongside the scones, then looked across the table to where Phoebe was watching. 'Seriously though, Miss, apart from the jewellery there ain't nuthin' you couldn't get if you wanted to go to that ball.'

'I will not spend a great deal of money on . . .'

'You wouldn't 'ave to,' Lucy said quickly. 'Gloves you can get from Underwood's, ones that reach up over the elbow for no more than ninepence. An' they 'as feathers an' buttons. Eh, Miss, wi' your sewin' I reckon as you could make a lovely frock for little or nuthin'.'

'Hardly nothing.' Phoebe covered the scones then began to take cooked pies from the oven. 'How much is the material going to cost? Think how many yards it will take . . . Lucy, the whole thing is out of the question.'

'I don't know how many yards it'll take nor 'ow much the cost would be!' Lucy banged bowls and dishes together impatiently. 'An' neither do you 'cos you ain't asked so 'ow can you say it be out of the question? An' afore you says anythin' about shoes an' the costin' o' them you could always try John Kilvert's place.'

Phoebe straightened up, her cheeks reddened by the heat of the oven. 'A pawn shop!' she exclaimed. 'A pawn shop is not going to have dance slippers.'

'There you goes again!' Lucy rattled spoons and knives into the large mixing bowl. 'You'm a right one for reachin' a answer afore askin' the question, Miss Phoebe. Who's to say what old Kilvert 'as got stored away in that pawn shop . . . it ain't always the ones looks down an' out is down an' out, there be others 'ad to visit 'im, others popped pledges as they couldn't redeem.'

'But dance slippers?' Phoebe shook her head. 'Really, Lucy, I can't see there being such as that in a pawn shop.'

'You said that when that old brown cloak o' your'n got to be too bad off lookin' to go into town in any more, but you found that good green suit in one. What I says is if you don't try you won't know. Time to say a thing can't be done after you 'ave tried an' not t'other way round.'

She could always ask, she didn't have to buy anything. Ninepence for gloves . . . say threepence for second hand slippers . . . twopence for a dozen buttons . . . trimmings . . .

Gathering the rest of the used dishes from the table, she followed Lucy into the scullery.

Maybe it could be done, but jewellery, what of that? Phoebe smiled inwardly. Perhaps the Queen may have pawned the Crown Jewels.

'Lucy,' she asked, 'you did say the satin you saw in Underwood's shop window was a *pale* yellow?'

'Yes, Miss.' Lucy looked up from scouring pots. 'A lovely colour it be, like butter fresh from the dairy. Set your colourin' off to a tee it would.'

Pale yellow. Phoebe picked up the drying cloth and began to wipe the dishes Lucy had stacked on the board beside the sink. At least it wasn't pink.

Annie Pardoe wrote quickly, her well-formed copperplate hand rapidly covering the sheet of paper. She had bought the ink and the pen in Birmingham, that way she did not have to use that which was on the desk in the study, and the paper together with its envelope was the last of a birthday gift she had received from Abel many moons ago. She had kept one sheet of paper and one envelope, hiding them away for so many years, hiding them away but never forgetting them, knowing only that one day they would serve to hit back at him. Abel had died before she had found a way to strike, but that would not rob her of the revenge she had longed for all these years. Abel might be beyond her reach but his flesh and blood were not.

Folding the sheet of anonymously white notepaper she slipped it into the same self-effacing envelope, sealing it before writing an address across it in the same sure style. Abel was in his grave but his daughter was not. Slipping the envelope into her bag, she replaced the top on the bottle of ink, wiped the pen nib on a scrap torn from a corner of the newspaper, then slipped both into her bag alongside the letter.

Tearing the advert from the newspaper she slipped it into the drawer of the washstand, burying it beneath the towels. Abel was beyond her vengeance but she would destroy his daughter.

Thrusting a long hat pin through her hat, fastening it securely to her head, Annie checked her bedroom with a long seeking stare. The newspaper was folded neatly against her bag, the scrap of ink-stained paper was in the pocket of her coat, there was no sign of a letter having been written. Taking up her bag and the newspaper she left the room, passing that of her brother without looking in.

'Mr Samuel is still sleeping,' she said as she entered the kitchen, the lie sliding easily from her tongue. 'I thought it best not to disturb him. Take him a breakfast tray at eleven o'clock. I am going to ask the doctor to call, I am not at all sure Mr Samuel's health is improving despite the medicines.' Going into the scullery she deposited the newspaper with others kept in a wooden soap box alongside the stove to be used for lighting the house fires, then carried on, leaving the house by the rear door.

'Don't think Mr Samuel's health is improving?' Maudie watched from the scullery window. 'O' course it ain't improvin' an' you don't care for all you pretend to. You don't fool me, Annie Pardoe, you don't fool Maudie Tranter not for one minute you don't. You tell me you be going to fetch the doctor but it be my guess you be about more than that. You be up to summat, that much I be certain sure of, up to summat as sure as God med little apples.'

Standing to the side of the window so her watching presence would not easily be seen from outside Maudie waited until Annie had left, driving her small trap around to the front of the house. And still Maudie waited. She wouldn't put it past that sly bitch to come back into the house from the front. For several minutes she stood listening then, assured her mistress had gone, crossed the scullery to the soap box. Picking up the top newspaper she checked the date printed on the front page and smiled mirthlessly. 'You 'ave to get up early o' a mornin' to catch me, Annie, ma wench,' she murmured, then scanned the date on several papers until she found the one delivered to the house the day before. Turning to the page number she had made a mental note of, she smiled again. The advertisement for Pardoe's Patent Locks was missing.

Annie drove the trap at a steady walking pace, she was in no hurry and had no desire to draw attention to herself. She spoke to no one and none spoke to her, her long practice of ignoring people producing in them an almost total disregard for her. Passing to the left of Oakeswell Hall she skirted the black and white Tudor house, following the track across open ground the locals called the Mounts and coming around towards Hill Top. At the foot of the swell of ground Annie reined in the horse and sat looking at the black-grey water. Millfield Pool had formed when several gin pits had flooded, their vertical shafts filling with water which merged at the surface to form a large pond. The flooding of those shafts had taken many men, drowning them in their sludgy surging tide before they could scramble free, and it had taken others since.

Taking pen and ink from her bag she climbed from the trap and walked to the rim of ground overlooking the pool. 'You robbed me, Abel,' she whispered to the still menace lying at her feet, 'you robbed me of my life. Now watch while I rob your daughter of hers.'

Throwing the small bottle she saw it wing outward then thump into the water. She sent the pen after it, standing watching the spreading circles mark their watery grave. Taking the scrap of paper from her pocket, she stared at it for several moments. 'Vengeance is mine, Abel,' she whispered, rolling the paper between her fingers and letting it drop into her palm. Slowly raising her arm, stretching it out towards the water in macabre benediction, she tipped her hand, letting the balled scrap roll off the tips of her fingers. 'Vengeance is mine!'

Chapter Sixteen

'I wrote me name for it, Miss, I 'opes as that be all right? I 'ad no way of knowin' 'ow long you would be like, an' the postman, well, 'e 'ad other letters 'e 'ad to be deliverin'.' Lizzie Ingles's features struggled between a worried frown and an uncertain smile. 'I thought as if I wrote me name to say as I 'ad taken it in place o' you it would be all right.'

'It is all right, Lizzie, thank you.' Phoebe smiled and the other woman's face brightened. 'I wonder who it can be from?' She turned the white envelope but apart from the address written in neat flowing copperplate it bore no identifying mark.

'Only one way to find that out, Miss,' Lizzie said. 'That be to open it an' read it, an' that be best done over a nice cup o' tea.'

'I agree with you there, Lizzie.' Phoebe picked up the brown paper-wrapped parcel she had set down at her feet as Lizzie had met her. 'It's a fair walk from the Tipton Road. I got a ride from the carter as far as there but even so I am ready for a sit down and a drink.'

'Would you like me to make it for you, Miss?'

'That's good of you, Lizzie, but you must have work enough without waiting on me.'

'Nothing as will take 'arm from waitin' a while.' Lizzie opened the door that led into the mill house through the scullery and waited for Phoebe to pass inside. 'Bert an' Mark be in the workshop an' the babby be playin' around the back there.'

'Then you have time to join me. I will enjoy a cup of tea the more for having your company.'

Phoebe placed the parcel on the table in the kitchen, the letter beside it, unbuttoning her coat and hanging it beside the old brown cloak she kept now for working about the yard. 'I will take it upstairs later,' she said, seeing Lizzie eye the coat she needed to keep looking its best.

'I'll run it up for you, Miss.' Lizzie released the coat from its nail, her boots rattling on the stairs as she whisked up to Phoebe's bedroom.

'You really shouldn't,' Phoebe said as the woman skipped back in to the kitchen. 'You will have me too idle to scratch myself.'

'You, idle!' Lizzie poured boiling water on the fresh tea leaves waiting in the pot. 'That'll be the day. I've yet to come across a wench as works 'arder'n you an' I've met a few in me time. You sews most o' the day, then you 'elps with the filin' down o' the locks in the workshop, then o' nights you 'elps Lucy wi' 'er cookin'. No, you ain't idle, Miss. Whatever thoughts you might be 'oldin' about yourself that 'un be wrong.'

'I bought the most beautiful material for a gown.' Phoebe began to untie the string securing the parcel, Lizzie's compliment painting her cheeks a ripe pink. 'It is every bit as lovely as Lucy said and not nearly as expensive as I would have thought.'

'Eh, that's real pretty!' Lizzie made to touch the delicate lemony-cream fabric then pulled her hand away. 'An' it be just the colour for you with your hair.'

'There were others.' Phoebe added milk and sugar to the tea Lizzie poured for her. 'Green, blue, a really deep scarlet and a soft sugary pink. They were all so nice I was spoiled for choice.'

Sweetening her own tea, Lizzie sat opposite Phoebe in the warm kitchen. This girl must have had silks and finery, all the comfort and luxury her father's money could buy, and yet it hadn't spoilt her. There was nothing bay-windowed about her, and nothing vicious either. Even the months spent in that rat hole of a gaol hadn't altered her nature. Lizzie drank her tea. That son of Dartmouth's came visiting too regular for it to be a way of apologising for what he had done. His sort might say it once if you were lucky but not a couple of times a week. There was more to his coming than that. He was looking to make this wench his wife and if he got to do it he could count himself fortunate. This one would be no high-faluting, sit-on-her-arse lady of the manor. This one would care for the folk who worked for her.

'I got these to go with it.' Phoebe delved into the basket she had carried, taking out an assortment of buttons and lace. 'I thought feathers might be a little too much, what do you think?'

'I think you made just the right choice.' Lizzie admired the lace and touched a finger to the pretty pearl buttons. 'You'll be pretty as a picture, Miss, an' no coddin'.'

'But a ball gown,' Phoebe said, holding the elbow-length gloves she had bought against the material, then looking worriedly at Lizzie. 'I hope I haven't taken on more than I can handle. A ball gown . . . it's so different from a child's dress.'

'A bit fancier, Miss, I'll give you that,' said Lizzie, gathering the teacups, 'an' a bit on the bigger side, but that be all an' that ain't different, not really.'

'You make it sound so easy,' Phoebe called after her into the scullery, 'I almost believe it myself.'

Lizzie returned from the scullery drying her hands on her rough apron. 'You believe it, Miss, 'cos it be the truth. Lizzie Ingles wouldn't lead you up the garden path, 'er tells you the way 'er sees things an' no lies. Now you best be gettin' that there cloth up to your workroom afore summat be findin' itself spilt on it.'

'Did the metal come?'

'Ar, Miss, brass founders delivered it about an hour after

the three of you left this mornin'.' Lizzie watched as Phoebe gathered her purchases into one parcel. 'Bert says as there be enough for a couple o' dozen doublers an' p'raps a bit left over as'll make a few close shackle padlocks, an' 'e says as it be good quality metal an' all.'

Thank heaven for that, Phoebe thought, remembering how she had declared to the brass founder that any dross delivered to her would be returned unpaid for and her business taken elsewhere. She had trembled inside, seeing the scorn in his eyes as he had listened to a woman trying to play at business, but the scorn had faded as she had declared the price she was prepared to pay for brass or steel, changing to veiled admiration as she stated she would pay not a penny more.

'Don't forget your letter, Miss.' Lizzie nodded to the envelope that had become hidden beneath layers of brown paper. 'I'll be off now.'

'Thank you, Lizzie,' Phoebe said as the other woman left through the scullery. 'I will just take these upstairs and then I will see what it is.'

'. . . *one gross of Invincible locks to be delivered by the close of business on the last day of the month* . . .'

Phoebe stared at the words written neatly across the sheet of notepaper, its heading boldly proclaiming James Greaves, Hardware and Ironmongery. An order for one gross of locks, the first in answer to her advertisement. She read the remainder of the letter: '. . . *should you find yourself unable to comply with my requirements please notify me by return post.*'

The end of the month. Phoebe made a swift mental calculation. That left twenty-one days all told, including Sundays. It could not be done. She sank heavily to a chair, the letter in her hand. Her very first order and it could not be met. The start she had prayed for and it was over before it had begun. Folding the letter, she returned it to its envelope.

'It is as I have told you before, your brother's constitution has been weak from childhood.' Alfred Dingley pulled on his chamois leather gloves. 'I can prescribe medicine to help him sleep or to relieve pain should he have any, but there is no real cure for what truly ails him. You know it, Miss Pardoe, and I know it, and sadly so does he.'

Picking up the black Gladstone bag that was his constant companion, the doctor pressed a hand to his patient's shoulder before leaving the bedroom. 'He is getting weaker,' he said as he reached the front door. 'You can try him with beef tea or with some chicken broth but nothing too heavy.'

'My brother eats so little,' Annie said with mock solicitude, 'I worry so for him.'

'Worrying heals no wounds.' The doctor raised his tall black hat the merest fraction. 'And seeing you fret will only add to his suffering. My advice is to treat him the way you have always done – give him no intimation of how things really stand with him, though it is my guess he needs none.'

'How do you mean?' Annie asked, her hands shaking just enough.

Placing his valise on the seat, the doctor climbed into the carriage. 'I mean your brother is probably already acquainted with the fact that he has just a few years left on this earth.' Taking up the reins, he raised his hat again. 'Good day, Miss Pardoe. I will call one week from today.'

A few years? Annie returned to the house. Alfred Dingley was wrong. Her brother Samuel did not have a few years left on this earth, he had less than a few days.

She had taken so much care. The seeds of yew and laburnum painstakingly collected from the garden of the Bescot house. Several seasons' worth gathered and stored before the shrubs had been rooted out and burned, leaving nothing that could be traced. Dried and ground to an ultra-fine powder and added to water, the seeds had produced a liquid that held death in its pale golden heart, death that had slept within a perfume bottle waiting the time to strike. That time had come on the day of the burglary.

Annie stood before her cheval mirror admiring the sheen

of her pearl grey dress. Samuel had said how nice it was to see her in a colour other than black. How much more becoming soft shades were to her, how particularly well the grey suited her. It had suited well that day. She touched her fingers to the pocket in her skirt, concealed by the folds of taffeta. She had taken the bottle from the drawer and put it in her pocket. Samuel had been so taken up with examining the other rooms in order to ascertain whether anything other than the few silver ornaments had been taken he did not see her add the liquid from the bottle to the glass of sherry she had poured for him. Clinton had arrived just at that moment. He had heard of the burgling of her home, he said, and had to call to satisfy himself no one had been harmed.

It had not mattered to her then. She had almost smiled as she had poured a second glass of the pale golden sherry for Clinton. It had not mattered that he had met Samuel, theirs would be only a short acquaintance. Placing the glasses on a small silver serving tray she had been interrupted by the arrival of the constables and had left the two men to their drinks while she showed the policemen to the study.

Clinton had been taking his leave when she returned and she had walked with him into the tree-shrouded drive. She would have the deeds to her industrial properties the next day, he had told her, then kissed her cheek before leaving.

Turning from the mirror she crossed the room to the chest of drawers. Sinking on to her knees she pulled open the bottom drawer, taking the box with its amethyst ring from beneath the tissue-wrapped petticoats. Slipping the ring on to the third finger of her left hand she twisted and turned her wrist, admiring the dancing spurts of purple flame shoot from the heart of the stone. Soon she would wear it beyond this room, soon it would shine where all could see.

She felt no regret for what she had done to Samuel, for bringing early the death that Alfred Dingley foretold. Any regret she might have felt was gone, eaten away by her wasted years; nor did she feel any guilt. That must be Abel's for the shackles forged by his money.

Returning the ring to its box, Annie slipped it back beneath the petticoats and stood up. She would be Clinton's wife and Samuel would be gone from her life. Soon she would be free from all she had despised for so long, free from all that had held her prisoner while her youth slipped away, a freedom that had no place in it for Samuel and none for Abel's daughter.

Abel's daughter! Annie turned away from the chest of drawers, catching her reflection in the mirror as she did so. She had once been as Abel's child, young, pretty enough, full of happiness, eager for life and the promise it held. But the promise had been broken, life had not been given to her, it had been snatched away, snatched by a brother intent on his own happiness to the detriment of her own; a brother who could not himself be made to pay for what he had done to her but whose daughter would pay.

Annie smoothed her grey dress but her eyes were on the reflection of her face, on the tired skin, on the lines about her mouth, on the creases across her brow, on the look of age. The gall of bitterness rose within her. 'The sins of the parents shall be visited upon the children,' she whispered. 'She will pay, Abel . . . to the very last penny.'

'It's just impossible.' Lucy read the letter then passed it to Mathew. 'Six or seven locks a day . . . it can't be done.'

'I know.' They were in the kitchen of Phoebe's house, the evening meal having been cleared, the table holding only the letter Mathew had placed at its centre. 'The first reply to my advertisement and I can't fulfil the order.'

"Ave you talked of this wi' Bert?'

'What is the use?' Phoebe glanced at the tall young man, shirt sleeves rolled above the elbow, a broad belt about his waist. His sleeked back hair was still wet from a wash at the outdoor pump.

'Maybe none,' Mathew answered, 'but you should talk to 'im all the same.'

'Like Miss Phoebe says,' Lucy turned to her husband, 'it ain't no use talkin'. Talkin' don't make no locks.'

'It don't cost nothin' neither.' Mathew's retort was sharp.

'You think I should have shown the Ingleses that letter?'

'I don't think as 'ow it would 'ave 'urt none even if it didn't do no good. Seems only right to me some'ow that Bert be told.'

'I don't see as tellin' Bert will make no difference no'ow,' Lucy said stubbornly. 'It might only make 'im feel bad 'cos 'e can't do what that order asks.'

'Lucy has a point, Mathew.' Phoebe picked up the letter, folding it into its envelope. 'Bert works so hard, I would not want him to feel that losing this order was due to him.'

'Nor you should.' Mathew's lower lip came forward as it always did when he felt his argument was the right one. 'But it seems the bloke 'as the right to know 'is locks not just be sellin' well but could be sellin' a damn' sight better.'

'An' that be supposed to make 'im feel good, is it?'

'It would bloody well mek *me* feel good!' Mathew frowned at his wife. 'A bloke slaves 'is guts out, it shouldn't be too much for 'im to know the job 'e be doin' is a good 'un.'

'You are right, of course, Mathew.' Phoebe stood up, the letter in her hand. 'Bert should see the order. I will take it to him now.'

'I realise it cannot be done but we thought you should see the order, it shows how well your work is being received.' Phoebe waited while Bert Ingles read through the letter.

'It can't given the way we be now,' he handed back the letter, 'but that don't mean to say as it couldn't be done at all.'

"Ow be that then?' Mathew asked, his broad shoulders almost blocking the doorway of the small workshop. 'I don't follow.'

'It be logical,' Bert answered. 'One bloke on 'is own can't be doin' everythin', but give 'im a little 'elp . . .'

"Elp?' Lucy squeezed in against Mathew. "Ow can we 'elp? We be knowin' nothin' of lockmakin'.'

'Mathew do.' Bert smiled. "E's picked it up real well, an' Lizzie does most of the filin' down, an' Miss Phoebe there 'elps out wi' that, an' the lad works the bellows an' fetches coals up from the cut.'

'Coals!' Phoebe asked, perplexed.

'Ah, Miss, coals.' Bert turned to her. 'You needs coal to fire the forge an' we gets it from the barges that pass along the cut.'

'You mean the bargees give you coal?'

'Not gives,' Bert grinned, 'they comes 'ere for fresh water an' leaves a few buckets o' coal the side o' the cut afore they goes. It's fair trade.'

'But . . . but don't they get into trouble? It . . . it's like stealing.'

'No, it ain't, Miss.' Lizzie smiled. 'The coal bosses, they knows as cut men can't carry everythin' they needs for trips to London or the coast an' they makes allowances like. They knows a bit o' coal 'as to be swapped for water an' such.'

And may the Lord shut His ears to your lies, Lizzie Ingles, she thought, glancing away. Any hint of a bargee exchanging coal for any reason would have the coal bosses slamming him into gaol, but then, what the eye don't see, the heart don't grieve over.

'So if we all be already doin' what we can to 'elp, 'ow come you says the fillin' o' that order could be done?' Mathew asked.

'I reckons as 'ow it could be given another bloke or two, a few more hours workin' a day, an' a bit o' proper machinery to work wi'.'

'But we don't 'ave another bloke!' Lucy stated the obvious.

'Then there be the metal, Miss,' Lizzie added. 'You 'ave to

'ave money for metal. Bert sometimes gets carried away. 'E don't always see obstacles till 'e cuts 'is nose on 'em.'

'I see this order could be the start.' Bert looked at Phoebe. 'This could lead to others. Get this done an' I reckon you will be lookin' at the beginnin' of a business that could grow into summat big.'

'Buying brass and steel is one thing,' Phoebe was touched by the note of hope in Bert's voice, knowing how his dreams had ended with his father's death, 'but buying machinery is another.'

'You wouldn't 'ave to.'

'Then how?'

'I think as Bert be thinkin' of 'is own,' Lizzie put in. 'The rest of 'is tools still be in a out'ouse back of 'is father's place. They were never sold . . . nobody 'ad use for 'em seemed.'

'Until now.' Phoebe's mouth set in a determined line. 'We are going to use them. What has happened once will happen again and next time we will not have to refuse an order.'

'What you thinkin' of?' Lucy asked, recognising the determined expression.

'I am thinking we should discuss this further but not here in the workshop. Come across to the house, all of you. And with your permission, Lizzie and Bert, I would like Mark to come too. He helps in the workshop, he should be part of any decision that is made.'

'So,' Phoebe looked at the circle of people grouped about her kitchen, 'we need metal, we need men, and we need equipment. Where do we find them and how much will it cost?'

'The equipment be no bother,' Bert said. 'There be several bench vices, an anvil, 'ammers, tongs, chisels, files, the lot in my old place. They only needs bringin' 'ere, and findin' space to work be no 'eadache.'

'Then we must find a way of bringing them here.'

'Reckon a couple of Lucy's best mutton pies would see to that.' Bert grinned as he had in the workshop, the excitement of regaining his own equipment showing in his eyes.

'I see,' Lucy laughed, 'it's bribery now, is it?'

'Summat like that.' Lizzie looked up from her chair by the fire, her daughter on her knee. 'Bert be good at that.'

'See, Miss,' he went on, 'the 'ole lot, bench an' all, could be brought 'ere by barge.'

'But you don't work the barges anymore, Bert, so how does that help us?'

'No, I don't work the barges any more,' he answered, 'but I knows many who does an' there be one alongside towpath who be goin' up to Wolverhampton tomorrow. That will take him through Willenhall and right past my old place, an' 'e will be back 'ere the same afternoon. 'E would cart the lot for nuthin' more'n a couple of pies.'

'Could the man do that? Alone, I mean. Some of the things you need must be quite heavy?'

''E would need another man. I thought as I might 'ave to go wi' 'im.'

'Would there be anythin' I wouldn't recognise?' Mathew caught the flavour of the discussion. 'If you give me a good description, could I find the things you want?'

Bert thought for a moment before nodding. 'Reckon you could, ain't nothin' special.'

'Then why don't I go?' Mathew looked at Phoebe, her hands resting on the table, still holding the letter with its order for one gross of locks. 'That way Bert could carry on with the locks 'e is workin' on.'

'But what of your own work?' Phoebe asked.

'Ain't much of it at the moment,' Mathew answered wryly. 'Don't seem to be anybody wantin' odd jobs done right now an' what locks I'd be sellin' round the town could be countin' towards the gross we be needin'.'

'We are still left with the matter of employing another man,' Phoebe said.

'I've 'ad me brain on that one an' all,' Bert said again, 'if it's all right to say?'

'You've 'ad nuthin' but good ideas so far Bert so let's be 'earing what else you 'ave to say.'

Bert smiled at Mathew's words but his eyes were on Phoebe.

'Mathew has said what we all feel.' She smiled encouragement. 'Without you there would be no lockmaking business. You have solved all the problems so far, I am sure you will be helpful again.'

'Well, Miss, way I look at it is this. Mathew there 'as a good 'and for the locks, 'e 'as picked the job up a treat, 'sides which 'e as the strength needed for usin' 'ammer an' anvil. Now 'e 'as said as 'ow odd jobs 'ave dropped off so why not give 'im the job of workin' along o' me?'

'I had never thought of that,' Phoebe said, 'but how would Mathew feel about it? And what of Lucy?'

'I wants Mathew to be 'appy in what 'e is doin',' Lucy said as her husband's eyes turned to her. 'Whatever 'e chooses I know 'e does it for the best.'

Reaching for her hand Mathew folded it in his own, his smile broad. 'I'd like to work wi' Bert, Miss. Tattin' for jobs be no way to mek a livin'. Seems this lock business is goin' to tek off an' bein' in on it would give a man a reglar job like.'

'So we have our new hand,' Phoebe tapped her fingers against the envelope, 'now what we must do is work out the finances.'

Almost an hour later Phoebe pushed across the table a sheet of paper covered with figures and leaned wearily against the back of her chair.

'If only I had not bought that material to make a gown we might just have managed. I'm so sorry, Bert.'

'Ain't your fault.' Lizzie handed her daughter across to Mark who placed a protective arm about his sister's thin shoulders. 'You wasn't to know about no order comin' in.' Taking the pot from the dresser, she set about making tea.

'Of course it ain't no fault of your'n.' Lucy turned to help Lizzie with the tea. 'It was your money, you 'ad a right to spend it any road you wanted.'

'What say we goes through it once more?' Bert intervened.

Her calculations were correct, Phoebe knew. To go over them a thousand times more would only bring the same result: she just did not have sufficient money to buy the metal and pay the extra wages and no amount of checking the figures would alter that. But she leaned over them again, not having the heart to say no as she saw the dream dying in Bert's eyes.

'Let's all have a cup of tea an' p'raps things will look better.' Lizzie handed out the steaming cups while Phoebe buttered a scone each for the children.

''Scuse me, Miss.' Mark pulled a sultana from the edge of his scone, eyeing it with the look of a connoisseur, 'but you said as since I was workin' along o' me father I should be paid a reglar wage.'

'So I did, Mark.' Phoebe saw the astonished face of the boy's mother and the tightening of Bert's hand on his broad leather belt.

'Well, Miss,' Mark kept his eyes on the sultana, avoiding the warning glare that was in his father's eyes, 'I don't want it.'

'You don't want it?' Phoebe glanced quickly at the angry face of his father then back to the boy. 'But, Mark, we all agreed that a shilling a week was a fair wage.'

'It's a bostin' wage, Miss, only you can keep it toward payin' for metals. But when you gets paid for them locks, I will tek a shillin' a week.' His toffeedrop eyes gleaming with the air of a satisfied businessman clinching a deal, he popped the sultana into his mouth.

His anger forgotten, Bert touched a proud hand to his son's shoulder. 'He be right, what you reckon to pay 'im do be a good wage. Reckon lad 'as shown the way we was lookin' for,' he said. 'You can 'old my wage over till job be done an' locks paid for an' all.'

'I could not do that.' Phoebe looked up, astonished at Bert's words. 'Thank you, both of you, but you cannot work for nothing.'

"T'wouldn't be for nuthin',' Bert answered solemnly. 'Look at it my way. As things be Lizzie an' me 'as a roof for the children an' food for their bellies. Anythin' over an' above that be a luxury, an' luxuries can be gone wi'out. I know Lizzie will agree to what I says an' it be this. We will do as we did the first week we come 'ere. We 'ave enough to live on for the next three weeks so Mark an' me will tek no wage. You can make it up once locks be paid for.'

'Lucy an' me be of the same mind,' Mathew came in quickly, preventing Phoebe's refusal. 'We can manage same as Bert an' Lizzie.'

'I don't know what to say.' Phoebe's eyes glistened.

'Ain't nuthin' to be said, 'cept get these cups outa the way an' let's go over them figures again.' Bert came to stand at her shoulder. 'This time we're goin' to make 'em work.'

'We are still short,' Phoebe announced later as Lizzie carried her sleeping daughter out of the kitchen, Mark at her heels. 'I don't see there is anything more we can do.'

'I do 'ave one more suggestion.' Bert ran a hand through his hair. 'You 'ave down there the wage for another workman along o' Mathew. That be countin' for 'alf a crown a week. Now Mark, 'e knows lockmakin' inside out. Long nights on a barge leave a lad wi' little to do. 'E 'as a good brain, an' what's better 'e listens to what 'e be told. 'E can do all I do 'cept for the anvil an' that be a bit too 'eavy for 'im as yet.'

'So what are you saying?'

'I'm sayin' this. You got to pay 'alf a crown a week for summat my lad can do, and on top o' that you will need a coupla weeks to show a new bloke the ropes an' a damn' sight more'n a coupla weeks afore 'e can be left to work on 'is own, where the lad can do that now.'

Phoebe pressed a hand to her back, more tired than she wished to show. 'I don't understand, Bert.'

'I think I do,' Mathew said. 'You will be payin' a man's wage for a job 'e won't be able to do for weeks, the same job as Mark can do now, so why not let 'im work on the locks an' get another bloke to work the bellows an' bring up the coal, right, Bert?'

'Almost.' He grinned. 'My way you will be gettin' job done quicker an' for less money.'

'But if Mark is doing what a man would do he must be paid the same wage.'

'That ain't the way of things, Miss.' Bert straightened from where he had been stooped over the figures. 'Lad won't be doin' quite all a man would 'ave to, like I say 'e ain't up to 'ammerin' on a anvil, not yet. An' anyway, young 'uns gets paid less on account of the trainin' they be given. I 'preciates your thinkin' but I would rather 'e learned the usual ways of the world.'

'Bert be right in what 'e says,' Mathew nodded. 'This be one o' the facts you 'as to learn if you be goin' to run a business.'

'I expect so.' Phoebe smiled. 'And I understand we have no time to train a man in the skills of lockmaker, but we will still have to employ one to do what Mark was doing so where is the saving in that?'

'I said Mathew was almost right.' Bert pointed to the column of figures. ''Alf a crown for a bloke against ninepence for a lad, so why set a bloke on doin' a lad's work? Pumpin' bellows be a lad's work so why not get a lad to do it? It will cut nearly two-thirds off what you will pay in wages.'

Phoebe ran a swift eye over the figures, her tiredness evaporating as the import of what Bert was saying struck home. Mentally deducting the wages of Mathew, Bert and Mark, together with the revised wage of a youth, she felt a tremor of exhilaration. She could do it!

'Supposing you can make that many locks in a day, then we can accept our first order.' Rising from her chair, she held out a hand to each of the two men. 'Thank you,' she said simply, 'thank you both very much.'

'An' I'll thank you both to leave,' Lucy bustled into the scullery in search of baking tins, 'otherwise there'll be no mutton pies for that there bargee an' that'll put the cobblebosh on the lot of it.'

Taking his flat cap from his trousers pocket, Bert held it in his hand. 'I'll go down to towpath now an' 'ave a word wi' 'im, but 'e will bring my stuff right enough, no need to lose sleep over that. Night, Miss. Night, Lucy.'

'Goodnight, Bert,' Phoebe answered as he moved toward the scullery door. 'And, Bert, you have a good son in Mark.'

'Aye, Miss,' Bert fitted the cap to his head, 'Lizzie an' me, we knows that.'

Chapter Seventeen

'I instructed my own barrister to look into the affair of your time in prison.' Sir William Dartmouth looked at the young woman standing before him, hands folded across the front of a print dress, hair that was neither gold nor brown caught back in a knot that tried in vain to add years to her face. 'The result, I regret to say, showed a lamentable lack of justice. I have here a warrant signed by a magistrate – not, I might say, the one who consigned you to prison in the first place. What I ask is, will you return to Handsworth Prison for Women with me or would you prefer the constables to escort you there?'

Instructed my own barrister, I have a warrant, will you return, would you prefer the constables . . .

The words whirled together, dancing a crazy fandango, whisking in and out of her understanding. Phoebe clenched her hands together, hoping the bite of nails into flesh would stop the screams rising to her throat. He had not forgotten though he had been told of her innocence of the theft of his daughter's necklace, he wanted vengeance, never mind if the victim be free from blame. He had pretended friendship, even to the length of asking that his son be her escort to a farewell ball, and all the time he had been searching for a way to send her back to hell.

'You . . . you say you have a warrant?'

'Here.' He tapped the folded sheet against a gloved hand. 'Do you wish to read it?'

'No . . .' Phoebe breathed long and deep, fighting the nausea that was laying claim to her stomach. 'There will be no need, Sir William.' She could read it, Phoebe thought, fetching her coat, but she could not alter it. This time the Magistrate would not be wrong. This man would have his revenge and would make certain there could be no way he would be cheated of it.

Thanking the coachman for the hand he held out to help her up, Phoebe climbed into the carriage, her gaze on her home until it fell away below the rise of the ground.

How long had he been planning this? Phoebe watched the passing landscape but saw only the devils of fear dancing in her brain. Was it in his mind when she met him outside of the Magistrate's rooms in Wednesbury . . . was he thinking of it when he sent Edward and Sophie to invite her to the ball? And Edward, was he party to his father's action? Had he known of it even when he had asked her to marry him?

She closed her eyes, leaning her head against the padded upholstery of the carriage. No one save Sir William Dartmouth would know where she had gone or what had happened. Lizzie had watched from where she had been hanging washing on a clothes line Bert had set up beside the old windmill to catch the best of the breezes, but it had been too far for her to see any distress which might have shown. How long would Lucy and Mathew wait before making enquiries as to her whereabouts? Tomorrow? The next day? No, not that long, they knew she would not stay away from Wiggins Mill that length of time unless she had told them beforehand. And what if they went to the Priory? Would he see them, or would he have them dismissed without a word?

'Miss Pardoe, Miss Pardoe, we have arrived.'

This was not happening, it was a bad dream that would vanish when she opened her eyes, but it didn't and as she stepped from the carriage to be faced by that blank wall with its solid oak door Phoebe came face to face with the nightmare she had thought was over.

The door opened in answer to a knock from Sir William's malacca cane and they were inside. Inside the jaws of Hell.

Phoebe followed the grim-faced wardress in her grey soulless uniform, their footsteps sounding sharp in the carbolic-laden air of the narrow bare brick corridors. *I sentence you to fifteen years* . . . The words seemed to echo from the brickwork. How many years would it be this time? How much of her life would be spent paying for a crime she did not commit?

'Begging your pardon . . .'

The wardress had led them to a small, sparsely furnished waiting room Phoebe had heard of but had not seen and now stood looking at her, a faint shadow of near-forgotten concern on her long, drawn features.

'. . . but are you feeling unwell, Miss?'

Sensing Sir William move toward her, Phoebe stepped away.

'We do 'ave a infirmary 'ere, Sir,' the wardress looked at Sir William, 'if the lady would like to rest? She do look pale.'

'Thank you, but I am quite all right.'

Phoebe forced the words past a throat tight with fear. Resting in the infirmary would delay her return to the dormitory and the laundry only for as long as it took the man who had brought her here to leave. It had to happen, she had to return to the torture of long days and nights locked in this Godforsaken place, so why delay the inevitable? Let her sentence begin.

'Then I will tell the Governess you are 'ere.' The wardress bobbed the tiniest of curtsies. ''scuse me.'

'Miss Pardoe,' catching her arm as the wardress left the waiting room Sir William pressed her to a chair, 'are you quite certain you are not feeling unwell? You were very quiet during our drive here and now . . . as the wardress said, you are looking very pale.'

Looking very pale? Phoebe wanted to laugh but stared at him instead, rage at his treatment of her suddenly destroying the fear that had been suffocating her.

Pushing his hand from her arm she stood up, her features calm and icy as if carved from some glacial peak. 'I am looking very pale, how unwarranted of me!' Every word clipped into the quiet room like ice cubes falling into a glass. 'Please forgive my thoughtlessness. How ungracious of me to look so when you were kind enough to escort me here personally . . . how ignorant to repay that kindness by looking pale! So tell me, Sir William, how do you expect a woman to look when she is being returned to the grave?'

'Returned to the . . . I don't understand?'

'Of course you don't understand!' Phoebe spat, anger and fear overcoming her reserve. 'How could you understand? You to whom a girl dare not come with the truth for fear of tainting the name of Dartmouth. You who have been protected from reality all your life, whom the people raise their hat to, the powerful Billy-me-Lord, how could *you* understand what it is to be imprisoned? The degradation, the total lack of privacy, the utter soul-destroying mindlessness of it, the complete waste of a life . . . how would you know the torment of being accused of something you did not do, of having your life ripped away, of being condemned to a living hell, to be released only to be returned? To have the torment begin all over again!'

'Miss Pardoe . . .' He made to touch her then his hand fell to his side. He stayed where he was, watching the shades of passion flit across her face. 'I am sorry my bringing you here has caused you distress . . .'

'Sorry!' Phoebe glared contemptuously. 'You are *sorry* to have caused me distress? What did you expect returning me to prison would cause?'

'I did not think . . .'

'You did not think!' Phoebe cut across him, her tone lacerating. 'Do not insult me with lies, Sir William. You could have thought of little else all the time you were planning your revenge.'

'Revenge? I . . .'

'Yes, revenge.' She refused to let him speak, anger still uppermost. 'You pretended friendship towards me, you and your family, when all you really wanted was to have me re-committed to this prison. Why, Sir William? Why when you know I am innocent, when you have the necklace back? Why . . . is it to show the great Sir William Dartmouth is not to be played with?'

'Miss Pardoe, listen . . .'

'To what? More lies?'

'Call what I have to say lies if you will, but you shall listen. I brought you here . . .'

'Good day, Sir William.'

He stopped in mid-sentence, turning to see Hannah Price standing in the doorway.

'Miss Pardoe, my dear, how are you?'

Habit bent Phoebe's knee to a slight curtsy as she faced the Governess of Handsworth Prison for Women, fear surging up through the anger.

'I am well, Ma'am,' she murmured.

'But you look so pale.' She glanced at the man standing tight-lipped beside the young woman who had spent over a year locked behind the walls of this prison, a young woman she had come to like, whose loyalty and courage she had grown to respect. 'Sir William, perhaps the infirmary . . .'

'No, Mrs Price, thank you but we will get our business over. I want no further delay.'

'As you wish.' The governess nodded to the wardress who had remained at the door and she stood aside, allowing a third figure to enter the room.

'You wanted to see me, Ma'am?'

Everything stilled in Phoebe: her mind, her heart, the very blood in her veins.

'Yes, come in. Would you wait outside, Mrs Marsh?'

'Yes, Ma'am.'

Phoebe refused to let the exchange register, waiting only for the voice that had stilled her world to speak again.

'I think you know one of our visitors?' Hannah Price said.

In the stillness of her soul, Phoebe waited.

'Phoebe?'

The voice was uncertain but Phoebe was not. She knew that voice, recognised it from the long months of her captivity. 'Tilly!' She whirled to face the gaunt-faced woman, her hair tied in the compulsory plaits, the regulation grey skirts hanging loose about her thin body. 'Tilly! Oh, Tilly!'

'Sir William.' Phoebe stood at the front entrance to Wiggins Mill, her cheeks pink with embarrassment of what she knew she had to say. He had remained silent during the drive back to the mill, watching her hold a sobbing Tilly in her arms, then had waited until she had been settled with tea in a china cup, the kindly Lizzie in attendance. 'Sir William . . .' Phoebe began again.

'You do not have to say anything.' He placed a hand on her elbow, leaving it there as he added, 'It was thoughtless of me to act as I did. There is no need for apology.'

'There is every need,' Phoebe said, her eyes still holding traces of the tears of relief and happiness she had shed. 'It was wrong of me to speak to you as I did.'

'I think harsh words a mild punishment given the circumstances.' His grey eyes grew warm. 'Were I in your shoes nothing short of a horsewhipping would satisfy my feelings, I do not consider you at fault in any way.'

'That is kind of you, Sir William.' The colour deepened in Phoebe's cheeks, 'but I was at fault. I should have asked your reasons for taking me back to that place before I railed at you.'

'What did you think my reasons were?'

'Revenge.' Embarrassed as she was, Phoebe forced herself to meet his gaze. 'I thought you planned to have me returned to gaol, to have me serve the sentence originally passed upon me or perhaps an even longer one.'

'You thought the warrant I had was an order returning you to prison?'

'Yes.'

'But you had not been brought before a Magistrate, there

had been no new charge laid against you, how could you have thought you were being returned to serve that sentence?'

'Fear makes you suspect many things you would not normally think. I was afraid – afraid of being locked into Hell.'

'Miss Pardoe,' his eyes darkened and the fingers holding her arm tightened, 'I would never have you afraid because of me. Believe me when I say I was thinking only of the pleasure my actions would afford you. Causing you fear or concern never entered my mind. You told me of the circumstances of your friend's trial, of how you suspected there had been a miscarriage of justice. I thought it would in some way make amends for the suffering my family caused you if I could get a review of Mrs Wood's trial. I put the whole of what I knew before my own barrister who set in motion a further investigation of the so-called murder of the husband. It appears that other occupants of the lodging house where they lived had witnessed the argument. They had seen the man strike his wife and her attempt to defend herself. They had seen him fall backward down the stairs, causing his death.'

'Why didn't they say so at Tilly's trial? Why didn't they tell the Magistrate that?'

'It appears the constables did not report there being witnesses to the fall.' He did not remove his hand nor did his eyes leave hers. 'Or at least that is what the prosecution claimed. My barrister pressed for a complete review of the trial on the grounds of suppression of evidence, with the result that Mrs Wood was given a Queen's Pardon. Had I thought to tell you of all this before we went to Handsworth Prison you would not have been subjected to so much worry. I am deeply sorry and apologise most profoundly.'

'You are sorry and I am sorry.' Phoebe broke into a smile. 'We are a sorry pair, you and I, Sir William.'

'Yes.' His fingers tightened fractionally and the grey of his eyes turned to smoke. 'A sorry pair,' he finished softly.

'Sir William,' she said as he withdrew his hand from her

arm and turned towards his waiting carriage, 'I will not forget what you have done, for Tilly and for me.'

I will not forget either, Miss Phoebe Pardoe, he thought, climbing into the carriage. I will not forget what you have done to me.

'Annie dear, tomorrow I would like to see James Siveter.' Samuel's fingers moved without hesitation. 'I told you I wish to return most of what Abel bequeathed me to Phoebe.'

Annie's mind moved like quicksilver. He could not know that Phoebe still lived here in Wednesbury. She scrutinised the newspapers closely before passing them to him, removing those advertisements that referred to Pardoe's Patent Locks, and there was no one who could communicate with him other than herself. She alone had learned to speak with her hands; even Abel had not troubled himself to do so, relying on her to relay what he wished to say to Samuel.

'I want the papers drawn up tomorrow.'

She caught the quick movements, her thoughts outstripping them. Let Samuel say all he wished it would achieve nothing. There would be no tomorrow. She had thought the poison she had concocted from the yew and laburnum seed would have acted more rapidly than this; she had tried it often in those early years, feeding it to mice then cats then a dog, and in every instance it had brought death in less than two days. But for Samuel it had not worked. He had shown no more than his usual signs of illness. Was that due to Alfred Dingley's potions? She doubted it. The medicines he prescribed were no more than coloured sugar water prescribed as a salve to his own conscience for the fees he charged.

'I will go to his office in the morning,' she signed. 'I will tell him what you want and ask him to bring the papers here to you when they are ready.' That way she could delay long enough, she thought. A day would be all she needed.

'No.' The shake of Samuel's head signalled his refusal while his fingers flashed the rest of his words. 'I do not wish Mr Siveter to call at the house. I intend to visit him in his office myself tomorrow.'

You may intend to visit him, Annie thought, but I intend you do not.

'Will you be kind enough to drive me there in the trap, Annie dear?'

'Of course.' She smiled, her hands moving nimbly. 'If you are feeling as well tomorrow as you are today then certainly we will visit Mr Siveter.'

If he was well. Annie resisted the temptation to laugh. He would not be!

Samuel looked about him, the colours of late summer glowing the borders to the lawns. He loved the garden in all its phases but perhaps this was his favourite time.

'Brunswick House is such a kind house,' he motioned, 'it is almost a shame to leave it.'

A shame for you, Annie's thoughts raced, but not for me. I shall not be sorry to see the last of this place, to see the last of Wednesbury. I shall have a home of my own at last, a home with Clinton.

'Like you say, Samuel,' her fingers answered, 'it will be a shame to leave, but if it will give you peace of mind then of course that is what we must do.'

'Thank you, dear,' he smiled his weary smile, 'you always were so understanding, I will ensure you are well provided for.'

'Nonsense,' she returned, 'whatever makes you happy is all I want. But tell me, dear, how do we go about finding Phoebe? We do not know where she went, she may not even live in Wednesbury any more.'

'I know,' Samuel answered, 'but I am sure Mr Siveter will have methods of enquiry. We may leave it to him to find her.'

'Then we will tell him to begin tomorrow.' Annie touched a hand to the pain below her breast. It troubled her more often as the days passed, forcing her to take the white tablets several times each day, waking her in the night with fresh demands.

'It's time for Mr Samuel's medicine, Ma'am.' Maudie Tranter set a tray on the wicker table set between the garden chairs. 'Will I measure it?'

'Yes,' Annie nodded, 'but carefully. Two dessert spoons, no more, we must not exceed the amount the doctor advised.'

Bloody hypocrite, Maudie thought, carefully filling the dessert spoon she had placed on the tray then pouring the liquid into a glass before repeating the process. 'Er wouldn't care if 'e swallowed the lot, bottle an' all. But the Lord missed nothing and he wouldn't be missin' Annie Pardoe's doings. There was evil in that one, an old evil that had festered from her mother's passing, an evil that wouldn't be quenched this side of the grave.

'Will I pour the tea, Ma'am?' she asked as Samuel took the glass, swallowing its contents.

'No.' Annie reached for the dainty flower-patterned milk jug. 'I will do it myself.'

Samuel would take his tea then would go to his room and rest, probably sleep for several hours. That would give her time. Annie took her own cup, sipping her tea as the seed of her plan germinated in her mind, temporarily banishing the pain from her side.

'I want you to go into town.'

'Yes Ma'am.' Maudie had answered the bell summoning her to the study.

'Mrs Gaskell Wheeler told me of a herbal tea she was sure would be of benefit to Mr Samuel,' Annie went on. 'I have written the name of it on this paper. Take it to the herbalist in Meeting Street and wait until it is made up, I want my brother to have it today.' She handed the paper to her housekeeper together with a florin. 'There will be change from that,' she said as Maudie turned to leave. 'That herbal tea will cost no more than sixpence.'

'I'll get 'im to mek a bill out,' Maudie said, and banged the door behind her.

Samuel had been sleeping half an hour, Annie looked at the fob watch she wore pinned to her dress, and Maudie had been gone five minutes. Opening the doors that led directly into the garden she walked its length, turning at the tall privet hedge that screened the brick boundary wall and making her way to the low bothy building housing garden tools.

It was not one of the days the gardener-handyman was employed at Brunswick House. What she was about to do would be observed by no one. Going into the building she searched quickly along the shelves. It was there, the cardboard carton the gardener had bought, a carton containing rat poison. He had shown it to her, labouring the importance of keeping it out of reach, stressing the potency of its contents.

Taking her handkerchief from her pocket, she tipped a little of the powder into it, wrapping it carefully in the folds of the small white square of cloth before pushing it deep inside her pocket. Then, after replacing the carton on the shelf, she left.

From his bedroom window Samuel watched his sister return along the garden and knew where she had been. The colour of the dress she wore had changed. She no longer wore black, but that was the only thing about his sister that was different. Inside the same bitterness that had plagued her youth plagued her still.

Entering the house through the scullery, Annie glanced at her fob watch, checking the time once more. Maudie Tranter would be another hour at least. She had time yet.

'What did you think when you knew there was to be a re-investigation?'

They sat together in the warm kitchen. The fire had settled low in the grate and one oil lamp spilled a pool of yellow light courted by shadows.

'I didn't know.' Tilly's eyes strayed for the hundredth time around the kitchen, not yet believing it would not disappear like some dream-built world at the chime of a clock.

'But you must have been given some hint? The Governess or the wardresses, surely they said something?'

'If they knowed they said nothin' to me.' Tilly returned her gaze to the glowing coals. 'You knows what it's like in that place. If anythin' good was goin' to 'appen then that lot would be as close-mouthed as a Jew in a presbytery. They'd keep it to theirselves on purpose, drag out the agony a bit longer.'

'I can believe that of the likes of Agnes Marsh but I had thought better of Hannah Price,' Phoebe answered. 'I always got the impression she acted fairly.'

'Ah, me wench, we all thought that, an' 'er was fair an' all. 'Er was a decent woman an' a good prison governess. You kept yer nose clean and you 'ad no worry from 'er.'

'Do you think she knew?'

'Can't say.' Tilly looked again to the rough wooden dresser, studying the motley assortment of cups and dishes. 'Maybe yes, then again maybe no. There was some comin' an' goin' about a week ago, 'er was off out somewhere two or three times, but we put it down to meetings wi' Prison Board.'

'Mary Pegleg heard nothing?'

'You can bet yer life 'er didn't.' Tilly stretched a hand to the lamp Phoebe had set in the middle of the kitchen table, running a finger over the gleaming brass body. 'Mary Pegleg gets to know summat an' 'er's like a cat wi' a maggot up its arse – 'er can't get it out quick enough.'

Phoebe bent over the spent fire, adding fresh coals, the move hiding her smile at her friend's rough language. Tilly had been in gaol a long time and the ways of others had touched her. It would take time for them to fade.

'If those meetings with the Prison Board concerned your release and Hannah Price said nothing of it to you, then she must have been told not to. I can't imagine there being any other reason for her to keep it from you,' Phoebe said, sitting down again.

'Like as not yer right,' Tilly nodded, 'an' come to think on it p'raps it were the sensible thing to do. I think if 'er 'ad told me there was a chance I'd be gettin' outta that place, then told me later that I weren't, I'd of got meself out another way.'

Phoebe looked perplexed. 'Another way? But surely there was no other way.'

'Oh, ar, there was, me wench.' Tilly looked up from the fire, her laughterless eyes haunted by the spectre of hopes long dead. 'A way I'd thought on many a time. A sharp knife across the throat gets you out of anywheer.'

'Oh, Tilly!' Leaning forward, Phoebe pressed the other woman's calloused hands. 'It's all over now.'

'For me it is.' Suddenly Tilly sounded far away. 'I'll never go back theer again, I'll put meself in me box first.'

Phoebe rose, kneeling before Tilly to put her arms about her. 'You won't ever go back, Tilly, I promise, I promise.'

Holding each other, the two women stared into the flickering flames of the rebuilt fire, each seeing their yesterdays in its heart.

'Phoebe,' Tilly asked after several minutes, ''ow come that man knowed about me an' what I'd done?'

'Sir William?' Releasing her, Phoebe stood up. 'I am afraid I told him after . . .' She broke off, the horror of the attack on her flooding back.

'After what?'

'Nothing.' Phoebe made a business of taking cups from the dresser and setting them on the table. 'Nothing.'

'Yer 'ands be shakin' an' yer face be the colour of a corpse. That don't be tellin' me it was nothin'.'

Locating a brown-coloured tin labelled 'Bournville', Phoebe spooned cocoa into the cups, spilling as much of the powder over the sides as went into them.

'A man came to the house,' she said, knowing Tilly would repeat her question until it was answered. 'I . . . I was upstairs. He thought I had been given money by Sir William and that I had it hidden somewhere.'

"Ad you?' Tilly watched the cocoa powder sprinkle like brown snow over the cups. It was her bet the girl had told nobody the full story of what had happened, and no matter what it had been it was better told and in the open; fastening it up inside herself would only see the fear grow.

'No.' Phoebe loosed the spoon into one of the cups, the clatter loud in the stillness of the kitchen.

'But 'e didn't believe you?' Tilly led her on, knowing each answer would relieve the pain.

'No, he didn't believe me. I thought if I could get him out of the house I might somehow escape him so I told him the money was in the old corn barn. He made me go there with him and while he was searching among the sacks I managed to run out into the yard, but he . . . he . . .'

Tilly rose from her chair. This was the part that was buried deepest, the core of the pain etched across that young face. Taking the tin from Phoebe's trembling hands, she stood it on the table then drew her into her arms. 'Get it up, ma wench,' she said softly, 'let it all come out, Tilly's got you.'

Slowly, between long shuddering sobs, the full story of the attack came out. Tilly listened without intervention. The dam was broken, let the water flow.

'I thought it was Liza,' Phoebe sobbed against her shoulder, 'I thought it was Liza!'

'Ssshh.' Tilly stroked her hair. 'Liza won't 'urt you no more, an' neither will anybody else so long as I be livin'.' She stood with Phoebe in her arms, holding her as she would a child until the sobbing had stopped.

'Now I think we're both ready for that cocoa,' she said, pushing Phoebe into a chair. 'An' I thinks I'll be meking it, you spills too much.'

'I never thought Sir William would do anything to help you,' Phoebe said, sipping the hot frothy liquid.

'An' why should 'e?' Tilly held her own cup cradled between both hands, savouring the heat on her fingers. ''E don't know me from Adam, so why put 'isself to all that bother?'

'He said he did it to try to make up for what his family had caused to happen to me.'

'Well, whatever 'is reason, I thank the Lord for it. 'E got me from Handsworth Prison when I never thought to see the outside of it never again.' She looked across at Phoebe, sudden concern in her eyes. 'Eh, wench, I've just thought! I never even said thank you. 'E's gonna think I'm a right 'un.'

'You didn't say anything as I remember,' Phoebe smiled at last, 'but I am sure Sir William will understand.'

'Do yer think as I might see 'im agen?' Tilly asked. 'Might 'e call 'ere agen sometime?'

Phoebe dropped her eyes to her cup, surprised at the answer rising silently within her. I hope so, Tilly, I hope so.

'P'raps it might be better to write 'im a note, just in case like,' Tilly went on. 'Would you 'elp me, Phoebe?'

'Of course.' She looked up. 'We will do it tomorrow and Lucy will post it for you in Wednesbury. The post office is just a stone's throw through the Shambles.'

'Is there work in Wednesbury?' Tilly asked. 'For a woman like me?'

'A woman like you!' Phoebe said sharply. 'What does that mean?'

'It means, will anybody employ a woman they know 'as been along the line.'

'If you are referring to a certain Tilly Wood,' Phoebe adopted her most cautionary tone, 'I advise you speak of her with respect. She happens to be one of my greatest friends and one who stands in no need of employment for she is to live, and work I might add, here with me at Wiggins Mill.'

'Oh, Phoebe, me wench!' Tilly choked. 'Phoebe!'

Carrying the cups to the scullery Phoebe washed them then returned them to the dresser, giving Tilly time to regain her composure, then she asked, 'Tilly, what happened to Liza?'

'Huh!' She snorted. 'A bad 'un that if ever I met one. It seemed for a long time as 'er wouldn't get over 'ittin' 'er face agen that wall, but 'er did. 'Appen there be no stoppin' the Devil's own, an' Liza Spittle was that all right. 'Er 'adn't been outta that infirmary no more than a fortnight when we 'ad a new inmate, pretty little thing wi' 'air the colour of corn fresh scythed an' eyes blue as a kingfisher's wing. Well, I don't need to tell it but Liza took a shine to 'er an' you won't believe this but so did Emily Pagett. You know, wardress as took Sally Moreton's place.'

'I remember.' Phoebe took a chair on the opposite side of the fire, resting her feet on the hearth.

'Well,' Tilly smiled sardonically, 'that pretty little thing looked like a angel but 'er weren't none. 'Er played them two women one agen another, lettin' both touch 'er up then tellin' each in turn the other 'ad forced 'erself on 'er. It would 'ave been summat for the rest o' we to laugh at if we 'ad any laughter left in we. Any road up, outcome was Liza 'ad the blue devils an' went for Emily Pagett wi' a knife.'

'Did she kill her?'

'No, me wench,' Tilly shook her head, 'though 'er nearly did. Knife just missed 'er lung so Mary Pegleg 'eard the doctor tell the Governess. Anyway, they took Pagett off to some 'ospital in Brummagem an' that be the last we seen of 'er.'

'And Liza?' Phoebe stared at the fire, seeing in its redness the birthmark that spread across the woman's face.

'Prison Board dished out thirty strokes of the cat.' Tilly's voice was devoid of emotion. 'No more than 'er deserved.'

'But is she all right?' Phoebe had to ask. 'She did get over it?'

Tilly was silent for a moment before answering the girl Liza Spittle had tried so many times to assault. 'Might 'ave been,' she said quietly, ''cept 'er 'ung 'erself wi' laces out of 'er own stays.'

Chapter Eighteen

Letting the fob watch drop back into place over her left breast, Annie listened. The house was silent, no movement from overhead. She breathed slowly. Samuel must still be sleeping.

Going into the pantry she brought out the one small chocolate-covered cake delivered to the house fresh each day. Samuel had never liked the taste of medicine, any medicine, complaining of the bitterness after every dose and the cake was a treat that took the taste away.

Annie placed it on a plate. Shaped like a cup, its thick chocolate sides daintily fluted, it was filled with a generous depth of fresh cream and topped with a thick chocolate lid embedded in which was a walnut. Working quickly, Annie removed the lid, scooping out the cream on to a saucer. Taking the powder from her pocket, she tipped it into the cream, mixing the two together. Would Samuel detect the taste? What if he left it uneaten after the first bite? Annie thought for a moment, then going back to the pantry brought out a box of finely powdered sugar. Adding a large spoonful to the cream, she folded it in then carefully returned it to its chocolate case, replacing the lid.

It was done! Putting cake and sugar back in the pantry, Annie cleared all traces of her activity from the kitchen then carried the plate to the scullery, washing both it and her hands and rinsing them in several bowls of water before drying them. Replacing the plate on the dresser in the kitchen, she returned to her chair in the garden, dropping her handkerchief in the stove as she passed through the scullery. Tomorrow she would not be talking to James Siveter, tomorrow she would be talking to Thomas Webb, Wednesbury's undertaker.

'The 'erbal tea, Ma'am.'

Annie opened her eyes, blinking rapidly, pretending to chase sleep from them. But she had not been sleeping though she had been dreaming – dreaming of her life with Clinton.

'The 'erbal tea.' Maudie held out a bottle in which a sludgy brown mixture reached almost to the cork. 'The 'erbalist said to give a small wineglass o' this twice a day.'

'Was that all he said?' Annie hitched herself straighter in the chair.

'No.' Maudie still held the bottle at arm's length.

'Then what else did he say?'

''E said we was fortunate to be 'avin' such fine weather though like as not we'd be payin' for it come winter.'

Snatching the bottle, Annie glared at her housekeeper. The woman deliberately tried to anger her. Was she hoping to be dismissed? Hope or not she would be in very few weeks from now. Rising from the chair, Annie stalked into the house, a smirking Maudie at her heels. 'I will leave this here.' She put the bottle of herbal mixture on the table Maudie kept well scrubbed.

'Will I be tekin' a draught up to Mr Samuel?'

'No.' Annie looked at the bottle then at Maudie, busy fastening the straps of her long white apron. 'No, you can bring a glass with the afternoon tray.'

'The bill for that be there on the dresser an' the change from the florin alongside o' it. You best count it.'

'Didn't you count it when the herbalist gave it to you?'

'Oh, I counted it,' Maudie looked bland, 'but then I ain't the one was worried over it.'

Sweeping to the dresser Annie snatched up the bill, reading the words 'One eight-ounce bottle of herbal mixture, sevenpence'. Scanning the change, one shilling, a threepenny bit and two pennies, she scooped them into her hand. 'Mrs

Gaskell Wheeler was confident this mixture would help Samuel.' She moved across the kitchen toward the door linking it to the rest of the house. 'And Mrs Gaskell Wheeler is most knowledgeable in the use of herbal remedies.'

Mrs Gaskell Wheeler this, Mrs Gaskell Wheeler that! Maudie grabbed the tea tray from beside the dresser, her thoughts acid. Annie Pardoe was possessed by that woman. Would kiss her arse if asked to.

'I think Mr Samuel would quite like his afternoon tea in the garden,' Annie went on. 'It is still so pleasant out there we should take advantage of the warm spell while we can. It is not often we get the chance with a climate such as ours. I will see if my brother is awake yet.'

She had thought of everything but as she moved up the stairs Annie went over it all again in her mind. The herbal tea had been Violet Wheeler's idea and Maudie Tranter had collected it. She, Annie, had left it unopened in the kitchen and would leave it to Maudie to administer it as she would leave it to her to give Samuel the cake. Should anyone question the cause of his death there would be no finger pointed at her and there would be no trace of poison having been added to either the herbal tea or the medicine Alfred Dingley prescribed.

And the cake? Who could prove poison had been added to that? Annie paused at the head of the stairs, pressing a hand to the pain that shot upward through her breast. The cake would be eaten. Samuel was too fond of sweet things to leave any of it uneaten. What if anyone asked the reason for there being just one cake? Annie pressed harder, clenching her teeth against the fire clawing at her side. Maudie Tranter would answer that. She could tell them Annie Pardoe never ate cake or sweet desserts. And the doctor? He would not look too closely, he had been expecting Samuel's death for too long. Pulling in a deep breath, she walked along the corridor to Samuel's bedroom. Yes, she had thought of everything, just as she had with that letter.

* * *

'They all be so pretty,' Tilly fingered the dainty dresses and lace-edged petticoats Phoebe had ready for market, 'an' they sells well, you say?'

'They have up to now.' Phoebe held a strip of ribbon against a length of delphinium-sprigged cotton cloth, matching the colours. 'Lucy says we could sell more.'

'Then sell more is what you must do!'

'It is not that easy.' Phoebe changed the ribbon for one of darker blue. 'I can't sew any more than I do already. I was hoping to buy one of Mr Singer's new sewing machines – I read about them in a newspaper Lucy had wrapped around some fish.'

'Bet that made a change from the smell o' brass filin's.'

Phoebe glanced across at Tilly, noticing the smile about her mouth, a smile that came more easily as each day passed.

'Then why ain't you?'

'Why haven't I what?' Phoebe went back to her first choice of ribbon.

'Why ain't you bought one o' Mr Singer's newfangled machines?'

'Money.' Phoebe spread the flower-strewn cloth on her workroom table and began laying paper pattern cut outs over it. 'I haven't got enough money. My clothing sells well but buying metal for locks swallows it as fast as I get it. I use every penny either on that or cloth or food.'

'An' what does this be for?' Tilly touched the delicate cream-yellow satin still lying in its paper wrapping.

'It was to have been for a ball gown.' Phoebe glanced at the gleaming satin then returned to her cutting.

'Was to 'ave been?' Tilly questioned. 'Why "was to 'ave been"? Why ain't it still goin' to be?'

'Because I will not have the time to make it,' Phoebe said, her lips pursed as she cut around a tricky piece of pattern.

Tilly waited until the manoeuvre was finished then asked,

'But won't the woman it be for be put out wi' your not mekin' 'er gown after gettin' that cloth an' all?'

'I don't think so.' Phoebe gathered the paper pattern pieces together, laying them aside. 'You see the woman was me.'

'You was mekin' yourself a ball gown?'

Phoebe gathered the pieces of cloth she had cut out. 'I had intended to do so but sometimes plans have to be set aside.'

'That means you ain't no longer goin' to mek it.' Tilly covered the cloth with its paper wrapping. 'Why?'

Sitting at her work table Phoebe began to pin the pieces of cloth together, matching sides to sides. 'Because it would be wrong of me to spend time sewing something that was not intended for sale, something that was bringing no money to Wiggins Mill when everyone else was working so hard.'

'But it must 'ave been special for you to 'ave spent money buying that cloth in the first place.'

'I have been invited to the Priory,' Phoebe explained. 'Sir William is giving a farewell ball in place of the more usual Advent Ball, the reason being Lady Amelia is leaving for the continent earlier than she would normally do. Her Ladyship took the influenza some weeks gone and is not yet over the effects.'

'An' you 'ad accepted the invite?'

'Not exactly.'

'Cockeyed way o' carryin' on, ain't it?'

'What is?' Phoebe asked, her mouth half full of pins.

'Buyin' stuff to mek yourself a fancy frock an' you not accepted the party invite exactly.' Tilly retrieved a pin from the floor, dropping it into the tobacco tin Phoebe kept them in. 'Strikes me you 'ad every intention of goin' to that ball. P'raps it could still be done if I 'elped you with the sewin' of it.'

'I did not know you sewed?' The words pushed past the pins still locked between Phoebe's teeth.

'There be a lot you don't know about Tilly Wood, me wench.'

Phoebe removed the pins from her mouth, putting them in

the tobacco tin that had once belonged to Mathew. 'This much I do know, you already work hard enough. You have taken on the running of the house and preparing the meals . . .'

'Lizzie does a fair share o' all that,' Tilly said quickly.

'And you do a fair share of the filing down of the locks.' Phoebe smiled gently. 'I wanted you to rest, Tilly, I didn't want you working just as hard as . . .'

'As hard as I had to inside.' She took up the words Phoebe couldn't say. 'Phoebe, wench, what I does 'ere at Wiggins Mill be paradise compared to Handsworth Gaol. I thank God every minute I breathes for what 'e done for me, an' 'elpin out wi' a bit o' sewin' ain't too great a burden. I'd like to see you go to that there ball.'

'Very well,' sorting a needle Phoebe broke off a length of blue thread, 'we will do a little each evening.' She looked up from threading the needle, her eyes smiling. 'Unless, of course, a fairy godmother should exist somewhere and decides to bring me a gown already made.'

'Oh, they exist all right.' Tilly picked up the tin of pins, staring into it. 'An' not all o' em be old neither. You be my fairy godmother, Phoebe. What you did for me be nuthin' short o' magic.'

'It was not I who got you released from prison, Tilly,' Phoebe reminded her softly. 'It was Sir William Dartmouth. He is the one who worked the magic.'

'Ar, wench, 'e is, an' grateful I be to 'im.' She replaced the tin on the table close by Phoebe's hand. 'Only some'ow I can't see 'im wi' wings an' wavin' of a wand.'

'Bert says the new lad Mathew got to work the bellows is doing very well,' Phoebe said when they had both stopped laughing.

''E is. Lad works like a little Trojan, nuthin' ain't too much trouble for 'im.'

'Do you think carrying coals might be too heavy?'

'No, wench, I don't. The lad be strong enough, Bert wouldn't set 'im no task 'e thought too much.'

'No, he would not.' Phoebe examined her line of stitching. 'Bert is a kind man.'

'They'm a nice family an' willin' workers the lot o' 'em.'

'Including Ruth. I have seen the way she gets under your feet, you can't do anything without her being there.'

'Ar, you be right.' Tilly smiled. 'But I don't mind that, 'er be a pleasant little thing, an' Lizzie 'as seen to it 'er knows 'er manners, never forgets a please or a thank you. An' talkin' of folk gettin' under other folks' feet, I better be off an' leave you to get on wi' what you be about.'

'How are the locks coming along?' Phoebe called after her.

'Nearly 'alf done,' the answer came back. 'Bert says you will 'ave 'em all on time.'

'How can you be certain?'

The evening meal finished, Lucy and Mathew sat for a few minutes before starting their evening's work.

'I can't, but it do seem strange me not seein' 'im once since 'e started.'

Mathew lit his pipe, sucking the stem much as his father did. 'P'raps 'e's found some other way.'

'Such as what?'

'Such as followin' the cut.'

'Could be as you're right but it wouldn't make a lot o' sense,' Lucy said. 'Cut would take 'im right out o' 'is way – 'e lives other end o' Wednesbury. Least that be what 'e told you, wasn't it?'

'Ar.' Mathew tapped his pipe against the heel of his hand. 'Then why would 'e be followin' the cut 'ome?'

'Who knows why kids do 'alf the things they does?'

'They does some daft 'uns, I'll give you that,' Lucy began to clear the table, 'but to go a mile or more outta your way 'ome after a day's work don't strike me as no kid's lark.'

'So what do you reckon?' Mathew blew down the stem of

his white clay pipe. 'You've got some bee in your bloomers, wench.'

'You watch the way you be talkin', Mathew Leach, I ain't no fish wife to be listenin' to your vulgarities.' Lucy flicked out with the cloth she had taken to the dishes but she was smiling.

'You ain't seen 'im, not once?' Mathew resumed, sucking his pipe.

'Not once,' Lucy affirmed. 'An' I thinks that be more'n strange. You know what I really thinks? I thinks 'e ain't goin' 'ome at all.'

Several puffs of blue-grey smoke curled into the room, suspended like a delicate veil above Mathew's head. 'Then where do 'e be goin'?'

Carrying the enamel bowl with its washing up water into the yard, Lucy emptied it into the drain running along its width then stared at the old windmill, secretive and brooding against the fading light. ''E be goin' there,' she whispered. 'It's my guess 'e be goin' there.'

Back in the outhouse they had made into a comfortable home Mathew finished his pipe, knocking the burned ash of the tobacco out against the bars of the fire. ''Ave you said anythin' to the others?'

Lucy fitted the cups and plates on to the rack Mathew had made and set on the wall, then folded the cloth she had dried them on and hung it across the length of string set across the grate. 'I thought as I would talk to you first.'

'You am sure?' Mathew put his pipe alongside the tin of shag tobacco on a cupboard that had come with a job lot of furniture from a tat man who had delivered it all for a shilling.

'Sure as I be talkin' to you.' Lucy reached for the white apron she wore only when baking, fastening the straps around her waist.

'Then we best tell the others.'

Phoebe listened, concern deepening on her face as Mathew spoke of Lucy's suspicions.

'He could not have crossed the heath without you seeing him?'

'I swear 'e couldn't, Miss Phoebe. A body can see for miles across there, it bein' mostly flat ground, an' I ain't seen 'im nowhere on it, not when I've been goin' in to Wednesbury on a mornin' nor when I've been comin' back at night. I be tellin' all o' you, that lad ain't passed me an' I says that shows 'e ain't goin' 'ome nights.'

'But his parents would have enquired before now surely?' Phoebe said. 'They must know where he is employed.'

'Maybe not,' Bert said. 'Maybe the lad 'as got no parents.'

'Was nobody wi' 'im that day I picked 'im out o' the line,' Mathew put in. 'Leastways nobody spoke to 'im when we set off.'

'If 'e don't 'ave no parents it could follow 'e don't 'ave no 'ome.' Lizzie looked at Phoebe. 'That would explain Lucy not seein' 'im on the way to an' from the town, wouldn't it?'

'It would.' Phoebe nodded. 'But if he is not going home at night, where is he going?'

Lucy's glance strayed to the rise of high ground, to the silent windmill painted black against the sky. 'I thinks 'e be goin' nowhere,' she said, 'not for the 'ole night anyway.'

'Then where is he spending his nights?' Phoebe asked, worry plain in her voice. 'I hope he is not sleeping on the heath.'

'I don't think 'e is,' Lucy glanced again at the windmill standing tall into the glow of the setting sun, 'I think 'e be sleepin' in there.'

'The windmill?' Bert followed the line of Lucy's eyes and her reasoning. 'Could well be. I could think of worse places a lad might get 'isself 'oled up in. You women wait indoors, Mathew an' me will go look.'

'You have been sleeping in the old windmill since the first day Mathew brought you here?' Phoebe said ten minutes later when the bellows boy stood in her kitchen, Mathew and Bert to either side of him.

'Yes, Miss,' the boy answered, chin on chest.

'But why? Is the walk from Wednesbury to here and back too much for you?'

'T'ain't too much!' The boy's chin came up defiantly. 'Ain't nuthin', that tiddly walk. I could walk six time further'n that wi'out feelin' tired.'

Bert placed a hand on the boy's shoulder, feeling the bones through his ragged coat. 'Tell 'er, lad.'

'Ain't nuthin' to tell.'

'If there ain't another reason you be sleepin' in that mill then Miss Phoebe be right in thinkin' the walk be too much for you, an' that bein' the case 'er might give you your coppers, lad, an' that means you'll be out o' a job.'

The boy looked quickly to Phoebe, the subtle warning Bert had given bringing fear to his eyes.

'You wouldn't, would you, Miss? You wouldn't go givin' me the sack?'

Phoebe looked at him. The sleeves of his threadbare coat were short of his wrists by several inches, his trousers halfway up his legs with more holes in them than sultanas in one of Lucy's scones, and her heart twisted with pity. What was it drove him to sneak back to sleep in the mill?

'I would have to if I thought it too far for you to walk, Josh.'

''T'ain't, Miss. Honest 't'ain't.' He looked down to where his toes peeped through boots that lacked the laces to fasten them. 'It's . . . it's . . . I ain't got no 'ome.' The reservoir of pride breached, the words tumbled from him. 'Me dad 'e buggered off years ago, left me mother to fend for 'erself an' me. We managed not too bad while she could tek in washin', then when 'er got sick we couldn't pay the landlord an' 'e chucked we out. It was the work'ouse or the road an' me mother wouldn't tek the work'ouse, least not till 'er could 'ardly walk no more. 'Er died the day after 'er went in. So you see, Miss, I ain't got other than the 'eath to sleep an' that windmill be a shelter from the wind.' He looked up at Phoebe. 'I didn't think as you would mind, Miss, I meant no 'arm, really I didn't.'

'And you did none.' Phoebe resisted the urge to take him in her arms, knowing that his fierce pride would resent any offer of childish comfort. 'But I wish you had told me.'

'You would 'ave chucked me out if I 'ad.'

'Miss Phoebe wouldn't 'ave chucked you out,' Mathew said.

'Mebbe 'er wouldn't,' the boy remained stubborn, 'but it was a chance I wasn't tekin'. Long as nobody seen me go in I 'ad a place to sleep.' He twisted free from Bert's hand. 'Who told you I was in there anyway?'

'Nobody told we,' Bert answered. 'Well, p'raps that's not strictly true. It were Mrs Leach not seein' 'ide nor 'air of you not comin' to work in the mornin's nor goin' back of an evenin'. Seemed strange to 'er that did, set 'er to wonderin' just 'ow you did get to Wiggins Mill.'

'I couldn't 'ave missed sight o' you, Josh,' Lucy said apologetically. 'The 'eath be mostly flat 'tween 'ere an' Wednesbury. You could spot a grass'opper a mile off.'

'I knows you didn't mean to drop me in it,' the boy tried to smile as he looked from her to Phoebe, 'an' I'm sorry to 'ave been the cause o' trouble, Miss. I won't go in the mill any more, you can be 'sured o' that. Just let me keep me job an' I'll bugger off every night cleaner than me father did.'

'You won't go nowhere every night, same as you won't be usin' that foul language no more.' Lizzie pushed further into the kitchen. ''E can't be sleepin' on that 'eath, Miss Phoebe, so unless you 'ave any objections 'e could bed down the side o' our Mark. There be room a-plenty in the corn loft, an' 'im an' Mark, they gets on well together.'

'Bert?' Phoebe looked at the man standing beside the young boy.

'That be all right by me, Miss Phoebe. Lad can stay wi'

Lizzie an' me long as 'e as a job at Wiggins Mill. An' if I knows Lizzie, 'er will look after 'im.'

'What do you say, Josh?' Phoebe asked.

A smile splitting his face, the boy looked at Lizzie. 'Bostin',' he breathed. 'I say that be bostin'.'

'I thought we would have afternoon tea in the garden, it is still quite warm enough,' Annie signed, finding her brother in his studio. 'And you do so enjoy the garden.' She stopped speaking, her mouth half open with surprise as she caught sight of the canvas on the easel. It was a finished portrait of Phoebe, only the paint that formed the signature still gleaming wetly. The face looked serenely back at her, a calmness beyond its years radiating from it. It was also the image of Abel's pretty wife, she realised.

'I . . . I did not know you had painted this.' Annie caught her brother's eyes on her and struggled to regain her composure. 'It is very good, especially considering you have seen so very little of Abel's daughter.'

Samuel's long narrow fingers moved rapidly. 'I worked from this more than from memory.' Going to a drawer set in a long bench-top table on the opposite side of the room, he drew out a photograph, handing it to Annie. 'It was in among some of Abel's papers. I found it when I went through them.'

Among Abel's papers? Annie stared at the photograph. She'd thought she had weeded everything out but obviously she had missed this and Samuel had said nothing of it, as he had said nothing of the portrait he'd now finished. What else had he said nothing of? What other secrets lay hidden from her? None that mattered, surely. She had held his Power of Attorney long enough to take everything from him save this house, and now it was too late for him to make good his intention of naming Phoebe his heir. She handed back the photograph. Their niece would get none of the wealth that had once been her father's.

'It is a very good likeness,' Samuel signed. 'We must hang it opposite the one of her father, they will look very well together. Perhaps James Siveter will find her and persuade her to come home. It would be nice to have her here with us, don't you agree, Annie?'

'Of course, dear,' Annie's fingers carried the lie. 'Nothing would give me more happiness than to have Phoebe return to us. We must pray that God will make it so.' She watched Samuel clean his brushes, immersing each in a jar of turpentine then wiping the bristles on a soft cloth. He could pray as much as he liked but he would find God as deaf as himself. She looked at the lovely painted face, her fingers curling into her palms. The portrait could hang with that of Abel but his daughter would never again live here.

She would sell this house, she thought as Samuel poured water from a tall flower-twined jug into a matching basin and washed his hands. She would sell it and give the money to Clinton to invest in more tube works. After all, there would be no need to keep this place on when she became his wife.

Clinton's wife. The thought stayed with Annie as they walked downstairs to the garden. How long would it be before they could marry? Not for several months that was certain, a suitable period of mourning for her brother must elapse before they could be wed, the proprieties must be observed. But Clinton would not mind the waiting, not when he saw her grief for Samuel's passing.

'Will you be wantin' tea now?' Maudie followed them into the garden.

'You have not mashed it yet, have you?' Annie asked sharply. 'I have no taste for stewed tea.'

You've no taste for anythin', if you asks me! Maudie sucked in her cheeks, looking at Annie's lavender dress with ill-concealed disdain.

'Tea ain't been mashed, not yet,' she replied. 'I knows 'ow you likes yer tea, an' so I should after all the years I've spent mekin' it.'

That won't go on for much longer, Annie thought. Once I am married you can count yourself dismissed. Aloud she said waspishly, 'Not long enough to do it graciously but I suppose we must make do. You may bring the tray now.'

Sour-faced old cow! Maudie returned to the kitchen. But then, that one had never had a good word for the doings of anybody other than herself – not that she had ever done good in her life.

'You have forgotten the herbal tea.' Annie looked at the tray her housekeeper set down on the wicker table.

'I ain't forgot nothin',' Maudie replied. 'I set it on a sep'rate tray. Seein' as 'ow Mr Samuel don't care for medicines I thought it might suit better for it to be on another tray altogether.'

'I see.' Annie began pouring milk into the cups. 'Then bring it out. It will do Mr Samuel no good left sitting in a bottle.'

'Yes, Ma'am.' Maudie turned away. If that mixture were only poison, she would gladly pour the lot down Annie Pardoe's throat!

'It is just a herbal tea, dear,' Annie's fingers signed rapidly to her brother. 'Mrs Gaskell Wheeler recommended it, she is convinced it will help you build up your strength, and I am sure Mrs Tranter has something that will relieve the taste should it prove unpalatable.' She looked at Maudie, carefully measuring the mixture into a cup, adding a little of the hot water from the tea tray. 'Have you something sweet?' she asked.

Maudie nodded a smile to Samuel, knowing he could not hear but wanting him to understand. 'Yes, Ma'am,' she said. 'I took a chocolate cake from the baker this mornin'. It be Mr Samuel's favourite sort.'

'Bring it for him then,' Annie said, 'he will take the herbal tea much easier with a chocolate cake to follow.'

Pouring the tea, she watched Maudie set the cake at Samuel's elbow then hand him the herbal mixture. Swallowing it in two long gulps, he handed the cup back to her.

'There now, that didn't be so bad, did it?' Maudie crooned to his silent ears. 'Now eat up your cake an' you'll soon forget the swallowin' o' that stuff.'

Annie picked up her own cup as Samuel took the cake, sinking his teeth into the chocolate-covered mound. Eat his cake and Samuel would soon be forgetting everything!

Chewing the last vestige of chocolate, Samuel touched his mouth with his napkin, eyes straying to the privet hedge that shielded the end of the garden. Annie had walked the length of it and when she had walked back she had held a hand close against her skirts.

It had gone as she'd known it would. Annie stood beside the four-poster bed that had been her brother's marriage bed. Samuel had eaten the cake. The ground yew and laburnum seeds had not worked, why she could not guess, but the poison she had mixed in the cream of that cake would. This time there would be no mistake. Come the morning Samuel would be dead and she would be free to enjoy her life as Mrs Clinton Harforth-Darby.

The pain that had gnawed at her all day spiralled up from her side and into her breast, the rawness of it stealing the breath from her lungs. Sinking on to the bed, she groped for the bottle of small white tablets, taking two into her mouth even as she poured a glass of water from the carafe on her night table. Waiting for the pain to pass, she checked the fob watch pinned to the shoulder of her dress. It wanted a quarter of an hour to nine o'clock. Samuel always retired at eight-thirty, he would already be in his bed.

Annie forced herself to stand. She must say goodnight to him as she always did. Tomorrow he would be beyond remembering whether she had or not but that sharp-nosed Maudie Tranter would remember the least thing that was different, and though you may not see Maudie Tranter, you could be certain the woman missed nothing.

Tapping on Samuel's bedroom door as her mother had

insisted everyone must though no sound passed his barrier of silence, Annie pushed open the door.

'Goodnight, dear,' she signed.

Samuel's hands rose like white wounded birds. 'Goodnight, Annie,' he signed, a slowness in his fingers. 'You always did what you thought best. Thank you, dear.'

What did he mean? Annie asked herself, leaning down to kiss his brow. Then in the soft glow of the oil lamp she caught the look in his eyes. He knew! Samuel knew what she had done. He was thanking her for giving him death!

Chapter Nineteen

Dead!

Phoebe walked across the heath toward Wednesbury, her mind still trying to reject the news Lucy had brought with her the night before. Her Uncle Samuel was dead.

She had not seen him since the reading of her father's will. In all that time he had not tried to contact her, not even when she was in prison. True she had never seen a great deal of Uncle Samuel, even as a child, but for him to ignore her very existence seemed somehow unnatural.

Reaching the town, she walked along Lower High Street, taking the turning that would lead her past Oakeswell Hall. She glanced at the black and white half-timbered building as she passed its curtain wall. Would Sophie live there when she married Montrose? The thought brought a twinge of pain, but it was pain for Sophie not for herself.

At the gate of Brunswick House she paused. This had once been her home, a place of happiness and love. Now it held neither. She had always been so glad to return here yet now she wanted only to turn and run. But she had to go in. Uncle Samuel was her father's brother and she must show her respects.

At the door she tugged the bell pull, her eyes avoiding the mourning wreath set at its centre. Her aunt hated her, that much had been made plain, but she was not here for the sake of her aunt.

'Eh, Miss Phoebe!' Maudie Tranter looked at the girl standing on the doorstep. 'What be you doin' 'ere?'

'Lucy told me my Uncle Samuel has passed away.'

'Ar, Miss, 'e 'as. In the night it was . . .'

'Who is it, Mrs Tranter?'

Inside Phoebe shivered at the sound of her aunt's voice but she stepped determinedly into the hall. 'It is me, Aunt.'

Annie Pardoe's hand flew to her side. She had not expected this, had had no intention of informing Abel's daughter of his brother's death. 'What are you doing here?' she rasped. 'You are not wanted in this house.'

'You made that clear enough more than two years ago,' Phoebe replied.

'That will be all, Tranter.' Annie glared at the listening Maudie, waiting until the door leading off to the kitchen had closed behind her. 'If I made it so clear,' she said, turning back to Phoebe, 'then how come you are here now?'

'I was given the news my Uncle Samuel was dead. I have come to Brunswick House to pay my respects, and that is the only thing I am here for.'

'Respects!' Annie let her gaze travel slowly over her niece. 'What respect does it show to come dressed in green? You have not even the respect to adopt mourning.'

'I apologise for the colour of my clothing,' Phoebe's chin came up, 'but this is all I have. You did not allow me an extensive wardrobe, did you, Aunt?'

'I want you to leave.' Annie placed a hand on the door handle.

'And I want to leave, Aunt, very much, I find you a most unpleasant person to be with, but I will not leave until I have done that for which I came.' Phoebe walked to the foot of the stairs. 'Is Uncle Samuel in his room?'

'No,' Annie looked towards the door of the parlour, 'he is in there.'

Phoebe stood for a moment, unmoving. Uncle Samuel had not wished her to visit him in life. Would he wish the same in death? Was her presence in this house an intrusion he would have resented? Somewhere deep in her heart she felt that to be untrue. He had been so kind to her on the few occasions they had met. Taking a long breath, she walked into the parlour.

Nothing had changed. The chiffonier held the same Staffordshire china figurines, the same high-backed sofa stood against the wall, only the mahogany table below the central ceiling gasolier was different. It stood where it always had but its heavy Brussels lace cloth was gone and in its place was draped the black velvet that had lain beneath her father's coffin and now lay beneath Samuel's.

Phoebe stared at the features that seemed to be cut from marble, her heart full of tears that would not reach her eyes. Though his eyes were closed and no smile lingered at his mouth the strange haunted look that had constantly drawn his face was no longer there. Her uncle seemed to have found a peace in death he had never known in life.

'Aunt,' she said softly, 'why do you hate me so much?'

Stood on the opposite side of the coffin Annie felt the breath catch in her throat but the rising gall of bitterness was too much for her to swallow.

'Your father stole my life!' she screamed. 'He took it, him and his fancy wife, and gave me this in return.' She struck the side of the walnut casket with her hand. 'I have had no life of my own now for nearly twenty years, I have known a living death all that time and it was your father's gift to me. He made me responsible for Samuel – Samuel who could not be cared for by any other than his own family, who could not be taken into your father's house for fear of causing distress to his pretty wife. Oh, yes, *she* must be shielded from his affliction.'

Phoebe looked from the face of her dead uncle to that of her aunt, twisted with bitterness. 'Affliction?'

'Yes, affliction!' Annie spat. 'That which kept him from leading a normal life, which kept him from taking a wife, which used up my life in keeping his secret.'

'But surely Uncle Samuel's deafness was not a good enough cause to turn him into a recluse.'

Annie's eyes burned as she answered, 'No, it was not a good enough cause. But it was not only deafness my brother suffered from – it was this!' Reaching into the casket she lifted the long white robe that covered her brother's body, snatching it open to the waist.

Phoebe gasped then turned away, her senses stunned.

'That was what made my brother a recluse!' Annie cried viciously. 'That was the shame that must be kept hidden from the world. That was what kept him from taking a wife for what woman would marry a man who was no man, who was neither male nor female, but had the genitals of both!'

'How strange we meet in the same place, Miss Pardoe. Miss Pardoe!' Sir William Dartmouth caught the arm of the young woman whose eyes set in a chalk-white face seemed to look straight through him. 'Are you feeling unwell?'

'Uncle Samuel,' Phoebe mumbled. 'Uncle Samuel, he . . . Lucy will . . . I must . . .'

Supporting her with his arm as she sagged against him, he helped her into the George Hotel. 'A doctor, quickly,' he ordered the attentive manager. 'Then a brandy. Move, man!'

'Nothing physically wrong,' Alfred Dingley said an hour later. 'She is suffering from some sort of shock, though . . . I have given her a sedative that will help but she needs rest and will get that better at home than she will here.' He nodded towards the door of the upstairs sitting room Phoebe had been taken to. 'I will have a carriage sent round to take her. Was there anyone with her, do you know?'

'She was alone when I met her in the street,' Sir William answered, 'so I presume no one was accompanying her, and as for a carriage there will be no need. I will see Miss Pardoe gets home. Send your account to the Priory.' He stood aside for the doctor to leave. 'Good day, Doctor.'

Tapping first at the door he went into the room where Phoebe sat, the wife of the hotel manager hovering at her elbow.

'Are you feeling better, Miss Pardoe?' he asked.

She looked up, the shock still showing in her eyes. 'Yes,' she said. 'Thank you, Sir William. I am sorry to have been so much trouble.'

'You were no trouble.'

'That is kind of you to say.' Phoebe stood up, her legs still not quite her own. 'But I have delayed you. I thank you again for helping me. I can manage on my own now.'

'Were you alone?'

'Yes.' Phoebe smiled at the woman handing her her bag.

'You said something about an Uncle Samuel and Lucy, were they not with you?'

Phoebe breathed deeply, her fingers curling tightly about the bag. 'My uncle is dead, Sir William. I have just come from paying my respects and I was going to speak to Lucy.'

'Lucy?' He frowned slightly. 'Is that the Lucy you told me was once in the employ of my wife?'

Phoebe nodded.

'Mrs Leach, so where is she now?' he asked.

'She will be in the market place.'

Sir William looked at the woman still hovering close to Phoebe. 'Send to the market place. See if Mrs Leach is there.'

'I know 'er, Sir,' the woman bobbed a curtsy, 'I'll fetch 'er.'

'There is no need,' Phoebe protested, 'I can go there myself.'

'Go to Mrs Leach,' Sir William spoke to the woman, ignoring Phoebe's protest, 'ask her to be good enough to come here, and tell your husband to have my carriage brought to the door.'

'Yes, Sir.' The woman bobbed again then disappeared through the door.

'I am sorry to hear of your uncle's death,' he continued to Phoebe, 'please accept my condolences. If I can be of assistance, do not hesitate to contact me.'

Phoebe walked from the room and down the stairs to the lobby. 'My aunt will be handling everything,' she said. 'She has cared for my uncle for many years.'

'Miss Phoebe, are you all right? What happened?' Lucy rushed in from the street.

'Lucy!' Phoebe caught her hands, holding them tightly. 'Lucy, I am so glad you are here.'

'Miss Pardoe has suffered something of a shock,' Sir William answered Lucy's enquiring glance. 'The doctor says she will be all right but she is in need of rest. Will you see her home?'

'O' course.' Lucy put an arm about Phoebe. 'You take a seat, Miss, while I finds the carter. 'E'll be 'avin' a drink in the Turks 'Ead round about this time. 'E'll give us both a ride as far as the Tipton Road.'

'Do not trouble yourself with the carter, Mrs Leach,' Sir William said as Lucy made to get a chair. 'My carriage is just outside. My driver will take you home and return for me here.'

'I'll collect your things from the market, Mrs Leach. They will keep 'ere till you collect them.' The manager's wife hovered nearby, eager to be seen offering assistance.

'Ta, Mrs Jinks.' Lucy led the way out of the lobby. 'I'll pick 'em up tomorrer.'

'Sir William, there is no need for me to take your carriage,' Phoebe hesitated at the door, 'a ride with the carter will do as well.'

He smiled suddenly, a light dancing behind his grey eyes. 'Miss Pardoe, you once told me that I should never use the word "must" to you again, but I will if I have to. Now spare me the retribution that would bring by accepting my carriage.'

Phoebe smiled. 'I would not have retribution fall upon you, Sir William, so I will accept. And thank you.'

Inside the carriage Phoebe leaned back, her eyes closed against the horror of what had taken place at Brunswick House, a house that had once held so much love and laughter and now held so much unhappiness.

Poor Uncle Samuel. She flinched as the picture of his thin disfigured body flashed before her closed eyelids. To have spent a lifetime with such a deformity would be terrible enough for any man to suffer, but knowing his sister's resentment, thinking that he was responsible, albeit indirectly, for her solitary life, as he must have done, could only have added to that suffering; and Aunt Annie, so consumed with her bitterness, so twisted with hate for her own family, had she ever made any attempt to hide her true feelings or had she shown them to Samuel as she had shown them to Phoebe?

Behind her closed lids a pale finely drawn face smiled back at her, a gentle kindly face, but one whose blue eyes held the shadow of pain.

'Are you all right, Miss Phoebe?' Lucy asked, feeling the shudder that passed through her.

Phoebe saw again the figure of her aunt standing over the casket which held that malformed body, her face distorted with the hate she held for her brother's child. All right? Phoebe turned her face, pressing it into Lucy's shoulder. Would she ever be all right again?

Five days to the end of the month. Phoebe looked at the calendar. She had crossed off each day as it ended, making a note of the number of finished locks. Now less than thirty were needed to make the gross. They had all worked so hard; even Ruth had helped put the finished locks in the wooden soap box Josh had got from the carter.

Brushing her hair, Phoebe remembered the grin on the boy's face as he had related his deal with the man. She had sent Josh with twopence to pay for the box. He had offered the carter one penny.

'A penny!' Zach Coates had laughed. 'It cost me more than that to cart it out 'ere.'

'It'll cost you twice as much if you 'as to cart it back,' Josh retorted. 'You might as well let me 'ave it.'

'Not fer a bloody penny I ain't. I might as well use it fer firewood, at least it'll keep me warm.'

'Why not swap it for this?' Josh had opened the sack he had carried with him across the heath, displaying the lumps of coal. 'It'll burn a lot longer than the few sticks that old box'll mek an' give off a lot more 'eat.'

'An' where 'ave you pinched that from?' Zach had demanded.

'Never you mind,' Josh told him. 'If I tell you you'll only get a 'eadache worryin' about it an' you'll 'ave to pay tuppence for a bottle of Aspro to cure it. So you see, you'll still be outta pocket.'

'You be a right bloody smart arse, don't you!' Zach grumbled, handing the soapbox down to Josh.

'Ar, an' you'll be a right 'ot 'un if you stands too near that coal,' Josh returned, handing over the sack. ''Eat that gives off is more than the fires o' Hell you've 'eard talk about.'

Tying a ribbon to the plait in her hair Phoebe could not resist a smile. Josh had bounced into the workshop, placing the box on the floor, his grin wide as the heath as he handed back the two pennies.

He was a nice boy. Phoebe climbed into bed, the smile still warm on her lips. Things were going so well, maybe he could stay on after the locks were finished.

Climbing into bed, she turned off the oil lamp that stood beside it on a table and lay back, staring at the moonlight filling her window. It was the same moonlight as filled the windows of Handsworth Prison only the spectres it held were different. In gaol the moonlight had brought memories of her life outside. Now it often brought memories of her life locked away behind those walls. How many women were lying behind them now, their freedom snatched away, and how many were staring at the moonlight?

She would never forget. Every moment spent in that place was etched deep in her soul, every word and every blow. No, she would not forget, nor would she forget Sir William. He had brought the release she thanked God for each night, but more than that he had shown her kindness at every opportunity. But why? For what reason? If he had been indebted to her because of her imprisonment he had more than made up for it. Or could it be her friendship with his son, did he know of Edward's feelings toward her? Phoebe looked away from the light of the window but the tall figure of Sir William Dartmouth remained lit in her mind. No, that was not the reason behind his kindness to her. A man with an ancestry graced by the best families in the county for so many generations would not allow his son to break with tradition. Whatever reason lay behind his friendship she was sure her possible marriage to Edward played no part in it.

Edward . . . Phoebe closed her eyes. Was he blind to his illustrious name? Could he honestly not see his parents could never accept her as his wife, a woman who had been in prison, or was he just too stubborn to accept it? He had asked her to marry him again when he and Sophie had called, bringing their mother's regrets that Phoebe would not be attending the ball and also her condolences for Uncle Samuel's death.

Phoebe turned restlessly, her eyes returning to the moonlit window. She had refused as gently as she could, trying not to hurt Edward, and now he was gone, left for Europe with his mother and sister. Painful as she knew it would be to him, she had felt bound to tell him she did not love him, her feelings were not those of a girl desiring to be his wife. He had smiled then, masking the hurt, and Phoebe had seen the strength of his father in him. Edward Dartmouth had been hurt but that hurt would never be allowed to affect his friendship toward her. Phoebe closed her eyes again but it was not Edward who stayed with her as she drifted into sleep. It was not his mouth that smiled or his eyes that watched her. The face that bent toward her was that of Sir William Dartmouth.

'That is the last of them, Tranter.'

Annie Pardoe folded the sheet of paper, slipping it into the envelope she had just finished addressing. There had been more messages of sympathy for the death of her brother than she would have expected and she had let a suitable time elapse before answering them. Let people believe her too grief-stricken to write replies before the two weeks that had gone by. Gathering the envelopes together, she handed them to Maudie.

'People will understand why it has taken so long before I answered their messages,' she said, wiping the pen nib clean of ink before moving from the desk. 'They will realise how much pain it causes me.'

Pain my arse! Maudie thought caustically. The only pain Samuel caused you was the pain of wanting him out of the way, and that pain worsened with the arrival of that Harforth-Darby!

'Take them to the post office now.' Annie took half a crown from a small black lacquered box, handing it to her housekeeper. 'That will be more than enough to pay for stamps.'

'Yes, Ma'am.' Maudie did not bob a curtsy. 'An' there'll be change an' all, I know that wi'out yer tellin'.'

Annie bit back the anger that rose in her as Maudie walked from the study. Maudie Tranter knew a lot of things and in a very few weeks she would know one more. She would know she was out of a job.

Following her from the study, Annie walked up the stairs. Maudie had seen her leave the study, she would think the last of the letters written as she had been told, but there was one more yet to do. Watching from the window of her room she saw Maudie leave the house by the rear door, crossing the yard and taking the path that led through the grounds to a door set in the garden wall. Looking at her fob watch, Annie remained at the window. She would give Maudie five minutes before writing that last letter.

The minutes gone she took the sheet of writing paper from where she had slipped it into the packet of her skirts. It was not exactly the same as the one that had lain so long in the drawer of her washstand but it was white and that was near enough. Going to the wardrobe she took her bag from the shelf, taking out a fresh bottle of ink and a new pen. She had thrown the others into Millfield Pool not thinking of the letter she must write now but her visits to Alfred Dingley's consulting room had afforded the opportunity to purchase more. Stress, the doctor had called the pain in her side, stress due to the passing of her brother but it would cease with time. She'd known it had to come, he had told her, slipping tablets into a small brown glass bottle. They had all known, even her brother himself. Annie levered the cork from the bottle of ink. Yes, Samuel had known. The look in his eyes as she kissed him goodnight had told her so.

Reaching once more into her bag, she took out the bill she had been given when she went back to that shop near Birmingham railroad station. It had been clever of her to pretend to have forgotten to buy pot menders when she bought those mousetraps. It had given her two receipts.

Fetching the small nail scissors she kept in a drawer of her dresser, she carefully cut the heading from the receipt. Quickly pouring a small amount of water from the carafe on her night table she placed it beside the ink then, drawing her handkerchief from her pocket, tipped into the water the spoonful of plain flour she had taken from the pantry while Maudie Tranter had been on her half day off. Using the long handle of the pen she mixed the flour and water to a paste then, with the tip of one finger, smoothed a little of it on to the back of the heading she had cut from James Greaves's receipt, attaching that to the top of the sheet of white paper. That done, she carefully washed pen and glass in the bowl on the washstand, wiping them on the towel folded beside it. Opening the window, she emptied the water she had used on to the flower border below. Maudie Tranter would find no trace when she came to clean.

Annie sat at the table and began to write. Tomorrow she would post this letter herself and the ink and pen would follow the others to the bottom of Millfield Pool.

The letter finished and sealed, all trace of its having been written hidden away, Annie returned her bag to the wardrobe, caressing the silk of the pearl grey gown and the rustling lavender taffeta. She must wear black for appearance's sake but once the period of mourning was over she would never wear it again. She would wear only gowns of coloured silk, the colours Clinton liked. Soon she would be with him. But how soon would that be? Annie tried to push away the thoughts that held sway in the shadows of her mind but they would not be denied.

Three weeks and more, it had been all of that since she had given him the money which the sale of the last of Abel's bequest had brought. Three weeks and she had heard nothing from him. He had told her she would have deeds of ownership to land on which to build her tube works in a couple of days, but those days had grown into weeks and she had seen nothing of him or the papers. But he would come, he would! She closed the door of the wardrobe, gritting her teeth as a spasm of pain bit upward to her breast. Clinton would come.

'Change from the post office.' Maudie entered the sitting room where Annie now sat, a newspaper spread across the table.

'Leave it there.' A nod of her head indicated the opposite side of the table but Annie did not look up.

'Do there be any mention of the Wheelers' trouble in the paper, Ma'am?' Maudie asked.

'Trouble!' Annie looked up sharply. 'What trouble? What are you talking about?'

'I 'eard it when I was comin' from the post office.' Maudie stood with hands folded in front of her. 'Two women was sayin' as 'ow Oakeswell 'All be in mournin', said as they 'ad it from one o' the maids.'

'In mourning?'

'That be what them women said, I 'eard for meself.'

'But for whom?' Annie asked, not quite believing what her housekeeper had said. 'Is it Gaskell?'

'Don't know, Ma'am,' Maudie replied. 'They said as nobody knowed.'

'How ridiculous! There couldn't be a death in the house without its being known who had died.'

'No, Ma'am, but there could be one as 'adn't took place in the 'ouse. That way could be the maid wouldn't know who it was 'ad died.'

'Well, it is no member of the family,' Annie glanced at the newspaper, 'otherwise there would have been an entry in the Obituaries column and there is none. Most probably it is a remote aunt of Mrs Wheeler's. She did sometimes talk of one living in southern France.'

'Likely that be who it is then.' Maudie turned to leave then paused as Annie spoke again.

'Nevertheless it is only polite to call and offer my sympathy, I shall go to Oakeswell Hall now.'

Fastening her cloak, Annie thought rapidly. She would go to the post office first and post the letter she had written. Then she would make her way to Oakeswell Hall, passing Millfield Pool where she would dispose of pen and bottle of ink.

From childhood she had been used to harnessing pony to trap and needed no help with either. Twenty minutes from hearing the news Maudie had brought, Annie was driving across the open ground that skirted Millfield Pool.

'I heard it being talked of in the town,' she said when she was shown into Violet Wheeler's sitting room, 'and felt

I must call and offer my condolence were it true for I saw no announcement in the newspaper.'

Violet Wheeler sat down, her black skirts flowing over the edges of her chair. 'Gaskell made none.'

'Then your husband is still with us, thank the Lord.'

Ordering tea from the housemaid who answered her ring, Violet looked at her visitor. 'Gaskell? But of course he is still with us.'

Uncomfortable beneath the other woman's gaze, Annie apologised. 'Forgive me, but with there being no announcement . . .'

'Of course,' Violet cut in, 'but as you say, Gaskell is still with us, thank the Lord.' Waiting as the maid reappeared with the tea tray, then with a bobbed curtsy left again, she went on, 'My husband is recently returned from London.'

'It is not Montrose, I hope?' Annie said. 'Not your son?'

Violet poured the tea with the grace of long practice. 'If you mean you are hoping it is not my son's death we are mourning, Miss Pardoe, then your hopes are fulfilled. My husband was in London on a business trip, not concerning our son.'

So it was Violet Wheeler's aunt who had died. Annie took the cup held out to her. 'It relieves me to hear your son is well.'

'Yes, Montrose is quite well though he is disappointed that given the circumstances we will not now be holding a farewell reception for him before his regiment leaves for India.'

Replacing her cup on the tray, Annie stood up. 'I will not intrude upon you any longer, Mrs Wheeler. I came only to offer my sympathy in your loss.'

'Before you go there is something here we believe was intended for your brother.' Crossing to an elegant mahogany sideboard she took a large envelope from a drawer, handing it to Annie. 'Gaskell saw his name on this but it bore no address so he brought it back with him from London.'

'Oh!' Annie turned the envelope in her hand but it bore no mark other than the name 'Pardoe' scrawled shakily across it.

'It was among Clinton's effects.'

Effects! Annie's hand tightened convulsively on the envelope. Why was Gaskell Wheeler dealing with Clinton's effects? Why was Clinton in London when he had told her he would be in Wednesbury? The answer was staring her in the face. Clinton had gone and her money had gone with him!

'Thank your husband for me.' Annie's lips struggled with the words.

'Gaskell's cousin was so ill before he left Oakeswell Hall . . .' Violet Wheeler's words followed Annie to the door.

'Ill?'

'Yes, it all came upon him so suddenly,' Violet answered the query in Annie's voice, 'stomach cramps and symptoms so akin to fever he thought it a return of the malady that struck him when he lived in the Caribbean. He went to London to consult his doctor there and we heard no more until a mutual friend wrote to tell Gaskell that his cousin was dead. Who would have thought it?' She fluttered a handkerchief to her eyes. 'A man as vital as Clinton, dead in a couple of days.'

Clinton was dead! Annie stood in her own bedroom with no memory of the drive back to Brunswick House. He had died after so short and so unexpected an illness. Clinton was dead! Taking the scissors she had used earlier that afternoon, she opened the wardrobe door. Clinton was dead and with him her dreams. Stabbing the scissors into the cloth, she slashed the grey and the lavender gowns. Clinton was dead, she would have no need of colours. The gowns in shreds about the floor, Annie slumped to the bed. *Such a short illness, so sudden, dead in a couple of days* . . . Violet Wheeler's words reverberated in her brain, circling round and round. What was it that had caused the death of a man who had appeared the picture of health when he had last called on her?

When he had last called on her. . . . Annie stared at the remnants of the pearl grey gown. She had been wearing that when he had been shown into the sitting room, when she had handed sherry to him and to Samuel. She had given Samuel the glass she always used for him, the glass with a small air bubble in the stem, one that she could not confuse with her own. She had handed it to him as Maudie had announced the arrival of the constables. But she hadn't! Fear closed her throat as memory returned. She had not handed Samuel his sherry. The tray had been taken from her by Clinton.

So sudden. . . . The words seemed to scream in her mind. Stomach cramp followed by fever, the same symptoms the powdered seeds of yew and laburnum produced. She had not handed Samuel his sherry, Clinton had after she had left the room. That explained why her brother had not fallen ill as she had expected. He had not drunk the poison, Clinton had. She had killed Clinton!

Pain surged into her breast but Annie ignored it. She had killed Samuel for nothing, she had sold his inheritance for nothing, she would never be Mrs Clinton Harforth-Darby. And the money she had handed over to him, what had happened to that? Was it in some account that would most likely pass to Gaskell Wheeler? And the envelope Violet Wheeler had handed her, what lay in there? Reaching for it where she had dropped it on the bed, she looked at the name sprawled across it. Was it some lies as to her money or did it contain the barefaced truth? He had played her for a fool and now thank you, Annie Pardoe. Thank you and goodbye.

Breaking open the seal she drew out a letter, the writing spidery. '*Annie, my dear,*' she read, '*I wanted to bring you these myself but I am afraid I feel too ill. I will post them to you from London. You will be in my thoughts until I return. Yours, Clinton.*'

Taking the rest of the contents from the envelope, Annie looked at the stylised wording . . . *land and buildings appertaining thereto the property of Annie Mary Pardoe* . . .

Slowly she began to laugh, a low empty laugh that echoed round the room, laughing as her soul died.

Chapter Twenty

'They be a fine job, Miss, you'll 'ave no trouble wi' them.'

'Thank you, Bert, you have worked so hard.' Phoebe looked at the wooden soap box filled almost to the top with shining brass locks.

'I couldn't 'ave done it by meself, everybody 'as worked 'ard and that includes yourself.'

'Four days, Bert,' she reminded him, 'four days to delivery. Do you think we will do it?'

'We be good as done now,' he smiled. 'Mathew an' me we be on the last batch. Tomorrow will see the lot finished.'

'I must admit I had doubts when we started. It seemed impossible for you to have made so many in the time we were given.'

'Would 'ave been if Mathew 'adn't stepped in, an' them two lads 'ave worked like Trojans. I tell you, without that pair there would 'ave been no order to deliver in four days' time.'

'I wish I were the Queen."

'The Queen?' Mathew glanced up from the lock he was freeing from a vice attached to the work bench. 'Whatever do you want to be 'er for?'

Phoebe's eyes danced. 'Because then I could give you all a medal. You certainly deserve one.'

Josh looked up from pumping the bellows, his face red from his efforts. 'Medals be no good, you just 'ave to keep on cleanin' 'em. 'Sides, like me mother used to say, you can't eat medals.'

'In that case, Josh, I will make yours a fish supper.'

'That be more like it.' He looked across to where Mark was working alongside Mathew. 'What you say, Mark?'

'I say mek that two suppers, an' mek me eat both.'

'Them pair, eatin' be all they think on,' Bert joked. 'I swear neither of 'em 'as a bottom to their belly.'

'Hard work makes men hungry, which reminds me – Tilly and Lizzie said to tell you the meal was ready and waiting on the table.'

'I would rather 'ear news like that than that the Queen was to visit.' Josh laid the brass-studded bellows aside, running his palms along the sides of his trousers.

'Well, I might not be Queen, Josh White, but rubbing your hands on your trousers will not do for me nor will it do for Lizzie. You know her rule: no hands washed, no dinner given.'

Josh looked at his hands then at Phoebe, his grin cheeky. 'I might 'ave known there'd be a price to pay! Mind you, I wouldn't mind 'avin' a bath for one o' Mrs Ingles's dinners, only don't tell 'er I said so.'

''Ave you thought on what you be goin' to do wi' them locks when they be finished?' Mathew asked as they ate their dinner.

'Do with them?' Phoebe asked, a certain amount of surprise in her voice. 'I am going to deliver them to Mr Greaves, of course.'

Mathew chewed on some cheese. 'I know that be your intention but 'ow?'

'I've been wonderin' the same, Miss.' Bert looked up from his plate of cheese and pickles. 'Carryin' two or three o' them locks be one thing. Carryin' a gross on 'em be summat else.'

'Carryin' 'em be summat you ain't never goin' to do. You needs transport.' Mathew cut a slice of onion, sliding it into his mouth from the blade of his knife.

Across the long trestle table that the men had set up at one end of the corn barn, and where Lizzie and Tilly had laid the midday meal, Phoebe looked at them both, her brows drawing together in a worried frown. She had been so busy, so preoccupied with her sewing and with helping in the workshop, she had totally forgotten the need to arrange transport of the locks to Birmingham.

Mathew continued to eat. 'So what be you goin' to do?'

'I don't know,' Phoebe admitted. 'That part of it never seemed to enter my head.'

'We could 'ire a 'andcart?' Mathew suggested.

Bert nodded. 'We could, but it be a long push to Brummagem. It be all o' ten mile.'

'What about Zach Coates?' Mathew took a pull from the mug of beer he had brewed himself. 'If we could carry 'em between we up to the Tipton Road, 'e could put 'em on 'is cart down into Wednesbury and then on a train from there.'

Phoebe's frown turned to a look of dismay. 'That would mean paying carriage charges and a return fare for one of us to go with them.' She spread her hands on the table, defeat in the gesture. 'I just do not have the money.'

'Would it tek more'n four shillin', Miss?' Josh asked through a mouthful of food.

'I would not have thought so, Josh,' Phoebe answered, 'but I do not have four shillings.'

'I 'ave,' he swallowed noisily. 'Least I 'as three an' another 'un this comin' Friday'll mek four, so if as you says four shillin' be enough to pay to get them locks to Brummagem, then they'm as good as there already.'

'Those three shillings,' Phoebe looked at the tousle-headed boy regarding her with eyes like molten bronze, 'are they the same three shillings you have been paid as wages since you came to Wiggins Mill?'

'Ar.' He took another bite.

'And the fourth shilling is the one you will be paid for the work you have done this week?'

He nodded, the food in his mouth leaving no room for his tongue to manoeuvre.

'Thank you, Josh,' Phoebe said, her eyes grateful though her mouth would not smile. 'But I cannot take it. You will need that money to keep you until you find other employment.'

The boy's grin faded at her mention of finding work elsewhere but his eyes lost none of their brightness. 'I managed afore I come 'ere,' he said, allowing the food in his mouth to slide past his throat, 'an' I can manage when I be gone so you tek them shillin's an' get them locks to Brummagem. Could be when the bloke as 'as ordered 'em sees what 'e be gettin', 'e will up an' order another gross on the spot.'

Phoebe shook her head. 'No, Josh.'

'Why!' the boy demanded. 'That money be mine. I've earned it so I can do what I likes wi' it, an' I wants you to 'ave it.'

Pushing herself up with her spread hands, Phoebe rose from the table. 'You are right, Josh, that money is yours. You earned it and you are going to keep it, I . . .'

"Ang on, 'ang on!' he cut in on her refusal. 'I've been 'ere near a month as meks no odds an' in that time I ain't paid no board nor lodgin', I've 'ad three good meals a day an' supper besides, an' on top o' it all I've 'ad a bed. Now then.' Putting aside his knife, he held up his left hand, fingers curled into his palm. 'Three meals a day would cost tuppence a go an' they wouldn't be 'alf the tucker I've 'ad from Mrs Ingles neither, so wi'out supper I would 'ave been set back a tanner a day.' Two at a time he raised the fingers of his left hand, counting slowly before raising one finger of his right. Satisfied with his numbers he went on: 'A penny to 'ang the line in Joe Baker's lodgin' 'ouse would mek it seven.' He raised another finger. 'Sevenpence a day that would be, an' nowhere near the comfort I've 'ad 'ere so I reckons I owes you that money, Miss, an' a damn' sight more aside it.'

'If you owe anyone, Josh, it is Mrs Ingles. She is the one who has given you food and found a bed for you to sleep in.'

"E don't owe me nothin'.' Lizzie smiled at the boy. "E 'as

earned more'n a meal or two, the 'elp 'e gives me around the place, an' as for a bed, 'tain't nothin' outta me way lettin' 'im lie in the loft along o' me own so 'is money be 'is own to do whatever 'e likes wi' it.'

'There you am!' Josh grinned triumphantly. 'Now will you tek it?'

Phoebe shook her head. 'No, Josh, I will not.'

'What about the cut?' Mark had remained silent until now. 'You could get them locks straight into Brummagem if you sent 'em along the cut.'

"Course,' Bert nodded, 'I never give a thought to the cut.'

'What! An' you workin' the narrow boats this three year?' Lizzie smiled across at her husband. 'Some bargee you be, Bert Ingles. Back at the locks for a few weeks an' you forget the cut exists.'

'I 'ad forgot it an' that be no lie,' Bert said sheepishly, 'but Mark be right. Get that box o' locks on a boat an' you could bring 'em right into Gas Street Basin. An 'andcart from there an' you as 'em delivered.'

'It sounds easy, Bert,' Phoebe said, the worry in her tone not diminished, 'but will there be a barge going to Birmingham in the next day or two?'

'Sure to be.' The words were Lizzie's. 'Barges be up an' down to Brummagem as often as a barman serves beer on a Friday night.'

'Might be one comin' now.' Josh jumped up. 'Shall I go an' see?'

'Ar, lad,' Bert nodded, 'an' if one passes as ain't due for Brummagem ask if 'e knows when one is. An', lad,' Bert pointed a finger at him, 'no dawdlin'. There be work still to do.'

'Can I come?' Ruth scrambled up from the table. 'Take me wi' you, Josh, I want to come.'

"Old on to 'er,' Lizzie said as Josh looked at her for permission. "Er can be off like a ferret down a rabbit 'ole if you leave go of 'er.'

"Er'll be all right wi' me, Mrs Ingles.' Josh caught the girl's hand. 'We'll be back quicker'n a navvy sups a pint.'

'There be a boat along o' the towpath.' Josh was back at the bellows in under five minutes. 'Bloke says if it be on for 'im to fetch water from the pump, 'e'll cart your locks up to Brummagem.'

'Can you carry on if I goes for a word wi' 'im?' Bert asked from the yard.

'Ar,' Mathew nodded. 'Mark 'ere can put me right should be I needs it.

'Settled?' he asked when Bert returned to the workshop later.

Sitting in his place at the workbench Bert took up a lock, removing it from the pattern mould. ''E goes up to Brum' wi' an empty boat, 'as a load to pick up from Gas Street in the mornin'. 'E 'as agreed to lay up 'ere for the night to give we the time to finish the last o' the order.'

'That be a bit o' good news for Phoebe.' Mathew put the lock he had finished on the pile set aside for filing down. ''Er was worried, you could tell that.'

'Well, the worry be groundless now,' Bert answered, 'but somebody 'as to go wi' them locks an' I don't think as Phoebe be the one. There be no other woman on that barge an' while I ain't sayin' as it be the bloke would touch 'er, I am sayin' as 'ow it wouldn't look right.'

'So what you reckon?'

'What I reckon is one o' we men should go wi' 'em.'

'It be the sensible thing,' Mathew agreed, 'an' that one should rightly be you, Bert. You can talk locks better'n me and you knows what they be worth. A bloke won't find it so easy diddlin' you as 'e would me.'

'Mmm.' Bert reached for a screwdriver. 'I'll go tell 'er when I've finished this, but we'll 'ave to bide by 'er decision.'

'It would have been the answer to our problem,' Phoebe said when Bert told her the reason for his being in her kitchen, 'but it will no longer be necessary. The locks are not going to Birmingham.'

'Not goin' to Brummagem?' Bert looked surprised. 'Then where do they be goin', Miss?'

'They won't be going anywhere, Bert. Perhaps you had better read this.' She handed him a white envelope. 'It came just a few minutes ago.'

Drawing a folded paper from the envelope, Bert read the neat copperplate hand. 'But why?' he asked. 'There be no reason given an' the month's end be three days clear away.'

'I do not know why.' Phoebe took the letter from Bert, her eyes scanning the heading James Greaves, Hardware and Ironmongery. He had given no reason in his letter, merely stating the gross of locks ordered on the second day of the month would no longer be required.

'I don't believe it!' Bert pushed a hand through his hair. 'I just don't bloody well believe it! Three days from finishin' an' the bloke 'as the gall to say 'e no longer wants 'em, an' not even a reason.'

'I am afraid we have to believe it.' Phoebe folded the letter, returning it to its envelope. 'But we do not have to accept it without a reason.'

'What you be goin' to do?'

'I am going to Birmingham, Bert.' Phoebe's chin came up. 'I am going to see Mr James Greaves.'

Phoebe sat on the slatted wooden seat of the steam tram, her bag with the one lock in it held close in her lap. The journey would take longer by tram but the fare by train was more than she had. The tram moved along Holloway Bank, complaining at the rise in the ground.

'Nice day, ain't it?'

A large woman in an even larger flowered hat nodded at Phoebe.

'Very nice,' she replied, her thoughts not with her words.

'It'll get nicer an' all if it don't get no worse.' The

woman's head bobbed, setting the flowers on her oversized hat wobbling dangerously.

'My rheumatiz says it be a-goin' ter rain.' A second woman joined the conversation.

'Oh, ar!' The flowers wobbled again. 'My old man says as 'ow 'e's goin' to get up off 'is idle arse tomorrer an' find isself a job – only tomorrer never comes, an' when it does 'e ain't in, so don't you go believin' all you 'ears.'

'You 'ave one o' them sort an' all, does you, wench!' The second woman laughed wheezily. 'I thought as I was the only woman wi' a bloke too idle to blow the froth off 'is beer.'

The large woman's assortment of chins wobbled in rhythm with the flowers on her hat. 'You knows what thought thought.' She laughed. "E thought 'e weren't dead till they buried 'im!'

'Boundary,' the conductor of the tram called loudly. 'Boundary, all change.'

'Change?' Phoebe had been to Birmingham several times but always in her father's carriage. Now the conductor's call confused her.

'You 'as to get off 'ere, luv.' The large woman eased herself out of her seat. 'It's the boundary, did you want to go further?'

'I want to go to Birmingham.' Phoebe got out of her seat as the conductor called again.

The woman began to move along the narrow aisle separating the wooden bench-like seats, her ample hips brushing both sides. 'Wednesbury tram only runs as far as West Bromwich,' she said as Phoebe followed. 'To go on to Brummagem you 'ave to change at the boundary.' Alighting heavily, the woman eased her basket more firmly on to her arm then pointed. 'Just go a bit further down the road an' you'll see the tram for Brummagem. It be navy blue an' cream where this one be red, you can't miss it.'

Murmuring her thanks, Phoebe followed the way that had

been pointed. It took several more enquiries before she found the shop front announcing James Greaves, Hardware and Ironmongery. Taking a deep breath, she pushed open the door.

'Mr Greaves,' Phoebe took the letter from her bag, placing it address uppermost on the smooth polished wood of the counter that ran the length of the small dark shop, 'can you please explain to me why you have cancelled your order for one gross of Invincible locks just days before that order was due to be delivered to you?'

'I beg your pardon!' The man's smile faded to be replaced by a bemused look.

'I have no doubt you do,' Phoebe replied tartly, 'but begging my pardon is not enough. I require an explanation.'

'Are you sure you have come to the right shop?' He sounded almost apologetic. 'I have ordered no locks.'

'Yes!' Phoebe glared, her mouth tight with anger. A reason with or without an apology she would accept, but not bare-faced denial. 'You are Mr James Greaves, are you not?'

'I am, Miss,' the shopkeeper answered politely.

'And this, if I am not mistaken, is a Hardware and Ironmongery store?'

'It is.' He nodded, following Phoebe's cursory glance at the various articles of hardware hanging from every available space.

'Then this must be yours. Please read it and tell me if I am wrong.'

Taking the letter from the envelope, he fitted a pair of wire-framed spectacles to his nose, looking first over them to Phoebe's angry face then through them to read the words written on the paper. 'I am afraid you are wrong,' he said, after reading it through, 'I did not send this letter and neither have I sent any order for locks.'

'But it has your name and business address.' Phoebe took the letter, tapping a finger against the heading.

'I do not deny that,' he answered levelly, 'but I deny having written that letter. If you would care to look at this ledger you will see the handwriting is not the same as is on that letter.'

He could have disguised his writing. Phoebe glanced at the ledger. But why should he go to so much trouble? What did he have to gain from ordering a gross of locks then cancelling that order days before delivery?

'Then who?' Phoebe's hand fell limply on to the counter.

'I don't know who,' the man answered gently, seeing misery slowly spread across Phoebe's face, 'but it must be somebody who holds a grudge against you.'

Drawing in a deep breath, Phoebe folded the letter returning it to her bag. 'I apologise for having accused you of such an action, Mr Greaves,' she said, 'I should not have spoken as I did.'

'I understand, Miss. You pay it no more mind. These locks you spoke of, what be they like?'

'I have one here.' She took the lock from her bag, laying it on the counter where its polished brass gleamed against the dark wood.

'That ain't no botched up job.' James Greaves took the lock in his hands, examining it closely. 'This be a good bit o' work. Man as made this knows his job.' He looked up at Phoebe. 'Bet they teks a bit o' time making and all. And you have a gross, you say?'

He examined the lock again as Phoebe nodded. 'A man can be proud of making something like this,' he said. 'He's a craftsman and no mistake. Look here, Miss . . .?'

'Pardoe,' she supplied.

'Miss Pardoe,' he handed back the lock, 'I will be willing to take some locks off your hands.'

Phoebe sat on the steam tram, finding the journey home no less a strain than the outward one had been. James Greaves would take some of the locks but to whom could she sell the remainder? She looked through the window towards a sky that was already darkening. But it is not as dark as my horizons, she thought miserably. How do I tell

Mathew and Bert and Mark, and Josh there is no money to pay what I owe them?

'So there you have it.' Phoebe looked at Bert and the others grouped in her kitchen, their faces solemn. 'It appears that James Greaves did not send us an order for one gross of locks and neither did he send the letter that cancelled that order.'

'Then who the 'ell did?' Mathew had listened silently to all Phoebe had said and now his temper broke. 'Some stupid bugger wi' a twisted mind, an' if I finds out who it be 'e'll 'ave a bloody twisted neck to go wi' it . . .'

'You said as this Greaves bloke showed you a ledger of 'is 'andwritin'?' Bert said, interrupting Mathew's explosion, his own voice still level and calm. ''Ow good a proof do you take that to be?'

Phoebe looked up with eyes shadowed with disappointment and worry. 'Well, the ledger did go back several years and all the entries were in the same hand, quite different to this.' She touched the envelope lying on the table in front of her. 'I can't believe a man would go to so much trouble as to disguise his own handwriting to play a practical joke on someone he does not know, on someone he never even met before today.'

'There be no tellin' what folk'll do if they 'ave a mind,' Mathew cut in, his anger still hot.

'True,' Bert agreed soothingly, 'but what would the bloke be gainin' by doin' such? There was nothin' in it for 'im.'

'P'raps 'e thought 'avin' been turned down once 'e could get them locks cheap,' Tilly ventured her opinion. 'Mebbe 'e thought you would be only too glad to get shut of 'em.'

'There is no telling,' Phoebe answered wearily. 'The fact is I am left with a gross of locks for which I have no sale, and whether the ordering of them was a practical joke or not will not pay wages.'

'The ironmonger did offer to buy some of 'em and at the

price you first said. 'E made no attempt to cut you down, you told me?'

'None.'

'Well, to me that seems to say 'e wasn't tryin' to buy more on the cheap,' Bert thumbed the buckle of his broad belt. 'But like Tilly says, you never know 'ow a man's thoughts be turnin'.'

'Mine be turnin' to murder,' Mathew growled. 'Whoever it be 'as done this, pray God I never comes across 'im 'cos I won't be responsible for what I does to 'im – but it'll be a long time afore 'e walks again.'

'It's done now an' what's done can't be undone.' Lizzie took her daughter's hand. 'Best for all of you to get some rest. The problem will still be wi' us in the mornin', it can be talked on again then. Might be as you will see a way out when you be feelin' calmer.'

'Lizzie be right, Miss.' Bert followed his wife through the scullery to the yard. 'P'raps summat will make itself plain come mornin'.'

'I hope so, Bert, goodnight.' Phoebe stood as the Ingleses and Josh followed by Lucy and Mathew crossed the mill yard to their respective dwellings. They had all worked so hard, and for what! She looked up at the night sky, its inky void strewn with stars heavy with light. It could not all be for nothing, there had to be a reason. Why would someone want her to throw her last penny into a venture, only to see it sink? It didn't make sense. But then sending her to prison for a crime she had not committed had not made sense. She drew in a deep breath of the night air, carrying the sweet smell of the heath to her nostrils. She had been imprisoned but not defeated, and the failure to sell her locks would not defeat her either. Bert and Mathew had put their trust in her and it was up to her to ensure that trust was not in vain.

'But what can you do, wench?' Tilly asked later as she handed Phoebe a cup of steaming cocoa. 'It's all right you sayin' it's up to you to mek things good, but what do you reckon to do? You 'ave no money to pay the men an' none to buy more metals wi'. Not that you needs 'em with so many locks unsold.'

'I don't know what I can do,' Phoebe's hands shook as she put the cup on the table, 'I only know I have to do something. Mathew and Bert need their money to support their families and somehow I have to find that money.'

'Somehow, somehow!' Tilly fussed about the grate, banking down the fire for the night, the kettle already filled with water for the morning sitting on the hob above the oven. 'You can go on sayin' somehow till the cows come 'ome but it still won't put money in yer purse.'

'There has to be a way.' Phoebe closed her eyes, a thin film of tears glistening along the edge of her dark lashes.

'You could let James Greaves 'ave the dozen locks 'e said 'e would tek. That would be little, I know, but a little be better'n none at all.'

'And if I can't sell the rest, what then?' Phoebe spoke more to herself than Tilly. 'The Ingleses can't stay where there is no job to support them. They will have to move on, and that means being on the road for God knows how long, on the road with Ruth and Mark. And then there is Josh, what will he do? Go back to the streets of Wednesbury, standing in line for a job that breaks his back for a penny, sleeping under a hedge because that penny is not enough to buy him food and a bed. I can't let that happen, Tilly, I can't.'

'Mebbe you won't 'ave to, wench.' She rested a hand on Phoebe's slumped shoulders. 'The good Lord only lets we tek as much as we can bear then 'e teks the rest. 'E as give you a burden an' it be 'eavy for you, but 'e won't let it break your back. 'E'll lift it, you'll see. P'raps 'e won't tek it away altogether but 'e'll lift it enough for you to mek your way.'

'I don't mind for myself, Tilly,' Phoebe looked up, 'you and I have known worse, but I feel I have let the others down.'

'You've let nobody down, my wench!' Tilly said fiercely. 'You found 'em food an' a place to live when nobody else would 'ave 'em, an' they won't go blamin' you for what's 'appened. If it be as the Ingleses 'ave to move on then that will be 'cos the Lord is wantin' it that way.'

'No, Tilly,' Phoebe pressed the hand resting on her shoulder, 'the Lord has no desire to see children suffering on the streets or men dragging their families from town to town in search of work. While we have food in the house we will share it, and with God's help we will stay together.'

'Amen to that,' Tilly answered fervently. 'Amen to that!'

In the moonlit shadows of her bedroom Phoebe slipped her nightgown over her head. They would go back to selling Bert's work one or two a day as before, but the profit from that would not be enough to keep his family and pay Mathew for toting them around Wednesbury. That in turn would mean extra work for Lucy, trying to cover the shortfall with her baking, and the strain of the past month was already showing in her face. She could not go on like this much longer. And then there was Josh. The Ingleses could not go on feeding him when they had next to nothing to keep themselves with.

Going over to the window she stared out over the silent night: over the windmill, its folded sails thrust out like a cross stark against the dark sky, over the corn loft into which she had been forced by the man who had come to rob her, and to the spot in the yard where he had almost raped her. 'Why?' she whispered softly. 'Why is all this happening to me?' But out of the quiet shadows there came no answer.

'Can I see you for a minute, Miss Phoebe?' Bert stood cap in hand at the doorway to the scullery.

Leaving the breakfast dishes she was drying as Tilly washed them, Phoebe laid the huckaback cloth aside. 'Of course, Bert. Come in, please.'

Nodding a greeting to Tilly, he followed Phoebe to the kitchen but as she made to go through to the parlour he held back. 'It will do 'ere, Miss.'

Phoebe's heart skipped a beat. She had lain awake the

greater part of the night trying to find a solution to their difficulties but none had come. If her burden was to be lifted it seemed the time was not yet, and if Bert had come to tell her that he and Lizzie must move on she had nothing to offer that would hold them to Wiggins Mill.

'It's like this,' he twisted his cap between his fingers, 'Mathew an' me, we been talkin', an' we thinks as 'ow p'raps them locks would be better taken down to Liverpool.'

'Liverpool!' Phoebe exclaimed.

'Ar.' Bert looked at her, his eyes candid. 'Mathew an' me, we says we got nothin' now so if we get nothin' there then we lost nothin'. We thinks it should be given a try, but we 'ad to ask what you thought. 'Ow you felt about it.'

'Liverpool.' Phoebe sat down, her hands together on the table. The night had brought her no idea of what to do with the locks but the same could not be said of Bert.

'Ar, Liverpool, Miss.' He reinforced the theme, his voice enthusiastic. 'You see, Liverpool be the docks from where ships sail to America. Mathew an' me reckon if we can get them locks over there, they will sell.'

'How do you reckon that?'

Bert shuffled from one foot to another, his hand nervously throttling his cap. 'Well, Miss, from what I 'ear tell, you can sell spectacles to a blind man in that country.'

Trying but failing to hide the smile his words brought to her mouth, Phoebe asked from whom he had such information.

'Word gets round the docks,' he told her. 'Sailors comin' in from America an' the West Indies talks of 'ow the country be growin' that fast an' 'ow they be 'ungry for all sorts o' goods. They tells the cut men you can find a market over there for anythin', an' if they be buyin' goods fast as we can ship 'em over seems reasonable they 'ave to be stored for a time in warehouses. An' warehouses need locks – good locks as can't be broken.'

'And you and Mathew think our locks will sell over there?'

Bert smiled. 'Like Mathew says, they might not be the first locks to 'it America but they'll be the best.'

'But it will take weeks, Bert, maybe months, and you have already gone a month without wages. You can't go for several more. It is different for Mathew, he can go back to oddjobbing in the town and they have the money Lucy makes selling pies, but you and Lizzie will have nothing and I have not enough money to buy more metals for you to carry on while you are waiting – not unless we let Mr Greaves buy the one dozen locks he offered to take.'

'We've thought of that, me an' Lizzie, an' we both say the same. Leave the gross of locks intact an' send 'em off to America. We will find a way to manage till we gets word back.'

'But if they should not sell as you think, Bert,' Phoebe added a cautionary note, 'Lizzie and the children . . .'

'Lizzie an' Mark knows the score,' Bert said quickly. 'They also knows that should it fail to come off we will be back on the road, but if we never takes a chance then we'll never 'ave the answer, one way nor t'other, so the final word rests wi' you, Miss.'

'Has Mathew discussed this with Lucy?'

'They spoke of it this mornin' as he walked 'er to the crossroads.'

'And Lucy was in agreement?'

'Sees 'er was,' Bert nodded, 'but t'would be better all round to talk the matter over wi' all concerned brought together. That way everybody gets to 'ear all the fors and all the agens, and gets to say their piece fair like.'

'Agreed. But in the meantime have you thought of the cost involved in transporting the locks to America? It is going to be a great deal more than getting them to Birmingham and I did not have sufficient money to do that.'

'I 'ave thought of it.' Bert stopped mangling the cap he had taken to wearing to keep the dust of the workshop out of his hair. 'An' if you agrees then I think as we 'ave the answer. You see, while you was off to Brummagem to see James Greaves I went down to the cut side an' a mate of mine was takin' a load o' coal up to London. From there 'e 'as to pick up a load that'll take 'im to Liverpool. 'E will call 'ere day after tomorrow an' if I asks 'im 'e will take them locks wi' 'im. Won't cost no more'n a couple o' pies.'

'A couple of pies might get them to Liverpool, Bert, but it will take more than that to get them across the Atlantic. How do you propose we do that?'

'This way.' Bert stuffed the cap in his trousers pocket. 'The bargee as will be passin' 'ere in a day or two 'as a brother-in-law who is first mate on a cargo steamer that makes a regular run to America. 'E takes aboard various items to sell over there.'

'What sort of items?' Phoebe asked.

'Anythin' the bargee picks up along 'is route.' Bert grinned. 'Anythin' they think will sell, which seems to be most things. An' this brother-in-law sells them for a cut of the profit.'

'Is he allowed to take things aboard the ship to be sold for his own profit?'

'Put it this way,' Bert smiled, ''e is allowed to take aboard anythin' that nobody else knows about.'

Phoebe looked at him, uncertainty in her eyes. 'There is something that does not seem quite honest about it, Bert. He is taking things on board to sell for himself and not for whoever is paying for the ship to carry cargo, and that can't be right.'

'Crew be allowed to take their own box aboard,' Bert explained. 'Don't nobody ask if it be 'olding clothes or anythin' else. One box be all they be allowed, it be up to them what they 'ave in it, so if this first mate wants to fill it wi' things 'e wants to sell that be 'is concern so long as 'e don't overdo it. It be a recognised thing, Miss Phoebe, that be 'ow seamen makes up for the low wage they be paid, same as do cut men.'

'This brother-in-law of your friend,' Phoebe asked, 'is he

to be trusted? I do not wish to call his honesty into question but . . .'

''E won't do the dirty, Miss Phoebe.' Bert's grin faded. ''E knows the cut men, an' 'e knows to cross one o' them is to wake up one mornin' wi' a knife in your ribs. No, if 'e sells 'em you'll get your money, an' if 'e don't sell 'em you gets the locks back, 'e makes nothin' an' we makes nothin'. That way benefits nobody so you can rest your mind easy: if them locks will sell at all in America then 'e will sell 'em. You tell 'im 'ow much you wants for 'em, that way 'e won't bring you less, then you pays 'im for 'is part.'

Phoebe sat silent, thinking over what Bert had said. She had little to lose either way. 'Very well.' She met Bert's quizzical stare. 'We will discuss it together this evening and if everyone is agreed, we will send the whole lot to America.'

Chapter Twenty-One

It had been a month. Phoebe picked up the bucket of water she had filled from the pump in the yard. A month since the locks had gone off to Liverpool, a month in which the small workshop had been silent.

She carried the bucket into the scullery, emptying it into the copper to heat for washing the household linen, feeling the empty pull of her stomach. The food stocks had diminished quicker than she had expected due to her giving more than a share to the Ingleses and she would take from Lucy only the small amount her needlework paid for. How much longer could it go on? she thought, slicing thin slivers of Sunlight soap from a thick bar and dropping them into the copper. A few shillings a week to feed herself, Tilly, the Ingleses and Josh.

Josh! She stirred the soap slivers into the water with a wooden stick. She had not yet found the courage to send him back to the town yet she knew she was merely putting off the moment, that it had to come. 'But not yet,' she whispered staring into the soap clouded water, 'not yet.'

'What be not yet?' Tilly came into the scullery, her arms filled with sheets.

'I was thinking we cannot keep Josh much longer.' Phoebe felt almost relieved as she said the words she had admitted to no one but herself. 'Lizzie is finding it hard to feed her own even with our help.'

'I've known that for some time, my wench.' Tilly took the wooden stick, using it to push the soiled linen into the wooden tub that stood beside the copper, pressing the sheets beneath the soapy water. 'An' I knows you won't be able to 'elp much longer. There be almost nothin' left in the 'ouse.'

'Has Bert gone looking for work?'

'Ar 'e 'as.' Tilly took the wooden maid to the clothes in the tub, banging it up and down on the linen. ''Im an' the two lads, same as they does every day, but it be a waste o' time. There be no work, not even in the foundries seems like.'

Phoebe watched the other woman pound away at the washing, her thin body bent by the weight of the heavy wooden wash tool that pressed the dirt from the linen. 'Do you think he will wait much longer before taking to the road?'

'Who can say what a man like that'll do?' Tilly brushed a wet hand across her brow. 'All I know is you can see it's gettin' 'arder day by day for 'im, comin' 'ome wi' nothin'.'

'But Lizzie and the children, he wouldn't take them on the road again, would he?'

Using the wooden stick she had taken from Phoebe as a rod Tilly fished the pounded sheet from the wooden tub, lifting it across to the brownstone sink, sloshing clean water over it and rinsing away the soiled soapy suds before carrying the sheet across to the copper to be boiled. 'Could be Lizzie would refuse to stay behind,' she said, recovering from the effort of carrying the water-soaked fabric. 'A woman like Lizzie Ingles ain't easy separated from 'er man.'

Nor from her children, Phoebe thought, lifting another sheet into the wooden tub. Lizzie would not leave her children at Wiggins Mill while she and Bert went to look for work.

'When you goin' to tell 'em?' Tilly took the maid to the sheet in the tub, pounding it with a steady rhythm.

'Yer goin' to 'ave to,' she said as Phoebe turned away. 'You 'ave to tell 'em that sewin' night an' day you still ain't got the means to support 'em more'n another couple of weeks at the outside, an' you try to do more'n you be doin' already an' you'll work yerself into the ground an' that'll be a lot o' good to nobody.'

Tilly was right. Phoebe made her way slowly to her sewing room. She would tell them tonight. To tell Bert and Lizzie she could help them no longer would be painful but what would she say to Josh? How do you tell a young boy he must leave the home and people he loves? That would not be painful, that would be heart-breaking.

Pausing before the brown paper that held the creamy yellow satin, Phoebe ran a finger over the cloth. She was to have worn that to the Dartmouths' ball where she would have been Edward's partner. Edward who loved her and wanted to marry her. Her life would be so different had she said yes, had she loved him as he did her. But she did not love Edward, she did not love any man. Closing the brown paper back over the satin, she walked to her chair, taking up the petticoat she was making, but the stitches were blurred by the face in her mind. The face of Edward's father.

Her thoughts going again and again over the problem of keeping the Ingleses and Josh, Phoebe sewed until the light from the window was too dim to see the tiny stitches clearly. The whole day and only one petticoat to show for the hours of work. She smoothed the narrow pin tuck pleating that wound around the skirt above the flounces of cotton lace. If only she could afford one of Mr Singer's sewing machines! Laying the petticoat aside, she stood up, stretching the aching muscles of her back. If only she could buy just enough metal for Bert to make one or two locks it would help, but money would stretch just so far and buying brass or steel out of what little she earned was that much too far.

Maybe I don't need money. Phoebe stood stock still, the words singing in her brain. Maybe she did not need to pay for metal when it was ordered. Maybe she could pay at the end of the month like her father's customers always had. She could but ask. Tomorrow, she would ask tomorrow.

She had walked across the heath from Wiggins Mill and now stood in the ledger room of Thomas Bagnall's iron foundry, conscious of the dust on the skirt of her green coat.

'This way, Miss.'

Phoebe followed a small man, his shoulders permanently stooped from bending all day over ledgers.

'In 'ere, Miss.'

The man stood aside, holding a door open for Phoebe to pass into an inner office.

'Miss Pardoe.' Heavy-jowled, his hairline way back from the front of his head, Thomas Bagnall pushed himself to his feet as the door closed behind her. 'I 'aven't seen you in a long time. Sit down, my dear, sit down.'

'Thank you.' Phoebe perched nervously on the chair he indicated, aware of the glance that took her in from boots to hair.

'So, my dear, you're well, I 'ope?'

'Quite well, Mr Bagnall,' Phoebe said, unable to furnish the words with a smile. There was something in Thomas Bagnall she did not like and the sooner their business was finished and she could leave the greater would be her relief.

'Then what is it Thomas Bagnall can do for you?' He smiled, the heavy folds of flesh on his face shuttering his small eyes. 'Nothing 'olds more pleasure for me than serving a pretty woman.'

'I want to order some metal.' Phoebe tried not to wonder how his eyes would re-emerge from the enfolding flesh.

'That's easy done,' Thomas Bagnall's eyes stayed buried by his broadening smile, 'you only 'ave to say what it is you want.'

'Twenty-four pounds of brass and half that of steel.'

'That don't be much.' The folds of flesh gave a little ground, allowing his eyes to show.

'No, Mr Bagnall, it is a smaller order than my previous one but it will suffice for now.'

Dropping a thick-fingered hand on to a bell set on his desk he bawled the requirements to the same stoop-shouldered man who came in answer.

'We will 'ave that out to you tomorrow, Miss Pardoe,' he said when the clerk had left for the second time, 'if you will pay Simms on your way out?'

'I wish to speak to you about that.' Phoebe fingered her bag, her nerve threatening to run out on her. 'I – I wish to settle my accounts monthly in the future.'

'Monthly!' He smoothed the whiskers that ran the length of his flabby cheeks, at the same time coming from behind his desk to stand beside her chair. 'Now that be a different arrangement . . .'

Phoebe eased her knees away from the figure standing so close his legs touched hers. 'I am aware of that, Mr Bagnall, and though I have always paid in advance when purchasing metal from you, I believe it is not unusual to pay a month after delivery.'

'It's not unusual,' his small eyes glittered, 'not unusual at all between men. But you don't be a man.'

'I do not see that it makes any difference, I can pay as well as any man.'

'Except you ain't got any money.' Thomas Bagnall's smile registered triumph as he saw Phoebe wince. 'If you had the money you wouldn't be asking to pay at the end of a month, now would you, Miss Pardoe? And that being so we need to talk terms.'

'Terms?' She hitched herself further from him, sitting almost sideways in an effort to avoid the touch of his legs. 'Do you mean a charge for interest?'

'Some might see it that way.' The small eyes hovered about her breasts and his podgy hands pulled at his side whiskers as if tearing away her clothes. 'I see it as a way of saying thank you for a favour.'

'Do you charge a man interest for the privilege of settling his account after a month?' she demanded.

'How I conduct my business is my business.' He smiled, sending waves of flesh coursing toward his eyes. 'And if you want my metal without paying cash on the nail, you must meet my terms.'

'Which are?'

He touched a finger to her face, stroking it across her cheek and along the side of her throat. 'A little of your company, a private dinner somewhere secluded. Not much to pay for a month's credit.'

Not much to pay? Phoebe felt her stomach reach for her throat. A little of her company? Thomas Bagnall would want more than that.

'I find your terms too much!' Phoebe pushed to her feet, moving quickly to the door and snatching it open.

'P'raps you do but when you find nobody'll give credit to a woman then come back to Thomas Bagnall. You'll find his terms easier to fulfil when you've no money in your pocket and no food in your stomach.'

Phoebe walked back across the heath. She had not gone to visit Sarah or to see Lucy at her stall in the market place, knowing the contempt and disgust she was feeling would show in her face. But why had she avoided both of her friends? She sat on a half-buried stone, her feet aching from the long walk to the town and halfway back again. Why did she not want either of them to know what had gone on in Thomas Bagnall's office? Turning her face to the sky she closed her eyes. She had not gone to visit them for fear of their finding out what she only now admitted. She could not let the Ingleses take their children out on the road nor could she allow Josh to sink back into the poverty and misery of living in the streets. She had to go back to Thomas Bagnall, she had to agree to his terms.

* * *

'You have no need to take me.' Phoebe smiled at the stoop-backed clerk who looked up as she entered the ledger room. 'I know where Mr Bagnall's office is.' Knowing his eyes were following her, she went along the corridor that led to the comfortably furnished room she had been in less than an hour before. Pushing open the door without knocking, she stepped inside.

'Well, now!' Thomas Bagnall's self-satisfied smile obliterated his eyes. 'You've come to your senses, I see. I thought you would so I didn't cancel your order for steel and brass.'

He moved around the desk to stand close, his body brushing hers, bringing a fresh surge of revulsion to Phoebe's throat. If she were to help Josh and the others she had to do it now for she would never have the courage to do it later. Her voice little more than a whisper, her legs trembling with weariness from her long walk but mostly from fear of what she was about to agree to, she said, 'Dinner with you one evening, that was what you proposed as payment for extending me credit, was it not?'

He lifted a hand, stroking his knuckles across her breast. 'One evening for brass,' he said thickly, 'an' one for steel.'

'But you said one evening!' Phoebe pushed his hand away, her cheeks flaming.

'So I did,' he agreed, his tiny fat-shrouded eyes sweeping the length of her before settling on her face, 'and I'm still saying one. One evening for brass, one evening for steel. Those be my terms. You may take 'em or leave 'em.'

She had no choice. Trembling she turned to the doorway, stumbling through it in her eagerness to get away from a man who revolted her, yet a man to whom she must submit. 'Mr Bagnall,' she said, her voice low and shaky, 'I agree to your terms.'

'And what terms might those be?' Sir William Dartmouth caught Phoebe's arms as in her haste to be gone from the office she cannoned into him. Steadying her, he released her, asking again, 'What terms?'

'Miss Pardoe an' me had business together.' Thomas Bagnall's eyes receded behind their barrier of fat as he glanced warningly at Phoebe.

'How interesting!' William Dartmouth looked from one to the other, his glance pausing on Phoebe's flushed face. 'I am always interested in business and in the terms that conclude it. Perhaps, Miss Pardoe, you will tell me of yours?'

'It was nothing of consequence.' Thomas Bagnall stepped back from the doorway, leaving it clear for the other man to enter the office, but he did not move.

'What do you call "nothing of consequence" Thomas?' Sir William asked the question of the iron founder but his eyes were on Phoebe.

'Twenty-four pounds of brass and half that of steel, a piddlin' little order!' Bagnall snapped, annoyed at being questioned.

'Little indeed,' Sir William nodded, 'though it could have been more politely described in the presence of a lady, don't you think Thomas?'

What little could be seen of his eyes glittering venomously, the iron founder looked at Phoebe. 'I beg your pardon, Miss Pardoe,' he ground, 'a slip of the tongue.' Then to Sir William, 'Miss Pardoe was just leaving.'

'So I see.' William Dartmouth remained blocking Phoebe's way in the narrow brown-painted corridor that smelled strongly of the foundry. 'And hurriedly. Is that because you have other business, Miss Pardoe, or is it due to the terms you have just agreed with Thomas Bagnall?'

'I . . . I asked Mr Bagnall to allow me to settle my account at the end of the month from the date of purchase.' Phoebe straightened the quaver from her voice though her cheeks still flamed.

'That is the usual practice.'

'Not for me, Sir William.' Phoebe raised her head, a mixture of pride and despair in her green eyes. 'I have always paid the full amount at the time of placing an order but today it is not possible for me to do that therefore I asked for the month of credit I knew it was usual to extend to customers.'

'And the terms?' he asked, the temperature of his voice dangerously low.

'There were no terms. She asked for a month. I . . . I gave her a month, that's all we agreed.' Thomas Bagnall glared at Phoebe. 'There were no other terms.'

'And there will be none!' Sir William glanced past Phoebe to the other man, a world of meaning in his cold grey eyes. 'Miss Pardoe's order will be delivered in the morning and paid for one calendar month following that day and there will be no extra charge any sort whatsoever. The same terms will apply to any and all future orders she may wish to place.' He turned to Phoebe. 'Do you find those terms acceptable?'

'Most acceptable,' she nodded, 'thank you.'

Inclining his head so slightly his eyes did not leave her face, he answered quietly, 'Then your business here is settled. Good day, Miss Pardoe.'

The brass and steel would be delivered tomorrow! Bert would have the means of earning a living again! Phoebe walked home across the heath, her tiredness forgotten. She had a month in which to get the money to pay for the metals and thanks to Sir William she would not have to dine with Thomas Bagnall or suffer the attentions she knew would have followed. It was more than fortunate Sir William had arrived when he did, it was heavensent. She breathed a long deep breath of air flavoured with the scent of ling and wild flowers. It had been many months since her release from Handsworth prison but she still felt the same wonder and relief at being free to walk across the heath, just to stand and listen to the hymn of a skylark rising to the sky or the chorus of crickets in the grass. William Dartmouth had brought her that freedom just as he had brought another different kind of freedom today. 'Thank you,' she murmured using her inner eyes to look at the tall dark-haired man whose grey eyes seemed to smile back at her. 'Thank you.'

'When did he go?' Phoebe asked Tilly, her voice throbbing with concern.

'About a hour after yerself,' she answered. ''E come swannin' into the kitchen an' said 'e was off somewheres else to find work 'cos there was none to be 'ad in Wednesbury. It wasn't till later I found that in the parlour.'

Phoebe glanced at the coins lying on the table, a tiny pool of silver glistening in the last of the daylight.

'Did he say where he was going?'

'I've told you what 'e said, word for word,' Tilly answered patiently, ''ad 'e said more I would 'ave told you more.'

'I know, Tilly, and I am sorry to keep on questioning you, it's just that I am so concerned.'

'We all be that, my wench, but I don't see as worryin' yerself sick will do any good – you already be worn out wi' walkin' to that town an' back. Sit yerself down an' wait for Mathew gettin' in. Could be 'e was told more'n me.'

But Phoebe could not sit down. The meeting with Thomas Bagnall had unnerved her, and now this.

'Has Lizzie said anything?' She looked at Tilly peeling potatoes in an enamel bowl, black chip marks leaving a pattern of dots around its white edge.

'Nuthin' 'er can say.' Tilly hacked a hole in a potato, digging out the brown rottenness attacking its heart. ''E be gone an' that be all there be to it. Talkin' will mek no odds to that.'

Phoebe had talked yesterday of not being able to keep them all together at Wiggins Mill; now she had found a way, only she had found it too late. If only he had waited just one more day.

'That be Lucy and Mathew 'ome.' Tilly dropped a half-peeled potato into the bowl, rubbing her hands on her apron. 'Could be they seen 'im somewheres.' Following Phoebe into the yard she heard Lizzie already asking the question and Mathew's answer.

'I seen 'im this mornin' afore Lucy an' me went into Wednesbury an' I ain't seen 'im since.'

'Neither 'ave I.' Lucy shook her head.

'It ain't 'ardly dark yet.' Mathew glanced at the golden-red rim of the horizon. "E'll be back soon, you be worryin' over nuthin'. It ain't as if 'e ain't never been out in the dark on 'is own afore.'

'Mathew's right,' Lucy agreed, "e 'as most like gone into the town an' met up wi' somebody 'e knows. Give 'im an hour or so an' 'e'll be back.'

'I 'ope you be tellin' true, Lucy,' Lizzie said tearfully. 'I 'ope you all be tellin' true.'

'Tell you what,' Mathew scooped Ruth into his arms as she came squealing with delight into the yard, 'let me give my best girl a cuddle and then I'll go look for 'im.'

'Who you goin' to look for, Uncle Mathew?'

Kissing the little girl's cheek he set her down beside her mother. 'I'm goin' to look for the prince who will marry my little princess, but not till you be older.'

'Can I come? Can I, Uncle Mathew?'

Mathew smiled at the child, her tumbling red-gold hair caught with a strip of cornflower blue ribbon Lucy had bought for her. 'We can't 'ave a princess walkin' the 'eath an' gettin' 'er royal feet dusty.'

'You could carry me,' she answered, her eyes wide and serious.

'I might be able to, Ruthie,' Mathew hid his smile, 'but I be gettin' very old. Could be as I couldn't carry you back.'

Catching his hand the girl smiled up at him, craning her head back on her neck. 'Don't worry, Uncle Mathew, I will carry you back.'

'Come along, miss.' Lizzie caught her daughter by her free hand. 'You can carry yerself to the wash bowl and wash yer 'ands an' face ready for bed. Say goodnight to everybody.'

'You will let me know if you find 'im?' Lizzie asked when the goodnights had been said.

'Don't worry,' Lucy smiled sympathetically, 'I'll come right over.'

'I think I'll go wi' Lizzie,' Tilly said quietly. ''Er 'as took this 'arder than I would 'ave thought. I'll stop with 'er till Mark be 'ome then I'll be back to finish them 'taters.'

'I will finish them.' Phoebe looked towards Lizzie leading her daughter to the corn barn that had become their home. 'Stay with Lizzie as long as she needs you.'

'Who would 'ave guessed Lizzie would 'ave been 'it that 'ard?' Mathew lifted his cap, running a hand through his hair.

'When you grow to love somebody it be 'ard when they ups an' leaves wi' 'ardly a word,' Lucy answered. 'Beats me why 'e did it. 'E ain't goin' to find no better 'ome than 'e's got 'ere.'

'He did it because he thought we could not keep him at Wiggins Mill any longer,' Phoebe said. 'He was no fool, he knew how long it had been since any money other than the few shillings my sewing brings had come into the house. He knew I could not support them all for much longer so he left.'

'Poor soul!' Lucy sighed. 'An' now 'e is Lord knows where, but at least 'e as *some* money in 'is pocket an' 'e is well used to mekin' it stretch as far as it'll go so at least 'e will eat for a week or two.'

'But he does not have any money.' Phoebe turned towards the house. 'He left what he had in the parlour.'

'What, all of it?' Lucy asked as Mathew set off to search the heath.

'All of it,' Phoebe nodded. 'All four shillings.'

'Poor soul!' Lucy said again. 'Poor little Josh!'

'If only he had waited, we will have brass and steel tomorrow enough for Bert to start again.'

'Eh, Miss Phoebe! How did you manage that?'

'It's a long story, Lucy.'

Catching her arm, Lucy hustled her towards the house. 'Then let's 'ave a cup o'tea wi' the tellin'. I'm that parched I couldn't spit a tanner.'

'Eh, the dirty old bugger!' Lucy exclaimed when Phoebe finished relating the happenings of the afternoon. 'I wonder 'ow the 'oity toity Rachel Bagnall would take to knowin' 'er old man be no better than a lecher!'

'I hope she never has to know.' Phoebe poured tea for both of them, handing a cup to Lucy.

'Prob'ly wouldn't worry 'er none.' Lucy blew indelicately into her cup to cool the steaming liquid. 'From what folk tell 'er ain't no better than 'er should be.' She looked up suddenly, shock slackening her mouth. 'Eeh, Miss Phoebe, you wouldn't 'a gone, would you? Wi' old Bagnall I mean!'

'I think that at the time I was prepared to do anything, Lucy,' Phoebe admitted.

'You would 'ave been called on to do more than eat a dinner wi' that dirty sod!' Lucy's shock retreated before an onslaught of indignation. 'Thank God Billy-me-Lord turned up when 'e did. Which reminds me,' she put her cup on the table, 'there was talk in the market today about the Dartmouths.'

'Sir William?'

''Im an' all,' Lucy said quickly, 'but mostly 'is family, about them comin' 'ome to England.'

Edward was coming home. The thought was pleasant but it brought no rush of excitement. It had been the truth when she had told him she was not in love with him but he had said that would change while he was in Europe, that when he returned he would ask her again to become his wife. But her feelings for him had not changed. Edward Dartmouth was a kind attentive man who would make a wonderful husband but she could never marry him.

'When are they expected?' Phoebe asked.

Across the table Lucy's eyes were bright. 'They ain't!' she said bluntly.

Phoebe's brows drew together with a hint of puzzlement. 'But you said they were coming home?'

'They *was*,' Lucy emphasised the last word, 'but it seems there was a almighty storm at sea somewheres an' the ship they was on was sunk. 'Pears there was quite a few of the passengers didn't find a place in them lifeboats an' was drowned.'

'No!' Phoebe's face blanched. 'No, not Sophie, she was to be married . . . she . . . she can't be drowned!'

'That seems to be what 'er father said,' Lucy continued. ''Cordin' to what be told in the market the ship was sunk some time ago but 'e wouldn't 'ave it that 'is family was drowned. 'E kept on waitin' for word that would tell they was still alive.'

'But it did not come?'

'Seems not.' Lucy picked up her cup, sipping the tea. 'Seems he 'eard to the contrary. 'E must 'ave for word to be goin' around.'

'I never thought when I saw him in Thomas Bagnall's foundry today, it didn't seem to register.'

'What didn't?' Lucy looked up from her tea.

Phoebe frowned as though trying to recall some inner picture. 'He, Sir William, he wore dark grey. The collar of his coat was faced with black velvet and he had a narrow ribbon of grosgrain about the sleeve. He was in mourning and I never noticed.'

'Don't blame yerself, Miss,' Lucy said soothingly, 'after what you 'ad just been through wi' old Bagnall, 't'ain't surprisin' you never noticed.'

'But *he* noticed.' Phoebe condemned her own oversight. 'He noticed my discomfort even in his own sorrow and I . . . he must think I am so heartless!'

Rising from her chair Lucy went to stand beside the girl she had once served as a maid, the girl whom life had moulded into a woman. "E won't think nothin' like that,' she said, bending to place her arms about Phoebe. "E could see you was upset an' 'e won't tek no insult from you not offerin' 'im sympathy. Billy-me-Lord be too fine a man to 'old a grudge, 'specially from summat 'e knows full well to be not meant.'

'I hope you are right, Lucy.' Phoebe turned to her friend, hiding her tears against her waist. 'He was so kind to me, I never wanted to hurt him.'

'You ain't 'urt 'im, Miss Phoebe.' Lucy stroked a hand across sherry-coloured hair, her voice gentle. 'You ain't 'urt 'im, an' when you be feelin' more like yerself you can write to tell 'im of yer sympathy wi' 'is loss, but for now go an' wash yer face while I finishes peelin' these 'taters. You will feel better for it.'

'Ain't no sign o'the lad,' Mathew was saying when Phoebe returned to the kitchen. 'Bert an' Mark went over towards Tipton way an' I went towards the Lyng but it be blacker than the devil's tongue out there an' wi' no moon I couldn't see no more'n a spit in front o' me an' same wi' Bert an' Mark. Ain't no more we can do tonight.'

'But he might be sleeping out in the open,' Phoebe protested.

"E might an' I can't say as 'e ain't,' Mathew answered, 'but it be no use our lookin' any more. 'Sides if it be as 'e left the parish like 'e told Tilly 'e was goin' to do 'e could be anywhere by this time. We can't tell whether 'e 'eaded for Brummagem or took Walsall way, an' in any case, even if we does find 'im we can't force 'im to come back to Wiggins Mill, not if 'e don't want to.'

'But he was happy here and the work with Bert interested him.'

'Ar, the work interested 'im,' Mathew looked from Phoebe to Lucy, 'but who knows 'ow long a lad's interest be 'eld by anythin'? They changes their minds quicker'n a kingfisher flaps its wings. One minute they be fascinated by one thing an' the next minute they wants no more to be doin' wi' it.'

'I don't think Josh was like that,' Phoebe said quietly. 'I think he left because he saw it as the only way to help the situation. He thought one less mouth to feed was one less to worry over. Why else would he have left every penny he had earned in my parlour?'

'You be right, Miss Phoebe.' Lucy added salt to the potatoes she had placed in a pan set over the coal fire. 'But so is Mathew. If the lad 'as med up 'is mind to go then there be nothin' we can do about it. We just 'ave to accept it.'

'Lizzie has taken it so hard you would almost think it was Mark had left.'

'Lizzie be a good soul,' Mathew said, "er treated that lad like 'er treated 'er own. 'Tain't surprisin' 'er be tekin' it 'ard.'

'And Bert?'

"E were the same, treated Josh as 'e treated Mark.'

'One as worries me be Ruth,' Lucy said. 'That little 'un thought the sun shone out of 'is eyes, 'er followed 'im every chance 'er got. 'Ow do you explain to a child as young as that the one 'er took to be God 'as up an' left?'

'Lord!' Mathew breathed. 'Nobody thought about Ruthie.'

Phoebe stared at the window. The night sky had lightened into dawn and still she had not slept, her mind living and re-living the times spent with Sophie and Edward. Edward had loved Phoebe, and he had died knowing her love for him was not returned. And Sophie . . . she was so full of marriage plans, so happy at the thought of becoming Montrose's wife, and now she was lying somewhere on the sea bed. Son, daughter and wife, all taken in one swoop. Phoebe closed her eyes against the picture her mind formed yet again, a picture of people helpless against waves that engulfed then swallowed them. His whole family lost together, what must Sir William Dartmouth be feeling?

'Ruth . . . Ruth, where am you?'

Phoebe's eyes snapped open as Bert's voice rang across the yard.

'Ruth . . . Ruth, my girl, ah'll tan yer arse for yer if you don't come 'ere this minute!'

This time it was Lizzie's voice that rang on the dawn stillness. Flinging aside the covers Phoebe jumped from the bed, crossing quickly to the window that overlooked the yard. Bert and Lizzie, still in their nightclothes, were looking around the outhouses. Raising the sash, Phoebe called to ask what was wrong.

'It be Ruth.' Lizzie looked up at the window, her face a mask of concern. ''Er be gone from 'er bed.'

'Have you searched the barn thoroughly?' Phoebe realised the futility of her question only after asking it.

'We looked just about everywhere,' Lizzie said, her voice near to breaking, 'me and Bert been lookin' an hour or more.'

'I'll be down in a moment!'

'What be the matter?' Tilly came into Phoebe's room as she withdrew her head, leaving the sash open.

'Ruth.' Phoebe reached for her dress and petticoats. 'She is not in her bed and Lizzie and Bert cannot find her in any of the out buildings.

'Lord, not summat else!' Tilly threw up her hands in despair. 'If it ain't one thing it's another. When is it all goin' to end? I'll get me dress an' then I'll be down. That poor woman . . .'

Phoebe threw off her nightgown, scrambled into her day clothes. Unmindful of her unwashed face or her uncombed hair she thrust her feet into her shoes and ran downstairs to the yard.

'How long has she been gone?' she asked, reaching Lizzie's side.

'I don't know for true,' Lizzie answered, her face crumpling. 'I put 'er into 'er bed last night like always an' when I woke this mornin' 'er were not in it no longer.'

'Try not to worry.' Phoebe held the crying woman, realising the unreasonableness of her request but hoping it at least sounded confident. 'We will have her home in no time. She has probably gone over to the windmill to pick you some flowers. I noticed some very pretty ones around there the other day.'

'Or 'er might 'ave gone across by the cut.' Lizzie's body shook. ''Er might 'ave 'eard we talkin' after 'er 'ad been put to 'er bed. We said about Josh 'avin' left, an' Bert was sayin' 'ow 'e might never come back.' She stepped out of Phoebe's arms. 'You know 'ow 'er 'ad taken to the lad,' she said, her eyes darkening with fear. 'Summat tells me 'er 'as gone lookin' for 'im an' 'er'll 'ave little fear o' the cut. 'Er'll 'ave no understandin' o' the danger of it.'

'But she may not have gone to the canal.' Phoebe tried to sound reassuring. 'Why should she have?'

'I know 'er 'as.' Lizzie spoke more to herself than to Phoebe. ''Er 'eard Bert say the lad could well 'op a barge somewhere an' barges means the cut an' that be where my babby 'as gone! My Ruth be somewhere in the . . .'

'Don't talk like that!' Tilly snapped, coming into the yard in time to hear Lizzie's fear. 'That babby o' your'n be up to 'er arse in flowers over by that windmill an' 'er father will 'ave 'er back 'ere afore you 'ave time to blink, so stop yer snivellin' an' go mek 'er some breakfast to come back to!'

'Tilly is right,' Phoebe said as Mathew and Lucy joined them. 'Ruth will be back before you know it. Leave it to the men. You come with Tilly and me, a cup of tea will help.'

'Will it?' Lizzie sagged against Tilly. 'Will it 'elp that?'

Phoebe turned, following the line of Lizzie's stare. 'Oh no!' she whispered. 'Please God, no.'

'Ruthie!' Bert's agonised shout rent the quiet sky as he caught sight of his daughter, her white nightgown clinging to her small body, her red-gold hair a bright splash against a dark jacket. 'Ruthie!' he shouted again, running towards the boy who carried her in his arms . . .

• • •

'I were a few yards, along the cut,' Josh explained as Lizzie held her daughter, dry and in a fresh nightgown, tight in her arms. 'I know I'd said as I was leavin' Wednesbury altogether but when it come to it I couldn't, I just wanted to be near all of you, especially Mrs Ingles.'

'But why go in the first place, Josh?' Phoebe looked to where he sat, his fingers curled about the girl's hand.

'I knowed you was short o' money, Miss, an' 'ad been for some time. It sort of makes sense, don't it? One less body in the 'ouse meks one less mouth to feed so I went, but I come back when it was dark. I found a place to sleep the other side o' the lock. I would 'ave liked to have slept in the old windmill but I wouldn't 'cos I 'ad promised Miss Phoebe I wouldn't never sleep in that place again an' there were nowheres else so I kipped along o' the cut.'

'Thank the good God 'e put you there, lad.' Bert took the child from his wife, carrying her into the loft to her bed.

'But if you was sleepin',' Mark asked, ''ow come you knowed our Ruth was in the cut?'

'I was sleepin',' a puzzled look crept over Josh's face, 'an' I was dreamin'. I was dreamin' o' me mother only it were not me mother. Well, the face were not me mother's, it were Mrs Ingles's, but 'er were wearin' a lovely white frock an' 'er face were all shinin' like a light were on it an' 'er called me name.' He paused as if living the dream again. ''Er called me name two or three times an' then 'er told me to get up an' bring Ruth 'ome. I said as Ruth already be 'ome but 'er just smiled an' said it again. "Josh, get up and bring Ruth 'ome."'

He looked at the group of people watching him. 'I 'eard 'er say it plain as day an' then I woke up. I looked all around but I couldn't see nobody an' I was just goin' to lie down again when the water up along the canal by the lock went all bright wi' the sun an' I seen summat white floatin' in it. Well, I run like buggery to see what it might be an' . . . an' it were Ruth. I went in 'ead first an' brought 'er out but I couldn't bring 'er to wakin' so I carried 'er back 'ere to 'er 'ome like I was bid.'

'You did well, lad.' Tilly pushed a dish of thick porridge to each of the two boys.

'You did that.' Lizzie caught her husband's hand as he came down from the loft. 'An' don't you ever go leavin' we again, Josh, or I'll 'ave Bert 'ere belt the 'ide off you. This place or any other the Ingleses might find theirselves in be your 'ome an' we be your family.'

Josh looked up, a spoonful of porridge hovering at his lips, his eyes filled with something near to longing. 'Mrs Ingles,' he asked, 'could . . . could I call you Mother?'

'It was a strange dream Josh had,' Phoebe said as she walked with Tilly across the yard toward the mill house, 'strange but very fortunate.'

'It were fortunate all right an' a dream it might 'ave been.'

'Might?' Phoebe stopped walking and looked at the woman beside her. 'Now just what does that mean, Tilly Wood?'

'Mek on it what you will,' she answered, 'but to me that were no dream young Josh 'ad.'

'What else could it have been?'

'I ain't sayin',' Tilly's mouth set in a straight line, 'but the lad said as the sun shone on the water just about where that little wench was floatin', didn't 'e?'

'Yes,' Phoebe answered, puzzled by Tilly's attitude.

'Well, it 'pears to 'ave escaped everybody's notice but there ain't no sun, leastways none as can be seen through clouds that be thicker than a grorty puddin'.' She glanced skyward. 'There's been no break in them from first light. I knows 'cos I ain't been to bed. I sat watching against that lad comin' 'ome.'

Chapter Twenty-Two

'But this is more than I expected.' Phoebe looked at the banknotes on her kitchen table then to the man shuffling from one foot to another, clearly uncomfortable at being inside the house. 'It is more than I asked.'

'Ar,' he nodded, 'I knows that but my brother-in-law says they Americans were willin' to pay more for such good locks so 'e sold 'em for more. That bill 'e sent along wi' 'em be from man as bought 'em an' tells the price 'e paid. You will see when you check that it all be there.'

'I am sure of it,' Phoebe smiled, 'but why has your brother-in-law not taken his percentage?'

'You trusted 'im, Miss. Now 'e be trustin' you. If it be as you be satisfied wi' the deal 'e struck then you will be sendin' 'im what 'e earned, that be the way 'e looks at it.'

'I am more than satisfied and I think Bert and Mathew are too.'

'It be a right good deal so far as I sees it.' Mathew grinned delightedly. 'Bert was right to suggest it.'

'There be a market for many more, so I was instructed to tell you, an' they can cross over same way as before.'

'Take some time,' Bert said thoughtfully. 'We couldn't go on workin' flat out like we did to make that gross, not all the time we couldn't.'

'Well,' the man shuffled again, his clogs loud on the red scrubbed flags of the kitchen floor, 'I be away up to London termorrer and back this way along o' a week. I will call, if you allows, for water an' you can be givin' me yer answer then. An' if you don't mind, Miss, would you keep me brother-in-law's cut till I be comin' back 'cos it don't be doin' to 'ave money wi' you on the barges?'

'It'll be 'ere when you wants to pick it up,' Bert said, following the man from the kitchen, 'an' there'll be some for you an' all for the 'elp you 'ave been.'

"Elp where you can,' the bargee refastened the muffler wrapped about his neck, 'that's what me mother learned all 'er kids, an' if you can't be a 'elp then don't be a 'indrance.'

"Er couldn't 'ave learned you better,' Bert said, shaking the other man's hand. 'Safe journey to London an' I'll see you a week from now.'

'That went better'n I'd guessed,' he said as he re-entered the kitchen. 'Seems you 'ave a solid market if you wants to follow it up, Miss Phoebe.'

'We *have* to follow it up, Bert.' Phoebe glanced at the bill signed 'Hiram B. Rosmeyer'. 'It would be foolish not to. The only thing we have to decide is how many locks we can make in a month. As you have said, you can't work at the pace you were before so how many would you expect to make?'

'That depends,' he mused. 'As we be now I would say between a dozen or dozen an' a 'alf a week.'

'Half a gross a month,' Phoebe calculated quickly, 'two months before we could ship another worthwhile batch.'

'The market could be gone in that time,' Mathew said, 'could be somebody else will get a notion to do the same thing an' if they be quicker at it than we . . .' He shrugged his shoulders.

'I don't see we can do anything about that, Mathew.' Phoebe looked rueful. 'You all do your best and no one can do better than that.'

'Might be a way o' speedin' up the makin' . . .' Bert touched a hand to his chin. 'Mathew an' me 'ave both spoke o' the way young Josh picks things up. 'E be a quick learner an' already knows near as much of locksmithin' as do Mark. Now if we could tek 'im off the bellows an' set 'im to work on the benches along o' we three then you could turn that dozen an' 'alf into two dozen or more a week.'

'But who would work the bellows? You need those to keep the forge burning, don't you?'

Bert nodded. 'We need the bellows, that be right enough, but they don't need to be sat over full time. What I was thinkin', if Mathew be agreeable, was for each o' the four on we to tek the bellows to the forge when we uses it an' the two lads to tek a turn when Mathew an' me be too busy. An' as for the coal, I was of a mind to suggest that Mathew an' me hauls a load up from the cut each night.'

'Easy done,' Mathew grinned, 'I could knock up a cart on a couple of wheels to mek it less of a task.'

'I think though, Miss, in all fairness Josh should 'ave the same wage as Mark, learn the way o' the world ain't paved wi' gold like fairy tales would 'ave 'em believe.'

'Whatever you say, Bert.' Phoebe smiled her thanks. 'Pardoe's Patent Locks are in the export business.'

She had smiled confidently at Bert and Mathew but counting the banknotes later that evening Phoebe felt that confidence seeping away. Deducting the wages owed to the men and to Mark, and the money she would pay Bagnall tomorrow, plus setting aside even a minimum for food and household expenses, left the sum much depleted. Then she would need to order a further supply of metal if the workshop was to be kept in full production and that she would pay for in advance – she would take no more chances with the odious Thomas Bagnall. Phoebe counted in her mind. She was playing near the edge but she had done that before. Folding one of the white five-pound notes she shoved it deep into her bag. Perhaps it might be enough for what she wanted.

Leaving the iron foundry Phoebe smiled to herself. Thomas Bagnall had been surprised to find her settling one account two days before it was due to be paid and paying for a further, larger supply in advance.

With the five pounds in her bag she walked along Dudley Street, turning left against St James's Church, following Holyhead Road toward the Lodge Holes coal mine.

Joseph had given her the idea when she had visited on Sunday. He had mentioned that the old pit ponies were to be brought out of the mine and sold. Phoebe shuddered to think of these animals, most probably condemned to the glue works after years toiling underground, but that was the way it had always been.

Joseph had somehow seemed more than usually lame, needing Mathew's arm to walk around Sarah's tiny vegetable plot, and Phoebe knew they were worried for his job. If the new mine owner sacked him then they would have to leave their home.

Holding her skirts free of the dusty ground Phoebe left the road, striking left across open ground that gave on to the mine.

But Joseph had not been sacked as yet, and if she could only keep a supply of locks going to America, then maybe in a couple of years she could help Joseph and Sarah to find a new home.

'Please let things work out this time,' she breathed to the morning. 'Please don't let this order be a hoax.'

It was going to be hard work turning out the number of locks Bert had specified every week and she really ought to be at the mill helping all she could or at least busy on her needlework, Phoebe thought, feeling guilty at being away from the house. But for a few hours things were going to have to take their chances.

Reaching the large wooden gates that closed off the pit yard from nothing but open land, Phoebe saw her father's name, not painted out as yet. Nothing moved fast in Wednesbury. Loosing the skirts of her green coat, she took a deep breath and stepped hesitantly across the yard trodden black with coal dust. Today she would not be dealing with Joseph Leach, as she would have a few years before, now she would be doing business with a new yard foreman. Joseph had been dismissed when the mine had changed hands.

'Can I 'elp you, Miss?'

Phoebe smiled at the man who answered her knock on the door of the office. Of medium height but powerful across the shoulders, his splendid moustache wiggled as he spoke.

Phoebe swallowed the smile the dancing moustache threatened to bring to her lips. 'I have reason to believe you are bringing several ponies out of the pit today?'

'Ar, Miss, so we am.'

'Then I would like to purchase one of those ponies.'

'Purchase!' The moustache jigged. 'What do you mean, Miss?'

'May I step inside?' She glanced about the yard, seeing the heads of several men turn in her direction. Maybe Joseph would be in the office.

'Well, it be all dusty in 'ere like, it ain't clean for a lady.' The man hesitated, clearly unused to his working domain being encroached on by a woman.

'We won't let that worry us.' Phoebe stepped inside, glancing about the shed she remembered so well: at the heavy ledgers on a bench to one side, the row of nails hammered into one wall, each with a numbered tag that indicated a man underground, and the table where the dead Norton boy had been laid by his father. Pushing the image away she looked at the man who stood as if trying to bar her entry into a holy sanctum.

'As I said, I wish to purchase one of the ponies that are to be brought up from the pit.'

'You can't, Miss,' he said. 'Them ponies ain't to be sold.'

'What do you mean, they are not for sale!' Phoebe demanded.

'What I says, Miss.' The moustache danced indignantly at her question. 'Them ponies ain't to be sold, not to you anyway.'

'Not to me, but they are to be sold?' Phoebe pressed.

'Mebbe,' the man conceded grudgingly.

'Then why not to me? Why can I not buy one of them?'

"Cos you can't, that's all I know.' He touched a hand to his top lip as if to prevent the moustache leaping from his face. 'The ponies ain't to be sold.'

'You mean perhaps they have been sold already?'

'Maybe they 'ave, then maybe they ain't.' He held on to the moustache that seemed to want to lead a life of its own. 'All I know is what I'm told, an' I was told them ponies was not to be sold.'

'But they have always been sold,' Phoebe defended her case.

'They might 'ave bin, but that were before. This be now an' things am different. Seems new bloke don't want them ponies sent to no glue works.'

A tiny frown formed over Phoebe's eyes. 'Then what does he intend doing with them?'

'Look, Miss,' the man began to sound exasperated, 'I already told you I only knows what I'm told an' I ain't bin told that.'

'Then if you do not know perhaps you will direct me to someone who does?'

'You best talk to the manager,' he said stiffly, 'if anybody be told diff'rent it'll be 'im.'

Phoebe was taken aback. The pit ponies had always been sold off at the end of their working life to any who saw fit to buy them. It had nearly always been the glue works but others had never been barred from buying. 'Then please show me to the manager. Perhaps, as you say, I had best speak to him.'

'Can't do that.' The man grinned, triumphant in his small victory. "E ain't 'ere.'

'Then where is he?' Phoebe felt a strong desire to slap both moustache and its owner.

'Could be anywheres in the pit, might be one place might be t'other, ain't no tellin'.'

'It is clear you did not win a Sunday school prize for honesty nor one for helpfulness,' Phoebe snapped.

'Maybe not, Miss Pardoe, but *I* did so perhaps you would do better to talk to me?'

Phoebe turned at the sound of a voice that echoed almost nightly in her mind, a faint hint of pink staining her cheeks.

'Might I ask what you are doing here?'

'Sir William,' the blush on her cheeks deepened at the unexpected encounter. 'I – I was told some of the pit ponies would be finished today.'

He waited, eyes taking in the bloom of her face.

'Oh!' His well-defined eyebrows lifted quizzically. 'Were you also told the ponies were to be sold to the glue works?'

'No.' She looked away awkwardly. What was he doing at the mine? Why did she suddenly feel like an erring child?

'But you presumed they were?'

Phoebe lifted her head, re-engaging his eyes defiantly. Wanting to buy a pony to save it from the glue works was no crime. 'Is that not what always happens to ponies taken from the pits?'

'Not all pits, Miss Pardoe.' He glanced at the yard foreman watching them covertly and the man turned back to his ledgers. Sir William led her out. 'Certainly not those belonging to me.'

'You bought my father's mines?' Phoebe asked, surprised.

'I did,' he nodded, 'and that means no more ponies from here or the Crown at Moxley will go to the glue works. Once their working life is over they will be returned to pasture at Sandwell Priory.'

'Then if they are to be put to pasture, why can I not buy one?'

Almost at the gates that closed off the pit head from the open heathland, he halted. 'Why do you want a pit pony?' he asked bluntly. 'When these animals have served so long underground they are virtually worked out. They will not be useful for heavy work.'

'I do not want a pony for heavy work.'

'Then what do you want it for?'

She did not have to tell him, of course, chances were he would not sell her a pony if she *did* tell him, but then she had nothing to hide.

'I wanted it for Ruth.'

'Ruth?' His brows rose again.

'She is the Ingleses' daughter – they live at Wiggins Mill,' Phoebe explained. 'There was an accident and she fell into the canal and though she seemed to suffer no serious injury she has not been the same child since. She used to be so full of life, always playing about the mill, but now she seems so withdrawn. I thought a pony of her own, one she would have the caring of, would give her something of interest.'

'How old is Ruth?'

'She is just a child, no more than eight years old.'

'Would she be able to handle a pony?'

'I am sure of it,' Phoebe answered. 'Her family worked the barges along the canal so she is well used to horses – that was why I thought a pit pony used to being handled by young children would suit her.'

He smiled, his eyes taking on a new warmth. 'Then perhaps we should discuss the possibility of furnishing Ruth with a pony, but here is not the most suitable of places.' He looked at the film of black dust covering her shoes and edging the hem of her coat. 'Might I suggest we go to the Priory?'

'The Priory is at least an hour and a half's walk and I have little time to spare, as I'm sure is the case with yourself, Sir William.'

'You are sure of so many things,' he said. 'Sure my ponies are to be sold off to make glue and sure I do not have time to discuss the provision of one for Ruth.'

'I beg your pardon,' Phoebe coloured afresh at his mild rebuke, 'but I have so little time and a walk to the Priory will take a great deal of it.'

'Not so much if you will accept a ride in my carriage.' He

smiled again. 'It would also relieve me of walking there as I must if you refuse.'

'But could we not just agree a sale here?' she protested.

'I think the pit ponies deserve the peace of the pasture,' he answered, 'even though Ruth would cherish one of them.'

'Then there is no cause for me to accompany you to the Priory.'

'There is every need if you wish the child to have a pony. Please,' he said, seeing the query on her face, 'there is a pony there that will answer your needs perfectly if only you will take enough of your precious time to look at it.'

It would take more of her time than she had accounted for. Phoebe thought of the others working at the mill. She really ought not to be away so long but Ruth seemed so dejected, so apart from them. If two or three more hours would serve to restore the child's interest in life then it would not be too much to pay.

'She's beautiful,' said Phoebe later, stroking the sand-coloured pony nuzzling her hand. 'What's her name?'

'Pippin,' Sir William answered quietly. 'Sophie gave her that name when the mare foaled. She said the newcomer was the colour of the pippins in an apple she fed to the mother.'

'I was so very sorry to hear of what happened to your family.' Phoebe saw the sadness shadow his face. Then in an effort to chase away a little of the shadows, she asked, 'Was this Sophie's horse?'

'The mother was Sophie's so I suppose the foal was too.'

'Then I cannot possibly take her from you.'

'Why not?' He signalled a groom who came and led the horse back to its stable. 'Sophie would have wanted the child to have it, and I want her to have it. I also want her to have this.' Leading the way to a long stone building set with graceful arched windows, he swung open a pair of heavy doors showing a line of broughams and carriages at the end of which stood a small blue-painted governess cart. 'This was my daughter's when she was a child,' he said, going over to it. 'Now I wish it to be Ruth's.'

'But I can't!' Phoebe thought of the five-pound note at the bottom of her bag. It could not possibly be enough to purchase horse and cart.

'Would the child not like it?' he asked, turning to her.

'I'm sure she would.' Phoebe glanced again at the cart, its blue-painted side edged with a pattern of daisies. 'But . . .'

'Once more you are sure,' he said gently, 'so why the "but"?'

'Ruth would love the horse and the cart would be her delight,' Phoebe decided only the truth would conclude this discussion, 'but five pounds is all I have and I know that to be insufficient to pay for them.'

'I am not selling you the horse or the cart, they are a gift.'

'No!' Phoebe's mouth set in a straight line. 'What I cannot pay for I will not take, whatever the need. Thank you for your kindness but I must refuse.'

Touching a hand to the pretty cart he seemed to see into the past, to the child who had once ridden in it so happily. 'If you will not accept a gift from me, accept it from Sophie,' he said softly.

Seeing the droop of his shoulders and hearing the pain in his voice, Phoebe's heart twisted with pity. If only she could take him in her arms and hold him until the pain had gone but she could not. Offering a gift on Sophie's behalf then having it refused would add to the hurt he was feeling. But such a gift . . . Phoebe hesitated, torn between her wish to spare him any more hurt and her decision to accept no man's charity.

Almost as if he sensed her thoughts he turned suddenly, a half sad, half amused smile at the edges of his mouth. 'I will make a bargain with you, Miss Phoebe Pardoe. You are, I take it, familiar with the handling of a horse?'

'I both rode and drove my own governess cart until . . .' She paused. 'Until a few years ago.'

'Then you take this.' He touched the prettily painted cart. 'Tell the child's parents I wish to make a gift of it to their daughter. With your permission I will drive over to Wiggins Mill tomorrow and if they do not wish to accept it I will have it taken away and no more will be said on the subject. Agreed?'

'Agreed.' Phoebe smiled, a part of her already looking forward to tomorrow.

'I ought not to have said I would do it,' she said that same evening.

'Then why did you?'

Why had she? She pondered Lucy's question. Was it because she wished to repay a kindness? Part of her owned to that but the greater part denied it. She had agreed to William Dartmouth's request, not to humour him but out of a desire she could not acknowledge.

'Why did you agree to be 'is 'ostess at the staff Advent Ball?' Lucy asked, her hands deep in flour.

'I suppose it was because he might otherwise have cancelled it,' Phoebe answered, 'and that would have been disappointing to his workers. It is the one really big celebration in their working year.'

'Why 'ave to cancel?' Adding water to the bowl, Lucy began to knead her pastry.

'Sir William explained he has no female relatives, no one he could call upon to fill the role of hostess for the evening.'

'An' so you said as you would do it?' Tipping pastry on to a board, Lucy began to roll it out. 'Was it 'cause 'e gave that 'orse an' cart to the Ingleses?' She looked up, her eyes asking a question she did not speak.

'It seemed churlish to refuse when he had been so kind.'

Phoebe avoided Lucy's eyes, knowing her own would betray the secret she had only fully recognised in the long reach of a sleepless night, a truth that had hit her like a bolt from the blue. She did not feel only pity for William

Dartmouth – she felt love. She had felt it for a long time, she realised, hugging the truth, trying to drive it from her mind as the hours passed. She could not love Edward because she had always loved his father!

'I reckon the ball'll do you good,' Tilly joined in. 'A chance to meet folk and mix a while wi' others will bring you no 'arm.'

'Perhaps not.' Phoebe spooned filling into pastry cases. 'But have you two thought about my gown? Brown grosgrain is hardly suitable for an Advent Ball.'

'Seems like that there satin'll 'ave a use after all.' Tilly carried pies to the oven, packing them inside in neat rows. 'And before you starts on about tekin' time from yer other sewin', I will tek that on till yer frock be done.'

'I don't have much choice, do I?' She smiled at Tilly.

'Not lessen you wants an argy bargy,' her friend replied, 'an' Tilly Wood don't lose no argument – 'er be determined to win.'

'An' you can forget 'elpin' in the workshop.' Lucy lined a fresh batch of pie tins with pastry cases. 'Me an' Lizzie can see to the filin' down.'

'Did I ever tell the two of you?'

'Tell we what?' Lucy asked.

'Tell you how dear you both are to me,' Phoebe said softly.

Annie Pardoe pressed a hand to the pain eating away below her breast. It was constant now, sometimes vicious, sometimes bearable, but always with her. Taking the bottle with its white tablets from the drawer of her bedside table, she eased the cork from its neck then angrily banged the bottle down on the polished mahogany surface. The pills did no good, they did not ease the pain, nor did the laudanum that fool Dingley had prescribed.

Her steps slow and heavy, she crossed the room, drawing a large brown envelope from the chest of drawers and carrying it held to her chest as she returned to sit on the huge bed. Her breathing regulated by spasms of pain, she stared at the sprawled writing before her. Her name in Clinton's writing, his hand shaking as a result of the poison she had given him. But it was not meant for you, my love! Her heart screamed. It was not for you. But he had taken it and had died and with him had died all her hopes, all her reasons for living. But Clinton would not be forgotten. Pressing the button mounted on the panelling beside the bed, she waited until Maudie Tranter entered the room.

'I . . . I have some letters . . . to write,' she said, pain interlacing the words so they came out haltingly. 'Bring . . . bring me pen and ink from . . . from the study. I . . . I will write them here.'

'Yes, ma'am.' Maudie glanced at the pill bottle, its cork still removed. 'Will you be wantin' paper an' envelopes?'

'Yes.' Annie paused, a sudden jab of pain forcing her eyes shut. 'Yes, bring paper and envelopes.'

It's a doctor you be needin', Maudie thought as she went to get the things Annie had asked for. And if you don't be callin' on one soon it won't be a letter you'll be writin' – it'll be yer will.

Drawing the documents from the brown envelope, Annie stared at the titles to properties Samuel's legacy had paid for, properties she was to have built a new life upon, a life shared with Clinton. But now he was gone and without him her life no longer held meaning.

'Will you be wantin' a tray in the garden, ma'am?' Maudie set the writing materials on the table that had been moved near the grate in which a fire was laid but as yet unlit. 'Or will I fetch a pot o' tea up to you 'ere?'

Annie glanced at the fob watch pinned to the left shoulder of her black dress. 'I will have tea here in . . . in about . . . an hour,' she said, pain snatching at the words.

'Very good, ma'am.' Maudie left the room. There don't be many hours left to you, Annie Pardoe, she thought, making her way to the kitchen. With or without the potions of old Dingley, you be walking the last stretch and how far that be only God in Heaven be knowing, and he won't tell.

Alone once more, Annie glanced at each of the documents Clinton had intended to post to her. She had doubted him, had judged him guilty of theft. But you will have it all, my love, she thought. You will have it all, every penny, as you would have had when I became your wife. I would have given it to you then as I give it to you now.

Crossing to the table she sat down, her black skirts rustling in the quiet room. Dipping the pen into the ink, she began to write.

Slicing cucumber sandwiches, Maudie placed the wafer thin triangles on a china plate, arranging a few sprigs of watercress across them before covering them with a food net. It had been an hour since she had taken the writing materials to Annie's bedroom and though she knew her mistress would probably not touch the sandwiches or even drink the tea she would take it up to her nonetheless. Annie had eaten less and less every day since hearing of that man's death. Maudie filled the tiny flowered jug with fresh milk, setting a dainty bowl of sugar beside it on the tray.

I guessed you would not be getting him to no altar, Annie Pardoe, she thought, scalding tea from a kettle bubbling softly over the kitchen fire. But I never thought he would avoid it by turning up his toes.

Taking the tray upstairs, she tapped at Annie's door with the toe of her boot, waiting for the call that would give her permission to enter and tapping more loudly when it did not come. Balancing the tray awkwardly on one arm when her second tap went unacknowledged, she turned the door knob and pushed open the door.

Annie sat on the bed, her voluminous black skirts spread over the cover like a storm cloud.

'I brought your tray.' Maudie crossed to the table set before the fireplace but seeing that the letters Annie had written were still open upon it, she took the tray to the washstand, setting it down beside the jug and bowl.

'Will I clear the table or will you take yer tea on yer bed?' she asked, shoving bowl and jug a little further along the marble top of the washstand. 'Do you want to tek yer tea at the table?' She turned, repeating her question when Annie did not answer.

'I'll pour you out a cup.' Pouring a little milk into the fragile china cup, Maudie filled it with tea then carried it across to where Annie sat on the bed, a large sheet of paper in her hands.

'Drink this up while it be 'ot.' Maudie held the cup towards Annie. 'C'mon, tek it.' She offered the cup again. 'It be fresh brewed, the way you like it.'

Annie carried on staring at the paper in her hand and Maudie tutted with irritation. Maybe she didn't fancy the tea now she had it but it was only good manners to answer a body. But then, when had good manners ever bothered Annie Pardoe? Never, unless that Clinton be about, and then it was all please and thank you. Clinton Harforth-Darby! Maudie put the cup beside the open bottle of tablets on the bedside table. What kind of a name had that been to go to bed on?

'Don't leave yer tea standin' there,' she said, the irritation she was feeling colouring her tone. 'It'll get stewed an' you knows you don't like stewed tea.'

Pausing as she turned to leave, Maudie looked at the woman seated on the bed. She hadn't spoken but that in itself was no surprise. Annie Pardoe often ignored her. But she hadn't moved either, not even to shield the paper she was holding from the possibility of being seen by another. That boded no good. But her eyes be open, Maudie told herself, 'er be readin' that paper so 'er be all right!

'Yer tea be to the side o' you,' she said again. 'Leave what you be doin' an' drink it afore it gets cold.'

Returning the few steps to the bedside table, she took up the cup with one hand, the other touching Annie lightly on the shoulder – only to draw away again quickly. Annie Pardoe was holding a sheet of paper and her eyes were open but she was stone dead.

'Oh my Lord!' Maudie breathed. 'Oh my dear Lord!'

Her hands shaking, she set the cup back on the table beside the still full bottle of tablets. Whatever had killed Annie Pardoe, it was not an overdose of them. She looked to where the body had fallen backward at her touch, the head lying a little sideways on the pillow, the open eyes seeming to watch her.

'I thought you was on the last stretch,' she murmured into the stillness, 'but I little thought you was *that* near thy end. May the Lord rest you, Annie Pardoe.'

Bending to lift the dead woman's legs on to the bed, Maudie noticed the hand that still held the paper had dropped palm down across her breast, showing a large amethyst ring on the third finger.

'That be yer weddin' finger!' she said as if Annie could hear. 'That must be a engageyment ring but I never seen you wi' it afore.'

She bent to look closer at the ring. 'Did 'e give you that?' she asked the silence. 'Or did you buy it yerself to mek it look like 'e was goin' to marry you?' Ignoring the open eyes, she eased the paper from the already cold fingers, reading the letter Clinton had written. *In his thoughts till he returned* . . . Carefully she replaced the single sheet of paper. Then he was going to marry her, seemed like. But if he was, it was unlike Annie to have let the fact go untold.

Glancing around the room, her eyes lit on the letters Annie had written that afternoon. Picking them up she read the neat copperplate hand. *The Last Will and Testament* . . .' Maudie continued to read to the last word.

'You bitter, twisted old bugger!' she gasped, her hands falling to her sides. 'May the Lord see fit to forgive you for I never could.' She lifted the letters, looking unbelievingly at the second one. She could understand the feeling behind the first, if a woman wanted to leave her all to a man then that was her prerogative, but to write a letter like this to a girl who had done her no harm! Still unsure of what her eyes had told her, Maudie read again the letter addressed to Phoebe.

I want you to know whose was the hand behind the one that signed you to prison. I paid the Magistrate £100 to have you put behind those bars. It was I told Lawyer Siveter to advise Lucy Baines not to take what she knew of that necklace to the Dartmouths, and it was I paid John Kilvert to testify that you had pawned jewellery once before in his shop— jewellery he knew to have been stolen from another town altogether. But you were released, released from your prison though there was no release for me from the prison that held me. Abel's child was free but Abel's sister remained in the prison he had paid for.

Then there was the order for one gross of Pardoe's Patent Locks. How did you feel when you received that? I cut the heading from James Greaves's bill and pasted it to my own letter, and I did the same to the one you received cancelling that order.

And why? I will tell you why. Your father took my life. To me fell the task of living with Samuel, of ensuring no one would ever discover the twist of fate that held him and me prisoner in the same house, that none would ever learn of the affliction the medical world held out no cure for. Your father took my life so he might live his to the full. I could not make him pay so I exacted that payment from you, and though you might still live after I do not you will not have a penny of that which was first your father's and then Samuel's, for everything of that is for my husband that was to have been.

Signed, Annie Pardoe.

"Ow could 'er do all that to 'er own flesh an' blood?' Maudie said when she had finished reading. "Ow could 'er do such

335

bad things to a young wench who 'ad never done 'er no 'arm?'

Glancing at the first letter that was Annie's will she scanned the words again: '. . . *all land, property and jewellery belonging to me shall be sold, the realisation such land, property and jewellery shall produce is to be used for the erection of a monument to be dedicated to Clinton Harforth-Darby and is to bear the inscription, "Dear to the heart and to the memory of his betrothed, Annie Mary Pardoe . . ."'*

Maudie dropped the letters back on to the table. How could there be a spite so strong as to strike at a wench from the grave, as Annie Pardoe was here striking at her own niece? She had turned her from her father's house and even now was denying her the last of what should rightly be hers.

Maudie looked again at the figure on the bed and the papers spread about her. Going to the bed, she picked them up, quickly scanning words she did not understand but guessed to be legal proof of ownership of the properties they named. And all this was to be sold to build a monument to a dead man and feed the pride of a dead woman!

'An' Phoebe be to get nothin',' she said aloud. 'P'raps that be what you 'oped, Annie Pardoe, an' for all I know you may be 'opin' for it still but you reckoned wi'out Maudie Tranter. An' if you wants to stop me now you 'ave got to get up from that bed to do it!'

Seating herself at the table, Maudie began to copy the wording of the will until she reached the words 'shall be sold'. Careful to spell each word correctly, she changed the text to read 'shall become the property of my niece, Phoebe Mary Pardoe', then she signed Annie's name.

Taking both of Annie's letters, she pushed them into her pocket. They would burn on the kitchen fire. 'If what I be doin' be wrong, Lord, then you must punish me for I'll not change it,' she murmured. Then, slowly and methodically, she searched the room for any other paper Annie might have written and that could be compared with the Will now on the table.

Satisfied the room held no other documents she went to the rooms Samuel had used and searched them, finding nothing. She would collect the tray then search each of the downstairs rooms. Only then would she go for the doctor. Once more in Annie's bedroom she looked again at the dead figure, feeling no pity for the woman who could plot so much wickedness against her own kin. Reaching for the cup, she changed her mind. It would look more natural for it to be there; she would tell them she had left the tray earlier and on going back for it had found Annie lying on the bed and the letter she had said she wished to write on the table.

'You 'ave 'urt that wench enough, Annie Pardoe,' she murmured, leaving the room to go downstairs. 'You'll not 'urt Abel's daughter no more.'

It had been a month since Phoebe had agreed to William Dartmouth's request for her to stand as hostess for the annual party he gave for the household staff. The creamy satin falling in soft folds about her feet, Phoebe wondered if she had done right to consent to attend this evening at Sandwell Priory. Sir William had called at Wiggins Mill several times since the day he had shown her the little cart and the horse, each time saying he wished to enquire after Ruth's well-being, and with each of those visits she'd had to try harder not to read more into his grey eyes than friendship. That she loved him she could not deny, but to imagine that love returned was foolish as well as hopeless. Sir William Dartmouth might take another wife but he would not look for one at Wiggins Mill.

'You look beautiful, Miss Phoebe,' Lucy said, adding the last tiny yellow silk rose-bud to Phoebe's hair.

'Do you think he will expect jewels?' She looked at her reflection in the cheval mirror. The gown held her body in a close sheath, the satin drawn to the back in heavy swathes and the front of the skirt relieved by a trail of yellow roses

Lucy had spent hours making. The décolleté neckline was ornamented with one yellow rose, showing the swell of her breasts.

'That man 'as more sense than to go lookin' for jools other than the ones that be shinin' in yer eyes,' Tilly said, taking the gloves Phoebe had bought so many months before from the drawer and handing them to her. ''E don't need no finery – 'e can see what a woman be wi'out artificial 'elp.'

'Tilly's right,' Lucy added, 'you don't be needin' no jewels. They couldn't mek you look any more beautiful than you do now.'

'I hope you are right.' Phoebe took up her gloves and after checking one last time in the mirror, followed the two women downstairs.

'Afore you go, Miss,' Lizzie came hesitantly to the door of Phoebe's front parlour, 'the lads an' Ruth 'ave somethin' for you. Would you mind if they come in?'

'Of course I would not mind.'

'Eh, Miss, you look bostin'!' Josh was first through the door, his eyes round with admiration as he looked at her. 'Don't 'er, Mark?'

'Good enough to eat,' he grinned. 'I might even be tempted to tek you out meself, Miss.'

'Cheeky young sod!' Lizzie cuffed her son but could not help smiling.

'I think you looks like a princess!' Shy at being in the front parlour, Ruth pressed against her mother's side.

'Go on, Ruthie,' Josh urged the child, his hand gently taking hers, 'give Miss Phoebe what we got for 'er.'

The little girl looked up at her mother and at her nod allowed Josh to pull her forward. 'We buyed this for you, Miss,' she said, shyly holding up a fan of the palest lemon lace, each of its struts tipped with a tiny yellow crystal. Then as Phoebe bent to take it she piped, 'It be a new one, it ain't from the pawn shop.'

'Oh, you sweetheart!' Phoebe felt a rush of tears as she took the child in her arms. 'That is exactly what I needed.'

'We thought you might like a fan,' Mark's cheeky lopsided grin stretched across his mouth like a wedge of melon. 'You can 'ide yer yawns be'ind it if you gets bored.'

'I don't think I will be bored, Mark,' Phoebe said, giving Ruth one last hug before turning to him. 'Though I might need it to hide my embarrassment at having no jewellery.'

'No need for you to feel embarrassed,' Josh said gallantly. 'There ain't not one thing you could do would better the way you look.'

'Josh be right, Miss.' Mark wasn't to be outdone in the field of compliments. 'Ain't nothin' would mek you look prettier'n you look now. Ya looks real beautiful an' that be no lie.'

'When experts such as them two agree you look beautiful then you can be sure it's beautiful you look,' Lucy said.

'You could marry a prince,' Ruth said solemnly, 'you be beautiful enough to be a princess.'

'If I do,' Phoebe smiled, 'it will all be because of my lovely fan.' She flicked it open, holding it below her eyes. 'Any prince would be glad to marry a princess with a golden fan.'

But she did not want to marry a prince, Phoebe thought as she rode in the carriage sent to collect her. The man she loved held a title, albeit not a royal one, but he did not want her for his wife.

'Good evening, Miss Pardoe,' William Dartmouth greeted the young woman alighting from his carriage. 'Ruth is well, I hope?' He escorted her into the great hall of his ancient house.

'As well as she was when you called three days ago.' Phoebe smiled up at him, glancing quickly away as she met the look in his eyes, a look she so wanted to be saying what she knew he never would.

'And the boys?'

'Cheeky as ever.' Phoebe held out the fan. 'They bought me this.'

'Rogues, the pair of 'em.' He smiled. 'But rogues with good taste.'

'Mark said he might be tempted to take me out himself.'

'Did he!' Sir William laughed, the sound drawing the glances of his staff lined up to be presented to Phoebe. 'The young hound! There'll be many a man takes a horsewhip to that one before he settles, though I say again I admire his taste.' He glanced at Phoebe, seeing the colour steal the paleness from her cheeks. 'You look very beautiful, Miss Pardoe.'

'I think we should look to your guests.' She turned towards the line of waiting men and women.

'Our guests,' he murmured at her elbow. 'For one night at least allow them to be that.'

Later William watched the young woman dancing a waltz with his estate manager. For something like four hours she had mixed easily with the people of the estate, men and women alike, a smile and a word for each, her simple manner making her readily acceptable to them. Watching her now, the light from the chandeliers glistening on the bronze silk of her hair piled high on her head, tiny buds of yellow satin nestling in its coils, her slim body outlined by the lines of her gown, he felt a pang of jealousy that the arms holding her and the eyes looking down on her smiling face were not his. Impatient with his own thoughts, he turned to his steward.

'It is all going very well,' he said. 'Give my thanks to everyone in the morning and tell them I was very pleased at the effort they have all made.'

'I will, sir.' The steward smiled, pleased at these words of thanks.

'And now I think we should announce supper.' William watched the man make his way to the end of the great hall, to where the musicians were seated in a large alcove, not sure whether announcing supper or wanting Phoebe out of the arms of his estate manager was the real reason behind his having the music stopped. Watching the man escort her back to him, William carefully lowered his gaze, hiding the answer that throbbed in his heart.

'A glass of wine, Miss Pardoe?' he asked as the estate manager took his leave of them.

'I would find a glass of lemonade more acceptable,' Phoebe answered, a little breathless from the constant round of dancing.

'Lemonade it shall be.' He led her to the supper table. 'May I help you to a plate of something?'

Phoebe shook her head. 'Like the princess in the story, I am too happy to eat.'

'Unlike the princess in the story,' he said softly, 'don't disappear when the clock strikes midnight.'

'How does Pippin be gettin' along, Miss?' The groom who had led the horse from its stable to show to her smiled as Phoebe came up to the supper table.

'Being spoiled terribly.' Phoebe's own smile broke out spontaneously. 'She is loved by all of us but especially so by Ruth.'

'The master told us of Pippin's new mistress and with his permission we would like to send her an Advent gift.' He looked at Sir William and when he nodded permission the groom handed Phoebe a package. 'It be from all the 'ouse, an' we 'oped you would take it for we an' give it to the little girl.'

'May I peep?'

'Ar, Miss.'

The groom nodded and Phoebe peeled away a layer of brown paper, exclaiming with delight at sight of blue leather reins. 'How lovely! Ruth will be enchanted. Thank you all so much, it is so kind of you.' She smiled at the assembled staff, all of whom had their eyes turned to her and all of whom shared her delight.

Arranging for the gift to be placed in the carriage against her return, William Dartmouth accepted the glass of lemonade handed him by one of the housemaids, dressed now in a pretty print frock. 'You are a victim of your own popularity,' he said as Phoebe was kept continually busy answering the polite addresses of his staff, 'you have made too favourable an impression and I fear you will have to pay the penalty.'

'Talking to people as friendly as these is no penalty.'

'But you would like a quiet interlude before the evening resumes?'

She nodded. 'It would be nice. I have not been called upon to be hostess to a party before and it is tiring.'

'Exhausting would be my word for it. Let's go to the drawing room, it will be quiet there.'

He led the way to a room furnished with sofas and chairs upholstered in a deep cream brocade, the curtains over high arched windows echoing the same colour and the huge square of carpet patterned in cream and soft peach.

'I admit I prefer a glass of something other than lemonade.' Crossing to a large figured cabinet he drew out decanter and glass, filling the latter. Raising it to his lips, he looked at the young woman sitting on the sofa, her hair turned to glistening amber by the soft light, her lovely face smiling at him – and turned quickly away, staring into the fireplace.

'Miss Pardoe,' he said, the thickness in his throat not quite under control, 'I believe my son asked you to become his wife?'

Phoebe's smile faded. 'Edward did me that honour.'

'But you refused?'

'Yes.'

'Not once but several times, is that not so?'

Phoebe stared into her glass, the happiness of the evening draining away. Was this why he had asked her to come to Sandwell Priory? Was this why they were now alone in this room, so he could bombard her with questions? Glancing at a side table, she looked at the silver-framed photographs of his family, at Edward's face staring solemnly back at her. 'It is so,' she answered quietly.

He remained staring into the empty fireplace. 'Might I ask the reason or would that be considered too rude?'

Putting the lemonade aside, Phoebe took a long trembling breath. He had brought her to his home in order to question her and she would answer his questions, all of them, and then she would return to Wiggins Mill. 'No, I do not consider there to be any rudeness in your question. The reason for my refusals was simple: I did not love Edward in the way a woman should love the man she agrees to marry, and I would marry no man I did not love.'

'I see.' He waited for several moments, the silence marked by the ticking of a graceful clock on the mantel, above his head. Then: 'Was there someone else?'

Phoebe watched him, her emotions crying out to comfort him, knowing the pain these questions must be causing him, understanding his wish to know as much as possible of the son he had lost. 'When your son asked me to marry him there was no one else,' she said gently.

'And now?' He swivelled to face her, his question hard and sharp.

Phoebe hesitated, taken aback by the knife edge of his tone. 'I . . . there . . . no, I am not being called upon by anyone.' In the hushed light of the room Phoebe saw the play of emotion on his face, saw his fingers about the glass whiten with tension.

'I ask your pardon,' he said. 'I had no right to ask such a question.'

'No, you did not.' Phoebe looked at his face, still handsome behind the pain. 'But had I not wished to answer then I would not have done so.'

'Miss Pardoe . . . Phoebe.' He wrestled with the words, wanting to say them yet stubbornly denying them freedom. 'I, I . . .'

Phoebe remained silent. Whatever it was William Dartmouth had to say to her, he must say it alone.

'Miss Pardoe, had my family lived I would never have said to you what I must say now. Had Edward survived I would not have spoken, whether you had married him or not. You have told me there is no gentleman calling upon you, that you have promised marriage to no one.'

His fingers closed tighter, threatening to crush the glass in his hand, and a film of perspiration glistened on his forehead.

'That being so, allow me the honour of asking you to become my wife?'

Phoebe felt the rush of blood leaving her face, the fan falling from fingers suddenly without strength. Why did he want to marry her? Did he still feel Edward was somehow obligated to her, an obligation he must make good by making her his wife? That alone could be the reason, she decided.

'Sir William.' She spoke evenly though her heart was breaking. This was the thing she had dreamed of for so long; she loved this man deeply but he saw marriage to her only as a means of reparation. 'Edward was under no obligation to me, you have no debt to repay.'

'For God's sake!' He flung the glass from his hand, shattering it against the stone of the hearth. 'I love you. God help me, I love you!' He turned back to the fireplace, one hand on the mantel, his head bent, the anger in his voice replaced by a mixture of longing and recrimination.

'I have loved you since I brought you from that prison, may Heaven forgive me. It was wrong of me but I had no power to prevent it. I loved you even as Edward loved you, the thought of you married to my son or to any man haunted my days. I know it is useless to speak of it, I am afraid I allowed my emotions to override my judgement. It is unforgivable of me to have spoken to you as I have. I realise you would not dream of marrying me . . .'

'But I have dreamed of it,' Phoebe interrupted, her own voice soft with an answering surge of love. 'I have dreamed of it for many months and I dream of it still.'

'Phoebe!' He turned from the fireplace, his face lit with hope. 'You said you would never marry a man you did not love.'

She smiled across at him, her eyes tender with love. 'Nor would I, but I love you. I think I always have.'

'Phoebe!' He crossed the room with one bound, snatching her roughly into his arms. 'My love – oh, my love.'

He loved her, *he loved her*, and he wanted her for his wife. Phoebe leaned against him as he kissed her. But how would a wife who had been in prison be accepted among his circle? Would marriage to her slowly destroy his life? And children, what if they had children? What would they think of having a mother once accused of theft?

Pulling away from his arms Phoebe put her fears into words, asking each of the questions her soul told her she must.

He smiled at her, his grey eyes a deeper shade with the love he no longer feared to show. 'I want you for my wife because I love you. I love you so much I cannot conceive of life without you. I love your honesty and integrity, your loyalty and tenderness of conscience, your dignity and your constancy. I want more for my children than the emptiness of a society that prizes none of those qualities.

'The world is changing, Phoebe, and we must change with it. It might take some time for people to forget the past but give them that time and they will see for themselves that trueness of spirit that would never allow you to commit any crime.'

He drew her into his arms again, looking down into her radiant face. 'You told me once that I should never use the word "must" to you again, but I am going to do so one more time. Your father is unable to answer my request so you *must* do that yourself. Phoebe Pardoe, I ask for your hand in marriage. Will you marry me?'

Turning her face up to him, her eyes soft with love, Phoebe smiled. 'My father cannot answer you, William,' she murmured, 'but the answer would be the same. That answer is yes, you may marry Abel's daughter.'

A HANDFUL OF SILVER

For 'Our Wenches'. My sisters, Hilda, Phoebe, Ann and Joan, and the memories we all share.

Chapter One

'She is a what!' Morgan Cosmore's hands tightened about the arms of his chair, his long fingers whitening under the pressure. 'You would hand me a cripple for a wife! What am I supposed to do with that?'

Between cushions of fat his father's eyes were vicious. 'I'm handing you a bloody engineering works. What you do wi' the wrappin' be yer concern.'

'I will tell you what I will do with the wrapping, Father, I will leave it where it is and you can look for your salvation elsewhere. I will not tie myself to a cripple! I can't and I won't.'

'Won't?' Ezra Cosmore's eyes receded further into the puffy flesh surrounding them. 'Don't you bloody tell me you won't!'

'Father, please . . .'

'Don't bloody "Father, please" me. You'll do as I say!'

'No, Father, I can't, not this.'

'Oh, you can't, eh? Well, let me tell you summat. You marry that girl or you be finished in this 'ouse, do you 'ear me? Finished. An' then where do you go? An' where do you get the money to indulge yer fancy habits? You tell me no an' you be on yer own, an' then how would you earn a livin', eh? That would be interestin' to see, you as 'ave never struck a blow in yer life – how would you do it, eh? Tell me that, Mr bloody Smart Arse!'

'Well?' he demanded again when his question was met with silence.

1

Morgan's hands gripped the arms of the chair harder. He would have liked it to have been the throat of the stocky man standing facing him, legs straddling the hearth, his habitually florid face almost scarlet with temper. 'I . . . I don't know, Father.'

'"I don't know, Father. I don't know, Father,"' Ezra mimicked his son. 'Too bloody true you don't know! But know this – you marry Kerral's daughter or you'll find out, an' it'll be the quickest bloody thing you 'ave ever learned!'

'The girl, Father, what has she to say to this?'

'The girl! Who the bloody hell cares what the girl has to say? 'Er'll do as 'er's bid, same as you.'

'So she has been given the same choice as I have?'

'Arrh, Hobson's. God knows you be no catch, but you be the best 'er'll get.'

'Tell me, Father, how come I am the best Josiah Kerral's daughter can hope for?'

From his chair beneath the high window Morgan Cosmore watched the vindictive smile spread over his father's loose-lipped mouth. There was no love lost between them; his father had disliked him from the earliest times he could remember, always accusing his mother of namby-pambying him, blaming him for the fact she could bear no more children and on her death, ten years ago, marrying again and threatening to disinherit Morgan for the son his new young wife would bear. But there had been no son, only a daughter who had carried her mother with her to the grave.

'I 'ave already answered you on that one.' Ezra ran his tongue over his flabby lips. 'Who else would tek on a cripple?'

'Who indeed?' Morgan rose from his chair with a fluid grace that spoke of the strength in his well-muscled body. 'So I am to be the sacrificial lamb, eh, Father? Ezra Cosmore's lad will take the cripple.'

'You'll be tekin' 'er money an' that's all as need concern you. You won't be called on to do anythin' else.'

'Oh!' Morgan looked at the man who had fathered him,

feeling a potent mixture of dislike and contempt. 'Like what, Father?'

'Like . . . like . . . you know bloody well like what!' Ezra's scarlet face took on a deeper purplish shade. Morgan knew very well what was meant, he just wanted to be awkward the same as always, but he could be as awkward as he liked – he would still marry the Kerral wench. Everything depended on the money that would bring.

'Do I?' Morgan's mouth relaxed into a taunting smile. 'How can you be sure, Father, when you haven't told me? You have always said that if I am to get anything right, you must tell me how and when. So you had better tell me now. What is it I will not be called upon to do?'

'Go to hell, blast you!'

'I am very glad to do that, Father. I had a real fancy for going to hell.'

'Listen to me.' Ezra's head jutted forward on his thick neck and his piggy eyes gleamed. 'You may think yerself very clever wi' yer smart answers but they'll all end up the same. You'll say yes.'

'And if I do?'

'There's no ifs,' Ezra cut in sharply. 'You refuse an' we be done for. The business be up to its eyes in debt an' even this 'ouse be mortgaged for more'n it's worth, so you see, my lad, you give me any ifs an' buts an' we might well finish up wi' nothin'.'

'That's hardly likely, Father.' Morgan studied a perfectly manicured fingernail. 'After all, as you say, who else will take on the cripple? But what if the cripple should refuse? What if she refuses to exchange her fortune for me?'

'The girl will 'ave no say in the matter.' Ezra turned to a side table, selecting a cigar from a box, biting off the end and spitting the stub into the fire. ''Er will do as 'er father tells 'er.'

'Like all good little boys and girls should.' Morgan laughed drily. 'They should not object to being sold off and mated like cattle to satisfy their parents.'

'I never 'eard you object to spendin' my money.' Ezra stooped, pushing a wax taper into the fire. 'An' I doubt you'll object to spendin' that which the wench will bring with 'er.'

'I shall have no objections whatsoever to spending her money.' Morgan watched the older man light his cigar then replace the taper in a delft pot on the mantel. 'But what is in this marriage for you? What do you hope to get out of it?'

Blowing a cloud of smoke into the air, Ezra watched his son through the lavender haze. He was going to take some getting to the altar but get him there Ezra would – or break his bloody stuck-up neck in the trying! 'What do you think I 'ope to get?'

'I think you hope to get your so-called business back on an even keel,' Morgan answered evenly, his eyes watching every nuance of expression flicker across his father's face. 'But you will not do that through me. I will not be saddled with a cripple to save a business that hit the rocks years ago!'

'Then what will you do if you won't marry the Kerral girl? There be no more money left, it's just a matter of time before they foreclose on this 'ouse an' then you'll be out on the street. An' will yer fancy London friends tek you in, then? Will any one of 'em find you a home or finance yer trips abroad every fart's end? Oh, yes, they'll do all of that all right . . . like bloody 'ell they will!'

Morgan continued examining his fingernails as his father's temper suffused his face with a deeper shade of carmine. With luck he would have a heart attack here and now and then Kerral could keep both his money and his gimpy offspring. 'I was unaware Kerral had a daughter,' said Morgan quietly.

'That don't surprise me.' Ezra blew out another stream of smoke. 'You ain't bin aware of anythin' goin' on in Darlaston since you 'ave bin eight years old.'

'You can't blame me for that, Father.' Morgan smiled, showing teeth scrupulously cleaned with bicarbonate of soda. 'You had me sent away to school when I was eight years old.'

'A good job I did an' all,' his father shot back. 'Get you away from yer mother's namby-pambying. Christ! A few more years of that an' 'er'd 'ave 'ad you actin' like a big soft wench – not that that school made much of a job of turnin' you into a man. All you think on is fancy clothes an' fancy women.'

'Poor Mother,' Morgan sighed affectedly, knowing it would send the older man's temperature soaring. 'She always was your whipping boy, wasn't she, Father? She always bore the brunt of your mistakes.'

'Mistakes!' Ezra sucked in a mouthful of cigar smoke. 'What bloody mistakes?'

'Oh, you have made them, you know.' Morgan dropped back to the chair again, hand resting on his knees, eyes lifting to the man straddling the hearth. 'Not that you would admit to any, of course, but you have made mistakes – and perhaps sending me to boarding school was one of them. Maybe if you had kept me here with you, you would have done a better job of turning me into a man.'

'I couldn't 'ave done a worse one!' The words shot out on a stream of strong-smelling smoke.

'Of course you couldn't, Father,' Morgan continued his quiet needle-prick offensive, 'we both knew you were the best man for the job, whatever the job. Mother, I presume, learned so from the first day of her marriage. And I learned very early, Father. I learned that the best way to avoid your belt was to avoid *you*.'

'You needed the belt.' Ezra spat into the fire then turned back to his son, surveying him in the depths of the velvet-covered wing-back chair. 'To knock summat into yer 'ead beside drawin' bloody pictures. Yer mother was too soft wi' you. "Artistic" 'er said you was, when all the time you was too bloody idle to do anythin' else.'

'Yes, well, you soon put a stop to that, didn't you, Father?' Stretching out his legs in front of him, Morgan crossed one foot over the other. 'That school you sent me to gave me no lessons in art. Those periods were replaced for me with extra physical activity. That was on your instruction, wasn't it?'

'Yes, it was on my instruction.' Ezra flung the half-smoked cigar into the fire. 'What bloody good is paintin' an' drawin' in an engineerin' works, eh? Answer me that. An' if you can't, I'll tell you what good it is – none, no bloody good at all.'

'I am sure it isn't, Father.' Morgan smiled, watching the blood rise again in his father's face. 'If you say so.'

'I do say so! An' I say this an' all. It be time you stopped all this gallivantin' off to London an' Christ knows where else an' started to 'elp out in the business.'

'Oh, no, Father. I would not presume upon your territory.'

'Territory!' Ezra sat down heavily in a chair set beside the stone fireplace. 'What you on about? What territory?'

'The business, Father,' Morgan answered blandly. 'I would not presume to interfere with anything you do. What need is there when you do everything better than anyone else can? Besides you have made a perfectly good job of bankrupting us up to now. It would be foolish of me to try and prevent your finishing it. But I would ask this – merely from interest, you understand. How long has it been this time since the men were paid?'

'And let me ask this.' Ezra's eyes were almost obliterated now by the folds of flesh surrounding them. ''Ow long 'as it bin since you last bought one of them fancy suits? The price of one of them would pay every one of the 'ands for a month or more. You leave off yer fancy livin' an' mebbe we wouldn't be nigh on bankrupt.'

'Since we seem to be discussing my expenses and their effect upon the business, I think it only fair to cast an eye over yours, Father.'

'Mine?' The eyes widened pushing back the barricade of fat.

'Yours, Father.' Morgan flicked a finger along the seam of his expensive cashmere trousers. 'Your clothes . . .' He mimed a shudder designed to raise his father's blood pressure. 'I don't know the cost of them but I would advise your tailor to make more of an effort, so they look less like pawnshop rejects. Then of course there is the running of this house. Your table is not exactly that of a man close to bankruptcy though the costs of your wine cellar would bankrupt the old lady of Threadneedle Street. And, of course, we must not forget those regular visits to Birmingham. They do not come cheaply, I'll warrant.'

'Visits to Birmingham!' Ezra almost choked. 'What do you know of my visits to Brummagem?'

Morgan suppressed a yawn with a languid theatrical movement of his hand. 'I know a good deal about them, I have done for some years now. For instance, there is a certain dark-haired beauty name of Maria at the house of Mrs Morrison – though the nearest that woman came to being "Mrs" was lying on a bed with another woman's husband. Then we have the Conroy Club, private, for members only. A little more respectable with its air of gentility but offering the same amenities. You appear to have a favourite there too, Father, or should I say two favourites? Amelia of the baby blonde ringlets, and Consuela, the doubtful red head of equally doubtful South American origin. You prefer to have them together, do you not? And then . . . but need I go on?'

'I earn my money,' the older man parried, 'and I 'ave the right to spend it any way I want.'

Morgan fingered the seam of his trouser leg, smoothing its already perfect symmetry. 'Whereas I do not earn mine. My allowance is a symbol of your charity – a charity never graciously given but always gratefully accepted, and the spending of it always greatly enjoyed.'

'Arrh, well, the enjoyin' be about to stop for the pair o' we unless you bring 'ome Jos Kerral's money.'

'Not to mention his daughter.'

'Yes, well,' Ezra leaned back in his chair, eyes once more guarded, 'we can't 'ave one lessen we tek the other.'

'We being *me*, Father.' Morgan looked up suddenly, his gaze cold. 'You take the money while I take the cripple.'

'You won't 'ave to 'ave no truck wi' 'er once the weddin' be over.' Ezra's voice took on a placatory tone. 'You can carry on much as you 'ave bin doin' then.'

'So I can leave my crippled wife with you, can I, Father? You will spend your nights entertaining her whilst I am in London or abroad? A very different sort of entertainment to that you are used to. Are you sure you want to go through with it after all?'

Ezra understood his son's tactics. Threaten to leave the woman here in Darlaston, give his father the caring of her, and it would change his mind. If a soul could smile Ezra knew his was smiling now. 'There'll be little need for either of us to entertain 'er,' he said. 'A woman to see to 'er will be all 'er'll be wantin'.'

'And all she will be getting if it is left to me, Father.' Morgan's gaze lost none of its coldness. 'Tell me, how old is this prize I am to be presented with?'

'Just on twenty, so Jos tells me.'

'And did he tell you what she looks like? Or maybe you have seen her for yourself? Is she pretty, Father, as pretty as Maria?'

'I . . . I 'aven't seen 'er.' Ezra looked towards the fireplace, avoiding the accusation in his son's eyes. 'But what does it matter if 'er be pretty or plain, as long as the money be there?'

'No matter.' Morgan resumed his study of the seam. 'Seeing as I will not be called upon to look at her, at least not often, and maybe not at all if her face is marked by her disability.' He leaned forward, the seam forgotten as a new thought struck. 'Her face is not disfigured, is it? Because if it is you can kiss goodbye to all of your well-laid plans.'

''Er face be all right,' Ezra answered, hoping the gods would make it so. ''Er father assured me on that point.'

'If only he had assured *me*.' Morgan leaned back in his chair but his eyes displayed an inner wariness. His fox of a father would stop at nothing to get his hands on Jos Kerral's money. A little thing like planting a disfigured wife on his son would cause him no worry at all. 'So just what form does the girl's disability take? Exactly how is she crippled?'

'It's 'er legs.' Ezra faced his son. Cripple or no cripple, he was going to take the girl for his wife, and the sooner he accepted that fact the better. ''Er father says 'er be crippled in the legs. 'Er can't walk but apart from that 'er be all right.'

'And I am to be thankful for that, am I?' Morgan laughed. 'And what of the family line? What of the dynasty you dreamed of founding? Is she capable of bearing a child?'

'How the bloody 'ell should I know!' Ezra's temper reached breaking point. 'What do you want, a bloody doctor's report?'

'No, Father.' Morgan became colder, his own temper more controlled as that of his father ran wild. 'Neither do I want a cripple for a wife, pretty or otherwise. You want Kerral's money, you marry Kerral's daughter.'

'You think I 'adn't thought o' that?' Ezra shouted, his face contorted with a rage he could no longer confine. 'Well, you be wrong, but Kerral won't tek an older man. He wants a young buck for his daughter, though for what I don't know. Bloke as gets 'er will 'ave to spread 'er legs 'isself afore 'e can mount 'er.'

'That would not have bothered you, would it, Father? Though the fact she could not writhe and heave beneath you, or straddle you as you would a mare, might have detracted from your pleasure . . . But then, you will not be having the pleasure, will you? Seeing as her father deems you too old for the servicing of his daughter.'

'Watch yer mouth or I'll . . .'

'Or you will what, Father? Take your belt to me as you did every night for so many years? I don't think so, not any more. Those days are gone, finished, as this conversation is finished. I shall return to London in the morning.'

'And when the money stops,' Ezra glared at the man rising so easily from the chair, all the swagger of youth and good health in the movement, 'what will you do then?'

'I will just have to do what I have always done.' Morgan strode to the door of the oval-shaped room. 'I will have to wait for you to tell me!'

Yes, that's what you have done all yer life, Ezra thought as the door slammed behind his departing son. Waited while someone else did the grafting. Waited and let some other bugger do the thinking for you. Well, I have thought this out for you, my bloody smart arse son. You marry that wench and bring her money into this house, and after that you can go to the devil as quick as you like!

'Miri, how long have we lived in this house?' Esther Kerral turned to look at the middle-aged woman busying herself with clearing the table at which both of them had just taken their midday meal.

'That's a strange question.' Miriam Butler hesitated in her task, her quick glance taking in the girl seated now at the window of the small house set in the grounds of the larger, grander Rowena House. 'You know how long we've lived 'ere. Some sixteen years.'

'I was almost four.' The answer was quiet, musing.

'Arrh, nigh on.' Miriam resumed her bustling, loading dishes on to a serving trolley then removing the white cloth and folding it into a drawer of a long oak sideboard.

'Why?'

The loud agonised query took the older woman by surprise, causing her to stand a moment looking at the face of the girl she had reared – a face as beautiful as any she had ever seen but twisted now with hurt and pain. Dropping the table napkins into the drawer she quickly crossed the sunlit room, sinking on to her haunches beside the girl. 'Essie love, don't. Don't dwell on that, it does no good. What's done be done. Best to let it lie.'

'Best to let it lie?' Her soft brown eyes widened with fresh pain as she turned her glance to a line of tall conifers edging the bottom of the garden, masking the flat green of the lawns surrounding Rowena House. 'That is what he has done for sixteen years – let me lie here where I cannot be seen. Lie here, unwanted and forgotten . . .'

'Shhh, Essie.' Taking the girl in her arms, Miriam crooned softly, trying to ease the hurt, knowing she couldn't, that nothing could take away the pain of what Jos Kerral had done to his own daughter. 'Shh, my wench, try not to tek on, that man ain't worth yer tears.'

'No.' Esther pushed away from her arms, decision straightening her shoulders. 'That man is not worth any woman's tears.' She passed a finger over her cheek below her eyes and looked at the film of moisture that clung to it. 'And I vow before God these are the last I will ever shed on his account.'

'We could go for a turn in the gardens? It's a lovely day.' Miriam rose to her feet, a cold worm of fear nibbling at her insides as it did more and more often these days while watching Esther's disappointment turn to resentment, and resentment to cold, challenging anger.

'Yes.' Esther dried her finger on her handkerchief. 'A stroll in the garden would be nice, Miri.'

'I'll just wash these few crocks first.' She turned thankfully back to her task of clearing away the remains of their meal, yet even as she wheeled everything into the kitchen instinct told her there was trouble in the air. Esther had appeared calm at her suggestion of a stroll but Miri knew better. Rejected and despised for all these years, the girl was close to breaking point.

Left alone in the dining room, Esther stared at the row of conifers standing like a line of green-uniformed dragons, guarding the house she was not allowed to enter, the house where she was born, the house her father had lived in for sixteen years without once seeing his daughter. The last time she had seen him she had been four years old. It took no effort for her to look back over the years to the day her mother had died.

Despite the sunlight tumbling in through tall windows, the house had seemed dark for days. She remembered asking so many times to see her mother but each time she had been shushed by her nurse and told her mama was sleeping. Then had come that afternoon. She had woken from her nap to find the nursery empty, her nurse nowhere to be seen. At first she had played with ... yes, with large gaily painted wooden blocks, placing one on another until the line had fallen, sending one tumbling across the floor towards the open door. Her mama was through that door, her child's mind had told her as she went to retrieve the block, she would go to see her. The fact that she met no maid as she made her way along the curved corridor that led to her mother's bedroom held no significance for her four-year-old mind. She had been a few feet away from the door when it had opened and her father had stumbled out, a hand held across his eyes.

'Papa.'

She had laughed up at him, her high piping voice echoing through the stillness of the house, and he had dropped his hand and turned towards her.

'That *thing*!' His voice had been evil in its low intensity, his face twisted with disgust as he watched her drag herself along on her bottom, her useless left leg trailing behind her. 'That thing killed my wife!' Suddenly he lunged forward, his booted foot kicking viciously at her legs and back. 'That thing killed my wife ... that thing killed my wife ...'

'Mr Kerral, stop!' A woman in a white apron over a blue dress, a white cap standing high on her head, had run out of Mama's bedroom, catching at Papa's arm, trying to pull him away. But the foot had gone on kicking her until Miri had come flying along the corridor and scooped her into her arms, running with her back to the nursery, locking the door behind them. And all the time his frenzied shouts had followed: 'That thing killed my wife ... that thing killed my wife!'

That had been the last time Esther had set eyes on her father or he on her. She had been brought here to this house with only Miri to care for her, and here they had both stayed. It was only recently that she had learned the reason for her mother's death. The doctors, it seemed, had diagnosed a malaise caused by her child's crippled condition but Miri had declared that Mama had died from the consumption she was already suffering from on her marriage. Those doctors had been wrong, Miri said. The same doctors who had said Esther would never walk.

He had made sufficient allowance for the running of the house he had banished her to, that father of hers. Esther smiled coldly. Henry VIII had made allowances for the household of his daughters, Mary and the young Elizabeth, but that had not made them feel any more secure. They had suffered their father's rejection as she had suffered hers; they had waited for the knock on the door as she waited; they had longed to be sent for, to be told of the love their father held for them, as she had, and they, like her, had wept long hours when that call did not come. But she would weep no more, she had cried her last for Josiah Kerral.

There had been no questions about her well-being, as there had been none regarding Miri's household expenditure. Any extra items, such as the adult-sized bath chair Miri had requested when the one Esther had used for years finally became too small, were met immediately and Miri had managed to talk him into setting aside a tidy sum for Esther; she had dreaded the possibility of his remarrying and having other children and his first child being abandoned completely. The money had accumulated under the guidance of the owner of Long's Bank, until now she was fairly wealthy in her own right. No, her father had not denied Esther money, only his love.

She had been given to Miri lock, stock and barrel, and Miri had loved her as her own child. That love had been doubled when Miri had married a school master who taught the children of the town in St Peter's Church of England school on the green,

13

whenever the local families could pay the threepence a week it cost to send them there, or when the 'whipper in' could catch them playing truant – which it seemed was not often. Playing away was a skill nurtured by every worker's child in Darlaston and one that regularly defeated the school board man.

John Butler had taught Esther too, sitting at the table in the evening after supper, gently explaining when things seemed beyond her understanding, going again and again over a mathematical problem that threatened to defeat her until at last she defeated it; but mathematics and book learning had not been all he had taught her. He had taught her to use her brain to look logically at a problem, to search for its cause as well as its cure, and she had soaked up his teaching like a sponge soaks up water.

The only thing he could not teach her was how to walk, how to make her useless leg obey her, but he had refused to let it wither like a rotting tree branch. Every morning and every evening he had massaged her leg, matching the movements of his hands to little rhymes he'd made up to sing as he rubbed the wasted muscles.

> '*I have finished with books,*
> *With slate and with chalk,*
> *Now with Esther and Miri*
> *I'll go for a walk . . .*'

Esther's lips moved to the remembered words of her favourite rhyme, one she'd sung so often with John:

> *Swing your leg high,*
> *Swing your leg low,*
> *Just one more swing and off we will go.*
> *Off through the garden,*
> *Down to the brook.*
> *I like that much better*
> *Than reading a book.*

14

John Butler. Esther looked away across the garden to where the green-clothed conifers halted her gaze. He had loved her, had been the father that man in Rowena House had never been, and John Butler had taught her more than he knew. He had taught her how to take revenge, and some day she knew with certainty, some day the opportunity would come for her to use that learning. Some day her father would pay for the pain he had caused her.

Chapter Two

Ezra Cosmore watched the carriage drive up to the house. He had waited for Jos Kerral to make a move. It wouldn't do to appear anxious for his son to marry the Kerral wench. That might cause the cat to smell a rat. No, better to let the overtures be made from the opposite side of the stage, let Kerral come to him with the proposals. After all, his child was the cripple. He was the one who would be hard put to find a match.

'Mr Josiah Kerral, sir.'

'Ah, Jos, 'ow bin you?' Ezra nodded a dismissal to his man, extending his hand to the caller.

'I'm well, Cosmore, well enough.' Jos shook his hand then took the chair he was offered.

'Glad to 'ear it.' Ezra held a decanter of brandy questioningly in the air. 'And your daughter?'

'Well enough.'

Liar, thought Ezra, pouring two hefty measures of brandy into a pair of lead crystal tumblers and handing one to Kerral. I'll bet you don't bloody know if the wench be well or not, and you care even less. 'To yer continuin' good 'ealth,' he said aloud, raising his own glass in salute.

Taking a mouthful of brandy, Josiah swallowed it then set the glass aside. 'I won't go all round the Wrekin, Cosmore, I'm here to talk about thy lad marryin' my girl an' I want the details settled now!'

'Details?' Ezra regarded him through wary eyes.

'Arrh, details. You know an' I know this weddin' won't tek place wi'out the wheels well greased. You won't be lettin' yer lad tek on a wife wi'out summat comes wi' 'er, so let's get that summat sorted out.'

Ezra took a pull from his tumbler, rolling the liquid around his mouth while appearing to think. 'I can't say as 'ow 'e would like me talkin' for 'im,' he said, swallowing the raw spirit.

'That's shit an' you knows it, Cosmore,' Jos said, an echo of the anger he felt at having to ask a man to marry his daughter showing through his words. If only she hadn't been born a bloody cripple . . . if only she hadn't been born at all. 'An' I don't deal in it. We both know it'll be yer word that is followed in the end, yer son'll do as you tell 'im, so let's 'ave no more about 'im talkin' for 'isself. I'm 'ere to find out what you 'ave in mind.'

What I have in mind is all you've got, Ezra thought, watching the anger burn in the other man's eyes. Aloud he said, 'We must both see the young 'uns all right.'

'How all right?' Josiah waited. Ezra Cosmore would want more than to see his son 'all right' as he put it; he would want a great deal more.

'I thought as 'ow when my son weds I would sign my business over to 'im. 'E would be the master of it an' the profit would be 'is. An' o' course it goes wi'out sayin' that 'e an' is'n would live in this 'ouse along o' me.'

'And you think I should make over my own business the same way?'

Ezra sucked more of the spirit into his mouth, swishing it through his teeth. 'I ain't sayin' any such.' He allowed the liquid to trickle down his throat. 'I can't tell a man what to do wi' what 'e owns.'

'No, you can't.' Josiah watched as the glass was refilled, his own remaining untouched. He knew the ways of Ezra Cosmore. He had watched the man build up his nut and bolt works from a tumble-down shed, had watched him cheat and steal from any who would let him, but he wouldn't cheat

Josiah Kerral. 'It'll be a long day before another man gets all that belongs to me.'

'Yer daughter belongs to you,' Ezra eyed him over the rim of his tumbler, 'an' if you expects a man to tek a cripple off yer 'ands, then you 'ave to be prepared to pay for it.'

Josiah's fingers curled into his palms as he pushed back the anger that sat in his throat like a hard ball. 'She will come with a fair settlement. The man that teks her won't lose by it.'

'Maybe not, unless you counts the drag a crippled wife can place on a man's social life. Then there be a family to consider. Who's to say 'er might not be able to 'ave children, Jos? Think of the effect of that. A man workin' all 'is life to build up a respectable livin', only to 'ave no child of 'is own to pass it on to.'

'That is a risk that comes wi' all marriages, yers and mine included. Women don't come with a guarantee of fertility pinned to their bodice.'

'True, Jos, true.' Ezra held his tumbler to the light, watching it glint on the amber liquid. 'But wi' some the risk be stronger than wi' others.'

'An' it'll tek my business to alleviate that risk?'

'It could go a long way towards it.'

The curve of Josiah's mouth could have been called a smile but Ezra had seen it before when the man had been crossed or pushed too far; he had seen it and now he recognised it for a snarl. 'You will find it easier to catch a cold in 'ell than to get yer 'ands on what's mine.'

Now Ezra smiled, eyes almost swamped by fat. 'That could also apply to yer gettin' a 'usband for that wench o' yern. Think on it, Jos. Lads won't exactly be kickin' yer door in, I'll be bound. 'Ow many 'ave asked for 'er, eh? 'Ow many?'

'Your lad be the first,' Josiah admitted. It would do no good to lie. Darlaston was a small town and Ezra Cosmore's influence reached every part of it one way or another.

'The first, you say, Josiah?' Ezra drained his brandy. 'Wouldn't it be more accurate to say the only one?'

'See here, Cosmore.' Josiah's anger mounted dangerously. 'We 'ave beat about the bush long enough. Either you say what is satisfactory to you to let this marriage go ahead or I'll tell you good day now.'

Placing his empty glass on an ornate sofa table, Ezra eyed his fellow industrialist. Josiah Kerral had started out as he himself had, without two halfpennies for a penny, working every hour God sent to build up his copper and brass foundry out near James Bridge then branching into axles and wheels for the building of new-fangled motors. He should be worth a copper or two now, and a few of them coppers were destined to pull Cosmore Nut and Bolt out of the mire. 'Well now, Josiah.' Ezra leaned forward in his chair. 'I'll tell you what be acceptable to me . . . mind, that isn't to say my son will find it so but it will sugar the pill as they say. I will settle all of my business on my lad if you settle half of yers on yer daughter. All of mine to only half of yer'n – that be more than fair.'

'As you say, Cosmore, more than fair.' Josiah got to his feet. 'More than fair on *yer* side. Half of my business would swallow yer'n an' leave no trace. I'll bid you good day.'

'The master said to tell you 'e wants to see you.'

'What for?' Miri looked at the young man, breeches tucked into gaiters that smelled of the stables.

''Ow should I know?' he answered her question with one of his own.

''E ain't never sent for me afore.'

The lad grinned, showing a gap between his two front teeth. 'I don't know about that, missis, but 'e be sendin' for you now right enough.'

'Did 'e tell you 'isself? To come 'ere an' tell me to go see 'im?' Miri was still uncertain of the message she had just been given.

'Not 'isself 'e didn't.' The stable boy stared around him at the bright kitchen with its plate-laden dresser and well-polished range. 'It were Evans – 'e be the butler, like – well, it was 'im told me to bring that message. An' 'e wouldn't 'ave said if'n the master 'adn't asked 'im to, would 'e?'

'No, no, o' course 'e wouldn't.'

'Well then, I've told you so I'd best be gettin' back. Shall I tell Mr Evans you will be callin'?'

'Yes.' Miri nodded, still bemused by the suddenness of the summons.

'Best mek it quick, missis,' the lad added, his grin fading. 'If old Kerral says a thing is to be, it 'as to be done fast. 'E don't tek kindly to bein' kept waitin'. Is'n ain't the easiest o' tempers.'

Miri could have told him she was well aware of the trend Josiah Kerral's temper could take but instead she merely nodded, watching the lad sprint towards the screen of trees that kept a daughter's life separate from that of her father. What did he want? She continued to stare in the direction of the conifers. Not once in sixteen years, and not often in the four that went before, had he enquired after the child born to his wife in the first year of her coming to Rowena House.

Jos Kerral was well on his way by then, his works thriving and thirty or more men labouring in them. Not for him a Darlaston wench. He was going up in the world and his marriage was intended to reflect that. But things had soon turned sour for Jos Kerral; the smoke-grimed air of the Black Country town had not suited his wife, coming as she did from the fields of Worcester, and soon after their child was born she had taken to her bed with consumption, and from that day he had blamed a helpless child. So why now? For it would be of the girl he would be wanting to know, Miri well knew. Questions mingling with her memories she turned back to her tasks in the kitchen. She would go to the house, but what would she do if he ordered his daughter to return?

'Where did you say you were going?'

Miri set the tea tray she had prepared beside Esther then poured out a cup, handing it to the girl. 'Across to

21

the 'ouse. I 'ad a message sayin' as I be wanted over there.'

Esther set her cup down sharply, making it rattle in its saucer. 'You are wanted at Rowena House? For what?'

'Lad didn't say.'

'Who has sent for you, Miri? Is it my father?'

'Can't be nobody else. That stable lad said as Mr Evans sent 'im across 'ere wi' the message, but stands to reason it can't 'ave bin nobody else tellin' me I was to call 'ceptin' yer father.'

Esther stared unseeing at the roses bobbing beyond the sitting-room window. Why now, after all these years? What had aroused an interest her father had never shown before? What were his intentions towards her, for it was a certainty the reason for his seeing Miri involved herself? She had been unable to speak for herself all those years ago when he had banned her from his home and his life, but things were different now. Esther Kerral was no longer four years old. She had lain awake at night planning what she would say, what she would do, should the opportunity to come face to face with her father ever arise. And now it had! Steeling herself for argument, she looked steadily at Miri. 'I am coming with you,' she said.

'You be what?' Miri looked up from pouring her own tea.

Esther kept her air of calm resolution. 'I am coming with you.'

Letting the teapot almost fall back on to the tray, Miri stared at the girl, seeing her lovely face tauten with determination. It would be madness to let her go to Rowena House, to bring her face to face with a man who despised her, who had done his best to eradicate her from his life. To bring them together now would only encourage trouble, for Esther had inherited his stubbornness, the same strength of will. She would not be so easily written off a second time. 'I don't think that be a good idea,' said Miri.

'Good or not, I intend to come.'

'But, Essie,' Miri employed the name she had used since Esther's baby days, 'we don't know what 'e wants.'

'What better way to find out than to ask?'

'Then let me be the one does the askin'.'

'No, Miri.' Esther shook her head. 'This time I intend to speak for myself.'

'But it be me 'e 'as asked to see,' Miri protested. ''E won't tek kindly to anybody else bargin' in.'

'You mean he will not take kindly to his crippled daughter having the temerity to show her face in his house? Then I am afraid he will have to take to it unkindly for I am going to see him, Miri.'

'Ee, Essie, me wench, you don't know 'im. You don't know what 'e be like when 'e's angered.'

Esther smiled but her brown eyes were empty. 'Then I am about to add to my education.'

'Esther,' Miriam sat down heavily, fear obvious in her face, 'think what you be about. For sixteen years I've done my best to keep you from his sight, thinkin' that be the best way to protect you, and my John agreed wi' me. For you to go to 'im now might undo all we've done. It can only provoke 'im, then God alone knows what 'e might do.'

Leaning forward, Esther touched a hand to that of the woman who had spent her life caring for her. 'You have always done what you saw as being in my best interests, Miri, you and John. But is it still in my best interests to go on hiding me away as though I were some cancerous sore? The two of you gave me love where my father gave me none. You gave me knowledge and guidance. Now I ask you to give me understanding. Facing my father is something I have to do if I am to have any self-respect. John would have understood that. He taught me that turning my back on a problem was no way to solve it, and the problem that exists between me and my father must be resolved if I am ever to have any sort of life.'

'I know 'ow you feel, me wench.' Miri's face reflected the

pity she felt for the girl whose life was bound to a wheelchair. 'But is this the right time? You go tacklin' 'im now an' we might both end up on the street.'

'Is there ever a right time?' Esther asked. 'And as for us finishing up on the streets, it might be all to the good. Let everyone in Darlaston know Jos Kerral has a crippled daughter.'

Miri took Esther's hand in both of hers, the fear in her eyes potent. 'Ee, me wench, I 'ope you knows what you be doin'. If only John was livin' . . .'

'It will be all right, Miri.' Esther smiled, and this time her expression was tinged with love. 'John taught me well, I know what I must do. Now, if you will get my shawl we will go to Rowena House. Oh, and Miri, you will tell my father nothing! Promise me?'

'I promise.' Miri stood up. ''E will learn nothing from me.'

'What did he offer?' Morgan Cosmore helped himself to bacon and devilled kidneys from the dishes on the sideboard. 'What did Kerral offer for me to act as stallion to his cripple?'

''E ain't exactly med no offer.' Ezra tucked into his breakfast. His son had delayed leaving for the pleasures of London on hearing of Kerral's visit; getting him to delay further depended on how convincing Ezra could make the next few minutes.

'Made no offer!' Morgan's plate hit the polished mahogany of the dining table with a thump. 'But you said . . .'

'I knows what I said,' Ezra cut in, 'an' I meant it. Jos Kerral will mek over half 'is interests to you on marriage to that wench o' is'n.'

'That's what *you* say.' Morgan glanced scathingly at the heavily jowled face of his father.

'Arrh, that is what I bloody say,' Ezra scowled, 'an' it will be that way. But we 'ave to play patient. Rushin' a fence can ruin the jump. Just give Kerral 'is 'ead an' we'll 'ave 'im clear over the top afore 'e knows 'e's left the ground.'

'And the purse for the rider?' Morgan looked up from

his plate. 'It's the guineas as well as the laurels, is it, Father?'

'O' course.' Ezra swallowed coffee that was half brandy. 'You won't go short in the cash stakes.'

'How much?' Morgan asked bluntly. 'How much for riding a crippled mount?'

''Alf of Kerral's engineering business.' Ezra swallowed the remaining heavily laced coffee and signed for his cup to be refilled from the tall silver pot placed beside him on the table. 'An' a cash settlement on the side.'

'What sort of cash are we talking?' Morgan asked, first swallowing a mouthful of kidney.

Ezra's eyes folded away behind a screen of flesh. How much would this work-shy, self-centred bastard of a son settle for? ''E talked of a thousand a year.' It was a lie but Ezra was gambling on its being swallowed. If Cosmore Nut and Bolt was to survive he had to have Jos Kerral's money.

'Not enough!' Morgan lifted a forkful of bacon to his mouth.

'Not e-bloody-nough!' Ezra adopted a tone of astonishment. 'Not enough! A thousand a year for sittin' on yer arse an' you tell me it ain't enough?'

'You have that wrong, Father.' Morgan touched his lips precisely with a perfectly laundered napkin, his movements calculated to annoy. 'The money will not be payment for sitting on my arse but rather for lying on my face. That is the more usual way of servicing a woman, though not the most stimulating. And in this case there will be little enough of stimulation, don't you agree?'

'No, I bloody don't agree!' Ezra's hold on his temper began to slip.

'Really?' Morgan folded his napkin, keeping his movements deliberately controlled, knowing they would serve to send his father's temper through the roof. 'Perhaps you know something I do not? Tell me . . . how well *do* you know Kerral's daughter?'

25

Ezra held the coffee cup to his mouth, the fumes of hot brandy wafting to his nostrils. He supposed there must once have been some sort of affection between him and the man sitting alongside him, but if there had been it had long since died. Were it not for the fact that he needed Kerral's money, he would tell this son of his to bugger off back to London and stay there. Darlaston might be a blot on the map but it would be altogether better off without him. 'You keep that kind o' shit between yer teeth or . . .'

'Now, now, Father.' Morgan flapped the folded napkin. 'No more threats, please, they don't frighten me any more.'

'No!' Ezra's face purpled as he fought to hold on to his sliding temper. 'But this should. Last month seen off the last of the money I 'ave, an' that means the last of what you can expect. The 'ands at the works will be laid off come Friday wi' bugger all of the wages owed to 'em, an' that won't be no party you would like an invite to. If I knows anythin' about that lot they be like to set the place alight then come 'ere an' do the same to this 'ouse, so if I was you I would forget tryin' to force Kerral to up 'is offer an' tek what you can while the tekin' be good for you.'

'Or for you.' Morgan added sugar and cream to his own brandy-free coffee, spoon tinkling against the china as he stirred. 'That is what you really mean, isn't it, Father? Take what is on offer from Kerral for *your* good, for without that man's money Ezra Cosmore is finished.'

'Arrh, I'm bloody finished,' Ezra roared, smashing his cup into its saucer, sending fragments of china flying like wind-blown spume across the polished surface of the table. 'But what 'appens to me 'appens to you, you'd best remember that. I finish up on the shit pile an' you'll be alongside me, listenin' to the same blue-arsed flies buzzin' round yer 'ead, each of us squealin' for money we ain't got.'

'Not we, Father.' Morgan reached for a toothpick from the silver container placed between them. 'My name, I am certain, will appear nowhere on the deeds for anything you possess, you will have made sure of that. It is true I will have nothing, and that will include taking no responsibility for your debts. So you see, Father, you can no longer gain advantage from using threats.'

He was playing near the edge and it would almost be worth losing to see his father go under, but almost was not quite. He wanted to see Ezra get his comeuppance but if his father failed in this latest venture, then Morgan's allowance failed too, and though it galled him to admit it, his friends in London would no longer be so friendly if he was poor.

'So what do I tell Jos Kerral?' Ezra's fist followed the cup, hitting the table hard. 'That you won't tek 'is wench, you won't marry 'is daughter?'

That was what Morgan wanted to say. He wanted to tell Kerral to use his money to buy some other stud, but to do so would be cutting his own throat; a thousand a year was far below the sum he had hoped to acquire on marrying any woman, the only drawback to his plan being that no other offer had been made. As yet it seemed no family was desperate enough to ally themselves with the Cosmores – and that, if he worked it right, could be his winning card. If Kerral had contacted his father with a view to arranging a marriage then Kerral had obviously reached the stage of desperation, and that in its turn meant he, Morgan, might be able to dictate the financial terms of the situation. He told himself he'd settle for twice what was currently on offer. Placing the napkin beside his plate he stared at it for a moment then looked up to see his father's eyes fixed on his face. 'You can tell Kerral that if he wants to buy a husband for his cripple it will cost half his business plus an allowance of two thousand pounds a year.'

'Two . . . two thousand!' Ezra spluttered, freckling plate and napkin with brown spots of coffee. 'Am you bloody mad? 'E'll never pay that.'

'How do you know if you never put it to him?'

'It's nothin' but a waste o' bloody time even thinkin' on

such a thing. Two thousand a year? Kerral will never stand for that.'

'Depends on who else he has asked, how many refusals he has been given.'

'I don't know as 'e 'as asked anybody else,' Ezra mused. 'If 'e 'ad approached anybody in Darlaston, or Wednesbury for that matter, I would 'ave got wind of it an' I ain't, not a breath.'

'Then perhaps we are not just the first to be propositioned, perhaps we will be the only ones?' Morgan smiled. 'Maybe ours is the only family Kerral is prepared to ally his daughter with. Now there is something I never thought to see.'

'What?' Ezra looked bemused. 'What is summat you never thought to see?'

'You and me, Father,' Morgan's smile gave way to a laugh, 'you and me selected above the rest.' He laughed again, the noise of it ringing off the panelled walls. 'How does it feel? How does it feel to be one of the chosen people?'

Chapter Three

Esther watched the walls of Rowena House emerge from behind their screen of trees. Though built less than thirty years ago its red-brick walls held a quiet, established beauty. Lifting her eyes to the second floor, she sought the stone-lined window to the west of the house. That would be the nursery, the place Miri had described to her so many times she felt she knew every corner of it.

'We best go round the back,' Miri puffed, the effort of pushing the heavy wooden wheelchair taking her breath.

'Why?' Esther turned her head sideways, trying to look at the woman who had carried her from this house sixteen years before.

'Well, we can't very well go marchin' up to the front, can we?' Miri wiped a hand across her brow, standing still to regain her failing breath.

'No,' Esther agreed, 'we cannot go marching in, at least I cannot. But march or crawl, we do not enter by the back door.'

'But if 'e should 'ave callers . . .' Caution lowered Miri's voice to little more than a whisper.

'If he has callers then they will meet his daughter.' Esther turned her head to look again at the house. 'It is about time some of them did.'

'I don't know.' Still Miri hesitated.

'I do,' Esther said quietly. 'He said to come and we have, but we will not skulk in the back way for fear of being seen.'

'He said for me to come,' Miri reminded her.

Esther continued to stare at the house. What had her mother been like? She had tried so often to peer down the dark corridors of memory but had remembered only a mass of dark hair on a white pillow and heard only a tired whisper that might have been 'I love you' though she could not be sure. But the memory of that night had stayed with her, its clarity never failing, its pain never fading – the memory of her father's voice calling her 'that thing', the memory of his kicks thudding into her body. 'Yes, he said for you to come.' Lowering her gaze, she fastened it on the studded oak of the front doorway. 'But it will be me he will discuss and this time I am old enough to hear for myself what it is my father holds in store for me. And this time I can speak for myself.'

'Essie!' Miri's voice sharpened. 'Now don't you go sayin' anythin' to upset 'im. Let's just hear what 'e 'as to say an' then leave. We don't want no argy-bargy.'

'Argument is the last thing I want, Miri,' Esther said calmly. 'I have no intention of upsetting anyone, any more than I have any intention of living a lie – the lie of my non-existence. This is my coming out whether my father likes it or not.'

Miri held the bar attached to the back of the wheelchair, throwing her weight against it to set the wheels once more in motion. 'I can tell you now,' she said, ''e won't like it, 'e won't like it at all, an' what's more 'e won't allow it.'

We will see, Esther thought, watching the gracious house draw nearer. We will see what my father will allow. Maybe it will be more than he thinks.

Reaching the house, Miri leaned for a moment against the chair, catching her breath, feeling the effort of pushing it across the rough grassland from their own house to this. 'I . . . I still think we should go round the back,' she said, the breath catching in her lungs. 'It . . . it would be less . . .'

'Obvious,' Esther finished the sentence, her mouth clamping shut on the word. 'My father would like that,' she added, 'the less obvious it is he has a daughter who cannot walk, the more at ease he feels. But that ease will not be his for very much longer. He is going to face the world and I will be at his side. I want to see him explain the last sixteen years.'

'You don't know what you be doin' . . .' Miri tried one more warning.

Esther stared at the heavy door. Behind it was the man who had kicked a four-year-old child into semi-consciousness then turned her out of her home, shutting her away in a separate house, a separate life. But now their two lives were about to merge once more. 'Maybe I do not yet know how I am to do it, Miri,' she said, 'but I do know what it is I intend to do and I will not begin by entering my father's house through the back door.'

'Well, I can't push you up there.' Miri nodded towards the freshly whitened steps leading to the door. 'An' you ain't a child I can carry no more.'

'He has men servants,' Esther said. 'Ring the bell and they will help me in.'

''E don't 'ave so many o' them no more,' Miri answered, trying to work out how to walk up the flight of three steps without setting foot on the sacred white surface. 'I've 'eard it said in the town as 'is business ain't what it was. There's even talk among the men of 'is packin' it in altogether, gettin' rid of the bit 'e's got left if 'e can find a bloke to buy it off 'im an' clearin' out – though I can't see any fool doin' that. Seems there ain't the call there once was for wheels and axles.'

'Perhaps I am to be part of the clearing out? Perhaps Josiah Kerral is about to rid himself of his daughter as well as his business?' Esther said, watching Miri dance a hesitation waltz on the first step. 'But unless you ring that bell we are not likely to find out.'

Lifting her dark skirts, Miri tiptoed to the door and after pulling the metal hoop that set a bell jangling inside the house, tiptoed down again, setting her feet in exactly the same places. Moments later the heavy door swung inward.

'Mr Kerral said to come,' she explained as the figure of the butler emerged. 'You sent a lad across, Mr Evans.'

'I did, Mrs Butler.' The years undermining his height with a stoop, the grey-haired man looked at the girl in the wheelchair. 'But I believe the message said for you to come, it did not include anyone else.'

'You mean it did not include his daughter?' Esther said, her head lifting defiantly. 'Why not say what you mean?'

'Very well, miss.' The grey head dipped but the movement was so slight as to be almost imperceptible. 'I have no wish to appear disrespectful but the master's message did not include you. However, I will tell him you are here.'

'No, Evans, you will not tell him I am here.' Esther's voice held a note of authority, as if she had been used to giving this man instructions all her life. 'You will kindly call the men to assist me inside.'

'But . . .' He hesitated, unsure how to react to a girl who held no place in this house yet was still the daughter of its master. 'I don't think . . .'

'I have not asked you to think,' Esther went on, her tone still hard with authority, 'I have asked you to call the men to assist me in entering this house. Do it, Evans. *Now*, please.'

'Yes, miss.' Glancing once more from her to Miri, he turned back into the house.

'Ee, I never thought to see old Evans tek orders from nobody but Jos Kerral,' Miri said with a laugh. 'An' I bet 'e didn't neither.'

Esther smiled but there was no humour in it. 'I think Mr Evans will shortly be seeing quite a few things he had never thought to see.' She stopped as the lad who had called earlier rounded the corner of the house, followed by a taller man, older by five or six years, followed in turn by Evans.

'We'll soon 'ave that there chair up the steps, miss.' The youngest of the three grinned, grabbing a wheel of the chair with one hand and the pushing bar with the other, waiting for the other man to do the same.

'There'll be no need for that.' The taller man looked at Esther but there was no pity for her condition in his grey eyes. 'If you will allow me, miss?'

Bending, he lifted her from the chair, no sense of strain in the movement, then carried her up the steps. He held her there until Evans and the lad had brought the wheelchair.

'There you go.' Setting her back in the chair, his glance held hers just seconds longer than was necessary, 'Mr Evans will give me a call when you be ready to leave.'

'Thank you.' Esther sought his eyes, smiling when she caught them. 'Thank you, Mr . . .?'

'Paige.' If he knew her relationship to the owner of Rowena House he made no reference to it, there was no trace of deference in his voice. 'Adam Paige.'

'That'll be all, Paige.' Evans stepped in, clearly wanting to be seen to be on a superior level to the younger man. 'You will be called when you be needed.'

Holding Esther's gaze for a moment longer Paige turned, cleared the whitened steps in one bound then walked swiftly away around the corner of the house.

'If you will wait in the drawing room, I will inform the master you are here.' Evans led the way, waiting until Miri had pushed the wheelchair into a long light-filled room fitted with tapestried sofas and deep arm chairs.

'I'd forgot 'ow lovely this room is.' Miri gazed about her at the fine Wedgwood china bowls and the gleaming mahogany tables holding dainty Worcester figurines, but Esther gazed only at the portrait above the ornate fireplace. A young woman gazed back at her, her deep chestnut hair caught in a knot of loose curls framing a small heart-shaped face whose mouth held the essence of a smile but whose bronze-coloured eyes spoke only of sadness.

'Do you know who that is?'

Miri turned her eyes up to the painting. Oh, she knew who that was, the girl with sadness in her eyes and pain in her heart, she knew all right, knew more than Jos Kerral could guess. 'She were beautiful,' she answered softly, 'an' too good for 'im who brought 'er 'ere. That there be Helen Kerral, 'er were yer mother.'

'Helen,' Esther whispered, her eyes on the lovely painted face. 'She was beautiful. I can see why my father went a little mad when she died.'

'Arrh, but not why 'e often went the same way afore 'er died.'

'What do you mean?' Esther tried to twist around to see Miri. 'Was my father given to violence?'

'You can ask that?' she said, her answer clearly revealing her contempt for the man they had come to see. 'You can ask that of a man who would kick a 'elpless child almost to death? Oh, yes, 'e were violent all right, an' always for no reason other than 'is own filthy mind . . .'

'What the bloody 'ell be you doin' 'ere?'

Miri stopped speaking as the question rang out raucously, shocking them with its unexpectedness.

'I sent for you, not for . . .'

'That thing?' Esther had often tried to imagine what her feelings would be should she come face to face with her father, but none of those imaginings had produced the icy calm she was experiencing right now, the complete severing of all emotions, the coldness that left her in control.

'You did not send for me,' she said, holding his angry eyes with a steady gaze, 'but I had no doubt I would be at the centre of your discussion. That being so, I wished to hear for myself what you had to say. If my surmise is incorrect then tell me so and I will leave.'

'Do you mek a 'abit of goin' where you ain't wanted?' Jos Kerral strode into the room, coming to stand beneath the portrait, his back to the fireplace, legs slightly apart, his once handsome face twisted with anger and with something else – something Esther could see but could not name.

'I do not make a habit of going anywhere, but of the places

and homes I have visited yours is the only one where I have been made to feel unwelcome.'

'Then that's because you *am* unwelcome,' he spat. 'You're not wanted in my 'ouse.'

'That hardly needs to be said,' Esther replied, her calmness in complete contrast to the fury shaking the man facing her. 'Every part of you makes that patently obvious, as I knew it would.'

'Then why bloody come 'ere?'

'I have told you, I have come because I want to hear at first hand anything you have to say concerning me.'

'You would 'ave 'eard soon enough.'

'Yes, but I would not have heard it from you.'

'An' that's what you want, is it? To 'ear it from me?'

Esther looked at the man who, were it not for an anger that seemed to be pulling him apart as she watched, would still have been termed handsome. His hair, still thick and plentiful, showed much of the brown of youth through filtering strands of grey, and though some of the colour of his eyes had faded they were still a vivid green. Her eyes lifting momentarily to the portrait above his head, she visualised him as a young man with that beautiful woman at his side.

'Then 'ear it you shall . . .'

His voice eradicating the vision, Esther returned her gaze to his face.

'. . . but we won't need no ear 'olin' from you!' He glared at Miri who had stood silent from his entering the room. 'You can tek yerself outside. I'll call you when y'am wanted.'

Esther pressed the hand Miri dropped protectively on her shoulder. 'It will be all right,' she murmured, 'I doubt this will take very long.'

His eyes following the dark-clad figure, Josiah Kerral waited until the door closed behind Miri. 'So,' he began, after hearing the quiet click that said the door was firmly shut and they were unlikely to be overheard, 'you want to 'ear my intentions for you? Well, I'll tell you – you be goin' to wed Ezra Cosmore's son.'

His words acted like a blow to the head, sending Esther's senses whirling. Marriage! He spoke as though the whole thing were cut and dried, an established fact, rather than a proposition.

'Why?' was all she could ask.

Shifting his weight on his feet, he looked down at the slight figure seated in the wheelchair, his anger giving way to a feeling of elation. She had come here to his house with an air of cocky bravado, a smart answer in her mouth almost before his own words had been said. Well, her answer to the last ones hadn't been so cocky. He had soon knocked that out of her.

'Why?' he answered on a half laugh. ''Cos I say so, that's why.'

The mockery and contempt acted like a restorative on Esther's spinning senses, drawing them back to her. He was enjoying this, enjoying seeing her struggle to make sense of a situation that held none. Drawing a steadying breath, she looked up at him. 'I am afraid that is not a good enough reason.'

'What!' The supercilious smile leaving his mouth, he stared back at her.

Calm once more, her thoughts collected, Esther repeated her words of a moment before. 'I am afraid that is not a good enough reason. I will not marry a man I have never met just because you say so.'

'You'll do as I bloody say!' The words exploded from him.

'No, I will not.' She watched the rage rise in his face once more. 'You have taken no interest in me from the moment I was born so why this sudden flowering? Why have you bothered to find a husband for me? One could hardly describe the action as one of parental love, or even concern, so why?'

'I'll tek no back answerin'.' He kicked out at a small table, sending it crashing to the floor. 'You'll wed Cosmore's son an' that be all about it.'

Esther repressed the memory of those other kicks so long ago, her tone level as she answered: 'And how do you expect to get me to the altar? Kick me there as you kick everything that incurs your displeasure?'

His face, dark with rage, seemed to highlight the colour of his eyes, their greenness holding an almost mesmeric glow as he bent towards her. 'I'll get you there,' he breathed, 'an' it'll be wi'out yer teeth if you backchat me!'

'That will only add to my already monumental drawbacks.' Esther refused to let his anger sap her confidence. Once he thought her defeated he would ride right over her. 'No legs of any use, and teeth the same. I should make for an interesting bride! And speaking of interest, what is that of the Cosmores in all of this?'

'None of yer bloody business!' Disconcerted by her calmness he pulled back. He was unused to being denied in his own house.

'It is every bit my business. What are you paying for their taking a cripple as a wife for their son?'

'Payin'!' He moved to a chair, dropping heavily into it. 'Who said anythin' about payin'? This be a weddin' I be on about.'

'A wedding that will not take place without payment to the groom or his family.' Esther saw a change of expression on his face and knew she was right. He was paying a man to marry her. 'I am crippled in the legs, not the mind. I know you would have to pay a man to take me.'

'All right then.' He banged a tightly clenched fist on the arm of his chair. 'So I'm payin'. 'Ow else would a man tek you?'

'How indeed?' Esther nodded, refusing to let the pain caused by his words strike home. 'How much are you to pay? What is my market value?'

He hadn't expected this. He could argue with a man, that was the way of the world, but to have a woman question and defy him – that was a thing altogether different, a thing he did not often encounter.

'Market value?' He felt around for an answer, knowing the girl watching him would have her own. 'You talk as if you was a cow up for sale.'

'The only difference being I am a woman, not a cow.'

'What way is that for a girl to talk?'

'The straight way,' Esther snapped through tight lips, 'the only way. No matter how you might like to dress the fact up, I am to be sold and I wish to know the price.'

'You wish!' he shouted, his cheeks purpling. '*You* wish! An' who the bloody 'ell do you think you am to be wishin' anythin'?'

Esther smiled coldly. 'It seems I am the answer to a problem you can see no other way of solving.'

'Oh, arrh.' He glared back, the sting of her words touching upon the truth smarting like an open wound. 'An' what problem might that be?'

'Well, it is not consideration for my future, is it? And from the look of this house it ought not to be money, but it is safer never to set too much store by what you see so perhaps it *is* money?' She paused, waiting for a volcanic eruption of temper, but when he made no answer continued, 'Is your business in financial difficulties? Am I to be the crab to catch an apple? Will the shilling you hand the Cosmores for taking your cripple turn into a pound in your pocket? Is that the reason for this proposed marriage?'

'Mind yer own bloody business.'

'I am minding it.' Esther recognised the tone that told her she had struck home. 'And unless I get the answers I want there will be no wedding and that most probably will provide an answer of its own.'

'Are you tellin' me you won't marry Cosmore?'

'I am telling you I want to know the reason for my doing so.'

His fingers curling into a fist where they lay along the arm of the chair, Josiah's glance flickered from the face of the girl in the wheelchair to that of the woman in the portrait and back again. They looked alike, mother and daughter, but there any resemblance ended. His wife had never dared defy him so where did her child get this streak of stubbornness?

'You'll know only what I want you to know,' he ground out between clenched teeth. 'An' that be that you'll wed wi' Cosmore's son, an' that afore the month be out.'

Esther shook her head. 'Again I tell you, I will not. Oh, there is no doubt you can carry me to the altar but even you must recognise you cannot force the words from my mouth. Now, as you would say to any business colleague, we have gone all round the Wrekin so let's not waste any more time. You tell me what I want to know or else call Miri so I can leave.'

His fists beating a tattoo on the chair, Josiah stared at her, the venom of years rising in his throat. This thing had been saddled on him, this cripple had taken his wife, and now she was here again, reminding him of the pain of yesterday, confronting him with the face of Helen.

'I don't 'ave to tell you anythin'!'

'If you want a union with the Cosmores you do.' Esther ignored his drumming fists. 'You have called the tune long enough, now it is time to dance to your own music.'

'Right, you asked an' now you be gettin'.' He smiled but the effect was more that of a snarl from an animal that knew itself cornered. 'I need money. The axle and wheel trade ain't what it was. Cosmore 'as money. If I can cod 'im into believin' 'e's gettin' more for 'is son weddin' you than 'e really is, my worries will be over. I get you married into that family an' they won't let my business go up the Swannee. They'll propose a merger.'

'With you at the head?'

'Arrh.' Josiah nodded. 'I be a better 'and at business than Ezra Cosmore ever knowed 'ow to be, an' from what I be told 'is son ain't got no likin' for matters concernin' work.'

'So you are the better businessman?' Esther's mouth showed

no inclination to relax its harsh set. 'Then why is it your business is in danger of collapsing? So much so you are ready to sell your own flesh and blood to redeem it.'

'Why, you bloody . . .' One fist shot out, halting inches from her face.

'Go on.' Esther's voice was unwavering though her fingers wove together as the fist hesitated. 'Or perhaps you prefer to use your foot as you did sixteen years ago?'

'Damn you!' He withdrew his hand, clenching it once more about the arm of his chair. 'I should 'ave 'ad you put away.'

'Isn't that what you did?' she asked, the knot of her fingers remaining fast. 'You had me taken from this house the night my mother died and put into one hidden away in the grounds, and not once in all that time did you send for me or come to me. For all you cared I could have been dead. How often you must have prayed I soon would be.'

'Arrh, I prayed for that all right,' he rounded on her viciously. 'Every night wi'out fail I prayed you would die as yer mother 'ad died, but my prayers went unheeded. You lived, you with yer crippled limbs . . .'

'And why are they crippled?' she flashed, anger shredding her assumed calm. 'Tell me that? Was it fate or judgement? I had committed no crime, but what of you? "The sins of the fathers", isn't that what the Book says? Just what sin was it that resulted in my being born crippled?'

His anger fading to a dangerous calm, Josiah regarded the face of this girl – a face that regularly called him out of sleep, a face whose every line would be with him till the day he died.

'I should 'ave 'ad you put away,' he said, his eyes locked on hers, 'but I was too bloody stupid. I kept you out of charity.'

'You kept me out of guilt,' she flashed back. 'Guilt that because of you my mother was dead.'

'*You* killed yer mother.' His voice was a whiplash, cutting deep with every word. 'You wi' yer legs all crippled up inside o' 'er.'

'It was you put me there.' Her words were hurled at him like stones. 'Deny that if you will, but you know the truth of it.'

'That much is true.' For a moment the hatred in him seemed to flag and his shoulders drooped, then his head came up and he was fighting again. 'But it was you killed 'er all the same. The shock of 'earin' you would never walk was too much for 'er. Would to God you 'ad died in the womb!'

Esther's breath caught in her throat. How could any man wish such for a child he had fathered? How could this one dislike her so much as never to give her the chance to be a daughter to him, to let her love assuage a little of the pain of losing a wife?

'But I didn't die in the womb.' Her words came out softly, floating on a slowly released breath, one that seemed to carry the very soul from her body. 'I survived – survived so that ultimately you could survive.'

'An' what the 'ell is that supposed to mean?'

'It means that unless I agree to marry Cosmore's son, you will be nothing in this town. You will go under – everything you once owned, everything that made Josiah Kerral a name to be reckoned with, will have gone. *That* is what I mean by survival.'

Temper and frustration etched on his face, he glared at her. 'You ain't of age yet. I could still 'ave you put away. It ain't too late.'

'I fear it is for you.' The softness of her words seemed to add to the threat they held. 'And we both know it.'

Chapter Four

'Here you are.' Adam Paige halted the wheelchair at the door of Esther's home. 'Will I take you in?'

'Thank you.' She smiled up at the clear-cut handsome features of her father's employee. 'But it's not necessary. John made most of this house easily accessible for a wheelchair. It was kind of you to come so far. I'm afraid it is a little too much now for Miri to push me any distance.'

'I can still push you,' Miri said, 'but that don't mean I ain't grateful, lad. It was a bit of a effort goin' over the open ground – wouldn't 'ave bin so 'ard 'ad there bin a path up to the 'ouse.'

'Any time.' The smile Adam gave Esther was more than mere politeness. 'If you want to go anywhere you have only to get word to me.'

'I wouldn't dream of imposing upon you.' She returned the smile, aware of a sensation new to her agitating her stomach.

'You wouldn't be imposing,' he said, his words so obviously directed at her that Miri might not have been there at all. 'And as for dreams, what would life be without them?'

'A lot nearer reality,' Esther said, her hands going to the wheels of her chair.

'Maybe so.' He nodded. 'But a lot less rich. Dreams are the wealth of the poor; take them away and you add to their poverty, reality is always with them, the dream just makes it easier to bear.'

'Well, me wench, let's get you inside.' Having opened the door, Miri bustled the young man aside, taking charge of Esther's chair and shutting the door behind them.

Untying her bonnet, Esther handed it to Miri. 'Adam Paige seems very kind. Is he a local man?'

'Eh?' Miri was already busy at the hearth, stoking the fire and placing the black-bottomed kettle over its red glow. 'Oh, arrh, a real nice lad. 'Is folks live over by Rough Hay, up against Katherine's Cross – mother's a little body an' the father works drawin' copper rods over at James Bridge, an' that ain't easy work bein' at them furnaces all day. I've 'eard John say they've bin too close to the crucible when the 'ot metal 'as bin tipped.'

'Darlaston is not an easy place,' Esther said, staring at the glow of the fire.

'It ain't that,' Miri agreed. 'Least not for the likes o' the Paiges. An' there be enough of folk like them workin' day an' night, an' 'ardly enough to show at the end o' the week to feed their families on.'

'Do the Paiges have several children?'

Miri poked the fire, dragging grey ash between the bars, clearing the way for the heat to reach the kettle beginning to steam on its bracket.

'They did 'ave, two lads younger than Adam. My John 'ad the teachin' of 'em when the parents could find the threepence a week to send 'em to school, which wasn't often same as rest o' the folk. Darlaston men don't mek wages to send kids to school. That sixpence a week to pay for two would keep a 'ole family two or three days wi' broth med from scrag end o' mutton. Speaks for itself, don't it?'

'Mmm,' Esther mused. 'It would be good if schooling were available to all, whether the family had money or not.'

'It would be good if the Second Comin' 'ad 'appened yesterday,' Miri answered irreverently, 'but I don't see no three kings go ridin' by.'

'Miri Butler!' Esther pretended to be shocked. 'What would your husband say to hear talk like that?'

'Well, it would be no use 'im tellin' me to write out five hundred times "I must not blaspheme", seein' as 'ow I never did quite get the 'ang o' writin' – an' you can't say as 'e didn't try 'ard enough to teach me.'

'You said the Paiges had two more sons?' Esther watched the older woman spread a white cloth across the table then set about laying it with cups and saucers. 'That seems to imply they are no longer alive?'

'They ain't.' Miri reached down flower-edged plates from the dresser, setting them beside the cups and saucers. 'They both o' them died – oooh, what? Some fourteen or fifteen years gone. Doctor reckoned it were fever though 'e never said the cause.'

'Do you think it was fever?'

Reaching a tin painted round with Chinese girls crossing an ornamental bridge, their kimonos bright against the dark background, Miri spooned tea into the brown platter teapot set warming on the hob.

'Ain't no question.' She replaced the lid on the tin then set it back in its place on top of the pine dresser. 'Only argument is what was the cause o' it? It wasn't as if the Paiges was the only family to lose children, or even adults. There was quite a few others as I remember.'

'Was there no official enquiry?'

'Official enquiry!' Miri laughed, an old bitterness threading the sound. 'That would be the last thing that lot at the White Lion would want. The fever was caused by those families living in their own filth, was what they said; they caused their own problems, living as they did.'

Esther waited while Miri fetched milk from the cool jar kept in the scullery, asking when she returned, 'But you did not believe their problems were of their own making?'

'I didn't an' I don't!' Miri poured milk into each cup. 'I know many o' them women as live against the Cross, an' though

45

I say it meself there be none in the country works 'arder to keep their families clean. But no matter 'ow 'ard they tries it's a losin' battle, what wi' some o' em wi' six and seven kids an' no more'n two bedrooms to the 'ouse an' no privy between 'em but an open cess pit. But for all that, it was no cause for the fever that took a good 'alf of 'em. I say it were rats: they was overrun wi' 'em after the buildin' of that iron works, wi' the discharge bein' piped straight into the old pit shafts. That attracted rats, foulin' the brook that provided the folk wi' drinkin' water.'

'Did anyone else have the same idea?'

Miri spooned sugar into her tea, her eyes on the cup as she stirred. 'Oh, arrh, there was others all right, an' there was a few who said as much out loud – my John bein' one o' em. But them as owned the works owned the 'ouses an' they didn't want no truck wi' folk as complained. They told the men straight out: you don't like it, you can bugger off an' the same goes for yer job. That settled complaints soon enough. It's 'ard enough to feed a family when you 'ave a job in Darlaston. It's impossible when you ain't.'

'So they are still living in the same conditions?' Esther asked, and when Miri nodded, added, 'And does my father know of this?'

''E be sure to.' Miri ceased stirring her tea, setting the spoon in her saucer. 'Ain't no secret nor never 'as bin.'

'So he is among those who allow it to continue?'

'Now don't you go gettin' yerself all riled up about that 'cos there ain't nothin' you can do.' Miri looked up sharply. ''Sides, seems to me you 'ave enough on yer plate, judgin' by the look on yer face when you come out o' that room. Ee, talk about a shemozzle! I could 'ear 'im shoutin' from the kitchen. 'E . . . 'e didn't 'urt you, did 'e?'

'No . . . no, he didn't hurt me,' Esther answered, knowing just how close that fist had come to her face. 'He just made a lot of noise.'

'You can never tell wi' that one.' Miri sipped her tea. ''E be like a snake – you don't know when he'll strike. You didn't say anythin' you'll come to regret, I 'ope?'

'We never know that until the time comes. Let's just say that at the moment I regret nothing and it just might be that *he* will come to be the one having the regrets.'

'Oh!' Miri paused in drinking her tea. ''Ow come? Just what did you say in there?'

Esther smiled impishly. 'I told him if I was to be sold then I wanted a share of the profits.'

'Sold!' Miri set her cup noisily in its saucer, her eyes wide and questioning. 'What on earth do you mean "sold"? People don't go gettin' sold no more.'

'Maybe not as you understand the word but they are sold nevertheless – at least people like me are.'

'I don't understand you, wench, how can you be sold?'

Turning her gaze to stare through the window towards the line of trees screening off Rowena House, Esther suppressed a sigh. 'Quite easily it seems, Miri. My father proposes to hand me over as a bride to the son of Ezra Cosmore. I think he hopes the Cosmores will then invest money in his business which, it appears, will go bankrupt if this marriage does not take place.'

'You, married!' Miri couldn't hide her surprise. 'I never thought . . .'

'No.' Esther's smile faded. 'Neither did I.'

'Eh, me wench, I didn't mean . . .'

'That someone would hardly marry a cripple? It's all right, Miri, I thought the same. Anyone would. After all, what good is a woman who can't walk to any man?'

'Walkin' ain't everythin',' Miri said stoutly. 'You be a good sensible girl wi' 'er 'ead screwed on right way round. Any man could count 'isself lucky to get you.'

'I wonder if Morgan Cosmore feels that way?'

Morgan Cosmore! Miri turned her attention to the kettle hissing above the fire, taking it from the bracket and carrying it through to the scullery, allowing time for the anxiety to fade from her face. The Cosmore lad had always had a bob on himself, lording it over the lads of the town whenever he came home from that fancy school Ezra sent him to. It covered a multitude of sins did that school, John had once commented, and though the meaning of his words was not entirely clear to her, Miri knew without a doubt it wasn't good. And now the lad was to marry Esther . . . Filling a jug from the water pump over the brownstone sink, she poured water into the kettle. No good would come of such a marriage. She walked slowly back to the fire, setting the kettle back over the flames. No good at all!

'So old Cosmore be wantin' you to marry 'is son?' The kettle settled in its usual place, Miri returned to her chair at the table. 'That be all well an' good but I be askin' meself what be in it for 'im? Ezra ain't one for doin' anythin' for nothin'. If there ain't a profit in it for 'isself then 'e don't do it, an' that includes marryin' off 'is son.'

'The thought had occurred to me,' Esther answered. 'It seems he thinks my father's business is on a firm footing and that he, or rather his son, is to get a very substantial share of it as my wedding settlement.'

Miri frowned, trying to come to terms with what she had heard. 'But you said yer father was after Cosmore's money?'

'So he is.' Esther smiled. 'He is banking on the Cosmores not knowing the situation his financial affairs are in.'

'I know I ain't none too bright . . .' Miri continued to frown '. . . but seems to me as 'ow if Morgan be tekin' you 'cos of the settlement 'e's bin offered, then Cosmore's business ain't none too 'ealthy. Nothin' agen you, Essie, God forbid, but if that man's finances was all they'm cracked up to be 'e wouldn't be turnin' to Josiah Kerral to mek a marriage alliance.'

'I realised that,' she agreed, 'and I can't believe it has escaped my father, even if Ezra Cosmore has not noticed it.'

'Oh, 'e'll 'ave noticed.' Miri shook her head slowly, the action adding weight to her words. 'Only answer as I sees it is 'e's too desperate not to tek the chance o' bein' wrong.'

'I think they both are, and both are going to be wrong in the end – both of them are after money that does not exist.'

'An' what 'appens to you when it comes out that neither of 'em 'as finished up wi' a prize? You be the pig in the middle, me wench, an' I know for sure young Cosmore won't give a damn what becomes o' you. 'E'll be off so fast you'll think 'is arse be afire.'

Wheeling herself to the dresser, Esther pulled open a drawer, taking out a blackbound book. Placing it on her knees, she wheeled herself back to the table and pushed her plate aside.

'That is why I demanded a pre-nuptial agreement,' she said, laying the book where her plate had been. 'If I am to be a pawn in my father's game, then I want paying for it.'

'But you can't force 'im to pay you to marry!'

'Why not?' For a few seconds Esther's eyes flashed defiance. 'Morgan Cosmore is being paid to do just that.'

'But that's different . . .'

'Why?' Esther flashed again. 'Because he is a man and I am a woman?'

Miri cast around in her mind for an answer that would take the heat out of Esther's gaze, but finding none simply answered, 'Yes.'

'It's so unfair!' Esther's fist crashed down on the table, setting the cups rattling in their saucers. 'When are people going to realise that a woman is equally as intelligent and capable as a man? When will they accept that she has a mind as well as a body? It is 1901. How many more years are we to be kept under? How many more years before we are accepted on an equal basis?'

Miri had heard the same cry years before. Esther and John had often discussed the chances of women being recognised as having the same mental abilities as men and being granted the same voting rights, but she knew it would never happen.

No parliament would ever go so far as that, no matter how loud women shouted or for how long.

'Unfair it may be,' Miri dismissed a desire to voice her thoughts, 'but that be the way o' it. An' 'sides you bein' a woman, you be under age by a twelve month an' that means you do as 'im over at Rowena House says you am to do.'

'Only if he agrees to my terms.' Esther's mouth set stubbornly.

'Now look you 'ere.' Miri's voice took on the tone it often had when as a child Esther had demanded to be taken across to the big house. 'You be Jos Kerral's daughter an' if 'e says you'll wed, then you'll wed. An' if you 'ave any sense at all you'll forget this daft carry on of demandin' pre . . . what you said. You go demandin' an' you'll find out 'e can do more'n you thought!'

'Like having me certified mentally as well as physically incapable?' Esther asked, the first flush of her anger receding into bitterness. 'Don't worry, Miri, my father and I have already been over that. He may have very little left in the way of money but I think he has more pride than to admit a daughter of his to a mental institution. No, it is my belief we understand each other, I get what I ask for or he gets nothing of what he hopes for.'

'An' what 'ave you asked for?' Miri looked at the girl she had tried to shield from her father's spite and anger, by keeping a low profile for so many years. 'Just what do you expect to gain from bein' so reckless?'

'A little of what should rightfully be mine, a little of what I would have inherited had I been born a son.' Esther opened the book, her eyes scanning the neat flowing script. 'John kept me advised of the different aspects of my father's business and taught me the value of each. He taught me to be conversant with the current market prices of iron and steel and the selling price of most articles made from them. I have listed in this book each works and its products, their amount of business or lack of it.

I think my father would be surprised at just how much I know.'

'But how?' Miri asked, surprised. She knew John kept himself informed as to the state of the town's many industries, and that they had formed a central part of many discussions between him and Esther, but John had been dead these two years so how could she have kept up with these things? 'How can you be sure of what happens in them works?'

'Did you think Ria Stedman came here last week only to say thank you for my sending her that white gown to cut up to make her youngest a confirmation dress? Or that Annie Gough called just to be neighbourly? True, they called for that reason too but another besides: they brought word from their husbands of the goings on at James Bridge copper foundry and at the Wheel and Axle works. And they, my dear Mrs Butler, are just two of our callers.'

'So that's 'ow you do it?' Miri found herself beginning to smile. 'And 'ere be me thinkin' all the time they just be 'ere to thank you an' pass the time o' day. You be smart, wench, I'll give you that. Get the women on yer side an' you'll know everythin' as goes on in Darlaston.'

'Like the fact that my father was selling off the gun lock works in Great Croft Street? Or that John Carless was winding up his screw-making workshop in Foster Street and that Ezra Cosmore offered for it but someone else offered more?' She lifted her eyes from the book and as they fastened on the other woman's face they were dark with something other than the bitterness that set her mouth into a hard line. 'It is all here, Miri, here in this book – what my father bought and what he sold, the gain and the loss. And it also shows which of the ones he sold now belong to me. What would he say if he knew, Miri? What would Jos Kerral say if he knew his crippled child, the daughter he never wanted, now owns the businesses he sold. That, pound for pound, she is quite possibly more financially sound than he is?'

'Arrh, me wench, y'ave done well an' I'm pleased for you.'

Miri reached for the plates neither of them had used and, rising from the table, replaced them on the dresser. 'But remember: the louder the cock crows, the better chance the fox 'as o' 'earin' 'im. Keep your mouth tight shut as to what you 'old for once 'e gets wind o' it, 'e won't 'esitate in tekin' revenge. 'E never could stand to be beat an' as for it bein' done by a woman . . .' She broke off, unable to contemplate his reaction.

'Oh, he will find out,' Esther said as Miri picked up the cup, tutting at the way she had left its contents untouched. 'I intend that he should.'

Glancing at her, Miri felt a tremor of fear as the darkness in Esther's eyes was revealed as the light of revenge. Reaching for the plate of scones she had added to the table as an afternoon snack, she replaced them in the food locker John had made a few weeks after their marriage. What a pity Jos Kerral had made his move just now! Given a twelve month Esther would have been of age and more or less free from any hold he had over her. But as things stood now . . . Miri carried the dishes to the scullery where she set about washing them, her thoughts still on what Esther had said about those businesses that were now hers. Please God, never let Jos find out that a certain 'E. Marsh' was in reality his own daughter.

It had been John who'd taught Esther to keep the household accounts. As soon as she was of an age to understand he had gone over income and expenditure with her. He had said that her income was her affair and she must learn to administer it. She had, noting carefully each month how much remained unspent. It was when she had heard that old Henry Jessons was selling his soap-making works in King Street, along by the Bull Stake, that she had questioned John as to the possibility of acquiring it without using her own name. He had then purchased it using the first part of his name, signing 'Edward Marsh', a form of 'Edward John Marsh-Butler', the full form which he never used, then had immediately willed it over to Esther; and so it had gone on. Under John's guidance, the profit from one business had helped to buy another until his death had ended the use of his signature. But by that time Esther had several of the workshops of Darlaston under her control. How long they would stay that way should her father discover it needed no guessing.

'I wished it 'adn't 'appened just yet.' Miri returned to the kitchen as Esther was replacing the book in the drawer of the dresser.

'You wish what had not happened?'

'Your father decidin' to get you married. I don't suppose he would settle for a twelve-month engagement, d'you think?'

Closing the drawer, Esther turned the wheelchair until she was facing Miri. 'I don't expect he would but why would you want him to?'

''Cos then you would be of age, you noggy 'ead,' Miri said, anxiety turning to impatience. 'Then you could 'ave told 'im you wouldn't tek the Cosmore lad.'

'But I *want* to take him.'

The coolness of the reply shook Miri. 'You . . . you mean you want to marry Ezra Cosmore's son?'

'If it helped me repay my father for his treatment of me, I would marry the son of the devil.'

'For all you know you could be doin' just that!' Miri snapped.

Preferring to remain in the kitchen rather than spend the long hours of the day alone in the small sitting room, Esther now manoeuvred her chair to her favourite spot at the window looking out from the rear of the house. 'Life is full of surprises,' she said, setting her wheelchair at an angle where she could see the whole room. 'That would simply be one more. But devil or no, I shall take Morgan Cosmore. After all,' she shrugged, 'who else would marry a cripple, settlement or no settlement? And think of this also. Supposing I refused what my father asks and he did have me sent to an institution, not only would all of my affairs be taken over by him as my legal guardian but this house also would be taken. I cannot for one moment see him allowing you to live here then.'

'But this is my 'ome!'

Esther's eyes softened to velvet. 'It is that only while I am here,' she said gently. 'You know my father, Miri, and you know that I am speaking truthfully when I say he would not hesitate to turn you on to the streets.'

'But you won't be 'ere when you be married,' Miri said, dazed by this threat to her home, 'I'll 'ave to go then.'

'No, Miri.' Esther spoke quickly, trying to calm the panic she could see already rising in her friend's face. 'No, you won't, not if I get my father to make your living here for the rest of your life part of our agreement.'

''E won't do that.' Miri's mouth trembled. ''E won't never do that.'

'We will see,' Esther said, the distress of the woman who had given her so much strengthening her resolve to gain agreement from her father. 'We will see. But even should his answer be no, you will be well taken care of, Miri, you have my word. You can come with me to the Cosmores' house, or if you do not want that, there is enough money to buy a small house in the town somewhere. Whichever way you choose, I will not have you worrying. Please, Miri.'

'You're right.' Miriam smiled faintly. 'Ain't no use in goin' to look for trouble, it 'as a way o' turnin' up on its own. An' I've got a strong feelin' it'll come in plenty.'

'Then we will be ready for it.' Esther's determination returned, setting the line of her mouth.

Going into the small kitchen garden she had made when first they had come to live in the house, Miri pulled several potato plants from the earth, shaking the fat white-skinned potatoes free of soil before dropping them into a wooden pail. That girl be too like him, she thought, moving to where a line of cabbages glowed green in the late-afternoon sun. She's every bit as stubborn. He might have thought that chucking her out of his house was all it took to get rid of her but he was mistaken in that. There be too much of her father in her for her to give in that easy.

She straightened up, closing her eyes against the gold of the sky. They would never be rid of one another, she told herself. Not till both of them were dead for Esther carried him in her veins.

Chapter Five

'I'll ask 'im, but I can tell you now the answer will be no.'

'But I've worked this ten year an' five of them has seen no raise in the wage I'm paid.'

'An' the next five am like to reap the same reward.'

William Evans looked at the tall man facing him across the table of the kitchen at Rowena House, his eyes just a few shades lighter than the black hair that tumbled about his forehead. Adam Paige worked hard for the fifteen shillings a week he was paid for keeping Jos Kerral's horses – not that there were more than two of them these days, but that did not mean he took advantage. He kept the stables like a new pin and the yard much the same; no, the lad didn't take advantage but neither would he be taking away more money, Kerral would see to that.

'No disrespect to you, Mr Evans,' Adam answered him, 'but p'raps if I asked the master meself . . . if I told 'im about me father . . .'

'It ain't the usual way.' William Evans pulled at the lapels of his black coat, conscious of his position as butler.

'I know that, Mr Evans,' Adam said, respecting the other man's responsibility for the servants working under him, 'but if like you said there's not much likelihood of the answer being yes – well, Mr Kerral knows me from comin' into the stable and maybe he just might agree if I approach him polite like.'

'You approach 'im any other way an' yer arse will 'it the street so 'ard there'll be two cracks in it.' William Evans touched the sideburn that descended to his jaw. 'Kerral don't tek no old buck from nobody, much less them as 'e pays.'

'Don't worry, Mr Evans.' The grey eyes showed no humour, and no surprise at the other's words. 'I won't give any cheek. I'll just ask, an' either he'll say yes or no.'

And no prizes for guessing which it'll be, Evans thought, but aloud he said, 'Well, you can give it a try an' I 'opes for yer mother's sake 'e will up it a little bit, but I don't 'old out much hope.'

'Thanks, Mr Evans.' Adam jammed his flat cap back on his head. 'I'll see him next time he comes into the yard.'

That had been an hour later. Now, making his way towards his parents' house, Adam went over the scene again in his mind. Jos Kerral had come home in a stinking temper, jumping down from his sweating stallion and throwing the reins to Adam, catching him across the face.

'Raise!' he had shouted when Adam had nevertheless asked for his weekly pay to be increased. 'You get bloody fifteen bob a week now for doin' bugger all, an' you 'as the cheek to ask for a raise?'

'My pay hasn't risen in five years, Mr Kerral,' Adam pointed out. 'I get the same money now as I did when I was twenty.'

'Arrh, you do.' Josiah's face darkened, the red of his angry face taking on a purple hue. 'You get just as much money for doin' 'alf as much graft. What do you do round 'ere all day?' He glanced about the yard. 'I'll tell you what you do . . . nothin'! You do bloody sod all, that's what you do, an' you 'ave the gall to ask for a raise!' He paused, glaring at Adam, eyes filled with spite. 'Well, since you've asked, I'm goin' to give you a raise – you can raise yer arse off my land. You be finished 'ere!' He raised the whip he still held, bringing it down across Adam's shoulder, barely missing his head. 'Bugger off right now an' don't let me catch you 'ere no more.'

Dropping the horse's reins, Adam caught the ebony whip

as it rose for the second blow, snatching it and snapping it across his knee. Holding out the two pieces, he spoke quietly. 'You ever make to strike me again, Mr Kerral, and that will be your back.' Throwing the broken whip at the man staring open-mouthed at him, he had turned to walk away from Rowena House.

Now what was his mother to do? Adam kicked at the rough heath, three miles of which lay between the house of Josiah Kerral and the damp rat-infested one his parents occupied. He had wanted more money to give to them while his father was laid up with the fever that seemed to strike more and more often, but as it was they now had nothing. Maybe he could get work at the foundry over at James Bridge. He halted, watching the evening sky turn a fiery red as the furnaces of the foundries opened one by one. No, he would get no work at James Bridge. Jos Kerral owned those foundries and wouldn't allow Adam to be taken on, not after what had just happened. He watched the crimson rise from the horizon, spreading in a great glowing arc across the sky. He would have to look elsewhere if he were to save his family from starving.

Reaching the edge of the town a half hour's walk over the open heath, he turned into Wolverhampton Street. Passing the rear of the Victoria iron works, he hesitated. Josiah Kerral didn't own every works in Darlaston. Perhaps there might be a job here? Retracing the last few yards, he turned into the dingy little passage depressingly named Factory Street that separated the sprawling sheds and buildings that were the iron works, coming to the large wooden gates half hanging from rusty hinges. Entering an unpaved yard filled with rusting pieces of iron, he approached a low shed, its unpainted walls black with the dust of endless iron smelting.

'What you after, lad?'

An old man, a muffler about his throat, unsuccessfully trying to hide the absence of a shirt, stepped from the doorway.

'I thought there might be a job going?' Adam felt the reply before it was made and it hit his stomach like cramp.

'Ain't nothin' 'ere, chap,' the old man wheezed from lungs three-quarters filled with iron dust. 'Already laid ten men off last week and rest'll foller soon. Place be closin' down an' what'll 'appen to the blokes as depends on it then, only the Almighty knows.'

'Well, I had to ask,' Adam said, turning away. Then turning back again to the old man wheezing his way into the shed, he asked, 'Who owns this works?'

'Richard Tulley.' The man coughed deep in his dirt-filled lungs then spat on to the ground. 'You know 'im?'

'No.' Adam winced as the cough rattled again. 'But why is he closing the foundry?'

The old man hacked in his throat then spat again, wiping his mouth on a well-grimed coat sleeve. 'Won't nobody buy the iron 'e puddles.'

Adam looked at the man, his face etched with lines deep enough to run a steam tram on. 'Why is that?'

'I ain't sure,' the answer wheezed out. 'Still, it meks no difference now whether I be right or no but some months back Tulley 'ad a good ode ding-dong wi' Ezra Cosmore. Seems that one said 'e was payin' over the odds for iron an' either the price be dropped considerable or 'e would buy from somewheres else. Tulley told 'im to bugger off an' buy 'is iron somewheres else if 'e could get it cheaper – an' it seems like 'e 'as an' all 'cos we've sent no more to Cosmores.'

'Was Cosmore the only customer you had for your iron?'

''E was the biggest.' He paused, spitting again.

'T'others don't mek no odds – a bit 'ere an' a bit there. Not enough to keep this place goin'. So Tulley be gettin' out while 'e still 'as a few coppers left.'

'Who supplies Cosmore now?'

'Don't know, mate.' The old man spat again, this time out of habit more than necessity. 'All I do know is 'e 'as put Jake Tulley outta business an' is well like to do the same to a few more in the future. What 'e 'as done once 'e'll do again, an' if 'e gets away wi' it often enough 'e'll 'ave this town by the balls an' every bloke's eyes'll water. They think they be 'ard done to wi' wage they gets now but wait till they finds what they be offered should 'e come to be their gaffer. I tell you, lad, there'll be real 'ard times in store if Ezra Cosmore gets 'is way, so if it's work you be after then tek my tip an' don't look for it in Darlaston.'

'Thank you.' Adam turned away once more and this time kept going, the old man's gurgling phlegm-filled cough following until he turned again into Wolverhampton Street.

Another factory closing its gates. He touched a finger to his cap as a woman clad in black skirts and brown chequered shawl hurried past, the metal studs hammered into her boots ringing on the cobbled street. He had overheard Evans telling the housekeeper that Kerral too was on the verge of closing the Wheel and Axle works, which would mean another fifty or so men out of work. Adam thought of his father. With those numbers searching for work, what chance would a sick man have? And the Parish would pay him nothing when they found he had a son to support him.

The stench of discharge from the iron works reached him long before he turned off towards the huddle of tiny ramshackle houses that lay to the west of Katherine's Cross, stinging his nostrils and lungs with abuse of its filth as he came nearer. Foleys Croft! God, how he longed to take his parents away from this place! He had tried so hard to save but giving his mother twelve shillings from the fifteen he earned had afforded him little chance, and now that little chance was no chance at all. Standing still, he stared at the line of houses leaning drunkenly against each other as the abandoned mine shafts they were built over slowly subsided; at the lines of washing hanging in the dust-laden air, and the children, their bare feet covered in the black oozy sludge that filtered over everything, squabbling over a can filled with hot coals. Adam Paige was back where he'd started.

* * *

'Has he been back?' Morgan Cosmore stretched out a fawn-trousered leg, admiring the boots that had arrived that day from his London bootmaker.

'Not yet.' Ezra tipped back the brandy he had poured, refilling the glass from a heavy decanter. Holding the glass, he watched the facets of light dance their rainbow of colours in the lead crystal. He had become used to the finer things of life, enjoyed all that his money had once bought, and did not intend to forego them now. Get this marriage to Kerral's wench sorted and he could stop fretting. Jos Kerral had enough money to keep them both in clover.

'I thought he was anxious to get his cripple off his hands?' Morgan changed legs, raising the second booted foot into the air and running a discriminating eye over the supple Italian leather.

''E's anxious,' Ezra swirled the brandy in his glass, 'but don't want to show it. Thinks that way 'e can keep the price down.'

Lowering his leg so both boots rested on the carpeted floor, Morgan pretended disinterest. 'Did you tell him my price, as you so delicately put it?'

Ezra's small eyes surveyed his son over the rim of the brandy goblet. He was a waster, an idler and a spendthrift. He took what he could without making any effort to earn it, and Ezra knew he would take all he could squeeze from Jos Kerral, blow the lot on his London crowd then come back for more. He should have kicked the lazy, self-centred bugger out years ago and wiped his hands of him. He'd do it now except he needed Morgan to get Kerral's money. The thought was like gall in his throat. He gulped a mouthful of brandy but it didn't wash away the taste of his son.

'Don't matter which way you put it,' Ezra answered sourly, 'it comes to the same thing in the end. 'E wants 'is daughter teken off 'is 'ands an' we want payin' for doin' it.'

'We?' The inspection of his hand-made boots over, Morgan turned his attention to his hands, scrutinising each fingernail in turn. 'I fail to see the *we* in all of this. Might I ask how you have arrived at such an assumption?'

'Don't come yer bloody smart-arsed talk wi' me!' Ezra banged his empty glass on the table beside his chair, his already congested face darkening with the anger he always felt when talking to his son. 'Say what you 'ave to say in plain English.'

'Very well.' Morgan polished his fingernails against the cuff of his shirt. 'Since I am the one who will be doing the marrying, the one who will be tied for life to a cripple, just what will *you* be doing to count yourself a part in the proceedings? To put it in even plainer English, Father, why should any of the money Kerral pays go to you?'

'Why?' Ezra barked, his colour deepening to a blood red. 'I'll tell you bloody why! 'Cos it's been my money 'as bought you yer fancy education an' yer fancy clothes an' yer fancy friends. My money y'ave throwed around like chaff in the wind. Me . . .' he paused, poking his chest with a thumb '. . . I'm the bugger 'as kept you all these years. It be my bloody back y'ave rode on.'

Morgan smiled, enjoying the roller-coaster ride of his father's temper. 'Wasn't that what you were supposed to do, Father?' he asked, the smoothness of his tone increasing the older man's patent irritability. 'Is a father not supposed to keep his son?'

Reaching for the decanter kept always near to him and finding it empty, Ezra punched a small brass bell keeping it company on the inlaid mahogany side table. 'Arrh, it be a man's duty to keep 'is son. It's also 'is duty to see that son be equipped to earn 'is own livin', an' 'ow be you set up for that? Only equipment you 'as that can earn you anythin' be that that 'angs atween yer legs – an' I'm beginnin' to 'ave me doubts you know 'ow to use that!'

Morgan remained silent as the door to the large oval room opened, admitting the stringy figure of Evan Gittins. He had been with Ezra from the early days and the sight of his master's angry face was nothing new to him.

'Where the bloody 'ell is the brandy?' Ezra demanded, a sweep of his podgy hand tumbling the cut glass decanter on its side. 'What the bloody 'ell do I pay you for? It ain't for workin' 'cos I never sees you doin' anythin'. Sittin' on yer arse all day be what you lot call work. Well, it's gonna bloody stop, you 'ear me, Gittins? You tell 'em out there they either pulls their bloody trousers up or it's the sack for the lot of 'em. An' that includes you.'

'There is no more brandy in the cellar.' Gittins moved to the table, picking up the heavy glass decanter.

'No more brandy!'

Morgan disguised the smile his father's angry bark brought to his mouth. Ezra was in fine form. A little more of this and it would be a funeral the Cosmore house would be celebrating rather than a wedding.

''Ow d'you mean, there's no more brandy?'

The tray with its decanter and goblet safely in his hands, Gittins replied, 'I mean the cellar 'olds no more brandy. The last bottle was opened at dinner last night.'

'Last bottle was . . . no more in the cellar?' Ezra spluttered, trying to get his words out in his rising temper. 'Why ain't there no more? Why didn't you order more? You was so bloody busy shaggin' that 'ousekeeper you forgot, that's it, ain't it? That's it in a bloody nutshell!'

Morgan lifted a hand to his mouth, unable to disguise his smile any longer. The picture of the string-thin Gittins straddling the ample form of his father's housekeeper was too much for him.

'There's no more brandy 'cos Palmer's won't deliver until their bills have been paid.'

Evan Gittins was well aware Ezra would get no one else to stick his temper as *he* had done for so long; he was also aware Ezra knew it too and the knowledge enabled him to speak bluntly.

'Won't . . . won't bloody deliver!' Ezra's colour was dangerous by now and the veins in his neck stood out like thongs.

'Who do the bastards think they be bloody dealin' wi'? They'll whistle 'ard an' long afore they see a penny from this 'ouse. They can whistle till they blows their bloody teeth out. I'll get what I want elsewhere.'

'If it be wines and spirits you be wanting then you'll 'ave to go further afield.' Gittins glanced from father to son. How could two men both carrying the same blood be so different? Ezra, for all his temper, was a plain-speaking, hard-grafting man who had pulled himself up from the gutters of Darlaston, working side by side with his men then going on by himself into the small hours. Ezra Cosmore wasn't afeared of getting shit on his hands – not if that shit brought trade to his works, employment to the men in them and money to his pocket. While his son . . . Gittins looked back to the fuming Ezra. No matter what the old man's temper or his back-dealing ways, he didn't deserve a son who thought only to spend without once considering the cost or lifting a finger to help, coming home only when the need forced him.

'Why further afield?' Morgan brought himself to ask, though not quite bringing himself to clear the smile from his mouth.

"Cause you have used the wine merchants in this town and them in Wednesbury an' not one has been paid.'

Gittins saw the fractional tightening of the younger man's mouth, guessing at the thoughts racing through his mind. But Morgan Cosmore would never know the satisfaction of sacking him. Once he became master here at Addenbroke then Evan Gittins would be leaving of his own accord.

'Then go to 'ampton!' Ezra roared, aiming a kick at the chair opposite him. 'Go to bloody 'ell if needs be but get that cellar stocked up. An' while we be waitin' for that, bring owt that's left down there . . . well, go on, shift yer arse!'

'I will try Wolverhampton.' Gittins walked sedately to the door. 'Meantime it will have to be a bottle of hock – there is nothing else.'

'Then bring that!' Ezra swiped the brass bell from the table, cursing as Gittins closed the door behind him.

'The hounds are beginning to howl, Father,' Morgan said, the click of the door showing him they were not being overheard. 'The quicker you get Jos Kerral to agree my terms, the better it would seem.'

'Best for whom?' Ezra snapped. 'There ain't gonna be nothin' in it fer me. You said yerself, why should I be gettin' any o' Kerral's money? So I'm sayin' – why should I be the one settin' it up – settin' *you* up – for you to spend the rest o' yer life in bloody bone idle luxury like you 'ave the fust part o' it? You be doin' the marryin' an' you'll be doin' the spendin' so you can do the dirty work. See Kerral yerself. See 'ow far yer smart talk gets you wi' 'im.'

'It would . . .'

Morgan left off as Gittins entered the room again, carrying a freshly opened bottle of hock and two fine crystal glasses on a silver tray.

''Bout bloody time,' Ezra grumbled, grabbing one of the glasses even before the tray was laid at his elbow. 'Now bugger off an' see about that cellar.'

Waiting once more for the click of the door, Morgan began again. 'It would serve little purpose, my seeing Kerral. I have nothing in common with the man.'

'Oh!' Ezra laughed, filling his glass to the brim. 'Marryin' 'is daughter ain't 'avin' summat in common wi' the man? What you mean, you snotty-nosed git, be that if it come to argyin' you ain't got the tackle, whatever the size o' that 'as swings atween yer legs it be a damn sight more'n y'ave got atween yer ears cos when it comes to brains y'ave got nowt worth talkin' on but you 'ave to use the second if'n you 'opes to use the fust so go on an' talk to Jos Kerral it'll gie wi' all a laugh for it's a safe bet it'll gie wi' no more.'

Morgan knew he was beaten. He could not talk on the same level as his father, and Josiah always on the look out for the loophole he could close about the other man's neck, wheeling and dealing, looking for the last halfpenny he could squeeze; his was not their way, that of two men reared in the hard environment of the Black Country, their veins running with coal and iron dust. Rising from his chair, he walked to the door and held it ajar. 'I will leave that to you, Father. Talking is your forte. You always were the mouth of the family.'

Ezra's laughter boomed out as the door closed behind his son, the insult eradicated by the pleasure of victory. A bloody smart-arsed education did him no good when it came to argy-bargy with a Darlaston bloke.

She wouldn't be sold, she'd said. Josiah Kerral scowled at the plate set before him on the dining table. Not unless she got a share of the profit. Wanted a part of his business signed over to her . . . whoever heard of a woman demanding payment for taking a husband? He waved a dismissive hand at the offer of the vegetable dish, lifting his glass of red wine as it was withdrawn.

She should be glad he had got her a husband. The red wine warmed his feeling of self-righteousness. Especially at that price: a cool two thousand a year, they'd asked, plus a part of the business he had worked so hard to build. It was bloody robbery! He gulped the wine, feeding his growing sense of injustice. Sheer downright bloody robbery! He would have made a settlement but this was more takeover than settlement – yet do it he would have to to buy that cripple a husband.

Refilling his glass, he threw back the contents, drowning the truth surfacing in his mind. It wasn't the buying of a husband that motivated his agreement to such a payment; he would not have paid out threepence to see that thing married. No, it was the future of his business, his own future, that would set his signature to that paper. But to get Ezra Cosmore's money he had first to settle with his own daughter.

She wouldn't get half of what she wanted, though. He was back on the old track. She thought to take him for all she could get, but she would get precious bloody little, he would see to that.

'Evans!' he bawled. 'Send Paige across to that 'ouse. Tell 'im to fetch me . . .' He paused, unwilling even now to name Esther as his daughter. 'Tell 'im to say I want to see Miriam Butler and 'er charge.'

'Paige is no longer with us,' Evans said, noting the filling of Josiah's glass yet again. The coming meeting would obviously be no quiet affair.

'Not with us?' Jos looked up, his eyes clouded by wine fumes. 'What are you sayin'?'

'You finished 'im a week ago.' Evans removed the decanter, placing it on the sideboard.

''E must 'ave bloody asked for it.' Josiah rose unsteadily, leaning against the dining table. 'Send somebody else – the lad from the stable, anybody – but send for 'em.'

And who is to carry the girl in when she comes? Evans thought, removing himself and the decanter from the room. I can't and the lad hasn't the strength.

Miri arrived an hour after the summons, pushing Esther in her wheelchair.

'I can't carry you, miss,' Evans said apologetically. 'I wouldn't want to risk droppin' you. I ain't as strong as I once was.'

'Where is Mr Paige?' she asked.

''E ain't wi' us no longer, miss. The master sacked 'im last week.'

'Oh!' Esther's smile slipped. 'For what reason, Evans, do you know?'

'Arrh, miss, I do.' Evans glanced at Miri, unwilling to discuss his master's business. This girl was his daughter though Jos would not own to it, but should he find out his butler had discussed any household matter with her or anyone else he would not hesitate to deal him the same hand he had dealt Adam Paige.

'My father would not have sacked him because he asked for a rise in his wage, would he?'

Esther saw by the swift glance again at Miri that her intuition had proved correct.

'You have no need to say any more, Mr Evans.' Esther's bronze-coloured eyes met his. 'I think I have my answer. So,' she half turned towards Miri, standing behind the wheelchair, 'as Mr Paige is not here to assist me inside, we will just have to enter the house from the rear.'

'There be only the lad, miss,' Evans continued to apologise as Miri guided the chair towards the back of the large Georgian house. 'I'm sorry to 'ave to see you in like this. I knows 'ow you feel about goin' in the back.'

'Think no more of it, Mr Evans,' Esther answered him firmly. 'It will not occur again, you may be sure of that.'

Not knowing what to make of the quiet confidence in her tones, Evans preceded the chair, opening doors for Miri to wheel her charge through.

'I ain't goin' to beat about the bush,' Jos growled a minute later as Miri and Evans withdrew, leaving him and Esther together in the room with the portrait. 'If I'm to keep my business you 'ave to marry Ezra Cosmore's son, an' I'm tellin' you now I aims to keep it.'

'That very much depends on your first meeting my conditions.' Esther glanced up at the lovely face in the portrait. Her mother . . . what part had this bully of a man played in her death?

'Conditions!' Jos stood straddle-legged before the fireplace, his face a mask of anger. 'If there be any conditions to be made, *I'll* be the one who meks 'em.'

'Then make them instead of bellowing,' Esther snapped, watching shock at the way she'd spoken register on her father's face. It gave way to an anger so intense it seemed to draw his face in on itself, lips disappearing into a fine white line. Only his eyes, glittering like a beacon, stayed the same.

'Why, you bloody crippled bitch!' He stepped forward, right hand already swinging outward as he came towards her. 'You bloody, cankered, no good . . .' Taking his hand high, he swung it back and struck her hard across the mouth. 'I'll tell you the only condition I be prepared to mek – the condition that you keep yer mouth shut an' do as you'm told.'

The blow caught her full across the mouth: the force of it throwing her head back against the chair, the pain of it swimming in her brain. Pulling air fiercely into her lungs, Esther fought the shock of the blow, staring into eyes that held a maniacal gleam. There was no telling if he might strike her again, and if the next blow would be with a closed fist.

She glanced upward at the face looking out at her from the portrait above the fireplace and blinked away tears of pain. For a moment it seemed the lovely face came alive, pleading that she do as her father demanded, acquiesce without argument. Was that what you did? Esther asked in the silence of her heart. Did you give in every time he made a demand of you? Did he use the same bullying tactics with his wife that he is now using with his daughter? And what did your giving in to him bring but more fear? He likes that. Yes, he likes that a lot.

Esther brought her glance back to the man standing over her, his right hand opening and closing convulsively. He may have seen fear in her mother but he would see none in her. Resisting the urge to lift a hand to her stinging mouth, tasting blood against her teeth, she said, 'And if I don't?'

His hand jerking open and closed, like a puppet controlled by some hidden string, he stared at her, hatred and disbelief combined in his face.

'If you don't,' he whispered, the strength of his anger robbing him of his voice, 'if you don't . . . I'll tell you what if you don't!' With an effort that showed he stepped back, pushing his hands against the small of his back, an agitated flick of his fingers lifting the tail of his coat, then letting it fall against his backside.

'If you don't do as I say, an' that wi'out a song an' dance, you can get yerself outta that 'ouse I've let you live in, you an' that Butler woman. Then we'll see where yer mouthin' gets you.'

Blood warm and salty on her tongue, Esther kept her eyes on his face. 'That is your sole condition?'

Jos Kerral's still sharply green eyes sparkled. He had got what he wanted. This runt, this cripple, had found he was not a man to be messed with. He had soon put her in her place. 'Arrh.' The satisfaction showed in his voice and his fingers flicked, flapping his coat tails as if waving a victory flag. 'That be my sole condition.'

Esther directed a quick glance towards the portrait, swallowing the blood in her cut mouth, then returned her gaze to the man strutting before the fireplace. 'Very well,' she said, all her contempt and loathing, all the hurt of rejection turning her words to ice. 'I have heard yours. Now you hear mine. You make over to me ownership of the Leys nut and bolt works and I will consent to become Morgan Cosmore's wife. Refuse and I will see you go down until there is nothing left of you. And believe me,' she smiled bitterly, 'I would enjoy every last moment.'

Chapter Six

'My Jake says as 'ow it be closin' down.'

'That makes the second one in as many weeks.' Miri stopped the business of mashing tea, returning the kettle to the hob.

'It do that, Mrs Butler, an' there be no place'll tek the men on. Seems every works in Darlaston be layin' men off or closin' its doors altogether. I tell you, folks am real worried.'

'But what will people do?' Miri poured milk into three cups, replacing the cover with its pretty blue glass beads over the milk jug.

'The Lord only knows. Trouble be, 'E don't tell we.'

'When are the men to be finished, Mrs Stedman?' Esther looked at the starved-looking woman accepting the cup of tea Miri offered her across the table.

'My Jake says it can't 'old out no more'n a week or so. Reckons the blokes'll all get their tins by that time.' The woman looked at Esther over her cup, worry evident in her eyes. 'Seems old Ben Corns 'as bin 'avin' money troubles for some time now, an' reckons to throw 'is 'and in afore 'e loses the last bit 'e's got.'

Esther took her cup from Miri, her mind working quickly. Benjamin Corns had started up fifteen years ago, turning out nuts and bolts from his ramshackle tin workshop, never once struggling out from the depths of debt in all that time. He took so much pride in the making of his product, every one being hand-made, that profit barely came into it. If she bought the Sovereign nut and bolt works, could she hold on to it until demand picked up?

'Thank you, Mrs Stedman. And will you tell your husband thank you for me?' Esther pressed two silver florins into a calloused hand, the woman's twig-like fingers closing over them almost before her own were withdrawn.

'God bless you, miss.' Ria Stedman smiled, showing teeth that had never known the ministrations of a toothbrush. 'My Jake'll be pleased. An' if 'e gets to 'ear of anythin' else, anythin' at all, no matter what, I'll come an' tell you right away.'

'I would appreciate it.' Esther felt concern well up inside her as the woman turned to leave, her bare feet shuffling to hold on to her husband's work boots. They worked so hard, the men and women of Darlaston but no matter how hard or long there was never enough money at the end of it all to feed their children or clothe themselves properly.

'I'll be away then, miss.' Ria Stedman pulled her disintegrating woollen shawl, its many holes held together by rotting threads, about her shoulders, passing it around her thin back and fastening the ends together in a knot beneath her sagging breasts. 'G'night to you. An' to you, Mrs Butler.'

'Ee, that be bad news an' no mistake,' Miri said, returning from seeing Ria Stedman out of the house. 'Ben Corns might only 'ave 'ad a couple o' men workin' for 'im in that works o' his'n, but that be two more families wi'out bread in their mouths. If things goes on as they'm doin', then Darlaston is gonna become a desolate place.'

'I know, Miri, and the thought terrifies me.' Esther watched as she collected the cups and saucers, putting them beside the earthenware teapot on a wooden tray. 'All those men without jobs . . .'

'To say nothin' of the women an' kids who'll go 'ungry.' Miri carried the tray into the scullery then returned, taking the kettle with its remaining water from the hob and bustling back to the scullery with it.

Wheeling her chair across to the dresser, Esther pulled open a drawer, reaching for the slim blackbound book. Placing it on her knees, she returned to the table. With the book in front of her, she ran a forefinger down a long column of figures. She could do it! She could buy the Sovereign nut and bolt works provided the selling price was reasonable.

'Now what be you thinkin'?' The cups and saucers washed and dried, Miri came back into the kitchen, the tray in her hands.

'I was thinking, if I were to buy Ben Corns's place . . .'

'You can't do that, Essie.' Miri let the tray down on the table with a thud that rattled the platter cups. 'You can't go round feelin' responsible for every man that's thrown outta work.'

'I know, Miri, but if I can help . . .'

'It ain't goin' to 'elp them none, you buyin' the place, if you can't keep it goin',' Miri interrupted again. 'An' 'ow do you propose to do that when Ben Corns couldn't?'

'Ben never moved with the times.' Esther ran her eyes over the columns of figures.

'Oh, I see!' Miri's hands went to her hips, as they always did when she felt affronted. 'Ben Corns is old-fashioned. 'E ain't got the know 'ow you young 'uns 'ave, is that it? Well, you listen to me, Essie Kerral. We might not be as young or 'ave the education you've got, but that don't mean we be stupid. Old age an' a soft brain don't always go together.'

'I'm sorry, Miri.' Esther looked up, a smile creasing her face at the sight of her friend, hands on hips, the light of battle in her eyes. 'I didn't mean Ben was old-fashioned. It's just that he is a craftsman more than he is a businessman. The making of a fine nut and bolt is more important to him than getting a fair price for it. He's proud of what he produces, and rightly so, but pride doesn't feed a man. I think it's that pride that is making him bankrupt.'

Miri dropped her hands from her hips, already placated. 'But you just said it were a fine nut an' bolt Benjamin meks?'

'And so it is, and so it will have to go on being. But it can't go on being sold for almost nothing.'

'But will 'is customers be willin' to pay more? Could be they will tek their money elsewhere.'

'They more than likely will.'

'Well, if you knows that, why in the name of all that's holy be you talkin' about buyin' the place?' Miri said, banging cups onto the dresser in her agitation. 'Strikes me it ain't the old 'uns whose brains 'ave gone soft.'

'Miri, sit down for a minute . . .'

'I ain't got time to go sittin' down!'

'Please,' Esther insisted. 'I want to help the men who have been sacked, but I too need help if I am not to make matters worse. Talk it through with me, Miri, as John would have done.'

She sat down opposite Esther, uncertainty clear in her face. 'I don't know as I can 'elp, Essie. I ain't got the brain as my John 'ad, I've no sense o' business.'

'You have a great deal of sense.' Esther smiled. 'And it's that down-to-earth common sense I need now.'

'Well, wench, you know if I can do anythin' to 'elp, I will. I just don't see what it can be?'

Glancing at the book, Esther remained quiet for a moment and then, looking up, said, 'I have asked my father to make over to me the Leys nut and bolt works.'

So that was it! Miri made no answer. That was the reason she had come out of that room with her mouth the size of a threepenny cauliflower. She had tried to tie that swine to an agreement an' he had struck her. And a right cockaver it had been, with her barely able to talk for a week afterwards.

'He has not said he will do so yet,' Esther continued, 'but it is my belief that he will.'

'But what d'you want that place for? I remembers John sayin' it were almost finished an' that be some years gone.'

Esther leaned forward across the table, her fingers plucking the white cloth Miri had laid before setting out the teacups and not as yet removed. 'The Leys nut and bolt works is on the point of closure because my father made the same mistake as Benjamin Corns has with his Sovereign works. But whereas Benjamin's shortcoming was the pride he took in manufacturing a good product, my father's was not having enough pride in what he made; he had no interest in the works and as a result it has gone even further downhill.'

Miri shook her head. What the girl had said made absolutely no sense to her. 'So why be you wantin' it? Yer father must 'ave wanted to laugh when you asked for that pig in a poke.'

'Maybe,' Esther looked down the misty road to the future, 'but if all goes as I intend, he won't laugh for long.'

'So what *do* you intend? Always supposin' 'e gives you the clapped out place.'

'To modernise.' Esther brought her thoughts back to the present. 'John taught me to look for more in the newspapers and journals than just returns on the stock market. I have been reading of machines that can put a thread on a nut or a bolt in a fraction of the time it takes to turn one by hand.'

'A machine that can put a thread on a metal bolt?' Miri sounded and looked incredulous. 'Ee, Essie, be you sure, love? You ain't made a mistake? Ain't no such can put a thread on metal but a man's 'and.'

Esther leaned back, resting her hand once more on the slim book, its columns of figures gliding down the pages like sleek black worms. 'I have made no mistake, Miri. The machine is called a capstan and they are made in York by a firm called Ward. Apparently there are many different tools which can be fixed to what they call the turret, and one of those tools is a tap.'

'A tap!' Miri frowned. 'Do they be needin' water then?'

'No, Miri,' Esther laughed, 'tap is the name given to the tool that puts a thread on metal.'

'Ee, whatever next?' She shook her head again. 'An' you say it can do the job quicker'n a man?'

'Much quicker,' Esther confirmed.

Miri still looked doubtful. 'It might be all very well in its way but I don't see it bein' any use 'ere, what wi' works goin' outta business left an' right. There just ain't the call for nuts an' bolts, otherwise the closin' downs wouldn't be closin' down.'

'But they won't stay closed,' Esther said earnestly, 'I know they won't. Just look at the things that are being made: cast-iron bridges, trains, trams, the huge cast-iron balcony that is planned for the town hall that West Bromwich is thinking of building . . . the list is endless. And then there is the horseless carriage. They are going to replace the horse, Miri, I am certain they are, and the firm that supplies the nuts and bolts for those will lead the market – and that firm is going to be mine.'

Miri still looked puzzled. 'But if there's goin' to be all that call for a nut an' bolt, 'ow come yer father an' one or two others ain't seen it?'

'I have told you – my father has no real interest. He wants instant returns on what he makes, and if he doesn't get them then he no longer wants to know. I only wonder why he did not sell the Leys works years ago.'

'I wish 'e 'ad.' Miri stood up, pulling the white table cloth clear of the table. The accounts book coming with it, she shoved it back in place before Esther then proceeded to fold the lace-edged cloth with her. 'Then you couldn't 'ave got the crackpot idea of 'avin' it for yer own. An' it *is* a crackpot idea, Essie. 'Ow can a girl run a nut an' bolt works?'

Watching Miri place the cloth in the linen drawer of the dresser, Esther couldn't help but smile. They had had the same argument so often before when Miri had listened to her and John discuss the advantages or disadvantages of buying a business – and in Miri's eyes the disadvantages always won. Her eyes twinkling, Esther asked softly, 'How could a girl run a soap works or a candle works? To say nothing of a screw works she bought off John Carless in Pinfold Alley, or Harrington's stamping works down by the Green.'

Pushing the drawer closed, Miriam Butler turned to look at the girl whose crippled leg kept her prisoner in a wheelchair.

'You 'ave done well, me wench, an' glad I am for you. I just pray to God that one over at Rowena 'Ouse don't find out about it, nor them Cosmores neither.'

'There is nothing they can do.' Esther held out a hand towards the older woman, and when she took it, squeezed her fingers gently. 'Those businesses are not legally mine yet. John willed them to me but only after your death. Until then, Miri, to all intents and purposes they belong to you.'

'Arrh, an' that's another thing I ain't 'appy about.' Releasing her fingers, Miri resumed her seat opposite Esther. 'The way things stand, all you 'ave be in my name. You be named only as my heir.'

'I don't understand.' Esther's brows met in a frown. 'Why do you find that worrying?'

'Well . . .' Miri shrugged, searching for a way to put her feelings into words. 'It . . . it just don't feel right somehow, my 'avin' a 'old over what be rightfully your'n.'

'Miri,' Esther asked softly, 'if the businesses had in truth belonged to John and you, who would you have willed them to?'

'You should know the answer to that wi'out askin'.' Miri was sharply herself again, all her searching for words gone. 'You be the child me an' my John was denied, the Good Lord 'avin' 'Is reason for that, an' we couldn't 'ave loved you more if'n our two bodies 'ad the makin' of you. So who but you would get all we 'ad when our time be up?'

'So I would have been your heir then as I am now.' Esther smiled. 'So where is the problem?'

'I don't know, me wench.' Miri still did not sound reassured. 'It just don't feel right somehow, I worries over it.'

'Then don't.' Esther's tone was firm now. 'As it is, you are doing me a service. By using your name we are safeguarding my property.'

'If you say so,' Miri answered, going to the fire to swing the screeching kettle away from the heat. 'I just 'opes you knows what you be about.'

So do I, Esther thought, turning her attention to the volume in front of her. So do I!

Picking up the iron poker, Miri cleared the dead ashes from the bars of the shining blackleaded grate then added fresh coals before brushing ash from the hearth into the hole beneath the fire. Satisfied that all was neat and tidy, she picked up the shawl she was crotcheting, taking it to work on beneath one of the three oil lamps that lit the kitchen.

It would have been nice to have had those new-fangled gas lamps they had over at the big house, she thought, wrapping the strand of fine white wool over the crotchet hook. But then, there was many a thing it would be nice to have, but they wouldn't get them from Jos Kerral. But speak the truth and shame the devil, Miriam, she reprimanded herself. He has paid money to this household regularly every month and never missed. You could have done a lot worse.

'I can do it.'

'Eh, do what?' Miri looked up as Esther spoke.

'I could buy Benjamin Corns's works. That is, if he isn't asking a silly price. And I can't see him doing that.'

Miri rested the shawl in her lap. 'Ee, me wench, 'ave you teken leave of yer senses?'

'I don't think so.' Esther's eyes travelled the columns of figures as they had done twenty times this evening.

'But what for?' Miri sounded exasperated. 'Why buy summat that's goin' down the nick fast?'

'Don't ask me *how* I know this, Miri, I just do. The lull in the demand for nuts and bolts will be temporary, and when business resumes the market will take as many as anyone can produce. That is why I want to buy now, while lack of interest is keeping the price down.'

'You really think you can mek that little place of Benjie Corns's pay?'

'Not right away, Miri.' Esther's eyes gleamed like huge drops of molten bronze. 'But given time, and some of the modern machines I have read about, then yes, it will pay.'

'Talk is cheap, Essie wench.' Miri tried to caution her. 'But when the tongue be stilled the 'and 'as to pay out – an' wheer is that kind o' money to come from?'

'From you, Mrs Butler.'

'From me!' Miri started up, the white shawl spilling from her lap like a sudden snowfall. 'Ee, but Essie, I ain't got two halfpennies for a penny.'

'Maybe you have not,' Esther smiled, 'but Mrs Edward Marsh has.'

'Edward Marsh? We . . . we can't use that name, Essie. My John ain't 'ere any more.'

'No, John is not here any more,' Esther said patiently, 'but you are his widow, you are Mrs Edward Marsh, and as such you have the legal right to do as you wish with his estate. What was John's is yours.'

'But it weren't John's,' Miri answered, confusion making her stubborn, 'it were yers.'

'And I am asking now to use some of it to buy Benjamin Corns's place.'

'But I can't sign. A woman can't 'old property in 'er own right.'

Wheeling her chair around the table, Esther guided it to where Miri stood. Picking up the soft shawl, she pressed it into the older woman's hand. 'Sit down, Miri,' she said gently, 'and I will try to explain. Then, if you are still unhappy about it, we will forget the whole thing.

'It is only partly true, what you have just said about a woman owning property. On her marriage all that a woman owns becomes the property of her husband. If she remains single it is administered by her nearest male relative, becoming in all but name his property. But when a woman is widowed, all that seems to change. She is seen as being able to manage her own affairs; she can buy and sell. In short, Miri, she can do what she likes with her own money, and as John's widow you can do all that. You can buy the nut and bolt works in your own name.'

'Eh!' she breathed. 'An' that be legal?'

'Yes, Miri.' Esther's smile surfaced again. 'That is the law.'

Putting her crotchet work aside, Miri asked again if Esther was sure she had the funds to cover such a move?

'I am sure.' Esther wheeled herself back to where the accounts book lay open on the table. 'It is all here, what we make every month and what we spend. All of our businesses are doing well, Miri. We chose our managers carefully, John and I, though Rob Whitehouse was more than a little sceptical when we decided to add a range of perfumed toilet soaps to the soap works, do you remember?'

'Arrh, wench, I do,' Miri laughed. 'Said as 'is Mary accused 'im of bein' where 'e shouldn't!'

'But it paid off.' Esther looked again at the figures neatly recorded on the right-hand page of the book. 'Our sales trebled in little over two months. It is amazing what an advert in a women's journal can do.'

'Well, Essie, like me old dad used to say, there be nothin' for the dumb. If you wants it, shout for it.'

'I do want it.' Esther was suddenly serious. 'With that and the works I already own, the Leys works from my father, will provide more than a start.'

'Don't count on gettin' that.' Miri tried again to introduce a note of caution. 'Yer father won't part wi' nothin' if 'e thinks it'll do anybody else a bit o' good.'

Esther lifted a hand to her mouth, the backs of her fingers playing over her lips. 'He will give it to me, Miri,' she said quietly. 'He has too much at stake to refuse.'

In the grate the coals settled, sending a shower of sparks winging like miniature meteorites into the darkness of the chimney. Esther watched as one or two caught on the soot-lined brickwork, gleaming for one brilliant second before dying. Would it be like that for her? Would her flair for business gleam brilliantly then be snuffed out when her husband took her? After all, the businesses could only be hers for Miri's lifetime, and no one lived forever. But she didn't want forever – she wanted just long enough to avenge her father's treatment of her. And Miri would live that long, she had to . . .

'Supposin' 'e do?' The movement of Esther's hand to her face had not gone unnoticed. Miri felt the anger flame inside her as she remembered the girl's swollen face and bleeding mouth. "Ow will this give you that start you talk of?'

Esther lowered her hand but the memory of what it had touched burned in her eyes. 'The future of Darlaston rests on iron and steel, Miri. The town will be built upon it, and all that is made from it. And when it is I want to be a part of it. More than that – I want Josiah Kerral to see his crippled daughter do what he could not!'

'Ee, Essie, should you ought to go?' Miri cast a concerned look at Esther, fastening the buttons of her brown gloves. 'It ain't no place for a young woman.'

Making a final adjustment to her bonnet, Esther wheeled her chair determinedly towards the door of the kitchen. 'How can I see what the place is like if I do not go?'

'But even when you get there you won't be able to see inside. We can't get yer chair in the trap, an' even though you weigh no more than a handful of coppers you be too 'eavy for me to carry.'

'Even seeing the works from the outside will give me some idea.' Esther was not to be put off. 'Besides, it is Benjamin Corns I really wish to see and I could not risk his coming here.'

'I understands that.' Miri swung the door wide on its hinges but even so there was barely room for the chair to pass through. 'If just one whiff of what you be about gets to 'im over at Rowena 'Ouse, we'll both be done for.'

'He won't get to know. Why should he?'

"Cos folk ain't blind, that's why!' Miri's agitation got the better of her, putting a sharp edge to her voice. 'What if you be seen an' word gets back to 'im that way?'

'Who, apart from you and the staff at Rowena House, knows

83

of my existence? I have been nowhere but the grounds of this estate for sixteen years. How many people do you think remember Josiah Kerral even had a child, let alone would recognise her?'

'I still says it's risky.' Grumbling her uncertainty as to the expediency of what Esther was determined upon Miri pushed the chair close to the rear of the small governess cart she had harnessed earlier, calling softly to the mare standing patiently in the shafts. One hand holding on to the cart, the other across Esther's chest, she heaved upward, holding on grimly as Esther used her arms to lever herself to the edge of the trap's floor then hitch herself on her bottom further inside.

'Ee, me wench!' Miri leaned against the trap, her breathing short and fast. 'Give me a minute an' I'll lift you on to the bench.'

She should not have insisted on going to see the Sovereign works, Esther thought, guilt at causing Miri so much exertion coursing through her. She could have arranged something with Benjamin Corns, had him come to the cottage after dark perhaps? But even as the thought manifested itself in her mind, she knew she could not have taken such a risk.

'I'll just put the chair back inside.'

Miri cut across her thoughts and Esther watched her push the wheelchair back up the path and into the house. This was unfair. Miri was getting too old to push and lift her; she no longer had the strength of her youth. Seeing her walk back along the path a little more slowly than usual, lines of tiredness showing clearly in her face, Esther felt a great surge of love fill her soul. This woman had been the only mother she had ever truly known; she had loved and cared for a little cripple girl, hated and rejected by her own father, but now the physical side was beginning to become too much for her though Miri herself would be the loudest in her denial.

'Right, now let's get you on to the seat.' Miri hauled herself into the small trap.

Esther folded her gloved hands on top of her brown skirts. 'I am perfectly all right here.'

'You ain't all right.' Two sharp eyes stared indignantly down at her. 'I ain't 'avin' you sittin' on no floor . . . an' don't argue!' she said as Esther opened her mouth to protest. 'What would folk think, my lettin' a young woman sit on the floor!'

Brooking no more argument, Miri heaved her on to the low bench fitted around the sides of the trap then seated herself, taking up the reins. 'I only 'ope as we won't be seen,' she said, clucking the mare to a gentle walk.

Chances were strong that they would be, Esther thought as the trap rolled out of the rear entrance to the grounds of Rowena House, and there would be those who knew Miriam Butler. But how many of them believed the story given out by John and she that Esther was the child of Miriam's dead sister? Maybe there were some who had wondered, but life in Darlaston was hard. The wondering would not have gone on for long.

Happy to be away from the imprisoning grounds of her father's house, Esther remembered how John had tried to teach her of the mystical magnetic lines of the earth, the ley lines that were supposed to lie beneath the rough heath over which they were driving, but she had never really grasped their significance and now scanned the ground for the many varieties of wild flower which she had found it far easier to learn about. Deep blue cornflowers bent their heads modestly as the poppies flashed their scarlet skirts; purple-headed thistles stood tall and regal as kings with their feet on a carpet of golden buttercups. The whole scene delighted Esther and it was something of a disappointment when they reached a point where they came on to Wolverhampton Street, the town's main road, linking it to its neighbours of Bilston and Wolverhampton.

Miri guided the horse who pricked back its ears with each of her soft clucks of encouragement and Esther added her own smile as Miri nodded the time of day to drivers, their wagons filled with a variety of goods, who passed them on the way.

As they continued along the street, Esther watched the hurrying women: some of them bare-footed, ragged skirts brushing the ground, shawls covering their heads and tied beneath their breasts. None with time to stand and stare at a passing governess cart.

'Benjamin Corns's place be up along 'ere a ways, if I remember rightly.' Miri clucked again as a steam whistle from one of the foundries screamed of the intention to open the furnace, its sudden noise startling the horse.

Glancing in the direction of the sound, Esther watched as the whole bowl of the sky turned a fiery red. It never failed to impress her, seeming as if the very fires of hell had consumed the sky and were advancing across the earth.

'It's beautiful, isn't it, Miri?' she said, the breath almost still in her throat.

Miri glanced at the crimson stain but its beauty made no inroad on her practicality. 'Oh, arrh, it be beautiful all right, when you be standin' on the outside, but I bet it ain't so beautiful to the men standin' alongside o' them furnaces. The 'eat o' one o' them be fit to take the skin off yer body.'

It could not be easy and Esther felt for those who laboured in the steel and copper foundries, but still she could not quite deny the awesome majesty of a power that could turn the sky to blood.

'Steady, girl.' Miri returned her attention to the horse who tossed her head at the shout of a man heaving heavy corn sacks off a long-backed cart. They were coming up to the huddle of houses and buildings that surrounded Victoria iron works and there was more activity here than they had encountered so far.

'What do you think is happening?' Esther asked as a group of angry men spilled from the gates of the foundry.

'Can't tell,' Miri answered, tightening her hold on the reins, 'but summat 'as upset 'em.'

'You be as bad as all the bloody rest o' iron masters, Richard Tulley!' A man in a tattered open-necked shirt, string tied about the ankles and waist of his pair of moleskin trousers, picked up a stone and hurled it at the man closing the gates to the works.

' 'T'aint 'is fault,' a voice from the group answered. 'Things is bad all over.'

'Oh, arrh!' The first man picked up another stone. 'Bad for who, eh? Not for the likes o' Tulley who closes 'is gates fust time 'e loses a bob or two. No, it won't be bad for 'im. 'E's got 'is money tucked away. An' 'ow did 'e get it? Off the backs o' we men, that's 'ow, an' now we'm bein' throwed on the 'eap like iron dross.'

'You'm right, Jim,' another voice joined in, 'but we won't let 'im get off that easy. Let's get 'im. We'll give 'im a palin' 'e won't forget!'

'No, don't be so bloody daft.' This time it was a woman's voice. 'What good will knockin' the bloke's 'ead in do?'

'It'll do me a lot o' good.' The man called Jim hurled the stone, immediately grabbing another. 'It'll do me a lot o' good, missis, an' if you don't like what you be lookin' at, then bugger off.'

'Don't you tell me to bugger off, Jim Turner,' the woman rounded equally vicious. 'It b'aint yer Rachel you be talkin' to.'

'I knows that.' He grinned, showing gaps where teeth had once been. 'So does everybody else about 'ere. My Rachel knows 'er place.'

'Arrh, an' I knows 'er place an' all,' the woman retorted quickly. 'Under you every night while you'm gruntin' an' groanin', keepin' 'er belly filled, an' not wi' tucker neither.'

'Why, you . . .' Dropping the stone as laughter rippled through the group, he clenched his fists, moving threateningly towards the woman who stood her ground.

'Come near me, Jim Turner, an' you'll wish you 'adn't.' She shoved her arms free from her shawl, squaring up fearlessly to the threat. 'You'll 'ave no balls left to fill any woman's belly wi'.'

'You mouthy bitch!' the man roared. 'I'm gonna twist off yer scrawny 'ead an' stick it up yer scrawny arse!'

'You would need to be a man to do that,' the woman yelled back, 'an' you be no man, Jim Turner. You be nothin' but a bag o' piss an' wind!'

'Leave off, Jim.' A second man, dressed in moleskins with a scruffy muffler tied about his neck, grabbed Jim's arm, nodding for someone to grab the other. 'We ain't 'ere to fight wi' women.'

'Arrh, mebbe you be right.' Jim Turner glared at the woman, still standing with her hands on her hips, her expression one of defiance. 'I'll settle wi' you another time.'

'You do that, Jim, me old cock,' she laughed mockingly. 'But when you come, don't forget to bring yer lackeys wi' you. You'll need them to 'old you up after I kicks some o' that shit outta you!'

'There 'e is! Come out 'ere, Tulley, we 'ave a bone to pick wi' you!'

The woman temporarily forgotten at this shout, the men turned back towards the gates of the works where a middle-aged man in dark suit and derby hat stood nervously watching the huddle of men and women.

'That ain't Tulley,' came a voice from the left. 'Where's Tulley? Tell 'im we want 'im.'

'Mr Tulley has asked me . . .'

'Asked you!' The demand cut across the man's nervous speech. 'An' who might you be?'

'I . . .' The bowler-hatted man ran a finger between his rigidly starched collar and his throat. 'I am Mr Tulley's legal representative . . .'

''Is legal what?' a woman on the fringe of the group called.

''E said 'e was Tulley's legal representatit,' her female neighbour said loud enough for all to hear.

'An' what be one o' them when they be 'ome?'

''E be Tulley's sooliciter!' One of the men who had helped restrain Jim Turner aired his knowledge.

'Then why the bloody 'ell don't 'e say 'e be a sooliciter?' the first woman demanded. ''Stead o' tellin' folk 'e be a legal representatit.'

'Please, ladies and gentlemen . . .'

'Eh, 'ark at 'im, Sally, you ain't been called one o' them afore.' A woman's harsh laugh rang out, echoed by the rest.

'No, I ain't.' A small dark-haired woman with a red shawl draped about her shoulders tossed her head. 'But I knows the meanin' o' the word – which is more'n I can say for you.'

'Please,' the man at the gates tried again, 'Mr Tulley has asked me to tell you he tried to remain in business. It is no fault of his that the Victoria iron works is having to close its gates . . .'

'Whose bloody fault be it then?' Jim Turner roared. 'Our'n? Be that what Tulley be sayin'?'

'No . . . no.' The solicitor fingered his collar again. 'That is not what Mr Tulley is saying.'

'Then what *is* 'e sayin'?' Jim demanded to the applause of the others.

'He is saying . . .'

''E ain't sayin' it. You am!' an angry voice chipped in as the solicitor made another attempt at an explanation.

'We don't want to listen to you,' roared another man. 'You be a bigger bloody liar than Tulley.'

'Best sling yer 'ook now, mate,' said another, taking a step forward, 'afore we dishes you out a bit o' what Tulley 'as comin'.'

'Let 'im talk.' From the front of the crowd near to the gate a man waved his arms, trying to alter the mood of the angry men. ''Ow can we judge what be best to do if we don't listen?'

'I already knows what's best to do wi'out a sermon from you.' Jim Turner picked up a stone. 'I'm gonna get Tulley an' kick my money's worth out o' 'im. What d'you say, lads?'

'What Jim says be best,' one of Turner's henchmen shouted. 'Let's knock the bleedin' daylights outta Tulley an' anybody else who teks 'is part.'

'I tell you that breakin' into the works and doin' Tulley ain't the way . . .'

'An' I says it is!' Jim Turner let fly with the stone towards the man with upraised arms but it hit the gates, bouncing off into the crowd.

'That bloody 'it me!' a woman screamed, following up with a stone hurled accurately at Turner, catching him high on the left shoulder.

'Pity it weren't yer mouth!' He hurled a second stone after the first.

'Why, you stupid bastard, I'll smash yer bloody face for you!'

A smear of blood trickling down the side of his face, a wiry sandy-haired man of about thirty picked up a stone and hurled it towards Turner. It acted like a starting pistol and the whole crowd erupted, grabbing stones and throwing them at each other, as well as at the bowler-hatted solicitor who had seized the chance to nip inside the gates, locking them behind him.

In the street Miri jerked on the horse's reins, calling to the mare to walk on, but scared by the noise, she refused. Then, a stone striking her head, she reared violently, backing up in the shafts before rushing the small cart into a half-demolished building.

The force of the cart hitting the wall flung Esther forward, throwing her off the narrow seat as Miri struggled to hold the terrified horse.

'Hup, hup, girl! Hup, hup!' A figure hurled itself from the crowd, grabbing at the mare's halter, talking softly to it, bringing it slowly under control.

'Eh, lad, thank God you was there,' Miri said, her voice trembling. 'I don't know what I would 'ave done if you 'adn't come when you did. I ain't never seen 'er act up like that afore.'

'The noise startled her,' came the reply as the man stroked the mare's neck. 'She obviously isn't used to this kind of rumpus.'

'Neither am I.' Miri let the reins fall easy, allowing control of the horse to go to the young man still soothing her.

'Let's get you out of here.' Crooning to the horse, he led the animal gently forward and on along the street, his free hand going to her nose reassuringly as two uniformed policemen ran past, whistles blowing and truncheons held in full view.

'You will be all right now, Mrs Butler.'

'Why, it be you.' Miri looked properly at their rescuer for the first time. 'I 'adn't recognised you, lad.'

But I had, thought Esther trying to lift herself with her hands back on to her seat. I recognised you, Adam Paige.

Chapter Seven

'Essie . . . oh, Essie love, be you all right? 'Ere, let me
'elp you.'

Miri turned to Esther, still struggling to push herself back
on to the bench seat of the trap.

'No, Mrs Butler.' Leaving the horse, who stood quietly now,
Adam came to the rear of the trap. 'Will you allow me to lift
you, Miss Kerral? I think perhaps the strain might be too much
for Mrs Butler.'

'I got 'er in!' Miri said indignantly.

'So you did, Miri, and not until too late did I see just how
much of an effort that was and how wrong of me it was to
ask it of you.' She smiled at Adam. 'I would appreciate your
assistance, Mr Paige.'

Her weight no hindrance to his strong arms, he lifted her
back on to the seat. Held close to him, Esther smelled the
clean fragrance of soap.

'There you go.'

He had placed her on the seat but remained bent over
her, concern shadowing his grey eyes. Esther felt a sudden
quickening inside her.

'Are you hurt?' he asked gently.

'No.' She glanced away, conscious of the colour staining
her cheeks. 'At least, nothing more than my pride. That is
somewhat bent though I am sure it will recover.'

He smiled, showing strong even teeth, white against the
tan of his skin.

'I'm sure it will.' He swung down from the trap, going again to the horse and fondling its muzzle. 'She should be all right now, Mrs Butler. She was just scared, that's all.' Stepping away, he glanced at Esther. 'I'll say good day then.'

'Mr Paige.' Esther spoke quickly before Miri clucked the mare on. 'Are you busy . . . I mean, are you engaged upon some business?'

'Only the business of looking for work, Miss Kerral.'

'You are still not employed?'

He shook his head, sending a short black curl over his forehead, and Esther was surprised to feel she was glad he did not follow the fashion of plastering his hair with maccassar oil.

'I'd have more luck panning for gold in the Tame,' he said, the earlier smile dying on his lips. 'Seems nobody in Darlaston has jobs to give.'

'Then perhaps you would accompany us to Benjamin Corns's place? As you said a moment ago, lifting me in and out of this cart is becoming something of an effort for Miri, and I don't think Mr Corns would deem it very ladylike to see two women sprawled on the ground with their bloomers showing.'

'Essie!' Miri snapped, shock plain on her face. 'What way be that for a young woman to talk?'

'I beg your pardon, Mr Paige,' Esther apologised demurely, but her eyes sparkled with mischief, 'I forgot myself.'

'I should just think you did.' Miri's sense of propriety was still injured. 'We'd best get this business over an' done an' you back 'ome afore you says anythin' else that'll shame the pair o' we.'

'Well, Mr Paige.' Esther pursed her mouth, fighting back the laughter that would only annoy Miri more. 'Will you come?'

'Only if Mrs Butler feels my help is needed.'

Esther wanted to smile even more now. He was what John would have called a born diplomat.

'Well, we ain't got the chair,' Miri answered, 'so if 'er insists on goin' into the works, an' like enough 'er will, then I will be glad enough of 'elp. So yes, lad, I would think kindly of you comin', supposin' it ain't puttin' you out?'

'It is not putting me out, Mrs Butler.' He stepped once more to the mare's head, taking the bridle in his hand and leading her on. 'I am pleased to help.'

'How are yer parents, lad? Are they keeping well?'

'My father is still ill of the sickness he took a month ago,' he answered Miri's question. 'I fear his lungs are affected.'

'Has the doctor said as much?'

'There is no money for doctors, Mrs Butler, and my father will not go on the Parish. But his cough tells as much as any doctor could. He has spent too many years breathing in the dust of the foundry.'

'And you say you can't find work?' Miri tutted sympathetically. 'Yer poor mother must be at 'er wit's end.'

'I went to the copper foundry yesterday.' Guiding the mare, Adam turned into Mill Street. 'I asked if during my father's illness I could take over his job, but I was told they are laying off and to tell my father he was finished and not to go back even when he was well.'

'Ee,' Miri sighed. 'Things be 'ard right enough. What you gonna do?'

'The only thing I can do.' Turning into the yard of the iron works, Adam halted the mare. Taking the reins from Miri, he draped them securely over an iron bar. 'I shall keep looking for work until I find it.'

After he'd gone in search of Benjamin Corns and informed him of his visitors, Adam returned to lift Esther from the governess cart. To the surprise of the workmen looking on, he then carried her into the tiny works office.

'You must forgive me, ladies.' Benjamin Corns ran his hands down the sides of trousers shiny from wear and reached for the jacket hung on a nail inside the door. 'There be no niceties 'ere. A factory don't be the place for entertainin' women.'

'You pay that no mind, Mr Corns.' Miri accepted a chair

he found beneath a mound of paperwork. 'This be no social visit.'

'Oh!' Surprised, he looked from one to the other and lastly to Adam, standing just inside the door.

'I will wait outside,' he said, looking at Esther. 'Let me know when you are ready to leave.' Then to Ben, 'Perhaps, Mr Corns, you would allow me to look around the works?'

'Go right on in, lad. Get yerself a look while there still be summat to see. Come Friday them gates out there will shut fer the last time.'

Turning back to the two women, he waited until Adam had closed the door behind him. 'Well, I won't say as 'ow this ain't a new 'un on me, 'avin' women in the works, but why you be 'ere beats me.'

'I suppose it do, but like I said this be no social visit. We be 'ere on business.'

'Business?' He looked at Miri, one hand stroking side whiskers that might have been white were it not for the grey dust that had settled on them. 'I can't bring to mind any business you might 'ave wi' me, but if there do be anythin' . . .'

'There do,' Miri cut him short. 'We be after knowin' 'ow much you be wantin' for this place?'

'You be wantin' what?' Ben's face reddened, anger overcoming surprise. 'Y'ave got a bloody cheek, missis!'

'Mr Corns,' Esther interrupted quickly, 'my . . . my aunt meant no offence. We are not here to pry.'

Pulling his whiskers Ben looked torn between throwing them out or kicking them out.

'Mr Corns,' Esther tried a smile, 'we wish to know the sum you are asking for your works with a view to purchasing it.'

'You!' Ben pulled his whiskers again. 'You want to buy the Sovereign?'

Esther nodded. 'That is what I said, Mr Corns.'

'But . . . but you be two women.'

'Does that make a difference?' she asked. 'Have you something against selling to a woman?'

'No . . .' Ben was flustered, the proposition almost flooring him with its unexpectedness. 'I be ready to sell to anybody with the money, though I must say I never expected it to be to no woman.'

'Still might not be,' Miri said tartly. 'That be dependent upon what sort o' sum you be askin'.'

'You be serious?' Ben still looked unsure.

Esther looked up, her eyes steady though her heart raced and roared like a steam engine. 'I assure you, Mr Corns, we are very serious. And I also assure you that, should your price be acceptable to us, the money will be handed to you in cash on the day of the signing.'

Appearing to make up his mind that they were genuine prospective buyers, Ben left off fingering his side whiskers and reached down a ledger from a dust-laden shelf. 'You'll find all the figures for the last fifteen year in there.' He plonked the book unceremoniously on a rickety table. 'But I'll give you a rundown on things out there an' you can check wi' yer foreman when 'e finishes lookin' around. Not that there be a lot left to see. Some bars o' steel, a dozen one-inch and around two dozen 'alf-inch nuts wi' bolts to match of eight-inch and four-inch length. Add to that some files an' a couple o' vices an' that be all that's worth the talkin' about. All in all, given the buildin', I reckon to ask around three 'undred.' He left off as Adam came to stand at the office door, his silhouette visible though the glass panel was heavily coated with dust.

Not quite knowing why, Esther asked that he be re-admitted.

'So, lad, what dost think?' Ben looked anxiously at the younger man.

'You make a very good finished product, Mr Corns,' he answered. 'The steel you use is of high quality and the thread excellent. The way the nut runs up and down the bolt is a pleasure to feel. You know yer trade sir.'

'Arrh, I does, lad.' Ben beamed, knowing the compliment was truly meant. 'An' seems you knows a fair bit about it yerself. Who was you tied to?'

'I was apprenticed to no one.' Adam held a gleaming new-turned bolt in his hand, screwing the metal nut up and down the thread. 'I have never worked in the steel trade.'

'Never worked in . . .' Ben lifted his flat cap, running a hand through his grey hair. 'Well, all I can say is you knows a deal for a bloke as 'as never worked in the nut an' bolt. 'Ow did you come by the knowledge wi'out bein' in it?'

Adam turned the eight-inch metal bolt, examining the body, running his finger around the head. 'A good clean chamfer,' he said, feeling no roughness on the metal.

Ben nodded, watching the younger man's fingers caress the shining metal. 'Arrh, it is, an' that's summat else nobody but them turnin' a bolt would know. So 'ow come you does?'

'Evening Institute.' Adam laid the bolt aside. 'I went twice a week. It was not often Mr Kerral needed me in the evenings.'

'Oh, you worked for Jos Kerral?'

'I was his groom.'

'Was?' Ben eyed him, one hand abstractedly worrying a tuft of white whisker.

'Yes, he dismissed me some days ago and since then I have been looking for work.'

'It's a pity the trade be so low. There would 'ave bin a place for a lad like you if it 'adna bin. You seems to 'ave done well at that institute place.'

'I got my engineering certificates, but they won't stand me in very good stead now.' Adam pulled a wry face. 'Pity, I always fancied going into engineering.'

'Arrh, an' a good job you would 'ave made of it.' Ben picked up the bolt, turning it over and over in his hand, fondling the metal as if it were a living thing. 'You would 'ave med somebody a good foreman. In fact, I thought you *was* foreman in one o' Mrs Butler's places?'

''E don't work for me,' Miri said.

'Not at the moment, that is,' Esther came in quickly. 'But my aunt was hoping he would take charge of this works, supposing you and she agreed terms, Mr Corns?'

'Run this place?' Adam turned to where Esther and Miri sat, his grey eyes widening with surprise. 'But I have never actually worked in the trade.'

'Mr Corns seems to think you have the ability.' Esther smiled. 'As for actually becoming involved, you would be expected to play a part in the making as well as the supervising. At least, that was what my aunt had in mind. Is that not so, Aunt?'

'Yes.' Miri caught Esther's eye, questions in her own, but Esther turned back to where Adam stood looking as though he had been hit with a crow bar.

'So seeing as the matter has already been broached, will you consider the offer of working as my aunt's foreman here at the Sovereign works?'

'I do not need to consider,' he answered, still dazed by the unexpectedness of it all, 'I accept. And thank you, Mrs Butler. I just hope you find me satisfactory. You can be certain I will give you my very best.'

'I . . . I'm sure of it, lad,' Miri answered feeling the pressure of Esther's hand on her own.

'Eh, young 'un!' Ben thrust out a hand. 'I couldn't be 'andin' over to nobody wi' more of a feel for steel than you. An' if there be anythin' Ben Corns can do to 'elp, you 'ave only to ask.'

Adam grasped the old man's hand, shaking it warmly. 'I thank you, Mr Corns, I know I will be asking often.'

'Aunt.' Esther turned to Miri, her face the picture of innocence. 'Should Mr Corns be agreeable, why not ask him to stay, on a wage of course, to give Mr Paige the benefit of his knowledge?'

Giving her charge a 'wait until we get home' look, Miri nodded, the feathers on her black bonnet waggling remonstrance at Esther.

'That would be a fine idea. What do you think, Mr Corns? Will you stay on a while?'

'Arrh, I will that,' Ben beamed. 'For as long as lad feels 'e 'as need o' me.'

'In that case, Aunt, it only remains for you to say whether you accept Mr Corns's price. Is three hundred pounds acceptable to you?' Esther added as Miri turned a blank look on her.

'Eh! Three . . . oh, arrh.' Miri's glance held a promise of words yet to come as she looked at Esther. 'Three 'undred it is, Mr Corns. If you will be at Solicitor Burrows's chambers on Woods Bank at three o'clock tomorrer afternoon, you can sign the works over to me an' the money will be paid there an' then.' She stood up, her face telling Esther plainly she was not prepared to talk business any longer. 'If you would 'elp my . . . niece to the trap, Mr Paige?'

If Ben noticed the slight hesitation in Miri's speech he gave no indication, his smile wide as he opened the office door for them.

'Aunt is just a little tired, Mr Corns,' Esther said as Adam made to take her up into his arms, 'or she would have asked you to tell the men there will be no lay offs. Each may stay in his employment on the present terms, should he so wish.'

'I'll tell 'em that, miss.' Ben followed them to the trap. 'An' right glad they'll all be. There'll be one or two lighter 'earts in Darlaston tonight an' no mistek.'

'I have to admit my heart will be lighter along with theirs, and so will my mother's.' Adam settled Esther in the trap, his gaze travelling over her face those extra few seconds that caught at her heart.

'Arrh, it will be a relief.' Miri climbed into the trap as he jumped down. 'Off you go, lad, an' tell 'er.'

'My news will keep a little longer.' Adam looked back from the mare's head, the bridle in his hand. 'First I want to see you safely home.'

'I can manage.' Miri took the reins in her hands but allowed them to lie slack on the horse's flanks. 'There be no need for you to come so far outta yer way.'

Adam's grey eyes darkened as they held Esther's. 'For me there is every need,' he said.

'You took yer bloody time!' Ezra Cosmore glared at his son.

'Why, Father, anyone would think you'd missed me.'

'Then anyone would be bloody wrong!' Ezra spat. 'You need never come 'ome at all to suit me best.'

Smoothing his caramel-coloured coat, fashionably cut two inches above the knee, Morgan smiled. 'Then who would get you the money you need to save your business, Father?'

'*My* business arrh, the business be mine alright for you've never set foot near a workshop in yer life but it be yer own arse as well as mine, as marriage to the Kerral wench will be saving.'

'But mine alone that will be tied to a cripple, eh father?'

'If I know aught about you, the ropes won't be too strong.'

Ezra reached for the decanter, pouring a measure of brandy. Although the clock had barely reached eleven it was already his fourth that morning. Morgan watched as half the contents of the glass slid down his father's throat, wondering which town's wine merchants Gittins had duped into replenishing the cellar this time.

'And what of the little cripple girl?' Morgan saw the flush of liquor creep into his father's face. 'Has she agreed to the match?'

'Agreed!' Ezra kept the glass in his hands, cradling the balloon bowl. 'What's for 'er to agree? Wench'll do as 'er's told.'

Rather like me. Morgan wisely kept the thought to himself. If only fate would free him now before he had a cripple clinging to his coat tails! Why couldn't his father finish the business of drinking himself to death?

Morgan laid soft leather gloves of the same chocolate brown as the facings of his coat collar and lapels across his knee. Fate, it seemed, intended to play out her game, and if he wished to continue his present lifestyle he would have to be content to be Ezra's pawn – at least until a better hand was dealt at some other table.

'You have been in touch with Kerral, I take it?'

''Course I've been in touch.' Ezra glared, brandy putting a coating on his words. 'One o' we 'ad to an' you weren't 'ere to do it, you was gaddin' about London after the likes of 'er up there.' He glanced towards the ceiling.

'The outcome being?' Morgan ignored his father's hint.

'The outcome bein' you gets a thousand a year for life an' a percentage of 'is wheel an' axle works.'

'A percentage?' Morgan's green-gold eyes glinted coldly. 'What sort of a percentage?'

'Forty.' Ezra threw the remaining brandy down his throat.

'Forty per cent is not enough.' Morgan knew he was pushing, but the higher his father's volatile temper took his blood pressure, the less chance fate had of playing the winning hand. 'I want fifty-fifty or he can find himself another stallion to cover his crippled mare.'

'And don't think 'e won't!' Ezra slammed the glass on to a small table set at the arm of his chair. 'An' then where will you be? Where will the money come from to keep the likes o' that one?' He grinned spitefully, eyes lifting once more to the ceiling. 'There'll be no more from me, you knows that, an' you ain't exactly bin snowed under wi' wenches wantin' to marry you, 'ave you. Not even o' the sort you 'ave brought wi' you. I tell you, it's the Kerral wench an' 'er forty per cent or nothin'. So tek yer pick.'

There was an element of truth in his words, Morgan admitted. Without money from his father or another source he was as good as finished. 'Forty per cent is how much a year in hard cash?'

'I don't bloody know, I ain't seen 'is books.' Ezra's blood

pressure climbed another notch. 'But it's forty per cent more than you be gettin' now, not to mention the thousand on top. 'Sides . . .' He grinned again but this time cunning replaced spite. 'It will be yer forty per cent to do wi' as you likes. If it don't suit you to 'old on to it, you can always sell an' there be nowt Jos Kerral could do to stop you.'

His father was right, of course, Morgan realised. That forty per cent would be a Damoclean sword with which he could up his share of the profits every year for Kerral would not enjoy seeing part of his business, a large enough part if he owned to the truth, going to someone outside his family.

Retrieving the gloves from his knee, he stood up, smoothing his caramel coat. 'Very well, I agree. You may tell Kerral he has sold his cripple.'

Ezra reached for the decanter. 'Arrh,' he grunted, 'Kerral 'as sold 'is cripple an' you 'as made yer 'andful of silver.'

His glass half-filled, he paused as Morgan walked towards the door of the sitting room. 'Where do you think you be goin'?'

'I am taking Roberta for a drive. She has a wish to see this Black Country of ours – though quite why anyone should want to insult their eyes by gazing on this Godawful town eludes me.'

'Like workin' in it 'as eluded you all yer life.' Ezra replaced the decanter on the small pie-crust table. 'Well, I hates to disappoint Roberta but Jos Kerral be expectin' you over at Rowena House at one.'

One finger moving his caramel coat aside, Morgan took a gold hunter from his waistcoat of bronze-coloured silk, flicking it open. 'Make it three,' he said, returning the watch to his waistcoat pocket.

'But the arrangements be made!' Ezra roared in protest.

Smoothing his coat back into position, Morgan flicked a non-existent hair from his left sleeve. 'Then unmake them, Father. You are the businessman. You should be used to rearranging appointments.'

'Kerral won't tek kindly to yer puttin' 'im off to tek yer fancy piece carriage-ridin',' he stormed. 'If 'e finds out it could put an end to the 'ole deal. Why the bloody 'ell did you 'ave to bring that woman 'ere?'

'Why not?' Morgan asked blandly. 'God knows the place could do with cheering up.'

'An' 'er cheers you up, does 'er?'

'Yes, Father, she does. And rather more than you do.'

'Oh, I 'ave no doubt o' it. I might 'ave given you all you 'ave asked but I can't give you what you be gettin' from the like o' that one. But couldn't you 'ave done wi'out tumblin' 'er for a couple o' days? Couldn't you keep yer cock still in yer breeches long enough to settle wi' Kerral? 'Cos I tell you, if 'e finds out that'll be the finishin' o' it all.'

'That is a chance you will have to take, Father.' Morgan smiled, knowing it would annoy his father even more. 'Roberta is my guest. I cannot disappoint her.'

'An' 'er don't disappoint you, judgin' by the gold watch you 'as in your pocket.'

Morgan flipped the chocolate leather gloves against the palm of one hand, his smile bland as his tone. 'The watch was a gift, Father, though not from Roberta.'

'Oh!' Ezra leaned back in his high-winged chair, the brandy glass held between cupped hands, anger changing swiftly to sarcasm. 'So the watch was a gift but not from the lady? What sort of presents does that one give you, the sort that don't come wrapped in paper wi' a fancy ribbon tied round 'em?' Pouring more brandy into his mouth, he gurgled, 'That be the sort you be goin' to need, lad, when you be married to a cripple.'

Morgan gripped the soft leather gloves, his knuckles showing white against the brown leather. Going to the door, he opened it then turned to smile once more at the man laughing at him over the rim of his brandy glass. 'Three o'clock, Father,' he said. 'And Roberta will be coming with me.'

Chapter Eight

'I'll not push 'er across to that 'ouse no more.' Miri stood with hands on hips, her eyes hard and determined. 'You can tell 'im that from me, Mr Evans. An' 'er can't walk there so it be 'ere to this 'ouse 'e will 'ave to come, supposin' 'e wants to see 'er at all.'

''E won't like it, Mrs Butler.' William Evans looked from Miri to Esther. 'He told me to come meself, miss, so as nobody else would know 'is business.'

'So nobody else would know of 'is own daughter livin' 'ere an' 'im never ownin' to 'er,' Miri cut in, contempt written all over her face.

'I don't know about that . . .'

He tried again and again Miri cut him short. 'Don't play the devil's games, William Evans. That be lies an' you knows it. You 'ave known about the wench bein' 'ere these many a year, an' so 'as Letty Turner who 'as cooked over at that 'ouse since afore Essie was born.'

'I reckon that be the truth of it.' Evans looked crestfallen. 'But my job be as important to me as the next man's, Mrs Butler, an' should I not do as I'm bid then I can kiss that job goodbye.' He glanced again at Esther who sat in the alcove beneath the kitchen window. 'You understands, miss?'

'I understand, Mr Evans,' Esther replied. 'Please will you tell my father Mrs Butler is indisposed, and he must either send a man to get me across to Rowena House or else come himself to this one.'

'I ain't indisupposed!' Miri's eyes snapped but Esther ignored the anger in them.

'Tell my father Mrs Butler is indisposed,' she repeated.

'I will, miss,' Evans said. 'An' if 'e sends again I'll fetch you meself an' glad to, but I ain't up to carryin' you up them steps an' into the 'ouse. I would never forgive meself if'n I dropped you.'

Esther's smile broke out, lighting her lovely bronze eyes. 'I had said that never again would I enter my father's house by the back door. But for you, Mr Evans, I will make an exception.'

'You won't need to mek no exception.' Miri's mouth clamped into a firm line. '"Cos you ain't goin' an' that be all about it.' She glared at the butler. 'You seen the way 'er come from that 'ouse the last time. You seen it yerself, Mr Evans, an' you can't deny it – 'er wi' a mouth twice the size it should oughta be the way that swine slapped 'er. Well, 'e won't get the chance again 'cos 'er ain't goin' there.'

Wheeling her chair to where Miri stood, her eyes spitting fire, Esther took her hand. 'He won't do that again, Miri,' she said soothingly.

'Won't 'e . . . won't 'e!' Miri was not to be soothed. 'You don't know the man that got you, the man you calls yer father. You don't know 'im like we do. You ain't seen his moods, the way 'e swings an' turns like a kite in the wind. You ain't seen the things 'e can do when the blackness be upon 'im. You tell 'er.' She lifted her glance to the man standing beside the table. 'Tell 'er if what I says be truthful, Mr Evans, for you 'ave seen most, though not all, of the things I seen in that 'ouse. Tell 'er if 'er were daughter to you, would you let 'er go there?'

'I will give the master your message, miss.' Evans avoided Miri's question. 'And, miss,' he added softly, 'if you do come over to the 'ouse I will stay wi' you an' be buggered to the job.'

It was an hour later that Miri saw from the kitchen window

the tall spare-framed figure of Josiah Kerral striding towards the house. Grabbing the wheelchair, she pushed Esther into the small adjoining sitting room which she had long since turned into a bedroom for her. Shutting the door on the protesting girl, she rushed back to the table that occupied the centre of the kitchen, snatching open a drawer and taking out a long broad-bladed knife which she held hidden in the folds of her black skirts.

'Where is 'er?' The door to the cottage crashed back on its hinges, smacking against the wall. Josiah's body seemed to fill the gap, the black-clad menace of him bringing the blood pounding to Miri's throat.

''Er . . . 'er be sleepin'.' Miri felt fear of him seep into her bones like iced water.

'Don't you bloody give me no lies, Butler,' he roared. 'Get the crippled bitch or I'll drag 'er out meself.'

'There will be no need,' Esther's voice came quietly as she wheeled herself across the kitchen, 'nor is there need to shout.'

'This be my property.' He hit the table hard with his fist. 'An' if I wants to shout then I'll bloody well shout, an' it won't be no blighted wench'll tell me to stop.'

'If shouting like a spoiled child pleases you then carry on,' Esther said, her voice calm even though fear had every muscle taut in her body. 'But allow me to leave for I find the behaviour of a child unacceptable in a man.'

'Why, you bloody . . .'

'No, you don't!' Miri leaped in front of Esther, the knife raised as he lifted his hand to strike. 'Not again, Jos Kerral, not never no more. You 'ave struck 'er for the last time. Touch 'er again an' as God be me witness I'll put this knife in you. I'll kill you as I should 'ave killed you the times you lamped the other one near senseless. I'll stick this blade through yer gizzard an' be 'appy to swing fer the doin' o' it.'

'You get yerself outta this 'ouse.' Jos's face darkened thunderously. 'Find yerself another back to live off for you be finished 'ere. You'll be gone by mornin' or I'll 'ave you chucked out.'

Wheeling herself around Miri, Esther came to the table. 'Please say what you have to and leave so that we may pack.'

'We!' Jos glared at her, his usually clear eyes cloudy with rage. 'We! *You* be goin' nowhere.'

'I cannot stay here alone,' she replied. 'If Miri goes then so must I.'

His face pinched with anger, Jos turned slowly from one to the other, finally settling on Miri. 'The day 'er be wed, you goes from this 'ouse,' he said thickly. 'Mind what I says, the very day.'

'That had already been settled upon.' Esther folded her hands in her lap, giving a deceptive air of calm when in reality her whole being seemed to tremble. 'Miri will, of course, accompany me to my new home.'

'Got it all worked out, ain't you?' he said, the bile of frustration stinging his throat. 'You think you be so clever, the pair of you.'

'No, not clever, just prepared.'

'Prepared?' He seemed to gather himself inward, drawing together like a cobra preparing to strike. 'Then be prepared for this. Two weeks today you weds Cosmore.'

Two weeks! Esther saw the smile spread over his face at the suddenness of his announcement. He was allowing her no time to change her mind. 'Two weeks today will be quite acceptable,' she said, regaining her composure. 'Provided, of course, that the terms I put to you at Rowena House are fulfilled.'

Watching his smile fade slowly, leaving his mouth like a twisted gash in his face, she felt the cold fingers of fear grip her. He could so easily kill them both. Even armed as she was with a knife, Miri would be no real match for a man whose fury had driven him halfway to insanity.

'Oh, yes, yer terms,' breathed Jos, eyes narrowing. 'You think to get my works on the Leys.'

Esther saw his balled fists open and curl convulsively but refused to let him see her fear. Once he knew she was afraid all hope of revenge would be gone. He would break her as easily as crumbling a dried leaf.

'If you think to see me married, then yes.'

'It'll be married or buried,' he grated through his teeth. 'Either way it be the same to me.'

'Except the one way will not bring you the money you require.' Esther's own anger began to rise, burning away her fear. 'There is no premium paid on a corpse.'

Smashing his curled fists down hard on the table, he leaned forward, bringing his face as close to Esther's as Miri's knife would allow. 'Some things are worth losing money for,' he hissed.

He was so close she could feel his breath fan her face and the memory of that blow to her mouth reared in her mind. What he had done once he could do again but the pain of his fist against her mouth would be preferable to seeing him smile as she backed down. Breath tight in her throat, she looked levelly at the eyes searing her with their hatred. 'But are they worth losing a business for?' she asked.

For seconds that seemed to last half of forever, Esther watched the pull of his face, the searing anger that twitched the muscles into spasms then released them to snap back into place like an elastic band. Then, slowly, his eyes never leaving hers, Jos straightened up, drawing a folded sheet of paper from the inner pocket of his coat.

'There.' He flung it on to the table. 'There be the settlement you asked for: the title deeds to the Leys nut and bolt works, signed over into yer name. An' much good may they do you.'

'Thank you.' She made no move to pick up the paper, to read it and confirm the truth of his word. 'I am sure it will.'

'Enjoy yer moment of triumph,' he laughed, the bitterness

of it loud on the silent afternoon. 'For the minute that ring goes on yer finger I'll tell Cosmore you 'as that works, an' from then on it'll be yers no longer – it'll be 'is'n.'

Pushing away from the table, Esther wheeled herself to where the door still stood wide open, followed by a watchful Miriam. 'Do so, *Father*,' she said acidly emphasising the word. 'I would much rather he had it than you.'

'That is the truth of it, Mother. I've told it as it happened. I calmed her horse and led it to where she was going, the Sovereign nut and bolt works.'

'That place o' old Ben Corns's?'

Adam Paige smiled at his father, sitting in a chair drawn close against the low fire in the grate. 'Yes, Dad. Do you know it?'

'Know it?' Albert Paige coughed, the effort of it leaving him breathless. ''Course . . . 'course I knows it. I 'elped 'im get the place set up, me an' a few more round 'ere.' He coughed again, phlegm rattling in his throat. 'Makes a . . . a good nut an' bolt, do old Ben.'

'I know, Dad.' Adam went to his father, drawing the piece of tattered blanket closer about his thin shoulders, 'And I told him so.'

'You told 'im?' Albert laughed, then winced as a fresh bout of coughing seared his chest. 'I . . . I bet 'e 'ad summat to say about that.'

'He wanted to know where I got my knowledge of steel and to whom I had been apprenticed.'

'I bet 'e was took to when you said y'ad been tied to no iron master?'

'He was surprised, yes.' Adam reached for the poker, raking dead ash from the fire. 'But he said the Institute had taught me well.'

'An' so it 'as, but it were you did the learnin'. If you 'adn't 'ad the ability in the first place then no amount o' them instructors could 'ave got it into yer head. Y'ave a brain, Adam, an'

110

a good 'un. Mek sure you uses it. Don't finish up like me, coughing yer lungs up wi' slavin' in a foundry, breathin' in fumes an' dust till yer innards be clogged . . .'

'Take it easy, Dad.' Adam looked across at his mother, concern creasing his brow as a fresh bout of coughing prevented his father from speaking.

'I be . . . I be all right, lad.' Albert took the piece of white cloth his wife pressed into his hand, wiping it across his eyes and mouth.

'Did this Mrs Butler say 'ow much the job paid?'

Carrie Paige crossed the room to a small wooden cupboard set against the wall. Slipping aside the wooden latch that held the door closed she took down a white paper packet.

'I clean forgot to ask.' Lifting the iron kettle from a bracket above the fire Adam carried it to the table, one corner of its well-scrubbed surface covered with a piece of huckaback.

'A fine foreman you will mek,' his father laughed and coughed at the same time, the cloth held against his mouth. 'Too slow to ask his own wage.'

'I was that thunderstruck by the offer, coming as it did out of the blue, I never gave a thought to how much it might pay.'

Adam watched his mother carefully tip a third of the penny packet of balsam he had fetched from the herbalist's shop in Pinfold Street into an enamelled basin, chip marks showing like black stars around its rim and sides.

'I would 'ave thought that would 'ave been uppermost in yer mind.' Leaving the packet where she'd put it on the table, she carried the basin across, setting it on the square of huckaback. 'I know it would 'ave been throttling me to get out, seein' as we ain't got a penny piece left in the 'ouse.'

'I should have done, I know.' Adam poured boiling water on to the faintly brown powder, drawing his head back as the fumes of the mixture rose in the steam.

'Get you off out, lad.' Carrie stirred the mixture with a spoon.

'I'll help with Dad first.'

'Do as I say.' She looked at her son, the only one left to her of the three that had been her pride. 'I've managed yer dad all these months. I can manage a while longer.'

Waiting while her husband came and settled himself on a chair in front of the steaming bowl, she picked up a towel and draped it over his head, making sure the bowl also was covered, holding in the balsam-laden steam.

'Breathe deep,' she said, touching a hand to Albert's covered head. 'Five minutes an' then I'll shift the bowl. After that it's bed for you.

'Tek yerself away, son.' She smiled at Adam but there was no reassurance in her faded eyes. 'Rest is what yer father needs most an' 'e'll get that now you 'ave a job. That was what was 'ardest for 'im, knowin' there was no money comin' in. I think 'e was feared we might 'ave been for the work'ouse.'

Adam took his mother's hand, running a finger over the chapped, calloused skin. 'I will never let that happen,' he said softly. 'You and Dad won't finish your days in any workhouse, you have my word on that.'

'Adam,' Carrie caught her son's hand in both of hers, 'this Mrs Butler . . . 'er ain't the one y'ave been thinkin' on when y'ave talked of what 'appened up along Wolverhampton Street. 'Er weren't the one you kept in yer mind – it was the other one. But you must let it go, lad. Her sort ain't for the likes o' we. And God knows, life 'ere be 'ard for any woman, but wi'out the use o' 'er legs . . .' Carrie shook her head, her faded eyes soft with feeling. 'Leave the wench to lie in 'er own bed, son. It will be kinder to 'er in the end.'

Pulling his hand free, Adam walked from the tiny one-roomed house, the smell of open foul beds and rotting vegetation hitting his nostrils like an unseen fist.

It was right, what his mother had said. He picked his way along the unpaved road, sickened by the sewage floating in greasy patches along it. Esther had filled his thoughts, but even were she not the daughter of Josiah Kerral, iron master, he could never bring her here. But I won't always be here, he vowed silently. I won't always live in a rat's nest on Katherine's Cross.

The huddle of houses dropped away behind him, taking with it the stink of discharge from the iron works. There had been talk after the last big outbreak of the fever, the outbreak that had taken his brothers. Some had blamed the iron foundry, saying it was the rust and filth from there being channelled into the brook that was the cause of the sickness and there had been a promise of its being stopped – but like all promises iron masters gave it was never kept. Filth still poured day and night into the water the people of Foleys Croft had to use for drinking.

Somewhere in the near distance a lark rose, its heady song pouring out in praise if its own particular god. Standing still Adam listened, feeling the purity of the bird's carolling, letting it seep into him, soothing the hurt that nagged constantly at him. There was still beauty here in Darlaston, despite the factories and foundries that lay like black scabs over its once green fields. But it was a beauty that was fading as surely as his mother's had faded, eaten away by the spread of iron. But iron would be made to pay! He kicked hard at the ground, sending a tuft of grass curling into the air. Not that it would bring back the fields it had swallowed but one day it would pay for decent houses, streets that could be walked on without fear of filth, schools and hospitals that would be for the benefit of all – and there would be no more foundry discharge piped into the brook.

Silence settled over the heath as the bird lowered itself to the earth and Adam considered his dream. Was that all it would ever be? Would iron always rule rather than serve? Lifting his eyes, he gazed towards the pall of grey smoke that hung like a cloud; smoke that rotted buildings and ate away at people's lungs. How long would his town fester and puke under the gag of iron?

He pushed his hands into his trouser pockets, and walked

on. His mother had asked about the wage he would get as foreman of the Sovereign works and he had felt she wanted him to go to Mrs Butler and ask. But something in him had protested at the thought. Stubbornness? But Adam knew that was not the chain that held him; his fetters were forged from pride, one too strong to ask about money even when he knew how desperately it was needed. But was that his only reason for being proud, or was not appearing a pauper in Esther Kerral's eyes even more compelling?

He plucked a long blade of mugwort, smiling at the memory of the childhood game he had played with his brothers: running a stem between thumb and forefinger, pushing its feathery fronds to the tip of the long stalk, laughing if part of the squashed fronds stood proud for that signified a cockerel and pouting if evenness showed a hen.

But his mother had frowned on the game, her face serious and a little afraid as she'd warned of the magic held by the plant. To pluck it was to call on the spirits, she'd said. Ask for what it is you want, she'd advised, then lay the stalk back on the ground. If you took care not to bruise its delicate leaves the spirits would answer in kindness, but pluck it and crush it and their vengeance would be swift and certain. They had laughed at the tale, the three of them, but had nevertheless always raced home after playing that particular game, fear hot and spicy in their veins.

Holding the mugwort in his hand now Adam felt the uncertainty of youth touch his mind and laid the feathered stem gently back on the ground. He asked for nothing. The spirits could not give him what he wanted; there was no magic would give a girl the use of legs that were crippled, or grant him the daughter of an iron master. 'I'm sorry I plucked you,' he whispered, then smiling at his own foolishness he walked on. But the memory of brown eyes laughing at him from a face beautiful as the morning stayed with him.

Gaining Wolverhampton Street Adam halted, no clear memory of crossing the heath in his mind. His mother had told him to go, but where? He would not go to the cottage in the grounds of Rowena House.

'Want to earn a bob, lad?'

Adam looked over to where Arthur Foster had come to stand in the doorway of his small bakery, his plump red face streaked with flour.

'Empty that cart o' them sacks an' it'll pay a bob.'

A shilling! Adam crossed the street with quick steps. A shilling would buy food until he got his first wage from Mrs Butler. 'Where do you want them?' he asked, hitching a well-filled sack on to his shoulder, feeling the weight of it bite into him.

'Through 'ere.' The baker led the way, easing between sacks of various grains and seeds stacked around the walls, leaving little space to move in the tiny shop. Out in the yard, as cluttered with rusting wheels and old harness as the shop was with sacks, he pointed to a low-roofed brick building. 'In there,' he said. 'Drop 'em in there, lad, an' when you be done I'll be in the bakehouse.'

One after the other Adam carried in the sacks, enjoying the scents of corn, wheat, dried beans and peas that filled the small room which served as a shop, mingling with that of newly baked bread, the whole so different from the foul odours of Foleys Croft.

'Be you done, lad?'

Adam lowered the last of the sacks it had taken him well over an hour to shift and wiped his sweating face with the back of his hand.

'This is the last one.' He smiled at a woman as round as she was tall, her long skirts covered with a ruffled apron of spotless white.

'I'll just tell Mr Foster then, but meantime I bet you could bost a tankard o' summat coolin'?'

'I would much appreciate a drink, Mrs Foster.' Adam pushed a hand through his hair, lifting sweat-soaked strands from his brow.

'Come you into the kitchen then.' The woman smiled, eyes bright in her round apple face. 'Sit you there.' She motioned to a three-legged stool set against the open door of a room as small as the shop and equally as cluttered. A black-leaded range with ovens and hob was flanked on either side by four long wooden drawers topped by a cupboard that reached to the ceiling. Across from this was a door that Adam guessed opened on to stairs that would lead to a bedroom, while alongside it a small pine dresser held an assortment of dishes and cups. The centre of the room was given over to a large table, its wooden surface scrubbed white.

'There you go, lad.' The woman reappeared from the yard, a pewter tankard in one hand and a brown ironstone flagon hooked over the fingers of the other. Pulling the cork with her teeth, she poured a glowing golden liquid into the tankard then handed it to Adam before taking the cork from her mouth. 'You'll enjoy that,' she said, beaming. 'Though I says it as shouldn't it be a good drap o' cider. Get it down you, lad. It'll put a few 'airs on yer chest, will Polly Foster's cider.'

Setting the recorked flagon on the stone floor beside the dresser, she opened a small cupboard, its door patterned with a series of tiny punched holes, lifting out a large pie with edges fluted and crispy brown.

'I reckons a lad the size o' you could always eat a bit o' pie,' she said, slicing a wedge and handing it with a fork to Adam. 'Mr Foster says as 'ow I've got a way wi' pies an' such, tho' tis 'im as bakes the bread.'

Adam would have liked to take the pie home, it would have done his father good, but not to eat it might be interpreted as a slight. Laying his tankard on the floor beside his stool, he forked meat and vegetable robed in crusty pastry into his mouth, nodding approval as he chewed.

'I see my Polly got to you.' Arthur Foster entered the kitchen, wiping flour-dusted hands on an apron already covered with a thick creamy film. 'I swear nothin' pleases 'er as much as stuffin' folk wi' food.'

'It is very good food.' Adam reached for his tankard, swallowing the last of his cider. 'And so was that. My thanks to you, Mrs Foster.'

'You be welcome, lad,' Polly beamed, 'you be welcome.'

'An' now you be wantin' yer pay.' His boots leaving a trail of floured prints on the stone flags, the baker crossed to the dresser, taking a tin box from the drawer. Placing it on the table he removed the lid with a picture of a girl in a wide crinoline gown and ribboned bonnet ringed by the words 'Dainty Dinah Toffees'. Taking out a silver coin, he handed it to Adam.

'That be thine, lad,' he replaced the lid. 'An' you earned it.'

Adam curled the shilling into his palm. It was over generous for the job he had done. How long would the like of his father sweat in front of the foundry furnace for the same amount?

'Thank you, sir.' He could not smile though he wanted to. 'And thank you, Mrs Foster.'

'Tek this to yer mother, lad.' Polly pressed a bag into his hand, its brown paper thick as linen. ''Er'll find a use for it, I've no doubt. Now, now,' she urged as Adam tried to refuse, 'it just be a bit o' meat pie an' a few odds and sods that'll spoil wi' keepin' an' 'ave to be chucked out.'

'Thanks,' Adam said, but the look in his grey eyes said more. 'You are very kind.'

'Kind nothin'!' Polly's smile spread. 'You be doin' a kindness carryin' 'em away. An' there be a coupla loaves waitin' on you goin' through the shop.'

Adam walked slowly across the heath toward Foleys Croft. Perhaps the spirits of the mugwort had been kind after all? The vision of a heart-shaped faced surrounded by a mass of chestnut hair, a smiling mouth and wide bronze eyes, floated into his mind. For a second or two he looked at it with his heart's eyes before it faded. Some things the spirits of the little plant might give him but Esther Kerral it could not.

117

Chapter Nine

'I still don't think you should go to that house.' Miri smoothed Esther's maroon grosgrain skirts, covering her feet which rested on the footboard of the wheelchair.

'It is better that I do.' Esther secured the silk ribbon of her matching bonnet under her chin. 'I think it more suitable to receive them at Rowena House.'

'But you seen what 'e was like when 'e come across 'ere.' Miri stood up, her face anxious as she looked at the girl in the chair. 'I wouldn't trust 'im no further than I could throw 'im.'

'You are worrying for no reason.'

'Worryin' fer no reason!' Miri's voice rose a full octave. 'You can say that after what 'e did to you not a three week gone? I tell you, wench, there always be reason to worry when you be around that one. 'E ain't to be trusted – too 'andy wi' 'is fists, especially when it be a woman 'e be strikin'.'

'He won't do that again.' Esther pressed her hand.

'Don't you be too sure o' that.' And Miri's mouth clamped shut.

Esther smiled, trying to reassure her. It was natural Miri should worry for her safety but on this visit to Rowena House she would not be alone with her father and, untrustworthy as he was, it was hardly likely he would strike her in front of the Cosmores.

'Remember, Miri, Mr Evans said if I had to visit that house again, he would take care for my safety.'

'Arrh, 'e did that.' Miri nodded though the line of her mouth did not soften. 'An' I believes 'im. Jobs might be 'arder to find than gold in this town but when it comes to seein' a young wench smacked in the mouth then I thinks Will Evans would risk the losin' o' 'is.'

'So stop worrying.' Esther pressed her hand once more then released it. 'It will all be over in an hour and I will be back here.'

'I know you be right, Essie wench,' Miri sighed, 'but I still can't 'elp but wish it were done wi'. I won't feel safe till you be 'ome.'

'I know you cannot be with me in the drawing room but you will be close. They always make you welcome in the kitchen and you love having a good old gossip with Mrs Turner.'

Miri turned away, reaching for her cloak on the peg behind the kitchen door. Letty Turner did always make her welcome and it made for a pleasant change having a body her own age to gossip with, but the kitchen was not the drawing room. If Jos Kerral did take it into his head to strike Esther then neither she nor Evans would be close enough to prevent it. She tied the strings of her cloak, a quiet resolve already formed. If Jos Kerral laid one finger on Esther it would be the last day he would live. The kitchen of Rowena House had knives a-plenty and their blades were sharp. If he struck his daughter again one of them would find its way to his heart.

'Mrs Butler?'

The call following a knock at the door caused Miri's heart to skip a beat. It was time. When Esther returned to this house she would be promised to Ezra Cosmore's son.

'We be ready, Mr Evans.' Taking the push bar of the wheelchair, Miri propelled it to the door where the butler stood waiting.

'Good afternoon, Mr Evans.' Esther gave him her brightest smile. 'How nice of you to call yourself. This is kind.'

Will Evans returned the smile. The girl knew he had no option but to come to this house himself. He was Jos Kerral's paid man and as such must do as he said, but nevertheless it was good to be treated with a respect the father had never paid him.

'Have my father's guests arrived?'

'Not yet, miss.' Evans took the chair from Miri, pushing it towards the line of trees screening the view of Rowena House. 'Time arranged was three o'clock and it still needs a quarter of the hour. The master thought you would need that to get settled.'

Or to give him another few minutes to have a go at getting back the deeds to that works, Miri thought. But he stands more chance of flying in the air. Esther is every bit as stubborn as he is.

'You ain't to leave 'er on 'er own wi' 'im, Will Evans,' Miri warned. 'You ain't to leave that room till the others be there. If you do I'll go in there meself, an' to 'ell wi' what Jos Kerral says.'

'I'll 'ave to answer the door when they arrive.' Will glanced at the woman walking beside him, the feathers on her bonnet ruffled by the slight breeze. 'It'll be expected. But it'll take less than a couple o' minutes. 'E can't do 'er no 'arm in that space o' time.'

Oh, no! Miri's insides froze despite his reassurance. How long did it take a man to raise his fist and smash it into the face of a girl who couldn't move out of reach? Aloud she said, 'Just don't let 'im bully you into leavin' 'er wi' 'im afore you 'as to. Don't give 'im the benefit o' no doubt.'

'Y'ave my word, Mrs Butler.' Following the path that led to the rear of the house, he pushed the wheelchair through the door Letty Turner held open.

Once inside the kitchen Esther removed her bonnet, smoothing a hand over the thick chestnut hair caught in a ribbon at the nape of her neck. She had refused to let Miri dress it any other way. What was the use of that? Morgan Cosmore was not interested in her appearance, she had pointed out. He was interested only in her father's money.

'I'll tell the master you be 'ere, miss.'

'Thank you, Mr Evans.' Esther handed her bonnet to Miri who began nervously to twist the ties around her fingers.

'Let me tek that, Miriam.' Letty Turner released the bonnet gently from her hands. 'An' give my yer cloak an' all. You'll be 'ere some time. Best tek it off or you'll be over warm.'

Unfastening the cloak, Miri slipped it off, allowing Letty to carry it to the small room beside the butler's pantry.

'I give the 'ousemaid the day off,' she said, coming back into the large airy kitchen. 'What the mind don't know the tongue can't wag about, I always says.'

'That was right thoughtful o' you, Letty,' Miri said. 'Fewer folk as know about this day's 'appenings the better.'

''E said to tek you in now, miss.' William Evans returned as Miri spoke. 'So if you be ready?'

'Quite ready.' Esther smiled though her heart beat a rapid tattoo.

'Watch yerself, Essie,' Miri said, tears catching in her throat. 'An' remember, Will Evans. You waits till that doorbell rings afore you leaves that room.'

For the second time Esther found herself wheeled into the drawing room of Rowena House. Light streamed from windows that almost touched the ceiling with its huge ornate plaster rose from which descended a tiered chandelier, its crystal drops reflecting the light in a myriad of colours. Tapestry-covered sofas and chairs echoed the soft blues and powder greys of carpet and curtains. It was a room upon which a feminine hand had lain.

Jos Kerral stood beneath the portrait of his wife, legs slightly apart, hands behind his back beneath his black frock coat.

'Over there!' He jerked his head towards a deep armchair to the left of the fireplace then strode to the window, standing with his back to the room.

''Old on to me, miss.' One arm across the front of her, Evans lifted Esther from the wheelchair, hitching her sideways until he could lower her into the armchair.

Breathing hard from the effort, he looked into her face,

not sure if his handling of her had been too uncomfortable. 'Be you all right, miss?' he asked in a low voice. 'Sorry if I 'urt you.'

'You did not hurt me, Mr Evans.' Esther smiled. 'Thank you for your help.'

'When you 'ave bloody finished bletherin', Evans, p'raps you'll get that thing outta this room.' Striding back to the hearth Jos kicked viciously at the wheelchair, sending it rolling backward into a mahogany table. A Worcester porcelain group crashed to the floor.

'I'll just get Miss Esther a footstool, sir.' Evans half expected the next kick to be directed at him but when none came he crossed to a far corner of the room, taking a low footstool from before a wide spoon-back chair, bringing it to where she sat and positioning it beneath her feet. 'Allow me, miss?' he asked, and when Esther smiled her consent, knelt and positioned her feet on it, covering them with her skirts.

Standing once more, he turned to the man watching him, a scowl furrowing his face. 'I will just clean up the broken china, sir.'

'Leave the bloody thing,' growled Jos, glancing towards the open door of the room as the jangle of the front door bell sounded. 'Cosmore'll be seein' plenty o' that when 'e teks 'er into 'is 'ouse. Just get that contraption outta the way.'

'I'll tek it to the kitchen, miss.' Evans directed her a look that asked as clear as any words could have done if she felt up to being left alone with his master?

Esther nodded, more in answer to the look than his words, but her hand brushed nervously along the row of tiny maroon buttons that ran the length of her bodice.

Several seconds ticked by in the silence of the lovely room, seconds in which her father neither spoke nor looked at her. Esther glanced once at the face in the portrait then clasped her hands in her lap as Evans showed their visitors in.

'Good day, Cosmore.' Jos stretched a hand to the older man. 'Glad you could come.'

'Pleasure, Kerral, pleasure.' Ezra grasped the extended hand, shaking it warmly. 'This be my son.'

'Good afternoon, sir.' Morgan took his turn at shaking hands. 'Would you be kind enough to receive my friend, Mrs Roberta Vance? She is visiting us at Addenbrooke House.'

'You be the one doin' the kindness.' Jos tried to be gracious but no smile came to his lips. 'You be welcome in my 'ouse, Mrs Vance.'

'You are most gracious.' The woman's rather deep voice was soft, almost musical, and her movements graceful as she accepted the chair indicated by Jos.

'Let me present my . . . my Esther.'

Even now he could not say it without the word sticking in his throat, Esther thought. Even now he could not own to her being his daughter.

'Esther, eh!' Ezra grabbed her hand. 'It be nice to see you, an' this 'ere be Morgan, yer intended.'

'Good afternoon, Esther.' Rescuing her hand from his father, Morgan touched his lips to her fingers.

Esther looked into eyes whose colour she could not determine. Were they green flecked with gold or gold flecked with green? Either way they were a brilliant compliment to skin that was slightly bronzed. Releasing her hand, he stood tall and straight, shoulders wide beneath the cut of his dove grey coat. Handsome, Esther admitted, and a man who knows it.

'Allow me to present Mrs Vance.' He walked to the chair where the woman sat, standing beside it. 'Mrs Vance is on a visit from London.'

'How nice to meet you, Mrs Vance,' Esther smiled. 'I fear you must find Darlaston very different from London?'

'Different, yes, but Morgan makes it so . . . interesting.'

Roberta Vance smiled, a gloved hand reaching out to touch Morgan's arm. The minute hesitation in her words caught in Esther's ear and the smile that etched her full lips was not echoed in her cold violet eyes. I am being warned, Esther thought, watching the hand slide sensuously over Morgan's arm. Morgan Cosmore may be the husband my father's money will buy for me but he belongs to Roberta Vance.

'Will you take some tea, Mrs Vance?' Esther accepted the unspoken message. That Morgan might be, and most probably was, this woman's lover was of little consequence for theirs would not be a marriage born of love but of hatred – the hatred her own father held for her.

'Thank you, Esther . . . oh, forgive me, I have not asked if I may call you Esther?' Roberta fluttered her lashes as she looked up at Morgan. 'You will think my manners appalling, Morgan dear. You will feel shamed by bringing me here.'

'I would like you to call me by my name,' Esther put in quickly, wondering if the long curling lashes might not fall off with all the fluttering they received.

Roberta Vance reluctantly slid her eyes from Morgan's direction, making no secret of her possessiveness. 'And you must call me Roberta,' she said. 'We are going to be such good friends, I hope, Esther.'

'Tea?' She asked again, feeling the insincerity of the other's words and knowing herself untouched by it. Roberta Vance, if she but knew it, need have no fear of losing Morgan to his wife.

'That would be nice.' Roberta nodded. 'The drive here was somewhat dusty.'

'Would you, Father?' Esther looked at Jos for the first time since coming into the room, her smile a masterly pretence at a normal father-daughter relationship.

'What . . . eh!' Taken off guard, he fumbled then pulled a tapestried cord hanging to one side of the fireplace. Then, looking at Ezra added, 'The women be tekin' tea but you would 'ave a preference for summat else, eh, Cosmore?'

'Brandy, if you will,' Ezra answered as Evans entered the room.

Ordering tea, Esther gave an almost imperceptible nod of her head, seeing the look of anxiety fade from the butler's eye as he caught it.

'Are you staying in Darlaston long, Mrs Vance?' Esther asked as her father poured brandy into three cut glass goblets.

'I had intended to return to London tomorrow.' The violet eyes rested on Esther. 'But Morgan insisted I stay until he could take me home himself.'

''Ave you seen the copper foundry?' Josiah turned his attention to the woman Ezra had brought with him, annoyance at his bringing her today of all days niggling at him.

'Morgan's father offered to take me to James Bridge,' Roberta treated him to a fetching smile, 'but I would be terrified to go into such a place. The outside was frightening enough: tall chimney stacks pouring black smoke, and the thought of those furnaces Morgan told me of . . .' She touched a hand affectedly to her throat. 'They turn the whole sky to flame apparently. No, Mr Kerral, I am much too afraid to go inside a foundry.'

'Understandable, me dear.' Josiah sampled his brandy as Evans reappeared, wheeling a trolley set with a silver tea service and a cake. 'A foundry be no place fer a woman.'

'Arrh, it be understandable.' He resumed his stance in front of the fireplace. 'But then, Darlaston don't 'ave much more fer a visitor to see. It ain't got the entertainments that London can boast.'

'That might be true of the theatres . . .' Roberta Vance accepted the cup Esther held out to her, shaking her head at the offer of cake '. . . but it compensates for that in the friendliness of the people I have met.'

No doubt meaning the friendliness of Morgan in particular, Esther thought, taking a sip from her own cup and keeping up the pretence of a well-loved daughter.

'Roberta is seeking a rest from theatres,' Morgan said, glancing at the woman Esther guessed to be more than his friend. 'The social round can become quite exhausting.'

'Well, 'er'll get away from it 'ere all right.' Ezra gulped at his brandy. 'Only social round in this town be the beer 'ouses, and they be 'ardly the best o' places fer tekin' a woman o' quality.'

Returning her cup Roberta glanced at the portrait above the fireplace. 'I don't need to ask if that beautiful woman is your mother, Esther,' she said, her curiously deep voice almost husky. 'The likeness is very clear. You have her eyes and mouth and the same wonderful chestnut hair. In fact, my dear, you have inherited her beauty. She must be very proud of you.'

'My mother died when I was four years old.' Esther replaced her own cup on the trolley. 'I have very little recollection of her.'

'Oh, I am so sorry.' Pulling a handkerchief from the bag she carried about her wrist, Roberta Vance dabbed it delicately to her nose.

''As Morgan teken you to Brummagem?' Jos placed his glass behind him on the mantel above the fireplace. 'It be a much bigger town than Darlaston, more there to interest a woman.'

Replacing her handkerchief in her bag, she turned her violet eyes to him. 'Morgan has taken me to Birmingham, Mr Kerral, and though I found our trip interesting, I must admit I much prefer to spend my time in the garden – the one at Addenbrooke House is so very pleasant.'

'Not what it was in my mother's time,' Morgan said, 'but still pleasant enough.'

'Do you like gardens, Esther?' Roberta turned again to her.

'Very much so,' she answered, something inside beginning to prickle warningly as the other woman's smile swept to Morgan again.

'Then you will love the ones at Addenbrooke. They are so romantic, particularly in the moonlight with Morgan.'

'I don't really expect him to have much time to spend in the garden.' Esther glanced from Morgan back to his guest. If Roberta had thought to make her jealous she was sadly wide of the mark.

'But you enjoy them so much.' The violet eyes widened with pretend surprise. 'You said so just a minute ago.'

'My enjoyment of something will not make it incumbent upon Morgan to indulge in it.' Esther knew she was being led deliberately onward, that this woman's conversation carried a sting.

'Then perhaps I might prevail upon that enjoyment and ask you to show me your gardens? I am sure the men have some tiresome business they are itching to discuss. Will you walk with me, Esther?'

So this was the sting in the serpent's tail. Esther's hands tightened, pressing into her skirts. This woman must know, Morgan had to have told her, so why ask her to walk in the garden? Why unless to add to her pain or give embarrassment to Morgan . . . which was the answer, or was it both?

'That will not be possible.' Esther held her head high. 'You see, Roberta, I am crippled in the legs. I cannot walk.'

'I will go with you, Roberta.' Morgan was on his feet his green-gold eyes cold with anger. 'If, that is, we have Mr Kerral's permission?'

Why the bloody hell did he want to go buggering off into the garden when they had business to sort out? Josiah thought even as he nodded consent.

Roberta Vance stood up, lowering her lashes but not quickly enough to hide the glint of triumph in her eyes. So she had known. Esther felt her fingers throb with the pain of being pressed hard together. All this was for Morgan, she decided. Roberta is showing him what he is getting into, and what he could have instead. She is holding me up against herself. Oh, Roberta! She suddenly wanted to laugh. If only you knew, if only I could tell you. Once I become Morgan Cosmore's wife you can have him, take him where you will for as long as you like. My interest is not in him.

'No, Morgan.' The deep musical voice held a note of self-recrimination. 'I have made the most terrible faux pas and all I want to do is beg Esther's pardon then hide myself away until my embarrassment is gone.' She fluttered her lashes appealingly. 'Please, my dear, you must allow me to go alone.'

'You have no need to hide away.' Esther smiled, knowing the other woman's show of remorse was nothing but a sham. 'Even the most prudent of us makes mistakes occasionally.'

'Now then,' Josiah turned to the Cosmores as Roberta passed through the long window he had opened on to the garden, 'let's get to what you came for. I agree to give forty per cent of my business plus a thousand a year if yer son and my . . . Esther be wed. What d'you say?'

Morgan Cosmore crossed to Esther, looking into her upturned face. Roberta had been right when she'd said the girl had beauty. She was indeed easy on the eye, if only . . . 'It seems we both stand on the auction block, Miss Kerral,' he said softly. 'But say the word, say if you have no wish to go through with this marriage, and I will tell the auctioneers we have no need of their services.'

'I have no wish to withdraw,' she replied, unsmiling. 'If you are content to accept then so am I.'

'You could 'ave cocked things up good and well wi' yer big mouth!' Ezra snatched the brandy he had ordered Gittins to bring, swearing at him to get out. He had fumed all the way back to Butcroft, his temper finally spilling over as they reached Addenbrooke House. 'You gave that wench the perfect get out. "We both stand on the auction block, Miss Kerral,"' he mimicked.

'Is that not where we do stand?' Morgan asked, watching the older man tip more brandy into his glass.

'If that be the way you want to look at it then, yes, you stands on a bloody auction block. But there was no need to shout it out. We be less than a stride from the bankruptcy court but you don't go shoutin' about *that*.'

Morgan sank into a chair. Roberta had said almost nothing on the way home and had retired to her room as soon as they had reached the house, which was as well seeing the mood his father was in.

'You nearly put paid to the 'ole bloody business.' Ezra waved the glass in the air, slopping part of its contents down himself but ignoring it.

'And that would have put paid to your well-laid scheme, wouldn't it, Father? You would have had to find some other piper to play your tune. That's it, isn't it? That's what is making you so mad. Not the fact that I gave Esther Kerral an opportunity to chuck the whole thing in her father's face.'

'An' if 'er 'ad!' Ezra's face darkened. 'What then, eh? Then where would yer money come from? Money you 'as to 'ave if you am goin' to keep the like o' that upstairs. An' don't tell me you ain't doin' so. A man wi' no eyes could see what be goin' on there.'

'Let us leave Roberta out of this, shall we, Father?'

'Oh, arrh.' Ezra slurped more brandy. 'Let's leave yer smart-mouthed lady friend out o' it.' He glared at Morgan, his brandy soaked eyes receding behind rolls of fat. 'It be a pity you 'adn't left 'er out o' it altogether, but no, you 'ad to tek 'er, you 'ad to flaunt yer fancy woman in front o' Kerral.'

'But the deal still went through.'

Reaching for the decanter, Ezra eyed his son. It was a fool's game he had played, going to meet the woman he was to marry with a mistress on his arm.

'Yes, it went through.' He filled his glass till the golden liquid found an outlet over the rim.

'Was there ever any reason why it should not?' Morgan queried lazily.

'Reason?' Ezra's temper flared like a freshly stoked furnace. 'There was every bloody reason, seein' that piece you took wi' you. "Will you walk wi' me, Esther?" What the bloody 'ell possessed her to say a thing like that? You 'ad told 'er, 'adn't you?'

Yes, he had told her, Morgan thought. He had explained

everything: the reason for his marriage, the fact that the girl was unable to walk, the fact that it would make no difference to them. He had told Roberta and they had made love, laughing at the way the Kerral money had been tipped into their pockets. Yes, he had told her yet still they had been made to play that little scene.

'There was no risk of Kerral's pulling out,' Morgan answered, ignoring his father's question. 'Where else would he find a man fool enough to marry a cripple, a girl who cannot move from her chair?'

Ezra nodded his head. 'There be fools an' there be fools,' he said thickly. 'Old Kerral can find the sort 'e wants if'n 'e looks far enough, so you think on an' don't cook yer chicken afore the feathers be plucked.'

Morgan brushed one lazy finger over his hand-tailored grey trousers. 'You need have no worry. I will have Kerral's money and forty per cent of his business, which hopefully will amount to a fair sum. What you do need to worry over, Father, is that I shall also have your business – not just forty per cent but all of it, Cosmore Industries in total.'

Ezra hiccuped loudly, jerking fresh brandy down his waistcoat. 'Why . . . hic . . . why should that worry me?'

'Well, Father, think of it.' Morgan's lazy smile widened but his green-gold cat's eyes were icy. 'I might want to run the works myself.'

'You!' Ezra began to laugh, shaking jelly rolls of fat. 'You run the business? That'll be the day pigs fly over Darlaston. You . . . run my business . . .'

Laugh now, Father. Morgan closed the door softly as he left the lovely oval room. Laugh now and laugh long for you won't laugh once the James Bridge copper works and everything else you own is signed over to me. No, Father, you won't laugh then for I will not be running the business – I will be selling it.

The laughter still in his ears, Morgan entered Roberta Vance's bedroom. Crossing to the silk-draped bed he looked down at the figure, blue-black hair tumbling wildly over ivory-cream shoulders, violet eyes smoky beneath curling lashes, a wide full mouth smiling up at him while slender smooth legs, freed of cumbersome bloomers, parted meaningfully.

'I thought you had elected to stay with your father the rest of the afternoon.' The voice was throaty, reaching up to him, enfolding him like a caress. 'Such a waste, my darling, when you could be coming into me.'

Chapter Ten

'You be sure you wants to go through with it?'

Miri looked at the young woman in the wheelchair, her chestnut hair caught high on her head with a ribbon that matched her blue dress, her face a little too drawn despite her smile.

'Yes, Miri, I am sure.' Esther touched the other woman's hand. 'Would you get me my prayer book?'

She turned away towards the room Esther had used as a bedroom since John's death had meant she could no longer be carried up the steep narrow stairs. Going to the table beside the brass bedstead, she took up the book bound in soft white nappa, a cross incised in gold on the cover. This had been the prayer book Helen Kerral had carried on the day she had married; the book she had held in her hand as the breath of life slipped from her body; the book Josiah Kerral, in the fury of grief, had hurled against the wall and which Miri had carried hidden in her skirts away from Rowena House. So much grief, so much pain. Miri held back her tears as she went to where Esther waited to go to her wedding.

'It should 'ave been in church,' Miri said, her thin body arched forward with the effort of pushing the wheelchair. ''Ow can the Lord put 'Is blessin' on a match not made in church?'

'My father wanted it this way,' Esther said, hiding the fresh hurt her father's flat refusal of a church wedding had caused her.

133

'Arrh, I bet 'e did.' Miri sucked in a long breath. 'An' I knows why. Folk 'ere about 'ad forgot 'is wife give birth to a daughter an' 'e weren't wantin' to rouse no memories. Less known, soonest forgot be the way 'is mind works.'

'It is probably best this way.' Esther glanced at the book held in her lap. 'A more usual wedding would only have caused gossip and that can't do either of us any good in the end.'

'You might be right about it doin' no good an' I don't like tittle-tattle neither, but it'd shake 'im up if folk found out what 'e done to you an' the way 'e 'as treated you all these years.'

'It could have been worse, Miri. He could have had me admitted to the workhouse. He could have claimed I was the unwanted child of a runaway servant, there would have been none who would have denied it. As you yourself have often said, trouble hangs around every corner of Darlaston. You can find it easy enough without going to look for it, and at least he paid well for my keep.'

'Arrh, 'e did that.' Miri's admission was grudging. 'But to chuck you out of 'is 'ouse an' you no more'n a babby!'

'All of that is in the past.' In the past, yes, Esther thought, but not forgotten. She would never forget the nights she'd cried herself to sleep, longing for him to come for her, wanting the father who was so near yet never once showed himself; trying to understand when Miri told her he was a busy man who, because he was hardly ever at home, thought it best to leave her in the care of someone who loved her as much as he did. That had almost caused her to laugh when, as a teenager, she had at last realised he had no love whatsoever for her. Thank God Miri had not loved her just as much as he did!

'In the past, yes.' Miri rounded the line of trees that screened Rowena House from the cottage she must vacate before nightfall. 'An' what of the future? 'As 'e done any better for you there? Marryin' that Cosmore – pah! I 'ave me doubts. He only 'as the welfare of one at 'eart in the makin' of all this, an' that be Jos Kerral.'

There was no denying the truth of Miri's words even had

she wanted to. Her father had arranged this union with the Cosmores to suit his own purposes, but it would be made to suit hers also. Esther's hand tightened on the small prayer book. Somehow or other she would use this marriage to take her revenge on the man only a slip of paper acknowledged as her father.

'They already be 'ere, miss.' William Evans stood at the rear entrance as Miri and Esther arrived. 'Got 'ere some ten minutes back.'

'It is the prerogative of the bride to be late, Mr Evans.' Esther tried to keep her voice light. 'But let us not keep Parson Tranter any longer. Would you take me through, please?'

'Eh, miss, you look lovely.' Letty Turner bustled from the kitchen as Evans wheeled the chair along a corridor that led from the back of the house. 'Me and young Dotty, we . . . we 'oped you would take this, miss, just a little summat from the two of we like.' She pressed a dainty lace-edged handkerchief, a motif of blue forget-me-nots embroidered in each corner, into Esther's hand. 'Good luck, miss,' she whispered, tears edging down her plump face, 'an' the Lord go wi' you.'

'Yes, the Lord go with 'er,' Miri echoed as she watched the girl she loved as a daughter wheeled from her sight through the door that closed off this corridor from the main part of the house. ''Er be goin' to need 'Im.'

'An' you be needin' a cup o' tea.' Letty led the way back to her kitchen. 'Get a pot o' tea brewed, Dotty,' she called to the young housemaid. ''Er ain't really 'ere as kitchen 'elp,' Letty confided as she took Miri's cloak, 'but 'er don't be wanted upstairs for an hour or two so 'er might as well do a bit to earn 'er keep down 'ere.'

'You'll 'ave 'ad yer work cut out preparing a weddin' breakfast all by yerself, Letty.' Miri watched the girl, who was hardly more than fourteen years old but deft enough with cups and kettle.

'Weddin' breakfast.' Letty snorted. 'Ain't gonna be no weddin' breakfast.'

Miri looked aghast. 'But there's always a spread put on when there's a do in the 'ouse.'

'In any other 'ouse there be.' Letty waited for the tray complete with large flower-embellished teapot to be placed in front of her then waved young Dotty away to the scullery. 'Like I said afore, Miriam, the less the ears pick up, the less there be for the tongue to drop.'

'A wise course to take, Letty.' Miri accepted the tea poured for her. 'But 'ow come there be no spread laid on?'

Letty shrugged her ample shoulders, stirring two spoons of sugar into her tea. 'Left to me there would 'ave been but the master, 'e said no, there was to be no fuss. Everybody would leave when Parson did. Ee, that poor wench!' She shook her head. 'No church, no maids, no spread. What sort o' weddin' be that? Even poorest wench in Darlaston 'as a few flowers an' the blessin' of the Lord in 'Is own church when 'er be wed.'

'Poorest wench in Darlaston be one up on Esther,' Miri answered. ''Er don't 'ave Jos Kerral for a father. Way I sees it, 'e wouldn't dare put 'is nose inside a church 'case the Lord above struck 'im down for the way 'e 'as treated 'er . . . an' now this, a 'ole in the corner weddin'. I tell you, Letty, 'e should be made to pay – an' to my mind a thorough 'oss whippin' be what 'e should get.'

'Amen to that!' Letty lifted the cup to her lips. 'An' if'n the Lord grant my wish, I'll be the one to give it 'im.'

Reaching the drawing room, William Evans halted. 'You be certain you wants this, miss?' Going to the front of the chair he looked down at Esther. 'If you ain't really for goin' through wi' this marriage then say so an' I'll take you back. An' what's more, I'll tell the parson you be against it. Ain't much Kerral can do after that, an' as for this job of butlerin' 'e can stick it up . . . well, you knows where 'e can stick it, miss. You be the one who matters.'

'It is kind of you to feel that way.' Esther blinked away the mist before her eyes. 'But it is what I want. Yet there is one thing I would ask of you.'

William smiled at the girl he had come to like and respect. 'You 'ave only to ask an' if it be anythin' I can do, then I will.'

Esther smiled up at him, her bronze-coloured eyes clear once more. 'Then I will ask, Mr Evans. Please may I call you William?'

'You can that, miss, an' honoured I'll be.'

Opening the doors of the drawing room, he wheeled Esther in.

Her father occupied his usual position before the fireplace, legs apart, hands across his back beneath his coat. To his left the parson in cassock and gown perched like a nervous rook on the edge of a tapestry-covered chair while to his right Ezra Cosmore lovingly tended to a brandy glass; a little to the rear of his father Morgan Cosmore sat beside Roberta Vance. Esther felt the breath catch in her lungs. He had brought that woman to his wedding!

Watching them rise, she admitted to the woman's attractiveness. She was not pretty, no one could call her that; and neither would they call her beautiful with her slightly angular face, but there could be no denying an attractiveness that many men would find alluring. Dressed in smoky amethyst velvet jacket and skirt braided with violet, the exact colour of her eyes, shining raven black hair coiled thickly about her head, her full rouged mouth just curving into a smile, Esther could see the appeal she held for Morgan.

'Esther dear, you look enchanting, doesn't she, Morgan?' Just a few inches shorter than his five foot ten she fluttered a glance up at him before crossing to Esther and kissing her cheek.

'You can get out!' Josiah Kerral growled at his butler, and when the doors came together behind him, went on, 'Well, let's get this over. No call to stand gawpin'. Where do you want we should stand, parson?'

The priest jumped to his feet in his agitation, shifting the book he held in his hands. 'You as the bride's father will be at her left – if you will, Mr Kerral . . . and you, Mrs Vance, as her attendant matron of honour . . .'

'She is not my attendant,' Esther said coldly her glance lifting to violet eyes that laughed from under the cover of thick dark lashes.

'I . . . I . . .' the parson stuttered in confusion. He was used to marriage ceremonies being conducted within the hallowed precincts of the church, not in the house of an industrialist. While it was not illegal, it did not conform to what he as a servant of God approved of; was to his mind little short of sacrilege. 'The groom will take his place beside the bride.' Ignoring his mistake he left Roberta Vance to find her own place on a chair at the side of the room. 'Do you have a best man?'

'My father.' Morgan nodded to where Ezra still cradled his glass.

'I see. Then if he will come to stand at your left, we can begin.'

Making sure the goblet was well drained before he put it aside, Ezra took his place.

The priest opened his book. '"Dearly beloved, we are gathered here in the sight of God . . ."'

'We all know why we be gathered 'ere,' Jos interrupted, a scowl of impatience on his face, 'an' I for one don't care who be watchin' so you can cut all that bloody useless prattle an' get down to it.'

Finding the page he was looking for, Parson Tranter ran a finger down the centre then cleared his throat before beginning again. '"Dearly beloved . . ."' This marriage might not be taking place within a church but the service would be the same.

'Who giveth this woman to this man?'

Jos stepped forward but made no move to take Esther's hand.

Parson Tranter waited but Jos remained still.

'Take the bride's hand in yours.' The priest half closed his book, the glance he directed at Jos stern. This was his element and his domain, and he would have things done as they ought to be or not done at all. 'The bride's left hand.'

His own eyes fastened on the priest, obviously ill wishing him, Jos took Esther's hand, placing it in Morgan's.

'Do you Esther Helen take this man . . .' The parson, all earlier nerves forgotten, sailed on.

Esther's left hand, resting now on Morgan's, tingled but not with his touch. For the second time in her memory her father had touched her; the first had been only days ago when his hand had smacked against her mouth. Today, he had lifted her hand as if it were contaminated. She could almost imagine he had afterwards wiped his fingers down the side of his trousers.

'Do you, Morgan Winfield, take this woman . . .'

The priest droned on, the words washing meaninglessly over Esther. She had thought never to marry, that no man would take her, a cripple, for a wife, but it had not stopped the dreams of girlhood; dreams that saw her dressed in white, a chaplet of spring flowers in her hair, standing with her husband in St Lawrence's as the blessing was pronounced over them. Instead she had this, a furtive ceremony performed in her father's house. She was not being given as a bride to Morgan Cosmore, she was being sold for a handful of silver.

'. . . will you love her, honour her, in sickness and in health, keeping only unto her so long as ye both shall live . . .'

His stare passing over Esther's head, Morgan's eyes fastened on deep violet ones, his mouth curving into the shadow of a smile as he answered, 'I will.'

It was over. Esther looked at the thick gold band circling the third finger of her left hand. There had been no word of congratulation, no wish expressed for her future happiness, the ink had not been dry before her father had virtually pushed the priest from the room. She looked over to see him handing

Morgan a long brown envelope. Her bride price? The silver he thought to reap back as gold?

'That be it then.' Her father turned to Ezra who was looking hopefully in the direction of the decanter. 'I see no reason for delay. You can take yer daughter-in-law to 'er new 'ome. Will you push that wheelchair or do I ring for Evans?'

'Wheelchair!' Morgan had made a beeline for Roberta Vance as soon as Parson Tranter had pronounced the words 'man and wife'. Now he turned sharply, his look going to Esther. 'Do you mean she can go nowhere without a wheelchair?'

'Nowhere.' Jos Kerral glared suspiciously at Ezra, now forced to forego his hopes of more brandy. 'I told you, Cosmore, I told you 'er was a cripple.'

'Arrh, you did, Jos,' Ezra said placatingly, 'you did.' He turned to his son, his little eyes filling with anger. 'An' I bloody well told you so don't you go standin' there denyin' it. I told you the wench be a cripple an' I said it more'n once.'

'You did, Father.' Morgan stepped forward. 'But you made no mention of a wheelchair. I had not thought . . .'

'Then what did you think?' Jos asked harshly. ''Ow did you think 'er to be if not in a chair?'

'I thought perhaps a walking stick. I thought the chair to be a temporary convenience, no more.'

'A walkin' stick!' Jos exploded. ''Er be bloody crippled, paralysed in her one leg. 'Er don't 'ave a bloody sprained ankle!'

Morgan's face paled a little beneath its continental tan. 'I had not expected . . .'

'Makes no odds now what you expected,' Ezra roared. 'You shoulda made sure o' what you was gettin' afore you got it, 'stead o' bloody soddin' off to London after a bloody fancy woman.'

At last Morgan turned to Esther, in something like remorse. 'I beg your pardon for the embarrassment this must be causing you, Esther. The fact is I was not prepared for a wheelchair. I am afraid Addenbrooke House is not equipped for that. Had I known, I would have seen to it that alterations were made for you but as it is . . .' He broke off, turning his look to Jos, once more straddling the rug before the fireplace. 'As it is, I must ask that Esther remain here at Rowena House until such alterations can be made.'

'Stay 'ere?' Jos frowned, allowing his distaste for the request to show clearly. 'But 'er be yer wife, 'er place be wi' you.'

'That is quite true.' Morgan had recovered his poise and now met the undisguised anger of his father-in-law with a coolness that added to it. 'But until rooms can be prepared where she has ease of access with her wheelchair, then I think in her own interests she should remain in her former home.'

'If it be the stairs as is worryin' you, then surely there be somebody as can carry 'er up if it be too much for you?'

'I would not be prepared to count on my father to carry Esther,' said Morgan, ignoring Jos's deliberate snub. 'There are times he cannot be counted upon to get himself upstairs, and I am sure she would prefer not to have a manservant responsible for seeing her to her bed, the times I myself am not at Addenbrooke.'

Jos could see that continuing to argue the point would only serve to highlight the rift between himself and Esther, and though it could not alter the fact that she was Morgan Cosmore's wife, it could affect the way in which their money was made available to him.

'So be it then.' He gave way grudgingly. ''Er'll stay 'ere, same as before, but you see to it them alterations be done, an' quick.'

Turning back to Esther, Morgan bent over her, taking her hand and touching it to his lips. 'I am sorry, my dear, but I do think it best you stay here just a little while longer, until we can arrange a bedroom and bathroom on the ground floor of Addenbrooke House. Do say you forgive my lack of foresight?'

'You could not be expected to prepare what you did not know would be needed,' Esther answered, hoping that her not caring about being unable to accompany him to his home was not too apparent while wanting to smile at her father's chagrin at having her stay on, if only for a couple of weeks.

'We'll get a builder started today.' Realising the futility of his hopes that Jos's hospitality might stretch to filling the brandy glasses once more, Ezra determined on getting back to his own decanter as soon as possible. 'An' then we'll soon 'ave you to yer new 'ome, eh, me wench?'

'I look forward to it, Mr Cosmore,' Esther lied sweetly. It would suit her better never to have to go to Addenbrooke House, never to have to go to that part of the town that was known as Butcroft, but accepting Morgan Cosmore and becoming his wife was the only way she could see of freeing herself from her father. That of itself must compensate her for anything the future might hold.

'I think you are being very brave.' Silk and taffeta rustling beneath her velvet skirt, Roberta Vance came to stand beside Esther. 'I don't know how you can bear to be separated from Morgan. I know I could not were I his wife.'

But you are not, Esther thought, watching the long lashes flutter at Morgan, and for all your pretence at sweetness the gall of it shows. I wonder, Mrs Vance, I wonder what your feeling would be if I told you I do not care? That as a husband or otherwise Morgan Cosmore holds not one iota of interest for me.

'We must all bear what we have to, Mrs Vance.'

Roberta switched her deep violet gaze to Esther, her tight smile showing she had registered and understood the cryptic content of the sentence. 'Only until we elect to change it,' she said, her reply carrying its own veiled warning. 'Now, if you will forgive me, I really must return to Addenbrooke. I have a deal of packing yet to see to.'

'Leavin' Darlaston already, Mrs Vance?' Josiah flapped his coat tails. ''Ad enough of the Black Country, 'ave you?'

'Not at all, Mr Kerral.' The violet gaze switched to Jos. 'But I do have a long-standing appointment for which I must return to London. I hope to be invited back here in the not too distant future, perhaps when Esther is settled in Addenbrooke House.'

'You will be most welcome at any time.' Esther forced herself to smile. She was not jealous of Roberta Vance's obvious relationship with her husband, neither was she envious of her equally obvious attractiveness, so what was it? Why did she feel such a profound dislike and even mistrust of a woman she hardly knew?

'You may be sure I shall take up that invitation.' The reply was for Esther but the melting smile went straight to Morgan.

'We shall both look forward to it,' he said, taking her elbow. Seeing his hand go out to his guest, Esther wondered whether the 'both' of his answer meant himself and his wife or himself and Roberta Vance.

'I shall say goodbye then.' The velvet smile spread about the room bathing each of its occupants in violet warmth.

'Will you ring for Evans, Father?' Esther took the white prayer book in her hands as Roberta prepared to leave.

'Shall I wheel you to your room?' Morgan enquired. Esther knew there was no real desire to be with her prompting the question, and indeed why should there be? They both knew their marriage was solely one of convenience, a business merger in the strictest sense of the words.

'It might be best if I return with Miri,' Esther told him. 'We share a house in the grounds. I find it more suitable than this. My father had it specially adapted for me, and with his permission I will wait there until you send for me. It is not large enough to accommodate us both.'

'Then I will return to Addenbrooke.'

Esther nodded. She had not missed the relief in his face nor did she miss the gloating smile on Roberta Vance's.

'So you be back where you was not two hours since?'

Miri removed her bonnet and cloak, hanging them on the hook fixed to the kitchen door in the cottage. 'So much for the Cosmores. They 'adn't even the grace to get things ready for you.'

Esther glanced down at the prayer book still resting in her lap. Morgan had made no effort to take her to his home. Was that truly because no rooms had been prepared for her, or was it because of Roberta Vance? A crippled wife would pose no competition to that temptress yet it could be that the presence in the house of both wife and mistress might not be altogether to the taste of a man like Morgan.

'It could well be the truth,' she said lamely. 'Perhaps he was not told the full extent of my disability?'

'That could be the truth of it, I suppose, though I'd bank no money on it.'

'To be fair to the Cosmores it could be nearer the truth than we think. I would not put it past my father to have withheld the fact that I cannot move around without the aid of a wheelchair, and if he did do so then of course they were not to know I would require certain alterations to a house. After all, it is not as though they had ever seen me in a wheelchair. The one time we did meet I sat in an ordinary armchair, my father having my chair taken out of the room.'

'An' that be another thing that be mighty peculiar.' Miri drew the bracket holding the kettle across the glowing coals. 'To 'ave you wed after just one meetin' – it ain't decent!'

'Miri,' Esther looked across at the older woman, her voice low with resignation, 'we both know this marriage is not the result of two people falling in love. It was a match arranged by two men for their own ends. Beside those their children did not matter, and decent or not it is done now.'

'Arrh, it be done as you say, an' by two men who will answer to the Lord for this day.' Miri fastened her long white apron over her skirts. 'I can understand yer part in it. You 'ad no option, not bein' of age you couldn't refuse yer father's demand, but Morgan Cosmore be of age so why did 'e agree? What be in it for 'im?'

'I would say money.' Esther wheeled herself to the door of her bedroom. 'I think it quite likely that Morgan Cosmore has been well paid for taking himself a wife and most probably expects to go on being paid. It will be interesting to see his reaction when he finds there is no more silver in that particular pot.'

Manoeuvring her chair to the table beside her bed, Esther pulled open its one drawer, slipping the pretty lace-edged handkerchief and prayer book inside. This was all she had of her mother, she thought, tracing the gold cross with the tip of one finger: a prayer book and an almost forgotten memory of a face, its mouth forming words that could have been 'I love you'. She could have had a mother who loved her but instead she had a father who hated her and a husband who did not want her. Tears rising in her throat, she pushed the drawer hard shut. Why had this happened to her . . . why had she been born a cripple? 'The Lord 'as 'Is reasons,' Miri had often answered, the times she had put that thought into words, 'an' we must never draw the actions of the Almighty into question.'

Unfastening the buttons of her dress, Esther hesitated before calling Miri to help her change into her everyday brown. The Lord had His reasons and so had Esther Cosmore. She, like Morgan, had been given a choice. She could have taken a chance on her father having her placed in an institution but that way she would have been robbed of the one aim in her life, the one thing that had centred her very being for as long as she could reason: revenge. She would have been robbed of the chance to take her revenge on Jos Kerral, and weighed in the balance, marriage to a man she did not love and who held no love for her was of little consequence.

'It be as well that little in this 'ouse be mine to take away . . .'

The blue gown hung away, Esther sat in her chosen spot beneath the window of the kitchen watching Miri set about making her cure for all ills, a pot of tea.

'. . . least that way I ain't packed only to unpack. Ee, wench! I bet us stoppin' 'ere a while longer come to Jos like a smack in the face! I wish I'd been in that room to see it.'

As if the knowledge of having to leave this house soon had only just come to her she fell silent, her hands still as she gazed about the room that held so many memories. How long? A day? A week? How long before she must leave the home she had shared with John? The sudden feeling that what was left of her world was being snatched away overcame her and she gave way to the luxury she had always denied herself and let the tears slide unhindered down her cheeks.

'Miri!' Esther pushed herself forward, her arms reaching up and fastening about the older woman's waist as a child's might have. 'Miri, please, no more.' Her own tears burning, she pressed her face lovingly into the white apron. 'I can't take it, Miri, I can't take any more.'

'Oh, Essie, my little wench.' The words piercing the fog of her own unhappiness, Miri bent over the weeping girl. 'Don't you cry, don't cry. 'Ave faith in the Lord for 'E'll give you just what you can bear an' no more. 'E lets you walk clear up to the edge but never fear that 'E will let you fall for that ain't 'Is way. Y'ave 'ad life 'ard, me wench, but one day 'E will soften it for you.'

Standing there in the small kitchen, her heart rent by Esther's muffled sobs, Miri added her own silent prayer. Make the softenin' soon Lord, make it soon.

Chapter Eleven

'I hope it was not inconvenient for me to call here?'

'Not at all, Adam.' Esther smiled at the tall dark-haired figure facing her across the kitchen. 'Though I will not be here much longer and I do not yet know if it will be acceptable for you to call at Addenbrooke.'

'Addenbrooke?' A dark eyebrow rose questioningly. 'Do you mean Addenbrooke House?'

Esther nodded.

'Addenbrooke House over at Butcroft?'

'Yes.' She nodded again.

'But that is the Cosmore house. How come you . . .?'

He broke off, the question unfinished, as Esther pulled the accounts book nearer to her, the light from the oil lamps catching the gleam of gold on the third finger of her left hand. She was married! The shock of it seemed to strike him between the eyes, coming with a force like a physical blow.

'I married Morgan Cosmore a week ago.'

Adam swallowed a sudden crazy desire to laugh. Don't get involved, his mother had told him. The daughter of an industrialist was not for the likes of him even though she was crippled. But deep down had that not been the cause of his hopes? Had not the very fact of her being paralysed given him cause to think she might turn to him? But now she was married. How the spirit of that little plant on the heath must be laughing!

'When do you go to Butcroft?' he asked.

'In a few days. My . . . my husband is having alterations made to allow access for my wheelchair.'

'Then I will wait until I hear from you how you want to receive an account of the works in future.'

The bewilderment in his voice was sharp in her ears. He was wondering about her marriage, why it had not taken place in church, why been so sudden and so secretive. Not wanting to answer those unspoken questions, not wanting her own hurt to show, Esther bent over the accounts book.

'How many nuts and bolts did the Cammel carriage works take this week?'

'Five gross.'

'That is quite an increase.' Esther felt Miri's eyes on her and knew she was wondering why this terseness when other meetings with Adam had held all the informality of friendship.

'The men work hard, Mrs Cosmore.'

Esther kept her gaze on the columns of figures, their neat stiff lines running the length of the page. Mrs Cosmore. The words had come out harshly, a dullness in the saying of her new name that held a note of something deeper than bewilderment – a note that might almost match her own feeling of hurt and unhappiness, except there was no reason for Adam Paige to feel either of those emotions. She was a cripple and as such would never arouse those feelings in any man.

'I'm sure they works 'ard, lad,' Miri's words fell into the vacuum of silence, 'an' so must you for the turnout to rise the way it 'as this last couple of weeks. We was only sayin' this mornin' what a difference y'ave made to that place, the short time y'ave been in charge.' She turned to the kettle, seeing steam rattling its lid. 'Will you 'ave a cup o' tea, lad?'

'Thanks, Mrs Butler, but I won't stay. I told my mother I would be back in an hour or so.'

''Ow be yer parents?' She pushed the bracket holding the smoke-blackened kettle aside from the coals.

'Well enough, Mrs Butler.'

'I'm glad to 'ear it. An' you tell 'em both so from me when you gets 'ome.'

Miri's seemingly light conversation had been deliberate, thrown like a bridge across the chasm of her own wordlessness. Now Esther knew she must cross it.

'We have just acquired the Leys works.' She ran rather than walked across the bridge. 'And we intend to run it as a going concern. Do you think you could manage both that and the Sovereign works?'

Adam's grey eyes kindled with interest. 'The Leys as well as Sovereign?' He thought only for a moment. 'I reckon I could. Ben could see to the running of the Sovereign the times I wasn't there.'

'Mr Corns is getting rather old, Adam.' Esther looked up from the accounts, eyes begging for their old friendship. 'He might not always be able to stand in for you.'

'I've noticed his tiredness lately,' Adam acknowledged, 'but I wouldn't want to tell him he is not needed any more. I have seen too many men with broken spirits in this town to add another to their number.'

'That be right Christian o' you, my lad.' Miri looked up from the crotchet work she had carried to the chair beside an oil lamp. 'But you must bear in mind Benjamin Corns be no spring chicken. There's gonna be a time when 'e just ain't gonna be able to carry on, no matter 'ow much 'e might yearn to, an' you got to be ready for that time.'

'I realise that.' Adam looked back at Esther. 'That is why I have been training Barney Whitehouse. He is a good man at his job and gets on well with the other workers. And as for new ways, he is always ready to learn and picks things up well. I think you could rely on him to run things if the need arises.'

Esther turned the pages of the accounts book, stopping at a page with the heading Leys nut and bolt, her glance running over the few entries. 'If you think Barney Whitehouse can manage alone for a few days, we would like you to set about putting the Leys works into production. There is only a caretaker there at the moment so you will have to set some men on.' She smiled. 'I don't think you will have difficulty finding them.'

'None at all.' He answered her with a smile of his own. 'The Bull Stake is filled with them every day.'

'When you choose the ones you want,' she went on, 'look out for another of the Barney Whitehouse type.'

The smile faded from his lips, his eyes sharpening with the question: 'Is there any special reason?'

Esther glanced at Miri but her head was bent over her work. 'We do have a special reason though I do not expect it is the one you are thinking of.' She leaned forward, resting her hands on the table. 'Adam, the Evening Institute you attended – did they teach you anything about machinery?'

'Machinery?' He frowned. 'Some. Were you thinking of anything specific?'

'Did they teach you the working of a machine that can put a thread on a bolt or a nut?'

'A capstan?' The frown remained, furrowing his brow. 'Is that the machinery you are thinking of?'

Esther nodded. 'It is. Are you sufficiently familiar with the working of them to teach others the same?'

'The Institute didn't have the machine. What I was taught was from drawings, but I think, given a chance, I could soon get the hang of actually operating one.'

'Then will you organise the Leys and the Sovereign to take these machines? We would like you to travel to Mr Ward's works in York and purchase some of his capstan machines on our behalf.'

'You intend to buy some?' he asked, surprise plain in his voice.

'Only two for each of the works at the moment, but if they work as we hope there will be more. We intend to build nuts and bolts into an industry of note, Adam, and this is the beginning. There will soon be no more hand-made ones.'

'I trust you know how much quicker you arrive at the finished thing by using this machine?'

'I do not know, never having seen one.' Esther caught the warning in his voice. 'But I trust the speed of production will warrant their cost.'

'They will do that all right but how long could you hold the stock you will build up if there is no sale for it?'

Esther glanced down at the book lying beneath her hands then back at those questioning grey eyes. 'A good question, Adam, and one Miri and I have discussed. I can only tell you we feel the market will come back, that in a very few years this town will be able to sell every metal object it can manufacture. And we are determined our output will be well toward the top of that list.'

'Ours' meaning Cosmore, Adam thought. One way or another that family had always held half the town in their hands. Had marrying Esther Kerral brought them the other half?

'I will set about hiring men as soon as I have seen how many will be needed at the Leys,' he said abruptly. 'Perhaps you will send me word where my next report is to be made? Until then I will say goodnight to you both.'

The words were hardly said before he was out of the door, the sound of his boots on the flagstone floor fading quickly into silence.

'That lad 'as changed since leaving Rowena House,' Miri laid her crotchet work aside. 'Summat seems to 'ave got a 'old o' im an' it be throttlin' the spirit from 'im.'

At the table Esther closed the slim hard-covered book. There had been many changes these last weeks and Adam was not the only casualty.

Miri laid two cups on the table then reached a tin of Bournville cocoa from the cupboard. 'Ee, Essie, d'you reckon y'ave done the right thing, tellin' 'im to go buy some o' them fancy machines y'ave harped on about? Could be like the lad said, that you'll find yerself not able to sell what you make.'

'The only way we will find that out is to do it.' Esther watched the shower of brown powder fall from the spoon into the cups.

'But once y'ave spent yer money, it be spent.' Miri added a liberal two spoons of sugar to each cup. 'Ain't no way you can ask for it back.'

My whole existence has been a risk, Esther thought as Miri went to fetch milk from the cool jar in the scullery. A risk that my father would take me away from Miri; a risk he would have me buried alive in some asylum; risk is no stranger to me. It has stood by my shoulder from the day I was born and I expect it will remain there for many years to come.

'What money y'ave built up will be stretched mighty thin by the time y'ave paid out for machines.' Miri bustled into the kitchen. 'Don't you think you should wait till y'ave got a bit more by you?'

'No, Miri, I don't. The venture is risky, I admit that, but then my money is at risk both ways, and if I am going to lose it, I would rather lose it this way than have Morgan Cosmore take it.'

Smoothing milk and cocoa powder to a smooth paste, Miri added boiling water from the kettle. 'I'm wi' you on that score, wench, that one would 'ave the lot spent in a twelve month, but what be goin' to buy machines could be spent payin' men to do the same job.' She looked across at Esther, her face earnest. 'There be men in Darlaston wi' families an' no job to bring bread to their mouths, Essie. They should come before machines.'

Sucking in a long breath she held it for many seconds before freeing it in a juddering sigh. 'The people do matter, Miri,' she said, tears sparkling in her eyes. 'That is my whole reason for doing as I am. I could hire men and set them to work making nuts and bolts by hands but that would last only until someone else began to make them using machinery. Then it would be too late for me. One way or another these machines are coming but they are not going to take work away from the people of Darlaston, Miri – they will provide it. The time will come when nuts and bolts will be needed in their thousands and the manufacturer who can't produce them fast will go under.'

Miri handed her cocoa across the table, head shaking in disbelief. 'Ee, Essie wench, if only that could be true.'

Staring at the little cloud of steam spiralling from her cup, Esther saw her dream. 'It will be true, Miri,' she said softly. 'It will be true, and I will make it so.'

Coming to Wolverhampton Street Adam ignored it, striking off instead across the open heath, needing to be alone, not wanting to meet men finishing their shift, the few that still had work to go to, or women doing their shopping late, buying bruised vegetables and yesterday's unsold bread for a penny. Hands shoved deep into the pockets of his one good pair of trousers, he walked on, a prisoner of his own thoughts. Only weeks ago he had never even heard of Esther Kerral, never known of her existence. And now . . .

Above him the night sky reddened. The nine o'clock opening of the furnaces. He stood still, staring at the great scarlet bowl opening over him – scarlet from the blood and sweat of men slaving their guts out for the pittance paid by the likes of Ezra Cosmore. And now *she* was a Cosmore would she add to their hold? Would men continue to slave for her money? But Esther seemed to be all for helping the folk of the town, she genuinely seemed to care about people trying to eke out a living on next to nothing.

Appeared to care. Was that the nub of it? Was her concern genuine? He had to admit those factories she had bought had been kept in production with not one man being laid off, and she had given him a job with a wage that was more than fair. Oh, it was all done supposedly by Miriam Butler but his gut feeling told him it was really Esther Cosmore, hers was the hand guiding that business and hers the mind behind it and so far he had seen her do nothing but good

. . . but he had been wrong about her once already. He had thought . . .

He scuffed the ground with his boot, unwilling to acknowledge the rest of that thought, fighting it from his mind as it hammered at him. He had allowed it to happen, allowed himself to hope, to believe, and now the hope was gone he was blaming her, but that was wrong. She could not be blamed for dashing what she had never helped build; the fault could not be put on her for breaking a dream she had played no part in weaving. It was a fantasy of his own making. She had never once given him cause to think . . .

Overhead the sky spread like a vivid curtain of red slashed with gold and spiked with the black fingers of factory smoke stacks. Each in turn the steel works opened their furnaces, their brilliance turning the night sky to a carmine dawn, lighting the world around him.

Don't get involved.

His mother's words echoed like a distant warning.

Don't get involved.

Taking his eyes from the almost painful beauty of the glowing sky, Adam glanced down at the ground then, stooping, snapped off a stalk of the mugwort plant, half crushed beneath his boot.

Don't get involved.

He stroked a finger the length of the slim stalk, no urge in him to play the childhood game of pushing off the seed heads.

Don't get involved.

But it was too late for that, he was already involved, he was in love with Esther Cosmore. 'Yes, I love her,' he murmured, touching the stalk to his lips, 'and you did nothing to help!'

Flinging the stalk to the ground, he walked on across the heath. Nothing and no one could help him. The woman he loved was another man's wife, she was as far from him as heaven itself. He looked again at the sky, exulting in the great surge of colour. There was none could help, but there was none could be blamed either. Turning, he walked back to where the grassy stalk had fallen. Taking it in his hand, he looked for a moment at the tiny leaf-headed spike then laid it gently back among its fellows.

Foleys Croft lay like a smudge on the heath, deceptively beautiful beneath the flame-reddened sky. Adam hesitated. He didn't want to go on, didn't want to go back to the huddle of houses with their bleak damp rooms from which no amount of scrubbing took away the stench of refuse seeping into the brook. He didn't want to live the life of Foleys Croft but he knew he had to, for without him his parents might not live at all.

Each step a physical effort, he forced himself to move towards the hovels that housed the misery that was Foleys Croft.

What if she had not been married? He had a sudden vision of the cottage's small clean kitchen with its dresser and pretty crockery, neat bright rugs and sturdy furniture. And then there was Rowena House with all it contained. She might not have lived in it but it was her background, that was what she had been born to and one day it would all be hers. Adam laughed softly, emitting the bitterness of his soul into the quiet night. How could he have thought like that? How could he ever have dreamed of Esther? He looked down into the hollow that held his home, the faint anaemic glow of candles stippling the shadows. What had he to offer in place of Rowena House? A bed in a room so tiny it would hold nothing else but a stool? But then, they had no use for wardrobes in Foleys Croft. Folk owned only the clothes they stood up in.

His mother had tried to tell him of the uselessness of a hope he had not admitted to himself; she had tried to warn him of the folly of his dreams. And yet he had still hoped, deep in his heart he had thought . . .

Looking again at the silhouettes of the poor houses, he realised the truth of his mother's words: 'The daughter of an iron master don't be fer you, even if 'er do be a cripple.'

'You were right, Mother,' he whispered as he walked

towards the dim lights. 'I could never have brought Esther Kerral here.'

Reaching the door of his home, Adam took a last long look at the painted sky, the brush of a dozen searing furnaces streaking it with ruby, damask and vermilion. It was beautiful, but it was a beauty born of a hard taskmaster.

Pushing open the unlatched door, he walked inside.

A fire almost obscured by a thick mantle of grey ash burned low in the grate and a solitary candle stood in the centre of the table. His eyes already accustomed to the night shadows, Adam removed his jacket, hanging it beside his father's on a nail hammered into the door.

'You should not have waited up for me, Mother,' he said, not looking at her where she sat on her customary stool opposite his father's chair. He would have preferred to be alone, alone with the pain the sight of a wedding ring had caused. 'You should have gone to bed.'

Crossing to the fireplace, he took a poker to the ash-bound fire, raking away dead cinders.

'Did the balsam ease Father's cough?' He glanced at the empty chair.

'Arrh.' His mother stared at the pale fire. 'It seemed to do some good.'

'I'll bank the fire for the night.' Going to fetch the bucket he had earlier filled with slack, he threw the tiny chippings of coal and dust on to the dying fire, emptying half the contents of the kettle over it, cementing it into a crust, all the while willing his mother to go upstairs and leave him with his thoughts.

'I'll get you some tea, lad.'

'No. Thank you, Mother, I don't want any.' He spoke quickly. Having to talk while his mother brewed tea was the last thing he wanted.

Returning from replacing the coal bucket in the yard at the rear of the house, he glanced at his mother, still sitting hunched at the side of the fireplace. Usually she would be bustling about, insisting on his having the compulsory mug of tea, but tonight she had not moved when he came in, she had not even looked up. She looked so tired, sitting there, her shoulders slumped almost into an arc. Adam felt the hot surge of guilt race into his stomach. He should not have gone to Esther's house. He could have given his report of the works at any time, not gone off at night leaving his mother alone with a sick man she had fetched and carried for all day. Going to her, he placed an arm about her thin shoulders. 'Get yourself up to bed,' he said softly. 'I will help Father up when he comes in from the privy.'

''E ain't out the back.' Carrie Paige's voice was flat as she answered her son.

'He has already gone up then?'

'Arrh, 'e's already gone.' Eyes as dull and empty as her voice, Carrie looked up at the man beside her. 'Yer father's dead, lad, 'e died an hour gone.'

Outside his bedroom window the flame-washed sky held no interest for Morgan Cosmore. Taking a brown envelope from an inner pocket of his jacket, he laid the contents on the bed. Not what he had hoped for, but in his father's terms better than a kick up the arse any day.

Taking the folded sheet of paper he opened it, reading through the elaborate copperplate wording. Forty per cent of Kerral Wheel and Axle. Refolding the paper, he tapped it against manicured fingernails. He now owned forty per cent of Jos Kerral's business. What that meant in terms of cash per year he did not yet know, there would be time to go into that later. Right now he had one thousand pounds and he was going to spend it! Replacing the paper in the envelope, he laid it aside, a smile curving his mouth as he looked at the pile of banknotes.

His father thought to get half. Morgan's smile curved wider as he picked up the crisp white five-pound notes. Ezra would not get half though Morgan would give him something for arranging the match. Picking up the money, he held it in his hands, as if to weigh it. But there was no need. A smile parted his lips. Morgan had checked it a hundred times since the wedding, taking a greater pleasure with each counting.

Peeling one note from the pile he laid it back on the bed, putting the rest in a separate pile beside it. His father deserved to be paid for the effort he had put in.

Still smiling, he crossed to the long cheval mirror set in the sweep of the wide curving windows and stood admiring his own reflection. Hair the colour of beaten bronze curled softly over his velvet collar; green-gold eyes smiled lazily from fine-wrought features that showed nothing of his lifestyle. One hand checking the lie of his mauve silk cravat, he ran a practised glance over a body that was slim but still held the essence of strength. There was little of Ezra Cosmore in him except the love of money.

A few new clothes? Russet or aubergine . . . yes, something with a little colour. He always looked well in colours. Definitely some new clothes then, and he need pay for none if he patronised a new tailor. And then where? Paris . . . Rome? Either was pleasant at this time of year. 'Thank you, my little cripple,' he laughed, returning to the bed and scooping up the wad of notes which he crammed back into the envelope. About to leave the room, he hesitated, his glance falling on the solitary note he had placed aside for his father. What was Ezra's favourite line? 'Y'ave taken all yer life an' given nothin' . . .'

Taking up the note he looked at it, the same lazy, almost feline smile stretching his mouth. Then he placed it with the others in the envelope. 'We mustn't spoil the record now, Father,' he said, laughing softly.

'So y'ave decided to come downstairs at last, 'ave you?' Ezra turned brandy-soaked eyes on his son as he walked into the drawing room. 'I thought y'ad teken to yer bed for good.'

Ignoring the jibe, Morgan settled himself in a leather-covered wing-back armchair, carelessly placing one foot across his knee.

'Been countin' yer money again, I've no doubt.' Ezra smiled but the old distaste showed in his bleary eyes. 'You always did like doin' things in secret, waitin' till nobody could see what you was about. Sly little bugger you was as a kid, an' you ain't no different now 'cept you be a bigger sly bugger. Don't let 'im see, don't let 'im know what Jos Kerral gave me in that envelope. You forget, I already knows. I knows you 'ave a thousand quid in yer pocket.'

'Brandy does not affect your memory, Father.' Morgan stared coldly at Ezra and the almost empty decanter at his elbow. 'I do have exactly one thousand pounds in my pocket and I intend to spend it.'

'I never expected you to do otherwise.' Ezra reached for the decanter. 'Y'ave always been the same. Get a florin in you 'and an' it burns a 'ole in yer pocket till it be spent.'

'It affords me pleasure to spend money, Father.'

Ezra slammed the decanter heavily on the side table, his drunken eyes swivelling before focusing on Morgan. 'The money always comin' from somebody else. You couldn't afford to spend out o' yer own pocket 'cos you never earned a penny of yer own, not once in yer useless bloody life!'

'I agree, Father,' Morgan said coolly. 'If by earning you mean working in the James Bridge copper foundry then I have never earned a penny in my life, and what is more I have no intention of ever doing so.'

'An' 'ow long d'you think Jos Kerral will let you get away wi' doin' nothin' to 'elp keep 'is business goin'?'

Morgan ran a finger along the line of his costly leather boot. 'I think Kerral will act much as you have always done, Father. Be grateful that I stay out of his way.'

His hand shaking as he picked up the glass, spilling brandy down its sides, Ezra gulped a mouthful. 'As far as 'is business be concerned you be right in what you say, but what about 'is daughter, eh? What about that wench o' is'n? D'you think 'e'll be grateful for you keepin' out o' 'er way? 'Ow much longer d'you think 'e's gonna stand for you leavin' 'er over at Rowena 'Ouse?'

'He knows it is not practical to bring her here until alterations have been made.'

'Arrh, 'e does,' Ezra returned quickly, his brain sharp despite the quantity of brandy he had consumed. 'An' 'e also knows 'ow long them alterations should tek an' 'e won't stand fer you arsin' about over 'em. You mark what I be sayin' an' don't tek Jos Kerral fer a fool. 'E 'as only to think you be buggerin' around 'stead o' bringin' that wench to what be 'er rightful place, an' you can kiss yer thousand a year goodbye.'

'He wasn't so particular about her being in her rightful place before he married her off.'

The brandy glass halfway to his lips, Ezra paused. 'What d'you mean?'

Morgan straightened both legs, stretching them out in front of him. 'It means he was not particular enough to have Rowena House altered to accommodate her. Instead he put her into a house half the size of your stable. Why do you think that was?'

'I don't know, an' if you be 'alf so bloody clever as you think you be, you won't go askin' 'im. Keep yer mouth shut an' you might just go on gettin' yer thousand a year. Open it an' you be like to lose the lot. An' while we be talkin', I'll remind you I expects to get some o' that thousand you've already been paid.'

'I have already taken care of that, Father,' Morgan remembered the single banknote. 'You will get all you deserve.'

Ezra swallowed his brandy, coughing as the spirit clawed at his throat. 'Mek sure I do an' don't think I'll be payin' for them buildin' alterations out o' my share.'

Pretending a yawn, Morgan lifted a hand to his mouth, camouflaging a smile he could not discipline. His father had no real idea of the truth of the statement he had just made. There was no way Morgan would expect him to pay the builder out of his share of Jos Kerral's first payment!

'So when they gonna be finished?' Ezra was already holding the last of the brandy. 'All that row an' dust . . . they've been at it long enough to 'ave built a 'ole row of 'ouses.'

'They will be gone tomorrow. They finished the last of the structural work yesterday. That leaves only the clearing away of any rubble.'

'Better be cleared up properly an' all, I ain't 'avin' the place left like no rubbish dump.' Tipping brandy into his mouth, Ezra coughed, sending dribbles of liquid spewing from the sides of his mouth.

His own mouth tightening with disgust at the sight, Morgan got to his feet. Everything would be fit to look at – everything, that was, except his father. 'The house will be back to normal tomorrow,' he said tersely.

Not bothering to wipe his mouth, Ezra grinned, tiny globules of brandy dropping from his chin to his shirt, spreading their golden moisture over his chest. 'So the 'ouse will be ready to receive yer little bride? That'll put a stop to your gallivantin'. You can't go swannin' off 'ere, there an' everywhere wi' a cripple 'angin' from your shirt tail.'

Correct again, thought Morgan, the feeling of disgust intensifying as he watched the liquid drip from Ezra's chin. His father's level of intelligence appeared to rise with each glass of brandy he showered himself with. To have a wife holding on to Morgan wherever he went would be irksome to say the least; to have a cripple would be unthinkable.

Eyes clouded by alcohol peered at him from between rolls of puffy flesh and there was no mistaking the spite that lurked in them.

'Gallivantin' ain't all you'll be 'avin' to be doin' wi'out, is it?' Ezra slurred. ''Avin' a wife the side o' you, you won't be able to 'arbour the likes o' the Vance woman. You'll 'ave to do wi'out yer fancy women.'

Morgan looked at his father, slumped in his chair, his face flushed and brandy still trickling from his mouth. Drunk or not, he had been right in thinking that carting a crippled wife around wherever he went was not practical for Morgan but now his thinking was beginning to go wrong; if he thought bringing Esther Kerral to this house as a bride would affect Morgan's lifestyle in the slightest way, then Ezra Cosmore was very much mistaken.

Ezra laughed, sending brandy splashing down his front again. 'That wiped the smile off yer face!' he roared. 'Yer bloody thousand pounds don't feel so good now you can't spend it on your doxies, do it?'

'Oh, I dare say I shall manage, Father.' Morgan turned towards the door. 'You see, unlike yourself, I don't have to pay a woman to give me pleasure. They pay me.'

Slamming the door behind him, he made for the stairs. Women *did* pay for his company and were glad to do so, taking a delight in being seen with a handsome young escort. And he played the field, taking their little gifts of gold pins and pocket watches, gold Alberts and expensive rings – all of which he sold. Yes, women paid him. All, that was, except Roberta.

Reaching his bedroom door, he laughed softly to himself – a hard cynical sound. That particular lover played the same game, taking all he offered then wanting more. 'You'll 'ave to do wi'out yer fancy women,' his father had crowed. Turning the handle of the door, Morgan knew he could never do without Roberta Vance.

Chapter Twelve

'I'll take a cup of tea an' thank you kindly for it, Miriam.' Ria Stedman shuffled in her husband's boots, pulling her worn shawl close around her thin shoulders. 'Gets cool o' nights, don't it?'

'Yes.' Miri smiled, reaching for the kettle singing quietly on its bracket, 'You can smell autumn in the air.'

'Arrh.' Ria tugged harder at her shawl, tucking it under her sagging breasts as if already warding off cold. 'Pray the Lord winter don't come till it be summer. Some of the folk in Darlaston 'ave got 'ard enough times as it is wi'out 'avin' the bitterness of ice an' frost to put up wi'. Why, only last week young Adam Paige – 'e be the new gaffer over at the Sovereign works – well, only last week 'is father died. Some say it was the croup that killed 'im, what wi' workin' all 'is days in the copper, but I still thinks it was Foleys Croft done for 'im. God knows what be pourin' itself into the brook there but the stink alone be enough to kill. 'Ow them poor folk puts up wi' it is beyond me, it is an' all.'

Adam's father was dead! Esther's hands twisted together in her lap, a surge of pity swelling her heart. Poor Adam, seeing his father waste away in that place. And his mother, what of her?

'Thank you, Miriam, a 'ot cup of tea be right welcome.' Ria Stedman accepted the cup and the chair Miri indicated but Esther didn't notice. She had not seen Adam since asking him to take over management of the Leys. He had not come to this

house and she had sent him no word. If only she had known
. . . but supposing she had, what could she have done?

'. . . it seems to be goin' down the nick. What d'you
think, miss?'

'What? I . . . I am sorry, I did not quite catch . . .'

'I said as 'ow my Jake said to tell you old Cosmore be layin'
off. Ten men drawed their tins last Friday an' 'e says there's
like to be more doin' the same come this Friday. Seems the
copper works be just about finished, wouldn't you say?'

'Things be bad all over,' Miri cut in, 'an' they'm like to
get worse before they gets better. But don't bury the 'orse
afore it drops dead. Could be a few months will see the
worst over.'

'I 'opes you'm right an' you ain't wrong.' Ria sipped her tea.
'An' there be many a one in Darlaston as 'opes the same. Still,
there was two or three men took on last week in the nut an'
bolt so my Jake was told, took on at the Leys. An' surprisin'
thing was it were the same bloke signed 'em on as is gaffer
of the Sovereign, Adam Paige. That means 'e must be main
bloke at both places an' that be one fer the book, don't it?'

'Your Jake, 'e weren't laid off, were 'e?'

'No, 'e weren't, praise the Lord.' Ria put her cup on the table.
'An' wi' the blessin' of God 'e won't be one of the next. I don't
think I could stand no more wi'out sittin' down fer good.'

''Ow be that?' Miri continued to lead the conversation, seeing
that hearing of the death of Adam's father had upset Esther.
'Ain't nothin' serious, is it, Ria?'

''Pends on what you see as bein' serious. Some might not
reckon it so but Jake . . .'

'Your husband is not ill, Mrs Stedman?' Esther pulled her
thoughts away from Adam.

'Not in the body 'e ain't . . . well, not more'n usual, but I
can't say the same of 'is mind.'

'Ria!' Miri let the teapot fall heavily on to the table, her eyes
wide with concern. 'You don't mean . . . 'e ain't goin' out of
'is head, is 'e?'

Ria Stedman shook her head, her mouth pulling into a tight line. ''E goes out of it every time 'e claps eyes on our Sam.'

'Sam?' Miri thought for a moment. ''E would be yer eldest?'

'Arrh, that's right, Miriam, the oldest outta ten wi' four livin'.'

Esther asked, 'Is Sam still living at home?'

Shaking her head, Ria sighed. 'Arrh, 'e be at 'ome still. It shames me to say it but 'e is.'

'Shamed, Ria? Why be shamed, wench?' Miri refilled the other woman's cup. Hot tea was a wonderful inducement to gossip and she wouldn't want Ria leaving with this bit unsaid.

Ria drew the replenished cup towards her, lifting it from the saucer. 'I can tell you now for it'll be as plain as the nose on yer face in a couple of months. Sam 'as been knockin' about wi' a wench outta Dangerfield Lane an' now it be a case of visitin' the font afore they visits the altar. 'Is father warned 'im . . .' She sipped from her cup, her eyes closing appreciatively with each swallow. 'We both of we warned 'im but you know what young 'uns today be like, Miriam . . . beggin' your pardon, miss.' She glanced at Esther then back to Miri. 'They won't be gainsaid. The blood runs 'ot an' they 'aves to cool it. Well, Sam, 'e cooled 'is'n all right an' now wench be up the spout an' no ring on 'er finger. I tell you it's upset the 'ouse an' I can't see no end to it. 'Is father won't speak to 'im till 'e be wed and sets the wench in a place of 'er own and Sam can't do it lessen 'e gets a job – an' 'e 'as about as much chance of that in Darlaston as I've got of bein' Queen o' the May.'

'Mrs Stedman,' Esther gave the woman a thoughtful look, 'how old is Sam?'

''E'll be twenty-three come Advent Day.' The woman put down her cup, drained to the last tea leaf. 'That is, if 'is father don't put 'is lights out first.'

'And is he strong?'

'Strong? Arrh.' Ria beamed proudly. ''E be strong. Got some fair old muscles on 'im 'as our Sam. 'E could do a good day's work as well as any given the chance. But why d'you ask, miss?'

Esther pressed her hand into her lap, the right one covering the left, hiding the band of gold that now denied her the title Ria Stedman had used.

'Miri and I have decided to employ a man to lift me in and out of the pony trap and to push my chair should I wish to visit the town at any time. It is too much now for a woman, it needs a man's strength. The job, as I said, would mostly be lifting me in and out of the trap. There would be no need of help inside the house, though it would include caring for the horse. He could leave at seven in the evening and there is a small house with the post. Do you think Sam would be willing to take the job?'

'Willin'!' Ria Stedman's tired eyes sparkled with new life. 'Why, bless yer face, miss, 'e'll be a bloody sight more'n willin'. An' 'e'll take right good care of you or I'll 'elp 'is father doin' 'is lights meself.'

Esther smiled, her hands still pressed into her skirts. 'If Sam is interested, Mrs Stedman, would you ask him to come and see us in the morning, perhaps at ten o'clock?'

'Oh, 'e'll be interested, miss.' Ria stood up, pulling the ragged shawl over her tired hair, tucking the ends beneath her arms. 'An' I'm gonna look a right eyeful walkin' about wi' a May queen's crown on me 'ead!'

Going to the dresser, Miri took two coins from a tin placed inside the drawer that housed the accounts book and pressed them into the woman's hand. 'I tell you what, Ria,' she laughed, 'we will forget the wearin' of that crown till yer Jake be gettin' old Salisbury's job.'

'Prime Minister?' Ria chuckled, shoving her feet further inside boots almost twice their size. 'Now that would suit my old man to a tee. Tellin' other folk where they be wrong an' 'e be right is just up 'is alley, an' 'e 'as enough practice at it down at the Fryin' Pan on a Saturday night.'

Closing the door after the departing Ria, Miri came to stand at the table.

'What be this about a 'ouse goin' along wi' the job?' she demanded. 'You knows nicely we be off to Addenbrooke House any time now an' you don't know what there be there. I'm sure there ain't no 'ouse, small or otherwise.'

'I know, Miri.' Esther unclasped her hands. 'It was a lie and I should not have said it, but the thought of that poor girl being pregnant and not able to marry . . .'

'Pity 'er 'adn't thought of the same,' Miri returned tartly, ''er wouldn't be in that situation if 'er 'adn't been so quick at . . . well, if 'er 'adn't been so quick. A bit of 'oldin' back would 'ave avoided all this trouble, but then young folk don't think of nobody but theirselves an' gratifyin' their own feelings. Every other bit of sense goes out of 'em when they be rollin' in the grass.'

'Well, it is done now, Miri, and we must try to help.'

''Elp, yes, I be all for that!' She gathered the used crockery, stacking it on the wooden tray, the clatter emphasising her statement that Esther had acted rashly. 'But to say a 'ouse went wi' the job be goin' too far. What will you do if it turns out there be no 'ouse for 'im over at Addenbrooke?'

Listening to the sound of cups rattling in the enamel bowl as Miri washed them in the scullery, Esther thought over the problem her own hastiness had created. She had not forgotten their impending move to the Cosmores' house and didn't want Sam to live on the premises anyway, but just where was he to live? That was what she had not thought of.

Sweeping back into the kitchen, disapproval stamped firmly around her mouth, Miri set the china back on the dresser. 'Well, Essie?' she asked, her best 'I told you so' tone a clear indication of the expected answer. ''Ave you sorted out what you can be sayin' to the lad when 'e comes in the mornin'?'

'I have.' Esther smiled as she remembered. 'When we went to look at the Leys works before it was sold to Mrs Edward Marsh, do you remember the small cottage close by?'

'I remember.' Miri nodded. 'But surely that was used by the caretaker?'

'That is not the one I was thinking of. I mean the one opposite that. You must have noticed – it stood a little way off, just where the ground rises.'

'Now you come to mention it, I do recall seein' it. A little place standin' a way off from the works?'

'That's the one.' Esther looked triumphant. 'It is part of the property. Sam Stedman can live there.'

'I should 'ave known you would come up with somethin',' Miri said, disapproval fading from her face. 'Now get yerself over against the fire an' we will see about massaging them legs.'

If only her own problem could be solved so easily, Esther thought, wheeling her chair to the other side of the table. But all the massage in the world would not put life into her dead legs nor warmth into her dead heart.

'I thank you, miss, an' so will my Meggie.' Sam Stedman grinned. 'When Mother told me last night of yer offer of a job, I couldn't believe it. It seemed like a miracle.'

'No miracle, Sam.' Esther looked at the young man, his fair hair still damp from the scrubbing Ria had made him give it. 'And it will mean a fair walk for you if you take the house over at the Leys.'

'Ain't no walk, miss,' Sam replied, the thought that Esther might change her mind making him speak up quickly. 'It's no more than an hour.'

That could be pleasant on a summer evening, Esther thought, but in driving wind and rain . . .

'The job involves lifting me in and out of the pony trap. Did your mother explain that to you?'

''Er did, miss.' Sam twisted his flat cap nervously between his hands. 'Mother told me all you said.'

'I think I might prove rather heavy. Will you be able to manage?'

"Course I will.' Sam's hands stilled and his smile faded as though Esther's question somehow challenged his manhood. 'You don't seem to be more than a handful.'

'Appearances can sometimes be deceptive,' Esther laughed. 'According to Miri I am almost as heavy as a Christmas hog.'

'Beg yer pardon, Mrs Butler, but you be mistaken there.' Sam looked shyly at the wife of his old school teacher.

'Oh, am I?' Miri's smile escaped through her eyes. 'Just you wait an' see, me lad. Could be you'll change yer tune.'

'I will be able to carry you, miss.' He looked back to Esther. 'An' you need 'ave no fear of my dropping you. I'll take real good care of you, honest I will.'

'I am quite sure of that, Sam,' Esther said kindly. 'Now how are you with horses? The mare we have is a placid old thing but she will need feeding and grooming.'

Sam smiled, his eyes lighting up with pleasure. 'Me granddad was under-groom to Billy-me-lord over at West Bromwich, and I was allowed to 'elp whenever me mother could spare me. He showed me a lot, did me granddad, and I really loved being among them horses.'

'Then if twenty shillings a week plus the house is acceptable, Sam, you have yourself a job.'

'It's acceptable, all right.' Sam's smile threatened to split his face. 'An' I'll serve you well, miss. On God's honour, I'll serve you well.'

Catching the look Miri directed at her, Esther realised she had to say the words she had avoided saying to Ria Stedman. 'Sam, there is one more thing . . .'

'Just tell me, miss.' He looked keenly at her as she paused. 'Whatever it is, I'll do it.'

'It's just . . . I'm not . . .' She faltered, her whole being rebelling at the words. Miri's glance came again, sharp and determined. What was done was done and must be admitted to. Twisting the gold band on her wedding finger, Esther drew a short quavering breath. 'I think it will have to be

Mrs in future, Sam. Mrs Morgan Cosmore. And your duties will be at Addenbrooke House.'

'It be out now, wench,' Miri said, watching Sam stride away, his shoulders set square with relief. 'From now on all Darlaston will know you be Morgan Cosmore's wife.'

'Yes, all of Darlaston will know,' Esther repeated softly, but the only one who mattered already knew.

Closing the door, Miri turned to see Esther had wheeled her chair into the window nook; she herself felt just as sad as the girl she loved. 'It 'ad to be said, Essie,' she said tenderly, 'an' best to say it first as last. I know why you took 'im an' I know who you would rather 'ave taken, but it be done an' you must live wi' it.'

Yes, she must live with it. Esther stared at the trees blocking her view of Rowena House. Live with the pain of being married to a man she did not love. Live with the pain of being forever Mrs Morgan Cosmore and never Mrs Adam Paige. But she was used to pain; it had been her lifelong companion and it was what she would use to keep her going, to drive her on until she was paid her true bridal price: revenge.

Taking a china figurine from the dresser, Miri held it in her hands, studying the sculpted face and the gaudy blues and greens of the glazed dress. John had laughed when she had chosen this, saying she was daft to take it in preference to something useful, but he had smiled into her eyes as he placed it in her hands, the soft secret smile of love. They had been young then, she and John. Letting the memory slip away she picked up a piece of cloth, wrapping the ornament as carefully as if it had been of the finest porcelain, then laid it in the wooden soapbox standing near the kitchen door. So little, she thought, looking at the box while rubbing both hands across her aching back, so little for so many years, but then it meant there was not so much to pack.

'Sure you 'aven't left anythin'?'

Coming from her bedroom, Esther shook her head.

'Then I'll see if Sam 'as the trap ready.' Miri edged past the soapbox, going towards the small stable that housed the mare.

Slowly Esther wheeled herself to the window nook, glancing over her shoulder to the room where she had spent almost all of her life, a room that from today she would see no more.

Morgan would not come for her. She stared at the crockery, clean and shining on the pine dresser. She was not to be taken to her new home by a proud bridegroom. No, he would not come for her. Instead he had sent a note informing her that her rooms were ready. He might have been giving her permission to enter his household, as if hiring a servant. Her eyes rested on the fireplace, cold and empty now all the cinders and ash were removed – swept away as her sixteen years in this house were being swept away.

She closed her eyes, feeling the emptiness of the years behind her; the same emptiness that stretched before her the rest of her days. There would be no illusions between her and Morgan Cosmore. He intended to go on living his own life; she was an unwanted intrusion that would be quickly pushed aside.

'Is this the box, Mrs Butler?' Sam tapped politely on the door as he followed Miri back inside the kitchen.

'Yes, lad, that be it. I don't think there be much weight in it.'

'None at all.' Sam smiled, sweeping the box easily up in his arms. 'This ain't Christmas hog weight neither.'

'Be you ready then?' Miri fastened her eyes on Esther, refusing to let them stray around the bright little room, not wanting to admit even to herself how much it hurt to leave it; all of her life with John had been spent here, caring for him and for Esther. Now it was over, gone as he was gone.

'Yes, I'm ready.' Esther held out a hand, squeezing her friend's. 'Thank you, Miri,' she whispered. 'Thank you for coming with me.'

'I've put the box in the trap.' Sam tapped respectfully at the door, his interruption staving off the tears threatening both women. 'Will you be wantin' to be lifted in now, Mrs Cosmore?'

Esther hesitated then loosed her hold on Miri's hand. Sam had been using that name for the past few days yet still she was not on easy terms with it.

'I can wait. Old Queenie is in no hurry to be goin' anywhere.'

'Queenie never is. Unless, of course, there is the offer of a bran mash, then she can hurry well enough.'

'Yes, likes her food.' Sam cast an affectionate glance towards the mare waiting patiently beyond the gate. 'And it shows. Might be as well to cut her down a bit.'

'Let's not do that.' Esther wheeled herself to the doorway. 'She is such a sweet old thing, I couldn't bear to take anything away from her.'

'You know, Mrs Cosmore,' Sam took the bar of the wheelchair, pushing it along the narrow stone-flagged path, 'I couldn't neither.'

Esther seated in the trap, he turned to Miri. 'In you get, Mrs Butler. I will take the chair back inside and return for it when I've got the two of you to Addenbrooke.'

'No, you won't, lad,' Miri said, determination in every word. 'There will be no comin' back. We go from this 'ouse an' that be the endin' of it.'

Sam frowned, eyeing the small cart. 'But there's not room for both of you and the chair as well. I will *have* to come back for it.'

'No, lad, you won't.' Miri remained stubborn. 'I'll push the chair.'

'You can't walk all the way to Butcroft,' Esther protested. 'It has to be at least two miles.'

'Two miles, four miles . . .' Miri grasped the chair by its push bar '. . . makes no difference. I've said I'll walk, an' walk is what I'll do. An' it's no good you goin' on. There'll be no comin' back was what I said, an' no comin' back was what I meant.'

'If that's the way you want it, Mrs Butler . . .'

'It is, lad, it is.'

'Then we will take it steady. Just say if you find it becoming too much and we will put you in the trap and I will wheel the chair. Queenie doesn't really need me to lead her.'

'Yes, lad.' Miri turned her face from the cottage. 'I'll say.'

Sam led the mare at a steady walk but this time Esther took no pleasure in studying the flowers dotting the heath. Deep in her own thoughts, she remained unaware of the heath giving way to drab faceless houses huddled about the grimy soot-blackened iron works and the line of doll's-house-sized shops, their tiny windows peeping like eyes from smoke-smudged walls.

The stares of women hooded in shawls following the strange little procession, Sam led the way along Pinfold Street to the Bull Stake, dominated by the large brick building of the Darlaston Steam Tram Company. Following the tram route for a while he then branched right into Birmingham Street, thus avoiding the rise in the ground that, gentle as it was, had Miri breathing hard; she had resisted all his attempts at getting her to ride in the trap and he knew the futility of trying yet again.

Coming to the junction with Old Park Road, he took a narrow track to the right that ran along between ploughed fields, their hedges of hawthorn threaded with silken white trumpets of bindweed growing almost shoulder-high.

For over an hour Esther had sat in silence. Now the jolting of the trap over the rutted track seemed to jerk her from the lonely world of her own thoughts. Seeing Miri leaning hard against the chair, the effort of getting its cumbersome frame over the rough ground almost too much, she motioned Sam to halt.

'You all right?' Concern replacing the lines of fatigue on her face, Miri looked hard at Esther.

'No, I am not all right.' She tried to make her voice hard though her heart cried out at the tiredness in Miri's face.

'Has this track jolted you, Mrs Cosmore?' It was Sam's face now that clouded over with concern. 'Are you in pain?'

'No, Sam, I am not in pain though I do hurt – hurt from seeing Miri so tired with pushing my wheelchair. I refuse to let you go a yard further until she gets into the trap.'

'I said I would walk . . .'

'I know what you said,' Esther cut across her stubbornness. 'Now you hear what I have to say, Mrs Miriam Butler. I do not move from this spot until you ride. You have two choices: either you sit with me in the trap or I tell Sam to go on ahead and ask for a cart that will take both you and the chair.'

'I don't want them Cosmores sendin' nothin' for me!' Miri's tone was mutinous. 'When I get to their door, it will be on my own two feet.'

'Then we stay here.' Esther folded her hands in her lap, a look of determination settling around her mouth.

'Could I make a suggestion?' Sam looked tentatively at Miri.

'You can speak yer mind, Sam Stedman, you know that.'

'Well, Mrs Butler, seems to me you could ride until we come to Addenbrooke House then I could set you down at the gates and you could walk up to the door.'

'That ain't the way I wanted it.'

Sam glanced at Esther, asking her to leave the handling of this situation to him.

'Things don't always go just as we plan them.' He kept his voice firm, knowing how she would react if she thought he was patronising her. 'You know that as well as anybody. But it will do no harm to change yer plans this once.'

Miri gave him a sharp look. 'It'll harm me!'

'Begging yer pardon, Mrs Butler, but it's only yer pride will be harmed, and like my mother's forever telling me, it's a proud man has the hardest fall.'

'Yes, well, Ria Stedman always did 'ave 'er fair share of common sense.'

Sensing that she was coming round, Sam pressed home his advantage. 'Me and my brothers used to come this way when we were kids and got to know Butcroft. The old gun butt workshops had a real fascination for lads so I know the area pretty well, and I tell you – Addenbrooke House lies a way off yet.'

Across the hedge a man's voice called to horses pulling a binder, cutting across wheat waving tall and golden then throwing aside the bound sheaves.

Miri had been determined to walk but it had been further than she remembered. She shuffled, aware of the ache in her feet. And Addenbrooke still lay a way off.

'You're sure you can leave the mare to walk by herself if you push the chair?' She looked up at Sam, willing him not to laugh at her.

'Queenie knows what she's about, Mrs Butler.'

'Arrh, we all think that,' Miri answered, a little reluctant still. 'We all of us think we know what we are about till the time comes when we learn we ain't as smart as we thought.'

'Animals mostly have the good sense to stop when they realise it would be unwise to go on.'

'There's no arguin' with you on that, seein' as I don't know a great deal about animals,' Miri conceded. 'But I do admit Queenie 'as a lot more sense than many humans I've come across.'

Darting another glance at Esther, Sam moved to the back of the trap, one hand resting on its tail gate. 'So what do you say, Mrs Butler? Will you ride part of the way?'

'Tell the truth, lad, I think I'd welcome it. But mind . . . just as far as the gate and no further.'

Separated from the farmed land by broad sweeping meadows, Addenbrooke House stood like a red-garbed sentinel. Large square windows were set in plum-coloured brick; chimneys rose like startled rooks from its dark slate roof while before a heavy door the drive curved in a semi-circle, ending at high brick-built pillars surmounted by miniature iron anvils – a testimony to the iron master who lived there.

'Miri!'

Esther turned wide eyes to the older woman, but a glance from her made the girl bite back her frightened remark. There could be no going back, no undoing what was signed by man and sealed in the eyes of the Lord; for better or for worse the words were spoken, and for better or for worse this house was now Esther's home and she must live in it, whatever it might hold for her.

Trudging along the drive, Miri felt her own courage and determination flag. Ezra Cosmore and Josiah Kerral were cast from the same rigid mould; both had come from nothing, working their way up in the world by sheer hard graft – and in Jos Kerral's case that hardness had spread to his dealings with men and with his own family. Would they now discover that the same harshness applied to Ezra Cosmore? Did his family count for nothing where his own ends were at stake, and did he resort to blows when his demands were thwarted?

Waiting for her tug on the bell pull to be answered, Miri felt only cold premonition.

'Good afternoon. Mrs Cosmore?'

Esther looked up at the thin grey-haired man standing just clear of the opened door. 'Yes,' she said, her mouth dry with nervous fear, 'I am Mrs Cosmore.'

'The young Mr Cosmore is out but I will tell the master you are here.'

Morgan had not come himself to fetch her from Rowena,

but summoned her by way of a note. Now he was not even here to welcome her. Esther swallowed hard. It seemed her husband intended to carry on the way he had started.

Chapter Thirteen

'Come away, Mother. Let him go.' Adam Paige put his hands on his mother's shoulders, turning her away from the plain rectangular wooden box resting on the table before an empty fireplace.

'First yer brothers and now yer father . . . oh, Adam, son, what will we do? What will we do?'

Folding her bony body close to his, he wrapped his arms protectively about her, listening to the long agonised sobs. They would do what they had to do: go on living.

'The men be 'ere wi' the cart, Adam.'

'Thanks, Mrs Price.' He looked over to the neighbour who had slipped quietly into the room, its threadbare curtains closing out the light of day. 'Would you take my mother while I see to things?'

'Arrh, lad.' The woman's face creased with sympathy. 'Give 'er to me. I'll take 'er round to my 'ouse till you be done.'

The two women gone, Adam stood looking into the plain deal box at his father's body, dressed in moleskin trousers, a muffler round his neck tucked into a ragged jacket, hiding the absence of a shirt; Albert Paige would stand before his maker in the only clothes he had.

His touch gentle as if caressing a sleeping child, Adam removed the two pennies that had held the dead eyelids closed but the one his mother had placed on the tongue he left in place.

179

'I wish things could have been different, Father,' he whispered, 'but I guess this is the only way any of us will leave Foleys Croft. I wanted so much to . . .' He broke off, tears clogging his throat. Bending, he kissed the cold face that had been so carefully washed by his mother. 'I love you, Father,' he murmured. 'I love you.'

Taking the piece of unplaned wood that was standing at the side of the fireplace behind his father's chair, he lifted it on to the coffin then fetched a hammer and nails from a box in the wash house and nailed it into place.

'Ready, lad?'

Adam looked at the man with his flat cap held respectfully in one hand. He had entered silently through the open door.

'Yes, Mr Price, all ready.'

'I'll get the others then. You go next door and get yer mother.'

'Mr Price,' Adam called as the other man made to leave, 'will you share this between yerself and the others? I'm sorry it couldn't be more.'

'No, lad.' George Price looked at the four shillings Adam held out. 'We'll take no money for carryin' yer dad. We all be neighbours and we do for one another. We in Foleys Croft 'ave to 'elp ourselves.'

Reluctantly Adam returned the coins to his pocket; each of the men who would bear his father to his grave could have done with taking his shilling, not many in the Croft had work to bring in food, but they each of them had their pride and to press money on them for assisting in burying a man they had known and liked for fifty years would be taken as an insult to that pride. The men of Foleys Croft didn't have much in life but they had their loyalty. 'Thanks, Mr Price,' Adam said simply. 'Thanks.'

Bringing his mother from the neighbouring house, holding her close beside him, Adam stood behind the handcart borrowed from the corn chandler in Wolverhampton Street. Around them the people of the Croft stood in huddled groups outside their houses. The curtains would remain closed until the body of their neighbour was laid in the ground.

To a murmur of sympathy among the watchers, the coffin was carried from the house and laid on the handcart. Two of the bearers, flat caps folded into their pockets, grasped a handle of the cart while the other two placed themselves to either side of it.

The end and the beginning, Adam thought, his eyes fixed on the crude wooden box. They were the same in Foleys Croft. A man was born into poverty and he died in poverty. No great rejoicing welcomed his birth and no grand funeral marked his passing; there could be no mahogany casket with gleaming brass handles and no plumed black horses to draw a glass-sided hearse for Albert Paige, just the wild flowers of the heath picked by children and tied into a sheaf by neighbours.

The cart rumbled along Katherine's Cross, branching left into Pinfold Street. Passers by stood still and removed their caps, women crossing themselves and drawing their shawls across the lower half of their face in respect for the dead as the pathetic cortege went on its way; a steam tram rattled noisily along the rails, passengers paying the same respects as the driver sounded his steam horn in tribute.

Turning into the Chapel, Adam held his mother, feeling the sobs shake her body. Darlaston respected its dead but where was its respect for the living?

'What's that you say?'

Josiah Kerral leaned over the desk, his face thunderous.

'It is as I told you, Mr Kerral.' Marshall Thomas, the solicitor, edged nervously back in his chair, wanting to put more space between himself and the man glaring at him in fury. 'The first I knew of it was when I got a letter from a friend of mine. He overheard Mr Cosmore talking about the sale.'

'What friend . . . who told you?' Jos demanded.

'I'm sorry, Mr Kerral.' The solicitor held the arms of his

chair, the palms of his hands slippery with nervous fear. Josiah Kerral could quite easily strike out if he heard no satisfactory answer to his question.

'You'm sorry!' Jos banged the desk with his fist. 'You'm sorry? 'Ow do you think I feel! It be my bloody business he's sold.'

'Hardly *your* business.' Marshall Thomas tried a nervous smile then thought better of it. It might be dangerous to give Jos Kerral the slightest reason to think he saw the situation as amusing. 'You had signed it over, had you not?'

'Signed it over? Of course I signed it over. But that don't mean I gave 'im permission to sell.'

Breathing a breath of relief as Jos turned to stand at the window overlooking Church Street, Marshall shuffled the papers on his desk. 'He would not need permission,' he said after several seconds spent judging whether or not he should say anything at all. 'When you put yer signature to the document of conveyance it became his property to do with as he liked.'

'But surely I should 'ave been told?'

'It was signed over as a deed of gift.' Marshall avoided the other man's angry stare as Jos whipped round to face him. 'A man does not have to say what he intends to do with a gift.'

'When it be my bloody gift he does!' Jos shouted, one foot sending a chair scudding against the wall. 'Who was it sold to?'

'The note did not include the name of the buyer.'

'Maybe the note didn't include it,' Jos replied sarcastically then ground out the rest. 'But you'd better find out who or y'ave seen the last of my business.'

Slamming out of the office he climbed into his carriage and drove himself, snatching at the reins and laying the whip to the horse's flanks as he wheeled about. Oblivious of pedestrians, he drove furiously, the carriage lurching dangerously round the bend that gave on to Victoria Road. Hurtling past the park, he ignored the cry of a woman terrified by the galloping horse, laying on with the whip and sending the carriage flying across the railway bridge towards Bull Piece. Then, passing the road that would have taken him to Butcroft, he headed out for James Bridge. That no-good bloody son of Ezra Cosmore's might be nowhere to be found but he would get his answers from somewhere.

Driving into the yard of the copper foundry, he strode towards a huddle of buildings encrusted with the same rust-coloured dust that covered everything in sight.

'Mornin', Mr Kerral, sir. Was you wantin' . . .'

'Out of my bloody way!' Jos elbowed the gateman aside. He needed no help in finding the hole Ezra Cosmore called an office. He had watched this place rise shack by shack, seen every brick and every tin roof go into place – and seen some collapse with the same speed. But it wasn't the office he was looking for. What he wanted would not be there.

Striding into the foundry, he felt the stinging acrid smell of the outside air thicken in his throat, quickly laying a coating on his tongue. Heedless of the sparks rising in golden fountains from molten metal being tipped into moulds of rough clay, he crossed the beaten earth floor of the foundry, taking no heed of men shovelling coal into the gaping white-hot maw of the furnace. Sweat glistened like polished silk on bodies stripped to the waist. Some were just boys, barely more than children, labouring to drag away the spitting moulds to the cooling shed.

Climbing a rickety wooden stairway, he kicked open a door at the top.

'Cosmore!'

Jos's shout, carrying over the din of hammers against hardened clay, brought several glances from the foundry floor but he paid them no mind.

'Cosmore, I want a word wi' you!'

Stepping into a tiny room also liberally scattered with the thick red dust, Jos glared at the clerk inside, his long-handled pen poised in mid-air as he stared at the new arrival.

'Get out!'

Not waiting for the man who paid his wages to order otherwise, the clerk scrambled through the door, his feet echoing on the wooden stairs outside.

'Jos?' Ezra Cosmore frowned. Being bawled at in front of his workmen was not to his liking. 'What be this all about?'

'Don't try tellin' me you don't know.' He kicked out at the door, sending it crashing shut. What he had to say was for Cosmore's ears alone and not those of every man in Darlaston.

'All I know is you be 'ere wi' yer arse in yer 'and over summat. Either you say what it is now or you get yerself out of my foundry. I've got better things to do than mess around wi' yer bloody bad temper.'

'Yes, you got better things to do all right!' spat Jos, his mouth tight with anger. 'Things like sellin' off my business behind my back.'

'Sellin' off yer business? You be talkin' daftness, man. 'Ow can I sell off yer business?'

'Yer 'and might not 'ave signed the paper but I reckon yers was the mind had the directing of it, for I doubt that son of yers has the brain for it.'

'What's my lad to do wi' this?'

'I'll tell you what yer lad 'as to do wi' this.' Jos, his face livid with fury, banged a fist on the table that served for a desk, sending up a small cloud of the red dust. 'He's sold forty per cent of my business, forty per cent of Kerral Wheel and Axle. That's what 'e 'as to do wi' this. He sold it off, and not a single word to me.'

Ezra glanced at the door, satisfying himself it was closed, then through the window, ensuring the clerk was not hovering on the stairs. 'Be you sure, Jos?'

''Course I be bloody sure!' Veins stood out thick on his

neck as Jos roared his answer. 'I've just come from Marshall Thomas's place in Church Street.'

'Was it him 'ad the 'andling of the sale?'

'No. He would 'ave known better than to sell off what was mine without tellin' me first.'

'Then 'ow can you be sure that what 'e tells you be true? If 'e didn't handle it, 'ow come 'e knows about it?'

''E were told,' Jos barked. 'And afore you asks, I don't know who by, but this you can be sure of: Thomas wouldn't tell me anything 'e were not certain of.'

'But why?' Ezra swept back several wisps of sandy hair that had fallen over his face. 'I see no reason for it. Morgan had the thousand pounds you paid on the day of the marriage so why sell off his share in yer business? I tell you, Kerral, if it has been done then it's been done without my knowledge.'

'It's been done all right, I'll stake the other sixty per cent on that!' Jos wrenched open the door, slamming it back against the wall. 'And you can stake one hundred per cent of this place on this. When I come across that bloody nancy boy you call a son, I'll break his neck!' Stepping out on to the stairway, he turned back, glaring at the bloated, ruddy face watching him through hooded eyes. 'That is, if he ain't already sold this place as well!'

'The rooms are to your satisfaction?'

'Perfectly so, thank you.'

Esther looked at the tall figure elegantly dressed in aubergine-coloured coat, a pink silk cravat expertly tied about his throat, calf-length leather boots showing beneath breeches the colour of rich butter cream.

'I am sorry I was not here to meet you.' Morgan Cosmore smiled, showing even white teeth. 'I trust my father took care of you?'

'Your father sent word he was wanted at the foundry and would see me on his return.'

'How unfortunate,' Morgan glanced about the sitting room

that was part of the suite that had been adapted for Esther's use, 'that neither of us could greet you on your arrival, but I had no idea of what time you would appear.'

'Perhaps I should have made an appointment?' Esther replied acidly.

'An answer to my note would have been helpful.' He smiled charmingly, refusing to respond to her note of rebuke.

'Your coming to fetch me would have helped!' she replied sharply. 'Instead of leaving me to arrive as any freshly hired servant might have.'

Morgan flicked at one perfectly padded shoulder. 'My dear, there was nothing I could do that the competent Mrs Butler could not.'

'Including lifting me from my chair into the pony trap?'

'I trusted one of your father's hands would do that.'

'Fortunately for me my father did provide a man for that purpose,' Esther lied, 'for I could not see Gittins being able to carry me, and neither you nor your father was available.'

'Then if you had a man, I see no cause for complaint.'

There was no victory to be gained from argument, Esther realised. This man had no feelings for her, no interest in her other than the money she had brought him and any she might yet bring.

'The man who is employed to carry me,' she pressed, 'he will be allowed to continue that employment here?'

Morgan looked at her, his smile bland as he recognised an end to hostilities. 'Provided I do not have to pay for it.'

'You will not.' Esther folded her hands together, feeling the hard band on her finger, the band that would hold her to this house, to this man whose smile held no warmth and whose heart held no love.

'Then he is as welcome as you yourself.'

He walked to the wide square window that looked on to a walled garden ablaze with roses which his mother had planted on first coming to Addenbrooke – the only part that for him reflected her gentleness, for the rest of the house carried only the hard tasteless imprint of his father.

As welcome as you yourself. His words echoed in Esther's mind and she tasted their double edge. There was no welcome here for her; it would have suited him better had she stayed at Rowena House.

Turning from the window, Morgan glanced once more about the room which was furnished with the same dark heavy furniture as the rest of the house. 'Do you have all you need here? The bedroom and bathroom – are they satisfactory?'

'Quite,' Esther nodded, remembering the message implied by the small single bed. Morgan would not be sharing her bedroom.

'Then perhaps you will allow me to take you to the drawing room? My father is waiting to welcome you there and I have instructed Gittins to serve tea.'

If your father's welcome matches your own then I might as well stay where I am, she thought grimly, but remained silent as he took the bar at the back of her wheelchair and pushed it from the room.

She had been carefully tucked away from the body of the house, she observed as they passed down a long narrow corridor she guessed led to the kitchens and servants' hall. But then, where else to put a wife with whom one had no wish to be seen?

Why had she done this? Why had she entered into a marriage that at best could lead only to unhappiness? Why ally herself with a family that saw her only as a means to their own selfish ends? Waiting before a heavy panelled door, Esther heard the answer echo in her mind and owned her own reason as selfish as Morgan's. She had married him for one reason and one reason only: to bring about her father's downfall.

'So there you be, wench.' Ezra, his face already flushed with brandy, peered blearily at her as she entered the room.

'Welcome to yer new 'ome.'

'Thank you.' Esther smiled. At least the father had had

the grace to say she was welcome, even if he didn't mean it.

'Is everything all right for you? Yer rooms, I mean. They're comfortable?'

'Very comfortable, Mr Cosmore.'

'Well, if you wants anything, you just sing out.'

'I have everything I need,' Esther said, 'and I am sure I shall manage very well.'

'Good, good.' Ezra waved his brandy glass, his eyes going to his son. 'Don't keep the wench in the doorway. Bring her over against me where I can get a good look at 'er.'

Inspecting the brood mare? Morgan smiled inwardly as he wheeled the chair across the room, positioning it beside a table set with a tea tray and daintily cut sandwiches. Don't bother, Father. All the satisfaction you will get from this marriage will be seeing Jos Kerral lose everything he has.

Esther glanced about the oval room, beautiful in its design but marred by the heavy leather armchairs and elaborate chiffoniers that had been used to furnish it. Tall, almost ceiling-height cabinets were filled to capacity with china and figurines: an overly ornate mantel topped the large fireplace. Were all the rooms in Addenbrooke House as distressingly ugly as this one?

'Pour yerself some tea, wench.' Ezra took a pull of his brandy. 'You be the mistress of Addenbrooke now so the quicker you get settled to that, the easier it'll be for you.'

Easier for her? Esther glanced over to where Morgan was closing the door of the room. It would never be easy for her in this house.

'Do you take milk and sugar?' She posed the question as he took a chair opposite. How extraordinary, she thought, how unbelievable that she could be married to a man and not even know how he took his tea.

'Both.' Morgan smiled affably enough yet Esther found herself mistrusting it: it was a smile that hid something, and that something she felt instinctively would not be to her liking or advantage.

Passing him his cup, Esther glanced at his father.

'No tea for me.' Ezra read the question in her eyes and waved the brandy glass a second time. 'I've got all I want right 'ere.'

Pouring tea for herself, she felt a lull settle awkwardly over the room. Morgan, one leg folded across the other knee, balanced his cup precariously on it, his stare fixed somewhere in the middle of the once beautiful carpet. Ezra, on the other hand, reaching for the decanter, belched noisily as he refilled his glass.

'Has he showed you over the 'ouse?' He was first to puncture the silence.

'There was no need,' Morgan answered his father rapidly.

'No need!' Ezra banged the decanter down hard. 'What d'you mean, no need? Of course there be a need. This be 'er 'ome from now on an' 'er will 'ave to find 'er way around it. An' who better to show 'er than 'er husband?'

'Esther has seen that part of the house that was altered to accommodate her wheelchair, I see no reason for her to be taken into rooms she will never be using.' Morgan took the cup from his knee, replacing it on the tray.

'You see no reason!' Ezra's voice rose. 'So if you see no reason, nobody else 'as to either, eh, Mr bloody 'Igh and Mighty? It don't matter that yer wife might want to see the 'ouse y'ave brought 'er to.'

'You seem suddenly concerned for Esther, Father.' Morgan turned a cold glance on the older man. 'So much so I am wondering if the brandy is not confusing you a little more than usual.'

'Meaning?' Ezra's eyes withdrew a little further allowing the mounds of puffy flesh to almost close over them.

'Meaning she is not one of your Birmingham ladies.'

Ezra's face, already flushed and bloated with alcohol, turned a deep shade of red. 'You cocky bastard!'

'None could know my parentage, or lack of it, better than you,' Morgan smiled calmly.

'Forever the smart answer,' Ezra ground out. 'Well, 'ere's one for you. That wench ain't no Brummagem whore an' 'er ain't going to serve as no cover up for a London strumpet, so you'd best clear the shit outta yer stable!'

Esther stared at the two men, each glaring at the other, contempt in the eyes of one and hatred in the eyes of the other.

'After you with the shovel, Father!' Morgan hissed, his handsome features redrawn with the pen of fury. 'After all, you have been a stablehand longer than I have.'

'Being clever won't get you anywhere this time,' Ezra picked up his glass. 'This be my 'ouse and I'm telling you, get yer garbage out.'

'This *is* your house,' Morgan stood up his face white with anger, 'but for how long, Father? How long?' Turning his back on a slightly bewildered Ezra, he looked at Esther. 'You have my apologies for this display but I warn you now my father normally behaves this way whenever I am present, he exercises no regard for a lady. I ask your permission to leave? Would you care to return to your rooms now or will you call Gittins?'

'If your father does not mind, I would like to go to my room. I am feeling a little tired.'

'Go and get some rest, wench.' Ezra managed a smile. 'And if my talk has offended you, then you 'ave my apology.'

Taking the bar of the chair, Morgan pushed it across the room. *He exercises no regard for a lady.* Esther seemed to hear Morgan's words again. Ezra Cosmore's speech was rough and what he had said was not pleasant yet she felt that of the two it was he who held her in the higher regard. He had used the word 'welcome'; it was he who had asked if she had been shown over her new home. Morgan had offered neither.

Opening the door, her husband wheeled her out into the wide square reception hall of Addenbrooke House and at that moment Esther knew the reason he had not shown her the rest of the house. Coming down the oak staircase, her blue dress seeming to glow against its wood, was Roberta Vance.

'That didn't take very long,' Miri remarked after Morgan had left Esther in her rooms again.

In her own sitting room, Esther leaned her head against the back of her chair and closed her eyes, feeling the tension of the past half hour assail her.

With a wisdom born of many such moments, Miri went on quietly arranging the room; moving chairs and side tables, making clearer access for the wheelchair.

'At least he bade me welcome to my new home.' Esther vanquished the threat of tears and opened her eyes.

'Morgan did?'

Her smile barely a glimmer, Esther gave a shake of her head. 'No, not Morgan, Ezra.'

'Ezra Cosmore bid you welcome? Well, that's a turn up. I 'adn't thought that one to 'ave a civil word to 'is tongue.'

'I think that, despite his manner, he could be a kind man.'

'Mebbe you be right.' Miri pushed a chair away from the window, making a space where Esther could sit and look out across the garden. 'To be fair, life ain't been easy for Ezra Cosmore for all his money; first losin' 'is wife so soon after they wed an' then 'avin' a son that don't care tuppence for 'im. No, 'e ain't had life easy, but then 'ow many in Darlaston 'ave? Cosmore ain't one on 'is own there.'

No, Ezra Cosmore was not alone in that, Esther thought. She had first-hand knowledge of what it was like to have someone who did not care tuppence for you. Her father had always made his indifference to her very plain and now she had a husband in the same mould.

'So what *did* that 'usband of yers 'ave to say if 'e didn't bid you welcome?' The last of the furniture placed to her satisfaction, Miri turned to the girl she had reared and wished she had not asked the question as she caught a quick flash of pain twist her mouth.

Taking a long breath, Esther answered: 'I asked him if Sam could stay on here, doing the job my father employed him to do . . .'

'Yer father?' Miri interrupted, brows lifted in disapproval.

'A lie, I know, but I could not take the risk of telling him *I* pay Sam. Had I done so he would have wanted to know where my money came from.'

'Of course you be right,' Miri nodded, 'that 'adn't crossed my mind.'

'I'm afraid it is not the first lie I have told over the past few weeks. If I don't watch out I might well become proficient at it.'

'Not you, Essie,' Miri said emphatically. 'You ain't the kind. That be one thing you did not get from Jos Kerral. An' anyway, a little lie sometimes saves a big heartache.'

Esther's gaze dropped to the wedding ring on her left hand. Lies and heartache, that was to be the shape of her life from now on.

'So what did 'e answer when you asked if Sam could stay on 'ere?'

Her gaze still on her wedding ring, Esther replied, 'He said Sam was as welcome here as I was myself.'

Uncertain as to the exact meaning of what had been said, Miri decided to leave it, yet it rankled in her mind. There was something not quite right about it, a coldness she could almost feel. Had Esther felt the same coldness? Had she felt that in some way Morgan Cosmore's words held a double edge?

'So what more did Ezra say?' she asked, hoping to steer the conversation to safer ground.

Lifting her gaze, Esther looked around the room. 'He asked if Morgan had shown me the remainder of the house.'

'Which of course 'e ain't, but then if the rest of it be as unpleasant as these rooms, then it ain't surprisin' 'e be in no hurry to show it to you. This be the ugliest assortment of furniture I've seen in many a day.'

'I do not think it was the furniture he did not wish me to see,' Esther said quietly.

'Oh!' Bewilderment returned to Miri's brow drawing it down. 'What *do* you reckon 'e didn't want you to see then?'

Esther looked up, her bronze-coloured eyes bright, and when she spoke her voice was calm and steady. 'I think Morgan did not wish me to see what was standing on the stairs.'

'Standin' on the stairs!' Miri's frown deepened. 'What was it was stood on the stairs?'

'Not what,' Esther replied, 'but who.'

'Who! You mean it was a person stood on the stairs?'

'Yes.' Esther's smile surfaced at last but it was a smile without humour. 'It was a person who stood on the stairs – the person of Roberta Vance.'

'What!' Miriam's knees buckled and she dropped heavily into a chair. 'That woman be still 'ere in this 'ouse!'

'So it would seem.'

'But I thought . . . 'er said . . . didn't 'er go back to London?'

'It appears not,' Esther replied when Miri had stopped spluttering. 'Not unless she left and then returned.'

'But why should 'er come back 'ere? What for? An' why should 'e let 'er?' The questions tumbled out of a highly offended Miri.

Esther amazed her with a calm acceptance of the situation. 'Miri, we both know the answers to your questions. Let us be honest with each other at least. She is here because she is my husband's mistress.'

'I can't deny what you say, Essie.' Bewilderment gave way to anger as Miri looked at Esther, reading the unhappiness in the girl. 'But to 'ave 'er in this 'ouse . . . to 'ave 'er stay where 'is wife is . . .'

'He is being open about it, Miri, being honest not only

with himself but with me. Roberta Vance is his lover and he is making no pretence otherwise. Her presence in this house testifies to that and I am grateful to him for it – I would much prefer to know of her existence and her place in his affections than be the victim of deceit.'

'You be the victim of a damn' sight more'n deceit!' Miri cried, anger getting the better of her. 'You be the man's wife, for God's sake!'

'Yes, I am Morgan Cosmore's wife.' Esther still spoke softly, her voice holding no trace of recrimination, no hint of bitterness. 'But Roberta Vance is the woman he loves.'

'Oh, Essie,' Miri covered her face with her hands, 'what a' you goin' to do?'

Fingering the circle of gold on her finger, Esther looked out of the window. 'I accepted him for better or for worse. That included living here, and if he chooses to have Roberta Vance under the same roof too then I must accept that.'

But not forever, she added under her breath, not until death do us part. Only until I have what I set out to get: revenge on my father. In the deepest corner of her heart the flame of resolve burned higher. I will be Morgan Cosmore's wife only until revenge do us part.

Chapter Fourteen

'Everything going well, Barney?'

'It is that, Mr Paige.'

Adam smiled. He had asked many times that the man he had put in charge of the Sovereign works should call him by his given name but always he addressed him as 'Mr Paige'.

'See 'ere.' Barney Whitehouse picked a bolt from a box on the floor of the workshop, running a finger along its shining silver length. 'Just you look at the finish on that.' He handed it to Adam.

Just as Barney had done, he ran a finger along the bolt, testing the smoothness of the cut metal then touching the same finger along the edges of the head.

'It be a good bit o' chamfer be that.' Barney smiled, proud as a man with his first-born son.

'Smooth as butter,' Adam agreed.

'Arrh.' Barney turned to a separate smaller box, selecting a metal nut and giving that to Adam too. 'Just try that an' tell me y'ave 'ad better.'

Twisting the nut on to the scored end of the bolt, Adam ran it up and down, feeling the almost intimate cling of metal to metal.

'Telling you I have known better would be lying to you, Barney,' he said. 'That is as good a thread as I have seen on a hand-made nut and bolt. They run beautifully together, the fit is just about perfect.'

'Like a virgin on 'er weddin' night!'

'Better not let Mrs Marsh hear you talk like that,' Adam said, joining his laugh to the foreman's.

''Ave you told 'er yet, about the new enquiries?' Barney was serious again.

'Not yet.' Adam returned the nut and bolt to their respective boxes. 'I want to work out exactly what it will mean in terms of man power and extra machinery.'

'It'll need plenty o' both, I'm thinkin'.' Barney lifted his cap and scratched his head before pulling the hat back into place. 'These 'ere be goin' flat out the 'ole o' the day.'

Adam glanced around the workshop at the men working the new capstans. Others were collecting and counting the finished nuts and bolts while two more boxed them up and stacked them near the door, ready to be loaded on to the cart for delivery.

'How are the men settling to the machines?' he asked, raising his voice against the clatter.

'Took to 'em well,' Barney answered, 'though they didn't trust 'em at first – seen 'em as takin' their jobs away. But they soon forgot that when they seen what them machines put in their tins.'

'Their pay has been increased to match their output,' Adam said. 'They work hard and deserve to be paid for it.'

Barney gave a nod. 'They appreciates it all the same, Mr Paige, an' there's many a bloke in this town wishes 'is gaffer was as fair-minded.'

Adam led the way from the workshop into the yard. 'I wish that too, Barney,' he said, a vision of his father rising in his mind, 'but I fear it is a long way off yet.'

Leaving the yard, he turned left into Wolverhampton Street, following it until he branched off towards the Leys. He had been right to suggest Barney Whitehouse for the job of foreman of the Sovereign and when next he spoke to Esther he must propose a foreman for the Leys for he himself was as often as not absent from the workshop, either talking to customers or on some other errand – more

than was advisable if that works was to run as efficiently as
the other.

Yet he had to admit both were running well and productivity
was increasing as the men became more familiar with the
machines, but that increase could go only so far. They were
almost up to full capacity now and still new orders for nuts and
bolts arrived almost daily. Esther had said the market would
pick up and it seemed her words had been prophetic. Would
the rest of what she'd said prove true? Did Darlaston's future
lie in the steel trade and were nuts and bolts to be its birth
bed, and more significantly was a young crippled woman to
be its midwife?

He had not spoken face to face with Esther Cosmore
since the night she had told him she wanted him to go to
York and buy the capstans now operating in both works.
All her instructions to him since and all his reports to her
were carried by Sam Stedman in the form of written notes but
the importance of what he now had to impart could not be
conveyed in writing. He needed to see her, to speak to her;
but to see her with Morgan Cosmore . . . Adam looked across
the expanse of unbroken heath. That he could not bear.

He would write again this evening. That way the note
would be ready should Sam call again this week. It was to
be hoped he did for opportunities such as Adam had been
offered did not often come twice in a lifetime.

Approaching the Leys works, Adam halted, squinting against
the afternoon sun. There was a horse and trap in the yard, a
small pony trap, the trap he had led away from the crowd
that day – Esther Kerral's pony trap.

His step quicker than before, he walked into the yard,
crossing to the ramshackle workshop and making for the
tiny office overlooking it.

'Good afternoon, Mrs Butler.' He closed the door of the
office, shutting off only a little of the scream of tools cutting
into metal.

'Good afternoon, Adam lad.' Miri smiled at him.

'Miss Kerr— Mrs Cosmore.' Adam checked his mistake.

'Good afternoon, Mr Paige,' Esther returned his greeting. 'I was so sorry to hear of your father's death.'

'Yes, lad, I've no doubt it come as a terrible shock to yer mother. How is 'er bearin' up?'

'The shock was very great as you say, Mrs Butler,' he answered, 'and though my father had been ill for some time, the end coming so quickly was quite unexpected.'

'Arrh, well, the Lord never tells nobody their time be up till 'E be standin' on the doorstep waitin' on 'em. It be 'ard but it comes to everybody in the end.'

'Will you give our condolences to yer mother, Mr Paige? And if there is anything we can do, please tell her not to hesitate to ask.'

'My mother will appreciate your kindness.' Adam's smile was faint, fading quickly from his mouth. 'But there is nothing you can do. It is thoughtful of you to offer assistance, Mrs Cosmore, but the bottom has fallen out of her world. We can only hope that time will bring an improvement in her spirits.'

'It will, Adam, it will,' Miri said, sympathy soft in her voice. 'I know what yer mother be feelin' but it will pass. 'Er might not think as much now but, believe me, the pain will ease, at least to a point where 'er can live wi' it. Until then you needs to be patient wi' 'er.'

'I will, Mrs Butler, you can be assured of that.' He turned as the door of the little office opened and a man of about forty appeared in the doorway. A piece of sacking was tied about his middle with string and a dirt-streaked cap covered brownish hair.

'Oh, you be 'ere.' He looked at Adam. 'Old Tom on the gate said to come to the office 'cos there be two women come askin' to see you, an' wi' you not bein' 'ere 'e thought as it be best for me to come. But you am 'ere so weren't no need o' me comin' after all.'

'Thanks, Joe.' Adam nodded to him. 'Will you go and

see that the order for Maybury Carriages is ready for delivery.'

'It is ready,' the man answered, his glance going from Esther to Miri then back to Adam. 'I seen to that meself an hour gone. D'you want me to put the boxes in the yard?'

'No.' Adam shook his head. 'No sense in lifting them twice. Leave them where they are until they come to collect.'

'Eh up, Herdun! Maybury's wagon be in the yard.'

Giving a quick wave to the man who had shouted, Joe glanced enquiringly at Adam.

'Get them loaded,' he said. 'I will bring the delivery note in a few minutes.'

'No need, gaffer,' Joe grinned, 'I seen to that an' all.'

'He is a good man, reliable and with a head on his shoulders, though your being here twisted his tongue a bit,' Adam said to Miri as Joe left the office. 'I was going to suggest him as foreman for this place, Mrs Butler. There needs to be someone in charge when I am not here, which seems to be fairly often these days; it means someone who not only knows the job and can handle men but who can make decisions. In my estimation Joe Hadley is that man.'

'Joe Hadley?' Esther queried. 'I thought his name was Herdun? At least that is the name I think that man shouted.'

'It was,' Adam laughed, 'but that is not Joe's name — or at least it was not his father's name. It is a nickname given him by the men, referring to the sack tied around his waist. Joe is never seen to go anywhere without it. In fact, it is strongly believed he turned up at his wedding with a sack fastened about his middle!'

'Do you believe that?' Esther's eyes sparkled.

'I reserve judgement, Mrs Cosmore.'

'Well said, lad,' Miri replied, her own face filled with smiles. 'This town be full of rumours an' it takes a smart man to recognise 'em.'

'Well, I like the rumour,' Esther laughed. 'I think I shall believe it.'

'Well, Herdun or Hadley, I think you should consider Joe for the job of foreman, you won't get better.'

'You really think you need one?' Miri asked, remembering Esther's reminder to act the part of owner of the works.

'I do, Mrs Butler, and I think you will be more than satisfied with Joe.'

'Then do it, Adam. Offer him the same wage as you gave Barney Whitehouse.'

'Will you see him yerself, Mrs Butler?'

'No, lad.' She stood up. 'That be best done by you.'

'Do you want to see the books?' He turned to a shelf buckling under several heavy ledgers.

Looking quickly at Esther, Miri refused. 'No, we won't be hindering you any more, Adam. We must be off. If you would find Sam an' tell 'im we be leavin'?'

'There is no need to find Sam,' Adam's grey eyes burned as he looked at Esther. 'I will carry Mrs Cosmore.

'You are safe with me,' he whispered as he bent close to her. 'You will always be safe with me.'

Lifted easily into his arms, the strength of them holding her close against him, Esther felt the same sudden jolt of her heart as she had that day he had lifted her from the trap; a feeling she never had when Sam lifted her.

Seated in the trap once more she felt a strong desire to hold on to Adam, to keep his arms around her. Blushing at her thoughts, she thanked him, keeping her eyes lowered as Miri climbed in beside her.

'I need to talk to you, Mrs Butler . . .'

Adam gripped the side of the trap as if he would hold it there, his eyes meeting Esther's as she looked up.

'. . . I have something to discuss with you.'

Miri took up the reins, holding them slack in her hands as Sam came from the gateman's hut.

'If it be to do wi' the works, then you see to it.'

'It is to do with business but I can't see to it, Mrs Butler, it needs yer decision.'

'Y'ave always 'ad my trust, lad.'

Adam gave a brief nod to Sam, returning his greeting as he took the mare's bridle then turned again to Miri.

'I know, Mrs Butler, and I thank you for it but this time I need to talk to you before taking any action.'

Miri looked anxiously towards the street, her fingers twitching nervously on the reins. 'We can't . . .'

'Is it something important, Mr Paige?' Esther cut in quickly. She recognised Miri's agitation and knew its cause, but could also see something bordering on urgency in Adam's eyes.

'I think so, Mrs Cosmore. It is a matter that needs consideration and one which needs to be decided upon quickly.'

'I will talk to Mrs Butler when we get home and send you word with Sam when we can meet you. When must it be settled by?'

'A week at most I would say. To leave it longer would be to risk letting the opportunity go to another.'

'Then you will hear from us within a few days,' Esther said, seeing Miri's nervousness begin to show on her face. 'Good afternoon, Mr Paige.'

'We should never 'ave gone there,' Miri said later as she brought a tray of tea from the kitchen to Esther's sitting room. 'Them works be no place for a young woman like yerself.'

'Because I am crippled, is that what you mean?'

Miri let the heavy tray down on to a squat oak table. 'You know what I mean!' she said, her tone sharp. 'A woman of yer class don't go visitin' a nut an' bolt works, sittin' about in a dusty office. You stick out like a sore thumb. Them men be sure to talk of it in every beer house they goes into; they ain't exactly famous for bein' tight-mouthed in Darlaston.'

'I'm sorry . . .'

'No, you ain't sorry!' Miri banged the china milk jug loudly on the tray. 'You ain't sorry at all. You insisted on goin'. I told you not to, but would you listen? Oh, no! You 'ad to 'ave yer own way. An' what 'appens if their talk reaches the ears of Ezra Cosmore or 'is son? They ain't neither of 'em fools. They'll soon put two an' two together an' they won't come up wi' 'alf a dozen. They'll 'it the nail right on the head, an' when they do you will lose everythin'.'

'They couldn't take the business . . .' Esther tried soothingly. 'It is in your name.'

'Oh, can't they!' Miri refused to be soothed. 'Legally it be mine, that much I'll grant, but like I said – neither of the Cosmores be fools. It won't take them long to figure out the name be mine but the money be yer'n, and once they 'ave, yer life won't be worth the livin' till they've squeezed every last penny from you.'

My life isn't worth much of the living now, Esther thought, but what Miri said was true. They would wring every last penny from her, and then what of her revenge? She had acted foolishly in going to the Leys but the desire to see Adam had driven common sense to the wall. Adam . . . A picture of his face rose in her mind, his grey eyes burning into hers. If only she had not been born a cripple. But she had! Savagely she pushed the image away.

'Don't you see, Essie wench?' Miri slumped on to the chair she had placed beside the table, her anger evaporating. 'It be dangerous for you to be seen in either of them works. It only takes one man to open 'is mouth about it an' you could find yerself up to yer neck in trouble, so why go? Y'ave managed the soap works well enough without goin' there.'

'It was very foolish of me,' Esther admitted. 'I had not thought of gossip. I promise you we will not go there again.'

Miri picked up the teapot, filling both cups. 'Thank the Lord for that!' she said emphatically. 'Now all we 'ave to do is pray them men 'ave something better to talk about over their ale than our visit to that works.' And to herself she added, And let's pray even harder that the cat don't already be among the pigeons.

* * *

'What the bloody 'ell was you thinkin'?' Ezra glared at his son across the dining table.

'I was thinking to make a profit, Father.' Morgan helped himself from the vegetable dish Gittins held out to him.

'But did you 'ave to do it so quick?' Ezra demanded. ''Aven't you got enough in yer pocket?'

Taking a spoonful of vegetables from the tureen, Esther kept her eyes on her plate. This argument had flared the minute Morgan had entered the dining room and she knew Ezra's latest salvo referred to money taken from her father, money to ensure the marriage between them.

'A man can never have enough money in his pocket.' Picking up his knife and fork, Morgan began to eat.

'Not if 'e be as bloody greedy as you 'e can't!' Ezra flashed. 'So greedy you couldn't hold on to it for five minutes.'

Morgan looked up, eyes cat-like. 'Why hold on to something I did not want?'

Ezra gulped some brandy, enriching the colour of his cheeks. 'You 'ardly gave yerself time to find out whether you wanted it or not. No sooner 'ad you got it than you got rid of it.'

'Why burden myself with maybe?' Morgan watched the colour deepen on his father's face. 'Take what you want when you want it, maybe could prove to be too late.'

'That be yer philosophy all over,' his father roared. 'Take what you want an' pay no mind to anybody else.'

'A sound philosophy, I have always found.'

'Arrh? Well, you just 'ope it be as sound this time, for the mood Jos Kerral were in it would be no surprise to me if 'e killed you.'

Esther looked up, her glance going from one to the other. Ezra had spoken of making a profit and her father had talked of making over a percentage of his business to Morgan as a wedding settlement. Surely he had not sold his share?

Morgan touched his napkin to his lips. 'Why should Jos Kerral kill me?'

'Why!' Ezra spluttered, sending a spray of brandy over his untouched plate. 'You can sit there an' ask me why? I tell you, if you 'ad done the same to me as y'ave done to 'im, I would wring yer bloody neck!'

'I see no reason why he should.' Morgan resumed his meal. 'It was mine after all.'

Heat of anger spreading colour down his thick neck clashing with the white of his stiffly starched collar Ezra stared across the table.

'Then you be a bloody sight thicker in the head than I took you for. You think sellin' off 'alf a man's business behind 'is back don't be reason enough?'

Esther felt the blood drain from her face. So it was his share in her father's business which Morgan had sold? Looking up, she met the violet eyes of Roberta Vance, filled with mockery.

Returning his knife and fork to his plate, Morgan took a mouthful of wine, savouring it on his tongue before replying.

'Forty per cent of Jos Kerral's business was mine,' he said, holding up the glass to catch the light from the heavy crystal gasolier. 'It was given to me in payment for marrying his daughter.'

Opposite, Roberta Vance's expertly painted mouth curved derisively, the lovely eyes smoky with vindictiveness. She knew, Esther thought. She knew he had sold what my father gave him. She knew and now she is exulting in it.

'You watch yer mouth.' Ezra glanced quickly to Esther, seeing her face devoid of colour.

'I have said nothing with which Esther was not already acquainted, surely?' Morgan admired the rainbow-coloured points of light reflected from the facets of his wine glass. 'Your father did tell you of our arrangements, did he not, my dear?'

Feeling those violet eyes on her face, Esther lifted her chin proudly. 'He did tell me of your transaction.'

'And didn't you care?' Roberta Vance's voice flowed mellifluously. 'I mean, was it not painful to know yourself . . . well . . . traded off?'

Esther ran a slow deliberate glance over the attractive face then down to where a necklace of amethysts lay against the pale grey silk of an exquisitely fitted gown.

'Traded off!' She kept her voice clear and patient as if dealing with a backward child. 'My dear Mrs Vance, I am afraid you have the wrong idea – but then, perhaps you never had a parent love you so much he willingly gave half of all he owned as your marriage gift? Had you had such a father you would have known there could be no pain in his giving you to a man he held in such high esteem.' Glancing at Morgan, Esther caught a quick gleam that looked suspiciously like congratulation in his tawny eyes.

'Jos Kerral made it plain to all involved, an' them as don't be should keep their nose out,' Ezra said bluntly, his little eyes going straight to Roberta Vance before darting back to Morgan. ''E made it plain that his business an' mine be merged as the families were merged, an' not to be sold off as soon as the ink dried on the paper.'

Putting his glass down on the table, Morgan leaned back in his chair and looked steadily at his father, now refilling his brandy glass yet again.

'There was no mention of that or anything like it in the agreement I made with Jos Kerral.'

'Did 'e 'ave to bloody spell it out? Did 'e 'ave to tell you in words a babby of three would understand?' Ezra's fury mounted. 'Ain't you got enough of what it takes to know a man don't make a gift of summat it 'as taken almost the 'ole of 'is life to build, only to see it sold off behind his back!'

Morgan had seen the colour deepen in his father's face and his eyes withdraw behind their barricades of flesh, now he surveyed his own fingernails in the lazy fashion he knew would add to the fires of his father's anger.

'If you admit that forty per cent of Jos Kerral's business

came to me as a gift, Father, then you should also accept that it was mine to do with as I pleased – to sell if and when I saw fit.'

'Oh, an' you saw fit all right!' Ezra gulped at his glass, half the contents disappearing in one swallow. 'An' you sold it.'

Morgan surveyed his fingernails calmly. 'Yes, I sold it, as I had the right to do.'

'The right? Arrh, you 'ad the right. But did you 'ave to do it behind the man's back? Couldn't you at least 'ave given 'im the chance of buyin' it back?'

'What makes you so certain I did not?'

Had he given her father the chance to buy back what he had signed away? Esther kept her eyes on Morgan's face. And if so, had her father had the money to buy it back?

'Well, did you?' Ezra held his glass in mid-air.

'I did.'

'So why did he turn up at James Bridge breathing bloody murder an' sayin' you 'ad sold yer share behind his back?'

'Because while he was trying to raise the money, I had a better offer from somewhere else. In short, Father, Jos Kerral was too late.'

'Too late? Why too late? Surely you ain't in that much of a hurry for money? You couldn't 'ave spent that thousand you got for . . .' Ezra broke off, glancing awkwardly at Esther.

'Morgan,' Roberta Vance turned a violet glance to Esther, 'was the money you spent on me part of your wife's marriage gift? If so it was naughty of you, darling.'

'Wouldn't surprise me if 'e spent the 'ole bloody thousand on you,' Ezra exploded in a fresh wave of fury. ''E never did 'ave the sense to know shit from chocolate.'

Morgan's face paled and he brought himself slowly upright in his chair. 'Mrs Vance is our guest, Father. I think she warrants an apology.'

''Er ain't my guest an' it ain't no apology 'er be warrantin'.'

'Please make allowances for my father's rudeness.' Morgan

turned to Roberta. 'He drinks far more than his tongue can handle.'

'I can 'andle my tongue better than you could 'andle that thousand pounds. An' what about what you got from that sale? Did you spend that an' all?'

'No, Father, I have not spent it.' Morgan smiled sardonically. 'I need that to pay for my honeymoon.'

Honeymoon? Esther looked quizzically at her husband. He had not mentioned a honeymoon, but then he had mentioned hardly anything. In fact she rarely saw him except at dinner, and then only briefly. It seemed he was always about to take his attractive guest some place or other. But a honeymoon! Surely he would have discussed that with her?

'So you need it to pay for a honeymoon? It's a bloody great deal to pay, ain't it? Just 'ow much do a honeymoon cost?'

'As much as it takes.'

Ezra squinted blearily over the top of his glass. 'An' then you'll be back with me.'

Morgan smiled coldly. 'You know me so well, Father.'

'Arrh, I do, an' you better know this – you get no more money outta me.'

Morgan's smile remained, cold and hostile. 'I shall have no need to ask you for anything in the future for I already have everything that was yours. Surely you remember, Father, Jos Kerral was not the only one to sign a paper? But then, he was smarter than you. He only signed away part of his holdings. You signed away the lot.'

Ezra's glass crashed to the floor. 'You wouldn't dare to sell my business!'

'You have always been so sure of my behaviour, haven't you? Well, this time I advise you not to take anything for granted. It's highly probable you will be in for a bitter disappointment.'

'You would do it, wouldn't you, you bastard? You would sell everythin' I've ever worked for an' never blink an eyelid!' Ezra looked at Esther, and his furious expression gave way to sympathy. 'Well, wench, you be the wronged one in all of this. We married you to a no-good bloody fool. The least I can do is wish you a pleasant honeymoon, even if it is yer father's money pays for it.'

Pushing back his chair, Morgan moved around the table. 'Signing away your all was not the only mistake you made,' he said sourly, 'and I did advise you not to take anything for granted.' Coming to where Roberta Vance was seated, he dropped a hand on her silk-clad shoulder. 'You see, Father, it is not Esther who will accompany me on honeymoon – it is Roberta.'

''E's takin' that woman!' Miri said in amazement. ''E be takin' 'er on honeymoon in yer place?'

Esther nodded. Morgan's words had stunned her. Theirs was not a love match in any sense of the word but she was his wife and surely deserved his respect? There had been none in the way he had announced his intention. She had no wish to accompany him anywhere and no objection to anyone he might choose to travel with, but she bitterly resented his telling her in that way; resented the triumph in Roberta Vance's violet eyes.

'Ee!' Miri knelt, removing Esther's shoes and proceeding to massage her legs. 'Ee, Essie, I can't believe it of 'im. I knew 'e were no good but I would 'ave bet me Sunday bonnet on 'is good manners.'

'He is not altogether to blame,' Esther said tiredly. 'His father went on and on until Morgan lost his temper.'

'I take it Ezra had been on the bottle?'

'Most of the afternoon by the look of him, and he filled his glass several times during dinner.'

'A man ain't in proper control of what 'e be sayin' when 'is brain be soaked in alcohol,' Miri said, kneading the muscles of Esther's calves. 'But that son of 'is 'ad not drunk 'is senses away and 'e knew full well 'e intended to go on honeymoon wi' that ... well, 'e knew and 'e 'ad plenty of time to tell you of it instead of throwin' it in yer face the way 'e did.'

Of course he had had time to tell her privately, so why hadn't he? As Miri had said, Morgan's manners were usually impeccable.

'It does not really matter.' Esther leaned her head against the chair, her eyes closed. 'I have no interest in what Morgan Cosmore does or who he does it with.'

'But surely you asked him whether he had intended tellin' you?'

'I thought it better for me to say nothing, Miri. For all I know he could have come here to my rooms while we were at the Leys. What would I have told him had he enquired where we were?'

Miri slipped Esther's shoes back on her feet then leaned back on her haunches, looking up into her pale drawn face. 'You did right, Essie wench. No questions requires no answers, an' that's the way we wants things right now.'

Pushing herself to her feet, Miri went into the room adjoining the over-furnished sitting room, turning down the sheets of Esther's bed then making sure the hand bell was close beside the lamp on the side table before returning to where Esther still sat, with eyes closed. 'What about lettin' me 'elp you to bed?' she asked, crossing to the wheelchair. 'Then I'll go down to the kitchen and make you a nice cup of cocoa.'

'You get on well with the cook and with Gittins, don't you?' Esther opened her eyes. 'I mean, they don't resent your going into the kitchen?'

'Bless you, of course they don't,' Miri laughed. 'Dolly Foster an' Evan Gittins an' me all growed up together. Went to the same school – least we did when our mothers 'ad the half-penny a day it took to put we there, which weren't very often. And as for that little maid, Peggy Deeley, well, 'er be too frightened of Dolly to call 'er name 'er own much less say anythin' against my bein' below stairs. And I'll tell you somethin' else – they 'ave all taken a shine to the new Mrs Cosmore.'

'Me?' Esther asked, surprised. 'I have not seen them more than half a dozen times.'

'Maybe, but each time you 'ave you've spoken civilly to them, you 'aven't treated them as though they be naught but dirt, an' they respects you for it. Believe me, Essie, you be well liked by the staff in this 'ouse.'

'In that case, perhaps they won't mind if I have that cup of cocoa?'

Alone in her bedroom, Esther lay back on the pillows, staring at the shadows on the ceiling.

Morgan had come to her just as Miri had left to make cocoa. He had apologised for imparting his news at the dinner table but offered no regrets for the fact that the partner sharing his holiday would be Roberta Vance. Esther had asked for none. He was leaving tomorrow, he had told her. Of his return, he made no mention. That would be when his money ran out, doubtless.

Esther smiled to herself. How had she had the nerve to sit at that table and tell him her father had signed away almost half of his holdings to her plus giving her an extra one thousand pounds as a sign of the love he held for her, when the truth of it was he had used it and her in a bid to gain Ezra Cosmore's financial assistance to save his own failing business. What would Jos do when he found his scheming was to no avail, and that Ezra Cosmore had made the same mistake? He too had gambled on his child saving his business and to this end had placed everything in his name – and Morgan Cosmore was not one to give any of it back. As far as James Bridge copper works was concerned, Ezra had signed his own death warrant and Roberta Vance would be the only inheritor.

In the shadows Esther saw again that attractive face framed with thick dark hair, the full seductive mouth and wonderful violet eyes – the face of her husband's lover. A lover whom she knew instinctively would take every penny of Ezra's money.

She shouldn't care, she thought, closing her eyes. Like her father, Ezra deserved what he got. But in a strange way she did care, and in the same inexplicable way she cared about Morgan; but as sleep settled on her eyes it was another face that filled her mind. *You are safe with me, you will always be safe with me.* Drifting into sleep, Esther smiled back into the clear grey eyes of Adam Paige. She shouldn't care for him, but she knew she did.

Chapter Fifteen

'The young Mr Cosmore and his guest left for London an hour ago.' Gittins's voice held a strong note of contempt. 'He left no message for anyone.'

Esther nodded. She had expected no word from Morgan. After the events of last night, what else was there to say?

'Thank you, Mr Gittins.' She accorded him the same courtesy she showed her father's servants. 'And Mr Ezra?'

'The master left for James Bridge some time ago.'

'Did he say what time he would be back?'

'He will not be back, madam,' Gittins informed her. 'The master is going from James Bridge to Birmingham. Said he would be staying the night there.'

'I see. Does he often stay in Birmingham?'

'Quite regularly.' Gittins picked up the tray the timid little housemaid had left with Esther. 'Sometimes twice a week.'

'And he will not be returning this evening?'

'Definitely not, madam. It will most likely be tomorrow afternoon, after he has checked that everything is running smoothly at the works.'

Both of them gone, Esther thought as Gittins left the room. That gave her the opportunity to find out what it was Adam found so pressing. She would ask him to come to Addenbrooke House.

'I want Sam to take a note to Mr Paige,' she said as Miri came in. 'I thought today would be the perfect opportunity for us to discuss the matter he mentioned at the works.'

'You mean, you intend askin' 'im to come 'ere to this 'ouse? Be that wise, Essie?'

'Morgan has left for his honeymoon and his father is away in Birmingham until tomorrow so I see no danger in asking Mr Paige to come here.'

'Mebbe you don't,' Miri said, a cautious note in her tone, 'but askin' Adam Paige to this 'ouse in daylight ain't the safest thing y'ave done. What if 'e be seen? An' what if them that sees 'im should speak of it to Ezra Cosmore? 'Ow would you explain it? What reason could you invent for his bein' 'ere? I tell you that what you be about best be thought carefully on, if 'e must come then make it night, folks see less in the dark!'

Once again Miri was right. Wheeling herself over to an elaborate chiffonier, Esther took out notepaper, pen and ink, steadying them in her lap as she manoeuvred the chair back to the table.

'Then I will ask him to come about eight,' she said. A thought struck her and she asked, 'But what about the staff? Sam will have gone by that time but the others . . .'

'With Ezra away there won't be no call for them to be knockin' around, 'specially as they knows I see to you myself. An' even if they do see Adam, we can always say he be 'ere to see me.' Miri smiled. 'It's 'alf a truth anyway.'

I would rather not tell Adam half a truth, Esther thought. The idea of lying to him made her feel ashamed.

'Do you think we should tell him?' She looked pleadingly at Miri.

'Tell 'im?' Miri sounded puzzled. 'Tell 'im what?'

Esther placed the writing materials on the table, each movement slow and deliberate, as though giving herself time to think. 'The truth.'

'About what?' Miri prevaricated. She felt she already knew what Esther meant and could guess the girl's reason for it, but it worried her. She could see in Esther's face what she felt when she saw Adam Paige or even when his name was mentioned. But even had she not already been another man's wife, nothing could come of her love for him. She was crippled and no man married a crippled girl from love.

'The truth about the businesses being mine.'

'Adam Paige be a shrewd man,' Miri answered. 'It be my opinion he knows that already, but what ain't been spoken don't need to be denied. Take care what you tell him, Essie. You could lose it all yet.'

'It could happen,' she said, dipping the pen into the ink and beginning to write. 'But it will never be brought about by Adam Paige.'

'Thank you for yer confidence, Mrs Cosmore.' Adam Paige looked at the girl in the wheelchair and felt his heart swell. Sam had brought her note asking him to call at Addenbrooke and from then on he had found it difficult to settle to his work, wanting it only to be eight o'clock so he could be with her again.

Don't get involved. His mother's words had drifted regularly back to him over the day and each time he had smiled inwardly at the sheer futility of the warning; there had been no outward sign and no words exchanged between them but he knew himself to be committed. He knew as surely as he knew his own name that he would never be free from Esther Cosmore.

'Would you like some tea, Adam?' Miri, like every other woman in Darlaston, reached for the teapot as soon as any visitor set foot inside the door.

'No, thank you, Mrs Butler.' He smiled. 'My mother had the pot on before I left the house and she will have it on again when I get back.'

Turning to Esther, Miri asked the same question, and again receiving a negative answer, went on, 'In that case p'raps the pair of you wouldn't mind my joining the others in the kitchen for an hour or so? After all, there be no need for me to comment on the business, now Adam has the truth of it.'

Esther was a married woman and as such needed no

chaperone, Miri thought, going along the corridor that led to the kitchens. Let her talk to Adam alone. It was like to be the nearest thing to pleasure she would get in this house.

'Please sit down, Mr Paige.' Esther motioned him to a chair as the door closed behind Miri. 'Tell me what it is that concerns you about the works?'

'It is not the works as such I want to discuss,' Adam took the chair offered, 'but the orders I have been asked if we can fill. It seems you were right when you said the market would pick up. I have had enquiries from Metropolitan Cammel who need a supply for their railway coaches, and I was also approached by the new works in Booth Street that has been set up to supply components to the horseless carriage trade.'

'That's wonderful!' Esther said, her face alight with enthusiasm. 'It will mean so much more work for the men.'

'It would be wonderful had we been able to undertake to supply these firms,' Adam said. 'But as things stand we will not be able to.'

'But why?'

'The reason is simple enough – we cannot meet these new demands with the present workforce.'

'But that is what is wonderful about it.' She smiled radiantly. 'We can employ more men.'

'I've already thought of that, Mrs Cosmore.' Adam looked steadily at Esther, seeing the enthusiasm begin to fade from her face as he shook his head. 'Men making nuts and bolts by hand could not produce the quantity required and the machines are already working at full stretch, so either way you look at it we cannot take on more business and hope to keep it.'

'So if we cannot accept new business, why did you feel it so important to discuss it? Why not just refuse there and then?'

Adam leaned forward and Esther could see the fine lines about eyes that looked tired, as if sleep had not been a close companion for some nights.

'Because I have a strong suspicion these works will grow, they will become a big part of the industry in Darlaston, and as such you must grow with them. If you do not supply them, someone else will. And once you get left behind, you will have difficulty catching up.'

'But you have already told me the works cannot produce more than they are now so how can I grow with these new firms?'

'We cannot produce more working as we are at the moment, but when the men who operate the machines go home at the end of the day, production ceases until the morning.'

'I don't understand.' Esther frowned. 'Of course production ceases. The men can't work day and night.'

'The men can't but machines can.'

'Machines need men to work them.'

'Of course they do.' Adam's eyes lit up, determination chasing away tiredness.

'Mr Paige, forgive my not understanding but I don't. You will just have to explain.'

'It's simple, Mrs Cosmore . . .'

'Esther.'

'What?'

Her smile widened. 'I said, Esther. Please, I prefer not to be formal among friends, and "Mrs Cosmore" does sound so formal.'

'Esther.' He said it softly, as if rolling some well-loved treat around his tongue, reluctant to swallow it. 'Then Esther and Adam it will be between us, and friends shake hands, do they not?' He held out his hand and as Esther placed her own in it, said, his voice soft and throaty, 'Hello, Esther.'

There was no trace of tiredness now in his grey eyes. A glow seemed to rise from their depths, lighting them yet at the same time darkening them to dusky sable. Caught in their hold, Esther felt her senses reel and her breath catch in her throat.

'H-hello, Adam,' she murmured shyly.

217

He did not let go of her hand at once but held it fast in his own for several seconds while his look seemed to seek beyond her eyes, plumbing the deepest, most secret recesses of her heart.

'So will you explain, Adam, how machines can run without men to work them?' She released her hand, finding it more difficult to free herself from his molten gaze.

'They can't and I didn't.' He gave a slight laugh, almost as if he too had found it difficult to break his gaze. 'I said or I meant to say . . .'

He smiled and at once the slight feeling of tension that the touch of his hand and the glow in his eyes had caused was gone. Esther smiled back.

'Those machines need not be left idle. Why not start a night shift?'

'You mean, employ men to work through the night?'

'Why not?' Adam shifted position in his chair, hitching it closer to the table.

'But people do not work at night,' Esther protested, 'they would not wish to.'

'Men have worked at night in the coal mines ever since the first shafts were sunk,' he replied, 'and there are those in Darlaston will tell you so. As for not wishing to work at night – there are many who stand the line on Katherine's Cross every day with no hope of work who would jump at the chance. Don't you see, Esther? Starting a night shift would solve not only the problem of meeting those new orders but would give work and new hope to some of those men in the line.'

'If you think it will work then start this night shift, but who will be there to see things run smoothly?' She thought of the tiredness she had seen in his eyes. 'It can't be you, Adam. You can't work through the day and the night as well.'

'I realise that and I have someone in mind. Things will go as smoothly as in the day, I promise you.'

She could think of no more questions to ask but that meant

there was no longer any need for him to be here – no need except for the one burning inside her, and that was a need she could never acknowledge.

'Then if you are certain, you may employ the men.' She said the words reluctantly, not wanting their meeting to end, and as he rose felt the traces of a now familiar disappointment, almost unhappiness, begin to rise in her stomach.

For a few moments he stood just looking down at her, his dark hair shining like polished ebony in the light of the lamps while his eyes held a new intensity.

'Esther, a little while ago you did not deny it when I referred to us as friends. Now I am going to risk losing that friendship – and, believe me, I would rather risk everything I have than risk that. But there is something I must ask you, something that may anger you.' He dropped to his haunches so that his eyes were more on a level with hers. 'Esther,' he asked, his voice firm, 'why do you sit in that chair? Why don't you walk?'

The ticking of a heavy baroque clock on the mantel seemed to crash in Esther's ears, his words forcing the breath from her lungs. He could ask her that? Ask her why she spent her life in a wheelchair when he knew her legs were crippled?

'I . . . I . . .' She looked at him, her bronze eyes wide and deep, filled with pain. 'I do not walk because I cannot. My legs are paralysed.'

'No, they are not!' he said unflinchingly, though the pain in her eyes cut through him.

Why was he doing this? Esther asked herself. Why was he hurting her this way? He knew her legs were crippled, that she had never walked.

'Adam,' she said, the happiness of the last hours slipping away, 'why do you deny what you see to be true?'

'Because I know it to be untrue!' Still on his haunches he gripped both of her hands, his face intense. 'I have lifted you in my arms half a dozen times and each time I have felt movement in your legs. Only a faint movement but it was there.'

It was not true, how could it be? If there was movement in her legs she would have known it, she would have felt it long ago. She closed her eyes, fighting the urge to scream out her pain, scream against a fate that had decreed her life be spent in a wheelchair.

'Esther,' he spoke her name softly, 'it is true, believe me. Each time I lifted you I felt it, a faint tensing of the muscles in your legs, and if you can do that, you can walk.'

'No, Adam, I cannot!' She pulled her hands free. 'I would have known . . . Miri would have known!'

'Not necessarily.' He stood up. 'Who was it decided you were an incurable cripple? How long since then before you were examined again?'

'I don't know!' Esther's eyes widened. 'I don't know. I only know my father said I would never walk . . .'

'Your father!' Adam spat the words as though the taste of them on his tongue was foul to him. 'Your father told you so that makes it gospel. He never did get a doctor to examine you while you lived with John and Miri, did he?'

'No,' Esther whispered. 'He . . . he never even came to the house.'

'I should have guessed that. He cast you aside like a child would throw away a broken toy.' He dropped to his haunches again, his hands clasping hers. 'But not all toys are broken irretrievably, Esther. Some can be mended. All it takes is care and patience.'

'But I had those from Miri and her husband.'

'I'm sure they gave you both in plenty,' he answered her, 'but they, like you, expected you never to walk and that could have blinded them to what I know is there. Did they ever once try to get you to walk?'

Esther shook her head. 'They knew it was useless.'

'You think that because it is what you were told!' He jumped to his feet, anger flaring in him. 'Well, carry on believing it if you must, Esther. BUT I FELT YOU MOVE.'

Could he be right? She looked up at the man she had come

to care for, seeing his face taut with emotion. Could it be that her condition was not irreversible, that her father had been wrong?

'You are sure, Adam?' she asked.

'I wish I were so sure that you . . .' He paused, looking into her upturned face, into eyes that pleaded for the truth. 'I am sure,' he said.

You are safe with me. The words came to her softly, stealing into her mind. *You will always be safe with me.*

A smile curving her mouth, Esther held out one hand. 'Then will you be the first to help me?'

'Essie . . . Essie wench, you'd best get dressed quick!'

'Miri, what is it? What is wrong?' Esther pushed with her hands, driving herself up on to the pillows of her bed.

'It be Ezra.' Miri snatched open the heavy velvet curtain then turned to the wardrobe, pulling out a dress. ''E be poorly – right poorly, I'm thinkin'.'

'But he was well when I saw him yesterday.'

'That were yesterday.' In the bathroom Miri tipped water from a pink flowered jug into a large matching basin, then snatching a towel, carried them into the bedroom, putting them on the table beside the bed. 'Just give yerself a swill with that. You can bathe later.'

Washing just her hands and face, Esther lifted her white lawn nightdress over her head. 'Miri, will you please tell me what is wrong with Ezra?' she asked, struggling into her petticoats and then the brown dress Miri flung over her head.

'I don't know for sure.' Miri knelt, pushing stockings over Esther's feet, drawing them up her legs then fastening on her shoes. 'But Evan Gittins said 'e looked bad.'

'Has the doctor been sent for?' Esther pulled a brush through her hair, leaving it loose about her shoulders. She would braid it later.

'Not yet.' Miri took the bowl and towel, rushing it away into the bathroom. 'Evan said to wait for you.' Putting her arms around Esther, she helped her into the wheelchair. 'You be the mistress, and while Gittins be unable to ask either yer 'usband or 'is father 'e must wait for instructions from you.'

'Why can't he ask Ezra?' Esther felt a cold flicker of alarm.

Opening the doors to both bedroom and sitting room, Miri pushed the chair out into the corridor, turning it towards the main body of the house.

''E would get no answer,' she said. 'Ezra be unconscious.'

'I took the precaution of getting the master to bed,' Gittins explained to Esther as Miri wheeled her into the hall. 'I got Sam to help me.'

'I waited till you came,' Sam said. 'I thought you might be wantin' to go up to Mr Cosmore.'

'Thank you, Sam. Yes, please, I think perhaps I had better go to him.'

She had been in this house almost a year, Esther thought as Sam carried her up the staircase, and this was the first time she had been upstairs.

Gittins leading the way, Sam carried her to a room just off the wide landing. Inside, looking strangely small in the four-poster bed, Ezra lay with eyes closed.

'What happened?' she asked as Sam lowered her to the chair the butler had placed beside the bed.

'I cannot be certain.' Gittins's voice was hushed. 'He came home last night fairly late and I helped him to bed . . .'

'Helped him?' Esther glanced up.

'Yes, madam, he . . . he had been drinking. I put him to bed. I can only think he woke in the night and went downstairs to get the decanter from the dining room.'

'Downstairs?' Esther looked at her father-in-law, his usually ruddy colour less marked, his closed eyelids blue-veined. 'But you helped him to bed?'

'I did.' Gittins bent over, tucking Ezra's left arm beneath the covers. 'It wasn't till I went to wake him this morning that I found him lying halfway down the stairs, unconscious. I think he must have been there several hours. I'm sorry but none of the staff uses the main staircase first thing in the morning. I am always the first when I go to wake the master.'

'It is not your fault.' Esther touched her hand to Ezra's brow, surprised to find how hot it was when he looked so pale and cold. 'You were not to know. You did very well to get him to bed. And now, would you please send for the doctor.'

'I'll go, madam,' Sam said quickly. 'If it's all right I'll take the trap. That'll be quicker than walking.'

'Of course, Sam.' Esther smiled faintly. 'Ask him please to come at once.'

'Arrh, madam, I will that.'

Glancing at Miri as Sam left the dim room, Esther whispered, 'He is going to be all right, isn't he?'

'Only the Lord can tell that.' Miri shook her head. 'And I've a feeling 'E won't answer in a hurry.'

'How is he?' Esther wheeled herself forward as Charles Platt came down the stairs, a black Gladstone bag in his left hand.

'Not good, Mrs Cosmore.' He nodded to Gittins as he took the gloves and tall black hat the butler held out to him. 'I am afraid he has pneumonia, and coupled with what years of drinking too much brandy has done to him . . .' He shook his head. 'I wish I could tell you otherwise but I can't. Perhaps I might speak to his son?'

'My husband is not at home at present,' Esther answered evenly, though the words had shaken her. 'He is abroad.'

'Then contact him,' Charles Platt said bluntly, 'and let us hope he returns in time.'

'In time?' she asked softly.

'Yes, and in a short time, Mrs Cosmore. Your father-in-law is dying.'

Dying! Esther sat stunned. Ezra Cosmore dying? He had used her in the same way her father had, to gain his own ends, but since her arrival in this house he had treated her civilly, trying in his own bluff way to ease the lot he knew was not easy for her. In fact she had sometimes received the impression, in the rare moments they really talked together, that he felt a certain affection for her – one her own father had never shown.

'You will want me to send a nurse.' The doctor paused at the door. 'He will require round the clock nursing.'

'What? Yes . . . yes, of course.' Esther fought her way through the numbness of shock. 'Thank you.'

'I will call again tomorrow.'

Morgan . . . Esther watched the doctor leave. How could she contact him? He had not told her where he was going.

'Come away, Essie.' Miri turned the wheelchair. 'Come and have some breakfast, I will stay with Ezra.'

'No!' She dropped her hands to the chair wheels, preventing its moving. 'I will stay with him. Please call Sam.'

Once more in Ezra's bedroom, Esther sat looking at the face that suddenly seemed so old. She could not find it in her heart to blame him for what he had done to her; she could understand a man fighting any way he knew to save his life, and Cosmore copper works was Ezra's life.

'I brought you some tea, madam.' Gittins entered the room carrying a tray set with teapot and cup.

'That is very thoughtful.' Esther tried to smile but failed.

'Would you like me to pour, or perhaps I should send Mrs Butler to you?'

'No, leave Miri to have something to eat. And I would like you to pour. I . . . I feel so trembly.'

'That be understandable,' said Gittins sympathetically. 'It's the shock. You drink this while it's hot and you will feel better.'

Esther took the cup, hearing it rattle in its saucer. 'I don't know what to do,' she murmured. 'I don't know what to do.'

'The nurse will be here soon, she will know what to do.'

'It is not taking care of your master I am thinking of. He is in good hands with you and Mrs Foster, and I know Miri will help.' Esther looked up at him. 'Mr Gittins, I have to get in touch with my husband and I have no idea where he is. Did he by any chance leave an address with you?'

Gittins shook his head. 'No, madam, he gave me no address, and nor did he say where he was going.'

'Then what can I do?'

Looking at her stricken face, Gittins forgot his role as butler. She was still so young and had gone through enough without this trouble. 'You'll do all right, me wench,' he said, momentarily slipping back to the speech of his youth. 'You've done all right so far spite of what the Cosmores 'ave done to you, an' you'll go on doin' all right. Forget that tripe hound you be wed to. See that Ezra gets the lookin' after 'e needs, an' if it be as 'e dies, then bury 'im. Way I see it, you can do no more.'

She could do no more, Esther silently agreed, but maybe Ezra would not die. Maybe the doctor would prove to be wrong.

'I will bring the nurse up when she arrives, madam.'

'Very well. And, Mr Gittins . . . thank you.'

That girl be too good for Morgan Cosmore, Gittins thought, returning downstairs. What in the world was her father thinking of to wed her to such a grab-all as that one? He turned towards the kitchen. The day Morgan Cosmore became master in this house was the day Evan Gittins left it!

Esther looked around the room, lit only by an oil lamp near the four-poster bed and another on a table set beside the fire in the grate. All around shadows played about the walls, their ghostly shapes given life by the flickering flames. Ezra had not woken all day and with the coming of night Esther had known a new worry. If he did not recover, who would take over the running of his business? She knew nothing of the smelting of copper.

'Excuse me, madam?'

Esther started. She had not heard the tap at the door of

Ezra's bedroom nor noticed as the nurse opened it, admitting Gittins. Now she looked at him from tired eyes.

'Will you be wanting Sam to take you to your sitting room?'

Blinking, Esther tried to clear the weariness from her eyes and the mists from her brain.

'What time is it?'

'Almost eight o'clock.'

Eight o'clock and Sam usually went home at seven. Esther drew in a long breath, sweeping the last of the cobwebs from her mind.

'Sam says he will take word home and then come back. He will stay here until the master is recovered and things are back to normal.'

'No.' Now the mist had cleared, Esther thought rapidly. 'Please tell Sam there will be no need for him to stay. He must go home to his wife and child.'

'But how will you get downstairs?'

'I will not be going downstairs.'

Gittins threw a quick glance at the nurse who was preparing a hot poultice.

'There is nothing you can do here, Mrs Cosmore,' she said, her tone more sympathetic than brisk. 'There will be no change tonight.'

Esther would not question the woman's opinion, that she knew her job was evident from the efficient way she had dealt with Ezra, but if he should wake, Esther thought, then he should have someone of his family beside him. And if it could not be his son it had to be her.

'Mr Gittins,' she asked, 'is there a room up here where I can sleep?'

He was not surprised by what she asked. He had been expecting something of the sort. This girl was not the kind to turn her back.

'There is, of course. The young Mr Cosmore's room.'

He never referred to Morgan by his name or even as 'the

young master', Esther reflected. That he held no liking for the younger man was obvious.

'Or there is the old mistress's bedroom.' Gittins read the revulsion in her eyes at the suggestion of Morgan's room. 'Or perhaps madam would prefer one of the guest rooms? Mrs Foster could have one aired quite quickly.'

A guest room would be best. She would not want to be thought to be prying by taking Morgan's room. In fact, the thought of sleeping there repelled her.

'Give my apologies to Mrs Foster for disturbing her but I would rather take a guest room.'

'I will have one made ready immediately. And might I ask madam to take something to eat?'

That the nurse found something strange in her request for a guest room or in her sending an apology to a servant was plain in the glance she shot Esther.

'I will take a tray when the room is ready.' She smiled her thanks. 'And perhaps Mrs Foster will find something more than cocoa for nurse's supper?' She glanced at the woman who was placing a hot poultice on Ezra's chest. 'Mrs Foster makes delicious soup and her bread is a treat not to miss.'

'I'm never one to miss a treat.' Fastening Ezra's nightshirt over the poultice and pulling the sheet up over his shoulders, the nurse flashed her a warm smile.

'Your father-in-law will sleep most of the night, Mrs Cosmore.' She came to stand beside Esther. 'You really should go to bed yourself.'

'I've been tellin' 'er that for a couple of hours,' Miri said, coming into the room. 'Ain't no use in tirin' 'erself out.'

'I could not sleep if I went to bed.'

'No, no doubt you couldn't,' Miri said understandingly, 'but you still need to rest and you can't do that properly, sitting up all night.'

'Nurse needs rest too.' Esther looked at the woman, a starched cap covering her mousy brown hair, her apron brilliant white over dark blue serge skirts. 'I should have thought when the doctor said he would send a nurse that you could not be on duty throughout the night. I could have requested a second nurse to take over from you.'

'Knowledge comes quickest with hindsight.' Picking up the tongs, Miri placed fresh coals on the fire from the coal bucket the maid had brought in earlier. 'You never know you need something till you be without it. But Nurse will get 'er rest. I'll sit wi' Ezra tonight.'

'We will share,' Esther said quickly. 'I will sit . . .'

'No, you won't!' Miri replaced the tongs with a clatter. 'You will go to bed and stay there, even if it means my lockin' you in the room. I be quite capable of watchin' one night, an' after that you can either get another nurse or we will take it in turns to watch.'

Wheeling herself to the bed in the chair Gittins and Sam had carried up for her, Esther looked at the still form of Ezra, his breath rasping in his lungs. He was almost as rejected by his son as she was by her father. Did it cause him the same pain? Was he as lonely as she?

Touching a hand to a shoulder that somehow seemed thinner than before, she leaned over him. 'Goodnight,' she whispered, 'please get well.'

'Pneumonia be a funny thing,' Miri said later as they shared the meal Gittins had brought up. 'You can be mortal poorly one minute, and poof! The next you be almost over it.'

'I pray Ezra gets over it.'

'So do I, wench, so do I.'

'If I only knew where to find Morgan.'

'Arrh, it would be a 'elp.' Miri stacked the supper dishes on the tray. 'But don't blame yerself for something that be beyond you. He didn't tell you where 'e would be an' you're no mind reader, so pay no more heed to 'im.' She paused as a tap on the door heralded the return of the butler.

'Will there be anything else, madam?'

'No.' Esther shook her head. 'The soup was excellent.'

'And the room, is it to your satisfaction?'

'It will do very well.'

Taking up the tray, his eyes almost level with hers for a moment, he went on: 'It has not been used for several years but Mrs Foster keeps all the rooms regularly aired.'

She understood. He was telling her this was not the room used by Roberta Vance. Her own eyes speaking her gratitude, Esther smiled.

Almost at the door, he paused, looking back at her. 'Excuse me, madam, but earlier today you asked if I had been given an address where the young Mr Cosmore could be contacted.'

'Have you found one?' She twisted eagerly in her chair.

'No, madam, but if I might suggest – you could ask the master's solicitor?'

'Do you know his name?'

'It is Lacy, Patrick Lacy, and he has chambers in Bull Street.'

'I would never have dreamed of asking Ezra's solicitor,' Esther said as Miri helped her into bed later.

'There be lots of things a body don't dream less some other one tells 'em.' Miri folded the covers across the bed. 'Now you settle yerself down. If there be any change in Ezra, I'll call you.'

It seemed so logical, Esther thought as Miri left her, how could she not have thought of it? But as Miri said there were many things you did not think to try unless someone else suggested it first, as she had never thought to try to move her legs until Adam had vowed she could. Throwing off the covers, she pulled herself to the edge of the bed and, taking each leg in her hands in turn, lifted them over the side.

'Help me, Adam,' she whispered.

You are safe with me. The answer echoed in her head as, grabbing the bedpost, she hauled herself to her feet.

Chapter Sixteen

Patrick Lacy had not known where Morgan could be reached. Esther thought back on her meeting with the solicitor. Grey hair seeming to go in all directions, his black coat sleeves shiny from wear, he gave the impression more of an absent-minded schoolmaster than a solicitor. But there had been nothing absent-minded about him. He had not seen Morgan, he informed her, but he had heard from him and as sole owner of Cosmore copper works at James Bridge he had instructed that the said works be put up for sale.

Did Ezra know? Had that been the reason he had gone to Birmingham and returned too drunk to get himself to bed?

She looked at the sleeping form, the fat on his cheeks lying like deflated balloons, the puffy eye sockets now blue-lined hollows. Had his son not known what selling the works would do to Ezra? Or, more likely, had he known and not cared?

'I think he will sleep all morning, Mrs Cosmore,' the nurse said, turning away from the bed.

'Then you bloody well . . . think wrong,' Ezra protested, the words coming spasmodically.

'Don't talk, Mr Cosmore.' The nurse bent over him, touching a cloth to his lips drying the flecks of moisture his coughing dredged up from his lungs.

'Don't talk!' he wheezed, knocking the woman's hand away. 'Not talking be . . . be for the dead or . . . the dumb, an' I ain't neither, not yet.'

'Now, now.' The nurse tried tucking his arm back beneath the covers but Ezra pushed her away.

'Don't you bloody "now, now" me.' He coughed again. 'I ain't no child.'

'Mr Cosmore, you must not get yourself worked up. Please stay quiet.'

Ezra's eyes, bright with the light of fever, swivelled to where Esther sat. 'Esther,' he croaked, 'be that you?'

Taking his hand in hers, she answered gently, 'Yes, Mr Cosmore, it is me.'

'Send that one away.' Ezra glanced towards the nurse standing at the bedside.

'Come now, Mr Cosmore,' she said, having measured some medicine into a small glass. 'Drink this and . . .'

'Bugger off!' Ezra struggled to get up from the pillows. 'Get out an' leave me wi' my daughter-in-law.'

'Please leave us for a few minutes.' Esther looked at the nurse. 'I will call you if I need you.'

'Just a few minutes then, Mrs Cosmore.' The nurse put the glass beside her. 'Try to get him to drink this, I will just be next door.'

'Is . . . is 'er gone?' Ezra sank back, his head almost swamped by the pillows.

'Yes.' Esther squeezed his hand. 'She has gone but you must be better behaved when she comes back.'

'I don't want 'er back. Ain't no need for a woman flappin' round the room. Tell . . . tell Gittins to pack 'er off.'

Picking up the glass, Esther held it towards him. 'I want you to drink this.'

'Won't . . . won't do no good.' He closed his eyes as a fresh bout of coughing racked him.

'It won't if you don't drink it!' Esther said, a touch of Miri's firmness in her voice.

'I want to talk to you.' Ezra swallowed the medicine, his head falling back immediately on to the pillow. His eyes closed for a few seconds then opened again and Esther saw in them an urgency, a plea to speak to her while he still could.

Replacing the medicine glass on the table, she asked, 'What do you want to talk to me about, Mr Cosmore?'

'Mr Cosmore. It ain't never been anythin' else but that since you come to this 'ouse.' Laying his hand over hers where it rested on the covers, Ezra paused, dragging air into his lungs before he could carry on. 'An' I couldn't ask it of you but . . . but I wish . . . if things 'ad been different, it might 'ave been "Father".'

Esther felt a dryness in her throat. This man's son had taken her in marriage only as part of a business agreement – an agreement he, Ezra, had almost certainly engineered with her father. How could she have addressed him in any other way than Mr Cosmore? But he had not been the one who had forced her into agreeing to marry Morgan. Her own desire for revenge had played the greater part.

''Ave . . . 'ave you 'ad word from Morgan?'

Swallowing, Esther tried to keep the worry of what Patrick Lacy had told her from showing in her voice. 'Not yet but . . . but I have sent for him.'

'You be a good wench,' Ezra coughed hollowly. 'But you needn't lie. It be my bet you 'ave no knowledge of where 'e be. 'E be too sharp to let on where 'e goes.'

'We will hear from him soon, I am sure.'

'Oh, arrh, we will. We'll hear soon enough when 'is money be gone. 'E will be back sharp enough then but . . .' The cough rose in his throat, robbing him of the breath he fought so hard to drag into his lungs.

'Please,' Esther urged, 'don't talk any more.'

'Don't let a cough worry you,' Ezra smiled his eyes flaring with fever, 'it just be my lungs. They be rusty from the copper.' His fingers squeezed hers. 'Take care, Esther,' he said, the smile fading from his lips. 'Take care that son of mine never gets wind of what you 'old inside yerself.'

His eyes closing, he seemed to sink even deeper into the

pillows. Waiting until she thought him asleep, Esther began to withdraw her hand but he held on, his grip weaker but still discernible.

'Don't go yet,' he wheezed. 'Sit wi' me a bit longer.'

'As long as you want me to,' she answered softly.

'You be a good wench.' His eyes opened and he gazed at her. 'I be sorry for what we 'ave done to you, sorry for 'elping to tie you to my son. 'E will never be no good, 'e never 'as brought anythin' but worry. 'E be selfish through an' through an' I was the cause of it. I should 'ave kicked 'is arse and made 'im earn 'is own livin' long ago.' He broke off as a fresh spasm of coughing shook him then added, 'If . . . if I 'ad, you wouldn't be tied in wi' 'im.'

'If I had not become tied in with Morgan, I would not have met you.' Esther stroked back the strands of gingery hair from his forehead.

'We thought . . . we thought to get yer father's money,' Ezra laughed, bringing the cough rattling back. 'We thought by taking you we could save the business but . . . but yer father be as deep in muck as we. 'E ain't got two 'alf pennies for a penny. We thought to take 'im for all 'e 'ad got an' 'e thought to do the same an' all the time neither of we 'ad any money, not so much as a bent groat.'

'I know.' Esther touched her handkerchief to his mouth.

'You know?' He pulled her hand away.

'Yes.'

'You knowed before you was wed?'

Esther nodded again. 'I knew.'

'And you still went through with it! Why?'

Esther looked into the fever-bright eyes. 'Better to marry your son than spend the rest of my life in an institution.'

'Kerral threatened you with that!' he wheezed, will-power keeping the cough at bay. ''E threatened you with an institution, his own daughter! The bastard be no better than me. We traded you for a handful of silver! We both deserve to sit in hell with a blanket round we. I'm sorry,

Esther wench,' he spluttered as the cough took him again, 'I be truly sorry.'

Reaching for the glass of water kept at his bedside, Esther tried to get him to drink a little of it.

'No, me wench,' he refused, a gurgling in his throat, 'it will do no good, but . . . but I tell you . . . I could bost a brandy.'

Esther smiled into the fading eyes. 'Then a brandy you shall have . . . Father,' she whispered.

'You be a good wench, Esther.' Ezra's murmur was faint and his smile made no real impression on his lips. The hand which lay over hers had already lost its grip, lying still and heavy on her own.

'What do you think he could have meant, Miri? "Take care that son of mine never gets wind of what you hold inside yerself."'

'Well, something you hold inside is a secret. He meant you to take care of a secret, an' the only secret you 'ave is the one of owning yer own business, albeit in my name.'

'Do you think he knew?'

'Seems like nothing else to me.'

'But how?'

'Who can tell?' Miri mused. 'Ezra Cosmore was a sly old fox an' one as knew many tricks. He would know to set some things aside till the time was ripe for using 'em.'

'Like telling Morgan what I owned?'

'No . . . no, Essie, I don't think that. Somehow I don't think he would 'ave told. Anyway it seems by what 'e said that 'e 'ad spoken no word of it up to today for a man don't go tellin' you to keep secret what has already been told.'

'I feel so sorry for him,' Esther sighed. 'Dying without seeing his son.'

'You gave Ezra Cosmore more comfort in his last days than 'is son gave 'im in a lifetime, you got nothin' to reproach yerself with. If anybody should be sorry it should be 'is son but I doubt 'e would 'ave shed any tears even had 'e known. If 'e 'ad any kind of feeling for 'is father 'e would never 'ave gone in for selling the copper works while Ezra lived. Yet you say Patrick Lacy told you that's what 'e done?'

Esther nodded. 'He did, though why Morgan should be so much in need of money, I can't think. In just a year he has gone through what my father paid him and what he got for his share of Father's business. Why should he need so much? What on earth does he spend it on?'

'Don't take much thinking to answer that,' Miri said bitterly. 'An' if you be true to yerself you know the answer afore you asks the question: it be Roberta Vance 'e spends 'is money on. That one don't come cheap! Dressed like a duchess in silks an' velvets, an' them jewels round 'er neck an' wrists must 'ave cost near enough to 'ave kept all the folk in Darlaston fed for a twelve month. Arrh, that be where Cosmore's money goes an' where the money Cosmore's copper works fetches will go. All I can add is, thank God Ezra ain't 'ere to see it!'

'I think he already knew,' Esther said sadly. 'I think that was the cause of his death.'

'Could be you'm right.' Miri gathered up her crotchet. 'But it don't do no good to harp on about it. Ezra be laid to rest an' things will 'ave to stay the way they are till that son of 'is shows – an' when 'e does, you take extra care what you say to 'im. If Ezra did find out about you owning several works in the town, then chances be that Morgan can do the same.'

'I know Ezra has more than likely not *said* anything to him.' Esther watched Miri fold the shawl she was crocheting putting it away inside a large heavily carved sideboard. 'But do you think he may have something in his room or in the study, a note he may have left telling Morgan what he suspected?'

'You could always make a search. You could say you were looking for the address where Morgan can be reached.'

'I could,' Esther answered as Miri turned from the sideboard, 'but it would feel like going behind Ezra's back and I could not do that.'

'In that case you must wait, an' the longer that be the better I'll feel. I for one could do without the return of Mr Morgan Cosmore.' She glanced at the clock on the mantel. 'Adam will be along soon so I'll away an' 'ave an hour or so with them in the kitchen. Will you be wantin' anythin'?'

'No, thank you, Miri. Just relax and enjoy the gossip.'

'That I be sure to do.' Miri smiled. 'Dolly Foster can always be relied on to come up wi' something juicy, and that young Peggy ain't so shy as 'er used to be.'

Miri gone, Esther wheeled herself into her bedroom, going to the dressing table and checking her reflection in the mirror. Hair the colour of ripe chestnuts gleamed in the light of the lamp; eyes of bronze reflected its glow. Touching a finger to her high cheekbones, Esther thought of the portrait over the fireplace in the sitting room of Rowena House, the portrait of her mother. She had been beautiful and Roberta Vance had said Esther was very like her. She leaned closer to the mirror. Was there a resemblance? Was she like her beautiful mother? Did Adam think her beautiful?

Turning away, she returned to the sitting room which her husband had had altered to facilitate her chair and felt despair overcome her. What use to ask if he found her beautiful? What use to ask if he could ever have loved her? For what man would fall in love with a cripple!

'Good evening, Esther.'

She looked up as he entered the room and her heart soared. A smile curving his mouth, Adam Paige crossed the room.

'Good evening, Adam.' She returned his smile with difficulty, pain tugging at her heart. Adam Paige was a man any woman could take pride in as her husband, but that woman could never be Esther.

Taking her accounts book from the drawer of the chiffonier, she listened to his latest report on the works.

Profits were up again, she noted, entering the figures he produced into columns in the ledger. Up much more than she had expected. His idea of a night shift had worked well for all concerned.

'It could be more, much more,' he told her as she congratulated him. 'If only there were room to expand. We have the orders and there are still men on the line who would be glad of a job but there is just not room in either the Sovereign or the Leys, and Victoria works is no bigger.'

'Adam,' she kept her eyes on the book, 'have you heard any rumours concerning Cosmore Copper?'

He laughed, throwing back his head in the way she had come to love. 'There have been nothing but rumours since Ezra Cosmore died. Some say it has been sold, others say not.'

'So you know nothing?'

He looked at her, his grey eyes questioning. 'Why would I?'

Fingering the edge of a page, Esther kept her eyes averted. 'I thought perhaps you might have heard? You usually do if there is anything of the sort going on in the town.'

'I have heard nothing. Why do you ask? Have you had word from your husband?'

Esther shook her head. 'No, I have had no word from Morgan but Ezra's solicitor told me he is looking for a buyer for the copper works.'

'Morgan is selling out!' Adam leaned his weight on the back of his chair. 'My God, he didn't wait long! Thank heavens his father is beyond knowing.'

'I think Ezra did know.' Esther lifted her eyes to his face. 'I think he knew what Morgan had done and that it contributed in great measure towards his death.'

'I would not argue with that. The works was Ezra's reason for living . . . what kind of a man does Morgan Cosmore call himself!' Adam paused, allowing a frown to pull at his dark eyebrows. 'Esther, does your question mean you are interested in buying the copper works?'

Was she? Esther shook her head. If Morgan found out about her properties they would go to him, but his father's works would not be part of them. He would not get back what he had sold by means of his wife.

'I am not interested in that business,' she said, glancing at the columns of figures, their lines neat and regulated on the page. 'But I am interested in acquiring a piece of land.'

'Where?' Adam's frown deepened.

'Out past where the old Coronation coal pit used to be, where the cornfields give on to the heath. It is a pretty spot and not really so far from the town that people could not walk there and back.'

'I know the place. Heathfields we lads called it. But why do you want land there?'

'Because I intend extending the Victoria works.'

Adam gave a little laugh. 'What! Out there. That's some extension.'

'The works will be extended but I do not intend them to reach the Heathfields.'

'Then why buy land there?'

'Because I mean the people I employ to have a decent home to live in and I shall start building there. I got Sam to drive me to see it today and it seemed perfect for what I have in mind. Not close enough to the works for it to overshadow the houses but near enough for men to walk to work without being worn out before they get there.'

'And how many houses do you intend to build?'

Esther glanced again at the columns of figures, recalling the talk she had had with John Bartlett. He could build a small three-bedroomed house for one hundred pounds, he had told her.

'I want to begin with six.'

That would leave her with enough to extend the works and put in machinery, she calculated quickly, and if profits went on as they had she could add more within a year.

'It is a grand idea, Esther.' Adam reached across the table to touch her hand. 'I just hope it does not overstretch you.'

'My money, you mean.' She smiled, leaving her hand

beneath his. 'Far better to spend it on housing and work for people than leave it lying in a bank.'

Yes, far better this way, she thought. At least if Morgan does discover my businesses the houses will be built and the works can be sold to someone who will operate them. That way he would have the money but the people of Darlaston would have homes and jobs.

'So what will you call this street of houses you intend to build?'

'I shall not call it a street, Mr Paige,' Esther laughed, her bronze eyes shining. 'I shall call it a lane . . . Heathfield Lane. What do you think of that?'

'I think it is a fine idea, Esther,' he said softly, 'from a fine woman.'

Her hand still beneath his, she felt her heart swell, almost stopping her breath. If only she did not belong to Morgan Cosmore. But what then? Beneath the sweet pain, common sense held its own. What if she had not been married, would she have told him of her feeling? Could she have borne seeing pity in his eyes and hearing words of rejection from his lips?

Drawing her hand away, she returned the accounts book to the drawer of the chiffonier. When she was once more facing Adam, her lips were fixed into a smile.

Watching her wheel herself to the side of the fireplace, he asked, 'Have you told Miri yet?'

'No, not yet, she would worry so. I would rather wait a little longer.'

'You will have to tell her sometime.'

'Sometime but not now.' Esther's smile deepened as though she hugged some delicious secret to herself.

'Do you try when I am not here?'

'Yes, but not from the wheelchair. I am afraid of its moving. I need something that will not let me down.'

Leaving his chair, he went to her, arms extended. 'I won't let you down.'

Lifting her from the wheelchair, he set her on her feet, his arm around her back, supporting her as she stood.

'Just be still for a while,' he said, 'get used to it before you move.'

Get used to it? Esther's heart sang. Would she ever get used to this, to standing on her own two feet?

'Ready?' asked Adam moments later.

Nodding her head and drawing a deep breath, hands clenching together at her sides as he took his arm from around her, Esther stood alone.

Only inches from her but not touching her, he smiled, his voice calm as he coaxed: 'Come with me, Esther.' He took a step backward. 'Come with me.'

'Adam . . . I can't.'

'You can, Esther.' He said it softly, no trace of urgency in his tone. 'Come with me. You can if you want to.'

If she wanted to! She locked her eyes on his. There was nothing on God's earth she wanted more than to go with him. Pressing her lips together, she stepped into his arms.

'I knew you could do it,' he whispered against her hair, 'I knew you could.'

Not knowing if she were laughing or crying, and caring even less, Esther let herself rest in his arms. She would not be given this joy a second time. He would never again hold her in his arms as he was doing now, pressing her to him like a lover.

'Well done.'

Esther felt her legs tremble as he released her and stepped away.

'Now do it again. Come on, Esther,' he urged as she hesitated. 'Don't lose it now. Do it, Esther . . . come to me.'

'You are a hard taskmaster,' she gasped as after her third practice he lowered her into the wheelchair. 'Remind me not to ask you for a job.' She leaned back, her breathing rapid.

'How do you feel?' He smiled but there was concern in his expression.

'Wonderful, Adam.' Her eyes glowed with a feeling words could not convey. 'Though my legs feel shaky. That's probably the reason I still feel I need to hold on to the bedpost when I try to walk in my bedroom.'

'I thought of that.' Going to a table just inside the door, he picked up a bag she had not noticed. 'It could be that your legs need a little support until they get used to holding you up.'

Opening the bag, he drew out two narrow rods of steel attached to a sturdy leather strap about four inches wide.

'I know they are not attractive to look at,' he said, 'but fixed to the heels of your shoes, and the strap fastened just below your knee, they would give you the support you need. You would only have to wear them for a few months, just long enough for your muscles to strengthen. Will you try, Esther? Your skirts would hide them.'

'You were right when you said I could walk.' She smiled. 'Why not this time too?'

'I would have to try them against your legs. I could only guess what length to make the callipers.'

'Then try them.'

'We must wait until Miri is here.'

'Adam, who is there to see?' she chided. 'I don't mind so why should anyone else?'

'But, Esther . . .'

'But nothing! If you think it's going to be of any help to my walking, do it, Adam, and forget the proprieties.' So saying, she hitched her skirts to her knees.

Dropping quickly to his haunches, he held the strap in line below her knee, holding the steel calliper against her leg.

'Well, well! Not a sight I am accustomed to dropping in on but interesting just the same – very interesting.'

Intent on what they were doing neither of them heard the door of Esther's sitting room open and close. Now she looked up into the deceptively smiling face of Roberta Vance.

'How very romantic! A young man on his knees before you. Really, quite the twopenny novel, Esther.'

The violet glance swept over Adam as he rose, lingering on his face, the full lips curving into a smile.

'My name is Roberta Vance.' Her voice deep and sensual as her smile, Roberta stepped closer to Adam. 'How do you do?'

'Good evening, Mrs Vance.' He answered abruptly, no smile on his lips. Turning to Esther, who had pushed her skirts back over her knees to her feet, he said, 'I think I have the measurements for your callipers, Mrs Cosmore. I will fit them tomorrow, if that is convenient?' Slipping the supports back into the bag, he looked again at Esther. 'Will I wait with you until Mrs Butler returns?'

'No.' Esther shook her head. 'I . . . I have Mrs Vance to keep me company. Thank you, Mr Paige. Tomorrow will do excellently for a second fitting. Good night.'

'I don't think he likes me,' Roberta laughed as Adam left. 'Now I wonder why that is? Could it be because I walked in on your little game?'

'There was no little game, Mrs Vance,' Esther returned coldly. 'Mr Paige was measuring my legs so I may have callipers fitted.'

'Is that what he was doing?' Eyes hard and brilliant as gemstones were fixed on her. 'Well, you may claim that is all he was doing but will Morgan believe it?'

Esther felt her body tense, sensing the threat that lay beneath the words.

'You know, my dear, I don't think he will.' Mauve silk skirts swishing, she walked around the room, touching a figurine, straightening a lace cover, before coming to sit opposite Esther. 'In fact, your Mr Paige could well find himself on the other end of a lawsuit when Morgan hears of this.'

'But there was nothing wrong happening, nothing immoral, if that is what you are implying!' Esther protested, contempt for the woman rising like a flood tide. 'Adam . . .

Mr Paige . . . was merely fitting metal supports to my shoes.'

'And why is that?' Glancing at Esther's feet Roberta Vance's mouth lifted in a mocking curve. 'And where are they? Is Morgan supposed to believe that a woman who cannot walk needs supports fixed to her shoes? Or is the wheelchair part of the game too?'

'You know it is not, and once again I tell you, there was no game.'

Roberta Vance smoothed her skirts. 'That is not how it looked to me, and neither will it look that way to Morgan when he learns of it.'

The tension holding Esther tightened its grip. This woman, and doubtless Morgan too, had arrived unannounced and unexpected and there could be only one reason. Morgan still did not know of his father's death so there was little chance that had brought him back. The only reason he would return was money; Morgan was in need of money. Did Roberta Vance see this as a chance of making a little of her own?

'And you intend to tell him?'

The violet eyes widened in false concern. 'My dear, someone should!'

And that someone of course would be Roberta, Esther thought, watching mockery twist the other woman's painted mouth. 'Then let that someone be you, Mrs Vance. I would not deprive you of a pleasure you so obviously enjoy. Tell my husband what you saw here tonight and he will see the harmlessness of it and your stupidity for trying to make it appear otherwise.'

'Oh, Morgan will not think it harmless, my dear.' Roberta made an elaborate display of examining the huge topaz ring on the third finger of her left hand. 'Not the way I tell it. Would any man think it harmless to hear of his wife sitting alone in a room with another man, her skirts above her knees, legs wide apart, and the man with his head between them?'

'That is not true!' she gasped.

Roberta Vance laughed, a hard brittle sound. 'Who said anything about truth? I said Morgan would not think it harmless and he won't, not the way I'll tell him. And that, Esther, my dear, will spell grave trouble for Mr Adam Paige. That is his name, is it not? He will not be hard to find in a town this size.'

Esther gripped the wheels of her chair. Adam could not be involved. Morgan would see to it he lost his employment and in doing that could well discover his employer was Miri. And from that it was only a small step to discovering who truly owned those businesses.

'Where is all this leading?' she asked.

Her smile wider, Roberta looked at her. 'I think you know where it is leading, Esther. You want my silence. I want money.' She laughed, a short sinister sound. 'Isn't it all blissfully simple when we talk about it?'

So she had seen this as a chance to make money, seen it as a way to blackmail. And she must be allowed to succeed if Adam were to be protected.

'I have no allowance from my husband or my father,' Esther said stiffly. 'The only money I have of my own is three hundred pounds I got from selling a property my father made over to me before my marriage.'

'Not a great deal.' The smile remained but the violet eyes glistened malignantly. 'But then, I am not greedy. Everything a person has is enough for me.'

'I tell you, Cosmore, y'ave had all you getting out of me an' I was a bloody fool to 'ave given you as much in the first place. I could 'ave got any man in Darlaston to wed my daughter.'

'Then why didn't you?' Morgan surveyed his father-in-law. Jos had aged in the year and a half since that wedding day, the fine sifting of grey in his hair being more pronounced now, and his spare frame thinner. 'Was it because your daughter was a cripple or because no other man in Darlaston had the money you thought my father had?'

'That were a bloody lie an' all!' Josiah Kerral flapped his coat tails in a regular angry rhythm. 'Yer father had no money.'

'Did he claim to have?' Morgan asked, undaunted by the other man's fury. 'Or did you merely surmise as much? You both played the same game. You thought my father had money and he thought you had. You were both wrong but you made an agreement with me. An agreement whereby I would receive one thousand pounds a year. An agreement I intend you to keep.'

'You intend!' Josiah shifted position, spreading his legs like a boxer ready to defend himself. '*You* intend! An' how do you expect to enforce that? There were nothing set down on paper.'

Toying with the kid gloves lying on his knee, Morgan hesitated. There was nothing on paper, that part of their agreement had been purely verbal which had been a mistake on his part, but not one he could not rectify if he were careful. 'Talk can often prove more effective than a signature,' he said. 'A few words dropped in the right quarter . . .'

Throwing back his head, Josiah laughed. 'You must think one up wi' more to it than that. Talk never frightened me an' neither did any man, much less the gutless bloody spawn of Ezra Cosmore. You go on an' spout yer mouth off all over the town if you feel it'll do you any good, but you can talk till you be blue in the face – you'll get nothing more from me.'

'And what of your daughter?'

His mouth hardening, Josiah looked at the man seated a few feet from him. ''Er made 'er bed,' he rasped, 'an' now 'er must lie on it!'

'Do you really expect her to live without money?'

'I expect you to keep 'er,' Josiah spat, 'as I expect every man to keep the woman 'e marries. Same as you keep that bitch Vance.'

'Normally I might agree with you,' Morgan's green-gold eyes glinted, 'but in this case I do not. How can I be expected to keep Esther, much less Roberta, when the business is bankrupt?'

246

Josiah's coat tails flapped faster. 'A minute ago you reckoned you had ears you could talk into. Well, try asking them ears for a job. It'll be the only way you'll get money from this town.'

'Not the only way.' Standing up, Morgan drew the gloves slowly over his hands, smoothing them on a finger at a time. 'My wife is the daughter of a sick man, his only child, one who will inherit everything when that man dies.' He lifted his glance to Josiah, a glance that was filled with malice, and his voice lowered to a sibilant softness that reeked with threat. 'And with a town such as this, where sickness and accidents are so prevalent, who can tell when a man might die, or how?'

Josiah's coat tails ceased their flapping, his hand whipping out from beneath them to clutch Morgan's lapels. 'Young 'uns die as well as old 'uns, Cosmore,' he hissed, pulling Morgan's face close to his own. 'Some quicker than others. An' if you don't want to meet wi' one of them accidents you be talkin' of, get yer arse out of my house an' keep it out.'

Reeling from Josiah's backward thrust, Morgan steadied himself against a brocade-covered armchair. 'I shall be back for my thousand pounds before the week ends, Kerral,' he said coolly. 'And if you are a wise man you will have it ready.'

Chapter Seventeen

'Where did you hear that?'

The group of men standing in the smoke-filled Frying Pan Inn huddled closer.

'Toby Hackett told me.' The one being questioned moved his clay pipe about his mouth without removing it from between his teeth. 'An' what he don't know about what be goin' on in Darlaston ain't worth the knowin'.'

On the edge of the group another man nodded his head. 'That be right enough,' he muttered. 'If Toby Hackett said it you can take it as gospel.'

"Ow did 'e come to hear of it, George?' a man questioned him.

"Ow do Toby come to hear most things?' The clay pipe moved again. 'By keepin' 'is ear'oles open, that's 'ow.'

'Arrh, if Toby says the place be goin', then goin' it be.' A small man with his head swamped by a flat cap several sizes too big peered from beneath its brim. 'An' you all knows what that means!'

'You can't be sure of that, Cappy.' A third man took a drink from his tankard, wiping froth from his mouth with the back of one grimy hand. 'We ain't been told nothing yet.'

'No, nor we won't be!' Cappy replied. 'They won't tell we anythin' till they tells we to bugger off an' don't come back.'

"Ow do you make that out?' A man a little taller than the rest, his trousers held up with a broad belt, a muffler tied over his collarless shirt, sliced whisker-thin shavings from a stick of tobacco. 'They be goin' to need men.'

'Oh, arrh, they'll be needin' men.' The clay pipe glowed as its owner drew hard on the stem. 'But word 'as it they be bringin' their own from Walsall way.'

'I told you. I told you, didn't I?' Cappy shuffled from foot to foot as though performing some ritual dance. 'I said as much. It'll be a case of sling yer 'ook, we don't want you.'

'What do you think?' They all looked towards a man dressed as they were in moleskin trousers, jacket and muffler set off by a flat cap, a brown and white bull terrier at his feet.

'I think there ain't much sense in milkin' a cow without a bucket,' he said, his words wreathed in blue-grey smoke. 'I say, wait an' see what 'appens.'

His pint pot half hidden by the peak of his oversized cap, the little man snorted into his ale. 'An' when what 'appens be you all gettin' the sack, what then?'

'Buller be right.' Another man joined the conversation. 'Best wait an' see.'

'That always be your creed, Pigeon.' Cappy's pot emerged from beneath his cap. 'An' if we waits as long as you waits fer them birds of your'n to get 'ome, we be in fer a bloody long wait!'

The slicing of the tobacco finished, and the stick and penknife folded into his pocket, the tall man called for his pot to be refilled, pressing the tobacco shavings into his long-stemmed white clay pipe while he waited. Putting a penny on the wet wooden bar counter he nodded at the landlord. Holding a paper taper to the fire well back in the black grate, he used the flame to light his pipe.

'Pigeon Billy be right . . . an' Buller be right.' He puffed, drawing several times on the reluctant tobacco.

'So *you* says wait an' see an' all?' Cappy peered from beneath his cap. 'You be of the same mind as them. I'm tellin' you . . .'

'An' I be tellin' you!' The one called George clamped the

pipe between his teeth. 'Yer mouth be too big. If an elephant dropped into it we'd never find it. Hold yer peace an' give a man a chance to say what 'e feels. Go on, Jack, say what you started.'

'Arrh.' The others nodded as one voiced their joint opinion. 'Let Slacky say what 'e 'as to say.'

Slacky Jack, so called from his nightly habit of sneaking a bag of coals home from the foundry and vowing it were just the tiny fragments called slack, took several more puffs on his pipe. 'Well, to my mind they 'ave a point.' He squinted over the stem at the faces watching him through the haze of the smoke heavy room. 'An' I be right meself when I says they'll be needin' men, an' I also says there ain't no Walsall bloke comin' an' takin' the bread outta the mouths of my little' uns.'

'Nor mine.'

'Or mine!'

The words rang out into the smoky haze.

'Has anybody asked the gaffer?' Pigeon Billy's words dropped into the silence as the men fell quiet.

''E wouldn't tell you if 'e knowed.' Cappy's large hat jigged as he shook his head. ''E be too far up Cosmore's arse. Toby Hackett says the foundry were up for sale before old Cosmore snuffed it, an' the way 'e heard it is it's been bought by a bloke from Walsall an' 'e be bringin' 'is own men to work it.'

Looking to where the bull terrier lay at his feet, Buller Norton smiled grimly. 'Won't be no Walsall men settlin' their arses in the copper, nor in any other job in Darlaston.'

'It won't be that son of Cosmore's will be out of a job an' 'ome if they does.' Slacky Jack sucked on his pipe. 'That bastard won't go 'ungry, 'e'll be all right.'

'So! Be you lot goin' to stand fer 'im takin' yer jobs an' handin' 'em over to another, or be you goin' to do somethin' about it?'

'Ain't nothin' we can do, Cappy,' Pigeon Billy replied. 'If Cosmore be sellin' up, that be it. 'E be the gaffer.'

Cappy's head tilted back on his shoulders as he peered up at his companions. 'There be a bloody lot we can do!' he exclaimed. 'Cosmore only be the gaffer so long as 'e 'as a place to be gaffer of.'

'What you sayin'?' Once more George's pipe inched along his teeth.

Cappy glanced around the smoke-filled room, satisfying himself no ears but theirs were fixed on his next words. 'This be what I'm sayin'.' He lowered his voice. 'If we am goin' to be left with nothin', then let's make sure Cosmore 'as the same.'

'An' 'ow do we do that?'

The question came from the edge of the group. Waiting while the landlord slapped George's newly filled pot on the counter and scooped up his penny, Cappy answered, 'We burn the copper, set fire to it. We won't 'ave no job but at least Cosmore's git won't 'ave no foundry to sell.'

'We can't do that!' Pigeon Billy glanced nervously around the room.

'Why not? It's been done afore, eh, George!'

He clamped his teeth on the fragile stem of his home-made clay pipe. 'It's been done afore.'

'An' I say we does it again.' Cappy pulled the too large cap more firmly onto his head, bending his ears. 'Burn the copper an' then the 'ouse. Let's leave the bastard with as much as 'e would leave we.'

'I'm for it.' Slacky Jack downed the last of his ale. 'Let Cosmore taste what it be like to 'ave nothin', same as 'is old man made sure we 'ad nothin'.'

''Ow about the rest of you?' The peak of his cap hiding half his face, Cappy threw out his question.

Touching a boot to his watchful bull terrier, Buller Norton looked at the faces of his workmates. 'Be it fire or be it old Sam 'ere that puts a stop to Cosmore don't fret me none. Either way I be for it.'

'George?' Cappy peered through the thickening fog of

tobacco smoke that lay at head-height over the crowded little room.

'I be thinkin' along the same lines as Buller an' Slacky. If we don't work the copper then nobody does!' George set down his half-empty tankard. 'We do it but we sees to it nobody gets 'urt. You don't fire that foundry when men be workin' in it.'

'Then it best be done tonight,' Buller said. 'It being Saturday night the furnaces be damped down when the shift ends at nine o'clock. There'll be nobody on 'ceptin' old Jake at the gate an' Sam 'ere will fetch 'im out if needs be.'

'Then tonight it be.' Pipe rattling against his teeth, George spoke quietly. 'But we'd better not leave 'ere afore the usual time if we don't want to set anybody to wonderin'. We will do as our custom on a Saturday night an' 'ang on till the landlord chucks we out, then we'll meet about twelve up along where the mill stands on Bull Piece.' He hesitated, sending a wary glance towards the rest of the men filling the bar of the Frying Pan. 'Bring torches and matches an' make sure nobody sees you. Tonight will see the end of Cosmore.'

'I still thinks as this don't be right,' Pigeon Billy whispered nervously.

'Givin' our bloody jobs away don't be right.' In the moonlight Buller Norton raised one finger and the brown and white bull terrier sank soundlessly to its stomach.

Away in the distance the clock in the steeple of St Lawrence's church chimed midnight.

'Be everybody 'ere?' George looked at each face as the men that had been with him in the Frying Pan silently assembled.

'Right then,' he whispered, 'cut across Glovers Mound an' round the back of the Atlas works on to the heath. An' keep to the shadows. Could be others beside ourselves be out of their beds.'

Jackets buttoned across their chests, caps pulled low, the

men moved off in twos and threes, hugging the shadows until they cleared Whitton Street, passing the derelict Colonial works, its fallen stacks reaching up like deformed fingers. Crossing the junction of Bills Street they moved silently across the heath, keeping a straggle of buildings to their right. 'That be the Primitive Methodist Chapel.' George nodded towards a squat black shadow sitting apart from the rest on the skyline. 'We be only a mile or so from the foundry an' the heath be flat from 'ere so every man keep low.'

'Be Jake in there?'

Reaching the copper works, the group crouched just clear of the foundry yard. George looked towards the tiny brick building that housed the watchman, seeing Cappy's nod as he returned almost on his stomach.

'Buller!' George's whisper was soft.

'Sam, bring!' Buller Norton kept his eyes on the brick hut, not looking at the dog who moved silent as the footsteps of death.

'Gerroff, you bloody great bastard!' The watchman, wakened from sleep by the growls of the bull terrier, backed into the yard, retreating before the terrier's bared teeth until Buller Norton fastened a hand on his collar.

'You ain't seen nothin' tonight, Jake,' he murmured beside the old man's ear. 'Remember that. Y'ave seen nothin'! I wouldn't want old Sam 'ere to lose 'is temper, you understand, Jake?'

The old man nodded. Once a bull terrier fastened its teeth on anything, there was no prising it loose. 'I ain't seen nothin',' he said, throat dry with fear. 'Whatever you be about, I ain't seen you doin' it.'

'Sam!' The dog sank to its haunches, eyes fixed on the old man still as the group moved off towards the foundry.

Touching a match to his torch, each man used the light to set about gathering the rags the workmen had wiped their hands on and George and Slacky Jack threw out papers and ledgers discarded from the office to add to the heaps.

'Now!' George called when they could find no more, and touched his torch to the nearest bundle of papers and greasy rags. As if trained to it, every man instantly aimed his own torch, setting the rest alight.

Outside the yard George rolled the bundle of twigs covered in animal fat on the grass, extinguishing its flame. As the others followed suit, he turned to Jake. 'If you be asked, you was knocked out an' when you woke the foundry were burnin'.'

'Arrh, I was knocked out.' Jake looked at the dog's teeth which were still bared. 'An' I'll 'ave the bloody 'eadache to prove it!'

Returning the way they had come, the group paused in the shadow of the Atlas works. Behind them the night sky glowed yellow with flame.

'Now we make for Butcroft.' George turned to the others. 'Take the left fork when we reach Bills Street. That will take we through the old colliery straight on to Butcroft Fields. Cosmore's house ain't but ten minutes from there.'

'I ain't for firin' Cosmore's place.' Pigeon Billy hung back.

'You be in wi' the rest,' Buller muttered, 'old Sam there says we all goes together.'

'I tell you, I 'eard 'em plain as day. They thought as I was too far gone to be bothered about me.'

Staring at the night sky, Adam went over in his mind what Elijah Tucker had told him earlier. Elijah was a fixture in the Frying Pan. For over sixty years he had sat in a wicker chair set in the nook of the fireplace, forgotten nightly until the landlord chucked him out with the others at eleven o'clock closing.

'Are you sure?' he had asked the old man.

Tugging at white sideburns that melted with equally white whiskers, Elijah stared back at him with button eyes. 'I be in me dotage, lad, not in me coffin. I told what I 'eard an' I 'eard what I told. That lot were talkin' of Cosmore.'

'But Ezra Cosmore is dead.' Adam remembered the withering look the other man had given him.

'Arrh, Ezra be in 'is grave, but that son of 'is'n ain't.'

'Morgan?' Adam murmured.

'Don't know.' Elijah pulled his whiskers. 'But there be other ways of payin' a man out than layin' 'is entrails in the sun.'

'What more did they say?' Adam felt an icy stab in the deepest reaches of his stomach.

'They thought I couldn't 'ear 'em,' Elijah chuckled, 'they thought I was sleeping, but I wasn't an' there be nothin' these ears of mine miss. It were Cosmore they was talkin' of all right 'cos they said they was goin' to burn the copper, an' the only copper foundry 'ereabouts be Cosmore's.'

'Did they say when?' Adam grabbed the old man's arms as he put the question.

'Easy, lad,' Elijah had protested. 'Old bones break easy an' mend 'ard. Tonight was when they planned. Wi' the furnaces banked down there would be no men around to see 'em or to get 'urt. Arrh, it was tonight they meant to do it. Said if they didn't work the copper then nobody would.'

'Then it is the foundry they are going to destroy!'

'Not just the foundry, lad. They said they would go from there to the 'ouse an' do the same to that. If Cosmore could take away their job and their 'ome, they could do the same to 'im. They was all for payin' 'im in kind. Watch the sky, lad,' Elijah had said, shuffling away toward Katherine's Cross, 'watch the sky. Like as not there'll be more than the moon lightin' it tonight.'

Addenbrooke! Adam watched the figure of the old man merge with the shadows. Esther was at Addenbrooke and that was the house the men planned to burn.

Away across the Green the clock of St Lawrence's chimed midnight. His mother would be sleeping. She had gone to bed at her usual nine-thirty, an hour before he left the house. Why had he left? His back to the bole of an oak tree, its spreading branches cloaking him in shadow, Adam asked himself the question he had posed at least a dozen times while standing here, and still the answer was the same. He only knew that this was where he must be.

In the darkness Addenbrooke House rose like a spectre from the heath, its square windows staring blindly at the moon.

Would they come? Would they burn the house?

As if in answer a dozen pin pricks of light danced like fireflies in the blackness and Adam began to run.

'Pigeon an' you two,' George pointed at two of the men, mufflers tied over their noses and mouths, 'keep watch at the back. Buller, Slacky an' the rest of you, we'll put the torches in from the front.' Taking a box of Swan Vestas from his pocket, he drew out a match, dragging its head across the side of the box then holding the flame to the fat-encrusted twigs.

Waiting until the other torches flared, he whispered, "Ave you all got yer stones?' Seeing each of them nod, he signalled them to move. Within yards of the house he hurled his stone through a ground-floor window, sending the flaming torch after it. Like a series of pistol shots each stone found a window and each torch followed. In seconds the windows were brilliant with the light of blazing curtains and the attackers had melted into the shadows at the rear of the house.

'I'm off,' Pigeon Billy hissed nervously. 'I ain't waitin' for no fire wagon.'

'Won't be no fire wagon come out 'ere.' Slacky Jack watched the spread of flame. 'They knows by the time they 'ave them 'osses hitched an' they've got theirselves out 'ere, there would be no 'ouse left to save.'

'Eh up!' Slacky Jack crouched lower behind the banks of rhododendron bushes. 'Somebody comin' out.'

'That ain't Cosmore.' George squinted against the glare of the burning. 'That be Evan Gittins, 'e be butler for Cosmore.'

'Watch out, George. 'E could see you.' Slacky Jack pulled him into the shelter of the bushes.

'It won't make no difference what 'e sees, 'e won't be able

to tell nobody.' Pigeon Billy rose to his feet, letting fly with the stone he still held.

'You bloody fool!' George hissed. 'Y'ave probably killed 'im.'

'I meant to.' Pigeon Billy looked over to where Gittins sprawled face down at the rear door of the house. 'If 'e sighted one of we, the lot could go down the line.'

'Let's get out of it afore anybody else comes out.'

Turning away, Billy sprinted across the gardens, making for the open ground that gave on to Butcroft Heath. Seconds later the others followed, melting into the night shadows.

Mindless of the ache clawing at his lungs Adam kept on running, his eyes on the house, lit by the flames licking its walls. Esther was in that house.

Ignoring the front entrance he raced to the rear. That was where Esther had her rooms.

'Mrs Cosmore!' He found Gittins and heaved him over on to his back. 'Esther . . . where is Esther?'

Gittins groaned, his eyes rolling back in his head. 'I heard a window break. I . . . I came to see what . . .'

Leaving the barely conscious butler, Adam ran into the house. Smoke billowing from the front of the house filled his nose and throat as he stumbled along the darkened passage he knew led to Esther's sitting room.

She wouldn't be in an upper room, he thought, fighting the toxic grip on his throat, she never went upstairs unless Sam were there to carry her down again. But maybe Cosmore was home. Maybe he had carried Esther to an upstairs room.

The door of the sitting room in which she always saw him when he called to give his account of the works was open. He saw from the light of the flames licking down from the lobby of the house that it was empty. Coughing against the smoke torturing his already bursting lungs, he stumbled across the room. Esther had once referred to her bedroom and had looked towards the back of the sitting room.

Behind him the crackle of flames grew louder. One hand over his nose and mouth, he threw back the door. The bed was a mass of burning sheets and pillows where the thin makeshift ceiling had collapsed, sending burning laths into the room below, sparks turning chairs and rugs to miniature infernos.

Heat searing his eyeballs, Adam stared around the room. 'Esther!' he choked, catching sight of the still form lying a few feet from the bed.

Crossing to her, he dragged her further from the blazing bed. Looking across the sitting room, he could see into the corridor. Already there was a wall of fire advancing towards the sitting room. There was no hope of getting across that.

Jumping to his feet, he slammed the bedroom door shut. Maybe it would hold the fire long enough.

Grabbing a chair, he smashed it against the window, clearing the glass from the frame. Then, grabbing a smouldering carpet, he flung it over the window frame.

Returning for Esther he reeled as the night air flooded into the fire, feeding it so that it engulfed the door in one gigantic flame-filled explosion.

Heat and smoke tearing the lungs from his body, filling his eyes with smarting streams, Adam lifted the unconscious girl in his arms, carrying her to the window. Laying Esther half on and half off, he stepped over her, rubbing the scalding liquid from his eyes. Then, with the last of his strength, he gathered her into his arms and falling against the frame already covered in slithering flame rolled her through it letting her fall the few feet to the carpet.

The sharp night air swept the smoke from his lungs. Adam carried Esther to the safety of the lawn then peeled off his scorched jacket, wrapping her in it before going to where Gittins leaned against a stone sun dial.

'The rest of them,' he gasped, 'did they get out?'

'Young Peggy be at 'ome with her mother.' Gittins touched a hand to the blood trickling from his forehead.

'And Mrs Foster?' Adam urged.

'Dolly!' Gittins stared at Adam, his eyes bemused in the light of the flames.

'Is Mrs Foster in the house?' Adam shouted shaking the other man by the shoulders.

'Dolly.' Gittins stared at the house, his face lit by the incandescent glow, shock summoning the dialect of his youth. ''Er be 'avin' a night off, 'er be gone to 'er sister's.'

'And Miri?' Adam shook him again, demanding he hold on to his senses a little longer. 'What about Mrs Butler?'

Gittins swayed and his eyes shut as unconsciousness threatened to engulf him.

'Mrs Butler!' Adam shouted, shaking him ruthlessly. 'She was not in Esther's bedroom. Where does Mrs Butler sleep?'

Gittins lifted a hand, pointing to the room that had been above Esther's: the one that had collapsed as the raging inferno engulfed the house.

An arm supporting Gittins, Adam led him to where he had left Esther.

Miriam Butler was beyond his help.

'Do you feel up to sitting with her until I can harness the trap?'

Carrying Esther to the stable, Adam laid her on a pile of straw in an empty stall then grabbing a couple of horse blankets gave one to Gittins, wrapping Esther in the other.

'I'm all right now,' Gittins said, touching his brow where the trickle of blood had dried. 'It was that blow to my head knocked me out. I don't know what could have hit me . . .'

I can guess, Adam thought, remembering Elijah's words.

'Go see to the mare,' Gittins went on as the horse screamed in terror at the smell of smoke. 'I will stay with Mrs Cosmore.'

Gentling the mare, Adam knew she would bolt the moment he led her outside. The smoke already had her in a state of panic.

Taking his handkerchief from his pocket, he laid it across

the horse's eyes then led her out of the stable. Working as swiftly as he could, he harnessed her to the trap.

Calling to Gittins to come into the yard, Adam gave him the halter.

'Are there any more horses in there?'

'No.' Gittins glanced across to the house. Flames still danced crazily at its windows. 'The mare and the master's gelding were the only horses left.'

'The gelding!' Adam demanded. 'Where is it?'

'The young Mr Cosmore took it. He left yesterday.'

So Cosmore was not in the house. Adam glanced over his shoulder towards the burning building. Only Miri.

'Keep talking to the mare.' He turned back to Gittins. 'The stables are far enough away from the house, they won't be caught by the blaze. But the smell of burning frightens her. Luckily the breeze is carrying most of the smoke in the other direction.'

'Queenie is used to me, Mr Paige. She will hold still, don't worry.'

'Good.' Adam was already sprinting back into the stable. 'I will fetch Mrs Cosmore.'

'You're safe, Esther.' His face against hers, Adam held her pressed to his body. 'You are safe now.'

'I know, Adam.' Her whisper was faint. 'I will always be safe with you.'

Lifting her in his arms, he carried her to the trap, seating her inside. 'Will you ride with her?' He took the halter from Gittins. 'She is still very dazed.'

Nodding assent, the butler climbed into the small trap, taking Esther in his arms while Adam talked softly to the mare, leading her away. He removed the blindfold as they gained the heath. After walking in silence till they came to the Bull Stake, Adam turned to the butler.

'Do you have any place you can stay?'

'My brother has a place near here, just at the back of the steam tram depot. I can stay with him until . . .'

He trailed off, glancing down at Esther, still held against him.

'I will take you there.' Adam walked on, following Gittins's directions until he came to a row of small houses in a narrow cutting.

'This is it, Mr Paige, Corns Street. My brother lives in the house second from the end.'

His brother wakened and the butler safely deposited with the family, Adam politely refused their offer of hospitality for the remainder of the night. The little house was bursting at its seams. There would be no place where Esther might rest quietly.

Climbing into the trap, he took her into the crook of one arm, supporting her carefully while guiding Queenie with the other hand. Despite being wrapped in his jacket and a horse blanket, he could feel her shivering. That would be shock, and shock could be a killer, his mother always warned. He had to get Esther to a warm bed and get a doctor in to examine her. Clucking encouragement to the mare, he turned her back towards the Bull Stake.

'Adam, what happened?' Esther moved against him but his arm tightened, holding her still.

'There was a fire at the house.'

She struggled against his arm until she could see into his face, painted with moonlight in the shadows.

'Yes . . . yes, I remember. Was . . . was anyone hurt?'

'No,' he lied. To tell her of Miri now would only do more harm. 'Everyone is all right.'

'Thank God!' She sank against him, her whole body shaking. 'Oh, thank God!'

She did not speak again until he turned the mare in at the gates of Rowena House. Then her whole body stiffened.

'Not here, Adam.' She pushed free of his arm. 'Not here. My father will not take me in.'

'Of course he will.' Adam twitched the reins, urging the horse on as she halted outside the cottage that once had been Esther's home. 'Where else would he expect you to go?'

'I don't know.' She stared at the house coming into view beyond the row of trees. 'But he will not take me in here.'

Adam looked at her, face so pale it seemed to be carved from alabaster. Only the eyes were alive, gleaming like black pearls by the pale lustre of the moon.

What was it that lay between Josiah Kerral and his daughter? What was it made her think a father would turn away his only child? No man would do such a thing. Yet they had not lived in the same house, he remembered, they had not lived as father and daughter. Jos had kept himself apart, leaving Esther to live in that cottage with Miriam Butler and her husband, almost denying her existence, whilst he, Jos Kerral, lived alone in Rowena House.

Halting the mare before the steps leading to the front entrance, Adam jumped from the trap. Surely he would not deny her tonight? Not with her husband's house burned to the ground.

Banging with his fist, shouting at the top of his voice, Adam waited until the door opened.

'I have Mrs Cosmore in the trap,' he said to a startled William Evans, the oil lamp he carried spilling a patch of sallow yellow light across his long white nightshirt.

'Who?' Evans held the lamp higher, peering through its acid gleam.

'Mrs Cosmore.' Adam leaped down the steps. 'Jos Kerral's daughter.' Lifting Esther from the trap, he carried her into the house, elbowing Evans out of his way.

'What the 'ell be going on down there?'

Adam turned towards the stairs. Jos Kerral stood halfway down, a loaded shotgun in his hands.

'There has been a fire at Addenbrooke.'

'What be that to do wi' me?' Jos descended a few more steps. 'Why come bangin' on my door in the middle of the night?'

'Mrs Cosmore was caught in it.' Adam looked at the girl he held in his arms.

'What do you want I should do about that?' Beyond the narrow circle of the lamp's light he eased the shotgun in his grasp.

'Mrs Cosmore was hurt,' Adam said, his tone sharp. 'She needs help.'

''Er won't find none 'ere.'

'She needs a warm bed and a doctor.' Adam peered into the shadows shrouding the stairs. 'For God's sake, Kerral, you are her father.'

'An' Cosmore be 'er 'usband.' Out of the rim of yellow light the gun moved again. 'If 'er needs help, let 'im give it to 'er.'

'At least find her a bed for one night,' Adam begged, hardly believing the other man's answer.

'There be no bed 'ere for that *thing*!' Jos spat, stepping forward until the lamp gleamed on the barrel of the shotgun he now levelled at Adam. 'I told 'er 'usband to bugger off an' now I be tellin' you – get that cripple out of my house before I blow yer bloody 'ead off!'

'This be no place for 'er, Adam.'

He leaned wearily back in his father's chair. There had been no other place he could think of to take Esther.

'I know, Mother,' he said, eyes closed against the tiredness settling over him, pressing him down like a giant hand. 'But when her father turned her away . . .'

'Ee, son, I can 'ardly believe what y'ave told me tonight.' Carrie Paige pulled the chequered shawl draped over her calico nightgown a little tighter around her shoulders. 'To turn away 'is own wench an' 'er catched in a fire . . . may the Lord visit 'im with a 'ard callin' card!' Turning to the grate, she opened the door of the oven, drawing out the flat iron shelves. Wrapping each in a separate cloth, she carried them both to the door which gave on to the steep narrow stairs.

'I'll pop these in the bed at the side of 'er while you brews some tea.'

'Mrs Paige.' Esther opened her eyes as Adam's mother slid the hot shelves into the bed. 'It is very kind of you but I cannot take your bed.'

'Shhh, me wench.' Carrie touched a hand to Esther's brow. 'You get yerself to sleep, an' when it be mornin' I'll fetch you up a nice cup of tea.'

'Miri,' Esther murmured, already sinking into sleep, 'I should be with Miri.'

No, you shouldn't, Carrie thought, closing the bedroom door behind her. God forbid you should be where Miriam Butler be for many years yet!

Pouring tea into two platter pots, Carrie looked at the face of her son – too drawn for mere tiredness. There was a deeper strain etched there, a strain she recognised and feared. 'Don't get involved,' she had told him, but her words had fallen on deaf ears and now it was too late. Her lad was already involved. Though she felt in her heart he had not touched that girl lying upstairs with the hands of a lover, he was caught as fast. Her son loved Esther Cosmore. He loved another man's wife.

'When will 'er 'usband be back?' Carrie asked, handing a pot to Adam.

'I did not ask.' He passed a hand over his eyes. 'Gittins said only that he left Darlaston yesterday, and Esther was in no fit state to answer questions.'

Taking her own pot, Carrie lowered herself to her seat beside the fire Adam had stoked into life. 'What will 'er do till 'e gets back?'

'I don't know much of her background but I do not think she has any relatives other than her father.'

'Father? Huh!' Carrie said scathingly. 'I'd sooner call a snake "Father". He could at least have let you put 'er in that cottage 'er 'ad afore 'er wed. But to order her off with a shotgun pointed at 'er!' She shook her head. 'Well, there ain't no way 'er will be turned from my door as long as 'er be in need of shelter, though Foleys Croft be no place for a wench fetched up as 'er 'as been.'

Putting his cup down, Adam moved to his mother's side, sliding one arm about her and cradling her close to him. 'Foleys Croft might not be Rowena House or Addenbrooke,' he said tenderly, 'but there is more love and compassion here than in both of those places put together.'

'Arrh, lad.' Carrie reached a hand to his. 'We got little 'ere 'cept love but that wench sleepin' in my bed will be given a fair share of that. You need not be frettin' for 'er so long as 'er be under my roof.'

Bending, Adam touched his lips to her hair. The two people he loved most were here in this house but one could not stay.

The thought was like acid eating away at his soul.

Chapter Eighteen

Miri dead! Esther sat in Carrie Paige's tiny kitchen, the same two words beating over and over in her mind. How could it have happened? How had Addenbrooke caught fire?

'Adam said for you to stay 'ere. 'E 'as gone to the 'ouse to see to . . . to see to things.' Carrie looked at the girl her son had carried into her house in the middle of the night. Her small face was pale as a corpse in its coffin, dark shadows lay like pit pools beneath her eyes and only her fingers moved, twisting incessantly around each other.

Placing a piece of rough cloth on one end of the table, Carrie fetched an enamel bowl from the wash-house, setting it on the cloth then tipping water into it from the kettle steaming on the hob.

''E said 'e would pop into the works to check things was all right an' then come straight 'ome.' Fetching potatoes from a bucket kept under the sink, she tipped them from her apron into the bowl of water. ''E won't be long, me wench, try not to feel too bad.'

Reaching into a drawer set into the table, she took out a knife, its blade broken off some four inches from the handle, and set about peeling the potatoes.

'I'll get these outta the way an' then I'll make we both a nice cup of tea.'

Carrie carried on her one-sided conversation but Esther heard nothing save the drum roll of repetition: Miri is dead, Miri is dead.

Taking the bowl with peelings and dirty water to the midden pit at the back of the houses, Carrie turned at the approach of a neighbour.

'Mornin', Carrie wench.' Alice Perry threw her own vegetable peelings into the midden.

'Mornin'.' Carrie swished a hand around her bowl, scraping out the few strips of peel still clinging stubbornly to the sides.

'You be with visitors?' Alice gave an enquiring look.

'Arrh.' Carrie began to walk back to the house.

'I could see you was.' Taken unaware by Carrie's abrupt movement Alice had to take a couple of quick steps before she fell in beside her again. 'I seen that trap up against the wash-house and that 'orse tethered up by the brook. Be somebody to see yer Adam, be it?'

Disappointed by the set of Carrie's mouth, and knowing her neighbour's last word on the subject of her visitor had been said, Alice took a new tangent.

''Ave you 'eard about the fire over James Bridge way?'

'What fire be that?' Carrie allowed herself to be drawn on something the whole of Darlaston would know by this time.

'Last night sometime.' Alice looked pleased her story had found a new ear. 'Somebody set fire to the copper.'

'You mean somebody burned Cosmore's foundry?' Carrie congratulated herself. She sounded as shocked as if she were hearing it for the first time.

'Arrh, in the night sometime. Burned it to the ground so my 'Arry be told.' Reaching the communal wash-house, Alice waited hopefully for the regular invitation to drink a cup of tea.

'Do they know who done it?'

'Not yet.' Alice smiled, showing a row of teeth that looked as if they had been planted in soil. 'But the bobbies be on to it. Mind you, Carrie, that lot be too 'alf-soaked to catch cold, never mind the ones as set that fire.'

'Was anybody 'urt?' Carrie asked. It would never do to ask too few questions in Foleys Croft, especially about such a happening as the copper going up in flames.

'Old Jake Timmins seems to 'ave 'ad a knock on the 'ead but 'pears it ain't done 'im a deal of 'arm.'

'Thank the Lord for that.'

'I says Amen an' all, Carrie.' Alice glanced hopefully at the door leading to her neighbour's scullery. 'But seems they weren't satisfied with just burnin' the copper,' she said swiftly as Carrie stepped towards it. 'They made a bonfire of old Cosmore's 'ouse.'

'Never!' She kept up the charade.

'True as I be standin' 'ere.' Alice folded her arms, the bottom of her bowl tapping against her left hip, tiny circles of brown water spreading a line across her apron. 'Seems the 'ole lot of 'em was burnt to a cinder.'

'You mean there was folk inside?' Carrie's eyes grew suitably wide.

'A dozen at least, an' that wi'out Evan Gittins an' Dolly Foster.'

'The Lord rest 'em!' Carrie crossed herself. 'Dear God, what do folk in this town be thinkin' of to burn a man's 'ouse over 'is 'ead?'

'They likely be thinkin' to give Cosmore a taste of what that family 'ave dished out to the folk of Darlaston for many a year. An' more power to 'em be what Alice Perry says.'

'I will pop round this afternoon.' Carrie stepped determinedly inside her scullery. 'I'll take a cup o' tea wi' you. You might know more by that time.'

Arrh, could be I will, Alice thought, turning to her own house, but it won't be from you, you tight-gobbed bugger!

Washing the potatoes she had peeled, Carrie put them in an iron pot blackened from regular use over an open fire then carried them into the kitchen. Hanging the pot on the bracket, she swung it over the glowing coals then used the broken-bladed knife to hack a lump of salt from a block she took from a cupboard beside the fireplace, dropping it in with the potatoes.

Turning her attention to brewing a pot of tea, she glanced at Esther. The girl had not so much as moved an eyelid since Adam had carried her down the stairs that morning. It was proper to grieve, it was nature's consolation, but holding grief inside you, refusing to let it surface as she was, was not the way.

'Take a little tea, Mrs Cosmore.' Carrie placed her one china cup and saucer in front of Esther. 'It be like to do you good.'

Taking her own heavy platter mug, she carried it to the stool set in the corner of the fireplace, putting it on the hob as a knock sounded on the door.

'Adam told me I would find Mrs Cosmore 'ere,' Sam Evans said as she opened it.

'That be right, lad.' Carrie stepped aside in unspoken invitation for him to enter. Closing the door, she set the worn blanket that served as a curtain against draughts in place and turned to Sam. 'Y'ave seen Adam?'

He nodded. ''E were up at Addenbrooke.'

''E told you?'

Sam nodded again. ''E said . . .'

He paused, Carrie's warning shake of her head telling him to be careful what he repeated.

''E said that 'e 'ad fetched Mrs Cosmore to you an' that I should come to make sure you was both all right.'

Carrie nodded. It was not what Sam had been on the verge of saying. Now her look told him they understood each other.

'Is there anything I can do, Mrs Paige?'

'Arrh, lad.' Carrie was already stirring sugar into a second mug. 'You can get this tea down you an' then you 'ad best go see to that 'orse afore the kids round 'ere kills the poor beast with kindness. But mind,' she mouthed the last, 'don't say nothin' about 'er.'

Sam nodded, acknowledging the sideways shift of Carrie's eyes towards Esther.

"Ow be that babby of yours, Sam?' Carrie asked, unwilling for silence to settle on the tiny kitchen.

"E be a right little boster, Mrs Paige, an' bright an' all. You should see the way 'e grabs a pot.'

'Takin' after 'is granddad then. 'E be famous for the way 'e can grab a pot of ale.'

'Arrh.' Sam returned Carrie's smile. 'Me dad ain't never let one slip yet.' Drinking off his tea, Sam replaced the mug on the table, taking his cap from the pocket he had stuffed it in when entering the kitchen. 'I'll be away to Queenie then, Mrs Paige.'

'There'll be a bite of something 'ere for you to eat once you be finished.'

'Thanks, Mrs Paige.'

Gathering Sam's mug with her own, Carrie looked at Esther whose fingers were still clasped together then took her untouched cup, placing it alongside the mugs on a piece of board that did duty as a tray. There was nothing to be done but wait. The girl would speak in her own time.

It was mid-afternoon before Adam returned. After satisfying himself that Esther was showing no sign of physical harm, he washed before sitting down at the kitchen table.

'Sam Evans come earlier.' Carrie laid the plate of boiled potatoes and neck of mutton in front of him.

'Yes, I asked him to. Is he still here?'

'No.' Carrie went back to her stool beside the fireplace. 'He said the mare needed oats and hay, grass alone be not enough, so he took 'er back to the stable. Says to tell you 'e will be back 'ere in a couple of hours in case you 'ave need of 'im.'

'Has Mrs Cosmore eaten?' Adam glanced at her fingers, ceaselessly winding and unwinding.

'Not took a thing.' Carrie gave a shake of her head. 'Not so much as a drop of tea. But I won't be 'avin' you doing the same!' she added sharply as Adam pushed his plate away. 'You will be of no 'elp to 'er if you let yer strength sap.'

'That's the worst of it for me, Mother, I can't help her. I can run her business for her but I can't help *her.*'

Carrie's heart swelled with pain as she watched him drop his head into his hands. He meant he could not take that girl into his arms, could not ease her grief with his lips and his body, could not share her sorrow in the way a man would want to share with the woman he loved.

'I know you care for 'er, son,' she said softly. 'I know you 'ave feelin's that must remain unspoken. You might not think it now with yer 'eart in the turmoil it be in but you be 'elping 'er, you be the only one 'er can depend on. An' though 'er might not show it, 'er knows it; deep inside, 'er knows you won't go lettin' 'er down.'

'Oh, God!' He moaned softly like a child in pain. 'Oh, God, what can I do!'

Going to him, Carrie touched his shoulder. 'Only what you be doin' already. Watch 'er with yer eyes, love 'er with yer 'eart, an' keep yer sorrow a secret in yer soul.'

'I have to go back, Adam, I have been here with your mother for almost a week.'

'You can't go back there, the place is almost a ruin.'

'Nevertheless I must return, Adam, there are things still to be done.'

'Tell me what they are and I will do them.'

'Son,' Carrie Paige intervened gently, 'the only way to banish a fear be to confront it. Mrs Cosmore needs to see the place for 'erself if 'er is to overcome her fear of that night.' She looked at him, eyes full of meaning. ''Er 'as to come face to face with 'er sorrow, same as you will each 'ave to come face to face with our own.'

'Your mother is right, Adam, I have to go back to Addenbrooke.' Esther turned to Carrie. 'Thank you for your kindness, Mrs Paige, I really am most grateful.'

'No bother, me wench.' Carrie smiled. 'If you finds you can't be puttin' up with bein' in that 'ouse, then you come back 'ere to me.'

'I will see if Sam has the trap ready,' Adam said wearily.

Waiting until her son was clear of the scullery, Carrie took Esther's hands between her own. 'Mrs Cosmore . . . Esther,' she said softly, 'you can trust my lad. 'E don't be of yer class but 'e be a gentleman all the same. 'E won't do you down, an' whatever 'e says 'e will stick to it. But there be one thing 'e won't never be able to say so it be up to me to say it for 'im. My son loves you, Esther, 'e loves you deep an' that be the truth of it.'

Looking at Adam's mother, her brown eyes velvety with tears, Esther smiled. 'There is no division of class between Adam and me, and as for trust – I have trusted him from the first and will always do so, just as I will always return his love.'

Carrie kissed her cheek, whispering, 'The world 'as dealt you some bitter blows, me wench, but 'ave faith in the Lord. 'E 'as a way of turnin' things round when it 'pears to 'Im a body 'as suffered enough.'

After watching Adam lift Esther into the trap then walk beside Sam across the heath toward Katherine's Cross, Carrie turned back into the house, shutting the door on the enquiring looks of the folk of Foleys Croft.

'Did none of it escape?' Esther stared at the smoke-blackened walls, at the leprous spots of paint clinging to what was left of window frames and doorway.

'The front got the worst of it.' Adam turned as Sam halted the mare. 'The wind must have changed, blowing the flames in this direction before they reached the kitchen. That part of the house is unscathed apart from a few scorch marks on the door that closes it off from the passage.'

Waiting for Adam's nod, Sam continued to lead the horse around to the rear of the house then opened the door of the staff entrance for Adam to carry her through. 'I'll be in the stable, call when you be ready.'

'Have . . . have you been through the rest of the house?'

'I went through with the constable.'

'The constable!' Esther looked up as Adam settled her into a chair. 'The police have been here?'

'They had to come, Esther,' he said. 'A death always has to be investigated.'

A death! She felt the ache sweep through her. Miri had died in the fire.

'Do they know how it happened, what caused the house to burn?'

'Seems probable it was coals falling from the fire in the front sitting room.' Adam knew it was not the truth, but then again the men who had thrown those torches were never likely to be named so why add to her misery by speaking of them?

'But Mr Gittins and the others?'

'Safe, as I told you. Gittins is with his brother, Mrs Foster was visiting her sister and Peggy had gone home as she did every night. Look, Esther, being here is only making you unhappy. Please come back to Foleys Croft, at least until you can find another house.'

'I will not be looking for another house, Adam.' She glanced around the spacious kitchen. 'I am going to stay here.'

'You can't do that!' He frowned. 'You can't live here with the house in this state.'

'There is nothing wrong with the kitchen.' Esther met his glance calmly.

'You can't live in a kitchen!'

'Why not? Other women in Darlaston do, and theirs not a fraction the size of this.'

'Esther, please be sensible.'

'That is what I am being.'

'Not by proposing to live in the kitchen of a burned out house you're not!' Adam threw up his hands as he looked around. 'You could buy yourself a house tomorrow. Maybe not the size of Addenbrooke, but you could buy one. The business would stand it. So why stay here?'

'Adam, sit down and hear me out.' Waiting while he drew a chair closer to hers, Esther went on, 'Staying here is the sensible thing to do. Morgan knows my father would not give me the money to buy a house and he knows I have received nothing from him or his father since living here so if I buy another house he is immediately going to ask where the money came from. And how long do you think it would be before he found out? When he did he would also know that, with Miri's death, I no longer have her name to hide behind. I am named as sole beneficiary in her will and under the law that makes my property Morgan's. He would be entitled to take everything and would do so.

'And that, Adam, would be the end of my hopes for this town. He would sell it all off, little by little, until there was nothing left. But I won't let that happen! I will not let Morgan Cosmore take what I have built, not if it means living in a pit shaft on the heath.'

'I understand,' Adam said, worry darkening his eyes. 'But to live here . . .'

'Adam.' Esther leaned forward to touch his hand. 'If I leave here now, where do you think I would be living in twelve months' time?'

She was right, he thought. Her father had turned her away, and as for Cosmore – what thought had he given to her, spending every minute away from home as he did?

'This is the sensible way, Adam,' she continued. 'I have to keep Morgan believing I have nothing of my own, and the only way to do that is to stay on here.'

'I know you are right but you cannot stay alone. I shall sleep in the loft above the stable.'

'No, Adam, you must not stay here,' she said quickly. 'It would just cause gossip.'

'Then let it!' He stood up with a swift, almost angry movement. 'If folk want to talk, they will talk.'

'Yes,' Esther followed with her eyes as he moved restlessly about the room, 'but why add to that talk? Why give them the chance to see harm where there is none?' And why give Roberta Vance the chance to add to her lies? she thought.

'In that case you must get a woman to stay with you.' He turned to look at her, a half smile on his face. 'Though where you will get one to sleep with a horse, I don't know. That sort of woman is hard to find even in Darlaston.'

'She won't have to sleep in the stable.' Esther was glad to see the glimmer of a smile on his mouth after the sorrow of the past week.

'Then where?'

'Miri . . .' She paused, the sense of loss sweeping over her as it had so often since that fire. 'Miri told me that Mr Gittins sometimes slept in a room off this one.'

Doubt clear on his face, Adam went through a door in a corner of the large kitchen, coming back moments later. 'Miri told you true. There is a bed in there besides a table and a couple of armchairs. In fact, Gittins had furnished himself quite an acceptable room. But you still need one more place to put a bed.'

'What about the store room? There can't be a lot in there judging by the way Ezra ran his house. If it were cleared it should quite happily take a small bed.'

'You are determined to stay in this house, aren't you?'

'Yes, Adam.' Esther's iron hard resolve was unmasked by her softly spoken words. 'I am determined to stay.'

'You have been living here, in the kitchen?'

'My rooms were damaged in the fire and I had to live somewhere.' Esther met the green-gold eyes calmly. Morgan had arrived an hour ago and had gone through the burned out rooms of his childhood home, his rage increasing with every step.

'You should have returned to your father,' he said sharply, 'not set up home in the servants' quarters.'

'I was taken to my father but he refused to allow me to stay at Rowena.'

'Taken?' Roberta Vance returned from an inspection of the two makeshift bedrooms. 'You were taken to your father's house . . . by whom?'

To refuse to answer would appear suspicious and she could not say the person who had taken her to the Leys that night was Sam for Morgan might call him from the stable to question him.

Seeing the silent laughter in those deep violet eyes Esther saw Roberta Vance already knew who it was who had accompanied her on the night of the blaze.

'Mr Paige rescued me,' she said, catching the gleam of triumph in those watchful eyes. 'He took me to my father's house.'

'And when your father refused to have you . . .' The curiously deep voice washed over Esther like a douche of cold water, raising a shiver along her spine.

'. . . where did Mr Paige take you then?'

Esther glanced at Morgan but he seemed little interested in the exchange, going instead to the wine cellar.

'To the home of Mr Gittins's brother.'

Roberta moved from the dresser to the table, brushing the tips of fuchsia-gloved fingers together as if removing dust. 'Oh, yes.' She raised her eyes. 'The butler . . . if one could charitably call him by the title. And did this brother of his take you in?'

'There was no room, the house was very small . . .'

'And the family very large,' Roberta cut in, smiling. 'How wonderfully convenient. So where did Mr Paige take you next?'

The woman was almost beautiful, Esther thought, looking at the sensual mouth, a tiny brown mole to the left of it, and the fine-boned face crowned by gleaming black hair, but there was an evil behind the beauty, a venom beneath the mock concern, a poison she would use without compunction if it served her.

'He took me to his mother's home.' A quick triumphal lift of the head told her the woman had heard what she wanted to hear.

'He's still living there himself, of course?'

Esther didn't answer. Roberta Vance would fill in the missing parts for herself, adding as many embellishments as suited her.

'He didn't leave a lot in there.' Morgan emerged from the cellar, brushing at his knee-length chocolate-coloured coat.

'Your father did not take delivery of any wine for some time,' Esther told her husband.

'That is obvious. Half a dozen bottles of cheap claret is all that is down there. Why the hell didn't he pay his bills!'

Could it be because he spent most of his fortune on you? She asked the question silently the bitterness of it coating her tongue. Morgan was showing more feeling over the lack of a few bottles of wine than he had over his father's death.

'There is nothing left in the place that would fetch more than a few pounds.' He swept a hand through his bronze-coloured hair then across his face, removing traces of a cobweb.

'Except for this part.' The violet eyes stayed on Esther. 'But of course your wife is living here, is she not?'

'Until my husband finds us another home.'

A slight tightening of the other woman's mouth told Esther this answer had found her sore spot. It had never been a part of Esther's nature to rejoice at another's discomfort but in the face of Roberta Vance's she felt a distinct pleasure.

'Of course.' Roberta turned away, her fuchsia taffeta skirts rustling on the flagged floor as she crossed to Morgan, brushing a proprietorial hand across the shoulder of his coat, sweeping away a smudge of grey dust. 'You must buy another house, Morgan, Esther cannot remain here.'

'I will not be able to buy anything until the copper foundry is sold,' he answered, 'or unless Kerral comes up with that thousand pounds he reckons not to have – though that's a lie. He thinks to get out of paying, but pay he will. If I have to beat it out of him.'

So he had been to her father for money. Esther saw the anger in his face. And of course her father had no money. Kerral and Cosmore had both played the same game and neither had won.

'But I was told the copper works had been burned to the ground?'

'It was only thanks to their stupidity it was not!' Morgan returned curtly.

'I don't understand.' Esther frowned. 'Do you mean the copper works was not burned down?'

'Fortunately not. A few oily rags and a little paper collected in heaps on the floor blazed for a time, but no real damage was caused. A morning's clearing up and there will be no trace of the fire's having taken place. Whoever tried to destroy the place hadn't enough sense to realise it would take more than rags and paper to burn a foundry.'

'Do you really intend to sell?' Esther asked. 'Do you think that was the cause of what happened?'

Satisfied that the last of the cobwebs were gone from his clothes, Morgan stopped his brushing and looked at her. 'Of course,' he said. 'The men must have got wind of the fact and thought they would be out of a job so they took their revenge.'

'And would they have been?'

'Quite possibly, but who cares?'

Not you, Esther thought, watching the shadows of contempt play across in his eyes. The idea of men having no means to support their families worries you not at all.

'The buyer is still interested, isn't he?' It was Roberta who put the question.

'Patrick Lacy assured me he was when he contacted me to tell me of the fire. He said signing is to take place this afternoon.'

'There you are.' The woman turned triumphantly to Esther.

'Tomorrow Morgan will have the money to buy another house and you will no longer have to live in servants' quarters.'

'I will look around the area tomorrow.' Morgan walked to the door. He opened it and held out a hand to Roberta, elegantly gowned as usual, a feathered hat perched on her glossy black hair. 'Meanwhile, my dear, we must leave now if I am to keep the appointment in Lacy's office.'

He had not mentioned the death of Miri though he must have been told of it. Esther listened to the noise of his carriage die away. Nor had he asked if she had anyone living here with her, though doubtless Roberta Vance had thought of it. Leaning back in the new wooden wheelchair Adam had had made for her, Esther closed her eyes, a sudden weariness flooding over her. A new home, was that what she wanted? Morgan had not asked and she did not care. One home was as empty as another for Morgan Cosmore's wife.

Chapter Nineteen

'You sure you will be all right on yer own, Mrs Cosmore?' Peggy Deeley fastened the buttons of her grey coat.

'Of course I will.' Esther smiled at the girl. 'You go along to your mother's.'

'Well, 'er does like to see me,' Peggy said, pulling a flower-covered hat that was a cast off of Dolly Foster's on to her head and sticking it with a long hat pin. 'An' since I've been livin' in . . .' She broke off to look hesitantly at Esther.

'Of course she likes to see you,' Esther reassured her. 'It was quite a wrench for your mother, letting you take over from Mrs Foster, so it's understandable her wanting to visit when you can. Now off you go and don't forget to tell your mother how grateful I am that you did come, Peggy, and also how marvellously you are managing.'

And she was coping very well, thought Esther, listening to the girl's light quick footsteps cross the yard. She had been surprised when Dolly Foster had said she did not wish to return to her post as cook-housekeeper at Addenbrooke, even though with the house as it was there was little to do. She was starting a small business, she had said, in partnership with Gittins. They had taken a lease on a property on the Bull Stake where it joined the Wednesbury Road; with the trams coming and going from there they expected a brisk trade for their pie shop, Dolly said. Though she was sorry to be leaving, she and Mr Gittins had planned this for a long time, and, well . . . this seemed the proper time. But she had recommended

Peggy, telling Esther she was 'a good wench', and she had been justified in her faith. Peggy Deeley worked hard and willingly and her perpetual good humour was a bonus.

Esther listened to the silence all around her. It had been three days since Morgan had said he was to sign a deed of sale for the foundry, three days in which he had not contacted her. Was he still looking for a new home to which to take her?

She glanced at the row of copper pans adorning one wall, at the large pine dresser set with crockery taking up half of another, at the long range that Peggy kept gleaming like a huge black jewel, and felt a twinge of remorse. She had come to feel comfortable at Addenbrooke. Leaving it would be harder than she thought.

But was her regret at leaving this house due to how comfortable she had come to feel in it, or was it because this was where she saw Adam? This was the one place they were ever alone and that was what she feared losing.

Hearing his now familiar tap at the door, she smiled as Adam entered the kitchen. Since Esther had returned here he had checked with Sam every night that all was well, then had come into the house, insisting she walk a few steps at least.

'I saw Peggy as I came across the heath.' He came to the fire, holding out his hands to the glow. 'She isn't staying out for the night, is she?'

'No.' Esther watched him rub his hands before the heat of the glowing coals. The broad set of his shoulders, the dark hair left to tumble across his brow, the slow smile that creased the skin around his charcoal dark eyes – she loved them all. 'She will be back around ten. And before you say anything about her crossing the heath alone at night, her brothers escort her.'

'I'm glad to hear one woman has a smattering of sense.' He turned to face her. 'Not pretending she will be perfectly all right on her own, like someone not a hundred miles from me right now.'

'Why, Mr Paige, are you referring to me?' Esther smiled,

loving the ease that had grown between them since the night of the fire.

'Now why would I think that of you?' he teased, his smile matching her own.

'Adam,' Esther asked, serious once more, 'have you heard any news of the copper foundry? Has it changed hands?'

'Morgan hasn't told you?'

Esther shook her head.

'He has not been back since he told you of the meeting Lacy had arranged? He has made no further mention of getting you a decent place to live?' Adam's eyes darkened. 'I would not put it past him to take the money and run, leaving you here.'

'So the foundry *has* changed ownership?'

'Yes.' Anger making a hard line of his mouth, Adam smashed one fist against the iron range. 'And every man who had a job there sacked the next day. Cosmore is a heartless, self-centred swine. God, I could break his bloody neck!'

All those men. Esther felt the familiar tide of pity begin to rise within her. And all those women and children who would soon be without food.

'Can't we help?' she asked.

'Not by employing the men who were sacked,' Adam replied shaking his head. 'The works have as many hands as we can use, and though the demand for nuts and bolts grows by the week, to extend again would stretch you beyond your limit.'

'I feel so sorry for those families,' Esther said.

'So do I but there is nothing you can do. Had it been another few months, you probably could have.' He looked at her. 'Don't go brooding on it, Esther, that won't do any good either. Now,' he smiled, hoping to change the subject, 'how many steps did you take last night?'

'Eight.' Her face brightened. 'It felt so wonderful, Adam. To stand by myself was fantastic enough but actually to walk eight steps . . . oh, I can't find a word to express how I felt. I just know "wonderful" is not enough.'

'Eight!' He nodded, something more than congratulations lighting his eyes. 'That is good going.'

'The callipers you made for me help so much, their support gives me confidence.'

She glanced towards her feet, resting on the footboard of her chair, hiding the truth that was in her eyes. The callipers he had fitted to her shoes lent support to her legs but it was not those strips of steel which had given her confidence. That had come from him; from his strength and from the love she bore for him.

He held out his hands, dark eyes smiling into hers. 'Then let us make that eight into eighteen.'

Esther looked up. 'I think I told you once before, Adam Paige, you are a hard taskmaster.' But she put her hands in his.

'Fifteen . . . sixteen.' Adam stepped backward, keeping always within reach of her but never touching. 'Nearly there, Esther. Try . . .' He saw the effort of every step in her face. A stumble erased a little more of her colour and he knew he was pushing her but still he went on, his voice firm, encouraging.

'I can't, Adam.' She looked at him, her mouth tight with strain. 'I can't!'

He remained still, his arms outstretched but out of reach of her hands. Somewhere in the room a clock ticked its slow measured beat. 'Come to me, Esther,' he said softly. 'Come to me, my love.'

Morgan let the reins lie slack in his hands, his mind on Roberta. The money he had been paid for the copper works would last them barely a couple of years, she had said, and though he was loath to admit it, he knew her words to be true. Roberta liked the high style, both in England and on the Continent; she liked living well and would continue to do so, if not with him then with someone else. Roberta was never short of admirers, among them plenty of the sort who had the kind of money she craved and who were willing to spend it.

A peewit rose from the heath, disturbed by the horse's hooves, calling indignantly to its mate, but Morgan remained unaware of his disturbance of their tiny lives.

The money would not be enough, Roberta had said, and she was right. He needed more, and before he returned he would have more. Josiah Kerral had agreed to pay the sum of one thousand pounds a year for Morgan's marrying his daughter and that was what he was going to pay!

The horse shied nervously as the peewit swooped inches above its head. Morgan gathered the slack reins more tightly, speaking softly to the animal he had hired from stables adjacent to the Great Western Hotel where he and Roberta had a room.

He looked away across the rough open land towards the tall chimneys of the many factories, each belching a cloud of thick black smoke that dyed the sky pewter grey, lying like a veil all along the rim of the horizon. It would have been quicker taking the usual route to the Bull Stake then passing through the cemetery on to Leys Heath but that way he would have to pass those men who had stood the line and not been chosen for a day's work, and many of those would be the ones sacked from the copper works. Passing them could lead to an unpleasant confrontation. Morgan knew the men of Darlaston, knew their tempers were swiftly raised and dampened with difficulty, especially when their employment had been taken from them and given to others from a different town.

There had been fights and riots at James Bridge, so he had heard, and one or two Walsall men had gone home with broken bones.

Gaining the edge of Butcroft Heath he encouraged the horse as it picked its way over the tram lines and into Gordon Street. Passing the park, he raised his hat, acknowledging the nods of several matrons engaged on an afternoon's expedition to hear the town band play in the small flower-ringed bandstand.

'Damn!' he muttered, seeing a small group of men collected at the end of Victoria Road. They had obviously been drinking in the White Swan public house and now they turned at the sound of the horse's hooves.

'Well, if it ain't young Mr Cosmore!'

A thick heavy-set man, side whiskers running to his jawline, stepped into the road.

''Ow nice of you to come visitin'. We was 'oping you wouldn't leave afore we could thank you for takin' our jobs, weren't we, lads?'

The horse took several skittish steps backward, droplets of moisture spraying from its nostrils.

'Get out of my way!' Morgan ordered, bringing his plaited leather riding crop into full view across the animal's mane.

'Or you'll do what? Cane my bottom like a naughty schoolboy?' The thick-set man laughed, a vicious, half-crazy sound. 'You'll need more than that bloody 'obby 'orse whip to do it with.'

Holding the fretful horse with one hand, Morgan half raised the whip. 'I have warned you,' he said, 'I will not do so again.'

'Hear that, lads?' The man turned to his watching companions. ''Is lordship 'ere won't tell we a second time.' He turned back to Morgan as the group burst out laughing, ripping off his grease-stained jacket and throwing it to the ground. 'Well, just you let me tell you,' he snarled, reaching beefy arms towards Morgan, 'I for one don't need no second tellin'. An' when I be done with you, you won't 'ave no tongue to be tellin' anybody anythin'.'

'Get back!' Morgan brought the plaited leather down hard across the bare arms, causing the man to bellow from the sting of it.

'Why, you bloody shite hawk!' The whiskered face turned scarlet, eyes blazing with fury. 'I'm going to kick yer arse into yer ear'oles!'

'Gerrim, Jake.' One of the onlookers, trousers held at the

waist by a broad heavy-buckled belt and tied about the ankles with string, waved a heavy fist. 'Rip 'is balls off an' shove 'em up 'is arse!'

Lips white and set tight, Morgan raised the whip again and again, striking his would-be assailant on the head and arms, but still he came on.

'Go on, Jake, get the bastard!'

Encouragement in the form of a shove from another of his drunken cronies sent Jake stumbling against the horse and as the animal shied he caught at Morgan, dragging him from the saddle.

'I'm gonna bloody kill you,' he shouted, beery saliva and sweat running down his chin. 'You won't sell no more men outta their jobs.'

'That'll be enough of that talk, Jake Gaskin.'

The words followed two shrill blasts of a whistle as Morgan hit the ground with a thump.

'We all know how you be feelin', 'avin' no job an' all, but we can't 'ave no cussin' an' swearin' in the streets.'

Buttons gleaming in the autumn sun, truncheon swinging pointedly in his hand, a uniformed constable elbowed through the group who had formed a circle about the two men sprawled on the floor.

'Leave it, Jake!' The policeman spoke sharply as the man raised his fist above Morgan's face. 'Remember the last time? The magistrate sent you along the line for five years. You strike that one you be kneelin' on and like as not you'll go down for ten, 'im being a gentleman like.' He stepped up to the crimson-faced man, placing a hand on his shoulder. 'Let it go, Jake. It ain't worth seein' yer Lettie struggle on 'er own for ten years, just for the pleasure of giving a man a few bumps an' bruises.'

'I'll give 'im more than that, Bill Bootle,' Jake growled, still holding fast to Morgan. 'I'll break every bloody bone in 'is body!'

'Then I'll 'ave to break a couple of yers, Jake.' The truncheon swung, making a soft swishing sound as it disturbed the air. 'An' that will be painful for you if not for me. Now, do like I say an' let the man be, an' let's hope he is grateful for yer 'elping 'im up after he fell off his horse.'

Squinting up at the constable, truncheon still in his hand, Jake scrambled to his feet. 'You be right, Bill,' he muttered. 'Old Cosmore's spawn don't be worth it. But I reckon it would be ten years well spent if I could see 'im dead!'

'Be that as it may,' Bill Bootle raised his voice as the ring of men around them muttered their approval, 'you won't be seeing 'im dead on my beat. Now, all of you, get yerselves away out of it afore I gets me book out. There be laws against effin' and blindin' on a public highway same as there is against causing a disturbance to the King's peace.'

'The King 'as a bloody job!' a woman who had paused to watch the commotion shouted from the edge of the group. 'Same as you 'ave one, Bill Bootle.'

'Arrh, I 'ave a job.' The constable looked at the woman, a knitted shawl draped over her head and around beneath her breasts. 'And I mean to do it, Lizzie Noon, no matter whether it be arresting a man or a woman.'

'Oh, arrh!' The woman laughed mockingly. 'Well, you make sure my Paddy don't be at 'ome if you calls at our 'ouse or you'll find yerself carryin' yer balls 'ome in yer 'andkerchief.'

Ignoring the shouts of laughter as the woman turned away, Constable Bootle helped Morgan to his feet.

'I trust you ain't injured, sir,' he said as Morgan brushed the dirt of the street from his expensive dove grey coat. 'These cobbled streets don't be suited to horses. They lose their footing. A man is easily thrown, especially if it rains.'

Accepting his hat, retrieved from the street after being trodden out of shape by a carefully aimed foot, Morgan glared at the policeman.

'My horse did not stumble,' he said acidly, 'and I was not thrown. I was dragged from the saddle by that . . . that fool!'

'Arrh, I be a fool all right.' Jake stepped forward menacingly. 'A fool to listen to Bill Bootle when I could be throttling the daylights out of you. Well, I can still do it and to hell with the magistrate and his ten bloody years!'

'Jake!' The truncheon came down sharply on his right forearm. 'There be nothing more you can do to 'elp this gentleman so you best be on yer way.' Glancing again at Morgan, the constable went on: 'Lucky Jake was 'ere to be of assistance to you, Mr Cosmore. I'm sure you be grateful but like as not you will want to be on yer way, so we'll take yer thanks as said, shall we?'

Snatching the reins from a man who had thought to hold on to the horse, Morgan swung into the saddle. Antagonising these men further would get him nothing but a severe beating, and the subsequent prosecution would be a lengthy process he did not want to be bothered with. Pulling the horse's head sharply to the right, he laid the whip to its flank, sending it trotting rapidly past the church of St Lawrence then clattering along the narrow New Street, allowing it its head as they reached Leys Heath and headed for Rowena House.

'I will tell the master you are here, Mr Cosmore.'

William Evans discreetly ignored the traces of dried mud still visible on Morgan's clothing. It was possible there had been a rumpus in the town and he had been involved – not surprisingly when you thought how many men were hanging about the streets with nothing better to do than dream of giving Morgan Cosmore a hiding. Evans smiled grimly to himself. The pity of it was that he had escaped seemingly without hurt.

Opening a pair of double doors, he stepped inside the drawing room. 'Mr Morgan Cosmore asks to see you, sir.'

Looking up sharply from the newspaper he was reading, Jos Kerral's already bad temper degenerated even further.

'Oh, does 'e?' The newspaper crumpled to the floor, its pages crushed like the wings of a giant butterfly. 'Well, I don't want to see 'im. So you can tell 'im to bugger off an' not to call 'ere again.'

Pushing past the butler whom he had followed, Morgan strode into a room he had seen only once before – the room in which he had married Esther Kerral.

'I will be happy to leave, and much happier not to return, but that will only be when you have paid your debt.'

'What bloody debt?' Jos roared as Evans withdrew, closing the doors after him.

'You know very well what debt.' Still angry from the tussle in Victoria Road, Morgan swiped his short riding crop against his boot. 'You owe me one thousand pounds and I am here to collect it.'

'Then you 'ave had a wasted journey. I've told you before, you'll get no more money outta me!'

The whip slapped against Morgan's boot, leather against leather, a harsh and ominous sound.

'And I told you, Kerral, if you were wise you would have that money waiting for me when next we met. I hope for your sake you were indeed wise – wise enough to take heed of my words.' Morgan's voice was soft but a threat lay beneath it.

'Yer words!' Jos spat, rising to his feet. 'Yer words won't get you what I don't 'ave!'

'I married your daughter,' Morgan said, every syllable gritted against his clenched teeth. 'I took your cripple in exchange for a yearly payment of one thousand pounds and that you are going to pay!'

'How?' Jos folded his hands beneath his coat tails, head thrust forward. 'How can I pay you a thousand pounds when I would count myself wealthy if I had a thousand 'alfpennies? I tell you, Cosmore, there be no money. The wheel and axle business has been going under for five years. I thought to save it by marryin' you and the girl. It were my belief Ezra would put money into it sooner than see it die altogether, but it turned out 'e had little more than me.'

'There is always this house.' Morgan swept a glance around

the room with its tasteful furnishings. 'This has to be worth a pretty penny.'

'Oh, it be worth a penny or two,' Jos agreed, his own glance ranging around the room. 'But them pennies don't belong to me, they be the bank's. This house was put up as collateral against a loan that bought back the shares you sold off. I had to pay above the odds to secure 'em, so you might as well forget about gettin' money that way.'

'And the furnishings?' Morgan questioned, following Jos as he strode out of the house and into the stable yard where a young lad stood holding the bridle of a cob harnessed to a carriage.

'Same as the building,' Jos threw back over his shoulder. 'Every stick of it belongs to the bank!'

'Then you must sell the works.'

Jos stopped in his tracks and turned slowly, his face livid with rage.

'Sell the works!' he snarled. 'Sell the business I've poured my life into, to pass the money over to a bloody little jumped up snot who ain't never done a day's work in 'is life? I'll see you rot in hell first!'

'A bargain is a bargain, Kerral,' Morgan said, his green-gold eyes blazing with cold fire.

'Arrh, and some bargains be better than others. Seems you struck a bad 'un.'

'You believe that and you'll be making a bigger mistake than you did when you signed half your business over to me,' Morgan ground out through lips white with anger. 'I took a cripple in order to get that money . . .'

'Arrh, you took 'er,' Jos shouted, 'and now you must bloody well keep 'er. Ain't no use yer comin' snivelling to me for money. If I was up to my neck in gold sovereigns, I wouldn't give you a bent farthing. You're like yer father. You thought to take what another man had earned but you thought wrong. It didn't work. At least Ezra were man enough to accept his losses, while you . . . pah!' He spat contemptuously.

'Yes, Ezra was a man, more of one than you will ever be for all your talk of pouring your life into iron and steel. I might not have been my father's ideal son but at least he faced up to his responsibility for me. While you . . . you took the coward's way out. You saw what you had begot and turned your back on it. You threw a crippled child out of your home and out of your life until it suited you to fob her off on another man. Nobody can say of you "At least Jos Kerral was a man" because you are not. You are nothing but a cheat and a coward.'

'You bastard!' Jos bellowed, lunging to grab the other man's throat. 'You bloody, spineless bastard. I'll kill you!'

Stepping sideways, Morgan raised the plaited riding crop, bringing it down hard across Jos's face as he rushed forward then using both hands to push against his chest, sending him reeling backwards.

Arms flailing in an attempt to prevent himself from falling, Jos staggered back, hitting the horse's shoulder. Screaming in fear, the cob reared itself on stocky hind legs, a flailing front hoof catching his master on the back and spinning him to the ground. As Jos fell beneath him the cob bolted, rolling the wheels of the heavy carriage over his body.

'Mr Kerral!' the frightened stable lad called, bending over his fallen master. But Josiah Kerral made no move.

Roberta Vance stepped from the hansom she had hired at the railway station and, telling the driver to wait, walked into the office of Patrick Lacy.

A gold Albert spread across his grandiloquent chest, the solicitor rose at her entry, bright eyes darting appreciatively over her well-dressed curves.

'Good afternoon,' he greeted her, drawing a crown-back chair up to his littered desk.

'Good afternoon, Mr Lacy,' she purred. 'I am Roberta Vance, a friend of Mr Morgan Cosmore who has asked me to call on his behalf. And I am so glad that he did.'

Her eyes speaking volumes he avidly read, Patrick Lacy ran his tongue over his lips, moistening their dryness. She had not called at his office merely to make an appointment for Morgan Cosmore. This woman wanted something more than that and was prepared to pay with other currency than sovereigns. Curbing the excitement already twisting in his stomach, he returned to his chair behind the desk.

'It is my pleasure to receive you.' He smiled, lowering his heavy frame into the winged leather chair.

'It could be a pleasure for both of us.'

Her voice husky and musical, sweeping him a look from beneath long lashes, Roberta smiled to herself at the effect upon him. Patrick Lacy would tell her what she wanted to know.

'Then how may I help you?'

'Mr Cosmore wishes you to arrange a meeting with his wife's solicitor, and as I was to be in Darlaston today, I said I would give you his message.'

'I count myself fortunate that you were to be in the town. Please give Mr Cosmore my assurances that his wishes will be acted upon.'

'Mr Lacy, I was wondering . . .' One hand moving to the buttons of her smart mustard velvet jacket, she released the top two with slow deliberate movements, her eyes incandescent with promise. 'Would you give me the name of Mrs Cosmore's solicitor?' Two more buttons slid from their mooring, revealing a tantalising glimpse of ivory flesh. 'I would be most grateful.'

'Clients' affairs are sacrosanct.' The bright eyes fastened on the curve of ivory behind the loosened buttons.

'Of course.' Roberta's voice swept around the office like the softest of breezes. 'But to sin once in a while is a delicious diversion, especially when there is none to know of it save us two.'

'I know nothing of Mrs Cosmore's affairs, I am not her solicitor.' He watched the long fingers toy with the next button, tongue once more circling dry lips.

'I do not ask to be acquainted with her affairs.' The button popped from its button hole, only to be refastened. 'Merely with the name of her solicitor.'

Patrick Lacy's glance shot to the small window overlooking Bull Street. He had no appointments booked and it was against all odds anyone else would drop in unannounced as had this woman. His glance returned to her: to the violet eyes sultry with invitation; to the mouth with its painted lips parted seductively.

'Through there!' He nodded to a door at the back of the room. 'I will bring you the information in there.'

Turning as he joined her in the back room, a slip of paper in his hand, she went to him, arms closing about his neck, her mouth over his. Less than five minutes later she re-entered the hansom, directing the driver to take her to Woods Bank, leaving Patrick Lacy with his trousers around his feet.

It had been relatively simple to extract a name and address. He had virtually pushed the paper bearing it into the vee of her half-fastened jacket as she had unbuttoned his trousers, closing one hand over his jerking penis.

Leaning back against the upholstery, she watched the buildings slipping past: tall and narrow slotted between small and squat, houses and shops jostling public houses and non-denominational chapels along the confines of Pinfold Street. Yes, the first part of her reason for once more being forced to spend time in this smoke-blackened town had been easy to achieve, but what she still required to know might not be so easily come by.

Charles Burrows's chambers were furnished much as Lacy's had been. A large desk littered with papers took central place, two chairs and a wide bookcase stuffed with string-bound sheaves of documents keeping them company.

Roberta's smiling introduction of herself leaving her with little doubt as to his proving as amenable to her charms as his professional colleague, she perched delicately on the chair he held for her, smoothing the mustard velvet of her skirts.

'I believe you are the solicitor engaged to handle the affairs of Mrs Morgan Cosmore, formerly Miss Esther Kerral of Rowena House?' Her smile dazzling, Roberta watched him settle behind the desk.

'I do hold that brief.' He nodded but his glance fell below her attractive face, resting where the peaks of her breasts jutted against the fitted jacket.

Rising to her feet, she crossed the tiny room, standing with the window to her back, light shimmering on her sable hair and throwing her narrow waist into sharp relief.

'Mr Burrows.' The musical voice was low, its softness barely disguising the fervour beneath. 'Would you share a little information with me?' One hand moved to the neck of the jacket. 'For a suitable payment, of course.'

'It will be my pleasure to help you in any way I can, Mrs Vance, but a client's business . . .'

'And it will be my pleasure to thank you.'

Coming to stand beside him, eyes lambent with promise, mouth slightly open, the tip of her tongue running slowly over the ridge of her teeth she reached one hand to her throat, slowly releasing the top few buttons.

'What . . .' The promise in her eyes holding him like a rabbit in a snare, the solicitor gulped. 'What did you want to know?'

'Only a name.' Sliding a hand sensuously down over his chest and stomach, she took his hand and drew him to his feet, her body just close enough to give added fuel to the heat of her eyes, 'all it will take is a name.'

Sitting in her chair alone in the quiet kitchen of Addenbrooke House, Esther stared into the glow of the settling coals. Had she really heard those words? Had Adam truly whispered, 'Come to me, my love,' or had they been a figment of her imagination, an echo of the words her heart longed to hear? She had thought of them a hundred times, going over them again and again, testing her memory, forcing it to recall every detail of every moment they had been together. Yet always she arrived at the same conclusion: she could not be sure. She could not honestly tell herself that the words singing in her mind had actually been spoken, but of one thing she was in no doubt. She was sure of the way he had held her as she collapsed, laughing and crying at the same time, into his arms, the eighteen steps a reality.

Eighteen steps! She had actually walked eighteen steps. She rested her hands on her thighs, feeling the complaint of muscles forced into a use they had not known before and revelled in the ache of them. She had walked eighteen steps!

If only Miri could have known, if only she had told her. But she had kept it secret and the secret had lasted too long and now Miri would never know.

But she would not have held that against Esther, Adam had said. Mrs Butler was too fine a woman for that. She would have been as happy as Esther herself. Yes, being able to walk had brought happiness but at the same time it brought a new source of tension.

Being paralysed had in a strange way helped to assuage the bitterness of knowing she could never be Adam's wife, knowing that no man would willingly marry a cripple. But now she could walk . . . and she was Morgan Cosmore's wife.

'Good evening, Esther.'

Drowning in her own sorry thoughts Esther had not heard the quiet tread. Startled, she turned her head. Roberta Vance stood just inside the door.

'No, Morgan is not with me.' She stepped from the pool of shadow, the amethyst velvet of her frogged suit gathering the light of the oil lamp burning in the centre of the table. 'I came alone.'

'I see.' Esther watched the woman walk into her kitchen. 'Might I ask for what reason? I cannot see you coming to visit me simply for pleasure.'

'But it is always such fun to visit you, Esther.' The expertly painted mouth parted in a smile. 'And so rewarding.'

'As it was on your last visit. Three hundred pounds worth, was it not?'

On its bracket above the fire the kettle hummed its own particular lullaby but Esther ignored the unspoken rule of the town and offered no tea.

'A most welcome gift.' Velvet skirt rustling softly on the flagged stone of the floor, Roberta Vance moved further into the circle of light, its pale saffron gleam ringing her black hair like a halo.

'And one you wish repeated?' Esther said, knowing the woman behind the beauty. 'Is that your reason for coming here without Morgan?'

'Oh, I came for much more than that.' She walked to the fire and stood for a moment staring silently into its glowing centre. 'Did you know your father-in-law's solicitor has a predilection for entertainment?'

'Entertainment?' Esther frowned, wondering where Patrick Lacy fitted into the scheme this woman had obviously dreamed up to get more money out of her. 'That is not surprising, everyone enjoys entertainment.'

'Of course they do.' Roberta swung to face her, the same derisive smile on her mouth. 'But some more than others.'

'Mrs Vance!' Esther let both impatience and dislike ring in her tone. 'Let me tell you once and for all, I am not interested in Patrick Lacy and I have no more money to give to you.'

'Oh, but you do!' The smile faded and within the spill of lamplight the violet eyes took on a menacing gleam. 'And though you may have no interest in Patrick Lacy, you should have in Charles Burrows. You see, Esther, I called upon him today too. I know who Mrs Edward Marsh was, and I know who her heir is and the extent of the properties she has now inherited. And I want half.'

Fighting to stem the alarm coursing through her, Esther stared at the painted face of the woman who had already blackmailed her out of three hundred pounds.

'Mrs Edward Marsh and her heir?' she said, feeling her throat tighten. 'Who is Mrs Edward Marsh?'

'Don't pretend, Esther!' The deep voice lost its customary musicality. 'Mrs Edward Marsh was the wife of Edward John Marsh-Butler, in other words Miriam Butler, the woman who brought you up!'

How could she know? Esther felt her head spin. How could she have found that out?

'I told you, your father-in-law's solicitor likes to be entertained and doesn't mind paying for his enjoyment.'

Esther looked at her, bewildered. 'I do not understand?'

'There is really very little to understand.' Roberta's tone was once more carefully composed. 'I called at his office this afternoon. He was most co-operative.'

'And just how co-operative were you?' Esther asked, feeling her dislike and contempt for the woman grow by the word.

'Enough.' The glow of the fire silhouetting her figure, Roberta Vance stood looking down at the girl held prisoner by her wheelchair. 'He told me Charles Burrows was your solicitor, and he in his turn told me that Mrs Edward Marsh-Butler was your benefactor. It did not take much deduction to assume the same Mrs Edward Marsh-Butler was none other than Miriam Butler, and that you, my dear Esther, have inherited several nut and bolt works, a soap works, a candle works . . . need I go on?'

It was useless to deny what she said. Charles Burrows was the only one who knew the identity of the person behind the signature 'Mrs Edward Marsh'. That he had broken a confidence and divulged that information to Roberta Vance was obvious.

'So you seduced Charles Burrows into giving you details of my inheritance?'

'Oh, my dear, he enjoyed it.' Within the pool of light the sensuous mouth lifted in a contemptuous curve. 'They both did. Now you must decide. Either you give me half of what you now own or I give my information to Morgan. If you choose the former you will at least still have something, whereas if you follow the latter course then Morgan will lay claim to the lot and as the law stands you will have no choice but to hand it over. And Morgan being Morgan, you will get nothing.'

Sooner or later I will be left with nothing anyway, Esther thought, staring at that supercilious face. Roberta was only asking for half, but for how long? How soon would she return and how many times before there was nothing left? One way or the other, Morgan or Roberta Vance, it came to the same thing. She would lose everything.

'Do you really think Morgan would sell off the businesses I have built up to spend the money on you, knowing once it was gone there'd be nothing more?'

It was a futile question but Esther asked it anyway.

The glow of the oil lamp gilding her raven hair, tiny diamonds of yellow sparking from it as she tossed her head in a deprecating movement, Roberta laughed, a mixture of contempt and triumph soft in her throat.

'Do you really think he would not?' she asked. 'Ask him, Esther. Ask your husband for yourself which is more important to him, you and your businesses or me?'

Esther's fingers curled into her palms. Such a question needed no asking. Whether Morgan truly loved this woman or whether he was just besotted by her, it made no difference. He had spent every penny of the money he got from his father on her and there could be no doubt he would go on spending until the well ran dry. But if she had to hand over what she had . . .? Esther tried to reason it out then gave up. Whichever way she chose, Roberta Vance would be on the receiving end.

'Then I would rather Morgan got it all!' she said coldly. 'And I will make it perfectly plain to everyone I can that he destituted his own father to buy the favours of a common prostitute.'

'Not so common, Esther.' Roberta unbuttoned her jacket, slipping it from her shoulders. 'Tell them by all means but before you do, let me acquaint you with all the facts.'

Unbuttoning a mauve silk blouse, she draped it over the jacket she had slung across a chair. 'Let me show you why your husband's lover is not such a common prostitute.' Loosening the fastening of her skirt, she let it fall in a whispering amethyst pool about her feet, topped by the creamy foam of silken petticoats.

'I want you to know, Esther.' She laughed softly, snatching a cotton chemise over her head.

Bewildered, Esther stared then gasped at the realisation: the woman's chest was smooth and flat, she had no breasts!

'I want you to know it all!' Roberta laughed again as she lowered her lace-edged bloomers. 'I want you to know your husband's lover is a man!'

Sickness spurting into her throat, Esther closed her eyes, pressing the lids hard down. Roberta Vance was a man. Morgan . . . Morgan made love to another man!

'You can close your eyes, Esther,' the voice broke through her flimsy defences, smooth and poisonous as a serpent, 'but it will not hide what you know. You will never shut out what you have seen and once you tell your friends of Morgan's preference for spending his, or anyone else's, money on me, I shall tell them of his preference for having a man in his bed. Think of what the newspapers would make of that! And that is not all I will tell. They will be shocked but eager to hear how you yourself played our little games, how delighted you were to join in, how keen you were for your husband to lift you into bed for sex romps with himself and his lover.'

Vance smiled softly to himself. With any luck at all Esther would prove far too naive to realise he was bluffing. He could hardly risk involving newspapers seeing as his whole sexual relationship with Morgan was illegal, but she, silly girl, would probably never know that.

'And then there is your Mr Paige. How would he feel to find himself included? Who would care whether it were the truth or not? People much prefer scandal to truth, and how would you feel when he turned his back on you? Think it over, Esther.'

He will not believe you, she wanted to scream, he will not believe you. But there were those who would and the finger would always be pointed. Adam would be judged, tried and condemned by those who mattered, the ordinary people of Darlaston.

'There is nothing I can do tonight.' Opening her eyes, Esther stared at the figure now fastening its jacket, knowing she could not risk having Adam exposed to such lies. She would rather give up all she had than have this creature spread its filth – a filth neither she nor Adam could ever hope to eradicate from the memory of the town. 'I will see Charles Burrows tomorrow but I am sure it will take time to find someone who is willing to purchase a half share in the properties you have mentioned.'

'I do not expect things to happen overnight.' Robert Vance picked up his gloves. 'But I will not wait indefinitely, Esther. Don't think I will give up and go away. Whether it comes from you or through Morgan, I intend to have that money.'

Alone again in a silence broken only by the ticking of the clock, Esther stared into the coals. Had Roberta . . . Robert Vance come here tonight with Morgan's blessing? Did he even know about the visit? And if he did, was he a party to the demands the man had made? But why would he be? There was no need for Morgan to make threats or tell such blatant lies when he could quite easily claim in full every last penny she had.

It had all been for nothing. Esther leaned wearily back in her chair. A loveless marriage to a man who flaunted his lover in her face, and that lover a man who would rob her of everything; a father who detested her and had willingly bartered her on the chance of getting his hands on money that did not exist. She had taken it all, all that fate could throw at her for that one rea-son, to take her own vengeance, and now it had been snatched away.

Why? Esther stared at a flickering flame. Was it wrong to

desire revenge? Was it a sin against God to want to repay her father for his treatment of her?

'Vengeance is mine.' The words so carefully taught her by John and Miri surfaced in her mind and Esther smiled with resignation. Then God would have to find the way to wreak vengeance on Josiah Kerral for Robert Vance had robbed her of the chance.

Chapter Twenty

Esther fastened the buttons of her brown dress, a dull ache throbbing in her head. She had slept little and that fitfully, the scene between herself and Morgan's lover returning over and again to her mind. A man! How could Morgan be in love with a man?

'Breakfast, Mrs Cosmore.'

Peggy Deeley gave Esther's door a tap. Miri had insisted on her taking breakfast at the table and not in bed and it was a rule Esther continued to keep.

Wheeling herself into the kitchen, she smiled weakly at the young girl, busy with porridge and tea cups.

'Are you quite sure you be feelin' all right, Mrs Cosmore?' Peggy cast a concerned glance at her. 'You seemed real poorly last night when I got back from me mam's. I thought as 'ow I should 'ave got the doctor then.'

'I am perfectly well, Peggy, just a little tired.'

'Then why don't you stay in bed? It'll do no 'arm to 'ave one day restin'.'

'I think probably some fresh air is more what I need, Peggy.'

'Me mam would 'ave had you back in yer bed an' no messin'!' Peggy said forthrightly.

'And so would Miri.' Esther wheeled herself up to the table. 'But seeing as neither of those two is here, how about us following my suggestion and going out for an hour or so? They must have some new ribbons at Appleyard's or a new dress at Marston's. Looking at those would make a change from pots and a kitchen range.'

'That would be a treat, Mrs Cosmore.' The girl's smile broke out, lighting up her pert face. 'It's always a treat to look, even when you know you can't afford to buy.'

'Then we will have a cup of tea and afterwards you can tell Sam to harness Queenie to the trap.'

It was as good an excuse as any, Esther thought, watching the girl busy herself ladling porridge into a shallow dish. She had to go to see Charles Burrows and this way she could make it appear a casual call. The thought of giving Vance anything at all cut her to the quick but she could not take a chance; he would involve Adam in his lies otherwise. It obviously made no difference to him whose life he ruined.

Pushing the oatmeal around the dish, the very idea of eating causing her stomach to rebel, Esther at last pushed it aside.

'Not to worry, Mrs Cosmore,' Peggy said brightly, though the shadow of a frown between her brows showed she was still harbouring concern for Esther's health. 'There be a good hot broth for dinner. P'raps a blow of air will bring yer appetite back and you'll enjoy it?'

'I am certain I will, Peggy.' Esther's eyes followed the rapid movement of dishes and cups being loaded on to the wooden tray Dolly Foster had so often sent to Esther's room, loaded with a meal for herself and Miri. Her thoughts raced incessantly. What if she did not sign anything over to Vance after all? What if she simply gave everything she owned to Morgan? Either way it was lost to her but at least by giving it to her husband she would avoid seeing the triumph in his lover's eyes. True, Vance would reap a certain benefit, but that would only come via Morgan. It would have to be bought using the wiles of a lover. He would not know the pleasure of ever having her money in his own right.

And once her businesses were in Morgan's hands, what then? Would her husband provide her with another home? Out of the shadows of memory Miri's voice seemed to echo a favourite warning: 'Don't 'old yer breath, wench, don't 'old yer breath!'

Oh, Miri! Deep in her heart Esther felt an ache. You would have known what to do. You would have shown me the way. Miri . . . Miri . . . I miss you so. How can I go on without you? I need you, Miri, I need you so much.

But Miri was not here. Esther drew a long trembling breath. Miri would never be here again.

Peggy beside her in the trap, Sam leading the horse, Esther mulled over her thoughts again. There was no middle course, no way of keeping her long-held secret. Her mind made up, she gazed out across the ploughed fields edging the heath. She would wait for Morgan to come to her. He could have her property but he would have to ask for it himself. Like it or not, her husband must look her in the face when he claimed it for himself and his lover.

Reaching the Bull Stake, Esther nodded as Sam asked should he turn left into King Street? Halting the trap outside Appleyard's drapery shop, he helped Peggy to alight but Esther shook her head. She could see the window display clearly and had no real desire to go inside the shop.

Coming out several minutes later, Peggy's face held much the same concern it had at breakfast. 'Ee, Mrs Cosmore!' she gabbled, climbing into the trap. 'There be some women in there an' they be talkin' of fever.'

'Fever!' Esther felt alarm course through her veins. 'What do you mean, fever?'

'Just that.' Peggy glanced at Sam as he closed the little tail gate of the trap. 'They said as it broke out yesterday mornin' an' some of the folks be right poorly.'

'Where?'

'They said it were showin' no favours but were strikin' women, men an' kids alike.'

'Where, Peggy!' Esther demanded, feeling a coldness where alarm had been. 'Where has the fever broken out?'

'Out along Foleys Croft,' she answered as Esther shook her by the arm. 'The women . . . they said it was Foleys Croft.'

Foleys Croft! Esther felt the blood in her veins turn to ice. Adam lived at Foleys Croft. Young and old alike, Peggy had said. Maybe Adam was already ill . . .

'We best be gettin' you 'ome, Mrs Cosmore. We don't want you to go catchin' anythin'.'

The jolt as the trap moved forward brought Esther out of her stupor.

'No, Sam, stop!' she ordered. 'You and Peggy go back to Addenbrooke.'

'Sam an' me go back?' Peggy turned a sharp look to the woman whose face had gone the colour of fresh drawn milk. 'What about yerself?'

Esther held out a hand for the reins. 'I am going to Foleys Croft.'

'Eh, Mrs Cosmore, you ain't! I mean, you can't, not with the fever bein' there.'

'I can, Peggy, and I am,' Esther said, determination in her voice, showing she would brook no argument.

'Then I be goin' with you.'

'No.' Esther shook her head. 'I would not put your mother through the worry of that . . . no, Peggy!' she said sharply as the girl opened her mouth to speak. 'You go home to your mother and stay there until Sam comes to fetch you. And, Peggy,' she continued as he helped the girl climb down from the trap, 'I mean exactly that. Your brothers are not to bring you to Addenbrooke. You will wait for Sam.'

Obviously unhappy with Esther's order, the girl turned away in the direction of the houses that flanked the candle works in Crescent Road.

'You must go back too, Sam.' Esther still held out her hand for the reins.

'If you be going out to Foleys Croft then I be drivin' you there.' He held stubbornly to the reins.

Grasping the side of the trap, Esther leaned forward.

'Sam, you have a child. You cannot risk carrying home any infection.'

'Arrh, I 'ave a child. An' that child has a 'ome, thanks to you . . .'

'Sam,' she interrupted, 'do not have false ideas of duty because I rent you a house.'

'My ideas ain't false.' Coming to the back of the trap, he climbed inside. 'Don't matter what you say, you ain't goin' to Foleys Croft on yer own. And afore you says any more, my mother always reckoned fevers weren't caused by the folk theirselves. She always said them women kept their places as clean as was possible, given where they lived. She said it was summat as got into the brook an' from there into their systems when they drank the water. So, you see, I don't think I'll be takin' any 'urt back to my child.'

Flicking the reins, Sam turned the horse around, heading toward Katherine's Cross, the stench of chemical waste assaulting their nostrils well before the huddle of houses appeared in the hollow that was Foleys Croft.

'What the hell are you thinking of, bringing her here?' Adam had seen the trap coming down the swell of ground and come to meet it.

'She was set to come on 'er own.' Sam met his angry stare. 'An' I was 'avin' none of that. But to take 'er to Addenbrooke would 'ave done no good 'cos, with or without me, 'er would 'ave got here somehow.'

'You have to go back, Esther, there is enough worry here for me without that of your taking sick.'

Seeing the look that passed between them, Sam turned his attention to the horse. His mistress was a married woman and looks such as the one she had just given Adam Paige could reap her a whole crop of trouble. But if he were ever asked he had seen nothing.

'You could not expect me not to come,' she said as Sam

moved away. 'Your mother gave me her help when I needed it. How could I not do the same?'

'There is nothing you can do.' Adam covered the hand resting on the side of the trap with his own. 'There is nothing anyone can do short of knocking down this place.'

'Is anyone doing anything?' Esther looked at the houses tipping drunkenly against each other, at the road that was more a river of churned mud after yesterday's rain, and watched a small boy paddle across it, a chipped enamel bucket in his hand as he went to the brook for water. She felt the cool surge of controlled anger rise inside her. People should not have to live this way. The stables at Rowena and Addenbrooke Houses were far superior to this.

'I reported this fresh outbreak to the Parish yesterday morning,' Adam told her. 'They sent the Relief doctor. He said the only thing to do was to let it run its course.'

Her gaze still on the huddle of buildings, she asked quietly, 'How bad is it really, Adam?'

He looked across the trap, his gaze meeting hers. 'There are a few who are very sick but the women are handling it. It's nothing new to them.'

'Your mother, Adam, is she among the sick?'

'No, thank God,' he answered fervently, 'though how she stays well I don't know. She is in and out of neighbours' houses doing what she can for them. I feel scared coming back every night from the works in case I should find her ill, but so far . . .' He broke off, his face creasing with new lines of worry.

'I want to speak to her.' Esther drew her hand from his. 'Will you take me into the house?'

'Esther, there is nothing . . .'

'Please, Adam, I want to speak to your mother, and if you will not take me to her then I shall get Sam to do so.'

Inside the small room in his mother's house, Esther glanced at the stool set beside the fire and the chair that had been Adam's father's. A table in the centre of the room hardly left enough space between it and the one cupboard for a person to get through, yet everywhere shone from scrubbing and cleaning.

'You wanted to see me, Mrs Cosmore?'

Woollen shawl draped about her shoulders, the edge of her black skirts touched with mud, Carrie Paige entered the house followed by her son. 'I was just round at the Bartlett house lending a hand. Six little 'uns that wench has, an' 'er man sick.' Slipping off the shawl, she hung it on a peg set into the back of the door. 'Will you take a cup of tea?'

The question was really for form in Darlaston, the natural instinct of every woman being to stick the kettle on to the fire whenever a neighbour or visitor called. Carrie set about following that instinct.

'Mrs Paige,' Esther followed the woman's quick movements, 'what can I do to help?'

A cup in her hand, Carrie paused to look at the girl her son had carried into this very room the night Cosmore copper works had been set alight. 'You 'elp, wench? I don't see . . .'

'I know I could not help with the nursing,' Esther touched her legs, 'but there has to be another way. Do these people need food or bedding? Whatever it is there must be something I can do.'

Carrie glanced at her son standing at Esther's side. That was the reason she had come to Foleys Croft, the real reason. She had to prove to herself that Adam was not among the sick – but while he was not sick of the fever her son carried a sickness just the same, a sickness of the heart.

'Some of 'em got no food at all savin' what Adam brings. He more or less feeds the whole Croft on 'is wages. I tell 'im it be daft what 'e does, that 'e should save 'is money an' get 'imself off to a better place, but it be like talkin' to a stone wall.'

'And medicine?' Esther asked, sensing the look Adam sent to his mother. 'Has any been prescribed?'

'Oh, arrh.' Carrie turned to the kettle, steam rattling its lid.

'The Parish Relief doctor said to physic everybody wi' a bottle of extract of liquorice, but some of 'em be nigh physicked to a standstill already. Give 'em anythin' else an' it be like to see 'em off altogether.' Pouring boiling water over tea leaves generously heaped into an old thick china teapot, she placed it on the table. 'It don't be physic they needs so much as a full pantry and a heap of coal to heat the house against the damp that creeps in everywhere. I tell you, it would be a blessing if the devil dropped his clog on the Croft an' flattened it altogether. That way the Parish would 'ave to do summat.' Taking the tea Carrie poured for her, Esther stirred a spoon of sugar into it. She had taken tea and food in this house before and suffered no harm from them.

'Mrs Paige, would you make out a list of those things each family here is most in need of? Then have them delivered and the bills sent to me at Addenbrooke House.'

'Eeh, wench!' Surprise stopped Carrie's hand halfway to her lips. 'That be right good of you. It'll do a sight more good than the Parish doctor an' 'is physic.'

'And, Adam.' Half turning in her chair, Esther looked up into his face. 'The houses being erected out at Heathfield – I understand they are almost finished?'

'As good as.' He nodded, eyes asking what was to come next. 'A bit of rubble to be shifted and that's about all.'

Carrie looked at the tall dark-haired man who was her son talking with Esther Cosmore as if he had always been of her class, as though the gulf of money and privilege had never existed between them. She rose from the table, pushing away the thoughts that troubled her in the night.

'I'll be away an' do what you asked.'

Reaching for her shawl, she stepped into the mud of the street. She could have said down to the last grain of salt what each family in the Croft needed without leaving her kitchen but that way there could be no moment alone for a pair who must value even the shortest time together.

'Adam,' Esther said, as he came to stand facing the chair

he had placed her in, 'I want you to find which five families here are most in need of re-housing and offer them a place at Heathfield.'

'I guessed you had that in mind.' He smiled but it did not clear the worry from his grey eyes. 'But what of the rent? These folk won't be able to pay what those houses should be rented at, not until they have jobs anyway.'

'I will leave that to you to explain. A suitable rent will be fixed for each house as and when the breadwinner is in employment. But for now, Adam, just get them out of this place.'

'There are six houses built at Heathfield,' he said, 'but you only want five rented out.'

'Yes, Adam. I make one stipulation in all of this – one of those houses must go to your mother if she will leave here.'

'If she will leave!' He ran a hand through his hair, holding the black curls in his fingers. 'She has dreamed of nothing else since my brothers died. But, Esther!' He looked at her as a new thought struck him. 'You wanted those houses for the men you were to take on when the expansion of the works was finished.'

'Why not these men?' She smiled. 'I don't think we need look for any more.'

'It won't be an easy job choosing five families,' he mused, already busy with the task. 'Most of them have married children with kids of their own all pressed into a place no bigger than this, and each of those will be praying that one of your houses will be for them.'

'They will not have to pray much longer.' Her smile widening, Esther went on, 'I want you to take the soap works in Jesson Street in your name. I want the profits from that to build a whole lane of houses for people like these. I want to build the Heathfield Lane we talked of, Adam.'

'But why put the soap works in my name?' He frowned, loosening his hair, an unruly curl dropping stubbornly on to his brow. 'I won't have it, Esther, I will not take what is yours.'

'But it is the only way!' Her smile faded, replaced by earnestness. 'Morgan could find out I own several businesses and take them before he returns to London. Once he does there will be little chance of those houses ever being built. Don't you see, Adam? If I sell you the soap works for one guinea then that at least will not be stolen by . . .'

Adam's frown deepened as her words fell away. Stolen by Roberta Vance, was that what she had been about to say? If he agreed then the money the works earned would be a safeguard for her against being left to fend for herself. And he held little doubt that was what Cosmore would do; take her money and run, not showing his face in Darlaston again while a penny of it remained in his pocket.

'When?' he asked simply.

'Now,' Esther said, relieved. 'Come with me to Charles Burrows's office on Woods Bank and we will sign the papers right away, before Morgan has a chance to do anything to stop it.'

Lifting her in his arms, Adam held her gaze with his then slowly lowered his mouth to hers.

'Is there anything I can get you?' Having settled Esther in her wheelchair, Sam stood hesitantly in the kitchen of Addenbrooke House. 'I can make you some tea.'

Esther smiled. 'No, Sam, thank you, but no more tea. I think I will rest a while.'

'Will you need lifting?'

'No.' She shook her head. 'I can manage quite well for myself.'

'I'll be off to fetch Peggy then, will I?'

Esther glanced out of the window. It had been growing dark when they had finally come back across the heath. The transfer of the soap works had taken longer than she'd thought and now the sky was purple with evening.

'Stable Queenie for the night.' She smiled at Sam. 'And you could call at Peggy's mother's on your way home. Her brothers will bring her from there and that way you need not have two journeys.'

'Thanks, Mrs Cosmore.' Sam rescued his cap from the confines of his pocket, straightening it between his hands, 'I'll do that.'

Listening to the rumble of the trap wheels and Queenie's hoofs as she made her way into the stable, Esther leaned back tiredly in her chair. The people of Foleys Croft would have their houses, Adam would see to that. And she . . . what would she have? Eyes closed, she touched a finger to her mouth stroking it where other lips had pressed. She would always have the memory of Adam's kiss.

A wave of tiredness sweeping over her, she wheeled herself to the room that served as her bedroom, pushing the door closed behind her chair.

'I was beginning to think you were never going to return, Esther.'

Startled, she looked to the alcove beyond the bed. There, framed in its shadows, gowned in velvet, a smile on his mouth, stood the figure of Robert Vance.

'Why are you here?' Although she knew this man's sexual tendency favoured other men, Esther could not altogether dismiss the fear that had suddenly taken a grip of her.

'Why?' He laughed, a short hollow sound that began and ended in his throat. 'You ask that after our discussion the other evening?' He stepped out of the shadows. 'Very well, Esther, if we must play out your little charade then we will. I am here to collect my half of your business. I take it you have been to see your solicitor?'

Esther looked at the figure, slender and exquisitely dressed in eau-de-nil velvet suit, a matching feathered hat set at an angle on the jet black hair. A perfect picture of an appealing woman, except that this woman was a man.

'Yes.' She swallowed, trying to subdue her fear. 'I have seen Mr Burrows, I called on him this afternoon.'

'Good.' He moved towards her around the bed, his movements deceptively feminine. 'I was certain you would see things my way. After all, we would not really want to involve Mr Paige, would we? It always looks so bad when a woman becomes entangled with one of her employees.'

That looked bad! Esther could hardly believe the gall of it. How then did a man posing as a woman look?

'Darlaston is only a very small town but it still has its values and you do have to go on living here,' Robert Vance went on. 'Oh, yes, and I should perhaps tell you your husband will not be finding you another house and you yourself are already very well aware he will not be taking you with him when he leaves. So, you see, if you are to have any life at all here it is imperative you keep your reputation. After all, Adam Paige has the advantage of being able to walk away while you . . .' The elegant shoulders rose in the essence of a shrug.

'When is Morgan leaving?' Esther ignored the veiled insult of those last words, knowing he waited for at least a strangled gasp that would tell him his blow had found its mark. But that was one satisfaction he would have to do without.

'We are taking the morning train to London and from there we travel to Europe. Italy is superb at this time of year. Strolling about the piazzas of Rome, walking the Via Veneto . . . it really is such a pity you will never have that pleasure.'

'I have no doubt it is a most pleasant place to be,' Esther said, masking the anger that suddenly drowned her fear. 'The more pleasant when another man's money is paying for it all.'

Moving to the window Robert Vance stood against it, the pale green of his suit highlighted by the soft purple darkness outside.

'Why, Esther,' he laughed, 'do I detect a note of jealousy?'

She ran a slow deliberate glance over the figure framed in the darkened window. 'No jealousy, Mr Vance, only pity. I pity Morgan. If he had to live with a prostitute, even a male prostitute, I wonder he did not choose one with a little grace and finesse, both of which you singularly lack.'

The smallest of pauses emphasised the success of Esther's barb before soft laughter again broke the silence.

'Grace and finesse can be easily acquired – as easily as acquiring another woman's husband. I can have both, but you, Mrs Cosmore will never have the use of your legs!'

Esther's fingers tightened in her lap and she had to bite back the retort that she already had the use of her legs, and that it was growing with every day.

'Acquiring things seems to be something of a hobby with you, Mr Vance,' she said, self-control concealing the rage inside her. 'Though sadly the ones you came here to acquire this evening you will not be getting.'

The sharp hiss of his indrawn breath disturbed the silence that settled after her words. Half hidden by the long shadows of the room, he stood perfectly still. Esther tried to ignore her own fear but could not. He might be dressed as a woman but he had the strength of a man, one who could see a small fortune slipping from his grasp, and she was still more or less bound to a wheelchair.

'You said you went to see your solicitor this afternoon?' The words came slowly, dripping like acid.

'That was the truth.' Esther stared at him through the shadows. 'I did call at Charles Burrows's chambers this afternoon. He was most embarrassed to find I knew all about his amorous escapade with a certain Roberta Vance and almost fell over himself assuring me my instructions would be followed to the letter. You see, Charles Burrows also knows the value a town puts on reputation, especially that of a solicitor. You can take it from me, Mr Vance, he will not fall for your charms a second time.'

'What instructions?' he snarled, stepping forward. 'What instructions did you give Burrows?'

Unable to see his face clearly in the subdued light of the room, she was none the less aware what he was feeling.

Robert Vance had been so sure of his position, so sure of his hold over her, and now the threat of losing that hold was causing him to sweat.

'Why don't you call on Mr Burrows yourself?' Esther asked sweetly. 'Ask him what it was I said to him? Or could it possibly be that you too are thinking he would no longer prove susceptible to you?'

'What instructions?' he asked again the question strung out like a tightened cord.

Tension pulsed at Esther's temples but she stuck to her argument. 'I suggest that for your own peace of mind you ask Mr Burrows that question. At least that way you can be certain of hearing what you wish to hear, or as much of the truth as you yourself tell anyone.'

He stepped forward again, this time coming to within inches of her chair, and even in the half light she could see the fury distorting his carefully painted face.

'I will ask you again,' he grated, 'what instructions did you give your solicitor?'

How long would it be before Peggy arrived? Esther tried to calculate the time in her mind. Sam would go straight to her mother's house but even supposing Peggy left immediately the round trip would take two hours. There was no way she could stall this man for two hours. His temper was already seething. To stoke it with further taunts could prove very dangerous.

'My instructions were simple,' she said, following her own mental advice to tell him what he asked to know though it would not be what he wanted to hear. 'I informed him first of the consequences to himself should my wishes be ignored, then I told him that under no circumstances were any of my businesses to be transferred to my husband, or to be discussed with any person, whether male or female, claiming to be his representative, unless I am present.'

'Morgan has no need of your presence. As your husband, he is legally entitled to every penny you have.'

'Charles Burrows is aware of that,' Esther answered the snarl, 'but as we have both pointed out, the social value of a reputation is too high to be put at risk by public scrutiny. Morgan may have all that is mine but you will find it difficult to execute your own plan. I will sign nothing over to you, not so much as a pin head!'

Under cover of semi-darkness Robert Vance peeled the glove slowly from his right hand. He had thought to have this business over and done today, the title deeds to half of this woman's properties safe in his pocket. Now it seemed he would have to wait a little longer, but that wait would be of short duration. And this time it would not be half he would take. It would be all.

'You have been very clever, Esther.' He held the glove in his left hand. 'I congratulate you on your common sense, it is far superior to that of your husband, but then he is not alone in losing all common sense once he is in my arms. Morgan *will* give it all to me.'

'I am quite certain that he will,' she replied cuttingly. 'You are right when you say my husband has little common sense. And his father was also right when he said his son had even less taste!'

'That became patently obvious when he married a cripple!' Vance spat.

'And even more obvious when he failed to check whether or not that cripple's father did indeed have the money he had married her for.'

'I concede that Morgan may not always think things through as clearly as he might,' Vance replied, the anger seeming to have drained from his voice, 'but I can more than make up for his small shortcomings in that direction.'

'And who makes up for yours?' Esther retorted sharply. 'What are your own shortcomings that drive you to dress and act as a woman!'

'I do not always act the part of a woman,' he said softly. 'I am, and can be, a man in every sense of the word, Esther, as

317

you will find out in due course, a man who will not be played with. You have gained a small victory today but victories are often soon reversed, as yours will be. You have not seen the end of Robert Vance. I shall be back and when I am you can be sure it will be to give you much more than this.'

Raising the ungloved hand, he brought the knuckles of it hard down across her mouth.

'Oh, and by the way.' Already in the kitchen he spoke over his shoulder: 'Morgan called on your father earlier today. It appears they had a slight difference of opinion, a mere misunderstanding so I am told. Apparently it affected your father's horse more than it affected either of the men. It seems the creature kicked your father in the back and, not content with that, rolled the carriage wheels over him. Horses show such common sense, would you not agree?'

Her senses whirling in the aftermath of the blow that had almost stunned her, Esther heard the musical voice give way to harsh laughter.

'Poor Morgan.' His parting words echoed in the silent house. 'Now he is related to two cripples!'

Chapter Twenty-one

'I heard tell of it in the town, and thought I should come back an' let you know.'

'What happened, Sam?' Esther felt a twinge of guilt at asking what had caused her father's accident when she already knew, but to say as much would indicate Roberta Vance's presence in this house and that would serve no purpose.

'Seems yer 'usband called at Rowena House this mornin' an' 'ad a bit of a shindig with yer father.'

Esther felt her mouth dry. Vance had said the same thing. 'Who told you this?' she asked.

'I met William Evans along by the Bull Stake, he were just gettin' off the Walsall tram. He told me what the young lad in the stable yard says 'appened. The two of 'em, Mr Cosmore and yer father, were arguin' an' yer father went to strike out but Cosmore brought his riding whip across 'im an' he stumbled back against the 'orse harnessed to the carriage. The 'orse reared an' lashed out with a hoof, sending yer father to the ground, then bolted, rolling the carriage wheels over his back.'

So Vance had not invented the accident to her father merely to cause her worry. What he had said was perfectly true: Morgan had gone to Rowena House.

'Seems the argument was a follow on from the one they was 'avin' in the 'ouse,' Sam continued. 'Evans said he could hear yer father shoutin' from the kitchen, an' in a right old temper he seemed to be an' all.'

Bringing an extra lamp from the scullery, Peggy set it on the table, catching sight of Esther's cut cheek and swollen mouth by its light. 'Eh, Mrs Cosmore, what 'appened? Yer face be all swelled up.'

'It's nothing, Peggy.' Esther touched a hand to her smarting cheek. 'I leaned too far forward and my chair tipped and I hit my face on the corner of the table.' It was another lie but somehow it did not seem to matter.

'Ee, I knowed I should 'ave stopped with you!' the girl said, immediately blaming herself. 'I knowed I should never ought to 'ave gone to me mam's.'

'Peggy, stop that!' Esther said, anxiety lending her voice a sharpness it did not usually carry. 'You are in no way to blame. You did as you were told and let that be an end to it. Anyway, a bump on the mouth always looks worse than it really is so, please, no more fussing.'

The maid turned away but not before Esther saw the look on her face. She had been too sharp and the young girl's feelings were hurt. She should not let her own worries override her concern for the feelings of others, Esther chastised herself, especially when those others held her welfare genuinely at heart.

'Peggy,' she said gently, 'I'm sorry I spoke sharply, I just did not want you attaching blame to yourself for my own stupidity.'

'That's all right, Mrs Cosmore.' The girl's wide smile returned. 'Me mam always says I flap at nothin'.'

'What would your mother say to my bumping my face?'

'Ee, Mrs Cosmore, I couldn't be tellin' you that!'

'Might it be something like this . . . "It was yer own bloody soft fault for not watchin' what you be doin'"?'

The girl's eyes widened. 'Ee, how did you know that?'

Esther's mouth tilted and she winced inwardly at the pain the smile caused her. 'Because they were Miri's words exactly, and she would always turn to a cup of tea to make things right again.'

'I'll 'ave one made afore the devil bats 'is eyes.'

Beaming, Peggy set about preparing the local cure for all ills.

The girl's bruised feelings soothed and her attention taken by the ritual of tea-making, Esther looked again at Sam.

'Did Mr Evans say if my father was at home?'

'I asked 'im that.' Sam shifted uneasily, his boots scraping the flagged floor, sounding over loud in the quiet of the kitchen. 'He said as 'ow they 'ad carried 'im into the 'ouse and then sent for the doctor . . .'

'Go on, Sam, please. I must know!' Esther felt her heart jolt as he paused. Was her father dead?

'Well, the doctor, he . . .' Sam twisted his flat cap between his hands. 'The doctor said as he had to be taken into Sister Dora's.'

The hospital! Clasping her hands together to stop them shaking, Esther tried to make sense of her racing thoughts. They had taken her father to the Sister Dora hospital. That explained Sam's seeing Mr Evans get off the Walsall tram. He must have travelled in the bed carriage with her father and returned to Darlaston by way of the tram. But why could her father not be nursed at home?

Guessing her thoughts and seeking to spare her the pain of asking, Sam went on, 'Doctor Frost said yer father might need summat he called a spinal jacket but they wouldn't truly know till they had done some tests and them were best done in the 'ospital.'

A spinal jacket! Esther's heart lurched again, snatching the breath from her lungs. A spinal accident could mean her father was crippled as Robert Vance had said. No, please, not that! Much as she despised him, Esther prayed her father would not be crippled.

'Sam,' she tried to disguise the tremor in her voice, 'would you please harness the trap? I must go to see my father.'

'Will I come with you, miss?' Peggy reverted to addressing

Esther as a single woman, a habit she could not break whenever she felt nervous or worried.

'I will need to take my chair, Peggy,' Esther told her gently, not wanting to hurt the girl's feelings all over again, 'so there will not be space in the trap. I will have to sit beside Sam as it is. But we will walk with you to your mother's, I do not want you staying here alone.'

What if Vance should return? Esther thought, setting her lips firm against the girl's argument that she would be quite safe here at Addenbrooke. What if he lost his temper and harmed Peggy? That was one hazard she was not prepared to face.

'An' 'er signed the lot over to you?'

Carrie Paige looked at her son in amazement. First he had been made manager of all of Esther Cosmore's nut and bolt works, and now . . . now she had given him her soap works. Not made him its manager but *given* it to him, signed over in his own name!

'Yes, Mother.' He nodded. 'She also made over to me the houses she has had built up along the Heathfields.'

'Ee, Adam, lad!' Carrie shook her head wonderingly. 'That woman must think a deal of you.'

Think a deal of him? Adam looked into the fire glowing behind the bars of the grate. Esther trusted him if that was what was meant by 'thinking a deal of him', but that was all she could feel for him. He relived the touch of her mouth under his. She had made no response. Twice he had given himself away: once when he had called her 'my love' and again when he had kissed her. He would not make a third mistake. Esther Cosmore was given to another man; she harboured no feelings other than that of employer towards Adam Paige.

''Er give them 'ouses over to you?' Carrie said again. 'But what for? I mean, what be you goin' to do with 'em?'

'Just what Mrs Cosmore asked me to do.' Adam pushed his own thoughts aside. 'Find the five families from the

Fold who most need those houses and move them in straight away.'

'Five families?' Carrie took the poker from the side of the grate, scraping ash from the fire. 'But I thought as you said there was six of them?'

Looking at his mother, her woollen shawl fastened against the many draughts that found their way into the house, chilling it despite the fire, he felt new bitterness at the life she had been forced to lead in the Croft. But now she had the chance to leave, would she take it? He had been so confident when Esther had asked him that question; now he was not so sure. Foleys Croft was a living grave, but that grave held Carrie's memories.

'There are six houses,' he said, watching a shower of grey ash fall into the pan set below the well of the fire. 'Five of them are to be allocated as I told you. The remaining one Mrs Cosmore allocated herself.'

Carrie rattled the rolled metal bars, dislodging the last of the ash settled in the bed of the fire. 'Oh, who'd 'er give that to then?'

'You, Mother,' he said quietly. 'She gave it to you.'

'Me!' The poker clanged against the brick hearth, dropped by Carrie's suddenly nerveless fingers, but she did not move, only stayed crouched before the grate, the slight heaving of her thin shoulders the only display of the emotion contained in that one word.

'Yes.' Adam reached out to her, his arms folding about her. 'She wants you to have one of those houses.'

''Er said as much?' Carrie asked against his jacket. 'Mrs Cosmore, 'er said as much?'

'It was the one condition she made. Her words were that you were to be given one of the houses provided you wished to leave Foleys Croft.'

'Wish to leave Foleys Croft!' Carrie's worn fingers fastened in the cloth of Adam's jacket, pulling her face closer against it, fighting the tears of a lifetime. 'That's been the wish of years for me. Foleys Croft took yer brothers from me, it helped to take yer father and I 'ave a horror of its takin' you. All I 'ave asked of the Lord all these years is that He take you from the Croft afore the Croft takes you from me, an' now, praise be, He be giving us the chance.'

'Will you take it?' Gently pressing her away from him, he looked into her face. 'Will you leave here? I know it is a lot to ask of you. Three-quarters of your life has been spent here and that is a lot to leave behind.'

'Three-quarters of my life is naught but memory now, son.' Carrie smiled though her eyes were awash with tears. 'Those that are good will stay with me and those that ain't won't do no harm for the leavin'. I be willin' to up an' leave this minute, savin' for one thing only.'

'And what thing is that?'

Releasing his jacket, Carrie placed her thin hands over the ones cradling her face. 'I 'ave good neighbours 'ere, Adam,' she said softly. 'We've been through 'ard times together an' never once 'ave I known one turn their back on another. We be friends, son, real friends, the sort it be rare to come by. But they be sure to ask why me an' not them? That only be human nature an' none could be blamed for the sayin' of it.' She looked up at him. 'Much as I want to see the last of Foleys Croft, I won't risk the losin' of not one of 'em.'

'Carrie Paige, you take some beating when it comes to being a friend.' Adam's voice throbbed with quiet pride. 'But the ones who do not go this time will not have long to wait. Mrs Cosmore has instructed me to use the profits from the soap works to build more houses. In less than a year there will be a house along Heathfield Lane for any family who wants to leave the Croft.'

'Heathfield Lane?'

'Mrs Cosmore chose the name. She said it suited the location, it being just where the ploughed fields touch the heath.'

'Heathfield Lane.' Carrie smiled. 'I like it, Adam, I like it.'

* * *

Her whole body taut with the fear of what might await her, Esther kept her gaze on the brown-painted walls of the hospital corridor as Sam wheeled her in the wake of a nurse, who wore a starched white apron over long sleeved grey gabardine gown, a white thickly starched cotton cap covering her head and ears like a bonnet.

Yes, given the circumstances of her disablement Esther could see the patient, the nurse had told her, disapproval as thick as the starch on her cap. It was highly irregular, though. Visiting times were visiting times and must be adhered to if a hospital was to be run efficiently. It was highly unsuitable to have the public running around the corridors any time they decided to call. Five minutes was all she would allow. Five minutes and not a moment longer.

'Mrs Cosmore be 'ardly like to go runnin' around the corridors.' Sam had remarked stung by the woman's insensitive behaviour toward Esther.

The nurse had regarded him through eyes grey and cold as the colour of her uniform.

'You,' she had said to Sam, her thin straight lips hardly moving, 'will remain *outside* the ward. I will wheel the chair from there!'

And she had, charging forward using the wheelchair like a battering ram, leaving it beside a narrow-framed iron bed with a sharp command of: 'Five minutes!'

Esther looked at the figure of her father lying absolutely motionless beneath the bedlinen. The slightest crease had been smoothed from the sheets, their edges pushed ruthlessly beneath the straw-filled mattress. He was held immobile in their starched folds.

'Father?' she whispered. 'Father, can you hear me?'

Leaning towards him, she lifted a hand to the hair that was more grey than brown now but withdrew it, afraid his eyes would open and he would snarl at her to bugger off as he had the night Adam had carried her into Rowena House. He would not want her here, that much she knew, so why had she come? Why subject herself to a possible further tirade of abuse?

Esther sat with her silent questions, ones she could not answer for herself.

'Five minutes up!' The nurse, invincible behind the starched armour of her uniform, swung the wheelchair around without waiting for a reply, wheeling Esther out of the ward with its long rows of prisoners, none of whom dared to disturb his sheets by sitting up to watch.

'Visiting times are two to three p.m., Wednesdays and Sundays,' she announced, glaring challengingly at Sam as she handed him the wheelchair. 'Be sure to observe them from now on, we can make no exceptions for anyone.'

'Phew!' Sam snorted as they left the dull red-brick building. 'I wouldn't care to invite that one for a walk across the fields! 'Er be enough to frighten a brigade of guards. A couple more like that an' the King could do away with the whole British Army.'

'She was something of a dragon,' Esther answered.

'A dragon?' Sam lifted her into the front of the trap next to the driving seat. 'I'll say 'er is. St George 'imself could be forgiven for runnin' away from that one.'

Lifting the chair into the trap, he took a box of matches from his coat pocket and re-lit the candles in the small glass-sided lanterns set one to either side of the bodywork then took his place beside Esther.

'"Ow was yer father, Mrs Cosmore?' he asked after calling softly to Queenie.

'He was not awake, Sam, and didn't move at all.'

'I wouldn't go settin' too much store by that. Time you 'ad by 'is side weren't 'ardly enough for 'im to move.'

'Do you think he will be paralysed?'

'No, course 'e won't.' Sam tried to sound encouraging. 'It would take more than a kick from a horse to put yer father in . . .'

'A wheelchair?' Esther filled the awkward pause.

'Arrh, Mrs Cosmore. Beggin' yer pardon, but since you says in a wheelchair, I can't see Josiah Kerral comin' to that.'

But what if he has to? Esther watched the tiny pool of light dance among the shadowed grasses at the roadside. What if Josiah Kerral wakes to find himself a cripple?

Why didn't Morgan come? It had been a week since he and her father had come to blows in the stable yard at Rowena House. A week since her husband's lover had made his threat to return, and a week in which her father had neither moved nor spoken.

They did not know how long he would be this way. Doctor Frost had said in answer to her questions that Jos had obviously undergone some kind of trauma that had resulted in his becoming comatose – maybe the blow to the head when he had fallen. As for being paralysed, only time would prove or disprove that. For now all they could do was wait.

'Sam says the trap be ready when you am.' Peggy bustled in from the yard, her cheeks pink from the first kiss of winter.

'Thank you,' Esther said, her voice lacking enthusiasm. She called at the hospital daily for news of her father even though the strict visiting rules did not always allow her to see him, and daily she dreaded the possible news that he had woken to a world in which he could not move. But why should she care? Why, after the suffering he had inflicted upon her, did she care whether Josiah Kerral walked or not? Drawing on her gloves, Esther sighed inwardly. She didn't know why she cared, she only knew she did.

'You better 'ave a blanket to cover yer knees.' Peggy emerged from Esther's room, a dark blue travelling rug over her arm. 'I 'ave 'ad this airing for a couple of days in case of yer needin' it an' you'll be wantin' it today 'cos it be right parky out there.'

'You are so like Miri.' Esther smiled. 'You would think she had trained you herself.'

'It be me mam, Mrs Cosmore. 'Er says, keep the cold out of yer bones an' you'll keep the doctor out of yer 'ouse. It might not be true but it don't do no harm abidin' by it, do it?'

'No harm at all, Peggy, it is very sensible advice.'

'Oh, me mam is always comin' up with summat like that,' she said airily. 'Me dad says if we 'ad as much money as me mam 'as advice, we could all be livin' the life of Riley.'

'Ah, but do you all take her advice?' Esther asked, the girl's cheerful conversation lifting her flagging spirits.

Peggy's wide smile bordered on a grin. 'Oh, we takes it all right, but we don't always follow it.'

'That explains it then.'

'Explains what, Mrs Cosmore?'

Esther's own smile broadened. 'It explains why you are not living the life of Riley.'

Peggy's laughter rang across the kitchen as she placed the folded rug over Esther's lap before wheeling her out into the yard.

'Ah, Mrs Cosmore.' A portly man with a partly balding head turned from talking to a woman whose frilly cap and lack of apron over her grey gown marked her as a matron of the hospital. 'I was just discussing your father's case with Matron.'

Esther glanced at the woman, giving a nod to her quiet greeting, then back to the man who went on, a smile creasing his rotund cheeks: 'Well now, my dear, some good news for you after all your worry. Your father awoke during the night though he hasn't yet spoken. But that is nothing to be overly concerned about. We must remember he had a bad fall and give him time . . . give him time.'

'And his spine?' Esther asked. 'I was told my father might have injured his spine, that he might be . . .'

'Now, now, Mrs Cosmore.' The smile became a little too bright. 'It's early days yet. Let's not go looking for problems. We have not yet ascertained the depth of the injury your father has sustained to the spine and for as long as he is lying still we feel it best to let things stay as they are. After that, who knows?' He shrugged. 'As Matron will no doubt agree, the human body is a capricious thing. One day it appears useless and the next it has given itself a good shake and is once more in good working order.'

Then it is a pity mine never gave itself a good shake, Esther thought as Matron gave a prim nod.

'Now, Matron,' Dr Frost turned his smile on to the woman who quite visibly thought his were the words of God, 'I think we might persuade you to bend the rules a little and allow Mrs Cosmore five minutes with her father.'

'Certainly, Doctor Frost,' she simpered. 'If you think the patient is up to it?'

'Oh, I do, Matron, I do. A visit from a pretty daughter does a man more good than medicine.'

The reference to Esther's beauty tightening the matron's mouth to whipcord, she raised a finger. 'Five minutes!' she snapped to a young nurse who appeared like a silent wraith from an archway beyond which a gloomy brown-painted corridor stretched its depressing length.

'Mr Kerral will still be feeling quite weak, ma'am,' the young nurse cautioned as she wheeled Esther into the drab ward with its regimented lines of immaculately smooth beds, their occupants sitting on chairs beside them where they would remain until lights out at nine p.m. 'Please try not to tire him.'

Josiah Kerral did not move a muscle as the nurse wheeled the chair close beside his bed but his eyes swivelled to Esther and their glare was the green of an icy sea.

'How are you, Father?' She had to force the words out of her mouth.

'We heard from Mr Evans what happened,' she tried again as his glare seemed to intensify, its frigidity born of hatred.

'I did not know Morgan would come to Rowena House.' Were her words an apology? She tried to decipher her own feelings only to feel more unnerved by the animosity staring her in the face.

'Time's up, Mrs Cosmore.' The young nurse returned, her tread silent on the floor that reeked of carbolic. 'Matron said five minutes.'

Esther nodded, relief sweeping through her at being taken beyond the reach of her father's loathing.

Once more in the trap she breathed long and slow, the cold air washing her nostrils free of the smell of carbolic. But it could not wash away the memory of the expression in her father's eyes.

Why had she forced herself to go to the hospital? Why had she not been content to abandon him altogether as he had abandoned her?

Watching the white whorls of Queenie's breath curl into the chill of the day, Esther once more admitted she did not know.

'Be Mr Kerral still unconscious?' Sam asked guiding Queenie alongside the tramway that stretched the length of Walsall Street.

'He awoke in the night.' Esther watched a young woman, a baby wrapped in her shawl, drag away a toddler who squealed with delight at seeing Queenie.

'That be a good sign then.'

'Yes, a good sign.'

'Steady, wench, steady,' Sam crooned, reassuring the mare who was still not happy with the clang of a passing tram. 'Did the 'ospital say whether he be going to be all right, Mrs Cosmore? 'Is legs, I mean, will 'e 'ave the using of 'em?'

'Doctor Frost was not sure. He said it was too early to decide.'

'Arrh.' Sam nodded. ''E be right, I suppose, it do be early days yet.'

Reaching Cobden Street, he turned the trap left, trotting the mare between buildings fronting straight on to the narrow road. It was less busy here but several women with baskets over their arms and children clinging to their skirts stared as they passed, unused to seeing a wheelchair perched in the back of a small trap.

Esther tried not to feel like a freak in a sideshow of the Wakes, keeping her eyes deliberately on Queenie's rear until a hundred yards or so into the street Sam turned across an open patch of ground that gave on to Butcroft Heath.

'Mr Kerral will be needin' nursin' like as not once 'e be 'ome, 'specially should 'e come to need liftin', and Will Evans won't be up to doing that, not to my mind 'e won't. Letty Turner would be no 'elp in that direction neither.'

Esther had not thought of that. Sam's remark brought her thoughts away from herself. Her father would need care if he proved to be crippled and the staff at Rowena House could not provide it.

"Course somebody to lift be needed but there be none like yer own when a body ain't feelin' too bright,' Sam went on as Queenie picked her own way across the heath. 'An' with Addenbrooke half burned away, I suppose you will be going back 'ome to Rowena House to be with yer father, eh, Mrs Cosmore?'

Sam's words pricked her with the sharp shock of a wasp sting. Go home with him? That house had never been a home to her. And be with her father? Her stomach clenched with repugnance. The last person in the world her father would want at Rowena House was her.

The kitchen was warm when Sam set her chair close to the table, a warmth that eased the cold from her fingers and dispelled the chill his words had brought to her heart.

'I set a pot of soup against you bein' back.' Peggy took cloak, bonnet and gloves to Esther's room, returning at a run. 'I thought you'd be chilled to the marrow, comin' all the way from Walsall.'

'That was thoughtful of you, Peggy.' Esther praised the girl who tried so hard to please her, and though she had no appetite made a pretence of drinking it.

"Ow be that babby of yers, Sam?' Peggy watched as he gulped the soup she had ladled into a large platter pot.

'Growin' well, Peggy. Me mam says 'er be a fine little wench.'

Taking the pot from him, Peggy refilled it, the appetising smell of barley and onion wafting across the kitchen. 'You know what my mam always says of fine little wenches?' Her bright eyes sparkled with laughter as she handed back his pot. "Er says fine little wenches make troublesome big 'uns.'

'Be that right?' Sam grinned. 'So what 'ave you been up to, Peggy Deeley, that's been a trouble to yer mother?'

'I ain't tellin' you, Sam Stedman,' she chuckled, 'an' I ain't tellin' me mam neither or I be like to come back to Addenbrooke without a 'ead on me shoulders!'

Watching the two of them laughing together with all the ease of a childhood spent in one another's company, Esther felt regret for her own lonely years rise inside her. Miri and John had given her love and companionship but it was not the same as close friendship with children of her own age. They had been there for her whenever she needed them, teaching her, guiding her, but the learning gained from rough and tumble, from the exploration of things forbidden, was something they could not give.

'I'll be away to the stable and give Queenie a rub.' Sam handed his empty soup bowl to Peggy. 'If you be wantin' me, Mrs Cosmore, Peggy will give me a shout.'

'I won't be needing the trap again today, Sam.' Esther pushed away her own half-finished soup. 'You can unharness Queenie.'

'Right.' Fishing in his jacket pocket for his cap, Sam left the kitchen.

'I 'ope yer father was better this mornin', Mrs Cosmore?' Peggy set about gathering the used dishes on to the wooden tray.

'Yes, Peggy.' In her mind's eye Esther saw again the freezing stare of those hate-filled eyes. 'My father was more his usual self today.'

'I be glad of that.' She hustled the tray into the scullery where a rattling and banging told of pots being washed. ''E will soon be 'ome then?'

Yes, he would soon be home. Esther stared into the brightness of the fire. He would soon be home and then who would have the caring of him?

'Peg!'

Esther turned her chair towards the window, looking over the stable yard as a shout punctured the quietness.

'Peg!' The shout reverberated, urgency lending power to its volume. 'Our Peg, be you there?'

A lad Esther recognised as Peggy's youngest brother tumbled into the yard, his face red and his breath short and laboured from running too long.

'Peg . . . our Peg!'

'Hey up, young 'un!' Esther saw Sam stride from the stable and scoop the lad up by the back of his collar, holding him inches from the ground. 'What be all the noise about? Anybody would think yer arse was afire the way you was hollerin'.'

'I 'ave to speak to our Peg, Mr Stedman.' The boy squirmed, trying to reach the ground with his feet.

'Does that mean you 'ave to frighten the daylights out of everybody by shoutin' yer 'ead off?' Sam set the lad down but kept a firm hold on his collar.

'I ain't meanin' to frighten nobody, Mr Stedman, but I 'ave to speak to me sister.'

'Then speak to 'er you shall, but don't go deafenin' 'er with all that shoutin'.'

'Was that Sam I 'eard callin'?' Peggy came from the scullery, wiping the last of the water from her fingers on the corner of her apron.

'No, it was your brother.'

'Me brother!' She stepped quickly to the window, looking out over Esther's shoulder. 'Eh, it is our Georgie. I wonder if me mam knows 'e be across 'ere? 'Er will peel the skin from his arse if 'e be 'ere just to be a nuisance.'

'I am sure he is not here for that reason,' Esther replied, watching the boy's red face turn towards Sam.

'No, and 'e better not be or I'll be 'avin' the skin off him meself!' Peggy gave a determined sweep to her apron settling it in place over her skirts before going out to the yard.

The boy's voice, regulated now by the cautioning glare of an older sister, was too low for Esther to hear what he said but the swift look that passed between the girl and Sam alerted her that something was wrong.

Seeing Peggy wave a finger under her brother's nose and Sam take hold of the boy's shoulder Esther could not escape the feeling as her maid turned and ran indoors.

'It be me mam, Mrs Cosmore,' she said, her face ashen. 'Our Georgie says 'er's had a bad tumble an' 'er can't move. Ee, I'll 'ave to go to 'er.'

'Of course you must go to her,' Esther said.

'But what about you, 'ere on yer own?' Peggy had already grabbed her coat from the peg on the door, her fingers fumbling with its buttons.

'I am not a child to be afraid of being left alone, I will be quite able to see to myself.'

'If you be sure?' Giving up the struggle with the buttons, Peggy left the last two undone. 'I'll be off. I can be 'ome in half an hour if I run all the way.'

'And what good are you going to be to your mother arriving home entirely winded from running several miles?' Esther asked, feeling better for taking matters into her own hands. 'You are not going to run anywhere, Sam will take you and your brother in the trap.'

'But I can be well on the way in the time it takes to 'arness Queenie.'

'It will be time sensibly spent,' Esther answered the girl. 'Queenie can trot faster and longer than you can run so you will still be at your mother's in half an hour and in a state where you can help her. Now tell Sam to make the trap ready then call your brother to wait in here while you pack the rest of that soup and bread into a basket. A meal will help soothe everyone's nerves. And take some ham and cheese too. The boys can help themselves if you or your mother do not feel up to making supper for them.'

Following Esther's instructions, glancing all the time at the window overlooking the yard, Peggy ladled soup into a large lidded jar, placing it in the cane basket. Then fetching ham and cheese she wrapped them in a white cloth snatched from a drawer in the dresser, ramming them into the basket beside a large fresh-baked loaf.

'Queenie be in the trap.' Sam tapped at the door.

'Sam?' Esther called him inside. 'Would you please go for the doctor when you have delivered Peggy to her mother's.'

'Me mother can't go findin' money for to pay the doctor, Mrs Cosmore,' she said quickly, 'not even the eighteen pence it costs for Parish doctor to visit . . .'

'The doctor's fees will be paid by me,' Esther answered her. 'Now you go along home – and stop worrying.' Looking at Sam she added: 'If Mrs Deeley should need to go to the hospital, will you see to it?'

'Not to worry, Mrs Cosmore.' Sam took the basket from Peggy, standing aside for her to precede him into the yard. 'If the doctor says 'er needs to go to Sister Dora's, I'll take 'er meself in the trap.'

'Thank you, Sam.' Esther allowed herself a faint smile. 'And stay with the family for the rest of the day, or at least until Peggy's father comes home from the pit. Then you can take Queenie home with you. It will do her no hurt to be without a stable for one night. And, Sam,' she added as he turned to follow the girl and her brother out to the trap, 'tell Peggy she is not to worry about coming back here.'

'I'll tell 'er, Mrs Cosmore. If it be as 'er can't leave 'er mother, I will take the wife to 'er mother's 'ouse to sleep the night an' I will come back 'ere. Queenie won't mind sharing her bedroom with a man!'

Watching the trap drive away, Peggy and her brother in the back, Esther prayed silently: Please not another one, dear Lord, not another cripple!

Chapter Twenty-two

She had been alone here once before. Esther listened to the slow ticking of the clock in the darkening room. That night Robert Vance had revealed his true gender. What if he kept his later promise to return and came tonight?

Wheeling herself to the fireplace, Esther took the iron tongs and placed several lumps of coal on the slumbering fire. It would be a couple of hours at most before either Peggy or Sam returned, and it had been only a few minutes since Adam had left.

She placed the tongs back beside the hearth. Robert Vance would not come tonight, it was already too late. Going to the dresser, she took out a box of matches and proceeded to light the lamp left ready on the table.

'How nice of you to light my way, Esther.'

The deep, musical voice, issuing from the shadowed doorway, froze the blood in her veins.

'I told you I would return.' Robert stepped into the circle of light thrown by the oil lamp.

'How long have you been here?' Esther's voice was strangled by the fear rising to her throat.

'Long enough.' He smiled but in the lamplight his eyes gleamed slyly. 'I was already in your stables when Mr Paige made his appearance. There was no sign of the trap and I did not suppose the handsome Adam had called to see your maid. All I had to do was wait for him to leave.'

'Someone will have noticed you coming here.'

'A well-dressed woman alone would have given rise to speculation, but as you see I am not dressed as a woman. A man walking alone causes no comment. No, Esther, no one will give a second thought to my appearance tonight and I was extremely careful that no one saw me crossing the heath. So you see, my dear, we will not be disturbed.'

'What do you want?' she demanded, her tone holding a confidence she did not feel.

'It is not a matter of what I *want*.' He moved forward into the light. 'It is more a matter of safeguarding what I already have.' Reaching into the pocket of an immaculate lavender grey coat, he drew out a folded paper. 'This,' he tapped the sheet against the fingertips of his left hand, 'is Morgan's will. In it he names me his sole heir. Everything that is his – and of course that includes what you still refer to as yours – is to come to me at his death.'

'So why bring it here?'

'To compare it with the copy he has sent you. I must be sure my darling Morgan has altered nothing.'

'Morgan has sent me no copy of his will.'

'Don't lie to me, Esther.' Robert's voice dropped a shade lower. 'I will not take kindly to being lied to.'

'I do not care whether you take kindly or unkindly to what I tell you – Morgan has not sent me a copy of his will.'

Uncertainty in his eyes, Vance stared down at her. 'He said he was sending you a copy.'

'Did you see him post it? Have you two been separated long enough for him to come here and bring it personally?'

When he did not reply Esther guessed the answer to both of her questions was no. If she could keep him unsure of Morgan he might just go away, but to keep him in a state of uncertainty she herself had to portray a quiet confidence and how long she could maintain that was beyond her guess.

'I have no idea how long you have known my husband, Mr Vance,' she pressed her advantage, 'but it is a longer time than I have, and even I know he does not always do what he says he will. Perhaps you should have made certain he had sent me a copy of that paper you are holding before you made the journey to Darlaston?'

'Maybe.' He nodded, sending shafts of light dancing from his own fair hair, so different from the coils of his black-curled wig. 'But I have not left Darlaston yet. There is always tomorrow. Maybe your copy will come then.'

'You could always waylay the postman crossing the heath.' Esther glanced towards the window but beyond it the night was dark as pitch. Even if Sam or Peggy were coming into the yard, she would not see them. 'Then you could be positive you saw any letter addressed to me.'

'There is that possibility.' His mouth widened in a vindictive smile. 'Or I could stay here.'

'You could,' Esther agreed, though her brain screamed a protest. 'Sam will share the stable with Queenie but I am sure they could make room for you. And unlike you, Mr Vance, I would not broadcast to all and sundry that you had played three in a bed.'

Beyond the circle of saffron light dark shadows danced like puppets, their flickering movements matching the slow measure of the clock.

'Why has Morgan not come with you?' Esther asked, the silence jarring her nerves.

The fire at his back elongated Robert's silhouette in the dim light, seeming to widen his shoulders and add inches to his height.

'Morgan has been somewhat tired of late. He decided not to make this journey.'

'Has his striking my father caused this tiredness?'

Robert grinned at Esther's sarcasm.

'How is your father?' The soft quality of his voice only added to his air of menace. 'Is he to spend the rest of his life as his daughter will spend hers, tied to a wheelchair? I do hope so.'

'Why?' She could not prevent her surprise from showing.

'Why dislike him enough to make that wish? I can understand your having no liking for me, but why my father?'

'He agreed to pay Morgan one thousand pounds a year for tying himself to you and now he refuses to honour that agreement.'

'But that should be Morgan's grievance, not yours.'

'When it comes to money Morgan's grievance becomes mine. What he does not get I have to do without, and doing without money was never my strong point. Morgan only struck Josiah Kerral. If I have to call on him, I will kill him!'

In the dimness of the shadowed room Esther looked at the face of her husband's lover, knowing that the threat he made was real, that behind the pleasing features dwelt a mind that was totally evil.

'Which brings me to the second reason for my calling on you.' He moved forward, bringing the sulphureous gleam of the oil lamp to play across his face, turning the violet eyes a dull yellow topaz. 'Morgan is more than a little short of cash, which in turn means I am too. We both expect you to help.'

'I have said that whatever Morgan wants from me, he must come himself to fetch.'

Esther heard the sharp hiss of indrawn breath and as he half turned from her, watched his gigantic shadow climb as high as the wall.

'I warn you not to play with me, Esther.'

His voice held the same menacing softness of moments before and she felt herself tremble as she glanced again at the blackness of the night pressing against the window pane.

'It is no use your looking for help.' He followed her glance. 'There is no one out there. We would hear the horse and trap arrive long before you could expect assistance, and by that time, I assure you, it would be much too late to do you any good. You see, my dear, what I have promised to do to your father I can and will do to you should the need arise. Now, tell me where you keep your money and I will be gone.'

A pulse beating in her throat, threatening to choke her, Esther clenched her fingers, the nails biting into her palms. Why should she give in to this creature? Pay him now and he would return, sucking at her over and over again like a leech until he had taken every last penny.

'I . . .' she faltered. 'I have no money.'

'I warned you not to play with me!' Swift as a striking cobra his hand shot out, grabbing the front of her dress, using his hold to drag her to her feet. 'You *have* to have money.' He shook her, jerking her head back on her neck. 'Now tell me where it is or I'll knock it out of you!'

He shook her again, the force of it tearing the soft cloth of her gown and she fell backwards into her chair.

'Or perhaps that is not the best way to coax you to part with money?'

He leaned over her, eyes fixed on the pale skin of her throat, laid bare by the ripped dress. 'Perhaps I should employ another method . . .'

'Leave me alone!' Esther gasped, trying to pull together the torn edges of her gown.

'Later.' He slapped her hand away. 'But first . . .'

Clutching both hands to the bodice of her dress, he snatched it savagely open to the waist then seized her chemise, wrenching it from its delicate straps, leaving her breasts bare beneath his gaze.

'Is this what you want for your money?' he breathed. 'Shall I give you what your husband never has?'

Her eyes wide with fear, choking with revulsion, Esther struck out with both hands – only for her head to smash back against the chair as he slapped her hard on both cheeks.

'Relax and enjoy it, Esther.' He ran a finger over the nipple of her left breast, his violet eyes almost black with twisted passion. 'You will enjoy what I have for you, Esther.' He lowered his mouth to her throat, trailing his tongue over the soft flesh of her breast. 'You will enjoy feeling me thrust into you, just as Morgan enjoys it.'

'No!' Instinctively she pushed away but the back of her wheelchair held her a prisoner against his mouth.

Sliding to his knees before her, his mouth still fastened about her breast, he passed his arms around her waist, pulling her from the chair, rolling her beneath him.

Her ears filled with her own cries Esther did not hear the shout from the doorway, neither was she aware of the hands that snatched Robert Vance away from her, flinging him in one movement against the fireplace.

'Esther . . . Esther!'

Her name rising above the roaring in her ears, she felt herself lifted from the floor, arms holding her in a tight circle.

'Oh, Esther, my love. Thank God I came back!' His voice tight with fear and rage, Adam held her hard against him, feeling her sobs rack into his own body. 'It's all right, my love,' he soothed. 'It's over, it's all over.'

Holding her till her sobs stilled, he lowered her to her chair, snatching a cloth from the rail above the range and using it to cover her nakedness. Then and only then did he turn to the figure lying unconscious on the floor.

'Who is it, do you know him?'

Still unable to speak she nodded.

Going to stand over the fallen man Adam stared down at the still form. 'Is this . . .' He bent closer, looking intently into the face. 'Is he related to the Vance woman?'

Esther nodded again then forced her shattered senses to work. 'He is very closely related,' she whispered. 'That man *is* Roberta Vance.'

By the dim light of the lamp Esther saw disbelief flood Adam's face.

'It is true,' she murmured. 'Tonight is not the first time he has paid me a visit. He had been here twice before but each time in the guise of a woman. During the second of those visits he . . . he wanted me to know the truth of what lay beneath the gowns and the wig. He wanted to leave me in no doubt that my husband's lover was a man . . .'

'Did he . . . did he touch you then?' His voice sounded almost strangled.

Aware suddenly of her own tingling nerves and of the pain in his voice, Esther looked at the figure lying half propped against the shining black iron range then back to Adam, his face creased with deep lines. 'No,' she replied, eyes searching for his in the shadow, 'he did not touch me.'

'Then how?'

'He removed sufficient of his women's clothes. I . . . I saw the proof of what he really was.'

'And now the bastard has come back!' Adam spat, grabbing Vance by his expertly tied cravat. 'But he will think twice before he decides to call again.'

Pulling him forward as though to drag him to his feet, Adam paused then let the crumpled figure fall back. 'Esther,' he said, not looking away from the man he had thrown off her, 'whether this is Roberta or Robert Vance, he is dead!'

She clutched the cloth to her chest, the words whirling in her head. Robert Vance . . . dead . . . Robert Vance . . . dead.

'I will have to get the police.' Adam was on his feet and halfway to the door before she cried out for him to stop.

'Think what will happen.' As quickly as her brain had spun, now it cleared, leaving her calm and decisive. 'The authorities will view what has happened as murder, regardless of the circumstances surrounding it. You could well hang.'

'But it was an accident!' He looked back at the body of Robert Vance.

'Only the two of us know that for certain,' Esther argued calmly, 'and if we should not be believed, then you would die – die for that man. And what good would it do? Your death will not give him back his life but it would take your mother's.'

'The authorities have to be told,' he said, 'they will want to know what happened. We can't hide the fact that Vance is dead.'

'And we won't,' she said urgently. 'Only think of the

suffering it will cause to tell it as it happened. Listen to me, Adam, that man came here demanding money and when I refused to give it to him, he attempted to rape me . . .'

'Thank God I prevented that.'

'Yes, you prevented that, but in preventing it he was killed and that could be interpreted as murder.'

'That can't be helped.' Adam came to stand beside her. 'I killed him and must take the consequences if the magistrate does not see that it was an accident.'

'But he will if we tell them my way!' She caught his hand. 'We know he was bent on robbery and rape. If you leave now before Sam or Peggy returns, I can say that as he attacked me I pushed him and he fell back and did not get up. They can see my clothes are half ripped off me. There is surely no magistrate in the land would condemn a crippled woman for trying to defend herself against a rapist?'

'No!' Adam knelt, touching her hand to his lips. 'I was the one who did it and I will not have you take the blame.'

Esther's calm was beginning to slip. If she could not convince him to leave before the others came back then they were lost and a perfectly good life would be thrown away because of one that was dedicated to selfishness and greed.

'Adam, please!' she tried again, her eyes pleading for his agreement. 'An accident is an accident regardless of who caused it. Had there been any kind of malice on your part then I would say report to the police exactly what took place, but you had no intention other than to help me. That being so, let us tell them my version. It is almost all the truth.'

'And supposing you are not believed? Do you expect me to say nothing, to remain silent while you carry the blame?'

'No, Adam. If the police should decide there is a case to answer then you are free to say what you wish, but please . . . please don't throw your life away for Robert Vance, he was not worth it.'

Rising to his feet, he looked again at the motionless form. 'He was nothing but scum!' he said through clenched teeth.

'Then why waste your life and mine on him? Go, Adam,' she urged, 'go now before anyone comes.'

'If you are not believed, I shall tell what really happened.'

'I will get word to you. Now, *go.*'

Almost sobbing with relief as he left, she took a deep breath. She must not fail. If Adam were to live she must not fail in what she had to do now. Placing her hands on the armrests of her chair, the cloth covering her breasts fluttering to the floor, she pushed herself to her feet. Slowly, her hands clenched in concentration, she placed one foot in front of the other, each hard-fought step carrying her nearer the body sprawled across one corner of the fireplace, head lolling on the left shoulder. Reaching it, her throat dry with fear, she drew the folded oblong of paper from the pocket of the lavender grey coat and threw it into the fire. Then, fighting down a rising tide of nausea, she bent over Robert Vance, dragging her fingernails the length of both cheeks, leaving scarlet ribbons of blood in their wake.

The letter! She had almost forgotten the letter she had received that morning, the letter Morgan had written. He had told her of the will he had given to Robert Vance and of the different one, dated the day after and properly witnessed, a will that superseded the one Vance had, a will solely in her favour and safely posted to his solicitor.

The words she had read next flashed into her mind:

I apologise for the hurt I have caused you. You were used as a pawn in the game I played with your father but I will never be able to speak to you of my regrets for I have only a few days left to me. My way of life, my sexual proclivities, have to be paid for eventually. But there is one thing I can do for you, Esther, I can warn you of Roberta, only now perhaps I should call him Robert. He had his admirers once too often, he thought I did not know he deceived me, but there is little I did not know about Robert Vance. The money he hopes for is rightly yours, but he will not give it up easily. He is dangerous and will stop at nothing to get what he wants, and right now he wants money and wants it badly enough to kill for it. Take care, Esther, take care not to be alone.

Drawing the letter from the pocket of her skirts, she sent it after the other into the heart of the fire. She had not told Robert Vance of its existence. She would tell no one.

Nervous tension was beginning to take its toll of her strength. The muscles of her thighs and calves shrieked with the strain she was putting them under, threatening at every move to give up and throw her to the ground. She glanced around but there was no means of support other than the fireplace and she could not risk falling into the fire. A film of sweat breaking out across her forehead, she inched her right foot forward, wanting to cry out at the pain of it, but she had to get back to her chair. Everything depended on her being found in it. Slowly forcing one foot to follow the other, her legs screaming a protest, she moved towards the wheelchair, her brain in an agony of suspense as she listened for a sound that would say Sam or Peggy was back.

Two more steps . . . one more . . . Sobbing from the struggle, her breath coming in quick short rasps, she almost fell against her chair. Both hands grasping an armrest, she leaned forward, letting it take her weight as her head spun. She could not finish it! She could not force her legs to support her any longer!

Across the silence of the kitchen the slow tick of the clock insinuated itself into her brain. You must . . . you must . . . The words merged with the beat, becoming one with the sound.

She had to finish it! She sobbed aloud as her knees jerked, threatening to buckle beneath her. If Adam were to be safe she had to finish it.

Moisture ran from her brow as she pressed on the side of her chair, using her arms to force herself upright. Then, gripping the armrest, she heaved the wheelchair over on its side, the effort tumbling her down with it.

Relief enhancing her sobs she lay across the chair, exhaustion holding her in its grip but her mind clear. Who now would deny Vance had attacked her, or that he had pulled away when she had attempted to defend herself by scraping at his face with her fingernails and fallen back, sprawling into the fireplace where he had hit his head on a corner of the cast-iron range? Who would claim it was anything other than an accident? And even if such a claim were made, the police could not prove Adam was involved, that he had even been to Addenbrooke. If he told them he had, she would deny it. Adam's life would not be given to save her own.

'It is a rare occurrence but not entirely unknown.' James Frost closed the black Gladstone bag that carried the tools of his profession. 'I must say, my dear, you are fortunate to have come out of this business with nothing worse than a fall. It is fortunate you had the presence of mind to strike out at the man.'

'It only be a pity that tumble killed 'im,' Peggy said bitterly, adjusting Esther's skirts about her feet. ''E should 'ave lived so 'e could 'ave been 'anged! Goin' around breakin' into people's 'omes and tryin' to . . .' She stood up, fussing with her own skirts, the word she could not bring herself to say staining her cheeks pink. 'Well, you know what 'e was tryin' to do.'

'But he didn't, Peggy, and it's over now.'

'Arrh.' The girl nodded. 'Thank God. *An'* the use put back in yer legs. I still say it be a miracle.'

'Hardly that, young woman.' The doctor picked up his tall black hat. 'Stress, extreme stress, has been known to have many results. The human body reacts to the power of the mind. Mrs Cosmore obviously had a very powerful need to get away from that man, and her mind, in its highly active state, attempted to supply the means whereby she could satisfy that need.'

'You mean 'cos Mrs Cosmore told 'erself 'er could move 'er leg then 'er did?' Peggy's voice was disbelieving.

Dr Frost picked up his bag. 'Mrs Cosmore was still very badly frightened even when you and her manservant returned and helped her to bed. In that terrified state, and only semi conscious, she mistook her manservant for her attacker returning to relaunch his assault . . .'

Esther's fingers curled painfully as she remembered how he had shaken her so viciously, the sound of tearing cloth as he had snatched away her chemise, the slaps that had sent her head smashing against her chair, his tongue on her breast, the terror that had filled her throat as he had dragged her to the floor, rolling her beneath him; then Adam had been there, Adam . . .

'In order to get away from him,' the doctor's voice went on, 'she had to have the power of movement. Her mind simply supplied that power, causing her to twist her body so violently that it jerked her leg. And you my dear took that for a voluntary movement.'

'Eh!' Peggy murmured. 'Who would think a body's mind could do such a thing?'

'We should never underestimate the power of the mind.' James Frost glanced at Esther, watching from her wheelchair. 'As I explained to you several weeks ago, following that dreadful business, the mind is a Herculean force that can work for us or against us. It has properties as yet not fully understood by the medical world, but it is my personal opinion that it was your mind that prevented you from walking all those years. I had thought that perhaps something happened when you were very young, something that hurt you so deeply that in order to avoid it you mentally adopted the role of a cripple . . .'

'Get that thing out of my sight!' The words spoken so long ago returned with vivid clarity. Her father standing in that corridor, his face a mask of hatred, and her body winced as he seemed to kick out at her again and again; only now she saw there was more than hate in his eyes, there was pain.

'. . . and because you told yourself you could not walk, then of course you could not. I had hoped that another such shock, one you found equally abhorrent, would force your mind to countermand its order and thus return power to your legs. But . . .' he raised his shoulders expressively. 'However, try not to give up hope. While we have life we have hope, and you, my dear, have a long life ahead of you yet.'

'If it were fear that triggered movement in my leg could not that fear have caused me to walk?' Esther put the question into words. She had thought the magistrate who had heard her account of Robert Vance's death in private might have asked the same question, but he had not. The case had been closed immediately with a verdict of accidental death whilst engaged upon a task of a felonious and criminal nature, but she still dreaded someone asking it.

'It can be difficult for the untrained mind to comprehend the many complexities, as I explained to the magistrate.' The little man smiled smugly. 'Though in the first instance, Mrs Cosmore, you were undoubtedly alarmed, you did not then have the experience of that man's hands upon you. The second time, however, when you thought the attack about to be repeated, you already held the knowledge of what was about to occur. It was that knowledge that triggered your subconscious into returning to you the use of your leg, though for you to have actually walked . . . after so many years!' He shook his head.

'Well, it still seems like a miracle to me,' Peggy said, 'for all these fancy ideas.'

'Miracles do not always need a flash of lightning or a heavenly choir.' The doctor turned to the door. 'Our maker has mysterious ways, ways we do not always understand. Let us just be grateful for them.' At the door he turned again to look at Esther. 'Now remember, Mrs Cosmore, not too much to begin with. Those legs of yours have not been called upon to work for many years. Give them time to get used to the idea. I am certain you will find my opinion and hopes justified and eventually you will recover the use of both of your legs.'

'Doctor Frost be right.' Peggy returned from seeing the doctor out. 'A little bit well done be better than a lot botched up, so just you take things steady. And don't go losing hope, perhaps there be something to all this mind business.'

'I hope so.' Esther smiled at the young girl's advice. 'You need have no worries. I shall take your and Doctor Frost's advice.' She had to keep up the deception a while longer. Adam must be kept safe. The miracle must not happen yet.

'Ee, if only me mam 'adn't been so stubborn set against going to the 'ospital, Sam and me might 'ave been back in time to stop that 'orrible man attackin' you.'

'Then I might never have known of the possibility I might one day walk again.' It was a lie that caused Esther to look away from the girl's face, but it was a lie with Peggy's welfare at heart. She must never tell herself the blame for what had happened lay with her mother or herself and this seemed the most positive way of preventing it. 'It is as Doctor Frost said – sometimes the bad thing can trigger a good thing. And this has been a good outcome, has it not?'

'Ee, I 'ope so!' Peggy breathed vehemently. 'Please God I 'ope so.'

'I'll take 'er, sir.'

Hearing Sam call out, Peggy went to look out of the window.

'What is it? Who is Sam talking to?' Esther asked.

The events of that night still recent enough to cause her heart to pound at every unaccustomed sound, Esther's hands tightened in her lap.

'Don't know, Mrs Cosmore. But he be a gentleman and 'e be carryin' one of them fancy little cases.'

'Will you see who it is, Peggy?'

Esther's fingers twined about each other. A gentleman with a fancy little case! Could it be that the issue of Robert Vance's death was not completely closed after all?

'Mr Charles Burrows to see you, Mrs Cosmore.'

Esther's eyes fastened on the man following Peggy into the kitchen, apprehension building within her. Robert Vance had been to see Burrows that fateful day and the solicitor had revealed to him the name of Edward Marsh. Had the two of them planned something Vance had not told her of?

'Good afternoon, Mrs Cosmore. I apologise for presuming to call on you without first making an appointment but I felt my news could not wait.'

'Good afternoon, Mr Burrows.' She returned the greeting as the man's glance swept the kitchen. 'Forgive my receiving you in this room but I am afraid this is the only part of the house undamaged by the fire.'

'Ah, yes, the fire, a most unfortunate occurrence, most unfortunate.'

'Will you take some tea, Mr Burrows?'

'No . . . no, thank you.' He glanced at Esther then quickly away again, the embarrassment of her visit to his rooms following on the heels of his encounter with Mrs Roberta Vance obviously still painful.

'There be some things we be needin' from the town. I will go now 'less you be needin' me?'

Esther shook her head, recognising the girl's tact. 'I will not be needing you, Peggy. Go along and get what is necessary. Sam will take you in the trap.'

'Do sit down, Mr Burrows,' she invited as Peggy grabbed her coat then fetched the wicker basket from the scullery before making her exit.

Placing his valise on the table Charles Burrows extracted a sheet of heavy white vellum. 'I received this letter in the morning post.' He handed it to her. 'I thought, seeing the gravity of it, I should show it to you at once.'

Esther glanced at it, not recognising the small neat writing.

'Please read it, Mrs Cosmore,' Burrows said as she gazed questioningly across the table at him.

'"Sir,"' Esther read aloud, '"I write to you in fulfilment of the last wishes of my client, Mr Morgan Ezra Ashforth Cosmore. It is my sad duty to report to you the death of the said Mr Cosmore at five-forty a.m. on the eleventh day of this month of November, 1902. It was my client's wish that his widow be informed that all arrangements for interment were completed by himself and the burial carried out in Bromford Cemetery on the morning of the following day, being the twelfth of November, 1902. It was also my client's instruction that his will, which you hold in your possession, be read in the presence of his widow, Mrs Esther Helen Cosmore, née Kerral."'

Morgan was dead! The paper slid from her fingers to the table. Morgan was dead and buried and she had not known. He had told her in his letter that he had just a short time left to live, but she had not expected it to be so soon. Why had he stayed in London, why had he not come home? She could almost hear his mocking answer. *Why die in the kitchen of a burned out house when I can do the same in luxury?*

'I have your husband's will here.' Burrows drew out a long manilla envelope. 'Will you hear it now, Mrs Cosmore?'

First Ezra and now Morgan. Both had used her, both had hoped to gain through her, but the handful of silver the taking of her had brought was long gone and now father and son were dead.

Concerned by the sudden pallor of her face, the solicitor folded up the letter. 'I realise what a dreadful shock this must be to you, Mrs Cosmore. Maybe you would prefer that I called another day? I am sure the contents of your late husband's will can be safely held over until you are feeling recovered.'

'That will not be necessary, Mr Burrows, but I thank you for your kindness.' Esther swallowed but the lump in her throat remained. 'Please read my husband's will.'

Perching a pair of wire-rimmed spectacles on his nose, he withdrew a single sheet of paper from the brown manilla envelope, clearing his throat before reading.

'"This is the last will and testament of . . ."'

Looking over the spectacles at Esther, seeing her head slightly bowed, he asked, 'Would you prefer me to leave out the preliminaries, Mrs Cosmore? You will of course be at liberty to read this document for yourself at any time.'

At her nod the portly little man cleared his throat again then continued.

'". . . to my wife, Esther Helen Cosmore, I leave my apologies for the wrongs I have done her. This I do freely and sincerely and make no encumbrance upon her to forgive. In addition I bequeath to my wife, Esther Helen Cosmore, all that is left of my estate of Addenbrooke and ask that one day she might rebuild it; also I leave to her, and to her solely, the residue of my fortune, being the money made from the sale of Cosmore copper works of James Bridge, the same being one thousand three hundred pounds. To Mr Robert Vance, sometimes known as Mrs Roberta Vance,"' the puffy cheeks coloured, '"I leave my wishes that he meet with as generous a fool and patron as I proved to be."' He looked up. 'There follows only the signature of Mr Cosmore and the witnesses.'

'Thank you,' Esther whispered.

Tucking the papers back into the valise, he snapped it shut and rose to his feet, his fat cheeks still a clear shade of pink. 'I will contact your late husband's solicitor and see that the terms of the will are carried out. Perhaps I might contact you when everything is settled?'

'Yes, of course.' Her hand aching from the tight twisting of her fingers, Esther wheeled her chair around.

'Please do not bother to see me out, Mrs Cosmore.' Charles Burrows almost dashed for the door. 'I can do that for myself. Good day to you.'

'Be you all right, Mrs Cosmore?' Peggy was in the kitchen almost before the solicitor was out of it.

'I thought you had gone to town?'

'That were just an excuse.' She set the basket on the table while she removed her coat. 'I ain't leavin' you by yerself no more.'

'And what about your visits home?' Esther smiled. 'Your mother may not have suffered any broken bones from her fall but she did sustain a twisted ankle and I expect she still feels badly shaken.'

'Arrh, 'er does.' Peggy swept up the basket, returning it to the scullery. 'But our Georgie can fetch any bits an' pieces 'er wants from the shops, an' next door said they would look in when me dad an' the others be doin' their shifts.'

'The kindness of neighbours is always gladly accepted and appreciated but it does not make up for a daughter's care, Peggy. You will continue to visit your mother every day and I will not hear any arguments. Now get the tea brewed before Sam thinks we have both fallen asleep.'

Morgan was dead. Esther watched the girl move quickly about the kitchen. He had been no sort of a husband to her but she would not have wanted his death. *I leave you my apologies* . . . the words haunted her . . . *and make no encumbrancè upon you to forgive.*

But I do forgive, her heart whispered, I do forgive you, Morgan.

Chapter Twenty-three

'William Evans came to see me this morning.'

Esther finished looking at the production and sales figures that Adam had brought.

'Your father's butler?'

She nodded. 'My father is being discharged from hospital the day after tomorrow. The doctor says he can now be cared for in his own home.'

'That's good news.'

'I would have thought so too, Adam, until William Evans told me it is his belief my father has no home to return to.'

'No home?' Adam looked up from the last of the books he had brought for her to see. 'I don't understand, Rowena House is his home?'

'It was, until he mortgaged it to Paul Turner.'

'Paul Turner of First Trust Bank? But what makes Evans think that? Has your father said anything to you on any of your visits to the hospital?'

'No.' Esther answered the second question first. 'He refuses even to look at me when I visit, much less speak to me. And as for Mr Evans's suspicions, it seems two men calling themselves assessors for the bank were at Rowena House last week. It was they who intimated the house would be repossessed in a few days.'

'Rowena House sold?' Adam looked and sounded puzzled. 'But why?'

'Obviously my father took on a debt he was unable to repay and now the house is to be taken in lieu.'

'Losing Rowena House.' Adam shook his head. 'A kick from a horse and a carriage rolling across his back couldn't kill your father, but this very well might.'

No, that accident had not killed her father and neither had the abandoning of his only child, but the loss of his home . . .

'Where else can he go?' Adam interrupted her thoughts. 'He can't very well come here, there isn't another room.'

No, her father could not come to Addenbrooke, but neither could she see him become dependent upon the Parish.

'I shall go to see Paul Turner in the morning.' She looked at Adam. 'I shall ask the cost of redeeming the mortgage on Rowena House.'

He glanced towards the books lying closed on the table. 'Your finances are healthy but whether they will stretch to buying a house of that size . . .' He blew softly through his teeth. 'Don't count on it, Esther.'

'I don't have to. I have the money Morgan left me – that may be enough on its own. I will have to find out how much my father borrowed from the bank before I will know for sure. It will be ironic, Adam, don't you think?'

'How do you mean?'

'Ezra's works being sold and most of the money being used to buy back my father's house.' She smiled ruefully. 'At least we have something to thank Morgan for.'

Adam smiled suddenly. 'Yes, your father can thank Morgan Cosmore but listen out for rumblings from St Lawrence's.'

'The church? Why rumblings from the church?'

His smile widening to a grin, Adam leaned back in his chair. 'Not so much the church as the churchyard. The rumblings will be Ezra turning in his grave!'

As quickly as it had come his grin faded. 'Esther, now you are a widow you can hold property in your own right. No one can touch it. I want you to take back the soap works and the houses along Heathfield Lane.'

She felt a kind of quickening in her heart, a small sickening lurch as if something were being cut from her. 'But I gave those properties to you!'

'Only as a way of keeping them from Morgan,' Adam said gently, hearing the protest in her voice. 'But now he is gone the danger of their being taken from you no longer exists. Therefore I want you to take them back.'

The feeling of sickness in her stomach deepened. Was there more to Adam's wanting her to take back those properties? Was this a beginning, a first step in severing himself from her? Was he tired of working for a woman?

'If that is what you wish, Adam,' she said dully, 'I will see that it is done but would you wait until the business of Rowena House is settled?'

He rose, silence making no answer to her question yet answering it with resounding clarity as he left. Adam was breaking away. How long before he left altogether?

'You are to go home tomorrow.' Esther looked at the man sitting on a chair beside the narrow hospital bed, its covers smoothed to mirror evenness; a man whom the brief weeks since his accident had reduced to a faded shadow of his former appearance. Enveloped now in a thick brown dressing gown, his body thin and face haggard, he glared at her through dull eyes.

'But Rowena House is no longer yours, is it, Father?'

The eyes were venomous but today Esther had no fear of Josiah Kerral.

'You mortgaged it to First Trust Bank and they have now foreclosed.'

He still did not speak but stared at her with unblinking hatred.

'As a result you must find somewhere else to live.' Esther returned his stare coolly. 'Might I ask where you intend that should be?' When he still remained silent she went on, 'Why did you mortgage the house? Why take out a loan against it?'

'Why!' The bonds of silence ripped apart, his voice echoed through the silent ward. 'Why d'you bloody think? 'Cos there were nothing left after I paid that toe rag Cosmore to marry you. He took half of my business and a thousand in cash besides that, then when he had gone through the cash he sold his share of Wheel and Axle. Business had been going downhill for some time and when I came to buy back the share he had sold, I couldn't put my hand on that much money so I put the house up as collateral. And here be yer chance to laugh. I don't 'ave the means to redeem the mortgage so now it belongs to the bank. Now y'ave heard what you came to hear, bugger off. The sight of you in that wheelchair sickens me.'

'Mr Kerral, you must stop this unseemly shouting at once!' The nurse who had wheeled Esther into the ward returned almost at a trot.

'You bugger off an' all!' Jos roared, temper pumping life's blood back into his face. 'Mind yer own business and stay outta my way or I'm like to kick yer bloody arse.'

'Mr Kerral!' the nurse gasped, her eyes opening wide.

'Bugger off, I tell you!' he roared again, sending her scuttling away.

'I can help if you will let me?' Esther said as his glare fixed on her again.

'You!' He laughed, a short scornful sound. 'You be only a woman.'

'Women can sometimes be helpful.'

'They be useful for one thing only and you ain't even useful for that,' he snapped. 'You ain't even a woman, you be naught but a bloody useless cripple.'

'Stop that shouting at once!' The doors of the long ward opened and Matron sailed in, the nervous young nurse in attendance.

'So they've fetched you, 'ave they!' Josiah's temper flared

to new heights. 'Well, try comin' a bit closer and see what it gets you. 'Avin' my foot up yer arse will make a change from the noses of them spineless creatures you call nurses.'

Matron's nostrils flared as she prepared to attack.

'That's right, take a good breath,' Josiah shouted, 'it will make my kickin' it outta you that much more enjoyable.'

Her mouth thinning to obscurity as she re-drew her battle lines the Matron returned a stare equally as enraged as that of her patient. 'Mr Kerral,' she said, biting off each word sharply, 'if you shout just one more time I will call the police and have you removed from this hospital.'

'You do that,' he bawled even louder, the effort fanning the colour in his cheeks. 'Then I'll withdraw my donations to this bloody 'ospital, and see 'ow you likes that!'

'Mrs Cosmore . . .'

'Say what you 'ave to say to me,' Jos interrupted the matron's appeal. 'I be the one was doin' the shoutin'.'

'Then perhaps you would think of the other patients in the ward, Mr Kerral, and kindly stop shouting.'

'Bugger the patients in the ward and bugger you,' he yelled. 'If you wants me to shut up then take this . . . this thing . . . outta my sight!'

Her jaw sagging at his words, Matron looked at Esther.

'Mrs Cosmore, I am so sorry.'

'Sorry!' Jos laughed scathingly. 'What you be sorry for, you bloody hypocrite? You ain't in no wheelchair.'

'Will you let me wheel you out?' Matron asked Esther, her face registering disgust at what Jos had shouted.

'No, thank you.' Esther looked up into the woman's taut face. 'I have something to discuss with my father.'

'As you wish, but maybe you could get him to lower his voice? There are people in this hospital who need quiet.'

'If they be anything like the lot in this ward, then they need a bloody undertaker!' Jos shouted after her receding figure, smiling grimly as he saw Matron's back grow a shade stiffer.

'Behaving like a spoiled child does you little credit,' Esther said, making no pretence at disguising her contempt.

'What did you say?'

The question, low and grating, held far more of a threat than his shouting but Esther refused to let any fear of him show in her face.

'Has your accident affected your ears as well as your spine, or do you have some need to pretend you did not hear?'

'I 'ave no need to pretend anything to anybody, an' I 'ave no need of you so get yerself away!'

'There is no use in pretending, is there, Father?' Esther said, allowing her tone to sweeten. 'No use pretending you still have money to donate to this hospital when you have none, or pretending you can walk when you can't, or pretending you have a home to return to when you have none. Shouting like a child deprived of his favourite toy will not bring back any of those things.'

'I don't need you to preach to me,' he growled. 'Or has Cosmore taught you to kick a man when he's down? It's easy to see you be enjoyin' it.'

'And why not! If the Cosmores have taught me to kick then it is more than you ever did. And as for enjoying it, did you not enjoy kicking a four-year-old child? Did you not enjoy seeing me down for all those years? If I am enjoying seeing you as you are now, you have only yourself to blame!'

'I kept you fed. I made sure you wanted for nothing.' The colour still high in his cheeks and his temper only barely under control, Jos glared at the woman sitting opposite him. And she was a woman, he conceded to himself. The girl who had sat in his sitting room being exchanged for the chance of money was gone and in her place was a woman, cool and determined, one who showed no fear and who held him in little regard.

'Yes, you kept me fed as I shall you.' Her eyes on his, Esther answered, 'You made sure I wanted for nothing – I will do the same for you. You deprived me of a father's love, and you will be deprived of the love of a daughter.'

A shadow seemed to pass across his eyes at the last of her words, a darkness that was almost pain. But the acid in his reply was as stinging as before.

'*You* will keep me fed! *You* will make sure I want for nothing! And what will you do it with? Cosmore 'adn't a penny when he died and doubtless that son of his had none when he followed him to the grave. Huh!' he laughed, a hard sound devoid of humour. 'What the bloody hell have *you* got?'

'I have a great deal, Father. To begin with I have Rowena House.' Esther watched disbelief work the muscles of his face. 'Tomorrow I sign for the purchase of the Wheel and Axle works. I have all that was yours and a great deal more besides. I have enough to give you all you gave me. You will have the cottage in the grounds of Rowena House, a manservant, oh and one of these:' Esther tapped the arm of her chair. 'I hope the sight of you in it will not sicken anyone!'

Then, turning her chair she propelled herself from the ward.

Taking the box from the dresser, Adam walked from the house in Heathfield Lane. He had returned the properties to Esther months ago and now the last of the buildings was occupied. There were no families left in Foleys Croft. He had also wanted to resign as manager of her works, that way he would no longer need to see her, but as yet his courage had failed him. He did not want to be with her yet being without her tormented him. He had given over the task of presenting her with the accounts to Barney Whitehouse who now practically ran the Leys, knowing as much about it as Adam himself. That had freed him from going to Rowena House every week, a freedom he welcomed yet did not want.

Veering left he kept to the heath, not wanting to meet

workers finishing their shift and coming home to their evening meal.

Why did he not want the freedom he should welcome? Why did he feel he must end his employment with Esther? Why did he avoid seeing her when all the time he yearned for her?

He breathed deeply, the warm evening air scented with the perfumes of wild flowers, pleasant after the smell of slurry, the mix of oil and water that kept the capstan machines from overheating.

Was it still guilt at leaving her to explain away Robert Vance's death, even though she had insisted upon it again and again? Or was it the fact that with Morgan's death Esther was now a free woman?

The pull at his heart confirmed the answer he already knew, the answer he had known from the beginning. He had spent so many hours dreaming of Esther being freed from the bond of marriage, of his being able to tell her what was in his heart and ask her to be his wife. Now she was a wealthy industrialist in her own right, a status that would surely bring her a husband from her own class?

Away to the right above the roofs of the distant houses the canopy of the sky turned to flame as the steel works opened their furnaces. Pausing, Adam lifted his face to the scarlet veil, willing the fire that painted the sky to burn away the pain of his soul.

Tonight he would give in his notice. Tonight he would tell her they would not meet again.

Looking down at the box in his hands, his eyes went past it to the ground, lit now by the brilliant flush of the sky. A ghost of a smile touching his mouth, he bent, breaking off a tiny sprig of mugwort. The spirits of the heath would forgive him, he thought, threading the thin stem through the buttonhole of his jacket. If they could not give him the woman he loved, perhaps they would turn a blind eye to his taking a little of the plant that would always remind him of her.

But would he need any reminding? He walked on. Would the time ever come when her face faded from his mind or the need for her died from his body? *Don't get involved.* The smile on his mouth became a harsh, hopeless laugh.

Esther sat in the shelter of the line of trees that separated Rowena House from the cottage in which she had spent sixteen years of her life. Her father had lived there for six months now – six months in which she had provided him with all she had promised. And what of the promise she had made herself? What of the vow she had silently made to take revenge, to see him pay for the hurt he had done her?

That too had been fulfilled. She now owned all that had once belonged to Josiah Kerral. She had seen him fall from being a power in the town to being a man who had nothing: watched him depend upon others for movement where once he had walked free. Yes, she had been given her revenge, so why this feeling of emptiness? Why was there no joy in her victory? Was the bitterness she felt just that of an empty revenge or was it the old bitterness of craving her father's love?

So many times she had told herself his denial of her was of no consequence, yet always that denial rang false. It had been that way with her when she was a child; it was that way with her now.

The branches of the trees dipped and swayed in the light breeze of evening, leaves sending a flickering pattern across the walls of the little house. Inside a lamp gleamed though the sun had not yet set. He would be in that room, sitting alone with his thoughts as she had so often done. Was he as unhappy as she had been, even with John and Miri to love her?

'Don't let him be that unhappy,' she whispered to the breeze touching her face. 'Don't let him feel as I have all these years.'

Away in the distance the sky above the town flared to crimson, spreading like a great stain of blood as far as the horizon: the life blood of the Black Country, the blood of its industries.

Esther watched the brilliant display as gold-edged scarlet was slashed with violet and mauve. Her father had once been a part of the industries of which that coloured sky was the banner. Now he must miss it. How he must miss running the Wheel and Axle Works after so long.

'If only he would let me love him,' she sighed.

Across the expanse of ground that separated the two houses a gust of wind, a herald of night, blew among the trees, whispering behind the leaves. And to Esther's mind, caught up in her own emotion, it seemed to murmur: *Ask him . . . ask him*.

But how could she ask that? How could she give him the chance to hurt her again? Why give herself up to another onslaught of his hatred?

Ask him. The leaves echoed the message of the breeze and almost as if no longer conscious of her own movements, Esther wheeled herself towards the cottage.

Her father's wheelchair stood empty in the nook by the window that had been her favourite spot; it seemed that nothing had moved since she had left, that the house in some inexplicable way had stood still, encased in a bubble of time.

But it was not Miri sitting hunched in a chair staring into the heart of the fire, it was her father.

'Good evening, Father.'

He looked up as she spoke and the sight of his drawn face pierced her heart.

'Are you alone here?' she asked when he made no answer.

Returning his gaze to the fire he replied, 'As you see.'

'Your manservant, where is he?'

'A man needs the company of others. It don't do for him to be stuck with an invalid day and night.'

He stared into the red heart of the fire as if seeing pictures of the past, pictures of himself in the company of others. Esther watched him from just within the door. He had not shouted abuse at her, had not ranted or raved, he just stared quietly at the glowing coals.

'I should not have come,' she said as his silence became more unbearable than his bad temper had been. 'I am sorry for intruding.'

'It be yer house, you can come and go as you please.'

No, she wanted to shout, this is not my house, it is yours. It is *your* house. Instead she asked quietly, 'Is there anything I can do for you?'

'I be well enough taken care of,' he answered heavily. 'There be nothing you can do for me. There be nothing anyone can do.'

Seeing him there, shoulders drooping, all the fire and spirit leached out of him, her heart twisted and the bitterness and desire for revenge that had filled it for so long were suddenly gone. In their place she felt only pity and an overwhelming desire to help him. But how? He had refused her help before.

Across the kitchen the clock ticked, slow and regular. Tell me what to say, Esther prayed silently, tell me what to say.

'But you could do something for me, Father, if you would?' The words seemed to come from nowhere. She had not intended to say them nor did she know why she had.

'Help you? How do you reckon that? There be nothing you can need from me.' Still he did not look at her.

'There is something I need.' She crossed the room, coming to rest before him, words forming themselves without the help of her mind, coming easily from her mouth as if spoken by someone other than her. 'I need your experience. I know nothing of the Wheel and Axle trade. There has been a continued rise in demand for almost six months and I do not have the know how to meet it. I am afraid that if I do not, I will lose the business altogether. It needs you, Father. I . . .' Her voice dropped. 'I need you.'

Propping his elbows on his knees, he dropped his head into his hands. 'Don't give me yer pity,' he said thickly.

Esther's hands clenched at her sides and her mouth dried. 'I am not offering you my pity, Father,' she said, her voice reflecting the fear and longing of a lifetime. 'I am offering you my love.'

All around them silence ebbed and flowed in crashing soundless waves, surging over them, drowning them. Esther was left fighting for breath as her father sat with his head bowed in his hands, his only movement a heaving of his shoulders.

It had been useless to try. He did not want help, did not want anything that held even a small part of her. Wheeling her chair around, she started for the door.

'Esther!'

The half-choked cry was the last thing she had expected and tears already filled her eyes as she turned back.

'Esther . . . oh my God! Esther.' The hours given to following the advice of the doctor plus his own determination now paid off and he was on his feet, arms held out to her, his face a mask of misery.

'Esther, what have I done to us both!' He sobbed, dropping to his knees and drawing her into his arms. Her face against his shoulder, sobs shaking her body, her astonishment at his recovery lost in the sheer joy of being held at last in his arms, Esther too, sobbed.

'I've been such a blind, stupid fool,' he whispered into her hair. 'All I could see was my own pain, and all I could think of was myself, my own loss when yer mother died. I didn't want anyone near me, I didn't want you . . . oh, Esther! How you must have hated me.'

'There were moments when I thought I did, Father,' she said softly, 'but deep down I always knew I loved you.'

His arms tightening, he held her close for several seconds before letting her go. 'You might hate me more when you hear how your mother died.' He slumped back on to his haunches but before he could drop his face into his hands again, Esther took each of his hands in hers.

'Your mother was very young when I brought her here to Darlaston, young and beautiful, and I worshipped her. She was very popular with everybody and we were soon being invited to houses all around. That was when my love turned to jealousy. I grew resentful of the attention men paid to her, then as the months went by that turned to fear that I would lose her to another man – not that she ever showed the slightest interest in any of them apart from making polite conversation, but that did not ease my fears or calm the jealousy that began to eat me away. Often I would accuse her of having more interest in a man than social etiquette called for, until my mounting suspicion and mistrust turned to blows.'

He broke off, a long shuddering breath shaking the whole of his body as he relived former nightmares. Holding the silence, Esther waited.

'Then she became pregnant.' Jos went on in utter despair, 'I knew the child she carried was mine yet couldn't rid myself of the thought that maybe . . . then, in the eighth month of her carrying, I came home to find her in the company of David Blakely. He was the son of an industrialist colleague of mine from Birmingham and was on leave from his regiment of Staffords. Try as I might to control it, my jealousy mounted until I virtually threw him out of the house. Your mother was angry at my behaviour and for the first time in our marriage, she showed it.'

Jos drew another long breath, using it as a spur for his next words. 'I took her defence of him as a sign that there was more than friendship between them and in my fury I slapped her several times across the face, but even that did not calm the anger in me. I followed her up the stairs as she made for her room. I caught her at the top and shouted that she preferred Blakely to me, that she had invited him to the house as her lover. When she looked at me so pityingly, with her beautiful brown eyes filled with tears and told me he did at least treat her more considerately, I just went berserk. I remember her cry as I struck her . . .'

He breathed again, long and slow, holding it for several seconds before releasing it as slowly. 'She was on the floor moaning as I kicked out at her – I don't know how many times. Then Miri, her maid, was dragging her away. You were born that night, a cripple the doctors said would never walk. She did not once blame me but the fear never left her eyes from that night.

'Gradually, as you grew yet didn't walk, she seemed to withdraw into herself. The love that had been between us became a shadow, one that haunted me every waking hour and kept me company in my sleep. I had been the cause of her pain and of your deformity. Every time I looked at you I saw my own guilt; you were my accuser and my judge. Then came the night she died and I came out of her room to see you there in the corridor and the same madness as before took hold of me. She was gone and I could not bear the guilt, I could not face up to a lifetime of having you before me wearing my Helen's face.

'Miri got you away as she had your mother and later I realised my only salvation, and your safeguard, lay in avoiding you so I sent you to this house. For sixteen years you were here, and for almost two years after that you were at Addenbrooke, and through all of that time I carefully nurtured my grievance against you. I told myself I hated you and kept on telling myself that, because once I stopped I would have had to admit I loved you, that beneath the anger and pain and sorrow I had always loved you, and that would have been the end of Josiah Kerral. The knowledge that I had lost the two things I loved most in the world, my wife and my daughter, would have totally destroyed me. So you see now why I said you would hate me more than you could ever love me.'

'I don't hate you, Father.' Esther pressed her lips to each of his hands in turn, her heart swollen with pity. 'And I do not blame you. Neither would my mother. You hurt her, it would be senseless to deny that, but you did not kill her. Tuberculosis caused her death – that much at least Miri told me. Our emotions are powerful things, Father, and jealousy can, I think, be the most potent of all, but the past is the past and recrimination will not change a moment of it. I love you, Father, and I want you to love me. I want you to come home to Rowena House and share my life there as my father.'

Pressing her palms close against his face Josiah Kerral made no answer. Only his tears coursing over her fingers made his reply for him.

Esther smoothed the plum-coloured suit, the jacket trim about her waist. She had not enjoyed maintaining the lie, not telling her father or Peggy she could walk, albeit not very far as yet. But she had had to maintain it, she could allow no hint of suspicion to fall on Adam. Grasping the bedpost she pulled herself to her feet and stood looking at her reflection in the mirror standing against the opposite wall. If only Miri could have seen her walk.

'I love you Miri,' she whispered, tears misting her eyes. 'I love you both. Thank you, thank you both for loving me. I know you would have been so happy for me.'

But would Miri be happy with what she was about to do now? Slowly Esther walked from the room. 'I have to do it Miri,' she whispered. 'I must.'

'Oh my God!' Amazement rooted Peggy to the ground, staring as Esther walked into the kitchen. 'Oh my God, you be walking!'

'Yes.' Esther smiled, hoping the guilt she was feeling did not show on her face.

'But . . . but 'ow?'

'Later Peggy, just now I could do with my chair.'

'Eh? Oh, oh yes.' Grabbing the wheelchair from beneath the window Peggy rushed it to where Esther stood leaning against the door jamb.

'Has Sam left?' Esther spoke quickly, not wanting more of Peggy's questions just yet.

'He were in the yard but a minute since.' Peggy helped her into the chair. 'Will I fetch him for you?'

'No, no not right away. I would like a little time in the garden, but will you tell him I will need the trap shortly.'

Peggy grasped the handle of the chair. 'I'll wheel you into the garden then I'll tell him. Shall I say you'll call when you be ready? Eeh, I said miracles could happen!'

'Yes.' Esther nodded then to herself added, miracles could happen, but never twice.

'Ee, we 'aven't seen you in a long time.' Peggy smiled as she opened the door of Rowena House.

'No.' Adam returned the smile but it faded almost immediately. He should not have come here, he should have sent the box with one of the men.

'Well, come in.' Peggy stepped aside, holding the door wide. 'You'll be wanting to see Mrs Cosmore?'

'If she has the time.'

'Time!' Peggy closed the door, a puzzled frown settling between her eyes. 'Since when 'ave you had the need to ask that? Mrs Cosmore has always been pleased to see you.'

'Yes, she has, Peggy.' Adam realised he must have sounded churlish. 'But I try to remember that she is a busy woman nowadays.'

'Never too busy for friends,' Peggy retorted, 'and she can't 'ave too many of the right sort. And you 'ave always been the right sort, Mr Paige.'

Adam turned a mock serious look at the girl who had moved to Rowena House with Esther. 'Oh, it's Mr Paige now, is it? Just because you no longer live in a kitchen, you don't have to go all posh on me. What happened to Adam?'

'It be old Evans,' Peggy whispered. 'He insists that all callers be given their proper titles.'

'Titles?' Adam's smile returned, this time holding a little of its old warmth. 'I am not a member of the aristocracy.'

'The ari-what?' Peggy grinned mischievously.

'I am not a lord.'

'Thank the Lord for that,' she quipped. 'I 'ave enough trouble in rememberin' to call a bloke Mister without tryin' to remember to call one Yer Lordship.'

'What if we just go back to plain Adam?'

'I'd prefer that but old Evans would 'ave a face as hard as a fourpenny hock if he heard me call you that.'

'You leave Evans to me.' Adam smiled again, feeling happier than he had in some time. 'He might be butler in this house but he is not going to come between friends. I shall tell him that when I come here you – but only you – are to address me as Adam.'

'Ee! Old Evans won't like that, he be a stickler for what he call the proprieties.'

Adam leaned towards her, dropping his voice to little more than a whisper. 'My father used to tell me and my brothers when we were lads, if we were given something we did not like, not to roll it round the tongue but to swallow it down quick and get it over with. That way the taste did not coat the mouth.'

'Like burned onion and black treacle.' Peggy grimaced. 'Ee, the things me mam give us kids! Not to mention castor oil. The very thought of our mam's potions did more to prevent illness than they ever did to cure 'em.'

'But they helped you grow into a bonny wench, one the lads of Darlaston have an eye for, I'll be bound.'

'Ee, get away with you.' Peggy blushed. 'You 'ave a tongue would charm ducks off the water.' She turned, leading the way towards the sitting room. 'Will I take that box?' she asked, opening the door.

'No.' He glanced at the battered tin box, its once pretty lid and sides blistered and scorched, leaving tiny islands of coloured paint among the black. 'I will hang on to it.'

'Then if you wait in there, I will tell Mrs Cosmore you be here.'

'Is Esther . . . Mrs Cosmore . . . not in that room?'

''Er be outside in the gardens somewhere. Spends a lot of time out there 'er does, sometimes it be quite dark afore 'er comes into the house. I'll go look for 'er.'

Adam felt his determination leaving him. How could he look at her, knowing it would be for the last time? He had said for Peggy to call him Adam when he came to Rowena House, despite William Evans's instructions, but she would not have to risk the butler's displeasure for he would not be calling again.

'Don't bother, Peggy,' he said, 'I don't want you to disturb Mrs Cosmore. Just say I called when she comes in.'

The girl's eyes widened, showing her surprise. 'Ee, I'll do no such thing. 'Er would be quite annoyed if you left and I hadn't told 'er you be here. Now you hold on a minute while I fetch 'er.'

It could not be avoided. To insist on leaving without seeing Esther would give rise to suspicion, and suspicion fast turned to gossip. He would not have Esther open to gossip.

'You say she is in the garden?' he asked, and when the girl nodded, went on, 'then I will go out to her there.'

Esther breathed deeply, smelling the scents of spring blushing into summer. Her father had gone with her to Rowena House. With no need of his wheelchair, he had pushed hers across the ground that had so long separated them. She glanced up at the windows of the room where he now lay sleeping. She had the love and friendship of one of the two men who meant so much to her, but the love of the other would never be hers.

Returning her glance to the garden, she stared into shadows etched with silver. Why had Adam stopped coming to see her? Could it be that the evenings they had once shared were now shared with another? She had no claim on him save that of an employer and she would never use that to bring him to her. But she must go see him, and to do that she would walk, she must know why he no longer came to the house. Was it a woman that kept him away?

Adam with another woman . . . The pain of the thought cut like a scalpel into her heart but it was an idea she must accept. He would want to marry, that was only natural, and she must bear the unwelcome truth: Adam Paige would never marry her.

'Esther.'

Breath catching in her throat, she turned to see him standing a few yards from her.

'I was at Addenbrooke today,' he said, his words falling into the chasm of silence that yawned between them. 'I went to see how the rebuilding was progressing. One of the men gave me this, it was found in the rubble. I thought you might like to have it.'

She watched him, the rising moon bestowing his dark head with a coronet of silver light, the suddenness of his appearance robbing her of speech.

'It's a little battered but it survived.'

Yes, the little box had survived. Esther felt the lurch of her stomach and the sting that sprang along her veins. But how could she survive? What would her life be without him? The support of the callipers no longer about her legs they trembled as she rose from the chair she would never use again: from this day on she would walk unaided.

'What is it?' Just three words but the effort it took to say them was almost overwhelming.

'Open it.'

The translucent ivory of the moonlight touched his face and Esther dropped her eyes to the box, unable to stand the pain of wanting to lift her arms to him and knowing she could not.

Pushing the lid back on hinges buckled by heat, she gave an involuntary gasp. There, pale in the dimness of its interior, was the little white prayer book and the lace-edged handkerchief. A memory of her mother and a memory of her wedding day lying together in the box's dark heart.

'Thank you.' She lowered the rusting lid, closing away the memory of the day her life had meant less than a handful of silver; the day Morgan Cosmore had been paid to marry a cripple.

Would any other man have done it? She kept her gaze on the battered box. Would any other man have married a woman knowing she would never walk, even with that thousand pounds and a forty per cent share of an engineering works for recompense?

She said nothing. A misery he felt would crush the very life from his body swept over Adam as he guessed at the reason for her silence and bent head. After all he had done to her, she had obviously loved Cosmore and could not think of another man. He turned to go.

'Adam!'

His name was spoken as softly as the touch of moonlight on the trees. Esther had called him but she did not know what it would cost him to turn around; the price he would pay, and go on paying, for looking at her just one more time.

'Adam, may I ask you something before you leave?'

Turning, he saw her face lifted to his, the incandescent light adding to its gentle beauty. He felt it strike to the very core of him.

'You can ask me anything,' he said quietly.

Glancing once more at the tin box in her hand, she hesitated, searching her soul for the courage to ask her question and the courage to face the answer. Help me Miri, she prayed silently. Help me.

'Adam,' still she did not look at him, 'would you ever marry a cripple?'

In the shadowed reaches of the garden fireflies danced among the trees, their tiny points of light spangling the darkness.

He watched her for a moment, drinking in the picture he would not see again and he knew the unspoken meaning underlying her question, would he marry for money as Morgan Cosmore had. Then, his voice as low as her own, he answered: 'No, Esther, I would not marry a cripple. Not for position, not for property, not for money.' Stepping forward, he closed the gap between them. 'I would not marry a cripple for any of those reasons. But I would marry a cripple if I loved her . . . if I loved her as I love you.'

'Adam!' Her cry was lost as he lifted his arms and she walked into them, silenced by the touch of his mouth on hers.

'I love you, Esther,' he said at last, holding her away from him and looking down into her eyes. 'Could you ever be my wife?'

'Yes, Adam,' she whispered, 'it is all I have wanted for so long.'

He smiled, loosening his arms though he wanted to keep them close around her forever. 'Then would you allow me to choose the guest of honour at our wedding?'

Esther looked into his face lit by the moonlight and felt her love for him swell within her. 'Of course,' she said, 'who is it to be?'

Taking the sprig of mugwort from his lapel, he placed it on the lid of the box. 'Just a friend of mine,' he said softly. 'Just a friend.'